FORTUNE FAVORS THE BOLD

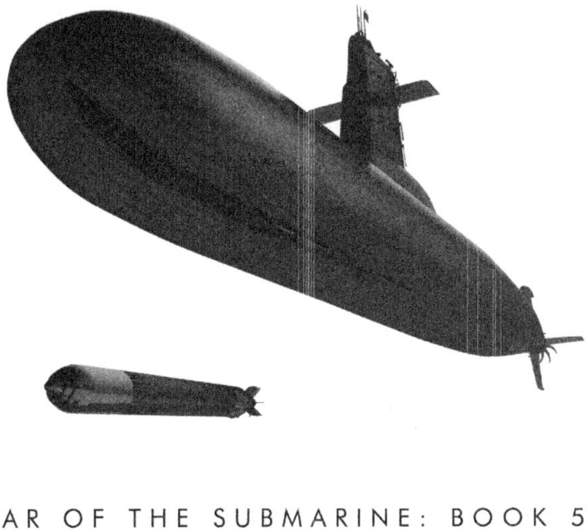

WAR OF THE SUBMARINE: BOOK 5

R.G. ROBERTS

Cover designed by MiblArt.

Edited by Jessica Meigs.

This one is to Shira, who is the best partner any writer could ask for. When this book refused to be written, her indefatigable support pushed me right through. I feel like I dedicate a lot of books to her, but let's be honest – I couldn't do this without her!

Contents

"'Fortes' inquit 'fortuna iuvat: Pomponianum pete.'"

"'Fortune,' he said, 'favors the bold: head for Pomponianus.'" Said by Pliny the Elder, Commander, Roman Navy, in his attempt to rescue his friend Pomponianus and others from Pompeii as Mount Vesuvius exploded. Pliny the Elder died in the attempt.

Prologue: The Best of the Best

12 December 2039, somewhere in the Indian Ocean

Jules Rochambeau was the best in the business, and he knew it.

So did everyone else. That was the sweetest part. Thirty-two months into the Third World War, there was no arguing that he was the best submariner in the world. With thirty-eight warship or gray-hulled kills—he counted military support ships but didn't bother adding up the merchant ships he was sent after, like the entire convoy he sunk months ago—Jules Rochambeau and *Barracuda* topped anyone's list.

Which was why it was particularly annoying when admirals ignored him.

"This is rubbish," he said to his executive officer, or second-in-command. Jules ran an annoyed hand through his brown hair, not caring that he mussed it. There were no cameras on his attack submarine except those he authorized, and certainly none inside his stateroom. "Admiral Bernard would not stand for this."

"Admiral Bernard died when the Alliance attacked Saint-Denis de La Réunion." Commander Camille Dubois pursed her lips. "The barbarians."

Jules sneered. "It was clear—if inefficient—revenge for the Indian attack on Diego Garcia. They attacked a target of opportunity the moment they had missiles to do so, waiting until most of our submarines were underway. The fools do not understand that we have other submarine bases now."

"They did catch three destroyers." She sighed. "A black day for us, for certain. Admiral Bernard was the navy's future."

"No longer, *m'ami*." Jules shook his head. "Now we must answer to Maxime Sauvageau. Your favorite admiral."

He resisted the urge to spit. Sauvageau was a surface ship driver who knew little about submarines, and worse yet, she hated Camille for reasons Camille would not go into.

No matter. Jules was still the best, and Sauvageau must recognize that. Even if she felt the need to hamstring him.

"She must not like you, either, if she has refused your request to transition to the north Atlantic." Camille shrugged in her artful way. The woman really was quite beautiful, and she wore her uniform like a model. Camille could make any man's heart race, but Jules preferred her professional skills to whatever her bedroom ones were. Camille had the heart of a killer. Men forgot that at their peril.

"Bah. She claims the British will keep Ursula North and *Gallant* here in the Indian Ocean." He flicked a finger at the electronic copy of their orders still sitting on his tablet's screen. "As if there were anything left to accomplish down here."

"Have they sent us after her, then?" Camille's eyes lit up.

"*Non.*" Jules sighed. "We are to hunt in the northern mouth of the Strait of Malacca, focusing specifically on submarines." He scowled. "Admiral Sauvageau does not even give us the latitude to sink surface ships. She wants us to strangle the Alliance's underwater effort, because she believes they are running out of missiles and that submarines are the real threat."

Camille sniffed. "It is nice to be appreciated, I suppose."

"They will build missiles if they cannot use torpedoes." Jules shrugged before catching sight of his own disheveled appearance in the mirror and reaching up to smooth his hair. "Still, we have targets, so we had best be about it, *ne devrions-nous pas*?"

"I will have the navigation team set a course." She stood and departed his stateroom.

Within minutes, the French Navy submarine *Barracuda* was in route to the Strait of Malacca, still the most contested waterway in the world. Currently patrolled by ships of the Grand Alliance—mainly American, British, and the stray Australian frigate—it was a fertile hunting ground for someone like Jules Rochambeau.

If only he was not on such a tight leash.

22 December 2023, near the northern approach to the SOM

"The contact is coming closer, *mon capitaine*," the sonar operator reported. Her voice was cool and professional, easily rising over the hum of activity in *Barracuda's* attack center.

No one flinched or sweated. His crew was calm and ready. *Barracuda* had prosecuted countless contacts and sunk eighteen of the eighteen underwater contacts they had engaged. Jules would not say his crew was overconfident, but they were rightfully assured of their skill and professionalism. Everyone knew *Barracuda* was the best in the world.

Today they would prove that again.

"Tonals match an *Astute*-class submarine," sonar said after another moment. "Likely match to *Astute* herself."

Jules smiled. "It seems our wait was worthwhile. Set action stations."

Moments later, his well-drilled crew arrived at their battle stations, each sailor well-rested and ready to face the enemy. Camille strode into the attack center right before the hatch closed, her smile picture-perfect and her eyes gleaming.

"Is it someone worth killing, *mon capitaine*?" she asked.

"Our old friend *Astute*," Jules replied, sitting back in his chair and sipping his latte. "I do not think you remember Lord Clifford Day?"

"I never had the pleasure."

"Oh, it was not a pleasure, I assure you. Never did I have a more boring partner in exercises, and the fellow is the *worst* kind of aristocratic ninny. More concerned with his self-image than his tactics." Jules grinned. "Sinking him will be a pleasure...and possibly a service to humanity."

Camille giggled. "Should we perhaps let him pass and make the Brits keep him?"

"*Non*, a dead submarine is a dead submarine. Besides, losing a member of their House of Lords will surely impact their public," Jules replied. "Truly, it's a miracle he survived this long."

He reeled through his memory, trying to think of where *Astute* spent the early days of the war. Had Day faced the Russians in the north? Surely not. If so, *Astute* would be on the bottom. There were some incompetent Russians, of course; their nation had fought several silly little wars and struggled through much turmoil this century, none of which had done their submarine community much good. But by and large, the Russians were good enough to sink this fool.

Jules eyed the tactical plot. "Is he even changing course?"

"*Non, mon capitaine*. He has turned to a least-time course to...Perdue Station."

"Perdue Station?" Jules cocked his head.

"Australian underwater station," Camille replied before the officer of the watch could speak. "Drills for oil, mines iron, and some miscellaneous minerals. Mid-sized. Decent gross station product. Recently retaken by the Alliance, and then some Indian *beauf* put two torpedoes in it."

Jules' eyes narrowed. Torpedoing underwater stations was a barbaric move; he had no love for the enemy, but innocents ought to be allowed to evacuate. Anything else only made it easy for the enemy to vilify the Freedom Union. "Am I remembering correctly that Perdue Station was also one of those places you instigated *incidents* at in our pre-war days?"

"*Exactement*."

"It is a pity we do not have marines to follow him in and steal Perdue Station back, but alas, such is not our orders." Jules shrugged. "Weapons Officer, prepare two torpedoes, but use the F21 on her. *Astute* is not worth one of the newer torpedoes."

"That will require us allowing the target within fifteen nautical miles for a good shot, *mon capitaine*."

"Make it eight miles," Jules replied. "Even a fool can outrun the F21 Artemis if we are stupid, and we are not." He winked. "I will bet they won't hear us. Does anyone disagree?"

No one took his bet. Two hours later, HMS *Astute* went to the bottom with all hands.

Unsatisfied, Jules Rochambeau resumed his hunt for a more challenging target.

Chapter 1

Course Change

23 December 2039, Perth, Australia

Leave it to Commander Wade Peterson to schedule a stores onload two days before Christmas Eve. On a Saturday. Lieutenant Bobby O'Kane tried to get his commanding officer to change the date, but Peterson had reminded him that he was "only" the navigator and not the real executive officer and ignored him. Again.

Bobby had been acting XO for months, ever since their real second-in-command fell down a ladder and broke his leg. As the boat's senior department head, Bobby inherited the job...temporarily, or so the captain promised. But that promise felt pretty darn empty while he supervised USS *Bluefish's* sailors passing eggs, frozen foods, and canned goods out of two trucks, up the brow, and down the open hatch into the submarine proper.

Meanwhile, Peterson lounged in his stateroom, talking to his wife on the phone. Or something. Bobby really didn't want to know what the captain was up to. He was just glad Peterson was gone. Without the captain here—Peterson's rank might have been commander, the navy called every submarine's commanding officer as "Captain" by courtesy—the crew might get through this stores onload without being micromanaged until their eyes bled.

Bobby glanced aft, giving the submarine a once-over. If Peterson found one line out of place, he'd rip someone a new one. That someone was usually Bobby. Everything looked all right, but Peterson was never satisfied. He should have been, though. *Bluefish* was a *Cero*-class submarine, commissioned just four years earlier. She was the seventh submarine built in the quietest and fastest class of attack submarines ever built by the U.S. Navy. Even if she wasn't an Improved *Cero*, she was still one of the best submarines in the fleet. The navy's demand for new submarines became insatiable once the war started, but *Bluefish* was still full of cutting-edge technology. With a top speed of almost sixty knots and room for twenty-eight torpedoes and twenty missiles, *Bluefish* was one of the most capable submarines in the world.

Her reputation said otherwise.

First, they'd missed out on what was now *the* engagement of World War III because Commander Peterson thought Convoy 57 wasn't important enough to escort. That humiliating episode left the crew both miserable and guilty, and now they were stuck pier side again. All because their captain was cautious to the point of ineptitude.

Oh, Peterson always put his best foot forward. If there was a tour to give or an admiral to impress, *Bluefish* was the first to volunteer. No speck of rust permitted. Every sailor should fit the perfect navy image. Drinking was forbidden because *liberty was a mission* and they needed to impress their Australian hosts. It was almost like Peterson hadn't noticed there was a war on. When he did, he adroitly avoided dangerous situations but rushed into anything that could make him look good without having to face too many enemies.

Bobby knew what the problem was. He'd read enough history to know that it happened in the Second World War, too. Back then, the navy needed years to figure out that peacetime captains often crumbled under the pressure of wartime decision-making, and now it was happening again. Peterson was a prime example of the kind of administrator a peacetime navy promoted. He performed fine in exercises, but when it mattered, he was better at avoiding combat than shooting. Still, it wasn't World War II, and Bobby had figured that the navy would have gotten its head out of its—

"Is there a problem, Lieutenant?"

Bobby jumped. "No, sir." He swallowed. "We're running ahead of schedule. The last truck just arrived, and they're breaking the pallets down now. Base Supply said we'll be done by fifteen hundred."

"Very well." Peterson sniffed like there was something rotten in the air. "Has the ice cream been onloaded yet? I don't want it to melt."

Bobby grimaced. It was eighty-plus degrees out, because the seasons were backward in the southern hemisphere, and *Bluefish's* current homeport was Perth, Australia. "Sir, did you, um, miss Suppo's email?"

"Email about what?" Peterson swung to face Bobby, his nose wrinkling.

"Uh, the base is out of ice cream." Bobby fidgeted. "Lieutenant Sonnen—"

"Who?"

"The new supply officer, Captain. She reported two days ago." Bobby shouldn't hint at how Peterson hadn't bothered to meet his newest, and most junior, department head. Being the acting XO had yet to save him from Peterson's wrath when he tried to do the job.

"I don't need *you* to tell me that." Peterson's glare made Bobby squirm more. "So, what is she going to *do* about the problem?"

That had been in the email, too. "The base should be able to fill our order when we get back from our next patrol, Captain."

"That's unacceptable. I'll talk to the commodore about it."

You do that, sir, Bobby didn't say. Because Base Supply could just crap out some ice cream to feed Peterson's stupid sweet tooth. Sure. Assuming they coughed any up, Bobby knew Peterson would reserve some for his use only. And if there wasn't enough, he'd claim it all, too. Even better, Commodore Banks might make someone give up ice cream for *Bluefish*. He and Peterson went way back.

"I'll, uh, be standing by for the results of that conversation, sir."

Peterson made the little frowny face that promised a storm. "If you were halfway competent, you would— What is *that*?"

Peterson gestured at the working party, his face growing more pinched. Then the captain strode toward the brow, glaring at a sailor wearing paint-splattered coveralls, crossing his arms and glowering. Bobby followed right on his heels, but there was nothing he could do to stop Peterson from yelling:

"Petty Officer Cecil!"

Cecil, a young machinist's mate third class, jumped. "Sir?"

"What *is* on your uniform?" Peterson snapped.

"Sorry, Captain. I was painting when the call for the working party—"

"And you thought it wise to represent *Bluefish* in a paint-splattered uniform?" Peterson cut him off, chopping his hand through the air to emphasize his point. The sailor-made conveyer belt stopped; Peterson was in the way of Cecil handing off his giant box of pasta, and the next sailor in line was staring. "Are you *trying* to make my submarine the laughing stock of Perth, MM3?"

"No, sir!"

"I doubt that." Peterson's sneer deepened.

"Go change your coveralls, MM3," Bobby ordered, not bothering to point out that the small splatter of white paint on Cecil's coveralls was hardly something to write home about. "Everyone else, carry on with the stores onload."

Cecil handed off the pasta and started to turn away, only to stop cold when Peterson added:

"Take your rank insignia off the coveralls you put on, Cecil. You're now a seaman. Lieutenant O'Kane will see to the paperwork."

"Sir, there have to be formal charges if you want to bring him to Captain's Mast," Bobby said. Peterson was a sucker for regulations. Surely, he'd rethink this?

Peterson turned to glare at him. "Then see to it. We'll hold Mast at seventeen hundred hours. All hands will be present."

Sailors exchanged murderous glances. Captain's Mast, the navy's version of non-judicial punishment, was a quick way for a commanding officer to assign punishment without sending someone to court martial. The penalties for going to Mast weren't as bad as those at a trial, but they were bad enough. Commanders like Peterson could put sailors on restriction, where they couldn't leave the boat, demote them, and even fine them a half month's pay. Most COs liked to conduct Mast in private, but Peterson always dragged things out twice as long as necessary and required the entire crew to be there. That meant no one would get off the boat for liberty before six p.m. Maybe later.

"Aye, sir." Bobby tried throwing Cecil a look of apology, but the young petty officer slunk off, his shoulders slumped and head down. Bobby wanted to say something, wanted to somehow save the kid from Peterson's wrath, but Peterson was already headed toward Lieutenant (Junior Grade) Sonnen, whose features were sharp with panic.

Bobby scurried after his captain, trying to figure out how he could get ice cream from somewhere other than base supply, even though he knew he couldn't.

Several hours later—after poor Cecil was busted down a rank and fined half a month's pay for two months—Bobby and his fellow department heads escaped to the base Officer's Club. The O-Club was a raggedy-looking building in the corner of an empty lot that was probably built during the Cold War. The place was scheduled for demolition before the war started and looked like it, but now it was the most popular club in town. Mostly because it was the only one you could walk back to the piers from.

"I think we just took the prize for the most miserable boat on the waterfront." Bobby leaned back in his uncomfortable wooden chair and groaned. He couldn't forget how the entire crew stood so stiffly, glaring at the captain they didn't dare defy. Something ugly was brewing on *Bluefish*, and Bobby couldn't figure out how to stop it.

"More like kept it." Rose Lange, the third person at their table, was *Bluefish's* Weapons Officer. She was even angrier than Bobby. Cecil was one of her sailors, and she'd tried to speak up for him. Not that Peterson had listened. Instead, he'd spent thirty minutes pontificating about what a horrible sailor Cecil was, all because the poor kid had spilled paint on his coveralls.

"You shouldn't say that." Louis Cooper, *Bluefish's* engineer, glared at him halfheartedly. Lou's eyes were dark with defeat as they followed a waiter carrying a pitcher of beer on its way to a nearby table. "Particularly not here."

"As if everyone in this place isn't already aware of it." Rose crossed her arms and leaned back to stare at the ceiling, which was dotted with water damage and rushed repairs.

"You're probably right." Bobby flopped back in his chair, wishing for a beer. Or straight-up vodka. Commander Peterson, in his glorious wisdom, had decreed all alcoholic beverages off-limits for his crew. In the middle of a *war*. Because that was the way to win friends and make your sailors happy. "At least the kids aren't here?"

Rose rolled her eyes. "Thank heavens for small favors."

"I'm actually a little worried about that." Lou's eyes darted around the O-Club, as if some of the younger officers from their boat would jump out at them. Not that any of them felt up to practical jokes. It had been a long war already, and *Bluefish* kept avoiding action while Commander Peterson looked for his weekly scapegoat. "Where *have* they gone off to?"

"Hopefully somewhere more fun than here." Rose shrugged, but Bobby couldn't quite ignore the sudden feeling of doom aching in his stomach. *Bluefish's* junior officers used to hang out at the O-Club, but not lately. Probably because Peterson liked to bring his wife here.

"You've got a bad feeling about this, don't you?" He had to ask, even if he didn't *want* to know if Lou knew anything. But he was the acting XO, which meant he had to care.

Lou shrugged. "Maybe I'm just being an idiot."

"And maybe I'm Mary Poppins." Bobby sighed. "I hate it when you're smart."

Rose grinned. "It's not hard to be smarter than you, Bobby."

Bobby rolled his eyes, but his cell phone's buzzing cut him off before he could retort. Slumping in his chair and *knowing* that the call would be from Peterson, he fished the offending phone out of his pocket. "Lieutenant O'Kane."

"Nav? It's Suppo. I've got the duty." The voice on the other end was high and nervous. What had their pencil-pushing micromanager of a captain had done this time? Had he stayed on board to torment the supply officer about the stores onload? Bobby should've stuck around.

He forced his tone to be light. "How's it going, Brigitte? Everything okay?"

"Um, no, sir. It's not. The ambulance is leaving now, but—"

"Ambulance? *What* ambulance?"

"The captain, sir." Brigitte Sonnen's voice was tiny. She took a shuddering breath before continuing: "Doc said it looked like a ruptured appendix. The captain fell down in the maneuvering room, and the base sent an ambulance to get him. Doc tagged along."

Bobby licked his lips. "Well, that's just...unbelievably fantastic."

"Yeah. Nav, what should I do now? I mean..."

"Just hold down the fort until I get back." Bobby sighed. It was so typical of Peterson to find the *worst* time to get hurt. They were supposed to get underway in four days, and no boat could do that without a captain *or* an XO. Bobby wasn't qualified for command of a tugboat, let alone a nuclear fast-attack submarine. The very idea made butterflies dance in his stomach. He swallowed. "I'm on my way."

"Thanks, sir." Relief made her voice gravelly.

"Just doing my job." Bobby forced a smile and then hung up. Rose and Lou were staring; he groaned. "Captain's on the way to the hospital. Time for us to head back to the boat, my lord and lady."

"Shit." Rose dropped enough money on the table to pay the combined bill as they all stood up. "What happened?"

"Ruptured appendix or something, Brigitte's not sure. Doesn't sound good." Bobby led the group out to the car that Lou had rented.

"Looks like you're the boss, then." Lou's words made Bobby stumble.

He chuckled to hide the sudden crush of responsibility. "Only until the captain gets back so he can yell at me again."

Knowing Peterson, that wouldn't be long. Bobby was sure a case of appendicitis wouldn't keep their dour captain down; nothing else seemed to. He was like a bad penny that kept coming back to get polished without ever being spent. Peterson would return to making everyone miserable within a few days. *Bluefish's* luck guaranteed that.

By the time the word made it up the grapevine to Submarine Squadron 29, it was just past four in the afternoon in Perth, Australia. Commodore Banks kicked the bad news upstairs to Commander Naval Submarine Force Pacific (COMSUBPAC) right away, and Vice Admiral Marco Rodriquez had never been one to let any grass grow under his feet. Within an hour, he called the Bureau of Personnel and cashed in a favor.

That led to a phone ringing in Groton, Connecticut.

"Yeah?" Alex Coleman had to pull his face out of the pillow to answer the phone. He was still on sixty days of leave after what happened to his last boat, and a four a.m. phone call was the last thing he expected.

"Captain Coleman?" The voice sounded familiar enough that Alex snapped awake.

"Yes, sir?" What the hell was COMSUBPAC doing calling him in Groton? He'd met the man nicknamed "Uncle Marco" once, but everyone knew about the navy's most colorful admiral.

"Did I wake you, Coleman?"

Saying yes wasn't the right answer. Alex was depressingly alone in the bed, anyway. His wife, Nancy, had returned to damaged destroyer in Perth already. "Not enough to matter, sir."

"I know you're on leave, but I've got a boat out in Perth needs a CO. You gonna fall the fuck apart if I give her to you, or do you think you can make magic again?"

Alex sat upright so fast he almost fell off the bed. Another boat? His chest felt tight, and for a moment, all he could see was the faces he failed to bring home with USS *Jimmy Carter*. Could he do that again? Three months ago, he'd been the redhaired stepchild of the sub force. Now *he* was the one that COMSUBPAC tapped when they needed a submarine commander in a hurry? What kind of ass backward world was he living in?

Maybe he should hang up and pretend this was all a dream. Alex glanced at the clock.

4:07

"I, uh, think I'll be okay, Admiral."

Rodriquez barked out a laugh. "Good. I need a captain yesterday."

"Give me a couple of hours to pack and I'll be ready to go." Alex hadn't unpacked everything leftover from *Jimmy Carter*; he'd been home less than two months and he hadn't been ready to deal. Still, he needed time to break the news to his teenaged daughters. Not to mention talking to his mother-in-law and calling Nancy. If he could get ahold of her.

This really hadn't been part of his Christmas plans. The girls would *kill* him. But there was a war on, and they were a navy family. They'd understand, even if they hated him going as much as he hated leaving. The U.S. hadn't done well in the war, and if Alex's particular skillset could help in any way...who the hell was he to say no? Besides, anyone who said no to command wasn't someone the navy would offer command to a second time. Or a third one, in Alex's case.

If he ever wanted another submarine, another chance, he had to go now.

"You're booked on a military flight out of Westover Air Force Base at noon. Can you make that?"

Alex took a deep breath. Westover was near Springfield, Massachusetts, almost two hours from Groton. It could have been worse. "I'll be there." He hesitated. "Anyone going to give me a copy of my orders before I go?"

"I'll have someone meet you in Perth."

"This was laid on fast, huh?"

"You think? Just get out to Perth, Coleman. I'll take care of the details."

"Aye, sir." How many questions could he get away with asking the notoriously short-tempered admiral? "Can you at least tell me which boat I'm going to?"

"That'd be *Bluefish*." He could hear Rodriquez frown. "She hasn't exactly covered herself in glory so far. I want you to change that."

Alex gulped. "Yes, sir."

The day went from bad to worse. By the time morning arrived, it was obvious Commander Peterson wouldn't return to the boat soon. Chief Waskow, *Bluefish's* independent duty corpsman, returned from the hospital and delivered the news in person, leaving Bobby to pace on the sub's aft deck by himself until Rose arrived.

They were free. At least for a while. He didn't have to defend the crew from—

Except Peterson would come back like the plague. A slow, creeping sickness that gnawed at your soul until there was nothing left. Worse yet, Bobby was in charge until Peterson returned. Not in command—no navy would hand *Bluefish* over to someone as inexperienced as Bobby—but the sub was his problem in the captain's absence. Joy. Peterson would take joy in tearing every single one of Bobby's decisions apart when he got back.

"I heard the captain's down for the count." Rose stopped next to him as Bobby ignored his rumbling stomach. He shouldn't have skipped breakfast. "HMC says that he spent hours in surgery."

"Yep." Bobby sighed. "Sounds like they're going to leave the toddlers in charge of the daycare for a bit."

Rose's laugh sounded hollow. "Aren't we just the best boat in the navy? We finally get even that broken outboard fixed—"

"Don't say it! The damned thing will hear you and break again."

"—we just *started* living down that Convoy 57 fiasco," Rose continued without missing a beat, "and now we can't go anywhere because we don't have a captain *or* an XO."

"And since this isn't World War II, we're not sending out subs with lieutenants in command. Thank God." Bobby tried to smile, but it came out as lopsided as a slip-n-slide.

They weren't that desperate, were they? World War III hadn't gone well for the Alliance, and yet... Okay. Yeah. Bobby wasn't sure. Submarines were at a premium; the bulk of the fight was underwater. The Freedom Union of Russia, France, India, and an assortment of smaller nations outnumbered the Grand Alliance by a ridiculously high margin. The loss of Japan's entire navy near the beginning of the war hadn't done them any favors, and their lopsided loss rate made it even worse.

Thinking about the naval drawdowns enacted by the U .S., UK, and Australia during the early 2000s in the name of *saving money* made Bobby nauseous. By the time money from underwater exploitation started changing America's GDP in a meaningful way, it was too late to catch up. Their enemies—and some old friends whose fundamental desires conflicted with America's—had built newer, better, and *more* ships and submarines.

Yep. Great war they were in.

"I think we'd do okay." Rose smirked; she loved a challenge.

Bobby rolled his eyes. "You can be crazy all day long, Rosie. I'll stick with common sense. For once in my life."

"Oh, come on. Where's your sense of—"

"Sorry to interrupt, Nav, but COS is on the phone for you." Poor Brigette wasn't on duty any longer, but she seemed like she was trying to make up for an accident that wasn't her fault by helping out.

"This early?" Bobby frowned, following Brigette to the quarterdeck, where all official calls came in. Rose trailed behind, and he exchanged a shrug with her before grabbing the handset. Bobby had no idea what the squadron's chief of staff wanted, but he bet it wasn't to commiserate with him. He took a deep breath and waited for Rose to shoo Brigette and the other watchstanders away before speaking into the phone.

"Lieutenant O'Kane speaking, how may I help you, ma'am?"

"I wanted to check on your readiness to get underway, Lieutenant," Commander Karla Reyes said without preamble. "You were scheduled to head out on patrol two days after Christmas, but a gap in coverage means we need *Bluefish* ASAP. Are you loaded out and ready to go?"

Bobby gulped. "We're topped off on stores and torps, but—"

"How does midnight tonight sound?"

"Ma'am, I don't think you heard about Commander Peterson." Bobby spoke quickly to keep Reyes from lurching into other plans. "He's in the hospital. From what our doc said, it doesn't sound like he's going to get out anytime soon."

"We'll have a new CO out to you by tonight. You can postpone your underway until they're on board."

"Wait, *what*?"

"Lieutenant, I realize this is irregular, but Convoy 3791 needs an escort. *Lionfish* cracked a blade on her screw, and that leaves you." Reyes paused. "Is there any reason you can't get underway?"

Bobby's mouth felt like he'd run a mile in the desert. "Um, not if we've got a captain. I guess not."

This had to be the worst idea in the history of the navy, right up there with Commander Peterson dodging getting underway for Convoy 57. But Bobby wouldn't run away from his duty. People were *dying* out there, and even if all *Bluefish* could do was scare the bad guys away, that was the job. They hadn't made a huge impact on the war so far, but Bobby knew the crew would rather be near the fight than tied up to the pier.

"Glad to hear it. Get in touch with the squadron if any additional needs come up." *Click.*

"Yes, ma'am." Bobby stared at the receiver in shocked silence after she hung up.

"Everything okay, Nav?" Rose stepped close, using Bobby's title since there were others around. They'd been friends since the Naval Academy, but Rose never let that interfere with her job.

Bobby let out a breath, feeling dizzy as his mind zipped through the thousand and three things he had to do for *Bluefish* to get underway on time. "Our underway's been moved up."

"What?" Rose jerked like someone slapped her. "Did they miss the memo on the captain?"

"Nope. Apparently, we're getting a new CO tonight. And then getting underway. All at the same time." Bobby hated his tendency to babble when nervous. "Midnight. Isn't it grand?"

"Merry fucking Christmas to us."

"You can say that again." Bobby looked around, glancing at the quarterdeck watch team. They all pretended to be engrossed in their jobs, but Bobby didn't care. Peterson would have. All Bobby noticed was how *young* they looked.

Hell, Bobby was just thirty-one. He only *felt* a million years old.

"Got any idea who they're sending out to be our new lord and master?" Rose asked, bringing him back to the present.

"Nope. COS didn't seem willing to share." Bobby shrugged. "Assuming she knew."

Rose groaned. "Fan-fucking-tastic."

"Yeah, it's like playing pin the tail on the piñata without knowing where the piñata is." Bobby needed to tell jokes; otherwise, he'd admit being terrified.

Commander Peterson was a terrible CO, surviving because he was friends with the commodore. But their incoming captain was unknown. There were plenty other of toxic COs in the service. How would *Bluefish's* crew cope if they got another one? Bobby knew he couldn't defend the crew from some mystery CO any better than he'd protected them from Peterson, so he did the only thing he could. Using his authority as acting XO, Bobby canceled work and cut the crew loose for a day of liberty. It was Christmas Eve. They deserved a chance to relax.

Within fifteen minutes, eighty-plus sailors—everyone not on duty, two-thirds of the crew—poured off the submarine. Bobby stayed behind, wishing that he didn't have such a sinking feeling in his stomach as he watched a group of junior officers laughing as they headed toward a cab. He didn't want to know if they were celebrating Peterson's early departure from command. If they were, who could blame them?

Chapter 2

I Will Try

COMSUBPAC Headquarters, Naval Base Pearl Harbor, Hawaii

"The opening events of the war matter very little in context," Lieutenant Commander Margaret Bennett said, pulling her final slide up with a flick of her fingers against the smart board. "Our assessment remains that the best route forward is to ignore those events and focus on the underlying root causes. The discovery of undersea resources—and our increasing ability to exploit them—continues to drive the war forward. So long as there is no international consensus concerning the ownership of resources and underwater stations in international waters, this war will continue." Maggie took a deep breath before going on:

"Therefore, the Office of Naval Intelligence's analysis is that the Indian and French Navies will continue to 'station hop' across the Indian Ocean—as the Russians are doing in the North Sea and the Sea of Okhotsk—until forced to stop. Attacks on convoys and land bases are secondary conflicts. Landward expansion is not the goal of this war. ONI rates the likelihood that the Freedom Union will withdraw from occupied countries at the end of the war as high. However, our estimate of the likelihood of a similar withdrawal from underwater stations remains low."

"Including Armistice Station?" a female commander asked.

The briefing room, full though it was, went quiet. Maggie could feel every eye on her, and it wasn't a feeling she liked. Oh, she didn't mind being the center of attention; she hadn't chosen gymnastics followed by a naval career because she hated the spotlight, after all. But years in the insular submarine community meant she preferred knowing her audience.

Providing a brief like this the day after reporting to a new command sent her stomach rolling like it hadn't since—

No. She wouldn't think about that battle. Not now.

Maggie shook herself and refocused on the commander. "Yes, ma'am. Armistice Station remains the most lucrative undersea resource station in the world. They won't give that back unless we force them to." She squared her shoulders. "Proceeding to active intelligence estimates, analysis of French and Indian signals intelligence indicates increased activity in the vicinity of Madagascar. This might be a precursor to an attack on the Comoro Islands..."

Twenty minutes later, Maggie wrapped her brief up, answered a few more questions for the assembled staff of Commander, Submarine Forces Pacific, known in navy parlance as COMSUBPAC, and generally tried not to look at the admiral sitting at the head of the table. In a just world, she would have had more time to unpack and adjust to the time zone before briefing the legend nicknamed "Uncle Marco."

Instead, she felt like a pretzel left out too long after midnight, and Maggie would've yawned if the fourth shot of espresso hadn't left her needing to use the head so badly.

But the bathroom was in sight, just one right-hand turn outside the briefing room, and then she'd—

"Commander Bennett! A moment."

Maggie froze. Admiral Marco Rodriquez had spent most of the briefing reading on a tablet and looked up only a handful of times. How'd he even know her name?

Too late, Maggie realized she was expected to answer, not leave her mouth hanging open like a blowfish. "Sir?"

"I was all set to ignore you until I noticed those dolphins on your chest," Rodriquez said, gesturing at the submarine warfare pin nestled over the ribbons on her dress uniform. The man sauntered up to her, and Maggie found herself looking down at the navy's second-ranking submariner. He was surprisingly short. "Then I spotted the Silver Star and it clicked. You were the navigator on *Jimmy Carter*, weren't you?"

"Yes, sir." Maggie made herself meet his gaze, even when her left wrist tried to ache.

"How the hell did you end up as my newest intel weenie?"

"I did a lat transfer to intelligence." Maggie tried not to fidget as she declined to mention how many times she'd applied for that same lateral transfer, only to be told the war was in submarines, so in submarines she'd stay.

"And they sent you to my staff." Rodriquez snorted. "Fucking idiots."

Maggie blinked. "Excuse me?"

"I don't need an analyst who appreciates submarine capabilities and limitations. I've got a big-ass staff to keep your idiot compatriots straight." Rodriquez gestured at the staffers trudging out of the briefing room, amongst them Maggie's boss of one-point-five days. He was a former aviator who didn't know a boomer from a fast attack, and it showed. "You'd do a fuck-ton more good at a SUBRON. Want to go back to Perth?"

"I just got here two days ago, sir. It's not like I'm unpacked." Maggie supposed she shouldn't be surprised; the navy's personnel system *still* hadn't caught up to the war a year and a half in. The orders sending her to Pearl Harbor were issued six days before she left. She was berthed in a room that looked like a shipping container and leaked like a sieve. Yeah. Australia would one-up Pearl, no problem. She didn't have any weird ex-boyfriends there, either. Avoiding Jack was hard when he worked upstairs.

Sure. Aside from the nightmares, this would be a win-win.

"Good." Rodriquez looked her up and down before smirking. "It's a damn shame you chickened out and went intel, but we might as well make use of your experience and brains while we've got them."

"I didn't 'chicken out' of anything, sir," Maggie snapped. "If I was going to do that, I would have done it during Convoy 57."

"Oh yeah?" He cocked his head, his dark eyes gleaming. "Plenty of people hang on just long enough."

"I put in my first lat transfer request two years ago, Admiral." He was baiting her, wasn't he? Only *part* of Uncle Marco's legend revolved around his foul mouth. Maggie clamped mental hands of steel around her temper. "I imagine it's still sitting in someone's queue somewhere. But it's amazing what kind of doors a Silver Star and a recommendation from a Medal of Honor winner open."

"Fair enough." The admiral grinned. "Good thing you've still got a backbone. You'll need it when I send you to work for Commodore Banks."

Wasn't that ominous? Maggie almost asked but decided that quizzing a three-star admiral about her new boss was a bridge too far to cross. She'd had bad bosses before and survived, so she just decided to appreciate the oblique warning. Even if it followed on the heels of an insult.

Admiral Rodriquez insulted everyone. Supposedly, it was part of his charm.

Maggie just shook her head, grabbed a copy of her new orders fresh off the printer, and went back to her leaky container for a nap.

24 December 2038, Royal Australian Air Force Base Pearce, Western Australia

The military air terminal at the RAAF base was bland, utilitarian, and almost empty. Alex paused exiting the jetway, trying to shake the sleep away and get his bearing at the same time. Twenty-three hours on a plane left him feeling like he'd been through a blender. He slept in the air, but his body wasn't sure what time zone it was in, and his brain had turned to mush somewhere over the Pacific. Military aircraft didn't have wifi, even when they were converted airliners, so he was left with the information he could download before takeoff.

There was depressingly little information he couldn't dig out of his own brain. *Bluefish* was a *Cero*-class attack submarine, just six years old. Although the *Ceros* were the newest and most numerous class of attack submarines in the American inventory, Alex had never served on one. His career had been spent in the older *Virginia*-class boats and then the even older *Jimmy Carter*. He knew a bit about the *Ceros*, at least in principle, but he'd never dug into the details.

Alex still felt like he was in the Twilight Zone. How had he even gotten command of *one* submarine after what he did at Armistice Station, let alone another? Part of Alex still couldn't believe the insane turn in his life over the last few months. He'd spent most of the war shepherding convoys around with *Jimmy Carter*, and then a super-secret mission sent them to rescue scientists out of the South China Sea. That seemed unimportant until Convoy 57 was attacked by Indians hunting those same scientists. And as for Alex...

Less than two months after his shattered submarine limped into Perth, he returned for a second command. *Jimmy Carter* wouldn't sail again, but Alex Coleman would.

"Captain Coleman?"

Alex turned, spotting a short, dark-skinned commander waving. She was in uniform; he wasn't. The rank he'd worn for just forty-nine days still sounded strange. How had she recognized him? Oh, right. She'd probably seen him on TV. He'd tried to avoid interviews while on leave following Convoy 57, but he'd been flat-out ordered into a few.

Shaking himself, Alex dredged up a smile. "I'm afraid you have me at a disadvantage, Commander."

"Karla Reyes, sir." She held out a hand, and Alex shifted his carryon bag to his left hand to accept it. "Chief of Staff for SUBRON Twenty-Nine."

"Nice to meet you." Alex tried to ignore the way she stared. Reyes was new in the job, since she hadn't been with the

Submarine Squadron the last time Alex was in Perth. The old COS and Alex fought over *Jimmy Carter's* age for months; that rat wouldn't have looked even an iota over-awed.

"It's an honor, sir." Reyes' smile flashed white teeth. "I know I speak for all of SUBRON 29 when I say that we're delighted to add you to the team."

Alex laughed. "Don't say that before you get to know me, Commander. I'm told I can be a real pain in the ass."

It had in fact been his new boss, Commodore Banks, who'd last called Alex that. Now wasn't the time to mention *that* tidbit. Or the fact that Banks, the famous stickler for details and the regs, now had to salute one of his subordinates. Alex bet that would go over like a lead balloon.

Reyes looked like she didn't know how to respond, so Alex continued:

"I assume you're here to talk about *Bluefish*." Apparently, being a captain meant he ranked the chief of staff for an escort. Back when he had been a commander, Alex would've been lucky to get a chief petty officer.

"I'm here to drive you out to the boat, sir."

"At this hour?" Assuming his phone remembered to change time zones, midnight was less than an hour away. Waking up an entire crew so he could get his feet wet felt pretty shitty.

"No one told you?"

"Told me *what*?" Alarm bells jingled in his head.

Reyes blinked. "*Bluefish* is scheduled to get underway at midnight, sir. Convoy 3791 needs an escort. The civilians got underway six hours ago."

A *Cero's* maximum speed was over fifty knots, which meant she'd be able to overtake the average convoy in six hours or so, but why the hell was this his problem *already*?

"Do I want to know whose brilliant idea this was?" Alex worked his jaw so that he didn't swear at her.

"*Bluefish* was already scheduled to escort the convoy." Reyes fidgeted but didn't back down. Good for her. "She was the only boat available before Commander Peterson's emergency."

"I see." Alex forced himself to nod. "Well, then I need somewhere to change after we grab my luggage. And since I'd hate to be late for my first underway, lead on, Commander."

"The captain's late." Bobby wanted to pace, but there wasn't room in *Bluefish's* sail. That small area was the topmost part of the submarine, with barely enough room for the people already there. Trying to pace would turn into marching in place, something he'd hated since the academy.

In port, people could stand on the submarine's deck, but underway—and not under water—they drove the boat from the sail. Where else could they? Standing on deck at any decent speed was a good way to drown. Bobby sighed. The Maneuvering Watch had been set for twenty minutes, and the crew was ready to get underway. All they had to do was send the brow ashore. Except for one crucial detail.

"I say we get underway at midnight if we've got a captain or not." Rose leaned back against the edge of the sail, looking serene. "You, me, and Lou can handle things just fine."

"You're crazy, you know that?" Bobby rolled his eyes. No navy in its right mind would let a submarine get underway with no one higher ranking than a lieutenant on board. Maybe that kind of stuff happened in the wild and woolly days of World War II, but things weren't that messy.

Yet.

He'd die of nerves if anyone even suggested he command the boat for real. No way. Bobby was not ready. Maybe he'd never be.

Rose shrugged. "We'd manage. It'd be easier than trying to work around Peterson's aversion to combat."

"*Rose.*"

"What? It's true."

Bobby twisted to glare at her. "You can't say that here."

"No one else is up here, Bobby. Unless you count the seagull." She gestured at the white bird perched on the back edge of the sail. The seagull had been there since they'd set the maneuvering watch, hanging out where the lookouts would be posted when Bobby called them up. It didn't seem interested in leaving.

"Frank is listening." Bobby crossed his arms.

"Frank? Who's—" Rose glared. "Really, Bobby? You *named* the seagull?"

"Everyone deserves a name." Bobby's foot left tapped. "And Frank is—"

His radio crackled. "Nav, Officer of the Deck, the pier watch just called. COS is on the way with the new captain in tow."

"Nav, aye." Butterflies reared up in his stomach as Bobby squinted down the pier. The tall and thin one looked like Commander Reyes, the squadron chief of staff. There were three people with her, one of which had to be their new boss. The other two carried luggage.

"Well, Mister Acting-Executive Officer, you'd better go greet the captain while I hold down the fort here." Rose winked.

Bobby scowled. "I could make *you* do it."

"Yeah, but then the captain would wonder why you weren't there, and while that might be fun for *me*, I doubt you'd enjoy it," Rose said.

"Fine, be smart about it. I'll be back." Matching actions to words, Bobby headed down the ladder from the sail to the sub's deck, walking aft to the quarterdeck. He arrived in time to see the officer of the deck wiping her hands on the legs of her coveralls. "Everything okay, Harri?"

Lieutenant (junior grade) Harriet Ainsworth was *Bluefish's* in-port officer of the deck, or OOD. Usually, Bobby trusted her to stand a good watch. Today, however, Harri kept yawning, her movements were sluggish, and the dark circles under her eyes screamed, "Hangover!"

Oh, great. Bobby was the idiot who approved the watchbill that put Harri on right now, wasn't he? Peterson's no-drinking rule had clearly been broken. Their old captain would have rained hellfire and damnation down upon *everyone's* heads if he was here. But Bobby didn't have time to deal with that. *Bluefish* couldn't afford a bad first impression.

"Yes, sir. Everything's fine."

Harri's crooked smile betrayed the lie. Bobby wanted to scream but didn't. Worst case, he could talk her through this, couldn't he? Announcing a senior officer's arrival wasn't hard; everyone in the navy knew their military courtesies. Harri wasn't some wet-behind-the-ears ensign who hadn't done this before. She could probably stand her watch while drunk. Hell, Bobby did that once as a junior lieutenant, not that he was admitting it.

The group reached the bottom of the brow. Judging by their uniforms, two looked enlisted, but the guy on Commander Reyes's right wore coveralls. His ballcap bore the fancy embroidery the navy called "scrambled eggs" on the bill, which only commanders and above wore. That had to be their new CO.

"All right, Harri." Bobby turned to give the OOD what he hoped was a reassuring nod. "Let's bong him on board properly. Four bells for a commander."

"Not as *Bluefish*?"

Bobby shook his head. While the CO of a ship or submarine was rung, or "bonged," on board using the name of the sub instead of their rank, their new CO hadn't assumed command yet. If in doubt, stick with the regs. Even Peterson couldn't yell at anyone for following the regs. "He's not captain yet. Let's do this right."

"Okay." Harri gestured to her petty officer of the watch, and the enlisted sailor picked up the microphone for the 1MC, ringing the bell with his other hand.

Ding ding. Ding ding. "Commander, U.S. Navy, arriving."

The stranger headed up the brow ahead of Commander Reyes, and Bobby stepped back to let Harri do her job. Their new captain was slender, blond-haired, and a little shorter than Bobby. He stopped at the head of the brow, saluting.

"Permission to come aboard?"

Harri's salute was a little too perfect. "Permission granted, sir."

The newcomer hopped down, and Bobby stepped forward to greet him, almost missing a step as he did so. *Oh, shit.* Their new CO was wearing a jacket over his coveralls, and ranks on his shoulders did glint silver...but they weren't the silver oak leaves of a commander. They were *eagles*, which meant Bobby just had the quarterdeck bong a full captain on as a commander. *Way to insult the new boss, Bobby. Good job.* He made himself hold his hand out.

"Welcome aboard, sir. I'm Lieutenant Robert O'Kane, the navigator and acting XO." He tried not to gulp. Better to take the blame than let the fallout find Harri. "I'm sorry about the mix up bonging you on board. We, uh, haven't gotten any orders for you and didn't know."

The captain laughed and took his hand. "It's not the end of the world, Nav. If it makes you feel better, I just got a copy of my orders twenty minutes ago. I'm Alex Coleman."

"Twenty minutes ago?" Bobby echoed. "This is really—Wait a minute, *what* did you say?"

His jaw dropped, and Bobby didn't care. Harri and the others on the quarterdeck were staring, too, every bit as starstruck as Bobby felt. By now, every submariner in the navy knew the story of how *Jimmy Carter* suckered the Indian Navy away from a convoy carrying thousands of civilians. They should have died; instead, *Jimmy Carter* turned in the best patrol of the war.

And Bobby had just demoted a medal of honor winner.

Coleman was also wearing a *Jimmy Carter* ballcap, which should have tipped Bobby off right away. The universe really hated him, didn't it? This was Alex *fucking* Coleman, the guy who ran the Indian Navy ragged. He was the first *living* submariner who'd won the Medal of Honor since World War II, and Bobby went and insulted him already.

He was the world's biggest idiot. The stupidest navigator to ever set foot on a submarine. Bobby wanted to smash his face into the nearest bulkhead. Rose was never going to let him live this down.

"Alex Coleman." The captain's smile got a little strained, like he was used to that reaction and didn't like it. Bobby made a mental note to remember that in case his new boss didn't already hate his guts.

"It's nice to meet you, sir." Bobby managed a nervous smile. "Welcome to *Bluefish.*"

"Thank you." Coleman frowned. "You said you're acting XO, too? What happened to the actual XO?"

"Oh, Commander Vanderbilt broke his leg a while back." The words came out in a rush. "The squadron keeps promising to get us a new one, but they haven't managed yet."

"I see."

Everything was jacked up here on the front lines. *Nothing* worked right, people were juggled like puzzle pieces, and round pegs never fit into diamond-shaped holes. Their pending underway was a great example of how off-the-rails things were.

Bobby could only shrug. It made him feel like a moron. "It's been an interesting war so far, Captain."

"You can say that again." Coleman sighed, glancing around. The two sailors carrying his gear had disappeared below while they were talking, but the pair reemerged and headed down the brow to join Commander Reyes. "So I hear we're expected to get underway before midnight?"

"Yes, sir." Bobby glanced at his phone. "I don't think we're going to make that deadline, though."

"No?"

"Well, the plant's lit off and we're ready to roll, but—"

"Then I'd best get to reading my orders so we can get this show on the road."

Bobby gaped.

Chapter 3

Minutes to Midnight

Alex never had a panic attack, but if the way his head was spinning was anything to go by, he was on the verge. How the *hell* was he supposed to get a boat underway when he'd never met the crew? His orders were to sail *Bluefish* into a war zone when he could barely remember the name of his navigator—or his XO, since they were the same damned person. Even better, that poor lieutenant looked like he wanted to die from embarrassment; Alex wanted to crawl into a hole. The way he'd taken command of *Jimmy Carter* had been merely unsettling. Now he was supposedly some Big Damned Hero.

Taking a deep breath, Alex turned toward the officer of the deck. She was a junior lieutenant with dark skin and bloodshot eyes, but she had the sense to hand over the mic for the 1MC, or general announcing system, before Alex could ask. Alex shot her a smile. "Thanks."

"Yes, sir." Lieutenant (junior grade) Ainsworth beamed, and something in that smile made Alex wonder about his predecessor.

"Ready to do this, XO?" he asked O'Kane. The lieutenant jumped.

"Ready like you wouldn't believe, Captain." O'Kane's smile was huge and showed too many teeth. "I'm really tired of being Acting Everything."

"Acting Everything?"

"Oh. Um, just a joke. Acting XO, Acting Captain...you know."

"Right." Alex swallowed. O'Kane's jitters made his nerves worse. What was O'Kane's first name again? Alex would have to ask somewhere more private.

This was insane. How in the world had he ended up taking command *twice* without meeting his predecessor? At least last time around he'd been at home in the U.S. Now he was on the front lines, and he didn't even know his XO's first name. Had he said Richard? Robert? Alex wished he could remember. *Time to get my ass moving.* Alex took a breath and nodded to O'Kane.

"Do you want to muster the crew, Captain?" O'Kane fidgeted. Alex tried to remember everything he'd heard concerning his predecessor.

Hell, he couldn't remember the guy's name. Just that *Bluefish*'s reputation sucked and she sure as shit hadn't been there when *Jimmy Carter* needed her.

Alex shook his head. "That's not necessary."

"Captain?"

"Let's not waste time on silly ceremonies." Alex tried to smile. At least skipping the formalities would spare him some public speaking and wearing a dress uniform with *that* medal on it. "Using the 1MC is faster, and we've got an underway scheduled."

O'Kane looked dubious. "If you say so, sir."

No one would blame Alex if *Bluefish* got underway late, but they'd given him another goddamned submarine. He wasn't going to screw this up.

While Alex was thinking, O'Kane took the 1MC microphone from his hand and cleared his throat. "Hey, *Bluefish*, it's the navigator. Contrary to how things looked a few minutes ago, we've got a new captain and we're going to get underway on schedule. Or something close enough for government work. So listen up."

Deep breath. Alex unfolded his orders and took the microphone. "To Captain Alexander G. Coleman, United States Navy, from Commander, Naval Personnel Command. Report not later than 24 December 2039 to SSN 843, USS *Bluefish*, homeport Perth, Australia, for duty as Commanding Officer." He looked at O'Kane, shifting the mic to his left hand to pop off a salute. "I am ready to relieve you, XO."

"I am ready to be relieved, sir." O'Kane returned his salute, wide-eyed.

"I relieve you."

Did O'Kane slump? "I stand relieved, Captain."

Alex lowered his salute, glancing around at what was now his boat. The topside watchstanders were gawking. He had to say something. Alex raised the mic again. *Don't say* Jimmy Carter, *you moron*, he told himself. *She's halfway to razor blades.*

Wasn't that a happy thought?

She hasn't exactly covered herself in glory so far. I want you to change that, Admiral Rodriquez had said. How the fuck was he supposed to do that if he stood here like a gaping idiot? Finally, Alex forced words out:

"*Bluefish*, this is Captain Coleman. I know it's not normal to get underway five minutes after the new CO walks on board, but I'm afraid that's what we've got." Great, now he was sprouting platitudes. Just what a confused crew needed. He cleared his throat. "So here's the short version. My name is Alex Coleman. Some of you may remember me from back when *Jimmy Carter* parked next door to *Bluefish.*"

There. That was out of the way. Judging from the navigator/XO's reaction to his name, he realized who Alex was, but now the crew would know. Alex couldn't hide his past, so he might as well own it.

"I'm sure we'll have plenty of time to get to know one another in the next few weeks. For now, let's concentrate on getting underway and getting back into the game."

Alex hung up the 1MC mic before he could say something stupid. Every eye on the quarterdeck was on him, but at least he'd finished the speech part. The rest he could handle. Having to look knowledgeable and impressive in front of strangers was just nerve racking. Shaking himself, Alex turned to the acting XO. At least O'Kane had a last name any submariner could remember.

"Let's get this show on the road, XO." O'Kane jumped when Alex used that title, but he nodded quickly.

"You want to take the conn, Captain?"

Did he *ever*. But Alex refused to let his ego outweigh his common sense. He shook his head. "I've never driven a *Cero*, so I'll leave that to you until I get to know her."

"Uh, as you wish, sir." O'Kane's smile was spastic. Alex followed him up to the bridge to get his new boat underway.

One pier down from *Bluefish*, a navy commander watched a pair of tugs ease the submarine away from the pier. Standing on the deck of his own command, USS *Kansas*, Chris Kennedy scowled.

It wasn't right. In a fair and just world, none of this would have happened. *He* was supposed to be the one in the limelight. Christopher Atticus Kennedy had never put a foot wrong in his nineteen-year naval career. He should have been a star. Instead, he'd been sent out time and again without proper resources, and sometimes without even a full crew. The war was a mess, the inmates were running the asylum, and people like Alex Coleman leapfrogged over their seniors to become captains.

He'd spotted the orders in message traffic an hour ago and almost choked on his late-night dessert. If *Bluefish* was underway, that meant Alex must've taken command. Wade Peterson wasn't exactly a loss to any submarine—he was a coward and a prickly grandmother—but why the navy saw fit to give Chris's old XO a second boat, Chris didn't know. Worse yet, *Bluefish* was a *Cero*-class submarine, the newest and best class the navy had to offer. Granted, *Bluefish* wasn't an Improved *Cero*, but she was still newer than Chris's own *Kansas*. And she was certainly newer than *Jimmy Carter*, the death trap the navy sentenced Alex to in the first place.

Yet that damned old boat—the one Alex hadn't even deserved, not after the stunt he'd pulled as Chris's XO!—had let Alex win the Medal of Honor. The *Medal of Honor*. Even thinking about it rankled. The rat bastard surpassed Chris's twelve kills in one day, rocketing himself to the top of the standings. Only Ursula North, the British superstar, stood above him.

They called *her* the Sea Witch. Apparently, North was an ironclad bitch. Was that what it took? Coleman was a piece of work, too. Maybe he'd get an insulting nickname, someday.

It wouldn't come soon enough.

Chris resisted the urge to snarl only in case someone was watching. No one had expected a war like this. Even when the Rush to the Ocean Floor started in 2034, no one had expected competition for undersea resources to add fuel to age-old territorial disputes. Minor shooting incidents at sea were supposed to be brushed away by the giant hand of diplomacy, but a series of supposedly unrelated provocations—including a wily French intelligence operative setting *Kansas* up to take the fall for sinking a civilian submarine—ended in a shooting incident in the Strait of Malacca.

Then diplomacy collapsed, and here they were.

"You're up late, Captain."

Chris turned to find his third XO approaching. Lieutenant Commander Mei Song had been with him for almost a year, and she was the best XO Chris ever had. Alex... Well, his attitude and disregard for orders said enough about him. Then the next one had been insufficiently aggressive. Allison had been a nice woman, and good on the administrative side, but Chris wanted an XO who would back him to the hilt. Mei tackled every challenge with enthusiasm and was in lockstep with her captain.

"I'm contemplating the eccentricities of the universe," he replied after a moment, trying not to frown too deeply.

Song cocked her head. "You mean why someone so lackluster that they gave him *Jimmy Carter* winds up being heralded as a hero, sir?"

"Something of that sort." Chris would never badmouth another CO, not even to his own XO. But he saw no reason to correct her, either.

"I suppose they're right when they say luck plays a part in these things." She shrugged. "Otherwise, we would have had better hunting."

"If there were any fairness in the world, yes." Chris tried not to grit his teeth. "Unfortunately, no one ever said war was fair."

"More's the pity."

It wasn't Chris's fault that he'd been handed dry patrol area after dry patrol area over the last year. Oh, *Kansas* had sunk a merchant convoy and a few scattered freighters, but fame came from facing off against warships. He'd started the war off well enough, with ten kills in the first eighteen months, but 2039 had been almost dry of warship kills. But it wasn't his fault! Enemy submarines and surface ships didn't come close enough to Perth. Idiot planners insisted on keeping *Kansas* closer to shore because she wasn't one of the shiny new *Ceroes*. All Chris needed was one stellar patrol. That could put him on top, but no one would give him one.

And that would keep him from ever achieving flag rank. His scowl returned. John Dalton got his chance to shine with *Razorback*. Where was his?

No one had ever handed him a target-rich environment like the Third Battle of the Strait of Malacca. If they had, Chris knew he'd have done at least as well as Dalton, and then *he'd* be the one with two Navy Crosses and the future as an admiral. Sitting on the sidelines when he knew he could do better stung, particularly when his defiant former XO sported a Medal of Honor. Dalton, at least, was an academy graduate and a gentleman. Alex Coleman was neither.

"Maybe it's time we made our own luck." The words were out before he could stop them.

"Sir?"

Did he really want to suggest this? Song would be on his side, Chris was sure. She wanted glory, too. They were both ambitious, and Chris wasn't the type to keep his XO from sharing the limelight. He frowned. "We'll have to see what our next patrol area is."

"And if it's more of the same?" Song asked.

"Then perhaps we have to be a little eccentric."

Chris wasn't going to say more. Not yet. Maybe someone at Planning would give them a different assignment, and if that was the case, he wasn't going to stick his neck out. Leaving their assigned operations area was technically a violation of regulations, but if Alex Coleman could get away with ignoring things like that, there was no reason he couldn't. With XO on his side... Well, logs could be edited.

Christopher Atticus Kennedy could go down in history, too.

Bluefish submerged and set the normal underway watch just after one in the morning. Bobby was dead tired, but he stuck around in control long enough to make sure that the officer of the deck wouldn't do something idiotic and humiliate them. Unfortunately, Lieutenant (junior grade) Rene Shorn was the oncoming OOD, and he looked almost as hungover as Harri Ainsworth. But Bobby didn't dare ask what the hell was going on with the new captain watching.

Peterson would have bitten someone's head off by now, but Captain Coleman just watched quietly, a cup of coffee in his hand. Finally, the new guy left, and Bobby eyed Coleman's back as their new CO disappeared into his stateroom. Rose, smart soul that she was, had already made sure that his network and email accounts were set up—she'd driven their chief electronics technician mad that afternoon—so hopefully there was nothing Coleman could find fault with. Maybe he'd even go to sleep and give them a quiet night. At least the navigation plan that Bobby and Rene drew up was solid, and

Coleman seemed okay with proceeding at best speed after the convoy. Peterson would have wibbled.

"Call me if anything comes up, okay?" Bobby knew he was fretting, but Rene's third cup of coffee didn't seem to be helping the way his feet dragged.

"You got it, Nav." Rene grinned. "I won't break the boat. Promise."

Bobby groaned before heading out of control. He took a quick spin around the boat. A *Cero* was only 389 feet long and had just three decks; even Bobby didn't need more than an hour to check everywhere. By the time he returned to his stateroom, Rose was there. Lou, his roommate, was sprawled on the top rack, pretending to read a book. Neither looked tired.

Sighing, Bobby dropped into his desk chair. "This is fun."

Rose snorted. "I find the lack of nitpicking disturbing."

"I didn't even get a call in Maneuvering." Lou chuckled. "I'm not used to being left alone to do my job."

"Yeah, it was weird in control." Bobby grimaced. "He didn't even try to teach Rosie the difference between right and left. She needs that, you know."

"Bobby, you're a dick." The insult was conversational, if drained. "But you're right. It was weird."

"If we're lucky, it's a sign of things to come." Lou untangled himself from his pillow and rolled over, tucking his tablet away on a shelf.

Rose rolled her eyes. "*Bluefish* is never that lucky."

"Hate to say it, roomie, but I'm with her," Bobby replied.

Lou shrugged.

Bobby hadn't known Lou as long as Rose, but he'd become one of Bobby's closest friends. The previous engineer had been Bobby's roommate, too, and they tolerated one another...usually. Except when he cut his toenails when Bobby was sleeping and left shards all over the deck. So, yeah, the last guy's firing left Bobby relieved. Lou was competent, friendly, and unflappable. All of which they'd needed under Peterson. He was also tall enough that his college advisors told him to choose *any* specialty other than submarines. A star basketball player at Tulane, he could've gone pro. Lou chose the navy instead.

Rose turned Lou's dark skin and height inside out. Shorter than Bobby by a head, she was blond, petite, and a fireball of energy. Lou approached problems with a calm even Peterson liked. Rose attacked them like enemies who needed murdering. Bobby, however, landed between the two. He was fit enough, and he liked to run when being acting XO didn't eat all his free time. Playing sports was better, but that wasn't an option on a submarine. *Bluefish's* treadmills were an okay way to work the edge off, but he'd seen little of them lately.

Maybe that would change with a new captain.

Bluefish swept forward into the night, steaming at over forty knots. That was faster than her best silent speed, but advances in sonar technology and sound dampening meant she was neither deaf nor blind. *Bluefish's* systems screened out her own noise, allowing the sub to keep a firm contact picture of the surrounding ocean. At this speed, they'd catch up with Convoy 3791 by early morning.

Bobby contemplated staying awake in case something went wrong, but once the stress bled off, he decided to hit his rack. He'd wake up jittery in the morning, but some shut-eye was better than none.

Alex didn't bother with sleep. His body still thought it was one in the afternoon. Experience told him the best way to sync himself with local time was to push through and stay awake until tomorrow night. So he grabbed a second cup of coffee from the wardroom and went to work. The computer in the captain's stateroom was set up with an account and password waiting for him, so Alex started by shooting an email off to his wife.

Hey Nance,

So I've got a little more news on the new boat than I had when I left. The good news is that Bluefish *is exactly as advertised, at least on the surface. They gave me a three-year-old* Cero-*class this time. My new baby can't even vote, let alone drink! Of course, she's got an embarrassing combat record with fewer kills than* Jimmy Carter *had even before Convoy 57, along with a reputation of avoiding every fight that she gets a sniff of. That's a big hill to climb, but hey, apparently I'm in the big leagues now.*

Best news is that we're homeported out of Perth, so I hope I'll see you soon. I miss you like crazy, but you knew that.

The bad news is that I'm already underway for a convoy escort. I did about a million of these things with Jimmy Carter, *though it was a bit of a surprise to get underway 5.2 seconds after taking command. More on that later. The other bad news is that there's something dysfunctional on this boat. I almost expected the crew to run away screaming when I arrived, and I'm hardly the most imposing guy you'll ever meet. I never met my predecessor, but something's wrong.*

The girls send their love, and your mom's still trying not to worry about your health. Stop skipping doctor's appointments, will you? Bobbie is still pushing for the three-year track at the academy, and I think Emily is serious about wanting to be a lawyer. She's still got a year to figure it out, but she's starting to talk about Norwich and...

Alex went on to tell a story about his brother, a Connecticut state trooper, chasing a would-be bank robber. Email was the way he'd shared news with his wife for the last year; during the war; he and Nancy saw each other less often than they wanted. They'd both chosen to stay in the navy, even after the war started, but that didn't make the separations easier. And both being in command made it even harder.

Nancy's destroyer, USS *Fletcher*, was still up on the blocks in drydock after taking damage from a "surrendering" French destroyer that exploded when *Fletcher* came alongside. Unfortunately, the private shipyard repairing Nancy's ship was about thirty kilometers north of HMAS Stirling, commonly known as Naval Base Perth. Alex knew that extra distance popped yet another challenge in their path...along with giving Nancy an excuse to skip her medical appointments.

Damn that stubborn woman he'd married. Alex loved her to bits, but she had a habit of being in the thick of the action. Not that he could cast stones, not after Convoy 57. Weren't they a pair?

Shaking his head, Alex clicked send and marveled at how the email went out almost right away. On *Jimmy Carter*, they'd had to go shallow for periodic uploads, but this boat was built for the twenty-first century. Their connectivity wasn't as good as what Nancy got on a surface ship, but this was still better than he was used to. Better yet, it was nearly impossible to detect a modern submarine while she transmitted, even at depths near eight hundred feet. *Nearly.* Unlike many of his contemporaries, Alex didn't put much faith in that. It was another thing he needed to address here on *Bluefish.*

Yeah, that was a good place to start. Alex opened his predecessor's standing orders and frowned. Every commanding officer personalized them from the same basic template, but these were abnormally long. Scratching his head, Alex flipped through the first dozen pages. Damn. Was this guy the biggest micromanager on the planet? Commander Peterson vomited nervous ego all over the pages. Requiring reports on friendly contacts every thirty minutes? Prohibiting watchstanders from answering external communications without the captain's permission? This was ludicrous. They were at *war*.

"Fuck me sideways," Alex breathed.

Updating his old standing orders from *Jimmy Carter* would be easier than editing this insanity out, even though the two boats had little in common. Groaning, Alex opened a new document and started typing.

Naval Base Pearl Harbor, Hawaii

"Freddie, I owe you an apology."

The words stunned the recipient—five thousand miles away in Norfolk, Virginia—into silence. "Are you all right?"

Marco Rodriquez laughed. "Better than you're about to be."

"This had better be pressing enough to interrupt my lunch."

"It's past two your time." He snorted. "Proper admirals eat at noon."

"So-called proper admirals don't spend all morning with the CNO talking about sub losses," his Atlantic counterpart retorted. Vice Admiral Marco Rodriquez was COMSUBPAC, the commander of all submarines in the Pacific Ocean. Vice Admiral Winifred Hamilton—Freddie, but only to her friends—was COMSUBLANT. That job also made her COMSUBFOR, Commander Submarine Forces, which meant she was the senior submariner in the navy. She was also sort of his boss.

"I suppose it can fucking wait."

It was just past eight a.m. in Honolulu, and Marco had been at *his* desk since just after six. He drove his staff mad; half of them wished they worked for Freddie Hamilton and half were marking time until Marco died of exhaustion. *She* was the politic one, the bright and shining star with four stars and a fleet written in her future. Maybe Freddie would become the chief of naval operations, someday. Marco Rodriquez made his third star when his predecessor as COMSUBPAC suffered an attack of the stupids and they needed someone who could handle pressure.

"If you say that, it's important. What in the world are you apologizing for?"

"I poached a captain." Marco started disassembling a pen. "Technically, he's more mine than yours, but since I twisted BUPERS into knots to steal him, I thought I should tell you."

Freddie sighed. "We have a personnel system for a reason."

"They're still shoveling shit out of the stables." Marco rolled his eyes. "Pull the other one."

"What did you do?" She didn't argue with his assessment, Marco noted. No one knew better than the navy's senior submariners that the detailing process couldn't keep up with submarines sinking left and right. It had a hard enough time scraping together crews for every new submarine.

"Put Alex Coleman in command of *Bluefish*."

"You *what*?" The sound of a jaw dropping was audible from five thousand miles away.

"Wade Peterson's appendix burst, and he's out for the count. Never was much fucking good, anyway. The man's as inspiring as a paper bag full of dogshit. We need a win."

"Not with him, we don't!"

"I know you don't like the man, Freddie, but even you agreed with giving him the Medal of Honor. No one's come *close* what he did with *Jimmy Carter*."

"No one else has come so close to destroying a submarine short of sinking it, either," she retorted.

"Yeah, but they fucking came back. He's been on leave for two months. That's too long to leave someone like him on the beach."

"Assuming he's not a one-shot wonder who'll go to pieces the second time around," Freddie said.

"So what if he is?" Marco shrugged. "We're not losing a damned thing. *Bluefish* hasn't done jack shit so far."

Freddie groaned. "I wish I disagreed with you."

"Glad to hear it! They got underway on Christmas Eve." Marco grinned when he heard her swear under her breath.

Yeah, Freddie didn't like Alex Coleman. Marco knew why: she hated cowboys. Coleman's actions at Armistice Station in 2037 might've been *right*, but he'd disobeyed orders. He'd been on Freddie's shit list ever since. Under normal circumstances, Marco might've agreed, but this war was anything but normal.

Judging from *Jimmy Carter's* video and audio logs, Coleman was a sound tactician and wouldn't hide when shit hit the fan. He'd also been damned lucky. Marco wasn't blind to the risks. *Jimmy Carter* was more durable than any other submarine in the American arsenal. If Coleman trashed *Bluefish* like he had *Jimmy Carter*, that *Cero*-class boat would break open like an egg. The navy needed someone like Alex Coleman, so Marco sent him back out again, but they needed him to take the fight to the enemy without getting his boat killed in the process.

Chapter 4

Logs in the Water

Rose was on watch, which meant Bobby felt safe going to breakfast. He was surprised to see Captain Coleman there; Peterson typically demanded breakfast delivered to his stateroom instead of eating with his underlings. Coleman, however, sat in the CO's seat at the end of the wardroom table, flipping through a tactical publication on a tablet while the other officers ate and talked.

"Mind if I join you, Captain?" Bobby asked, trying not to fidget. Tradition required asking the senior person at the table, regardless of their rank, but somehow having a new captain present made the idea anxiety-inducing.

Coleman waved him into a seat without a word, never even looking up. Gulping, Bobby plopped into an empty seat. Peterson—if he'd been there—would have said something cutting before Bobby ordered breakfast. Coleman just sipped his coffee and continued reading, oblivious to the wary-but-curious looks the junior officers shot his way. Bobby finished his breakfast in a hurry, throwing Lou a glance so that he ushered the younger officers out. Once the door closed behind Lou, Bobby cleared his throat.

"Uh, Captain?"

"Yeah?" Coleman looked up from the tablet, peering at Bobby over the reading glasses perched on his nose.

"Commander Peterson always wanted me to meet with him every morning so he could give me a work list." Bobby bit his lip. "And so he could, uh, 'set the pace' for the day."

"Did he." The glasses came off; Coleman sat back in his chair to study him.

Bobby fidgeted. "Yes, sir."

Coleman's face went blank. Had Bobby offended him? Already? *How*? The captain answered: "Today, sure. After that, you don't strike me as an idiot. Are you?"

"Well, no. but I'm also not really the XO." Bobby knew that Peterson had micromanaged the old XO, too, but had it been this much? Peterson made at least a dozen requests for a "real" XO, but Bobby was still here.

"You're what we've got." Coleman's smile was wry. "I'll trust you to do the job unless you prove you can't."

"Aye, sir." It sounded too good to be true, but—

The wardroom phone rang, and Coleman picked it up before Bobby reached for it. "Captain." Coleman listened. "I'm on my way."

Bobby jackrabbited to his feet. Why would Rose call in the middle of breakfast? There was almost nothing that pissed Peterson off more, unless it was waking him up, which his standing orders always required they do. In fact—*Crap.* Coleman got halfway out the door while Bobby fretted. Scrambling after him, Bobby followed his new captain up a ladder and forward into the submarine's command-and-control center. Control was *Bluefish's* beating heart, where the crew fought and navigated the sub. Right now, there was an air of tension in the air impossible to miss.

Rose was the officer of the deck, and Bobby knew her well enough to know that she was ready to jump out of her skin. With Rose, that meant she hoped action was imminent; she ached to make a difference even more than Bobby. Of course, with Peterson, their chances never panned out.

"What d'you got, OOD?" Coleman's brisk question made Bobby blink; Peterson was always formal in demanding reports.

"One of the civilian ships in the convoy reported seeing a periscope a few minutes ago, Captain," Rose replied. "It might be nothing, but I thought you'd want to know."

Coleman shoved his hands in his pockets. "Any other Alliance subs assigned this area?"

Rose shook her head. "No, sir. I checked."

"Nothing from sonar?"

"Not yet." Rose was braced to be yelled at, but Coleman just nodded, glancing down at the tactical plot. Unwilling to start fidgeting and unable to stop himself from pacing, Bobby headed over to sonar. It was just a little closet off control, closed by a curtain instead of a proper door. That curtain was open, so Bobby wandered in. STS2 Walkman was the senior sonar operator on watch, and Bobby touched her shoulder.

"Got anything, Walkman?"

"Not really, sir, but we're still aft of the convoy. It would help if we had the tail out, but..."

"Yeah." Bobby swallowed. Peterson never wanted to put out *Bluefish's* towed sonar array. The "tail" was a long string of hydrophones, a way of extending their passive, or listening, sonar reach. Subs depended upon passive sonar more often than active; active sonar involved pinging at their target, which everyone in the vicinity would hear.

Walkman glanced over her shoulder toward their new captain, whose eyes remained fastened on the plot. Coleman was chewing on the earpiece of his glasses, too.

"You think the new captain might let us stream the tail, sir?" Walkman asked.

"Maybe." Bobby wiggled. Unfortunately, it was his job to ask. No one else wanted to, and Bobby was still acting XO. "Gimme a sec."

Grimacing, Bobby turned away from sonar and back toward the captain. Coleman still looked thoughtful, but Peterson was good at looking like he wouldn't bite your head off, too. Bobby wiped his hands on his coveralls. All he had to do was do his job. He was good at that, right? Bobby believed that before he came to *Bluefish*. He cleared his throat.

"Uh, Captain, you want to stream the tail?"

This was where the lecture started. *Why would you want me to take such a risk, Mr. O'Kane? I'm sure even your limited understanding stretches to comprehending the fact that streaming the towed sonar array creates* noise, *and any noise can be deadly with an unknown enemy out there. No, we will remain covert and silent as doctrine dictates.* The accompanying glare always told Bobby that he was amoeba who'd amount to nothing and knew nothing about how to fight a submarine.

"Good call." Coleman turned to Rose before Bobby could comprehend the words. Had he just been complimented? "Officer of the Deck, stream the tail to a short stay."

"Stream the tail, aye, sir!" Rose lit up like the proverbial Christmas tree and relayed the orders to sonar.

Bobby tried not to sag in relief. Streaming the towed array wasn't that noisy. Sure, someone might hear it if they were close enough or sonar conditions were perfect, but Peterson still hadn't been okay with taking that chance.

A few minutes later, the tail deployed to its minimum length. They could string a half mile of hydrophones out in their wake, but doctrine said that was a bad idea if you were about to go into combat. Would they find something to shoot at? No way. Control was quiet as the sonar picture settled out. Volunteering unnecessary comments wasn't in vogue on *Bluefish.* No one wanted to be the first one to speak up.

"So this probably isn't the most opportune moment to ask, but I didn't see the convoy brief on the share drive. Are there any other escorts?" Captain Coleman asked.

"No, sir." Bobby wanted to smack himself. "We're it."

"Shocker." He turned to Rose. "All right, let's work our way around to the right. If *Emma Maersk* saw an actual periscope—and not a figment of someone's overworked imagination—relative motion says that's our best bet of finding it."

"Aye, sir."

Rose conned the submarine that way before glancing at Bobby. He met her eyes as Captain Coleman looked back down at the plot. Peterson would've been pissed because they hadn't found anything; their new CO was too quiet. It was unnerving.

"XO."

Bobby wished he could pace, but what would Captain Coleman think of that? Bad enough that they'd started by bonging him on wrong. Bobby'd gone and demoted the only living submariner Medal of Honor winner. Then he'd managed to forget to give the captain a copy of the convoy's details, making him appear uninformed in front of—

"Lieutenant O'Kane."

Bobby jumped. "Captain?"

"Let's have a chat." Coleman gestured, and Bobby followed him toward the hatch leading out of control.

"I'm sorry about the convoy formation message, sir," he said, wiping his hands on the legs of his coveralls. Again. "I should've made sure it was in your queue last night when you—"

"Never mind that." Coleman waved a hand. "At the rate this got laid on, it's a miracle you got me network access." His glasses went back on, and then his hands stuffed into his pockets. "But I could use a cheat sheet on *Ceros* if this goes in the crapper. I've never served on one."

"What?" Bobby hated the way his eyes went wide.

"It's been all *Virginias* and *Jimmy Carter* for me, I'm afraid." His new CO shrugged wryly. "I only know the basics."

"Oh. Um, I'm sure I can have someone put something together for you—probably out of the division officers' study guides, and, uh... Maybe an hour?" Crap. That meant he'd have to leave control, which was a bad idea if the captain wanted to hang around. Him and his big mouth.

"Sometime later today will be fine. For now, just give me the high points. Best silent speed, torpedo reloading time, and any other issues that might bite me in the ass."

Bobby blinked. "About twenty-eight knots, ten minutes, and the outboard always breaks." He paused for air. "The outboard is actually a huge problem. It never works." He hated admitting that, because he owned the thing, but *Bluefish's* bow thruster crapped out every few weeks. His people just couldn't figure out how to fix it.

"Is that the same outboard you traded away a sonar operator to get parts for?"

"Oh." Bobby's jaw dropped. Shit. "That...that was to *Jimmy Carter*."

Coleman laughed. "Yep."

Bobby wanted to sink into the floor. A little over a year ago, he and Master Chief Baker, the chief of the boat, conspired to trade a troublesome sonar operator for parts they *hoped* would fix the outboard. A frequently drunk, unfortunately creative, and *brawler* of a sonar man. And now the captain whose boat accepted said sonar man was his new boss.

Today couldn't get worse.

INS *Vagli* coasted along, shadowing the seven-ship American-Australian convoy from seven miles away. Captain Ranjeet Joshi had brought his *Requin*-E class submarine in close early on, just to see if he could spook any hidden escorts out of hiding. The *Requin*-Es were the export version of the French class of submarine Jules Rochambeau had made famous, slightly smaller and less powerful, but still a match for anything the Alliance had put in the water.

So far, no Alliance submarines had appeared, but he still waited. French Intelligence had a source that said the Americans thought themselves clever and were now only sending out single submarines to act as escorts for merchant convoys. That tactic was another strange example of the typical American combination of recklessness and procedure-following mania, and Ranjeet found it fascinating.

"Do we shoot, Captain?" his first officer asked, and Ranjeet forced himself not to scowl. Lieutenant Commander Kishan Kumar was a good officer, but he was new to *Vagli*.

"Not yet. I want to be certain there isn't an Alliance submarine guarding the convoy." Hopefully, an American. Shooting ancient Australian *Collins*-class diesel boats was easy in the open ocean, which was why the Australians kept them in the littorals. A *Collins* would struggle with the twenty-two knots this convoy moved at, anyway. Even the Australians' newer *Shortfins* lacked the longevity to keep up, although they did present more of a challenge for Ranjeet.

Kumar frowned. "Even one American could not keep us from sinking the entire convoy, sir."

"Of course not." Ranjeet chuckled. "But I don't particularly care about the convoy. Our orders are to find Alliance *warships* and sink them, not merchant ships. They're secondary targets."

He didn't bother mentioning that their government was more cautious about indiscriminately sinking merchant ships since the Battle of Samar Station, which the Alliance called Convoy 57. Those civilian ships had been passenger carriers, and while Ranjeet knew his government was after the Fogborne Research Team, the following media storm was regrettable. But that wasn't Ranjeet's concern. His job was to sink Alliance warships. If he could destroy another today, that would make two submarines this patrol.

"Surely we would have heard an American by now," Kumar objected.

"Perhaps." Ranjeet sighed, glancing at the sonar plot. "I went to their Naval War College before the war began, and I know their submariners. They're obsessed with procedure and convinced they are the best in the world. If there is an American SSN out there, they're running silent because they believe that will let them get the first shot in, no matter who we are."

"You're saying they don't know how quiet we are."

Ranjeet shook his head. "I'm saying that they're a bunch of old women. There is a reason why our navy—which has, sadly, no great submarine tradition—can hand them so many losses so easily."

"Our allies have helped with that," Kumar pointed out. He had trained with both the Russians and the French; Kumar was of the new generation, trained by India's current allies, not by the enemies who used to be her friends.

"They have, yes." Ranjeet had worked with those same allies, and he found many of them competent. The French were arrogant but cutthroat, and the new crop of Russians were innovative. They'd had to scrape out a new naval tradition out of the USSR's rust, just as Ranjeet and his fellows built one on their own.

But they'd done well. Ranjeet and *Vagli* had accounted for multiple surface ships, three Australian *Collins*-class submarines, one Australian *Shortfin*, and two American *Virginias* in just the last year. That, combined with his kills in the first year of the war, put him second on the list of warship tonnage killed by Indian submarine commanders. He was third amongst the Freedom Union, too, after India's own Avani Patel and—of course—that French hotshot, Jules Rochambeau. Rochambeau, however, was the best submarine commander in the world. Ranjeet didn't mind falling behind him. Patel, on the other hand... Perhaps he would overtake her this patrol.

"How long do we wait, Captain?" Kumar interrupted his thoughts.

"Let's give them one more chance to know we are here. Perhaps that merchant ship failed to notice our periscope." Ranjeet smiled. "Take us up one more time, Kishan. If no American shows himself, we will sink the convoy."

He wouldn't let a prime target like this go. Not when these ships were transporting iron ore to the United States so that annoyingly massive economy could build more warships to send against his country.

"You're a lifesaver, Harri." Bobby slumped against the bulkhead, thinking fondly of his rack. He'd left control to find a helpful division officer; luckily, Harri was awake and closer to sober than last night.

Bobby was *not* asking about that. Whatever made *Bluefish's* best division officers lose their minds and disregard the no-drinking rule wasn't a problem now with Peterson gone. Bobby didn't want to buy trouble. So he just leaned against the doorway to the stateroom Harri shared with three others and tried to act normal.

"I never figured that the captain would need my dolphin study guide, but hey, it's a crazy war." Harri grinned.

"You can say that about a million times," Bobby breathed. "Thanks."

"No problem, Nav. Or are you the XO, now?"

"Honestly? I've got no idea. I think I'm still Acting Most Things. Which is to say that I'm both." He was babbling again. Getting out of control didn't help Bobby's nerves. Nor had drinking another cup of coffee.

The problem was that the captain was still in control. Could Rose handle a cranky captain without flying off the handle after the way Peterson usually needled her? Coleman seemed more levelheaded, but Bobby had to get him the information he'd asked for. *Bluefish* needed a win with the new CO.

Hell, how unlucky were they? They got the captain that they sent the Menace to! Wilson. The chronic drunk who'd rented a car just to drive it off the end of the pier so he could swim out with scuba gear on. Rose would have kittens once she heard. STS1 Wilson had been her personal headache. Peterson had wanted to kick him out of the navy, but Master Chief Baker had talked him into sending Wilson to *Jimmy Carter*, instead.

Bobby bet Coleman had kicked him out of the navy. No way was Wilson along for Convoy 57—

Harri's stateroom phone rang, cutting into Bobby's thoughts. She answered but extended it to Bobby immediately. "It's Weps."

"Nav." Bobby tried to swallow the lump in his throat. "What's cooking?"

"*Emma Maersk* says she saw another periscope." Rose sounded ready to scream. "And I *really* want to tell them how fucking stupid they are."

"That's not real politic, Rosie."

"Don't call me that," she snapped. "Seriously, how many fake periscopes can they see in one watch?"

"At least one more?" Bobby sighed. "I'll be there in a sec, okay? Have you told the captain?"

"No. He left about twenty minutes ago, and I was relishing the peace and quiet."

"I'll tell him." Peterson would've had a fit if anyone neglected to tell him, but he'd also have a prissy little tantrum of you-should-have-known-better if the periscope sighting turned out to be a log. Bobby really hated being acting XO.

"That's what they pay you the big bucks for, right?" Rose's voice was light, but he could hear her relief.

"Yeah, except for the fact that I'm still a lieutenant making the same pay as you," he said. "I'll see you in a sec."

"Aye." Rose hung up.

Bobby handed the phone back to Harri, who asked:

"So how's the new captain so far? He seemed...nicer than Commander Peterson."

"Your guess is as good as mine at this point." Bobby sucked in a deep breath. "But you remember Wilson, right?"

Harri snorted. "Yeah, I was the unfortunate division officer who always got to tell the captain about the trouble he got in."

"Right. Well...do you remember what boat we sent him to?"

"*Jimmy*— Oh, shit."

"Yep! Makes the day great, doesn't it?" Bobby threw her a grin. "I've got to go earn my lordly salary, though, so try not to emulate him, will you?"

"Nav, I'm not—"

"If you think I can't spot a hangover when I see one, kiddo, you're dumber than my two-year-old nephew." Bobby paused, and Harri bit her lip. "You've just used your one and only get-out-of-jail-free card."

"Yes, sir." Harri was too smart to argue, so Bobby headed to forward toward the captain's stateroom.

It was a short walk, which at least meant that his stomach couldn't churn up breakfast. Maybe he had a fifty-fifty chance of not being yelled at? That was a happy thought. It was probably a stupid log, anyway. Even surface warships called in logs as periscopes. What were the odds that a container ship had seen two today? Not good, that was for sure.

The door to the captain's stateroom was propped open. That was a surprise.

"Um, Captain?" Bobby knew he was fidgeting, and it took a huge effort not to start playing with the stateroom doorknob. Fortunately, Coleman glanced up from the computer quickly.

"What's up?"

"I just talked to the OOD. She says *Emma Maersk* reported another periscope sighting." *Cue disapproving glare in three...two...*

Coleman's eyes narrowed. "Is there a reason she didn't call me?"

"It didn't come up?" How could you say that your old CO was someone that no OOD wanted to call? Bobby was used to being the guy who stole the strawberries.

"I see." Obviously, the captain didn't buy it, but he didn't argue. Instead, he rose and gestured aft, toward control. "Let's go check it out."

"Yes, sir." Bobby fought the urge to swallow. "I mean, it's probably nothing—probably a stupid log—but I guess it pays to look, right? Even if *Emma Maersk* is paranoid."

"Either that, or someone's screwing with us," Coleman replied, darting up the ladder.

Bobby's stomach rolled. "That's not very nice of someone."

Attack submarines were sleeker than they were large, so they reached control within a minute, Bobby still on the captain's heels.

"Captain's in the conn!" the chief of the watch sang out.

"Carry on." Coleman headed over toward the plot, and Bobby tagged along, afraid of what a frustrated Rose might say.

"Sir, *Emma Maersk* called again. They're insistent that they saw a periscope. I dropped a datum in the system at that location, but sonar's hearing nothing," she reported.

Coleman frowned. "Still on the same side of the convoy?"

"No, sir." Rose shook her head. "First sighting was just to the right of base course. Second one's to the left."

"Sounds like that's one hell of log, then." Coleman smiled wryly, pulling up data on the plot for the maneuvering solution. "Particularly if it's moving around fifteen knots."

Fifteen knots made a good silent speed for a submarine, Bobby knew. *Bluefish* wasn't going much faster than that. What were the odds of finding two logs out here in the southern Indian Ocean? The watch on *Emma Maersk* could have excellent imaginations, but—

"I think we've got a customer. Let's go to battle stations."

Bobby jumped. He'd been busy bracing himself for a tirade on the ineptitude of merchant captains, not a fight. Shaking himself, he walked over to relieve Rose. He was still the navigator, despite being Acting Most Things, which meant he had the deck at battle stations. His only consolation was that Rose looked as surprised as he did.

The donging sound of the general alarm sounded as Rose headed over to the weapons consoles, the chief of the watch's voice ringing out over the 1MC, or general announcing system. "*Man Battle Stations, Torpedo.*" The alarm rang for several seconds. "*Man Battle Stations, Torpedo.*"

The words repeated; Bobby ignored it, watching their new captain. His eyes were on the plot, unblinking and unflinching. *He did win the Medal of Honor for sinking an ungodly number of ships,* Bobby reminded himself. Commander Peterson was always nervous, afraid that shooting at the wrong thing might make him look bad. Captain Coleman probably didn't have a problem like that. *Even if he did trash his own submarine while he was busy shooting.* Bobby shuddered, remembering what *Jimmy Carter* had looked like pulling into Perth. Submarines usually *sank* with fewer holes.

Master Chief Baker, *Bluefish's* chief of the boat and senior enlisted sailor, stepped up next to Bobby. She was the diving officer at battle stations, and like Bobby, she'd been on *Bluefish* for over a year. She was also one of the few people who ever stood up to Peterson, even at his worst. "Battle stations manned and ready, Nav."

"Great." Bobby tried to smile while butterflies danced a samba around his small intestine.

"Left standard rudder, steady course two-three-zero. Ahead full for twenty-eight knots," Coleman ordered.

"Left standard rudder, steady course two-three-zero, aye," the helmsman, ET1 Yacono repeated. "My rudder is left fifteen degrees, coming to course two-three-zero. Ahead full for twenty-eight knots."

"Very well." Coleman let out a breath before reaching for the radio. Bobby blinked; Peterson always made someone else talk on the Convoy Command channel. Sometimes, he refused to talk to surface ships at all. "All ships, this is"—Coleman cut off, twisting to look at Bobby and taking his finger off the talk button. "What the hell is our callsign?"

Shit. "Silent Night, sir."

"All ships, this is Silent Night. Come right to new course three-one-five, increase speed to twenty-five knots."

The six ships of the convoy acknowledged the command, turning right as *Bluefish* hung a left underneath them. Assuming there was an enemy submarine out there, the maneuver put *Bluefish* between the civilians and the enemy, still running silently. Bobby burned to ask sonar if they had anything, but Peterson would have—

"Weps, make tubes one through eigh—shit, *four*—ready in all respects." Coleman hissed between clenched teeth. "Do not open the outer doors."

"Weps, aye." Rose grinned.

"Diving Officer, make your depth six hundred feet. Officer of the Deck, rig ship for ultra-quiet."

Bobby acknowledged the order, and *Bluefish's* deck sloped downward.

Chapter 5

One Shot Wonder

"I think I have something, Captain," INS *Vagli's* sonar officer reported. "Bearing about zero-seven-five. Submerged contact."

Ranjeet turned to Kumar with a smile. "It appears I was right."

"Indeed, Captain." Kumar's eyes gleamed. He was excited to be here, excited to take the war to the enemy. The Americans were once considered the best submariners in the world. *No more.*

"Set the shot up," Ranjeet ordered and watched his crew race to comply. He'd drilled them mercilessly over the last two years. *Vagli* was a well-oiled machine.

"Do you think it's a *Cero* or a *Virginia*, Captain?" Kumar asked.

Ranjeet shrugged. "I would prefer a *Cero*."

The American *Ceros* were newer submarines, and their loss hurt his enemy more than sinking a *Virginia*. But both classes had four torpedo tubes to his eight, and *Vagli's* weapons room still held thirty-two torpedoes, more than either of his enemies could carry. That was plenty to finish one pesky American submarine. Ranjeet only regretted there were not more of them.

Still, there was always the next patrol.

"Contact fading," sonar reported. "Tonals indicate a *Cero*-class submarine, but I cannot determine bearing or range. They're quiet, Captain."

"Hm." Ranjeet frowned. That remained something the Americans excelled at; they no longer built the deadliest submarines in the ocean, but they remained quiet. The Russians' *Yasens* were equal to the *Ceros*, and the French *Requins* perhaps better, but Ranjeet's own export *Requin-E* didn't have all the bells and whistles of their larger sisters. The French liked to keep *some* secrets from their allies, didn't they? He scowled. His enemy would hear him first if the American did not change speed, and the cautious Americans rarely exceeded their own best silent speed.

Ranjeet would have to change the equation.

It was worth the risk. He would have to be ready to shoot immediately, but hopefully he could surprise the American. After all, he wanted them looking for his submarine, and now the enemy was. It would not do to become shy at this late date.

"Go active, sonar," he ordered. "Flush him out."

"Conn, Sonar, active sonar bearing two-eight-zero, range approximately thirteen thousand yards!"

Alex's head snapped up. He couldn't afford to shoot at a friend. There weren't supposed to be any other Alliance subs here, but it paid to be sure. He hit the talk lever on the squawk box hard enough to hurt his finger. "Sonar type?"

"MGK-540, sir!" The young petty officer at sonar looked excited through the open curtain. Seeing her face was weird; back on *Jimmy Carter*, the sonar room had a door.

No time for that.

"Snapshot tube one, bearing two-eight-zero!"

A snapshot was a submarine's equivalent of a fire-and-forget missile; it was aimed down the threat bearing, shot, and then the torpedo did the work. *Bluefish* carried the same torpedoes as his last command, the Mark 84 ASV, or Advanced

Spearfish Variant. A merger between an American warhead and accuracy with British speed, the ASV had become the go-to for the entire Alliance. It wasn't the fastest torpedo in the world, but the Mark 84 was probably the smartest. Even with no guidance from *Bluefish*, the torpedo had a good chance of finding this enemy. The MGK-540 sonar suite was on late-model *Akulas* and on the *Requin-Es*. Both boats had tough hulls, but an ASV would bust them right open.

But his boat hadn't fired.

"Is there a problem, Weps?" Alex asked and then didn't give Lieutenant Lange a chance to answer, twisting back to the helmsman. "Left full rudder, steady course two-five-five."

The helmsman repeated the command and brought the submarine sweeping into a turn. That course meant *Bluefish* could close the *Akula* without paralleling it and wouldn't limit Alex to just firing tubes from one side. Alex had no idea how much of an off-bore firing capability a *Cero* had. Since he'd already been stupid enough to forget how many tubes his boat had, Alex didn't feel like making more rookie blunders.

"Captain, the firing key isn't here." Lange's face was white.

Alex's head whipped around to face her so fast his neck cracked. "Say again?"

"Commander Peterson used to keep it locked up, sir." That was O'Kane, who looked sick. Hell, half of the crew did—what the hell kind of jerk *had* his predecessor been?

"Conn, Sonar, torpedo in the water, bearing two-seven-zero!" Now the sonar watch sounded panicked. "*Second* torpedo in the water, bearing two-six-eight! Range twelve thousand yards!"

The first shots someone took at you were the hardest to handle; how was his heart only pounding at a thousand or so beats a minute, instead of hammering right out of his chest? Maybe it was easier the second time around. "Ahead flank! Hard left rudder, steady course zero-nine-two!"

Bluefish banked harder, and Alex felt the deck vibrating under his feet as his sub came around to match the torpedoes' course.

"Stand by countermeasures!" O'Kane ordered, and Alex gave him a quick nod.

"Sonar, what's the closing speed on those fish?" he asked.

"Um, system thinks it's about sixty knots, sir."

"Very well," Alex replied. A *Cero's* top speed was almost that high. With a six-mile head start, he'd outrun the torpedoes. Even accounting for the time it took *Bluefish* to turn, the torpedoes would run out of gas before they could make up those six miles. Shit, he was lucky the *Requin-E* hadn't gotten closer before firing.

To be fair to the Indian, they'd gone active because they hadn't known where *Bluefish* was. But Alex wasn't interested in being fair to the enemy. He swung to face his acting XO.

"Where the hell is the firing key?" Usually, firing keys were locked in the weapons safe—right there in control—while in port. Alex heard of COs who didn't want to bring it out unless combat was likely, but they were in the middle of World War III. When the hell *wasn't* combat likely?

"I, uh, think it's in the safe in your stateroom, sir." O'Kane gulped, wearing a kicked-puppy look that told Alex he expected to get his head ripped off.

Don't shoot the messenger, Alex told himself. "I assume you know the combo?"

O'Kane shook his head miserably. "The old XO did, but Commander Peterson told me I didn't need to."

"Well, fuck me sideways." Alex managed not to groan. "Too bad we can't step outside and call his cell phone. Anyone here an expert safe cracker?"

Uneasy laughter trickled around the space, but no one spoke. Not that he'd expected them to. This crew was too scared to volunteer for anything short of a winning lotto ticket. Alex wanted to smash his face into the periscope stand. Instead, he leaned into the squawk box, pushing the lever down to "talk."

"Maneuvering, Conn."

"Maneuvering, aye," was the immediate response from his engineer. He seemed competent in the thirty seconds of interaction Alex shared with him, but now was hardly the time to figure any of this out.

Thanks for the great Christmas present, Uncle Marco, he wanted to say. *I'm going to have to write you a card if this* Requin *doesn't get smart and sink me.*

"I'm need you to send someone with a PECU to my stateroom and cut the safe open," Alex said. A Portable Exothermic Cutting Unit was the navy's small version of a firefighter's jaws of life. The PECU was designed to cut through steel bulkheads and would make short work of his stateroom safe.

"Conn, Maneuvering, say again?"

"Steady course zero-nine-two," the helmsman interrupted. "Ahead flank for fifty-seven knots."

Bluefish might have had fewer tubes than *Jimmy Carter*, but she sure could sprint. Alex had never driven a submarine so fast. "Very well." He turned back to the squawk box. "I need the firing key. Get someone in there yesterday and destroy the fucking safe."

"Maneuvering, aye!"

Taking a deep breath, Alex asked sonar: "Torpedo range?"

"Eleven thousand yards, sir." Now the sonar chief answered. Alex really needed to learn her name. She was tall, dark, and lanky, wearing glasses, and wore a studious, no-nonsense expression.

"Very well." The Indian torpedoes were in a stern chase; *Bluefish* lost some ground when she turned, but now the torpedoes could only overtake her at about a hundred yards a minute. TEST 83 torpedoes had a range of thirteen nautical miles at sixty knots, which meant he only had to outrun them for thirteen minutes. They couldn't catch his boat before then, and the Indian CO had to know that—so what would he or she do?

The *Requin-E* had a top speed of something around fifty knots, which put the enemy a little short of *Bluefish's* top speed. Still, if the Indian CO sped up when he shot, he might be able to close the distance between them enough to get a hit in. And Alex couldn't maneuver crazily with two torpedoes in a stern chase. Doing that would let them cut a corner on him and get his boat sunk. Wouldn't that be a great way to cap off his first twelve hours in command?

There was nothing to like about this situation. He'd won the damned Medal of Honor for sinking enemy warships, and now Alex couldn't even pull the fucking trigger.

"Are we, uh, going to keep running, Captain?" O'Kane asked, gulping.

"Until those two fish run out of gas, we don't have a lot of options," Alex replied. "And until we can shoot back, we don't have a reason to look for another."

O'Kane's face closed off. "Yes, sir."

"You got a better idea?" Alex asked. He didn't know these people, but they were intelligent and well-trained. And traumatized by his predecessor. He couldn't afford to forget that gem. What the hell had he gotten himself into? Alex wished he'd asked more questions when he'd agreed to this assignment.

"Um. No?" O'Kane looked back at him with wide eyes.

"Pity. We could use a little crazy right now."

The look that earned him was almost comical in its terror.

Minutes ticked by; Alex watched the clock, doing math in his head and trying to ignore his bone-dry throat. The Indian torpedoes had five minutes of gas left, assuming they had the same capabilities as the ones he'd faced in October.

The silence in control was eerie; most of the crew tried too hard not to stare at him. Alex itched to call the Maneuvering Room and ask the engineer about the safe, but if Lieutenant Cooper didn't understand the need to hurry, they were all screwed, anyway. Instead, he glanced at the plot, glad to see that the distance between the *Requin* and Convoy 3791 opening. The range from *Bluefish* to the enemy, however, was much closer. Damn it! He couldn't even shoot to keep the bastard honest. What did the Indian think of Alex running and not shooting? Pity he couldn't pick up the phone and ask.

Taunting another submarine over a sound-powered phone wasn't his style. Jules Rochambeau did it to USS *Skate* last year, but Alex had no ambition to be that kind of asshole.

"Sonar, Conn, what's our range to the *Requin*?" he asked.

"A tick over thirteen thousand, sir," the sonar chief answered. Alex finally got a glimpse of her nametape, which read *Andreas*. She stuck her head out of the space, looking concerned. "He's out to starboard, not in a chase like his torpedoes."

"Aye." Alex pulled off his glasses to chew on the earpiece; he needed something in his mouth, and he'd forgotten his gum in his stateroom. Was this guy being clever? Was there something out here to make *Bluefish* change course, or was the *Requin* just hanging out until—

"Target is opening doors!" STSC Andreas said. "Torpedoes in the water! Two torpedoes in the water bearing one-eight-eight!"

"Very well." Alex scowled at the plot as his heart started pounding harder. "Damn. Fucker's smart, after all."

"Sir?" O'Kane sounded more worried about Alex's reactions than he did the incoming torpedoes, and didn't that paint a pretty fucking picture of what kind of boat he'd inherited?

Wait for it, Alex told himself. Half his job was to appear calm; if he started freaking out, everyone would. So he answered levelly:

"He's forcing us to turn or eat the second set of torps. Which we're obviously not going to do." Two torpedoes coming up from behind and two fired from off *Bluefish's* starboard beam. The second set would be aimed ahead of him so that *Bluefish* would have to turn and let the first torpedoes cut the corner to gain ground.

"That's *really* good to know, Captain," O'Kane replied.

Alex chuckled. "I take it you guys don't get shot at a lot?"

"Well, it's kind of supposed to be a bad day when that happens, right?" O'Kane's smile couldn't hide the way his toes tapped on the deck.

"Yeah. Just a bit." *Now.* "Left standard rudder."

"Left standard rudder, aye," the helmsman responded after a slight hesitation. "My rudder is left fifteen degrees, no new course given."

"You...don't want to turn any sharper, Captain?" O'Kane asked. Everyone else looked like they didn't dare ask the same thing. He missed having a crew who knew him.

Alex shrugged. "Sharper gives the first two fish a better chance at us. If we turn slowly enough, we might suck all four into a tail chase. At least until we run the first two out of gas."

"Yes, sir."

Damn. He'd hoped for useful input out of O'Kane. What were his options? Noisemakers or run. Wasting countermeasures was stupid while he couldn't shoot back. To shoot required a turn toward the *Requin*. For now, it could chase him.

"Conn, Sonar, torpedoes have turned," Chief Andreas reported two minutes later. "It looks like they're all following in our wake."

"Very well." Alex let out a breath. The first two turning like that meant that the *Requin* was wire-guiding the suckers. The other two had to have been cut loose, which meant Alex had a better chance of fooling them. A plan started forming in his mind.

If only he could shoot a torpedo this side of tomorrow.

He leaned toward the squawk box again. "Maneuvering, Conn, how's that government property destruction coming?"

"Conn, Maneuvering, stand by." It wasn't Lieutenant Cooper's voice that answered. A knot of worry formed in Alex's stomach. So much for playing it cool!

"Conn, aye." Alex's eyes flicked to the plot. The original set of torpedoes had gained about three thousand yards while *Bluefish* turned. Shit. Would his plan work, or was he about to hold command for the fewest hours in naval history?

Hinges squeaked; the hatch at the back control swung open. Glancing over his shoulder—wandering the boat at battle stations was forbidden—Alex blinked when his engineering officer rushed over. "Here's your key, Captain." Lieutenant Cooper's eyes widened as he looked at the plot. "Are there *four* torpedoes after us?"

"Yep." Alex managed a tight grin, grabbed the key, and spun to face the weapons consoles to the right. "Weps! Put this thing in so we can get to work."

Alex tossed the plastic key, lanyard and all. Lange caught it and, wide-eyed, inserted the key. "Key is green!"

"Firing point procedures, tubes two and four, track"—Alex checked the plot—"7703. Open the outer doors."

Lange repeated the command back, bending over the console as her team manipulated the computer to create the firing solution. At least this was familiar. No XO, torpedoes in the water, and Alex was a clueless rookie who might just get lucky. Before Alex could assign someone to verify the firing solution, O'Kane showed up next to Lange, going over the numbers. He was nervous, but the kid had a brain. That was a relief.

Hell, anything better than his last XO was a relief.

"Solution ready!" Lange said.

"Ship ready," O'Kane added.

"XO, stand by your countermeasures," Alex ordered, his eyes on the plot again as O'Kane scurried back to the countermeasure control panel. The first set of torpedoes was only five thousand yards astern, but they only had two or three minutes of fuel left. Screw those. The ones astern were the bigger concern. "Drop two...*mark!*"

"Countermeasures away!"

One, two— "Hard left rudder! Twenty degree up angle, make your depth four hundred feet, smartly!" He hoped this sub changed depth as well as she ran; Alex needed to generate some lateral separation to convince those torpedoes *not* to cut into the inside of his turn.

Alex ignored the repeat backs from the helmsman and planesman, instead watching the track representing the *Requin*. It was still astern of him, but *Bluefish* turned rapidly. She was agile, this new boat of his. His last one had turned like a drunk whale when damaged. *Almost there.* Alex took a breath.

"Weps, tubes two and four...*fire!*"

Lange slapped the buttons. "Tubes two and four fired electrically!"

"Very well."

"Two fish running hot, straight, and normal. First enemy torpedoes are at the countermeasures," Sonar reported, and Alex tried to pretend he wasn't holding his breath. "Torpedoes are pinging...aspect change! Both torpedoes are headed downward, sir!"

"Yes!" someone hissed from Alex's right. He thought it was O'Kane.

"Very well." Alex had to raise his voice over the quiet jubilation in control. "Don't get too excited, folks—we've still got two more to outfox. Rudder amidships."

"Rudder amidships, aye!"

"Our torpedoes are in acquisition, Captain." Lange's eyes shined.

"The *Requin* is turning, sir!" Chief Andreas reported. "He's coming hard right and cavitating—I think he's cut the wires to the other two torpedoes to evade!"

"Very well." Alex bit back a smile; he would've done the same thing, but it couldn't save the *Requin*. Cutting the wires meant that the *Requin* was free to maneuver, but it also meant the Indian had to trust his torpedoes' own sensors to find *Bluefish.* The enemy sub was moving at fifty knots, but the Mark 84 torpedoes Alex had fired had a maximum speed of eighty-seven knots. That was a hell of a lot more overtake than the ones chasing *Bluefish*. "Range to second set of enemy torpedoes?"

"Eight thousand yards, sir," Andreas replied. "They gained a lot of ground while we turned."

"Yeah, but it won't be enough." Alex grinned. "They've only got six minutes of fuel left, and they'll need some PFM to catch up to us."

O'Kane laughed. "Let's, uh, hope they don't have Scotty over there, sir."

"Huh?"

"Never mind, sir. Sorry." O'Kane went red. "Silly reference."

"Right." Alex shook his head. "Weps, how do our fish look?"

"Two and four in final acquisition, sir." Lange's voice was distant; she was leaning over her operator's shoulder, her eyes riveted on the screen.

A glance at the plot showed *Requin* corkscrewing along her course and dropping noisemakers. But both torpedoes were locked in, which meant it was Alex's job to look at the big picture. Quickly, he zoomed the display out, his eyes tracing back along *Bluefish's* original course. Convoy 3791 steamed along at a steady twenty-five knots, still heading northwest, fat, dumb, and happy.

"Impact!" Chief Andreas announced. "Underwater explosion bearing three-four-two!"

This time, Alex didn't stop anyone in control from cheering.

Chapter 6

Out of Place

25 December 2039, Western Australia

USS *Fletcher* (DDG 155) sat up on the blocks like a ghost ship, cold and dark without power. The holes in her port side were patched now, but Commander Nancy Coleman could still see the scars from where she stood on the edge of the dry dock. One coat of haze gray paint only hid so much when wartime shortages meant there was no primer, let alone enough for a second and third coat to make the new metal of the destroyer's hull match the old.

Nancy sighed. The French bastard who blew up his damaged destroyer in an attempt to take *Fletcher* with him remained in the brig in Perth, awaiting trial for war crimes. Faking a surrender was a crime under the Geneva Conventions, and thirty-two of Nancy's sailors died because of it.

The last two months had been a roller coaster. Between getting her ship blown to shit and her husband going missing in action with his submarine—only for Alex to miraculously reappear with *Jimmy Carter* in even worse shape than her destroyer, winning the Congressional Medal of Honor in the process—Nancy had barely had time to breathe. She'd gone home, ordered to recover from her injuries, grieve for her friends, and be there for her extremely shell-shocked daughters. Oh, and spend time with the husband she'd feared she'd lost.

Their stolen two months had felt like paradise, but Nancy and Alex were cut from the same cloth at the end of the day. There was a war on, and their friends were fighting and dying for their country. Neither could imagine being anywhere else.

So, thirteen days ago, she said goodbye to the girls, cried where they couldn't see, and exchanged no promises with Alex to be careful. They both knew what they were up against. They were still the navy's only married couple who were *both* in command—again, Nancy supposed.

She had a decision to make.

"Shitty place to spend Christmas, Nancy," a familiar voice said from her left, and Nancy turned to salute, her fingers brushing the plastic rim of her hard hat.

"Admiral." Her lips twitched into a smile.

"Good to see you with all your parts attached," Rear Admiral Julia Rosario said. "Seeing straight yet?"

Nancy chuckled. "Most days. Got piss-ass drunk once on leave as it sunk in that I really almost lost Alex, and I swear I could *see* sounds the day of that hangover, but other than that, I've been fine. Medical cleared me with flying colors."

"Glad to hear it." Julia's smile was wide and warmed Nancy's heart. Julia Rosario was both a friend and the best boss she'd ever had, a comrade who she'd shed blood and lost sailors side by side with. They'd faced the best and worst battles of the war together. It all started in the massacre called the First Battle of the Strait of Malacca, where the U.S. Navy first discovered how razor-thin their margin of superiority really was. Nancy had barely known Julia before that, but the then-commander of USS *Belleau Wood* had proven herself the best friend to have at your side in a fight.

Julia had taken care of *Fletcher* and Nancy's crew after the surrendering French destroyer blew a hole in *Fletcher's* side and took Nancy out of commission for a week, too. *And* she'd made sure Nancy had the time and space to go home on medical leave...which just happened to coincide with her husband's survivor's leave after Alex trashed *Jimmy Carter* in route to his Medal of Honor.

Her eyes drifted back to *Fletcher.* Her destroyer was still beautiful, despite the repaired damage. *Fletcher* wasn't the newest destroyer in America's arsenal, nor from the most capable class, but damn it, she was Nancy's.

Heaven help her, now she understood how broken up Alex was about *Jimmy Carter.* But at least *Fletcher* would survive her.

"You make up your mind yet?" Julia asked when Nancy remained silent, caught up in her thoughts.

Nancy scowled. "You're offering me a poisoned chalice. Trading away destroyer command to be XO on a cruiser. The navy's *worst* cruiser, no less."

"Technically, *Cape* exceeds most metrics."

"*Technically*, Connecticut residents are known as 'Nutmeggers,' but no one calls us that."

Julia laughed. "Rowling's on her last legs. You won't be her number two for long, and then we'll slide you right upstairs into command."

"Her last legs still sound pretty mean. I hear she's gone through three XOs in the last year," Nancy replied.

"Four. Cat Markham just threw in the towel. She's pregnant, and no full commander gets herself knocked up in wartime and *stays* that way by accident."

"Cat?" Nancy's jaw dropped. "I went to department head school with her. She's sharp."

Julia spread her hands. "It is what it is. She's not apologizing, and we've got to transfer her ashore."

"Shit." Nancy sighed. Getting pregnant to avoid sea duty was a time-honored way to skate out of a job you hated, but she'd thought better of Cat Markham. By the time anyone rose this high in the ranks, they were supposed to know better—particularly when their country was at war!

No way was that an accident. Captain Helen Rowlings of USS *Cape St. George* had a reputation as a jackass straight out of the pages of the *Arnheiter Affair.* Nancy always had liked that book more than *The Caine Mutiny*, at least in terms of sheer audacity.

"Rowling is a hardass, but she gets the job done. She's probably the best tactician we have in a cruiser." Julia grimaced. "I think she's better than I was."

"I doubt that."

"The gal's got what it takes, even if she is a little rough around the edges," Julia replied. "Her first XO checked himself in for a mental health evaluation and never came back. I'm not sure if that one's her fault or if the good old rumor mill just ran with it. The second got relieved for sleeping with the help—she and one of the department heads had a cozy little love nest in the XO's stateroom, so make sure you get it fumigated if you take the job." The admiral snickered. "The third one was the only one Rowling straight-up chased off, and I got those details from Admiral Bowman. Seems Commander Boguski liked to bully enlisted crew members and was embezzling from the morale, welfare, and recreation fund."

Nancy whistled. "Long list of misdeeds. But you know what they say: two's a coincidence, but three's a trend."

"I don't know what to tell you, Nancy, other than *Cape* needs an XO, and if you go there, you'll put on captain and she'll be yours within the year."

Nancy felt her spine straighten as she looked back up at *Fletcher*. Command of a cruiser within the year? Better yet, the *lead* cruiser of the newest, meanest, and fleetest class the U.S. Navy had ever built and sailed?

Cape St. George was the second ship to bear the proud name of the "perfect battle" commanded by the legendary Admiral Arleigh Burke. The cruiser Julia was offering—with a painful caveat—was commissioned one year ago, just long enough to work the kinks out. She was the first American nuclear-powered cruiser built in almost sixty years, and she carried almost twice as many missiles as the *O'Bannon*-class *Fletcher*, not to mention *four* times as many guns. Nancy had admired *Cape's* twin-gunned five-inch mounts from afar more than once; her class was the first time an American ship had carried more than two main guns since before the days of modern missile warfare.

"You really know how to make a girl swoon, don't you?" she asked.

Julia just laughed.

Nothing further needed to be said.

Bluefish quieted down after the attack on Convoy 3791. Alex's crew found no other lurking enemies, so he secured from battle stations. Retreating to his stateroom, Alex marveled over how normal things became after combat. Last time, the tension lingered for weeks as his broken submarine struggled her way to Perth. But this wasn't time for introspection; he had work to do.

Alex spent a few quality hours finishing his standing orders—and reading his predecessor's. Every page he turned made him shake his head. This guy made George Kirkland look inspiring! His XO on *Jimmy Carter* had been detail-oriented and pedantic, but Commander Peterson took that to a whole new level. Alex had never seen someone micromanage so inefficiently.

Not to mention locking the fucking firing key away where no one could get it. Alex scowled, glancing at the mangled safe. How the hell could any wartime captain be that stupid?

Unfortunately, idiocy and micromanagement didn't explain his crew's problems. Micromanagers were common in the navy. Yeah, they killed morale and efficiency and wore themselves out trying to nitpick their way through a war. But that didn't account for the beat down and frightened looks his new crew wore every time they thought he wasn't looking. A sinking feeling gurgled in his gut. Alex should've asked a lot more questions before getting this boat underway. Or *any* questions. Now he had to lead people who he knew jack shit and nothing about. This would've been a great time to be able to call his predecessor.

Then again, having read Commander Peterson's standing orders, Alex wasn't sure he wanted to hear what the man had to say.

Sighing, he leaned back and stared at the computer screen. What the hell was the number for the yeoman on this boat? No two classes of submarines were identical, including their phone numbers. *Jimmy Carter* had been a *Seawolf.* The navy stopped after building only three boats in that class—one of the worst decisions ever made, in Alex's opinion—instead opting to build cheaper *Virginias* and, later, *Ceros*. There were no *Seawolfs* left now. Yet his old command, ancient though she'd been, had been more capable than his new one. Not that it mattered. The U.S. Navy was in the middle of a war, which meant they'd keep building what they had...more *Ceros.*

Alex shook his head. This wasn't the time to ruminate on the navy's shipbuilding policies; he had a crew to meet and a boat to command. So he picked up the phone and dialed control.

"Officer of the Deck, Lieutenant J.G. Shorn speaking."

"OOD, it's the captain. Pass the word for all officers to meet in the wardroom at 1300, will you?"

"Yes, sir!" Shorn sounded a touch too motivated. Alex bit back the urge to ask what was wrong.

"Thanks," he said, and hung up.

Alex turned back to his computer. They'd gone shallow to receive message traffic after rejoining the convoy; lacking internet connectivity, messages were *Bluefish's* best source of information. The first few messages in his queue were boring but useful; Alex jotted down a few notes about low-acoustic mines deployed from *Yasen*-class submarines and a potential French subbase in the Antarctic. The fourth message, however, made his heart sink.

SUBMISS/SUBSUNK ICO
USS HYMAN G RICK-
OVER SSN 795.

Another friend gone. Jose Myers had been in Alex's Prospective Commanding Officer class in 2038. *Rickover* was an early *Virginia* class; like *Jimmy Carter*, she'd generally been relegated to convoy escorts. Despite that, Jose sunk six merchant ships and an Indian diesel boat along the way. Alex swallowed. There was nothing in the message indicating any of *Rickover's* crew got off. But there was something else:

> SUBMISS/SUBSUNK BOUY ACTIVCATION DETECTED AT APPROXIMATELY 32°09' 24.3" S 082°45'45.8" E. ALL SHIPS AND SUBMARINES ARE ADVISED TO PROCEED WITH CAUTION. POSSIBILITY OF A FREEDOM UNION ATTACK SUBMARINE IVO THIS POSITION IS HIGH.

Alex's head snapped up, looking at the position indicator on the wall. *31°28'26"S 080°50'53"E.* Quick and dirty math said they were approximately one hundred nautical miles away from *Rickover's* last position. *Son of a bitch. Bluefish* had already encountered one Indian *Akula*. Had he sunk *Rickover's* killer? Or was another enemy around?

His mind raced through possibilities. Either the enemy was nearby or already sunk. The call was Alex's. One running battle was easier than this. This was too routine. He had too much time to think.

Damn, he missed Maggie. Who the hell could he turn to on this boat? He didn't *have* an XO, which at least meant he wasn't saddled with a coward. His navigator looked ready to break down if Alex sneezed wrong, the engineer avoided control like herpes, and the weapons officer wanted to kill someone. As an extra-special bonus, the division officers were petrified, and the chiefs looked too worn down to object. His chief of the boat's eyes drooped from exhaustion, like she'd run fourteen marathons on not enough sleep. And Alex was the lucky bastard who got to fix this wrecked bunch.

How long would it take? Too long, Alex was certain. He sucked in a deep breath. He'd wait. Alex had a convoy to protect, not glory to find. He already had that, and it wasn't as much fun as people thought.

"Assemble all officers in the wardroom at 1300."

The chief of the watch's announcement blared out of the 1MC speaker to Bobby's right, making him cringe. Then he slumped against the stateroom wall. At least it was just him and Rose; Lou was doing what he did best, crawling around the emergency diesel, nicknamed "Georgie," after the first *Bluefish's* commissioning CO.

"Hey, we did good." Rose stuck her chin out. "We're not going to get a Peterson-style bitching out."

"I don't know." Bobby swallowed. His stomach was in knots. Rose's stateroom wasn't big enough to pace. Three steps one way, two steps the other; it sucked. "There's probably something he wanted us to do that we didn't. Or the stupid firing key being locked—"

"Stop it, Bobby. You're being stupid."

"Stupid? You're not the one who got to sit through daily lectures from our former glorious leader, generally concerning how unsuited yours truly was for the job." He groaned. "I guess I should thank my lucky stars that he waited before yelling at us? Maybe that's our Christmas present."

It was Christmas, too. Bobby *had* wanted to arrange a boat-wide Secret Santa, but Peterson axed that idea months ago.

Rose glared. "Even if you're right, we got to do something useful for once."

"I guess." It was sad how sinking one enemy sub made *Bluefish's* record better.

"Come on." Rose stood, grabbing his arm. "Time to face the music."

Damn. It was almost 1300, time to go to the funfest. Bobby was still acting XO, which meant he had to be there to back the captain up. At least Peterson was predictable. A man could get used to being treated like trash. Swallowing, Bobby followed Rose into the passageway and then into the wardroom. Lou was already present, wearing fresh coveralls—no one forgot how picky Peterson was about that—as were most of the division officers. Being late was fatal. Fortunately, Harri, Rene, Andrea, and Wallace—the foursome who'd been hungover—no longer looked like a fleet of semi-trucks ran them over. Maybe the captain hadn't noticed. It wasn't like he knew them.

Everyone popped to their feet when Captain Coleman walked in, and Bobby tried to tell his heart to stop doing the samba. Coleman missed a step and blinked at them in confusion.

"Sit." The captain matched actions to words, settling into the chair at the head of the table and dropping a tablet on the blue canvas tabletop.

Licking his lips, Bobby lowered himself into the XO's seat. Someone had to. The table only had room for eleven people, everyone except the three officers on watch. Coleman smiled crookedly and continued:

"For future reference, there's no need to stand on ceremony when I walk in here. That'll get old for all of us awfully fast. But I imagine that you're not all doing it for your health." His eyes slid sideways to Bobby.

"Uh, no, sir. Commander Peterson, uh, liked it." *Required it.*

"Well, I think we can kill that idea." Coleman sat back, looking around. "I called this meeting so I can meet everyone. There's usually a longer turnover process—during which I'd actually learn your names—but better late than never. The good news is that we didn't get sunk before we got a chance to play the introduction game."

A laugh wormed out of Bobby. Rose, however, blanched. "Captain, the firing key is still in control."

"It can stay there." Coleman waved a hand. "It's red, so we can't shoot anyone by accident, and I'd just as soon be able to shoot on purpose when I want to. Good job on the safe to the engineers, by the way. Your guys tore the shit out of that thing."

"Thanks, sir. I think." Lou looked torn between glee and embarrassment.

This time the laughter felt more natural, and a cautious smile tugged on Bobby's lips. He couldn't imagine Peterson joking with anyone, but the new captain's grin seemed genuine. It was too soon to hope, right? The last year on *Bluefish* had been miserable enough to make Bobby contemplate getting out of the navy.

More than contemplate. He had a job waiting for him at his brother's car dealership.

"All right, destruction of government property aside, let's get to the obligatory introductions. I think you've all probably heard of me after that...fun with Convoy 57. But, in case you haven't, my name is Alex Coleman. I come your way via *Virginia*, *John Warner*, *Kansas*, and then *Jimmy Carter*. I wanted to be an engineer, but the navy's infinite wisdom made me a Weps. I've been in the navy seventeen-and-a-half years, I have two daughters, and my wife is a surface warfare officer. So, if a Commander Coleman shows up when we're in port, don't freak out. She's in command of *Fletcher*." He looked at Bobby. "Floor's to you."

"Right. Um, Bobby—Robert—O'Kane, sir, but no one calls me that. I wanted to be a navigator, but the navy made me acting XO. My first boat was *Los Angeles*"—he didn't like thinking about how she sank last year—"and I like long walks in the moonlight and making too many pop culture references?"

Damn. He'd gone too far, hadn't he? Bobby gulped.

Coleman grinned.

One by one, the others spoke up, first Rose and Lou, and then the senior divos. Lieutenant (junior grade) Rene Shorn, Bobby's assistant navigator, went first, followed by Harri and then Wallace. LTJG Wally Hill was their damage control assistant, and he was Lou's senior division officer. He was also the wardroom's practical joker, fond of stealing uniform pieces and putting saranwrap on soup spoons. Their other partner in crime was Andrea Prince, the assistant weapons officer. *She* looked quiet and competent. Peterson liked her professional demeanor and never noticed the wicked sense of humor lurked under the surface.

Next up was Brigette Sonnen, their supply officer and thus half department head and half division officer. She'd had the misfortune of having the duty the day Peterson's appendix went the way of the dodo. To her right sat Ensign Tanya Chin, Lou's machinery division officer, who was almost always in company with Lieutenant (junior grade) Tien Nguyen, who was the CRA, or chemistry and radiological controls assistant. He was smart but shy, and Bobby had really liked him until he'd started hiding from Peterson about a month into his tour.

Ensign Charlie Maquire, Bobby's communications officer, sat next to Lou's electrical officer, Ensign Max Goldberg. Those two *wanted* to be trouble but weren't brave enough with Peterson in the seat. Bobby would have to watch them from now on, and wouldn't that be fun? Wouldn't it be nice to go back to worrying about just *his* division officers? Owning the whole ice cream sandwich as the acting executive officer meant they were *all* his problem. Somehow that hadn't seemed like such a big deal under Peterson. Everyone was too scared of him to be stupid.

Not that Bobby minded stupid. Stupid was okay in reasonable quantities. But stupid on *Bluefish* was anything fun or being downwind of someone drinking.

"Let's talk expectations," Captain Coleman interrupted his thoughts. "I like to think I'm pretty easy to work for, but I'd probably be the last to know. My standards are simple: do your job to the best of your ability, let me know if you have a problem, and remember that we're all on the same team."

Bobby managed not to swallow. Hoping at this early point would be foolish. Peterson sounded like a sane and normal captain when people were watching, too. Coleman continued, oblivious to the wardroom's concerns:

"Now, let's get some administrative matters out of the way. I've finished my standing orders—XO, will you make sure admin does their formatting magic and gets them out to everyone?"

Crap, that was him. "Yes, sir."

"Now, for the less pleasant part of this meeting." Coleman's smile vanished, and he slid the tablet over to Bobby without looking down. "I received an interesting email from the proprietor of a restaurant in Perth. Anyone want to take a guess at the name of said restaurant?"

Bobby didn't have to read the email to tell where this was going, not from the way the color drained out of Harri's face. His heart sank, and Bobby looked down, dreading every word of the short email. It read:

> *Dear Commander Peterson,*
>
> *I regret having to send this letter, since you are such a frequent and valued patron at the Mediterranean. However, we experienced a problem with four officers from your ship. These officers were responsible for $9500 worth of property destruction while drunk in my establishment. They also left without paying their bill, which totaled $539.27.*
>
> *I know you will deal with this situation expeditiously. I look forward to hearing from you, as well as to you and your wife's next visit.*
>
> *Sincerely,*

Dean Prendergast, Proprietor

Great. Just great. Bobby wanted to break the tablet and destroy the evidence, but the stupid email was on *Bluefish's* server. It was just delivered to the new owner of co@ssn843.navy.mil instead of the old one. And if Harri was involved...he knew exactly who the other three musketeers were. Every nerve in Bobby's body stood on edge, ready for the inevitable lecture. The silence in the wardroom was deafening.

For a moment, Bobby contemplated trying to talk around the problem. Peterson's no drinking rule said no one from *Bluefish* could be involved, right? He discarded the idea immediately. He just wasn't that into lying.

"I take it from the ominous silence that no one wants to admit to this little incident?" Coleman asked after a long minute or two ticked by. His face remained unreadable, but his glasses came off as he studied them.

Harri and Rene exchanged a look; finally, Harri cleared her throat. "I, uh, think that was us, sir."

"Define 'us,' please."

Four hands crept upward, confirming Bobby's theory: Harri, Rene, Wally, and Andrea. The fabulous foursome, the best division officers on board. Yet the truth was uglier than this mess. Those kids never would've gotten in trouble if Peterson's rules hadn't been designed to make them go crazy, but Bobby couldn't say that, could he? Even the department heads snuck in a drink or two. They were just old enough not to get drunk.

He should say something. A real XO would, but he wasn't the real XO. Was this covered in the Prospective Executive Officers' course? *Lesson number 482: how to diffuse things when your captain is mad at division officers who did the stupid.* Bobby almost groaned as he turned to meet Rose's eyes. This was where the tirade started, although Peterson didn't have this gift of making silences so heavy and uncomfortable. Pity Coleman was a good tactician. He only needed two minutes to demonstrate that he knew how to make everyone feel worse than they already did. Wasn't that just fantabulous?

"So. Ninety-five hundred bucks' worth of damage. Do I want to know what you did?"

Rene grimaced, his freckles standing out against his red face. "It wasn't really our fault, Captain. Or at least not entirely?"

"We wanted to make the Eiffel Tower." Wally's shoulders slumped. "It was just a silly thing. So we started stacking up plates and glasses..."

"And it all fell down." Coleman sighed. "That's supposed to be London Bridge."

The four divos looked at him like he'd gone out of his mind. "Sir?" Harri squeaked.

"Never mind. So you started in on French architecture because you were drunk. I assume you wanted to smash the thing in the name of victory?" Coleman pinched the bridge of his nose. "I still don't get where that adds up to ninety-five hundred dollars' worth of damage."

Andrea cleared her throat. "There was also a bottle of vodka—"

"A really expensive one," Rene said, earning a glare from Andrea.

"We wanted to use it as the spindle on top," Andrea finished. "But it fell on Wally, who ran into a waiter who dropped a big tray of someone else's food..."

"And they charged us for that, too." Harri heaved a sigh. "And the table. We didn't mean to cause any trouble, sir, really. It just got bad when the waiter tried to pick a fight, and we *knew* that we'd all end up in HAQ for fighting, so we left. We didn't think of the bill until we got underway."

"I see."

Bobby wanted to bash his head into the table. Peterson would've taken them to Captain's Mast and hammered them—which would've ended up with them on thirty days' arrest in quarters when not on watch—but *really*? Not paying the bill was stealing. He'd thought better of this group.

Another long moment of silence stretched out. Everyone fidgeted.

"All right." Coleman sat back in his chair again. "You four will send a letter of apology—one or four, I don't care—to Mister Prendergast. You'll also pay your bill and for the property damage. Again, I don't care how you do it; you are adults and naval officers. Figure it out."

All four division officers jerked upright in their chairs, eyes wide.

"I trust the four of you can handle that without me needle-dicking you into submission?"

"Yes, sir!"

"Then this is your one freebie. Figure out how to act like adults or I'll nail you to the wall. There's a war on, but that's no excuse to treat our Australian hosts like shit. Any more of these shenanigans and you'll all be looking for new careers. Understood?"

Four frantic nods. "Yes, sir."

The foursome practically ran out of the wardroom when the captain ended the meeting, with everyone else close behind. However, it was Bobby's job to deal with the *rest* of what they'd done, so he stayed. Damn, he wished he could convince himself to lie. Lying was the dark side, but Bobby'd heard they had cookies. He sighed, waiting for the door to shut before speaking.

"Captain, um, I don't know if you know that those four also broke *Bluefish's* no-drinking policy," Bobby said.

Coleman's pale eyebrows shot up. "No what-ing policy?"

"No drinking. Commander Peterson forbade everyone from having any alcoholic beverages, even on liberty." Should he mention that he'd broken that policy, too? Better to all go down together—

"Well, you can throw that horseshit away," Coleman said. "I don't think that's a legal order, anyway."

"Sir?"

"I'll hammer people if they're stupid. Until then, I don't care how much they drink or where they do it, provided they don't break local laws."

Was Bobby in the Twilight Zone? First, *Bluefish* sank an enemy submarine, and now the captain didn't care if sailors drank. Maybe they'd all died and gone to some weird version of heaven where there was still a war on. Weren't dogs supposed to be here?

Captain Coleman walked out, leaving a confused Bobby O'Kane in his wake.

Nancy's response to Alex's email took long enough to arrive that he'd started to worry. He always did, even when he should know better. War denied surface ships reliable internet access, too.

> *Bobbie emailed me not long after you*, Nancy wrote. *She's taking it better than Emily, though she told me Emily snuck off an early application to Norwich. I guess we shouldn't be surprised. We're both stubborn, and the girls got a double dose. I just hope Emily continues wanting to be a lawyer and stays out of the line of fire. Or the war ends before they can get out here.*

> *Speaking of the war, have you figured out what's going on with that crew of yours? It sounds like your predecessor was a real piece of shit. I know jack about submarines, but bad leadership is bad leadership. You're hardly the type to make people run in terror, even with that big scary medal of yours. I know you still hate it as much as you did when they pinned it on you, too.*

> *And now it's my turn to hand over some big news via email. Admiral Rosario offered me a transfer*

to a cruiser XO job...and I took it. I leave Fletcher *next week. The XO tour is promised to be short, and I'll be in command within the year. Then I'll only have to salute you because of the medal, not rank. That'll be nice. I'm not used to you outranking me!*

Alex laughed out loud despite the sudden tightening of his chest. It was true; Nancy had hit every career milestone before him, and she always promoted first. He'd never minded. He was *proud* of her, always. Even now, with her sticking her neck out onto the firing line again.

Lord, did he have any right to be angry, given where he was? After so long as the "safe" spouse, Alex was now anything but. Sure, he was on another convoy escort, but Uncle Marco's words kept echoing in his mind. *Bluefish hasn't exactly covered herself in glory. I want you to change that.* Telling Nancy to step out of the dance would make him a hypocrite.

I wish I wasn't used to saying I'll be as careful as I can and that I love you, Nancy's email continued. *I'm not used to us both being in danger...but we knew what we signed up for, didn't we? Try to stay safe. I'm not looking to redo the experience of you being thought dead for six weeks, okay?*

Alex swallowed. He didn't deserve Nancy. Hell, he never had. His wife was the most driven and dynamic woman he'd ever met; Alex would've followed her into hell about five minutes after meeting her their freshman year in college. He sure hadn't expected her to go to Regimental Ball with him, or *ever* to date a skinny nerd like him.

Almost nineteen years later, their marriage weathered everything the world could throw at it. Including this war.

Leaning back in his chair, Alex glanced at the clock. *16:00.*

Knock, knock.

"Come in!" Alex turned his chair away from his computer as Master Chief Ginger Baker walked into his stateroom. She was a tall and brown-skinned woman, with hair pulled back in rows of braids. She was built like she knew her way around a gym and might've done some "wall-to-wall counseling" with a sailor back in the day. Her expression was pure old school master chief, with wise eyes that had seen plenty of captains go by and were already judging him.

"You wanted to talk before you met with the chiefs, sir?" she asked, leaning against the doorframe with an expression that said she *dared* him to yell at her.

Alex grinned. "Yeah, sit on down."

He gestured at the other chair in his stateroom. It was luxurious compared to its counterpart on *Jimmy Carter*, despite being a utilitarian and metal thing, with the minimum amount of padding the lowest bidder could get away. Hell, the entire room was an upgrade. For one, the floor still had all its carpet.

Baker sat, eyeing him. After his meeting with the officers, her caution was almost understandable. And Baker wouldn't volunteer a damned thing, would she? If a crusty-ass master chief was beaten down, what chance did the kids have? This boat was an ever-loving disaster. Alex managed not to groan.

Fuck, it was almost as bad as public speaking. His old fear hadn't reared its ugly head since taking command, but now Alex felt the familiar butterflies dancing.

"All right," he said slowly, resisting the urge to chew on his reading glasses. The damn things really were useful, even if not for their intended purpose. "I don't know what kind of leader Commander Peterson is, but between you and me, I'm guessing it's not a very good one. This crew is a mess of problems, and I need you to help me solve them."

"I'll do my job, sir." Baker's face remained blank.

Yeah, Alex could see where this led. "With or without my help?" he asked.

Baker blinked. "I'd prefer to do it with, sir."

"That's good to know." Alex squared his shoulders. "Look, we can talk around this all day, but there's a war on, and I don't have time for that shit. So I'll be blunt. I can't fix what Peterson did if no one will tell me about it. But you're the chief of the damned boat. I need your help here."

"You're...not going to like it, sir." She crossed her arms. "Or at least I think you're the type not to like it."

"Master Chief, I don't like a damned thing I've guessed so far, so just hit me with it."

Baker took a deep breath. "It was mostly bullying, sir. And blaming others for his own mistakes. The old la—old captain, sorry—was afraid of his shadow, and he didn't like having anyone around who made him look incompetent."

"Was he?" Alex asked.

There were a thousand ways in which a captain could bully their crew; they possessed power over his or her sailors' everyday lives that a civilian couldn't imagine. The commanding officer of a warship controlled when their crew ate, slept, and could leave the boat. A control freak could even dictate what movies they could or couldn't watch or change the galley menu to suit their own tastes. Their power was nearly absolute, and sailors couldn't quit, not even in peacetime. There was no higher power to appeal to. The captain's word was law.

A bad CO could make a crew miserable without even trying. Alex had worked for one who demanded a ridiculous number of reports from the officer of the deck and had then yelled at said OOD when they woke him up to provide said required reports. The same one hated one particular junior officer and refused to let her qualify as a submariner until it got her kicked out of the navy. His last captain on *Kansas* wanted glory so badly he almost sank a civilian submarine. Yet none of Alex's previous COs had been toxic enough to traumatize the entire crew.

Had he just been lucky?

"I'm honestly not sure, sir," Baker answered. "He never did enough for us to tell."

"Glorious," Alex said. "All right. Hit me with the worst of it. I can't fix things if I don't know what's broken."

Her smile turned lopsided. "Just remember you asked for this, Captain."

"Noted."

Baker told Alex about broken equipment Peterson blamed on others, or maintenance problems he manufactured to get out of patrols he deemed too "unimportant" for his attention. She told him about a sailor demoted because he had paint on his coveralls, along with another who was put on restriction for sixty days for not clearing a clog in the captain's toilet within the hour. Then there was their old XO, Lieutenant Commander Vanderbilt, who fell down a ladder and broke his leg, only for Peterson to delay calling for medical attention when he thought his XO was faking.

One sailor opened a betting pool on if the XO fell on purpose, only to be taken to Mast for gambling and sent to a shoreside brig. Then there was the matter of Convoy 57, which Peterson flat out called their commodore to whine his way out of. The crew remained humiliated that they missed the most successful submarine action of the war...and mortified that their new captain had commanded the boat that *Bluefish* left hung out to dry.

The list went on long enough to make Alex boil. He was certain Baker left things out, too. She obviously wanted to protect the crew and hadn't decided if Alex was the enemy. He was all right with that; time would prove to her what kind of CO he intended to be.

On the bright side, Baker handed him a *Bluefish* ballcap on her way out.

It was a start.

Captain Jules Rochambeau
@JulesRochambeau
@RoyalNavy You shall have to build two more for me to sink.
#barracuda #HMSAstute #HMSAjax

Ursula wanted to kill someone.

The swine had sent off another tweet while she chased shadows and butterflies, this time in response to the sinking two British submarines in less than a week. *Astute* and *Ajax* were both *Astute*-class submarines, almost as quiet and as deadly as Captain Ursula North's own *Gallant*. She'd never been fond of *Astute's* lord and master; he was a tactical nincompoop who got his job through political connections and didn't have the sense to listen to his young and bright first officer. But *Ajax's* captain was competent. More than that. Losing one of her friends to her longtime rival burned.

Not that she could do anything about it. Not yet. Oh, her orders were simple; the Admiralty was surprisingly accommodating about the manner in which she was sent to hunt down the man whom she once trained with, back when the world was different.

Locate and destroy FNS Barracuda.

Nothing more. But then intelligence sent *Gallant* off to the southern Indian Ocean while Jules Rochambeau and *Barracuda* preyed on British ships further north. She wanted to scream. Or light Admiralty House on fire. So much for listening to admirals. Ursula threw herself into her desk chair with a sigh. It was time to use her own instincts and stop listening to the higher-ups.

She *knew* Rochambeau, unlike those political-driven fools. Before the Rush to the Ocean Floor, Britain and France were close allies, sharing tactics and technologies. Ursula perfected her trade back in those years, squaring off in exercises against France's rising star. They'd become acquaintances, even if she'd never felt comfortable befriending such an arrogant and self—

Her stateroom phone rang, cutting into her thoughts. Ursula snarled at the receiver. "Yes?"

"Captain, it's Lieutenant Commander Harrison," her first officer said. James Harrison was someone Ursula was pleased to consider her protégé. He was far quieter than her, but brilliant and steadfast. "I think you might want to come up to the attack center. We're receiving some unsettling transmissions."

"Pardon?" Then she blinked. "Never you mind. I'll be right there."

The walk to the attack center was a short one, particularly as her crew dove out of her path. Ursula knew there was steam rolling out of her ears, but after three consecutive months underway with nary a port or French enemy in sight, she felt entitled to a little anger.

Yes, she'd sunk plenty of Indian and even the odd Russian enemy. But they weren't bloody Rochambeau.

"Talk to me, Commander," she ordered.

Ursula North was no classic Briton beauty; she had a serviceable face, a rough northern burr of an accent, and dirty blond hair that she kept in a severe bun. Looking at her, one would never guess she bore the honorific *Lady* North. The nickname "Sea Witch" fit her much better, even if no one dared use it in her presence. Her father the earl hadn't wanted her to remain in the service with a war on, but the way Ursula saw it, she had a younger sister to inherit if she kicked the bucket. Dear sister Lydia was a politician and *far* from the line of fire.

Except that one time, but no one counted that.

James Harrison squared his shoulders. His height, easy smile, and dark skin made his warm presence a polar opposite to North's rough edges. It was easy to tell why the crew loved her second-in-command, but *Ursula* loved him for his competence.

"I put the radio mast up during our approach to Victoria, and the bridge-to-bridge radio transmissions we've detected are a mite worrisome, Captain," James replied. "They seem to indicate the Seychelles have discarded their neutrality."

"What?"

James spread his hands; Ursula stewed. The Seychelles were one of the few "friendly" ports left in the western Indian Ocean, at least to submarines. The Agalega Islands were technically part of the Alliance, but Mauritius had poorly disguised French roots and was right next door to Réunion, which *was* French. The Seychelles remained neutral so far, allowing submarines and ships from both sides to catch some R&R and buy supplies...so long as they kept the war far away from Victoria.

"I assume they have not suddenly decided in our favor." Ursula bit each word out, seeing red.

"No, ma'am."

She didn't even try to bite back her groan. "And, of course, this has not been announced."

"Not that I could locate online." James gestured toward the radio. "Although we overheard two French patrol boats speaking to the local police about setting up anti-submarine patrols."

"Bloody hell." As required by the local government, Ursula had already sent off a message detailing her arrival time and the stores her logistics officer wished to purchase from the locals. Now the locals wanted to kill her instead of making obscene profits, and better yet, *they knew she was there.*

James grimaced. "Indeed."

"I don't suppose those patrol boats have ventured out of the harbor far enough to sink them, have they?"

"Unfortunately, no."

Ursula felt her eyes narrow. "Then we will wait until they do."

"Are you certain, Captain? Although we have plenty of food, the crew is growing rather ripe, and—"

"Quite certain, Commander." Her lips twisted into a snarl. Ursula was *not* about to sneak away from enemies who wanted to sink her submarine. This patrol was *Gallant's* least successful yet, and she intended to use the torpedoes His Majesty's government had so kindly gifted her.

James knew when not to argue; that was why she liked him so much. "Aye, aye, ma'am."

HMS *Gallant* settled into wait.

Chapter 7

Snap Shot

4 January 2040

Bluefish dropped off Convoy 3791 without further incident, but Alex still had twenty-eight torpedoes and a burning desire to shoot something. On one hand, twenty-eight torpedoes seemed too few. *Jimmy Carter's* weapons room held almost twice that many before she went the way of the dodo, and Alex had used every one of them defending Convoy 57. But *Bluefish* only needed two to sink that Indian *Akula*, a fact Alex dutifully reported in a quick message to SUBRON 29 after handing the convoy to a pair of surface ships for their transit around the Horn of Africa. There were reports of a few Russian submarines hunting Alliance merchants in the Atlantic, but so far, no one dared brave America's front yard. News reports indicated things were heating up in the North Sea and the Baltic, but Alex's concern was the Indian Ocean.

2039 didn't end well for the Alliance; *Hyman G. Rickover* was the first sub sunk in the final week of December, but not the last. The British *Ajax* and *Astute* joined her just a day later, and then USS *Grunion* fell victim to India's rising star, Commander Avani Patel. *Grunion* was *Bluefish's* sister, commissioned just a year after Alex's own boat, which left a sinking feeling in his stomach. Next, USS *Washington* dropped off the radar on New Year's Eve. In return, Alex knew of only one enemy sub sunk by the Alliance: the *Akula* he sent to the bottom on Christmas. Those lopsided odds were still a depressing hallmark of this war. Even a year and a half in, they struggled to figure out why the enemy was so much *better* at this game.

That question took Alex's mind to dark places. They couldn't maintain this loss ratio.

A knock on his door made Alex glance up from his computer, only to see Bobby O'Kane there with a tablet in hand. "Sorry to bother you, Captain, but we got a SNAP SHOT message."

Alex sat up straight. "We did?"

"Here." Bobby extended the tablet, and Alex snatched it. SNAP SHOT messages came straight from Vice Admiral Rodriquez, who sent them only to subs in, or scheduled to be in, certain areas. They were only sent to subs COMSUBPAC thought had a good shot at hunting down enemy warships or high-value merchants. Rumor said Uncle Marco personally selected boats to receive SNAP SHOTs, too. Alex's heart hammered in his chest.

TO: USS BLUEFISH SSN 843, USS CERO SSN 837, USS LIONFISH SSN 841, USS MASSACHUSETTS SSN 798, USS BUMPER SSN 862//

FROM: COMSUBPAC//

INFO: COMSUBRON 29, COMSUBRON 13, COMSUBRON 7//

SUBJ: SNAP SHOT 1-2040//

RMKS/1. INTELLIGENCE INDICATES TWO (2) CRITICAL CONTACTS OF INTEREST, MV BLACK MARLIN AND MV MIGHTY SERVANT 3 EN ROUTE INS (INDIAN NAVAL STATION) VAJRABAHU, MAHARASHTRA, INDIA.

2. THESE HEAVY LIFT VESSELS ARE EACH ASSESSED TO BE CARRYING THREE (3) SCORPENE-III (KALVARI) CLASS SUB-MARINES.

3. MV BLACK MARLIN AND MV MIGHTY SERVANT 3 MAY BE ESCORTED BY UNITS OF THE FRENCH AND/OR INDIAN NAVIES.

4. LAST KNOWN CCOI POSIT 12°58'54.6" S 0 49°21'46.6" E 040215JAN34.

5. GOOD HUNTING.

VADM RODRIQUEZ SENDS.//

"Well, shit." *Cero, Lionfish, Massachusetts,* and *Bumper* were good company; all had stellar records. *Bluefish* didn't. An uneasy feeling stole down Alex's spine. He pushed it away. "Looks like we're in the cool kids club."

"I guess so, sir." Bobby's face twisted into an odd smile married to a scowl. Alex burned to shake him, but the last week only had brought *Bluefish's* crew around incrementally. They all still looked like they were waiting for heads to start rolling or Alex to start screaming.

"You ever get one of these before?" Alex never had.

"No, sir." A small, wry smile creased Bobby's face. "Not that Commander Peterson would've gone."

"No?" Alex cocked his head. He didn't want to encourage his subordinates to speak ill of his predecessor, but if this was the way to learn what was wrong on his boat, so be it.

"He wasn't big on taking...risks, Captain." A grimace. "Sprinting up to a likely intercept point could 'expose the submarine to lurking enemies.'" The way Bobby cocked his head and pitched his voice up spoke *eons* about Peterson, didn't it?

Alex ignored the odd lurch in his stomach.

"I see." It was easy to get gun-shy in this business; submarines operated blind, with only passive sonar as their eyes. In the old days, racing around near top speed meant *Bluefish* wouldn't be able to see anything. Now, her dampers filtered out most of her self-noise and gave them a decent idea of their surroundings. But running fast was always a risk. Someone quiet *could* sneak up on them. Pinging with active sonar guaranteed no one crept up on them, but sound worked both ways. "You already do the time-distance?"

"Yes, sir. About forty-one hours sprinting and drifting will take us to an intercept point," Bobby answered. "If they stay on the least-time course to Vajrabahu, we should beat them by a few hours."

"Sounds good. Tell the OOD to turn and burn."

Bobby fidgeted. "You, uh, don't want to check my course, sir?"

"Do I need to?" Alex asked.

"Well, I went over it three times with Rene, and had Weps check it for good measure—"

"Then let's not waste time." Alex's reply made Bobby blink, so he continued: "I believe in trusting people to do their jobs.

Don't run us into an underwater mountain, and we'll all be fine."

Bobby blanched. "I, uh, think I can manage that."

"Good. Let's get to work."

HMS Gallant, *off the coast of the Seychelles*

Even Ursula usually admitted patrol boats weren't worth wasting torpedoes on, but damn it all, she wanted to kill *something*! Her orders provided a remarkable amount of leeway to choose her patrol areas, so here Ursula would stay.

Every bloody captain liked the Seychelles. It was a damned paradise. Literally. The beaches were impossible to beat, and the water was the clearest Ursula had ever seen. Hell, she'd been proposed to here! She'd refused it, but the attempt had been romantic.

In peacetime, every ship wanted to come to the Seychelles so they could "Cross the Line," or the equator. Crossing the equator had particular significance in every navy Ursula knew of, complete with odd ceremonies, stranger humor, and some traditions that her navy no longer admitted having. The island was the best liberty port outside Australia and a hell of a lot closer to most shipping lanes.

Ursula had spent plenty of time here during her twenty-year naval career. This would've been her sixth visit, not including the one disastrous vacation that turned into the wedding proposal. However, the Seychelles' new alliance with the Freedom Union didn't change geography or tourists' desires, did it? She bet this would turn into yet another set of moneybags for the enemy. Worse yet, Quincy Mining Station had opened in 2031 right the bloody hell off Victoria, making cash flow into the small republic.

That was why the Alliance had allowed the fools to remain neutral, wasn't it? The Seychelles were rich...and sailors loved casinos.

Ursula ground her teeth again. Her father would've lectured her, but old Lord North could go jump off a cliff. He didn't want her out here, never had, and Ursula didn't give a damn. Maybe she'd email her sister and see if the prick had died of a heart attack yet. Lydia could have the damned seat in the House of Lords. Ursula knew where she belonged.

Right here, waiting for something worth shooting.

Eventually, a worthy target would present itself. She'd even take a high vale merchant or two; sinking even one container ship resulted in a clogged harbor for months.

USS **Bluefish,** *in route to SNAP SHOT coordinates*

Eavesdropping was rude, but submarines were small spaces, and it was hard not to overhear things when Sonar left the curtain open. Especially when you were a sonar officer who wanted to keep your people out of trouble. Harri had the mid watch that night, much to her surprise; Commander Peterson would've pulled her 0fficer of the deck qualification if he got that email from the Mediterranean, but Captain Coleman left her alone...so far. She, Rene, Andrea, and Wally sent off apology emails the day before, but they still dreaded the other shoe dropping. Harri's two-and-a-half years in the navy told her captains just didn't let shit like this go.

"Y'know, I have a friend who was on *Jimmy Carter*," a voice said from sonar as Harri wandered around *Bluefish's* small attack center. It sounded like Sonar Technician First Class Luis Perez, who was a good sonarman and the boat's biggest gossip. Harri couldn't count the number of times she'd caught her leading petty officer grinning and spreading rumors, true or not.

"Yeah?" That was STS2 Flora "Flo" Walkman, the sonar division's shining star. She was the best they had after Chief Andreas. Harri knew Walkman was on the fast track, no doubt.

"Yeah. She said that Convoy Fifty-Seven was fucking crazy, worse than the time she stole a plane and gave a few hookers a joy ride."

"Get out."

"I'm serious! We were on *Silversides* together before the war. I was at her Captain's Mast when she went up for that plane thing."

Walkman laughed. "Okay, so she's not *completely* full of shit. What's the story, then?"

"Convoy Fifty-Seven or the plane caper?"

"C'mon, dude, I don't care about the stupid plane."

"Jus' checkin'." Harri heard gum popping. Definitely Luis. Even fear of Prissy Peterson couldn't make him stop chewing gum. "So, yeah, Boxer says that it was fucking nuts. Says that the Indians smashed *Jimmy Carter* down to the bottom not once but twice and that the captain just picked the boat up and kept going back for more."

"Dude, you can't slam a boat into the bottom and get up again." Walkman snorted. "She's pulling your leg."

"I dunno. Did you read his Medal of Honor citation? It sounds like it was abso-fucking-lutely batshit. Boxer said they went to PD in the middle of the Indian formation when they didn't have any fucking torpedoes, just to pull the Indians away from the convoy."

"*What?*"

Harri gulped. She needed to read that Medal of Honor citation. She'd been on *Bluefish* when the other sub limped back into Perth and had seen how trashed *Jimmy Carter* looked, but she hadn't heard that last part. Hell, she hadn't known about them bouncing off the bottom, either. Harri wasn't sure how she felt about that. On one hand, it was nice to know that their captain could shoot—because nothing sucked more than working for a guy you were pretty sure was a coward—but on the other...

This was crazy. And now they'd gotten a SNAP SHOT—a fucking SNAP SHOT!—straight from Uncle Marco. *Bluefish* had been at the bottom of the navy barrel so long it felt like they were stuck there. Being somewhere else, and with someone other than Commander Peterson in command, was a strange feeling.

Perth, Australia

"Welcome aboard, STS1." LTJG Hewitt was Kansas' sonar officer and seemed like a decent sort. She also looked about twelve, with curly red hair and freckles for days, but Bud Wilson supposed that wasn't her fault. Hewitt shrugged. "Sorry we don't have a sponsor for you, but we just got your orders this morning."

"Well, ma'am, I'd had orders to Hyman G. Rickover, but that obviously isn't gonna happen, now." Bud felt a little guilty saying that so glibly, but Rickover wasn't the first sub America had lost in this war, and she wasn't going to be the last. He'd had a friend from A School on the boat, too, and really wanted to find out if any survivors had gotten off, but no one seemed to know. You'd think they'd figure that out in less than ten days, but apparently not.

Hell of a way to run a railroad. Or a war. Bud figured a war was probably harder, but the brainchildren in charge of this one probably couldn't make trains show up on time, either.

He shifted his seabag on his shoulder and snuck a surreptitious glance around *Kansas'* deck. The boat looked like it was in pretty good shape, which was nice. She was a shit-ton newer than *Jimmy Carter*, which was nice, too. Yeah, *Virginias* didn't have all the bells and whistles, but the late-model Block

Vs weren't exactly bad. *Kansas* was only ten years old, and in prewar days, that would've made her a spring chicken.

About a year ago, Bud would've had a count on exactly how many subs in the fleet were younger—or older—than his new boat. Now they sank too fast to keep up with.

Hewitt grimaced. "Probably not, no. But the XO likes to check all the boxes, so we'll get you hooked up with a sponsor this afternoon."

"Sounds fine to me, ma'am." Bud shrugged. "I guess that means I've got to do the whole check-in fun, doesn't it?"

"Is that a problem?"

"Nope. No, I mean." Bud managed not to grimace. He was back in the real navy now. It was time to pull his head out and act like it.

He missed *Jimmy Carter* already. Yeah, she was probably razor blades now, but he'd fit in there. Or at least he had once he stopped drinking. Heading to that old boat had probably saved his career, and Bud knew it. Being on *Bluefish* had been enough to drive anyone to drink, and he hadn't exactly needed encouragement. But now in the "proper" navy with an XO who liked to check all the boxes? Fantastic. It was time to remember how to smile at assholes.

Life on Smiley had gotten so much better when Commander Kirkland started hiding in his stateroom. Bud didn't suppose he'd be lucky enough to have that happen twice, though.

Maybe these idiots didn't know what kind of fuckup he'd been. Maybe they only knew about his shiny silver star. If so, this could be a fresh start. Did he want that?

Hell, he wanted to stay in the navy and do *something* worthwhile, so Bud supposed, yeah, he wanted them to treat him like he was fit to share air with real humans. Why did making a difference have to be so fucking addictive?

"Come on down to sonar and I'll introduce you to everyone. We're short a chief right now, so you're senior," Hewitt told him, and Bud perked up.

He hated chief petty officers, as a rule. There were a few who knew their shit and didn't get in his way, but most of them were full of themselves and thought they knew more about sonar than he did. Being the senior sonar operator, however, was something he'd done before and liked. So he followed Hewitt down toward *Kansas'* sonar spaces. He'd grab the rest of his crap out of the car and move aboard later. It was time to start a new chapter in his already colorful career.

Two days after the SNAP SHOT message flew, MV *Mighty Servant 3* and MV *Black Marlin* stumbled right into *Bluefish's* sights.

"Captain, we've got a good read on both heavy lift ships, and they've got two frigates for company," Chief Andreas's voice floated out of the intercom from Sonar. "Sounds like two FREMMs."

A FREMM was a common type of European multi-purpose frigate, built for various countries, including France, Italy, and Indonesia. A versatile and customizable hull form with some common systems, FREMMs ruled the seas from the 2010s onward. Designed in both anti-air and anti-submarine variants, they were solid and capable ships. Decades later, even the United States got into the game with the *Constellation* class. Nancy had served on *Chesapeake* earlier in her career, which meant Alex knew their capabilities very well.

"Very well." Alex took a deep breath. "Any helos up?"

"No, sir." Andreas sounded smug, and Alex couldn't blame her.

Submariners claimed the best way to kill a submarine was with another submarine, but that hid an ugly truth. Air assets, either fixed wing or rotary, almost always won. A submarine was within the same element as its prey, but a helicopter could use dipping sonar or sonobuoys to insert itself into that medium...and a sub couldn't shoot back at aircraft. Surface ships could be dangerous sub hunters if they carried helicopters, but these two frigates didn't have their helicopters in the air. *Is there something I'm missing?* Most French FREMMs were anti-submarine warfare specialists. He supposed that helicopters couldn't fly all day, but experience made Alex paranoid.

Was this too easy?

"All right, OOD, let's go up and take a look." He let Bobby conn the submarine to periscope depth, wanting to see his acting XO in action. Should he have worried? No, Bobby had a deft hand in a *Cero*.

"Level at eighty feet, Captain," Bobby reported after following all procedures to the letter.

"Up scope." Alex matched actions to words, raising the number two periscope. He was grateful the navy had finally moved away from the always-up type of periscope *Virginia*-class submarines sported. Those scopes were susceptible to proxy damage from nearby explosions; too many *Virginias* returned to port with their periscopes mangled. The *Ceros* did have a periscope camera display in control, however, which was pretty sweet. Alex could get used to that perk in a hurry, even if he was old-fashioned enough to prefer looking through the periscope proper.

A few of the younger officers gave his back strange looks for that habit, but Alex ignored them, slowly rotating the periscope to take in a 360-degree view of the outside world. *Bluefish* was three thousand yards off *Black Marlin's* starboard side, an easy shot. But the two frigates mattered more. As Alex swung the scope around, he spotted one ahead of the two-ship convoy and one further to starboard. *Perfect.*

"Come right to parallel *Black Marlin's* course and speed," he ordered, listening with half an ear as Bobby instructed the helmsman to bring the submarine around. Alex took one last look and then stepped back. "Down scope."

There was no reason to leave themselves open to being spotted; this wasn't World War II. Alex didn't need the scope to shoot. Even if he had done that before.

"Weps, set them up. Firing point procedures, tubes one through four"—he still hated only having four torpedo tubes—"for both frigates. Take the forward one with the port tubes. Make all tubes ready in all respects, including opening the outer doors."

"Firing point procedures, tubes one through four, Weps, aye!" Energy crackled around Rose as she and her team got to work; of all of Alex's new officers, she was the most charismatic, the obvious warfighter. She also seemed the least beat down by his predecessor, although that didn't say much.

Alex leaned into the speaker near the periscope and hit the talk switch, asking: "Sonar, Conn, got any surprises up there?"

The last time he targeted multiple ships, he'd gotten his sub pounded into scrap.

"Conn, Sonar, no, sir. Still no air assets up."

"Very well." Alex turned back to Bobby. "Raise the ESM mast. Let's make sure they aren't steaming along fat, dumb, and happy because they have P-8 support."

"Raise the ESM mast, aye." Bobby looked a little worried but didn't object. Raising the mast *did* cause a slight chance of detection, but it was worth the risk. Alex wasn't stupid enough to use *Bluefish's* small air-search radar. Active emissions were suicidal.

"Nothing detected but surface navigational radars, Captain," a watchstander reported a few minutes later.

"Very well. Lower the mast." Was he paranoid? Probably.

Now wasn't the time to think about the P-8 aircraft and helos that dogged *Jimmy Carter* with sonobuoys and depth charges. Or about how it felt when his last submarine hit the bottom. Alex shook himself. *Focus on the now, asshole.*

"Solutions ready, tubes one through four," Rose reported.

"Ship ready," Bobby said.

"Tubes one through four, fire." At least Alex couldn't overthink this. Convoy 57 taught him how to shoot, if nothing else.

Rose smacked the buttons. "Tubes one through four fired electronically!"

"Conn, Sonar, four fish running hot, straight, and normal," Chief Andreas reported a few moments later.

"Very well."

Minutes ticked by as Rose's team guided the torpedoes toward both frigates; Alex could've cut the guidance wires and let the Mark 84s search on their own, but he didn't dare do that against two ASW frigates. But guiding four torpedoes in meant Alex had nothing ready to fire if something happened. Here was hoping those two cats didn't have any underwater friends. "Whatever brainchild decided four torpedo tubes was enough needs their fucking head checked."

"Captain?" Bobby sounded concerned.

Alex jumped. Was his face on fire? Fuck. He made himself chuckle. "I'm just used to having twice as many tubes." As if he hadn't made that super obvious with his flub two days ago. "I'd rather leave a fish in reserve for any surprises, but four tubes don't offer a lot of flexibility."

"I guess not?" Bobby shrugged. "I've only ever served on *Ceros*."

"I was only on *Virginias* until *Jimmy Carter*, but having eight tubes is an advantage you get used to in a hurry." Alex shrugged. "She might've been old, but *Smiley* had a shit-ton of room for weapons."

"Makes you wonder why they went back to the 688 layout for the *Virginias*," Bobby said, and Alex could have cheered. His acting XO had a brain and wasn't going to pieces. Finally!

Alex spent hours walking around the boat talking to people in the last two days, but the wardroom was a harder nut to crack. Bobby O'Kane in particular.

"Probably because no one ever thought we'd get in an actual submarine war," Alex said. "And if so, the idiots thought we'd outclass our opponents by such a wide margin that it wouldn't matter."

"Yeah, that's worked out great for us." Bobby grimaced.

"Peacetime navies generally learn those lessons the hard way." Alex wasn't a historian, but he'd studied a lot over the last two years. It was a pity he hadn't spent more time on naval history in college than he had drinking, but he'd been an engineer and thought he'd never need it. "Look at—"

"Torpedoes are in final acquisition, Captain!" Rose said, and Alex twisted back to look at the weapons corner.

Wire-guided torpedoes almost never missed; why was his stomach in knots? Oh, right. The last torpedo he fired at a surface ship ended with *Jimmy Carter* depth charged into oblivion.

Alex steadied himself with a quick glance down to make sure his hands weren't shaking. "Very well."

"Impact!" Rose didn't quite whoop.

"Conn, Sonar, I have two surface explosions bearing one-niner-four and zero-eight-eight. We've got four good hits, sir!"

"Conn, aye." Alex smiled as he turned back toward Rose's team. "Well done, folks. Reload all tubes and get ready to do it again. Those merchants are going to run like hell."

Rose chuckled. "They can't outrun us. Why try?"

"Because they might get lucky and get air support if they split up." Alex made a face. "You never know who's going to show up and fuck up a battle."

"Yes, sir." Rose shot him a funny look, but Alex just shrugged.

Time dragged by as *Bluefish's* team reloaded all four torpedo tubes. Bobby started pacing, and Alex was tempted to join him. Not watching the clock was a chore. He needed to schedule drills. Ten minutes' reload time sucked monkey balls. But he wouldn't say that to his crew. Alex crocked a finger to beckon Bobby over.

"Captain?"

"Once we're done with these two, let's schedule some reload drills. We've got to get faster at this." Alex started chewing on his glasses. "Hanging around for ten minutes between shots is a great way to get dead."

Bobby fidgeted. "We've, uh, never trained to the wartime reload procedures. Commander Peterson preferred the older methods."

"He wasn't much for taking risks, was he?"

"No, sir."

"Well, nothing ventured, nothing gained. Big Navy is happy with the wartime procedures, and an enemy is more likely to kill us than our own torpedo misfiring. So let's implement them yesterday."

"Aye, sir." Was Bobby unhappy with this or unhappy in general? It was so hard to tell.

"All tubes reloaded, Captain," Rose reported after an eternity long enough to make Alex's hair go gray.

"Very well." Alex took a breath and looked over at the radio watch. "Dial me in to bridge-to-bridge channel sixteen, will you?"

The watchstander bobbed her head, her eyes too wide to show confusion. "You're up, sir."

"Thanks." Alex shot her a tight smile, wishing the butterflies in his stomach would listen to his rock-steady hands. Why was shooting people easier than public speaking? Alex shook himself and lifted the mike before he could stop himself.

"Merchant Vessels *Black Marlin* and *Mighty Servant 3*, this is U.S. Navy Submarine Eight-Four-Three. You are legitimate military targets sailing in a war zone. You have fifteen—I say again, one-five—minutes to abandon ship before I sink you." Alex repeated the words and waited for the protests.

He should've done this while he waited for his people to reload, but then they might've run while *Bluefish* was busy with the frigates.

"Captain, is this a new requirement?" Bobby crept to his side, frowning. Alex had broken stealth, a submarine's best defense.

"No." Alex chewed on his glasses for a moment. "But I'm not really a fan of killing civilians, are you?"

The closest he'd come to sinking civilian ships during the war was the pirates who came after *Jimmy Carter* in the South China Sea, but Alex hadn't felt a flicker of guilt over that. But these ships... These ships were legitimate military targets, but torpedoes broke unarmored hulls like eggshells. He didn't know how many civilians were on board each, just that merchant crews were usually small. But not small enough to not bother him.

"It's...the job." Bobby fidgeted.

"Yeah, it is. But when we can give them a chance to abandon before sinking them—without hazarding the boat—I plan to."

There was something strange in his acting XO's face, but Bobby nodded. "Yes, sir."

The merchants objected, but Alex merely repeated the same warning. Meanwhile, he brought *Bluefish* up to periscope depth to watch the merchant sailors abandon ship, looking at the trio of brand-spanking-new diesel attack submarines sitting on the deck of each ship. He had no qualms about sending those suckers to the bottom. He just wanted to get the civilians out of the way first.

Of course, if an enemy submarine stumbled upon *Bluefish* while Alex was busy trying to save enemy civilians, he'd look like a dead idiot. Fortunately, after his time limit expired, Alex shot a pair of torpedoes into *Black Marlin* and another pair into *Mighty Servant 3*. It was probably overkill, but the secondary explosions destroyed the *Scorpenes*, too.

Why was it so easy? Alex had just sunk one attack sub, two frigates, and two heavy lift ships in just this one patrol. *So much for boring convoy escorts.* That was pretty good record by anyone's measure, particularly if the six *Scorpenes* counted in his tonnage total. Less than three months ago, he'd been the CO of the navy's oldest and most forgotten submarine. Things really had changed.

6 January 2040, Naval Base Pearl Harbor, Hawaii

TO: COMSUBPAC//

FROM: USS BLUEFISH SSN 843//

SUBJ: SNAP SHOT 1-2040 RESPONSE//

RMKS/1. MV BLACK MARLIN AND MV MIGHTY SERVANT 3 LOCATED IVO 15°14'1 2.3" S 062°14'17.1" E WITH TWO (2) FRENCH FFGS ESCORTING.

2. ALL TARGETS SUNK 060845z JAN 40.//

"Well, I will be dipped in horseshit." Marco Rodriquez didn't bother to hold back his grin. "Guess that experiment paid off."

"Experiment?"

Ah. He'd forgotten his guest. Marco grinned harder, extending the old-fashioned hardcopy of the message his aide delivered. "You're not the only hotshot in the submarine business now, Dalton."

John Dalton scowled back at him; at least the man had guts. "You killed my 'hotshot' days when you pulled me off *Razorback* to give me a sub tender, Admiral."

"That's the price we pay for stars, sonny boy. You've got to stop banging the help and start acting like a responsible adult."

"I never—"

"Shut up and read the message."

Dalton did; it didn't take long before he started frowning. "*Bluefish*? Isn't that Wade Peterson?"

"No fucking way. His appendix burst, and he's still in the hospital. I gave *Bluefish* to Alex Coleman." Marco smirked. He knew the two were friends. He didn't remember how or why, but Dalton had wanted to be the one to call Coleman's wife when they'd thought *Jimmy Carter* lost. Something about serving together? It didn't matter.

"Seriously?"

Marco's eyes narrowed. "You got a problem with that?"

"No, sir." Dalton shook his head. "Just don't be surprised if you get the unexpected with Alex."

"Remind me how well you know him again?" Marco could gloat later. He'd only met Coleman once, when he'd surprised the kid—because damn, he'd seemed young standing next to the all-too-trashed *Jimmy Carter*—with a promotion. Marco attended the Medal of Honor ceremony, too, but even a vice admiral was small fry there. Dalton hadn't attended, but with *Nereus* underway, Marco couldn't hold that against him.

"He was my best man at my wedding, sir. I'm godfather to his youngest daughter."

Marco sat back in his chair, ideas swirling in his head. Captain John Dalton *was* the sub force's rising star; Marco gave him command of *Nereus* to groom him for a quick promotion...and to keep him from dying in a submarine. So far, *every* American superstar sub commander had died in the line of duty, except Dalton. Marco didn't think Dalton realized he'd yanked him out of *Razorback* to save his life, but the U.S. Navy needed future commodores—and admirals—with the right kind of combat experience. Marco didn't have a whit of it himself, and he didn't need tea leaves to see the future.

"Tell me more," he ordered.

If an up-and-coming son of an admiral and a general was friends with the unorthodox rebel that Admiral Freddie Hamilton was *so* very not fond of, Marco figured there was something to this.

Now he was starting to get ideas.

Chapter 8

Glory Hound

Bud Wilson had been on board *Kansas* for three days when they got underway, and he could read a chart well enough to know they weren't where they were supposed to be. Back in the olden days, the sonar room had been a dark and mysterious place, full of green-and-black monitors, speakers, and not much else. On a more-or-less modern submarine, however, sonar was just two consoles in the attack center, and there was a virtual chart display right next to Bud's station. He was also the senior enlisted sonar operator on board, which meant that he read message traffic and knew where *Kansas* was *supposed* to be.

"You got a minute, ma'am?" Bud asked as he got off watch. Coincidentally, LTJG Hewitt had just gotten off, too, which meant Bud might be able to grab a moment's private conversation with his division officer.

"Sure, STS1. What's on your mind?"

"Mind if we take a walk?"

She shrugged, so Bud led the young officer—she had to be at least twenty-four, but she *still* acted like she was in middle school—to one of the sonar equipment spaces. No one really liked to hang out in them, particularly since this one was too small to store even free weights, so the space was empty. Bud didn't bother to close the door; the last thing he needed was some stupid boat rumor about the new STS1 trying to boink the sonar officer. He sort of had a halfway decent career for the first time ever. Bud maybe liked the idea of being a top-notch sonarman.

Hewitt huffed impatiently. "Something going on down here that I need to know about?"

"I was about to ask you the same question, Ma'am." Bud took a deep breath. "I can read message traffic. I know that we're supposed to be filling in for one of the Australian diesels in boxes five-tac-three through five-tac seven...but we're nowhere near there."

In fact, *Kansas* was about two hundred nautical miles east of Australia instead of close to the coast, but Bud figured that his divo didn't need him to spell it out in very small words. When she sighed and studied the wall to his left, he was sure of it.

"You haven't gone talking about this with any of the guys, have you?" Hewitt asked.

"Ma'am, do I look like an idiot? I'm only an idiot when I'm drunk, and I quit drinking."

Hewitt's smile was wan. "You'd better have. The XO doesn't take kindly to liberty incidents, and you've got a bit of a reputation to go with that silver star of yours."

"Oh. Um." Bud hadn't told any stories, though he'd figured his new crewmates would've heard about the Silver Star he'd earned on *Jimmy Carter.* Unfortunately, his drinking escapades were equally well known. Maybe better. His finger painting with wine and the fort he built out of barstools was such a legend in Perth that he *still* heard people talking about it. "Yeah. I know I'm a bit of a menace, Ma'am, but that doesn't mean I'm wrong about this."

"No, it doesn't." She sighed. "Would you believe me if I told you that we got a change in orders?"

"Not if it wasn't in message traffic. I wasn't born yesterday." Bud wasn't stupid enough to point out that his divo looked like *she* was.

Hewitt's helpless shrug made Bud feel sorry for her. He was her leading petty officer, not to mention five years older than her, and *Kansas* was her first boat. She probably hadn't been in the navy for much longer than two years, and what did she know?

Hewitt cringed. "It's the name of the game, right?"

Poor kid. Bud could have said a lot of things, but this wasn't a battle he could win. "Fuck if I know, Ma'am. My job's to listen good and try to figure out where the bad guys are before they can shoot us."

"Just...keep this to yourself, okay, STS1?" The way she said it made the words sound like a plea.

"Sure. Who'm I going to tell, anyway?"

Bud sure as hell wasn't going to go to the captain. His check-in interview with Commander Kennedy had been yesterday, and if there was anyone who exuded the "rules don't apply to me" kind of attitude, it was that guy. And the XO, Lieutenant Commander Song, seemed even worse. *She* was a stickler for every regulation ever written—and had been obnoxious enough to ask how an extra-large Japanese-looking guy ended up with Wilson as a last name. But there was no way that the captain could do this without the XO playing along, which meant that Bud would have had to be the biggest idiot in the world to go whining to her.

And here he'd been thinking about how this boat would be normal. Great. It was almost enough to make him want to go back to *Bluefish*.

But almost only counted with depth charges, and Bud planned on avoiding those suckers from now on, thank you very much.

The patrol report for Convoy 57 was released a month and a half after the most famous battle of the war. Harri Ainsworth read it first and then came to the wardroom to pass it off to Bobby, her features a little ashen.

"Is this all true, sir?" she asked.

"It's supposed to be. Why?"

"They smashed *Jimmy Carter* into the bottom twice," Harri said. She swallowed hard. "That should have *sunk* her. For good, I mean."

Bobby knew that "they" was Captain Coleman, but no one on board wanted to call their captain out. Peterson taught them the error of even appearing to criticize *Bluefish's* captain. Wibbling, Bobby finally decided to turn this into a teaching moment instead of veering toward denigration of his superior. That was never good for discipline.

"I know the answer to that." He flashed Harri a smile. "I haven't read the patrol report yet, but *Jimmy Carter*—like all the *Seawolf* class—was constructed with HY-100 steel. Better stuff than they made this girl out of." Bobby slapped the nearest bulkhead for emphasis.

Harri frowned. "Why would they change that? If it's better..."

"All to save the almighty dollar, my child. HY-80 is cheaper."

"Oh," Harri said. She hesitated a moment before continuing, her eyes flicking left and right. "Do you think he knew they'd be okay?"

"Honestly? No idea." Bobby understood Harri's worries. No sailor wanted to ride around in a submarine whose CO was careless with their lives. Captain Coleman didn't seem like a maniac so far, but he hadn't been on board that long. The Convoy 57 patrol report probably told the truth. Captain Coleman had written it right after the battle.

Harri shifted uneasily. "Read it and let me know what you think?"

"You got it, kiddo."

"I'm not *that* much younger than you, Nav." She scowled.

"Sorry. I guess it's too easy to go into big brother mode. Got lots of practice and all." Bobby shrugged. "I'll read it. I promise."

Harri headed off, leaving Bobby alone in the wardroom. He liked hanging out there, liked being part of the team instead of hiding in his stateroom. Holing up there had been a great way to avoid Peterson, but now he didn't need to, right?

The Convoy 57 patrol report was longer than Bobby expected, way longer than the *Bluefish* ones Peterson never let him read. It was succinct, too, bold and straight to the point. It almost read like a video game script, except Bobby knew this had been very real—and an American submarine crew *lived* through it. *Jimmy Carter* sank one enemy after another, dodging torpedoes and depth charges until they were finally depth charged to the bottom. Most COs would quit at that point, even if they were reasonably certain they could coax their boat back up again. Hell, Bobby was pretty sure he never would've thought about getting into the fight after that! Any involuntary bottoming was practically being sunk!

Jimmy Carter did it twice.

However, what Bobby found the most interesting thing wasn't the details of the battle, or even *Jimmy Carter's* three-week struggle to make it back to port, damaged and unable to call for help. No, he was fascinated by Captain Coleman's honest assessment of his own mistakes. He didn't write like a megalomaniac, or even someone obsessed with success. He wrote like someone who wanted other people to learn from his experiences. He'd also listed the names of every sailor who died on *Jimmy Carter*...which meant he didn't want to forget them.

Did that mean *Bluefish's* new captain wasn't going to do something crazy? No. Coleman would do whatever he thought was his duty, and he'd do it in a heartbeat.

Bobby glanced back at the patrol report. He could live with that.

8 January 2040, Paris, France

It really was too easy.

Once, Captain Jules Rochambeau had respected the American submarine community. They'd redefined submarine warfare in World War II with USS *Wahoo* and Mush Morton and then moved into the silent days of nuclear submarines in the Cold War as the best in the world. Back then, his country had been a proud member of NATO, standing shoulder to shoulder with the Americans and British against the Russian bear. Now, the world had changed. Russia was France's friend, and American submariners had lost their edge.

Jules Rochambeau was the best submarine commander in the world, and he knew it. He'd almost lost count of the number of Alliance submarines he sank. But he didn't need to keep track, since the media did it for him. He *had* genuinely forgotten how many surface warships and merchants he'd sent to the bottom. He hardly needed those statistics at his fingertips. Even when called in for television interviews like this.

"Tell me," the lovely young interviewer asked next, brushing dark hair out of her eyes, "are the British *Astute*-class submarines as quiet and as deadly as they claim?"

Jules chuckled. "*Non*. Or perhaps sometimes? I did not find *Ajax* or *Astute* remarkably hard to kill, although I understand some of the sailors and officers were able to escape." He shrugged. "*Quel dommage*."

"And what will you and your crew do next, Captain?" Her smile told him that she didn't care about stranded Alliance sailors. So much the better.

"I cannot really say that, of course. Operational security." But he winked at her, and she blushed. She'd be open to a tryst, which meant he would have to remember her name. She'd probably ask him to tweet about it, which he'd regretfully refuse to do. But he might be open to a few celebrity photos or taking her to some event or another. She was stunning, and keeping the media on side was important. "But it is safe to say that we will be quite...busy."

In truth, *Barracuda* was long overdue for overhaul, which meant Jules's current task was to do interviews and keep his face in the public eye. Admiral Sauvageau was quite clear on that, and Jules hardly minded. He enjoyed the spotlight almost as much as he enjoyed his work. Upon joining the navy, he never expected to become a national star, but the sensation was addictive. Every camera flash sent a pleasurable chill down his spine, even when it was just someone's cell phone. The beautiful speed of modern communications meant warfighters could be stars again—and in real time!

What he couldn't understand was why his enemies were so slow to pick up on the ante. The Alliance rarely showcased their successful submarine captains. Ursula North was a legend amongst other submariners—second only to him—but the Brits seemed afraid to place her in front of a camera.

Then again, perhaps they knew dear Ursula too well. Lady North could blister the sound-deafening tiles off an attack submarine. That thought made him smile. As for the Americans...well, none of them had lived long enough to matter, had they? There was John Dalton, but the fools moved him to a submarine tender. Perhaps he would speak to Admiral Sauvageau about sinking USS *Nereus* next. That would be a nice blow to American morale. American industrial might was best restrained by their public's appetite for war, and no one in the Freedom Union wanted to awaken that sleeping dragon. If he could help them lose their taste for battle...

But for now, he turned his attention back to the beautiful woman interviewing him. She deserved nothing less.

Bluefish was less than two days out from Perth, four hours into the inbound lane between patrol sectors. Subs assigned to those sectors monitored the inbound and outbound lanes without actively patrolling them; they changed weekly and were classified. Even surface ships didn't know where they were. Attack subs were just expected to keep clear of their skimmer brethren or communicate with them. Attack subs assigned sectors close to Australia, on the other hand, were tasked with determining if incoming boats were friend or foe, which meant any sub captain with a brain was on edge during the transit.

Alex had held command of *Bluefish* for just seventeen days, but this was his twenty-first inbound transit to Perth. *Finally, something old enough to drink.* He smiled wryly, trying not to think of the nerve-racking mess his last transit on *Jimmy Carter* had been. They'd been lucky that no one heard them; otherwise, the limping and broken submarine would've been torpedoed straight to the bottom. Wasn't that such a happy thought? At least *Bluefish* was fully operational, even if he'd been warned that her bow thruster liked to break.

"Captain, do you have a sec?" Speaking of warnings, his acting XO stood in the doorway to his stateroom, there to rescue him from his dark thoughts. Bobby O'Kane still seemed like he was waiting to be yelled at, but he was a little better these days.

"Sure. Come on in and pull up a chair." Alex gestured Bobby into his stateroom with a smile. The younger officer closed the door behind himself, and Alex's eyebrows shot up.

"Sir, are you serious about revoking the old liberty policy?" Bobby fidgeted. "Cause, um, if so, it'll mean a lot to the crew."

Alex had almost forgotten about his predecessor's no-drinking brainchild. "I believe in treating adults like adults, yeah." He leaned back in his chair. "Speaking of which, I assume that our quartet of miscreants has made their apologies to the owner of The Mediterranean?"

"Yes, sir. All four blind copied me."

"Good." Alex finally let himself laugh. "They picked a really shit restaurant for those shenanigans. You ever been there?"

"Once? The food was, uh..."

"Crap. Being generous." Alex shook his head. "Overpriced and overcooked, too. A friend of mine—"

His phone buzzed, and Alex grabbed it.

"Captain."

"Good evening, sir, it's the officer of the deck," Harri—one of the aforementioned miscreants—said. "We're currently passing box five-three, and sonar reports that the assigned sub is nowhere to be found."

A cold chill raced down Alex's spine. "Who's meant to be there, and what are their other boxes?"

"*Kansas*, five-three through five-seven, sir."

Of course, it was *Kansas*. Alex still knew a lot of her crew and still exchanged emails with Master Chief Casey. There were a thousand and one reasons why *Bluefish* might not detect *Kansas*...but a *Cero* should be able to hear a *Virginia* under localized sonar conditions. They'd had good bottom bounce contacts just a little while earlier. "I'm on my way."

Alex filled Bobby in on the situation in the thirty seconds it took to make it up to control. The watch there was tense, but at least no one freaked out when he walked in. Baby steps. He'd take that. "All right, Harri, talk to me."

"It might be nothing, sir, but Chief Andreas is pretty sure there's no one in those sectors," his officer of the deck replied. Her eyes were a little wide, but at least she was worried about another submarine, not if Alex was going to rip her head off.

He hoped.

"And it might not be nothing," Alex agreed, absently chewing his glasses. He'd forgotten his gum when he'd packed, and his glasses were already paying the price. He needed more candy next patrol. Hell, he hated needing the stupid reading glasses, anyway. Nancy had bullied him into going to the eye doctor while on leave, but he wasn't even forty. Needing reading glasses felt like admitting defeat, even if she'd been right about what caused his headaches.

"Conn, Sonar, I've got a tick of something submerged on a bearing for the southern edge of five-tac-three," Chief Andreas' voice reported through the squawk box. Alex pulled his glasses out of his mouth.

"A tick of *Kansas*, or something else?" He missed STS1 Wilson from *Jimmy Carter*. Andreas seemed good at her job, but Wilson was just short of magical.

"Captain, Sonar, no positive ID, but it's not a *Virginia*. I've got something on the sixty-nine hertz line and there's nothing on *Kansas* that fits. It's not another *Cero*, either."

"Captain, aye." Alex glanced over at the nav display. *Bluefish* was dead center in the inbound lane and moving at fifteen knots. The southern edge of box five-tac-three was almost fifty miles from his boat's current position. He let out a breath. The Aussies had quiet diesel submarines. In fact, persistent rumors claimed that the U.S. was going to build a derivative of the newest Australian class of submarine. "Any chance it's a *Shortfin*?"

"No, sir. Not a *Collins*, either."

"Hm." Alex glanced at Bobby, who also bent over the plot, looking at the datum Andreas put in the system to signify the unknown contact's position. "You thinking what I'm thinking?"

"Well, if it's not *Kansas*, and it's not an Alliance submarine..."

"Bingo." Alex looked back at Harri. "Officer of the Deck, set battle stations torpedo. Silently."

"OOD, aye!"

Setting battle stations silently meant no one would pass the word on the 1MC speakers, instead spreading the word from one compartment to another. It took longer than using the general alarm, but with an enemy close, silence was *Bluefish's* best friend.

The usual chaos around Alex seemed muted; people whispered for no reason and scurried on their tiptoes. Smiling to himself, he headed into sonar to look over Chief Andreas' shoulder.

"Got anything more concrete, Chief?"

She shook her head, eyes riveted on the screen. "No, sir. Whatever's out there is fuc—really quiet."

"I've heard the word before, Chief. No need to worry about my virgin ears. I've even been known to use it from time to time." Alex grinned. "Any guesses?"

"We're not supposed to have any Brits down here, are we? The *Gallants* have an air compressor that operates at sixty-nine hertz." Andreas scowled. "But so do the Russian *Yasens.*"

"Russians? This far south?"

Andreas turned to look at him. "I think Brits would use the lane, sir."

"And the Japanese Navy ain't exactly what it used to be, yeah, I get you." Alex chewed his lip. They were *screwed* if the Russians sent boats down to play. The *Yasens* were the Russian version of the *Seawolf* class, subs built with one purpose in mind: killing other submarines. And they built a lot more than three of them, too. "Thanks, Chief."

Alex headed back into control, noticing that battle stations were manned. "Bobby, come left to one-zero-zero."

"You want to leave the lane, sir?" Bobby looked worried. Subs outside the lane were fair game.

"If this cat isn't a friend, we need to get a lot closer before we can shoot." Alex's eyes swept over the plot, watching the datum as it continued southeast. Where *was* this mystery contact headed?

"You think a hostile managed to get this close to Perth without being spotted, Captain?" Bobby sounded torn between worry and doubt.

"I think that's not *Kansas*." Alex scowled. "Anything more is speculation."

"So we follow until we know?"

"Yep." Alex turned to the squawk box. "Sonar, Conn, range to contact?"

"Forty-three miles, sir. Got a good bottom bounce track right now, designated track 7704. He's on course zero-six-zero, speed ten."

"Conn, aye." Alex's mind whirled through possibilities. If they heard the *Yasen*, could the Russians hear *Bluefish*? Sonar conditions made that likely, although American sonar was supposedly a bit better than even the newer Russian systems. Rumor said that the next Russian submarine class would beat the *Ceros*, but today Alex's boat *should* have a slight edge. He shoved his hands in his pockets.

"Okay, let's settle into a stalking position. Once we get within five miles, we'll match his course and speed. Hopefully, by then we'll know what this joker is."

Bobby blinked in confusion. "You don't want to shoot once we determine it's an enemy?"

"I want to know where he's going first." Alex's eyes traced the course indicator on the plot. "He's deep inside our defenses, but he's not heading toward any Australian ports. That could change, but..."

"You think he's got a friend out here?" Bobby asked.

"I think it's worth checking out."

Chapter 9

Mouse Trap

Six hours later, *Bluefish* reached ten nautical miles away from her prey and remained—presumably—undetected. The long stalk ate at Bobby's nerves and made him pace, even though they'd secured from battle stations hours ago. The nice thing about being acting XO was that it got him off the normal watchbill. He was still Officer of the Deck at battle stations, but he had nothing to do while they closed in on the (probable) Russian *Yasen*. That gave him too much time to think. To fret. And then think more.

It was like the Cold War, just deadlier. How the hell did the old timers do this without going insane? Even working for Peterson was less nerve-racking. At least you could count on Peterson to bully someone in his prissy little voice. This stupid enemy submarine just crept along, probably with its stupid cooling pumps off line to confuse them.

Or it was an oblivious friend, just tooling along.

"Still the same?"

Bobby jumped, wheeling to face his captain. "Um, uh, yeah. Yes, sir." He couldn't tell the captain not to creep up on him, could he? Bobby had stayed in control, hoping for something, *anything* to happen. So far, it hadn't. "Chief Andreas has been glued to the sonar console for five hours, but she still can't tell if this is a *Gallant* or a *Yasen*."

"Well, that sucks." Coleman chewed on his glasses again, making Bobby want to gag. Didn't he know how dirty glasses got? Eww. "Might be time to do something reckless."

"Sir?" Bobby's eyes wanted to pop out of his head. "You don't mean being stupid like that *Akula* and going active, do you?"

"No." Coleman snorted. "With my luck, it'll be Ursula North, and she'd pop off a torpedo."

"Is there a story there I don't know?" Bobby asked. Then he braced himself for the incoming lecture on how this wasn't his business.

"Something like that." Coleman sighed. "But—"

"Conn, Sonar, positive ID: this guy is a *Yasen*. System says ninety percent chance it's *Kazan*, second in class," Chief Andreas' voice blared out of the speaker. "He's sped up to fifteen knots."

"Conn, aye." The captain took the call, looking thoughtful. "That seems too easy, doesn't it?"

Bobby shrugged. "Hell, if I know, sir. This isn't the kind of thing we usually get here on *Bluefish*."

"Yeah, I noticed." Coleman's smile grew crooked, but he might as well have been speaking Wookie.

Bobby wasn't used to this, wasn't used to a captain who smiled, shrugged, and asked for his opinion. It wasn't *natural*. The last seventeen days were something out of a fever dream, or like someone popped Bobby into an alternate universe where being on board *Bluefish* didn't suck. Did they all get so used to living in *The Caine Mutiny* that they didn't know how to be normal submariners? Was this normal?

Bobby stepped on his urge to pace and chose to fidget instead, wiggling back and forth and making his sneakers squeak on the deck.

"Match his course and speed," the captain ordered. Bobby kept half an eye on Rene as he complied. Rene was a good officer of the deck, almost ready for his own department head tour.

Thinking about Rene meant Bobby needed a moment before the captain's orders sank in. "You don't want to just shoot him now that we know he's a *Yasen*?" he asked. "He's getting awfully close to Australia."

Close still meant five hundred nautical miles away, but against the ocean's size, that was chump change. And while *Peterson* not wanting to take risks was natural, Captain Coleman could shoot.

The way they'd sunk an *Akula*, two frigates, and those heavy lift ships still felt unnatural, too.

"He's not wandering around out here by accident." Coleman shook his head, gesturing at the plot. "Look at his course. He's come further left, like he plans to skirt the northern coast and head toward the Timor Sea."

"Maybe he's going home?" That was the only way back to Russia, unless this *Yasen* wanted to go through the Suez Canal. Going around the Horn of Africa was stupid.

"Maybe."

Grimacing, Bobby looked back down at the plot. Why *would* a Russian submarine come all the way out here just to head home? Unless they'd already sunk *Kansas*. Even then, one *Virginia* couldn't take that many torpedoes, and *Kazan* must have sunk her long before *Bluefish* came within sonar range. So they hung around for a while...only to what?

"I think this guy knows we're here." Captain Coleman got the words out before Bobby could think them, making Bobby's head jerk up. "And he's leading us around by the fucking nose, isn't he?"

Bobby swallowed. "Do you really think so, sir?"

"I wish I didn't." Coleman put his glasses on, crossing his arms. "But it adds up. Their sonar must be better than we thought, or we're louder than we should be. Either way, the question is where he's leading us."

"Shouldn't we just shoot him instead of trying to find out?"

"Nah." Coleman shook his head. "If he wants to lead us somewhere, let's be obliging."

Sometimes, Bobby missed having a coward for a captain.

HMS Gallant, *off the coast of the Seychelles*

Patience was not Ursula North's strong suit, but it paid off.

First, the French were kind enough to send two troopships to the Seychelles, where the army fools expected some rest and relaxation prior to boring garrison duty. It didn't take a genius to realize those ships were bound for Prince Edward Islands; the French had picked that South African property off the previous September. Ursula wasn't sure if anyone cared. The two islands were a nature reserve, strategically useless unless you killed a lot of local wildlife. Not that she'd put that past the French.

She still sent them to the bottom with a smile. Most of the troops waded ashore as she watched through the periscope, but that was fine.

Unfortunately, the two French destroyers sent to hunt down the dastardly submarine that dared sink two of their troopships proved a trifle more annoying. Perhaps they wished to rescue the ground pounders who swam ashore? The thought almost made Ursula laugh. They were welcome to them, but she'd make the soldiers go for a second swim if they boarded the destroyers.

"Captain, the two destroyers are splitting up," James reported an hour into their game of hide-and-seek. "One looks to be conducting a long-range search while the other draws closer to the island."

"That's a shame. I'd hoped to get both with one shot." Ursula shot him a grin. "But we shall simply have to shoot the closer one first. That should bring the other destroyer to investigate."

James' dark eyes studied her, and Ursula saw his first-rate brain working through the problem. James Harrison was night to her day: dark-skinned where Ursula was frigidly pale, quiet where she was brash, and the son of a laborer against her centuries-old title. But he was the most brilliant young officer she had the honor to mentor, and she valued his input and his instincts.

"Shall we take the shot, Captain?"

"Do so."

Gallant's torpedoes struck true, and while the second destroyer didn't exactly rush into her crosshairs, Ursula slid her boat into the open ocean and sank that ship before it found her. She refused to pull a Rochambeau and take pictures of the survivors in the water; Ursula found no joy in watching them struggle into life rafts. She refused to brag on Twitter. Her old acquaintance indulged in such bombastic swagger. Ursula let her results speak for themselves.

That didn't keep the British press from labeling *Gallant's* actions as the "One Boat Blockade" of the Seychelles after she sank an unsuspecting tanker and then the French submarine sent to kill her. Eventually, the Admiralty recalled her; the happy accident of her actions at the Seychelles was a distraction from the main war effort, no matter how well it played in the news. The One Boat Blockade added another layer to the legend of Ursula North.

Rochambeau, unfortunately, took out three more Alliance submarines in the meantime.

USS **Bluefish,** *tracking* **RFS** *Kazan*

"Conn, Sonar, *Kazan* is pumping and dumping."

Alex blinked. He had to stare at the squawk box for before words came. "Sonar, Conn, say again?"

"I've got overboard discharges." Chief Andreas' shrug was audible, and Alex knew why. Dumping trash, sewage, or anything over the side made *noise*, something submariners religiously avoided where anyone else could hear it.

"Conn, aye." Alex twisted to look at his XO.

"He can't be that stupid." Bobby cocked his head. "Can he?"

"Not if he knows we're following him." Alex frowned.

Kazan had sank Kurt Kins' *Darter*, hadn't they? Kins received a posthumous Medal of Honor for that patrol; he'd been one of the best in the business, but it hadn't saved him. And this was the guy or gal who sent him to the bottom. Alex frowned. "Unless he wants to keep us on his tail...?"

"I guess so?" Bobby scowled. "But why?"

"Except he doesn't want to make it too obvious." His mind whirled through the problem. "So why be stupid? Unless it's something else... Sonar, Conn, is he still pumping?"

"Affirmative."

"What if he's not dumping trash?" Alex's heart jackrabbited into his throat. "What if he's— *Make your depth eight hundred feet*!"

Bobby started. "Make my depth eight hundred feet, aye." He relayed the orders to the diving officer and then turned back to Alex. "Captain?"

"This guy has been smart enough to lead us right into his trap for hours. No way is he dumb enough to send trash and sewage overboard now. Not unless that's what he wants us to think he's doing," Alex said. He had to be wrong. Right?

The deck climbed under his feet as Alex tried to convince himself he was crazy. But the math didn't work. *Kazan* knew *Bluefish* was there. Were they trying to pretend they didn't? If so, pumping and dumping was a good way...but what was the point? His mind returned to that message on low-acoustic mines. Most submarines deployed mines out of torpedo tubes, but if the Russians had developed a new delivery system, maybe it sounded just like overboard discharges.

Bobby was quiet. Too bad Alex's acting XO still wasn't confident enough to ask too many questions. Alex needed to remember that. He let out a breath.

"I think this sucker is laying a minefield for us to stumble into, all fat, dumb, and happy," Alex said.

Bobby's brow furrowed. "You're thinking of their new low-acoustic ones, Captain?"

"I see you read message traffic." Alex grinned to hide his relief.

That earned him a grimace. "*Bluefish* hasn't exactly had good luck with mines."

"Ah." He'd have to ask later. "Come left to zero-four-five and man battle stations."

Bobby didn't need to be told to set battle stations silently. He had a good tactical mind when he wasn't afraid to use it, Alex decided. And at least Bobby O'Kane didn't shy away from combat. He might not be Alex's actual XO, but Bobby was doing better than the one real XO Alex had. Then again, Bobby *could* still go to pieces in a fracas like Convoy 57. Alex sure as shit had wanted to.

A few minutes later, Chief Andreas' voice came over the squawk box. "Conn, Sonar, *Kazan* has increased speed and come left. He's trying to get back in front of us."

"Well, isn't that cute." Alex shook his head. "Somebody's not pleased about his trap not working." Her trap? He thought *Kazan*'s commander was Katrina something. Or Katerina? Where had he read that?

"What do we want to do about the mines?" Bobby's toes traced circles on the deck.

"Put a marker in the system and stay well clear," he replied. "You how they say any ship can be a minesweeper."

"Once, yeah." Bobby snorted. "Though sometimes, if you get close enough but not too close..."

"I'm not sure I want to know." Alex had to pay attention to the plot. *Kazan* continued left, still moving toward them. What was he missing? He frowned. "Why here?"

"Captain?" Bobby sounded jumpy again.

"Why put the minefield there? And why come around like this if we're—"

"Conn, Sonar, surface contact bearing zero-nine-zero!" Chief Andreas' voice said through the squawk box. "New contact, must have just started moving—range eight thousand yards and closing fast!"

"Shit! That's right on the bearing from the minefield." Too late, Alex figured out what the Russians had planned—assuming they were both Russians. He hit the switch on the squawk box. "Sonar, Conn, got an ID on that surface ship?"

Chief Andreas sounded frustrated. "Computer's still working on it, sir."

"Very well." Alex glanced down at the plot, missing Wilson. That bastard had every ship class's blade count memorized. He chewed his lip, thinking. Hm. There was only a thirty-degree separation between the *Yasen* and the mystery surface ship.

At least they didn't have *Bluefish* boxed in. Had the surface ship moved too soon? Was there another surprise, something else he'd missed? Weight pressed down on Alex, and he felt like he was defending Convoy 57 again, where every move he made led to more danger. Decision time. *Fish or cut bait, Captain.* This was what he got for thinking things were easy. Uncle Marco asked if he'd going to fall apart if given another boat, hadn't he?

Now was not the time to think about how submarine commanders who burned brightly also burned *out*. Heart racing, Alex forced himself to take a deep breath. He'd already used ten of his twenty-eight torpedoes, which meant even pickling off all four in his tubes wouldn't leave *Bluefish* naked. But he had to make sure he wasn't shooting at an ally, first. It was possible that the surface ship was a friend who had been lying in wait for the *Yasen*.

"Conn, Sonar, tentative system ID on the surface ship is *Grigorovich*-class frigate— *Fuck*, splashes! Splashes bearing zero-nine-zero!"

"Well, I guess that tells us he's a bad guy." Alex grinned while Bobby paled. Now he knew what to do. "Weps, snapshot tube two, bearing zero-nine-zero!" He whirled toward the helmsman without bothering to listen to Rose's acknowledgment. "Ahead flank, left full rudder!"

Bluefish rolled as the helm repeated the orders. The *Grigoroviches* carried the Russian's newer 90-R1 rocket-propelled depth charges, which could dive deeper than he could. Worse yet, they were guided projectiles; the suckers could find *Bluefish* on their own with just a little programming. But they had one weakness: the 90-R1 was only good out to five thousand yards. All he had to do was stay outside that range—or scare the frigate away.

"Tube two fired electrically!" Rose's voice rose above the din.

"Very well. Cut the wire, close the outer door," Alex ordered. The Mark 84 would have to search for the frigate without help; he needed to maneuver. "Reload tube two."

"Weps, aye!"

"Conn, Sonar, one fish running hot, straight, and normal," Chief Andreas reported. "The *Yasen's* turned toward us, range now sixteen thousand yards and closing fast."

"I see it, Sonar." Alex turned his eyes back to the plot. *Bluefish* pointed almost straight at the Russian sub now. "Rudder amidships."

Boom! Boom-boom-boom-boom. Distant explosions echoed through *Bluefish's* hull, but experience told Alex they were outside the blast radius.

"Rudder amidships, aye!" ET1 Yacono's voice was octaves higher than usual, and his knuckles were white as he gripped the wheel. "My rudder is amidships, no new course given."

Alex put his glasses on and shoved his hands into his pockets. "Firing point procedures, tubes one and three. Get me *Kazan*, Weps." He glanced around the control room, noticing wide eyes and pale faces on almost every sailor. "Relax, folks. Those explosions would be a lot louder if they were close enough to get us."

A few people laughed nervously. Most stared at him like he was crazy.

"Solution ready!" Rose announced, teeth bared.

"Ship ready." Bobby sounded calmer than Alex expected; his face was a sickly pale shade of yellow, but his voice didn't crack.

"Fire!" Alex tuned out the responses, turning back to the squawk box. "Sonar, Conn, range to frigate?"

"Six thousand yards and opening," Chief Andreas replied. "He's running from the torp, sir."

"Finally, some good news," Alex said. But his closure rate with the *Yasen* was still far too high. "Ahead two—"

"Conn, Sonar, torpedo—torpedoes in the water, bearing zero-five-six!"

"Hard left rudder!" Turning right closed the range with the frigate and her depth charges. Or the minefield. He couldn't forget about the fucking minefield. "Cut the wires, close the outer doors, and reload tubes one and three."

Alex had hoped to guide both torpedoes in on *Kazan*, but in hindsight, it was a miracle that *Kazan* waited so long to shoot. Something still didn't feel right, but Alex didn't have time to think about it.

"Inbound torpedoes bearing zero-five-six and zero-five-five! Range thirteen thousand yards and closing at approximately sixty-five knots," Chief Andreas reported.

"That makes them Futlyar-twos, Captain," Bobby said quietly.

"At least they're not the three-hundred-knot variety." Alex shook his head. "Fuck! Remind me next time not to get cute and just shoot the bastard. Ease your rudder to left twenty."

"Ease my rudder to left twenty degrees, aye." Yacono still clutched the wheel in a death grip, but Alex didn't have time to explain. "My rudder is left twenty degrees, no new course given."

"Very well." Reducing the rate of their turn kept the torpedoes behind them; a sharp turn let the torpedoes cut the corner and gain on *Bluefish.*

"I'll make a note, Captain," Bobby replied, miming typing on a tablet. Was that a smile? Perhaps there was hope for Bobby yet.

Alex grinned. "All right. Stand by to drop countermeasures on my mark. Make it a pair of them."

Bluefish's arc put the torpedoes in a tail chase, and *Kazan's* turn toward the frigate meant the Russians couldn't wire-guide their torps in, either. Unfortunately, the Futlyars had longer legs than his own Mark 84s. Alliance intelligence estimated their maximum effective range at something around twenty-two nautical miles, and Alex had gone and let himself get suckered into less than half of that. Stupid captains got themselves killed. He couldn't make this mistake again.

"You don't want to outrun these guys, Captain?" Bobby approached slowly, creeping up like he was trying to tame a wild animal.

"It'll take too long. With their range and overtake, we'd need twenty-one minutes to run that torp out of gas. By then, the frigate and *Kazan* might be long gone." Alex grimaced. "We can't let them run around this close to Australia laying mines."

"Makes sense." Bobby twitched, but was that because of Alex's tactics or because torpedoes were chasing them?

"Conn, Sonar, more splashes," Walkman reported. "Aft of us, sound distant."

"Conn, aye." *Bluefish* continued her big turn. The two torpedoes were behind her, but not close enough to matter—if Alex played this smart. "Continue left, steady course zero-four-five."

That brought his boat through a full three-hundred-sixty-degree turn and pointed *Bluefish* at the frigate sprinting from right to left, trying to outrun *Bluefish's* first torpedo. The minefield was twenty degrees off the starboard bow and *Kazan* danced off to port. It wasn't a bad setup, except he had only one torpedo in his unused tube and two targets to choose from.

Tube four was on his starboard side; that decided it. "Spin up tube four for the frigate, Weps."

"Weps, aye!" Bobby darted over to Rose's side, and Alex wasn't surprised that she already had the solution worked up. "Solution ready!"

"Ship ready," Bobby said.

"Fire." Alex took a breath. "Estimated time to reload on tubes one through three?"

Rose bit her lip, glancing up from her console. "A minute for tube one and two, four minutes on three, Captain."

"Very well." Damn. They still needed to drill that down. "Guide this one in, Weps."

Rose grinned at him, turning to her chief fire control technician. "This one's yours, Chief."

"On it, ma'am," Chief Fire Technician Min Rhee replied, his eyes on the screen and hand on the joystick. Rhee struck Alex as one of the most competent chiefs on board, but he couldn't remember any details other than the fact that Rhee bred rabbits.

It was an odd habit for a submariner, but as long as Rhee didn't bring them on the boat, Alex couldn't care less. Now, Chief Rhee expertly guided the torpedo toward the still-maneuvering frigate, relying on *Bluefish's* sensors to steer it in without the torpedo's organic sonar. Alex watched the frigate's icon come left and slow down as the previous Mark 84 ran out of gas, and he almost felt sorry for the Russian CO. The poor bastard couldn't hear the newest torpedo...and he had no idea what was coming.

Thirty seconds later, the torpedo's track merged with the Russian frigate.

"Conn, Sonar, I've got a good hit! Implosions coming from the frigate's bearing!"

"Conn, aye." Alex glanced at Rose, but she shook her head. Why the hell weren't the tubes reloaded yet? He refused to turn into a CO who berated people mid-battle. "Close the outer door and reload tube four."

"Weps, aye," Rose said from between gritted teeth. She knew there was a problem. Good enough.

Bobby whispered from his right: "Countermeasures, Captain?"

"Not yet." Another glance at the plot told Alex that the torpedoes still dogged them. Damn. He'd need to come left to shoot again.

And, yeah, *Kazan* was still there. That boat could sprint as fast as he could, maybe faster if rumors were accurate. And she had ten torpedo tubes to his four. *Aren't those just great odds?* Alex sighed.

"Well, you can't win if you don't play." He turned to the weapons corner. "Weps, tell me we've got something to shoot."

Rose grimaced. "Tubes one and two reloaded."

Finally! "Well done. Set both up on *Kazan*. We're only going to have one chance at this, so we'd better hit him."

"You got it, Captain." Rose's grin returned. Was *Bluefish's* crew losing their terror of the new captain? Alex fucking hoped so.

"All right, XO. Stand by those countermeasures—we'll drop them as we turn."

Bobby chuckled. "And then we dodge the next set he sends our way?"

"Just be grateful he didn't gift us a spread of ten torps." Alex chewed his lip for a moment. "Then again, if he *was* shooting mines out of his torpedo tubes, maybe his tubes are fouled."

Bobby snorted. "Only if *Bluefish's* luck changes."

"Here's hoping." Alex glanced back at Rose. "Got her set up, Weps?"

"Solutions and ship ready."

"Very well." He turned to the helm. "Left full rudder, steady course two-three-zero." That pointed them ahead of *Kazan*. Alex eyeballed an intercept point, but he didn't want to ram the Russian. He just needed to close the distance quickly. "Standby to drop countermeasures—*now!*"

"Countermeasures away!" Bobby slapped the buttons, dropping two noisemakers to suck *Kazan's* torpedoes away from them.

Meanwhile, *Bluefish* raced toward where the Russian submarine would be in ten minutes if they didn't change course or speed. *Kazan* wasn't running all out; while Alex was busy dancing with Russian torpedoes, *Kazan* had avoided the first two he shot. But why weren't the Russians speeding up?

RFS Kazan

"Captain, the American has avoided our torpedoes," her sonar officer reported.

Captain Second Rank Katerina Revnik smiled thinly. She was a slender woman, built like the figure skater she had wanted to be before her war-torn country had other ideas. With dark hair, blue eyes, and a lovely pale complexion, she could have turned heads in any arena—but she didn't care about that these days. Her long hair was pulled back in a utilitarian French braid, and she wore her uniform like she was made for it.

Maybe she had been. Katerina was a rising star in the Russian Federation Navy, and although she was fully aware of that, she also knew that fame and glory were fleeting.

This American was good, far better than she expected. It was a pity that the initial plan had failed; she still didn't know what spooked the *Cero*-class submarine away from the minefield she laid. There was no time to dwell on that, however. Particularly not since eight of her torpedo tubes were loaded with mines, and now the American helpfully raced to intercept her. How close would he get before he tried to fire again? That was the important question.

"Come right to match his course, but remain at forty knots," she ordered her first officer. Vasili Viktorov complied without question. He was a good officer, and Katerina liked him—even if he was new at his job.

Then again, so was she. She'd inherited *Kazan* when the submarine's previous commanding officer came apart in combat; then, *Katerina* had been the first officer, and Captain Ovechkin Russia's future star. Now she owned the limelight, and Katerina was not disappointed. Her nation was fighting for its future. The Americans and their typical Alliance did not recognize Russia's legitimate need for resources. They never had.

So what if Russia's allies started the war? Katerina was farsighted enough to see how joining with India and France provided Russia with the excuse to take what she needed. Her nation was hungry for resources, space, and warm water ports. A resurgent Russia was inevitable, even if the world's blinder politicians could not see it. But her allies could. They all had selfish reasons for uniting. France and India were the convenient friends of today. As for tomorrow...who knew? No one thought the Freedom Union would last forever. For now, however, perhaps they could all regain some of their lost glory.

Kazan settled onto her new course, moving as smoothly as the figure skater Katerina once dreamed of becoming. The *Yasen*-class submarines, whose construction had been started, stopped, started, stopped, and then started again by the struggling Russian Federation, were truly the best hunter-killer submarines in the world. Katerina allowed herself a small smile. She may have achieved command in an unorthodox fashion, but her record spoke for itself...and she intended to go still further.

Watching the navigation display, Katerina noted how the American continued charging her way—and he wasn't changing depth, either.

Fool. A submariner who neglected to think in three dimensions died. She chuckled. "Begin deploying mines."

"Aye, Captain!" Vasili grinned wolfishly before doubt narrowed his eyes. "Do you think he'll wait before shooting at us, Captain?"

"He knows that his vaunted ASVs only have a twenty-knot speed advantage over us." Katerina shrugged. "He'll wait as long as he dares. Still...let's not make it too easy. Increase speed to fifty knots once the mines are deployed."

The American might have spotted the first trap, but Katerina knew he'd be overeager and miss the second one.

They always were.

"Conn, Sonar, *Kazan's* up to fifty knots."

"Conn, aye." Was Bobby imagining things, or did the captain sound perplexed? Then again, the *Yasens* could supposedly top sixty knots. Why so slow?

"Does *Kazan* need an overhaul?" Bobby blurted out. He braced himself, but the expected glare never came.

"Doubt it." The captain shoved his hands in his pockets, looking thoughtful. "Or there's something else going on." He leaned into the squawk box. "Sonar, Conn, any new sounds from our friend?"

"He's going too fast to detect any, sir." Chief Andreas sounded strained. But maybe they didn't need to worry? Ludicrous.

Even weirder, it felt like Captain Coleman *enjoyed* getting input from his crew. Everyone needed a lot longer than two weeks to get used to that. Rose glared at Bobby significantly from the weapons corner; he could tell that her trigger finger was itchy. Bobby bit his lip. Was it his job to say something? This acting XO stuff was for the birds.

"Range is down to eleven thousand yards, sir."

"Hm." Coleman focused on the plot again; Bobby wasn't sure he heard.

"Captain? Do you want to fire?" *Please, oh please don't let him freeze up.* Captains had a disturbing tendency to misplace their nerve these days. He'd heard rumors of COs losing it at all the wrong moments, but surely a Medal of Honor winner—the only living one in the sub community!—wouldn't crack up. Right?

"Not yet." Coleman shook his head. "We need to close within eight thousand yards before firing if we want to hit him. Otherwise *our* torpedoes will run out of gas before they get this sly fucker."

"That's assuming they can sprint as fast as we think they can." So far, *Kazan* hadn't.

When the hell had the Russians gotten good at this? The Cold War ended decades ago!

Oh, look! Rose wanted to light him on fire because he'd started fidgeting again. Bobby ignored her.

"I think we have to assume they can. Which means this cat is playing another game." The captain scratched his chin. Another beat of silence, long enough for Bobby's mouth to dry out. "Sonar, Conn, go active."

"Conn, Sonar, say *again*?" Chief Andreas sounded like she thought Coleman had gone crazy. Bobby wasn't sure she was wrong.

"Sonar, Conn, I say again, go active." There was an edge in Coleman's voice, one that made Bobby flinch. But he wasn't crazy, and he wasn't Peterson. What was going on?

"Sonar, aye." He could almost hear Chief Andreas rolling her eyes. "Going active."

Ping!

Bobby cringed. Going active on sonar meant sending sound waves into the water. Anyone in the area could hear them. No submariner liked that, and with modern passive sonar, it was rarely necessary, but...

"One ping, one ping only?" he asked, rubbing his sweaty hands against the legs of his coveralls.

Coleman barked out a laugh as a second *ping* reverberated through *Bluefish's* hull. "That only works in movies."

Okay. He got the reference. At least the new CO wasn't so boring he couldn't remember a quote from one of the best submarine movies ever made. Bobby wished he dared ask what was on the captain's mind. *Please don't be crazy.*

Chief Andreas interrupted his thoughts. "Conn, Sonar, I've got a return dead ahead, range four thousand yards. A few small returns—"

"Forty degree up angle, make your depth two hundred feet!" Coleman snapped.

Two hundred feet was damned shallow, and if anyone was on the surface— *Oh, God.* Bobby's jaw dropped open. "More mines?"

"Looks like." The captain's voice was grim as the deck sloped like a mountain under their feet. "Sonar, Conn, secure pinging."

Leaning forward for balance, Bobby looked at the new icons blinking to life on the plot. *Bluefish* climbed fast, sprinting for shallow water to get above the mines. Changing depth was a risky way to avoid them, but they couldn't gain on *Kazan* if they turned. He swallowed.

No, their new captain wasn't crazy. Crazy smart, maybe. But he was also single-minded about killing the enemy. Was that about to screw them over?

"She's changing depth, Captain," Sonar reported.

"*Chyort,*" Katerina hissed and then shook her head, chasing her disappointment away. "This American is clever. It looks like we won't be able to take him with the original plan, Vasili."

"Pity." Her first officer scowled. "I hoped for a quick kill. He is getting annoying, Captain."

"It does no good crying over what might have been." Katerina made herself smile. Her crew was watching, and showing her frustration would only make them nervous. *Bluefish* was a tougher target than expected, yes, but that did not mean *Kazan* could not trick him.

After all, she had already led one Australian submarine into her trap. It had not failed. That diesel submarine followed her right into a minefield and was damaged by the explosions, making her choose between surfacing and sinking. Predictably, her captain chose to live...and ended up right in the arms of *Admiral Golovko*. Even better, the Australian boat's damage kept her captain from getting word out, which meant she was a clean capture, allowing Katerina's second frigate ally to depart with one *Shortfin*-class submarine in tow.

Her navy wanted a good look at the newest Australian diesel/AIP—advanced independent propulsion—boat. Bagging one put a large feather in her cap, one Katerina knew would help her future career. The same could not be said for the unlucky *Admiral Istomim*, however. Thanks to the American torpedo, that frigate would be lucky to remain on the surface for another hour. Katerina shrugged. That was the price of doing business. *I'll see if they need assistance once I've dealt with this pest.*

"Do you want to reload with our last *Shkval* torpedoes, Captain?"

"No, it will take too long." She frowned. The *shkval* torpedoes were the pride and joy of the Russian Navy, but they were expensive and slow to manufacture. Katerina only had two left after sinking a pair of Japanese submarines on her way south, and now she wished she had not wasted them on diesel boats. Rumors from home said a production bottleneck would keep her from receiving more for months. "Better to save those for higher value targets."

A *Cero* was the best submarine the Americans had, but she preferred to sink an aircraft carrier with her precious three-hundred-knot torpedoes.

"Do we come up in speed, then?" Vasili asked. They could outrun the *Cero* and her torpedoes. Perhaps they'd creep back later, to sink the American when he least expected it.

No. Katerina would not leave someone this smart lurking in her baffles. "Come left until you clear the port tubes and then take him out."

"Aye, Captain!" His wolfish smile returned, and Katrina started to grin as *Kazan* swept into a sharp port turn.

"Torpedoes in the water! Range four nautical miles and closing fast!"

"Two fish running hot, straight and normal!" Chief Andreas sang out.

"I can't believe he was stupid enough to turn." Bobby looked like someone had hit him in the face with a frying pan, but Alex couldn't blame him. Turning was a singularly stupid move for an enemy who had played everything smart so far.

"I'll take it." There was some part of this equation Alex was missing, but the Russian had turned right after *Bluefish* avoided the minefield. That put *Kazan* safely within the eight-thousand-yard bubble from which she couldn't avoid Alex's torpedoes, and he fired right away.

"Conn, Sonar, he's turning and burning! *Kazan* is running hard, up past sixty knots and still climbing."

"Conn, aye," he answered automatically. "Try to tuck in behind her."

"You got it, sir." At least Bobby sounded more relaxed.

Alex's mind continued churning over why this wily Russian made such a mistake. Was this another attempt to suck *Bluefish* into a trap, or had their enemy finally mis-stepped? They were still "above" *Kazan* by about six hundred feet, which meant the mines in their path would have to float upward to meet *Bluefish*. But *Bluefish* would cross the eight thousand yards between them in less than five minutes, and the mines wouldn't rise that quickly.

Kazan was up to sixty-seven knots. That meant Alex's torpedoes had a good twenty knots of overtake...and the *Yasen* was finished unless he could outfox them.

"Keep your eye out for countermeasures, Chief Rhee," Alex said. "Weps, tell me when tube three is reloaded."

Both acknowledged the order, leaving Alex to watch *Kazan* and try not to fret about torpedo reloading time. If he followed closely enough, *Kazan* couldn't shoot at him—but that necessitated cutting the corner every time the Russian sub started to turn. That was the only way to stay within spitting distance with *Kazan's* ten-knot speed advantage.

Kazan had swung back right after *Bluefish* fired; anything else would've presented her broadside to the torpedoes. Now the Russian corkscrewed left and right, trying to turn enough to unmask her own torpedo tubes without giving *Bluefish's* torpedoes a bigger target.

"Come left another five degrees," Alex told Bobby quietly. "He's tracked left fairly consistently, and if we can get inside his turn, we'll gain ground."

"You think he's trying to lead us into another trap, Captain?" Bobby looked less tense, now; Alex hadn't missed how his earlier refusal to shoot had worried his XO.

"It's possible. More likely that he wants to further from Australia...and maybe closer to friends." Alex would do the same in *Kazan's* place, particularly if he couldn't get around and take a shot.

"Conn, Sonar, Torpedo range four thousand yards and closing."

"Conn, aye." Alex leaned back from the squawk box and did the math. That left about six minutes until the torpedoes intercepted—

"He's dropping noisemakers!"

Hearing that made Alex turn toward where Rose leaned over Chief Rhee's shoulder. The weapons corner was quiet; Chief Rhee and FT2 Kay were riveted on guiding the two torpedoes toward *Kazan* and Rose stood between them, quivering with excitement. Sometimes, Alex wondered about her. Rose was a warfighter, professional and focused, but he hoped her razor-sharp excitement was just a byproduct of too much time on the sidelines under Peterson.

Seeming to sense his gaze, Rose turned. "Not a problem, Captain. We've got her cold."

"Good." Alex grinned. "Let's take care of this so we can all go home."

All the corkscrewing in the world could not save them from Katerina's mistake.

"Five minutes to impact, Captain."

Katerina felt sick. This was her fault. She was the fool who forgot to check the range before turning, who let this American submarine get on her tail and stay there. She'd trapped his predecessor so easily that *failing* hadn't crossed Katerina's mind. Now her crew would pay the price.

"Take us to the roof, Vasili," she whispered.

"Aye, Captain." Vasili's eyes met hers, and they were so dark with sorrow that Katerina looked away. He didn't blame her—but he should have.

She swallowed. She had one trick left, and Katerina had no idea if it would work. Doctrine said that it was effective against the *previous* version of the American torpedo, but the enemy hadn't fielded the Mark 84 at the start of the war. Most of what Russia knew was about the old Mark 48 CBASS. Katerina had dodged *those* torpedoes with ease when the Japanese shot them at her. She hadn't let even the legendary Kurt Kins shoot at her submarine, so she had no idea what he'd carried to his death. Much to her sorrow, Katerina had assumed that the Mark 84 Advanced Spearfish Variant was more of the same, a slow enemy torpedo, easy to out-think and outmaneuver. Alas, it was a much better torpedo.

The capture of a *Shortfin* would let intelligence dissect those torpedoes, however, since the Americans shared with the Australians—not to mention getting a good look at one of the best Air-Independent Propulsion submarines in the world. AIP submarines were the children of diesel-electric submarines; they possessed diesel engines but ran on electric motors that could recharge without snorkeling. They were silent and deadly, although less capable than nuclear submarines like Katerina's own *Kazan*.

Yes, she'd captured the first intact submarine of the war. It was an undeniable victory, but Katerina would soon lose her own boat in exchange.

Was it worth it?

"Depth eighty feet," Vasili reported.

Katerina bounced on the balls of her feet. "Ready decoys."

"This close, Captain?" Vasili frowned in confusion.

"Time to impact?" she asked her sonar officer, ignoring Vasili.

"Three minutes!" The sonar officer looked green. The crew was too well trained to think Katerina would find some brilliant way to save them.

"Pass the word to brace for impact," she ordered, looking back at her first officer. "Drop the decoys at one minute until impact."

"That won't—"

"The American's torpedoes *will* sink us, Vasili," Katerina whispered. "It's only a question of if they explode against the hull or against the decoys."

Eyes wide, Vasili nodded. Katerina grabbed the periscope stand and tried not to lock her knees; no matter how this worked out, *Kazan* would die—and so would some of her crew. How much? She didn't know.

Hands shaking, she grabbed the microphone for the shipboard announcing system. A glance from her sonar officer told Katerina it was time.

"Impact in one minute," she said, surprised by how steady her voice sounded. "Prepare for impact. Prepare to abandon ship."

"Decoys deployed!" Vasili reported.

BOOM!

Bright lights flashed, and the world heaved out from under Katerina's feet.

"Impact!" Rose announced, only Chief Andreas to cut in:

"Conn, Sonar, I have explosions and hull popping noises—she's surfacing!"

"Conn, aye." Alex had to raise his voice over the cheering in control. Then he turned to Bobby. "Let's follow them up, XO. Periscope depth."

"Periscope depth, aye, sir." Bobby turned to relay the orders while Alex headed over to the weapons corner.

"That was quick, wasn't it?" he asked Rose quietly.

She chewed her lip. "They launched countermeasures at the last minute, sir. I'm not sure if the torps detonated against them or against the hull." Rose crossed her arms tightly against her chest, like she was trying to protect herself. "It shouldn't matter. Either way, the shock wave should sink them."

Shit, the way Rose stared at him, both defiant and tense, reminded him of his daughters when they misbehaved. But they were worried about being grounded. Rose expected to get reamed, and for what? Doing her job?

"It should." Alex smiled despite the disgust coiling in his gut. Thank goodness Wade Peterson wasn't there; he'd like to strangle the bastard. "Don't worry about it, Weps. You and your folks did good."

Her smile remained a little hunted, but Rose nodded. Alex turned back to watch his sailors bring *Bluefish* to periscope depth. Following wartime procedures, going shallow didn't take as long as in peacetime, but they still needed to pause and make sure there were no surface ships lurking. One surprise was enough for today. No way was Alex game for another nasty Russian shock.

By the time *Bluefish's* scope peeked above the waves, *Kazan* was low in the water. Her sail was visible, along with very little of her deck. This was one scene Alex didn't have the stomach to watch through a traditional periscope; instead, he leaned back and let his eyes find the periscope display camera.

Streaks of light colored the sky as dawn approached. The Russian submarine was little more than a black shadow against the horizon, with wave after wave crashing into her sail as a few sailors struggled into one last life raft. Other rafts peppered the water, the silhouettes of waterlogged sailors clinging to them.

Alex swallowed.

"Looks like she's going down, Captain," Bobby whispered.

"Yeah." He should have felt victorious. Part of him did. Yet guilt also tugged at his heart.

That could be his crew. He didn't need to say it aloud. One glance around control told Alex they all knew the odds of survival. One in every four Alliance submarines didn't make it home. Next time might be *Bluefish's* turn.

Kazan slipped beneath the waves as Alex and his crew watched. They were too far away to count how many sailors made it off...but it didn't look like enough.

"Radio, send a message to COMSUBPAC with their position," Alex ordered. "Someone should pick those poor bastards up."

"Aye, sir."

Perhaps the Russians would beat the Alliance there. The frigate probably got word out before she went to the bottom, and the Russians were loyal to their own. Or perhaps *Kazan's* crew would spend the rest of the war in an Alliance POW camp. Either way, it beat sitting on the ocean waiting for death to come.

Now he needed to think of his own crew's morale, so Alex forced himself to smile. "Do we have a broom anywhere on this barge?"

Chapter 10

Making Friends

12 January 2040, Near the grave of RFS Kazan

Twenty-six hours in a life raft made Katerina grudgingly respect her surface counterparts...or at least gain a passing fondness for the ones who abandoned their own mission to pull her crew out of the water. Properly defrosted and with some warm tea in her system, Katerina felt human enough to thank her rescuers. Wearing a borrowed uniform, she followed the young orderly to the bridge of the high speed "ferry" that had fished *Kazan's* fifty-two survivors out of the Indian Ocean.

Fifty-two. Her heart clenched, even though she knew she'd been lucky. Saving fifty-two people out of a crew of sixty-four was almost unheard of, but Katerina still knew the name of every one of her twelve dead sailors. She remembered their faces. She would always know that her mistakes led to their deaths.

Captain Third Rank Yana Pasternak saluted her, which Katerina returned with a wry smile. "Thank you for picking us up," she said. "I know it endangered your mission."

"No more than picking up the survivors of *Admiral Istomim* did." Yana, who she'd met in the Advanced Special Officers' Class at the Kuznetsov Naval Academy, shrugged. The other woman was short, burly, and with red hair and freckles that made her look younger than her years. "Sorry about the lack of accommodations. We're pretending to be a car-carrying ferry."

"Anything that isn't a life raft feels wonderful right now." Katerina tried not to shiver. The seas around Australia were warmer than those at home, but hypothermia could kill even in tropical waters. None of *Kazan's* life rafts got away from the wreck of her submarine without damage, and all had been taking on water faster than her sailors could bail with their bare hands. If Yana waited a few hours more...they would've been in for a very unpleasant swim.

Likely a short one, too, given how her muscles ached.

"Good. Did you see Marina?"

"Yes." Katerina scowled as she rubbed her upper arms to warm her muscles back up. Captain Second Rank Marina Naoumov of *Admiral Istomim*, the sunken frigate, was another acquaintance from the academy, but not exactly one Katerina would call a friend. "She felt the need to berate me for not saving her from the American submarine."

Naoumov hadn't *quite* inferred that Katerina left her on the receiving end of torpedoes out of spite, but she might have if her second-in-command hadn't possessed the sense to shut her up. It was a small mercy. Exhausted and offended, Katerina knew she might've said something that Naoumov's powerful patrons would use to sink her.

Or she might've punched the arrogant bitch right in the face, thereby ending her career forever. Katerina's fist still itched for that opportunity.

Yana barked out a laugh. "She always did have a way with words. You will note that I did not invite her to *my* bridge."

"May we all be grateful for small mercies." Her smile felt wan as Katerina forced herself to unclench her fists. Naoumov's face did not need rearranging today, and she had larger problems.

Eight months into her first command, her beautiful submarine lay on the bottom of the ocean. Her previous victories would mean nothing now. The Russian Navy remained a cutthroat organization for all its rapid growth. Captains who lost the submarines their motherland gave them were not offered second chances. At best, she'd drive a desk for the rest of the war. At worst...

"I've been ordered to deliver everyone to Malaysia for transfer home." Yana put a gentle hand on her arm. "Admiral Mikhailov asked for you to be on the first flight out."

Katerina focused on the horizon and managed not to swallow. "Well, if he expects me to be in my dress uniform, I'm afraid he'll be disappointed."

Yana's chuckle was as empty as Katerina felt. They both knew her career was doomed, simply because an American had refused to fall into the trap Katerina's orders created. It was a good trap and worked once...but that didn't matter. Nor did the fact that she'd managed to save all but twelve of her crew.

Time to face the wolves, then. Katerina squared her shoulders. She would meet her fate with her head held high. Her crew deserved no less.

Bluefish pulled into Perth, Australia, with a broomstick tied to her number two periscope. Under normal circumstances, Alex never would've imagined doing something so flamboyant, but his crew needed something to feel good about. He still wasn't sure what his predecessor did to them—and wasn't sure how to ask without sounding like an pretentious ass—but as far as Alex was concerned, *Bluefish's* crew had done damned well.

Tying a broomstick to the periscope was an old naval tradition signifying a "clean sweep" of all enemies. Legend said the Dutch Admiral Tromp had started it in the 1650s, tying a broom to his mast after a victory against the British. The U.S. submarine community embraced it with a vengeance in World War II, starting with the most famous submarine of them all, USS *Wahoo.* In the early 2000s, subs had started to use the broom as a symbol of successfully completed sea trials, but

Alex never could quite get behind that idea. But this...this was old school. Like *Wahoo*, *Bluefish* had sunk every ship and sub she had engaged, which merited a "clean sweep" in his mind.

Besides, the look on Bobby's face when Alex had asked about the broom had been priceless. Word whipped through the boat like lightning, and Alex noticed a bounce in his sailors' steps before they'd even surfaced. Now that *Bluefish* was pier side, it was even more pronounced.

Alex wasn't sure he'd ever felt so good about his actions in command. Pulling in with *Jimmy Carter* after Convoy 57 had been such a relief that he hadn't had time for pride; he'd been bone weary and worried his submarine might sink out from under him. Now, however, *Bluefish* was unscathed and the proud owner of an excellent war patrol. She'd downed three frigates, two heavy lift ships, and two attack submarines. It wasn't the best patrol of the war, but it was still damned good for a submarine whose previous reputation was centered on her ability to avoid battle.

"*Moored, shift colors.*" The words rang out over the 1MC as *Bluefish's* sailors received lines from the pier and tied them off. Watching from the sail, Alex ran a practiced eye over the evolution to make sure nothing was wrong, but his crew knew their jobs. Then he spotted a tall officer wearing khakis on the pier, with the telltale scrambled eggs on his cover. Squinting, Alex noted that it was a double row of scrambled eggs, which indicated a flag officer.

"Who's that?" he asked, turning to Bobby.

His acting XO couldn't quite hide his grimace. "Commodore Banks."

"Ah." Alex met Commodore Banks once, back when *Jimmy Carter* had limped into port following Convoy 57, and truth be told, he didn't remember much about him. Banks hadn't been particularly helpful, and Admiral Rodriquez had walked all over him. Somehow, it hadn't really sunk in that Banks was his new boss. Scuttlebutt on the waterfront said Banks wasn't the sort to go visit subs under his command, which made an uncomfortable shiver roll up Alex's spine.

"He and Commander Peterson were—are, I guess—pretty good friends," Bobby said after a moment. "I think they served together on someone's staff."

"Thanks." What was Banks doing here? He couldn't think Peterson was still in command; Banks' chief of staff had met Alex at the airport.

No one was that dense.

Alex shrugged. "Suppose I should go meet the boss, huh?"

"Good luck, sir." The smile Bobby flashed him plainly said, *Better you than me*, and Alex filed that away.

Quickly, Alex climbed down the ladder on the outside of the sail, standing back as a crane lowered the brow until it laid on *Bluefish's* deck on one side and the pier on the other. Sailors lashed it into place as Banks tapped his foot. He had an aide with him, a harried-looking lieutenant who kept walking over to talk to the crane crew. Alex could guess what the poor young woman was asking and pitied her. Finally, the brow was secure, and Banks headed across, barely pausing to salute the national ensign flying from *Bluefish's* stern.

The in-port officer of the deck barely managed to ring him on board in time. *Dong dong, dong dong.* "Submarine Squadron Two-Nine, arriving!"

Banks scowled.

Alex stepped forward, saluting his boss automatically, only remembering too late that he wasn't supposed to do that. One of the quirks of having the Medal of Honor was that *everyone* saluted you. Alex still wasn't used to that. Particularly when it came to flag officers. Banks didn't seem to notice. He was too busy pursing his lips in displeasure.

"Captain."

"Commodore." Alex tried not to shove his hands into his pockets. Banks stared at him like Alex had been dipped in shit, and that wasn't the way any sane captain wanted their new boss to look. "Is there a problem, sir?"

"*Bluefish* arrived three hours *after* your LOGREQ indicated."

Alex blinked. "As I explained in my subsequent message—"

"I value *punctuality*, Captain Coleman, not showboating." Banks glared at the broomstick, sniffing. "Glory hounds have no place in my squadron."

"I'll make a mental note, sir." Alex bit back the urge to say more.

"You'll do more than make a note," Banks snapped. "I expect my submarine commanders to exhibit proper adherence to standards and discipline and to set an example for all the sailors under my command. When you say you'll be in port at a specific time, I expect you to do so."

"Next time I'll tell the Russians to come back at a better time," Alex said. Not rolling his eyes took every shred of self-control he had.

"Don't start with me, Captain!" Banks hissed, his eyes narrowing. "Furthermore, in the future, I expect you to request permission before executing a SNAPSHOT message. I don't want to hear about it from message traffic you've sent to COMSUBPAC!"

Alex stared. "I...beg your pardon?"

"You heard me." Banks leaned in close, wagging a finger in Alex's face. "You were assigned a *convoy* escort. You hared off course to answer that SNAPSHOT without even consulting me!"

"Without—" Alex shook his head to clear it, feeling like he'd been punched in the face. The sensation made his spine straighten and chin come up. "Respectfully, sir, when underway, all subs are under the tactical command of COMSUBPAC."

"That's not my point."

Then what the hell is? Alex couldn't say. If this guy was good friends with Peterson, Alex began to see what kind of pedantic, pencil-pushing micromanager his predecessor was. Everything wrong with *Bluefish* started to make sense. Too much sense.

He couldn't say that to Banks, so Alex remained stonily silent.

"My *point* is that I want to be *informed.*" Banks gestured toward *Bluefish's* sail with one flailing hand. "And that I won't tolerate showboating or glory seeking. I run a tight and *disciplined* squadron, and I expect you to conform."

"I have no intention of seeking glory, sir." Alex met Banks' gaze. "I've had quite enough of that, thank you."

Banks flinched and then covered it up with a sneer. "I'm glad to hear that."

"Is there anything else you wanted, sir?" Alex asked as politely as he could. The glare he received in return told him that he hadn't done terribly well. "Unless you'd care to join me for a walkaround of the boat?"

Asking that was a calculated gamble; Alex didn't really want to spend more time around Commodore Banks, but he was willing to bet that Banks didn't want to hang around him, either. Besides, if Banks didn't visit subs often, he definitely wasn't the type to want to do a stem-to-stern walkaround. Unless he was just that spiteful.

Now there was a super-happy thought.

"No, thank you." The sneer returned. "I have better things to do. Good day, Captain."

"Good day." This time, Alex remembered to wait for Banks' salute, which the commodore offered grudgingly. He returned it quickly, not wanting to insult the man—but not willing to trample on military tradition, either. Alex turned to the officer of the deck. "Bong the commodore off, Max."

"Yes, sir!" Ensign Max Goldberg wasn't one of the miscreants who'd wrecked the Mediterranean, and he seemed to know his job. If his grin was a little too wide as their commodore stalked off the brow, well, Alex could guess that Banks was second in popularity to Peterson on *Bluefish.*

Dong, dong. Dong, dong. "Submarine Squadron Two-Nine, departing!"

Alex watched Banks collect his aide—who hadn't bothered to follow him on board—and head down the pier. Banks did pause to glare once more at the broomstick, but he hadn't ordered Alex to take it down. So Alex damned well wasn't going to.

"Stow that grin, Max," Alex said without turning. "It wouldn't do for people to think you're having fun."

"Yes, sir." Max snickered; Alex ignored it.

This was going to be an interesting tour.

Naval Base Pearl Harbor, Hawaii

"And *you* thought he was going to crap out on us." Marco threw his head back and laughed. So what if he was gloating? If an admiral couldn't call up his nominal boss to crow a bit, who could he call? Besides, Freddie Hamilton didn't like Alex Coleman for stupid reasons that had nothing to do with his tactical competence.

"*I* thought it was a risk worth taking," Vice Admiral Winifred Hamilton retorted from thousands of miles away. "There's no need to sound so self-satisfied."

"Self-satisfied, hell! I'm delirious. Three frigates, an Indian *Akula*, a *Yasen*, and all those *Scorpenes* on the heavy lift ships? The tonnage total is impressive." Marco wished he'd video called her, but it was five in the morning in Freddie's time zone, and they were both still at home. He was in his home office and mostly dressed like a human being, but there was no way Freddie would let him see her with her hair wild.

Marco remembered how bad she looked on wakeup back from their junior days in submarines together. Freddie faked being a morning person like an ace, but she hated waking up. Which was why he'd substituted in for her alarm clock today.

There had to be *some* perks to being Commander, Submarine Forces Pacific. The job was hell most days, so the man the sub force called "Uncle Marco" would take every victory he could get.

"I'll admit it's impressive." To Freddie's credit, she didn't even sound annoyed. "But don't get your hopes up. He still might burn out."

"Maybe. Or maybe he'll pull another Convoy Fifty-Seven. Either way, we—"

"You know that if he does that with a *Cero*, we'll be scraping him off the bottom for the funeral."

"Yeah, yeah, whatever. It's worth the gamble." Marco waved a hand and then remembered she couldn't see it. Damn. "*Bluefish* looked hale and hearty enough this time around, although Banks is hardly a fit judge of the thing. He's as useful as a waterlogged potato. "

"Quit complaining about him, Marco. Commodore Banks is perfectly competent."

"And his sea daddy is the chief of naval operations, I know," Marco growled. Bad enough that Banks was as uninspiring as the tape dispenser Marco reached for to disassemble. Now Banks had called Marco to complain about the navy's newest superstar. "Still, what kind of bleeding idiot *bitches* about being given a fucking Medal of *Honor* winner as one of his captains? You'd think he'd realize that some of the glory is bound to rub off on his dumb ass."

Freddie snorted out a laugh. "Not if Coleman remains the loose cannon I remember him as."

"You think that's a bad thing?"

"No, I'm just saying to be careful. I talked to Chris Kennedy two weeks ago, and—"

"Who?"

"Coleman's CO on *Kansas*." He could almost hear her rolling her eyes. "You know, the one that sent him to me for *Admiral's Mast*."

"Sounds like a fucking idiot to me," Marco said. "I've never heard of the man."

"You should pay better attention. He's still in command of *Kansas*, and last I checked, that submarine worked for you."

"What's this Kennedy creature say about him?" he asked. *Kansas* was middling to okay, probably because her captain was just competent enough not to get himself killed, but not daring enough to take risks. Did Marco care what such a fart thought?

"Chris says Coleman isn't great at tact. He said that he's not surprised that Coleman threw the rules out the window at the first opportunity. He's done it before."

Marco leaned back to glare at ceiling. The tape dispenser was in pieces and would need surgery later, but what did he need a tape dispenser at home for, anyway? "If Coleman played Convoy 57 traditionally, he'd be dead. So would've the entire crew of *Jimmy Carter*."

"Yeah, but that's a double-edged sword," Freddie replied. "I'm not going to say that we don't need some unconventional tactics, but that kind of thing also gets people killed."

"Yeah, well, I told you we need a Mush Morton. Even if he does die in the process."

"I know, I know. Just try to make sure he dies doing something *useful*, all right, Marco?"

"Yes, ma'am."

Freddie hung up without another word, leaving guilt twisting in Marco's gut. Against his will, his eyes tracked right, looking at the wall covered with copies of every SUBMISS/SUBSUNK released since day one of the war. Even ones from before he took this godforsaken job. Marco understood responsibility, and he fucking well refused to shy away from it. He sent subs to war, and some of them didn't come home.

But he knew in his bones that he was right. They *needed* a Mush Morton, needed a fucking legend with goddamned teeth, because somewhere in the ninety-ish years of peace between the two world wars, the U.S. submarine community had lost its mojo. Once upon a time, they'd known how to kick ass and take names, but peacetime inertia and carefulness smoothed down the nasty sharp edges necessary to win wars. Marco wasn't immune to the disease of peace, either; he'd been caught flat-footed more than once and hated himself for it.

Yeah. They needed a rebel, someone to turn conventional knowledge on its head and take the fight to the enemy. Commander Mush Morton's tactics had changed the navy in World War II. They needed someone to be his heir. Was it Alex Coleman? Maybe. Marco had similar hopes for other COs over the past year. None had survived, except John Dalton, who he'd thrown into a submarine tender to get him *out* of where the fire was hottest.

Maybe that had been a bad call, but Marco had been so damned desperate to save one of the kids, and Dalton had the makings of an admiral written all over him. He wasn't a rebel. Just a good tactician who somehow squeezed into both peacetime and wartime molds.

Freddie liked captains like Dalton. Marco...Marco wanted *more.* Marco wanted the superstar who danced on the razor's edge, who redefined tactics and inspired others to do the same. He needed a Mush Morton—and a Dick O'Kane, too, while he was dreaming.

Until now, every star he eyed had fallen.

Kirk Kins died on board *Darter*, winning a big damned medal but going down, anyway. Teresa O'Canas sunk with *Los Angeles.* Rico Sivers went down on *Guam* after almost singlehandedly stopping an invasion of the Mariana Islands, only to fall victim to dozens of Russian depth charges. The list went on. Kenji Walker. Jane Phelps. All burned bright and then burned out. Marco kept their SUBMISS/SUBSUNK messages near the door, just to remind himself that there was a *cost* to trying to put one submarine, one captain, on a pedestal.

He'd started to think he'd never find his Mush Morton, until a rebellious kid sentenced to the country's oldest submarine went out and made a difference.

Maybe Alex Coleman would burn out, but he sure as hell wasn't some one-shot wonder. Marco had skimmed his patrol report already—Coleman must've written it on the way into Perth, because most COs sure as shit didn't get them off so fast—and it made for eventful reading. He didn't doubt *Bluefish's* logs would back Coleman up, either. The two times he'd met the kid, Coleman seemed petrified of all the attention. No way would he embellish his actions. Hell, if Marco had a Medal of Honor hanging on his wall, he wouldn't need to embellish shit, either!

Picking up his phone, Marco shot off a text to his chief of staff. It was time to fly out to Perth again.

Perth, Australia

Having friends at Port Operations was the best way to know when subs pulled in, particularly when you had a husband who forgot to turn his cell phone back on. Most sailors couldn't wait to call their families, but Nancy had always known that her beloved idiot was cut from a different cloth. Yesterday's email hinted that *Bluefish's* patrol would end soon, however, so she'd asked her soon-to-be-former assistant operations officer, Lieutenant (junior grade) Blumenthal, to call up her girlfriend, who happened to work at Port Ops. A few minutes later, Nancy had confirmation that *Bluefish* had arrived shortly after three p.m. She gave it an hour before she headed over.

The nice thing about wearing a commander's silver oak leaves was that no one questioned her when she headed down the pier; the guard just looked at her I.D. and saluted. Security on base was tighter during wartime, but when you belonged, you belonged. Getting on board *Bluefish*, however, turned out to be a bit more of a challenge.

The ensign on watch almost jumped out of his skin when she headed up the brow. The kid was short and stout and probably lifted more weights than most football players to get that dwarven-muscled shape. One look at her seemed to petrify him.

Nancy bit back the urge to instill some discipline in the kid as her eyes swept over the sailors present on the sub's topside black hull. They were *all* staring like she was a harbinger of doom. Alex wasn't joking about how jumpy this crew was, apparently. Nancy was a sticker for discipline, but she didn't believe in yelling at people who didn't deserve it, so she just returned his razor-sharp salute and handed her I.D. card over.

"Is Captain Coleman still on board?" she asked.

The kid—his name tape read *Greenburg*—gulped. "Is there a reason you're looking for him, ma'am?"

Was he being protective? That was cute. Nancy managed not to smile. Alex inspired that kind of loyalty in people, but this was faster than usual. "Probably because I'm married to him and haven't seen him in a month."

Now was not the time to traumatize the kid by saying something about how she'd like to jump her husband's bones. Ensign Greenburg was already trying to swallow his entire foot. "Sorry, ma'am. I'll, uh, call him up right away."

"Thank you."

Nancy didn't have to wait long, and she spent that time looking over Alex's new boat. *Bluefish* looked spiffy; Nancy had seen enough submarines to know that this one was new and in good shape. She certainly looked better off than *Jimmy Carter* had, but that wasn't saying much. Still, it was nice to know that Alex hadn't gotten the shit kicked out of him this time.

"Hey, Nancy."

Hearing Alex's voice made her turn, and Nancy gave him a wicked grin before she saluted him. Nancy might've joked about how annoying it was to be junior to her husband, but she was proud of him.

"Oh, quit that," Alex grumbled, returning her salute.

"Your young officers are watching." Nancy dropped her salute. "I wouldn't want them thinking I'm some slacker who doesn't understand military discipline."

"Perish the thought." He rolled his eyes.

"Your new boat looks pretty good. I take it you managed not to bang this one up—unless there's something I can't see underwater?" She arched an eyebrow and grinned when he flushed.

"Trash a submarine *one* time..." Alex shook his head. "You've brought your destroyer back looking worse."

"*My* destroyer never tried to sink at the pier, thank you very much," she replied primly.

Alex snorted. "Not for lack of effort on your part."

"Darling, it's safe to say that I was the only unsurprised person in the navy when Admiral Rodriquez read that Medal of Honor citation." Nancy wished she could kiss him, but they were both in uniform. Still, they could walk aft on the submarine for a little privacy—and if she had her way, she was going to drag Alex off the boat for a little more than privacy. "How'd this patrol go? Another boring convoy escort?"

She knew Alex hated escort duty, but Nancy was secretly relieved. Getting shot at was bad enough without thinking about the same happening to your loved ones. Not that she'd had much other than boredom and a shipyard lately, but *damn*, the war got harder once her husband also started taking fire.

"It started that way but didn't end as one." Alex chuckled. "An *Akula* tried to ambush the convoy, and it got a little hairy—at least until I got them to cut the firing key out of my stateroom safe. Then things turned out okay."

"*What*?" Nancy's jaw dropped. "Who the hell leaves a firing key locked up in wartime?" Her destroyer's FIS—firing interdict switch, which was a removable plastic key—stayed inserted anytime they *weren't* up on the blocks in the shipyard.

And Nancy had thought very hard about leaving it in place even there, except her ship didn't have power...and no power meant no shooting missiles, so it was better to lock the key away.

"Let's just say there are plenty of things about my predecessor that haven't impressed me, and I've yet to even meet the guy." Alex sighed, glancing over his shoulder at the quarterdeck watchstanders. "At least they bonged you on board properly."

"More or less. I didn't mention *Fletcher*." Nancy shrugged. "It seemed the wrong time to be mean."

"Tell me about it."

"I'm missing something."

"I'll tell you the story later." He scrubbed a hand over his face. "You want to head out of here?"

"I thought you'd never ask." Nancy cocked her head. "You're not going to turn all workaholic and say you've got shit to do?"

"Nah. I've given the crew as much liberty as they can handle and written my patrol report. Let me just change out of my coveralls and I'm all yours."

"Be careful what you say. I might hold you to it."

He grinned. "Nance, I've missed you, too."

So much for the "one boat blockade."

Ursula's superiors ordered *Gallant* into port after she wrecked the Seychelles' best harbor, so she returned to Perth. Grudgingly. Luck being with her, she bagged a French *Scorpene III* along the way; the wanker was clever in his stalk of an Australian destroyer, but she caught him on the wrong side of the layer and put two torpedoes in his arse. No one came up after that, so Ursula continued on her merry way. Four days later, she brought *Gallant* into Perth for a much-needed rearm and resupply. Her supply officer's crocodile tears were on the verge of becoming real, and even Ursula, who generally didn't give two damns about what she ate, had noticed the sharp decline in food quality as their stores got low.

But three days of rattling cages failed to get her supplies onload scheduled for sooner than a week out, so Ursula set her crew loose for some well-deserved liberty.

For her part, she took her officers to the Perth Officers Club and paid for the first three rounds. They'd performed superbly, as always, and Ursula believed in fostering *esprit de corps*. She didn't much enjoy socializing with their less-civilized allies—drunk Americans were even more obnoxious than sober ones—but at least the Australians knew their way around good beer. They were cousins of a sort, and they were all in this fight together. Even if the Americans annoyed her.

Not that any of them got under her skin the way Rochambeau could.

"Penny for your thoughts, Captain?" James slid a foaming beer her way.

Ursula took it and sipped gratefully. She did love a good lager, even though her aristocratic relatives wished she'd drink more ladylike beverages. "Nothing charitable in them," she admitted. "Just thinking of an old acquaintance turned rat bastard."

"Rochambeau, then?" He chuckled.

"Am I so bleeding obvious?"

"Not tactically, but you are a wee bit determined where he's involved, ma'am," James said.

Ursula snorted. "Which is your polite way of calling me obsessed."

"I wouldn't go that far. The admiralty did give us—meaning you—the job of tracking the swine down."

"Yes, and that's worked out lovely so far." Ursula sighed. She wasn't accustomed to failure, and Rochambeau had evaded her for the better part of a year. She'd come *so* close last July, only for an American to blunder right into the trap she'd so carefully set, ruining everything.

After that, she promised herself there would be more chances, but here she was, six months later, without even a sniff of the fucker. Just thinking about it made her fury try to boil over, and Ursula quaffed more beer to cool her temper.

"We'll get him, Captain," James said.

She fought back the urge to scowl, to tell him not to make promises he couldn't keep. Ursula didn't mind optimism, but she felt like the devil was riding on her shoulder. Rochambeau had killed more Brits than anyone else, and her government depended on her to take him down. She wasn't nice, and she wasn't politically correct, but Ursula knew she was good at her job. She'd never doubted herself, and she wouldn't start now.

She shook herself. "Bloody right we will."

Movement from her right caught Ursula's eye, and she turned her head to watch a pair of American officers at a nearby table. The woman was almost as pale as she was, while the man was even darker than James. Both were lieutenants, but it was the woman who was easy to overhear.

"I thought the commodore was going to blow a gasket," the woman said. Her nametape read *Lange*, and she looked like a spitfire. "Who the hell gets pissed off when one of their boats does well? I mean, I know that *Bluefish* hasn't exactly made a habit of it, but Banks should be happy."

Her companion shook his head; Ursula couldn't read his nametape from behind his beer. "He's probably just annoyed on Commander Peterson's behalf, Rose."

"Those two really do define fraternization, don't they?" Lange—Rose, apparently—rolled her eyes. "I wish someone would remember that 'unduly familiar' isn't just about sex."

"There's a war on. They're ignoring that, too. You hear about the CO and XO on *Lionfish*?"

Ursula perked up. Shameful though it was, she loved gossip. And she loved hearing about how the Americans arsed things up even more.

Rose's jaw dropped. "They're sleeping together?"

"Their communications officer walked in on them together doing the dirty," her companion confirmed. "Friend of mine is their nav."

"Shit, Lou." Rose shook her head. "And Big Navy doesn't give a damn, huh?"

"Not as long as they get the job done. The cupboard's getting kind of bare, and they need people who can shoot." Lou shrugged. "Otherwise, they'd never have turned Captain Coleman around so quickly and given him *Bluefish*."

"True." Rose leaned back, but Ursula's head whipped around.

"Excuse me, did you say Coleman?" she asked the pair.

Both turned to look at her, confused. The male lieutenant's eyes swept over Ursula's own uniform. "Yes, ma'am. Is there a problem?"

"As in, Alexander Coleman? From *Jimmy Carter*?" Ursula kept her tone level, but rage began pounding in her ears. *Calmly, now,* she told herself. Two hapless lieutenants didn't deserve her ire.

"Yes, ma'am," Lieutenant Cooper—now she could read his nametape—repeated.

Ursula pursed her lips. "He's now in command of *Bluefish*, you said?"

"Yeah." Rose Lange was starting to look suspicious. "Can we help you with something?"

"No need." Ursula waved a hand. "Carry on."

The pair couldn't exactly argue; rank did have its privileges. Ursula turned back to her own crew without sparing Lange or Cooper a second glance, and she felt a small smile playing over her lips. Coleman had stopped her from getting Rochambeau, and Ursula never forgot a grudge.

She wouldn't sabotage an ally. That was...uncouth. Not to mention stupid. But there were many small ways to get revenge, weren't there?

And Alex Coleman was a *fine* target to work her frustrations out on.

Chapter 11

Bad Luck

14 January 2040, Perth, Australia

Two days after *Bluefish* pulled into Perth, Bobby still couldn't believe the wild turn life had taken. The idea of being on a *successful* submarine just wouldn't sink in, and not having a tyrant for a captain really took some getting used to. When they returned to port, Captain Coleman put down general liberty with no restrictions other than "act like an adult and I'll treat you like one" before Bobby could blink. That meant everyone aside from the duty section shot off the boat without looking back, half terrified that the captain would change his mind.

His luck being what it was, Bobby drew the duty for the first day in, but he was free after that. He spent some time with his older brother, a pilot on the carrier USS *Lexington*. Derek had plenty of free time while holes in *Lexington's* flight deck were repaired from a recent battle near Diego Garcia, which meant Bobby got to see him for more than an hour. He couldn't remember the last time they'd spent that much time together—it must have been before the war.

Derek offered to come with him to today's memorial service, but Bobby declined. He knew his brother meant well, but this was for submariners. Nothing short of a memorial for their dead would have convinced Bobby to strap on his dress whites, however, particularly since it still felt weird to wear whites in January.

Winter was summer here, he reminded himself for the hundred and seventh-seventh time. Weird was normal.

Glancing at himself in the mirror one last time, Bobby decided he was ready to go. Lou had the duty, and Rose was stuck in the base weapons depot for a meeting the schmucks over there wouldn't change, which left him flying solo. Bobby was okay with that. Most people didn't really want to go to these things, anyway; listening to the names of every submarine sunk and submariner killed in the last month was depressing. And yet...Bobby felt that *someone* should remember.

Grabbing his cover, Bobby headed out of his stateroom and climbed the ladders leading topside. Force of habit made him glance nervously at *Bluefish's* lines and the sailors on deck, but nothing seemed out of order. He'd talked to two chiefs about fixing the rat guards that morning, but that job was done. It was amazing how much faster people worked when they expected praise instead of punishment. Not having the captain fretting on board all the time helped, too. Captain Coleman slept on board—everyone was required to, since Commodore Banks didn't believe in having a caretaker crew take over when a boat came back from patrol—but he spent most afternoons off the boat. He'd even taken the time to remind the department heads to get some R&R of their own, which left Bobby wondering if their new CO was an alien.

"Heading over to the memorial, Nav?" Harri was Officer of the Deck again, and she wore a knowing look. It was a sober one this time, though.

"How'd you guess?" Bobby gestured at his uniform. "You know I get dressed up for all kinds of things, including taking a bath."

Harri shook her head. "Try not to hurt yourself with your sense of humor, okay? No one here wants a new acting XO."

"You know they'll give us a real XO eventually, right?"

"Don't burst my bubble, sir," Harri replied. "We kind of like things the way they are."

"Um, thanks, I think." Bobby wasn't sure if he should be happy about that; traditionally, the XO was the least popular person on board. The XO was supposed to be the disciplinarian, not that Peterson ever let him. Left at a loss for what else to say, he threw Harri a salute and headed down the brow, pausing to salute the national ensign.

Once on the pier, Bobby turned toward the parking lot. He didn't have a car in Perth—buying one seemed stupid when they were at war—but the base ran a few shuttles to the important places. The memorial was always held in a park not far from the base exchange, and Bobby had just enough time to catch the shuttle and then walk there.

If it wasn't running early. Two steps down the pier, Bobby saw the shuttle pulling away from the stop at the end of the pier, half full of sailors in their dress whites.

"Damn it!"

He was still more than a hundred yards away, and Bobby'd never been a sprinter, no matter how hard the academy's football coach made him try. Racing down the length of the pier in his whites would make him look like an idiot. Usually, Bobby didn't mind looking stupid, but he drew the line at doing it while dressed like a navy milkman. Besides, the white leather shoes were murder on the feet just standing. Running would be a nightmare full of rancid blisters.

He supposed he could walk to the memorial. He'd be late, but late was better than not going. Rose would say he didn't *have* to go, but Rose never had much time for ceremonies, even back at the academy. Sighing, Bobby trudged down the pier. The gate guards at the end saluted him, which he returned absently. He'd get there when he—

"Need a ride?"

Bobby jumped as the voice emerged from the Jeep parked in the spot reserved for *Bluefish's* CO. Captain Coleman, also in his dress whites, was in the driver's seat. Bobby gulped. "Sir?"

"I won't bite, and I can guess where you're going from how you're dressed." Coleman gestured at the passenger seat. "Hop on in."

"Beats walking, I guess." Bobby shrugged and got in. The Jeep looked like it had seen better days—a *lot* of them—but the seat was clean enough. That was important. Thirteen years of wearing this uniform taught Bobby to be careful with where he put his butt. At least he wasn't going to get a grass stain here.

Getting grass stains out of white trousers was *murder*.

Coleman shifted into gear after Bobby closed the door. Bobby tried not to fidget. When he caught sight of a pale blue ribbon with five white stars on it, that got even harder. He'd seen the ribbon that corresponded to the Medal of Honor before, but seeing someone wearing it was way different than one on the wall back home. His great-grandfather had died long before he was born. This was way more real than stories from World War II.

Crap, judging from the twitch in the captain's right cheek, Coleman had noticed him staring. Bobby gulped. "I thought, uh, that most COs felt coming to the memorials is bad luck."

"I always figured it was worse luck refusing to learn from our mistakes." Coleman shrugged. "You usually come?"

"When we're in port, yeah."

"I'm going to guess Commander Peterson didn't." The captain's tone was bone dry. Did Bobby detect a hint of derision?

"Not so much." Swallowing back the desire to say something uncharitable about his old captain was hard. Bobby *should* have felt sorry for the guy. Having an appendix burst was kind of horrible, but he was still relieved Peterson was gone.

And it was an easy surgery, right? Maybe Bobby should have the crew send him a card.

On second thought, there was no telling what people would write in it.

"He really was a winner, wasn't he?"

Bobby jumped again. "Sir?"

"Relax, I'm not asking you to speak ill of your old captain. Not unless you want to." A crooked smile. "He's out of the hospital, by the way. Got out yesterday."

"Oh. That's...good to hear." Bobby tried valiantly to make himself sound cheerful. It didn't work.

"Commodore Banks made a point of telling me that I should go see him for a 'proper' turnover." Coleman rolled his eyes. "I think I'll pass, unless there's anything you think he'll tell me that I should know."

Bobby swallowed. "I'm probably not the one to ask that, sir." *Not the way Peterson hated me,* he didn't add. Peterson blamed Bobby for a lot of things, including the time *Bluefish* stumbled right into a minefield that Bobby had warned Peterson might be there.

"No?" Stopping at a traffic light, Coleman threw Bobby a searching look.

"I wasn't exactly his favorite person." His foot was tapping. Why was it tapping?

"Did he *have* a favorite person on *Bluefish*? I'm getting the impression he hated everyone."

"Um, I think he liked Master Chief Baker. A little." Not that the chief of the boat liked Peterson, but she'd been damned good at hiding it. Bobby wasn't sure how much Baker said to their new captain, however, and he didn't want to throw her under the bus.

Coleman snorted, turning into the parking lot by the park. "Probably only because they tell you to trust your COB in the Prospective Commanding Officers course."

"I'm not sure he *trusted* anyone," Bobby said and then bit his tongue. Stupid big mouth! He was pretty sure that Captain Coleman wouldn't bite his head off, but Bobby still grimaced. Apparently, working for Peterson hadn't cured him of his honesty.

"His type usually doesn't." Coleman put the car in park. "All right, enough about him. Let's go pay our respects."

"Yeah." Throat tight, Bobby got out of the Jeep, pausing to make sure his shirt was firmly tucked in. Then he followed his captain toward the memorial.

Bobby wasn't sure what started this tradition, or why they always gathered by the fountain. It wasn't a very impressive fountain, but dozens of submariners assembled here every month. At first, a chaplain read the names, but after a few months, the senior COB on the waterfront took over, or sometimes a commodore if any of them could be bothered to show up. Today the list was held by an older man with a craggy face whose lines told several stories Bobby knew he wasn't cleared to hear.

The memorial was a no-salute zone and always had been, so Bobby and Captain Coleman joined the crowd without fanfare. A few minutes passed in silence, and then the master chief cleared his throat.

"Today we're gathered to mourn our brothers and sisters lost on eternal patrol," he said. "Since our last memorial, we've lost *Hyman G. Rickover*, *Grunion*, and *Washington*. All three sank with all hands, which means almost four hundred of our brothers and sisters are no longer with us." The master chief swallowed. "We've all lost friends out there, and I ain't the type for pretty speeches. So let me just say this: there's no taking back what happened. We're still fighting the fight, and it's our job to go out there and do it again.

"Honor their memory and raise a glass to them, but don't forget what we're fighting for."

Turning, the master chief nodded to the group of sailors standing to his left. Usually, they were sailors who recently transferred off the lost subs, or people who lost close friends on board. This month there were five. They took turns reading the names of each lost sailor and officer, and Bobby listened with a heavy heart. He'd been lucky this month and hadn't lost any close friends, but the war wasn't always so kind. He'd lost six classmates from the academy, along with his first department head, who died in command of USS *Missouri*. Two friends from his first boat had also been sunk on other submarines. They'd managed to escape, although one had lost her left arm because it was broken too badly to save.

The terrifying truth was that U.S. submarine losses were as high as they'd been in the Second World War, but subs were more expensive and crews were larger these days. No one had been prepared for a war like this. No one had been prepared for nations across the world to start gobbling up the undersea landscape, and Americans were slow to learn that they no longer had the best submarines in the world. They'd been overtaken by Russia and France, with India not far behind, and Bobby didn't know how they were supposed to get back to the top.

If that Yasen hadn't wanted us to follow them, we might never have heard them at all. He swallowed. The *Yasens* weren't even the quietest submarines in the world. The *Requins* were better, and the U.S. had nothing on them now that all the *Seawolfs* were gone. The *Ceroes* were good—and Bobby was biased in their favor—but after development of the so-called SSN(X) stalled, the class had been rushed into service, based in the *Virginia* class, a multi-mission class built to be *Seawolf*-light. And cheaper. True, more *Virginas* had been sunk than *Ceroes*, which at least meant that *Bluefish* and her sisters were an improvement over their predecessors. But they weren't good enough. Not with Russian *Yasens* and French *Requins* like *Barracuda* in the water.

The memorial ended, and people split up into quiet groups. No one thought their lost shipmates would mind friends talking.

"I didn't realize you were back in Perth, Captain. I haven't seen you since the ceremony." Much to Bobby's surprise, the master chief who had spoken for the memorial headed their way, holding his hand out to Captain Coleman.

Coleman took it with a smile. "I got out here just before Christmas to take command of *Bluefish*."

"Ouch. You've got your work cut out for you again, but Master Chief Baker's a good sort. She'll have your back."

"I figured you'd say that." Coleman chuckled and turned to Bobby. "Bobby, this is Master Chief Morton, my COB on *Jimmy Carter*. Master Chief, this is Lieutenant Bobby O'Kane, my navigator and sort-of XO."

"Sort-of XO beats being acting everything." Bobby grinned and extended his hand. Morton's handshake was firm, and he looked Bobby over the way only an experienced master chief could: just short of insultingly frank. "Nice to meet you."

"Likewise." Morton grinned. "You'll have fun keeping up with this one, Lieutenant. He's a little crazy."

"I'm still standing right here, Master Chief." But Coleman chuckled, which meant Bobby could laugh.

"Yeah, I think we've found that out already. Ask him about the firing key," Bobby replied.

Morton cackled. "I'll do that."

"Christ, I'm outnumbered already." Captain Coleman shook his head. "Don't believe everything this cranky bastard tells you, Bobby. Like any good master chief, he's two parts bullshit and three parts experience."

"Excuse me, Captain, but that's *four* parts experience to three parts bullshit. Your ratios are all off," Morton cut in. "I'll talk to Ginger about calibrating you."

Coleman chuckled. "You do that, Master Chief. I'm sure I need it."

The two continued joking, more at ease with one another than Bobby knew what to do with. Eventually, he wandered off to talk to an old friend. The idea of a captain who might joke with people and give a damn about them was enough to break his brain. Yeah, the last couple of weeks had been good, but Bobby still waited for the other shoe to drop and things to turn sour.

At least they hadn't given Peterson back to the crew. He was out of the hospital but not on *Bluefish*. Bobby counted that as a victory.

15 January 2040

Navy medical was the same, no matter where you went in the world. The same uncomfortable chairs. The same quiet waiting area. The same slightly late appointments everyone was still required to be fifteen minutes early for.

Sighing, Nancy slumped in her chair and returned her attention to flipping through the books available on her phone.

Watching the clock did no good, and it wasn't like she had anywhere to go. *Fletcher* was in her past as of yesterday; the change-of-command burned in her mind like a brand. And now one more medical evaluation stood between her and her new role on *Cape St. George.*

She resisted the urge to chew her lip. Julia Rosario was good for her promises. Nancy knew that. But going to be someone's XO again was no fun, even if it was the route to early cruiser command. Alex was the only person in her class to put on captain already. She might be the second if she assumed command of *Cape* before year's end.

A waspish voice drifted over from the check-in area. "I have been *waiting* for ten minutes already. My appointment was at eleven."

"I'm sorry, Commander. Doctor O'Halloran is backed up. You'll be up next," the receptionist replied.

"I'll be making a report to your superiors." The commander who spoke was a short man with olive skin and crossed arms. The way his chin jutted out told Nancy he thought he was important, as was the fact that he wore all his ribbons on his service khakis.

She shook her head and went back to looking for a new book to read. Who did that? No one wore more than their top three ribbons unless they were in a fancier uniform. No one with a normal-sized ego, anyway.

She'd just decided on *Beyond the Stars*, a new science-fiction epic, when a shadow crossed over her phone screen and the other commander plopped into the chair next to her.

"These people," he muttered, clearly intending for her to hear. "No respect for rank."

Nancy cocked her head, contemplating a mention of how it was eleven fifteen...which meant this egomaniac had shown up five minutes late for his precious appointment. But it wasn't worth an argument, not when she had her own poking and prodding to look forward to. "Everyone's busy these days. I hear they got a bunch of folks from a sinking in this morning."

"They should still keep to their schedule." He sneered. "The organization here is underwhelming."

Nancy shrugged. "I've seen worse."

"You have my pity," he replied. "But where are my manners? Wade Peterson, *Blue*—forgive me, formerly of *Bluefish*. Someone jerked her out from under me when I had a medical emergency, *against* my commodore's wishes."

"That sounds...disappointing." Nancy kept a straight face with an effort, studying her neighbor with new interest. So *this* was the guy Alex replaced? He seemed like a real peach.

He hadn't put his command-at-sea pin on the correct side of his uniform yet, either. Once out of command, that pin belonged *under* the ribbons instead of over the nametag. Alex had gone out to *Bluefish* a week and a half ago, which means this poser had been out of command for at least that long.

Nancy's own pin was firmly where it belonged, despite her giving up *Fletcher* less than twenty-four hours earlier. What an ass.

"It's beyond disappointing. First, a certain admiral takes a disliking to me and keeps me away from *any* mission where I could achieve success and glory in the war, and *then* he uses the excuse of a medical emergency to deprive me of command." Peterson sniffed, his eyes flicking to her own command-at-sea pin. "I sincerely hope you don't know how that feels."

"No, my change of command was yesterday," she replied, keeping her voice mild. Thank goodness Coleman was a common name.

"Lucky for you. Then again, perhaps the surface navy is less plagued by favoritism."

"I'd like to say competency always finds a way, but I've met a few folks..."

"Isn't that the truth?" Peterson's laugh was as unpleasant as the rest of his attitude. "Where are you coming from?"

"*Fletcher*. *O'Bannon*-class destroyer," she added when his face went blank. "Heading to a cruiser for a fleet up XO ride."

"Fleet up?" Peterson cocked his head.

"XO to CO, same ship. The surface navy still does those from time to time."

"I see." He pursed his lips. "Wouldn't that make you unduly familiar with the crew?"

Nancy shrugged. "That's never a problem I've experienced. Besides, it's wartime. The navy has to survive a lot worse than a little friendliness."

"Good order and discipline are *always* critical to a command's success."

"Of course. But in my experience, a good captain can balance the two." Nancy smiled, thinking of what Alex told her of the mess this idiot left behind. She'd met his type before, though maybe not quite as bad.

Peterson disguised bullying as discipline and petty tyranny as order. No wonder COMSUBPAC wanted him gone badly enough to override his own squadron commander. Alex hadn't mentioned that part, though, and Nancy made a mental note to tell him. Knowing his own commodore didn't want him would keep Alex armed against whatever shenanigans Banks might pull.

Fortunately, the nurse called her back before Peterson formulated a reply, saving Nancy from his response. She wasn't interested in playing match-the-ego today, so good riddance.

Toulon, France

"I desire to sink USS *Nereus.*"

Jules Rochambeau crossed his arms and sat back in his chair, meeting Admiral Savageau's eyes levelly. Most submarine commanders didn't get the chance to express such wishes to France's senior submarine admiral, but Jules Rochambeau knew he was a special case.

Sauvageau frowned, her eyes narrowing. She was newer in her job, and wholly unqualified in Jules' expert opinion, but he was stuck with her and must make do. Her reputation said she was a better operator in the back halls of politics than she was in a submarine, but Jules supposed that was useful in her current role...if he wanted to be generous. At least she was easy on the eyes, with blond hair, gray eyes, and fair skin that glowed in the afternoon sunlight. Pity she was an admiral.

"What for?" she asked. "Isn't that a tender?"

"Yes, but it is commanded by their Captain John Dalton." Jules shrugged, playing it cool. He did not know her the way he'd known the late Admiral Bernard, who usually let him have his head and choose his targets. "I missed him when he had *Razorback*."

"Perhaps later." Sauvageau smirked. "I have a more pressing target for you right now."

"Oh?" Jules hoped it would be something or someone interesting. He wasn't ashamed to admit that he liked media attention, and he aimed to remain the preeminent submarine commander in the world. France never had a true legendary submariner. Jules enjoyed being the first.

Yet would Savageau give him the chances he needed? She might resent him. Jules was not sure. She'd put him on shore to talk to the media, yes, and his ego enjoyed that opportunity...but what if Savageau wanted him out of the way? What if she was of the horrid mindset that she should *even* the playing field?

Jules' stomach lurched.

"Our new allies in the Seychelles are annoyed with Ursula North and *Gallant*," Sauvageau said. "She bottled up their harbor with shipwrecks, and no one can get in or out until it's cleared. I'm told it will be months."

Jules cocked his head, his heart beating wildly. "You are sending me after Lady North? Finally?"

"Do you think you cannot handle her?"

"Admiral, please. I know I can." Jules waved a hand. "This has never been the question. However, our leaders decided previously that my talents were better employed elsewhere."

He didn't mind racking up kills, but Jules would appreciate a challenge. Excitement made his chest tight. The Brits had been playing up the North v. Rochambeau rivalry for years. Would his government finally join in?

"That was before she antagonized our allies." Sauvageau sighed, rubbing her eyes. "The Seychelles are threatening to re-declare neutrality if we do not deal with her."

"They're a tiny island." He scoffed. "Who cares?"

"We care because we want to deny the port to the Grand Alliance." Now the admiral glared, but only a little. Jules was too important to be taken to task for something so minor.

"Of course." If only politics and politicians would get out of the way to let proper warfighters do the work. Jules tried not to sigh. Perhaps he was being uncharitable. His country finally had leadership with a backbone, a president who no longer danced to Britain and America's tune, who had struck out to make France a world power once more. They needed undersea resources and allies to accomplish that, so the warfighters fought.

And perhaps having a politician as the top submariner could work. Sauvageau certainly seemed able to sing the right songs.

"Hunting down Ursula North will give our allies the blood they want, eliminate a dangerous enemy, and provide our navy with a morale boost," the admiral continued. "We need all of those things."

"*Je comprends*," he replied. *I understand.*

"I intend to write your orders very liberally. Sink anyone who gets in your way, but if you can find Lady North, destroy her and her pesky submarine," Sauvageau said.

Jules grinned. "With pleasure, Admiral."

The conversation covered several other topics before Jules departed, but none of them were nearly as important as his newest challenge. He was tasked to kill his old acquaintance—or perhaps merely to sink her. Jules did relish the idea of Lady North penned up in a POW camp for the rest of the war. He didn't need her dead, after all, just out of the way.

Picking her up out of the water would be sweet. Perhaps he would surface and rescue her and her crew. The very thought made Jules shiver.

Ursula would make a fight of things, of course. It would be even better if she knew he was coming. That thought brought a wide smile to Jules' face, and he pulled out his phone. He knew how to be sure of Ursula's undivided attention.

> **Captain Jules Rochambeau**
> **@JulesRochambeau**
> @RoyalNavy You should tell Lady North that I am coming for her.
> **#Barracuda #HMSGallant #UrsulaNorth #BattleoftheCentury**

Perth, Australia

"Didn't you say that your predecessor was a Commander Peterson?" Nancy asked from the other end of the phone.

"Yeah, what about him?" Alex replied as he scrawled his signature across some routine paperwork on his tablet.

This set of documents acknowledged receipt for the torpedo onload they received that morning. The next page was for the stores onload they'd get that evening. It was almost dark already, but for some reason, the shoreside supply geniuses decided to schedule *Bluefish's* onload for six p.m. His crew was beat, and Alex was, too, but it was the only time available. With a war on, subs were expected to be ready at all times.

Not that he had a date for their next patrol. To be fair, *Bluefish* had only been back for four days. Alex knew that most subs averaged a week or two between combat patrols, but convoy escorts tended to come with a lot less rest. In fact—

"Alex, are you listening to me?"

"Shit. Sorry, no, I was looking at paperwork." He flushed, not that his wife could see it.

"I thought you said you had some down time while you were waiting for a stores onload?" Nancy asked.

Alex grimaced. "I do. Sorry, babe. I'll pull my head out. What were you saying about Peterson?"

"I was saying that he was even less charming than you implied," she replied. "I ran into him at medical and he was full of complaints about not being treated super special enough because of his rank. Also wanked about how 'his' boat got 'yanked' out from under him."

"Oh, joy." Alex pulled his glasses off to rub his eyes. "Should I expect a knife in my back soon?"

Nancy snorted. "Not from him. He doesn't seem brave enough. But I'd watch out for your commodore. If Peterson was being honest, he didn't agree with *Bluefish* being given to you, either."

"Having encountered Commodore Banks, I can believe that."

Believing Peterson was an all-around jackass was easy; every day, Alex found new ways daily in which Peterson traumatized his crew.

Yesterday, Alex spent four hours cleaning up the mess of how Peterson randomly decided fourteen sailors on board were not allowed to take their advancement exams. With no cause. The Bureau of Personnel was almost as displeased as Alex, and the disaster required six different long-distance phone calls to straighten out. It would've been much easier if the squadron lifted a finger to help, but Commodore Banks decided it was a boat problem.

Given what Nancy had shared...that was no surprise.

"I think you've stepped in a steaming pile, Alex," Nancy said.

"Certainly feels like it."

"God help me if I find something like this on *Cape*. I swear I'll scream."

He laughed. "You'll dig and dig until you're out of the hole. That's what you do."

"It's the job, right?" she replied. "But they couldn't just make fighting a war simple, could they?"

"If it was easy, everyone would play."

They changed the subject to family news, including their defiant but loveable daughters. The elder, Roberta—called Bobbie—was at the Naval Academy in Annapolis, while the younger, Emily, remained at home, applying for colleges. Emily was stuck on attending Alex and Nancy's shared alma mater, Norwich University, and while the very thought made Alex smile, he also worried. Would this war go on long enough that both girls might end up in the line of fire?

Nancy shared his concerns, but their daughters also shared their sense of duty. He could no more stop them from wearing the uniform than he could turn his own ranks in. Nor would Nancy. So all they could do was pray the war would end before Bobbie graduated in three years' time—or two, if she got her way and succeeded on an accelerated commissioning track.

After they got off the phone, Alex was left with nothing to do but turn his attention back to the stores paperwork. What fun. His supply officer, Lieutenant (junior grade) Sonnen, had forwarded a dozen forms for him to sign. Reading them took the better part of an hour, but Alex was done by the time the trucks were due to arrive. Then he waited.

And waited.

Six p.m. rolled by, and Alex called the quarterdeck to see if someone had just forgotten to tell him. Did Peterson feel stores onloads were beneath his dignity? Probably. At six fifteen, Brigette Sonnen called *him* to say that there'd been some sort of delay, but she'd investigate. Alex made himself sit on his hands and be patient; he hated being a micromanager and wouldn't start now. By six forty-five, the delay was *supposed* to be over, but the trucks still hadn't materialized.

At seven, Bobby stuck his head in Alex's stateroom. "Captain, I think I figured out our supply SNAFU."

"Oh, goodie. Enlighten me."

"It looks like HMS *Gallant* stole our stores." Bobby fidgeted. "I sent Brigette down to talk to the supply guys, and it seems like someone told them to go to *Gallant* instead of us."

"Someone." Alex knew his dry tone bordered on anger, and he swallowed his ire with an effort. He hadn't missed Bobby shifting from one foot to the other like he was expecting a flame spray. It had to be *Gallant*, didn't it? Surely that was a coincidence. He hadn't run into Ursula North since that day in the Perth O-Club where she accused him of ruining her shot at Rochambeau. She probably didn't even who he was. "Anyone have any idea who this 'someone' is?"

"Not so far, sir."

"Great." Alex groaned. "I take it Brigette didn't have much luck?"

"Nah." Bobby shook his head. "The chief in charge pretty much told her to suck it, only barely more politely. The Brits were even less help. They said *Gallant* needed the supplies more than we do."

"Well, isn't that just fucking ducky?" Alex forced back the urge to go have words with said chief. He couldn't protect his division officers from every asshole in the world. Like it or not, Brigette would learn from running across a bad chief. "All right, XO, what's your plan?"

"I thought I could go over see to the supply side guys and try to figure out who screwed everything up." Bobby squirmed.

Alex shook his head. "Nice though it would be to figure out whose idiocy caused this, the first thing we need to do is reschedule our onload. *And* we need to tell the squadron that we're not fully loaded, because they'll be counting on us to be."

"Right." Bobby flushed red. "I'll call the COS after I get Brigette to reschedule."

"Better you than me. I'm pretty sure I'm already on the commodore's shit list." Alex could have smacked himself the moment the words came out, but Bobby was his acting XO. The XO was supposed to be the captain's sounding board. Alex couldn't bite his tongue all the time.

Bobby surprised him by laughing. "Sir, I think that's just because you're not Commander Peterson."

"I'm hoping that's a compliment."

"Well, it'd be a stupid insult." Bobby's grin made the lieutenant look years younger, and Alex found himself grinning back.

Maybe they were getting somewhere. Finally.

16 January 2040, Rybachiy Submarine Base, Kamchatka Peninsula, Russia

Summons to see Admiral Dimitri Mikhailov just six days after losing your first submarine were never a good thing. Captain Katerina Revnik knew she was no exception to that rule, even if the admiral's aide ushered her through the door with unseemly haste.

Better to see her to her execution, she supposed. Though Katerina thought her navy was past that.

Weren't they?

"You requested my presence, Admiral?" Katerina asked, holding her salute until he returned it.

"Yes, sit down." Mikhailov was a tall man known for his bluntness. He took no prisoners and ruthlessly criticized mistakes. Katerina hadn't expected an invitation to speak in her own defense, let alone sit down privately with Russia's senior submariner. Particularly when he hadn't bothered to look up from the tablet lying flat on his desk and all she could see was his still-full head of silver hair.

Still, she was not a fool. Katerina sat.

"Shame about *Kazan*," Mikhailov said. "Good that you saved much of the crew, though. How'd you manage it?"

Katerina blinked. "I dropped decoys at one minute until impact. I believe the American torpedoes detonated against them instead of the hull."

"A wise way to save your lives. You'll have to write that trick up to be taught in the Advanced Special Officers' Class."

That needed a moment to sink in; Katerina had to stop her jaw from dropping. "Admiral?"

"Having you teach there is tempting, but you are needed elsewhere." Mikhailov finally looked up, lifting the tablet and extending it to her. "Look at this."

Katerina accepted the tablet, hiding her confusion. Then she blinked. The tablet displayed plans for an attack submarine, a distinctly Russian design she had never seen. The name on the top right corner read *Pictor* class, and Katerina's heart started to pound. Zooming in to inhale the details, she noted ten torpedo tubes, the same number of vertical launch cells for missiles, a large torpedo room, and an advanced set of sonar arrays unlike any current Russian submarine.

"What do you think, Captain?" Mikhailov asked.

Katerina shook herself. She had almost forgotten he was there. "This is... impressive, sir." She wanted to say more, but a disgraced submarine captain was not permitted such liberties.

"Good." Mikhailov smiled. "The third in class commissions in July. You will be in command."

"Sir?" Katerina hadn't even heard of a *Pictor*-class attack submarine. Surely, she misunderstood.

"Do you object?"

"No, obviously not. Just"—she swallowed—"why me?"

"You have a gift, Captain. The fact that you were able to save your crew tells me that." The admiral sighed. "And to be frank, our navy needs to learn from our mistakes, not sweep them under the rug like garbage. You are going to change things."

"Me?" Katerina did not squeak. Submarine captains were too dignified to squeak.

"Yes." He gestured at her. "It does not hurt that you are photogenic and popular within the navy. You are also tactically gifted. Your work capturing that *Shortfin* proves that, as do your previous patrols."

Katerina shivered. "I also lost *Kazan* to the next submarine I attempted to trap."

"No matter." He waved a hand. "That trick was never going to work more than once. The fleet commander who ordered you to attempt it again has been disciplined."

Oh. Katerina wasn't sure what to think of that. The days of *discipline* meaning a firing squad were more or less over, but failure when surrounded by wolves was still fatal to your career, even for admirals. And yet she was to be rewarded with a brand new submarine. Something did not make sense.

Anger prickled along her spine. He'd called her *photogenic.* Keeping her inner snarl behind a pleasant expression took so much self-control, but Katerina had not spent a year serving at the pleasure of the Russian Naval Command for nothing.

"I would still think the command would go to someone with a better record. Am I incorrect, sir?"

Mikhailov scowled. "Your record is one of our best. A sinking does not change that, particularly not when it came at the hands of an American medal of honor winner."

"It did?"

"Yes. Our sources brought that information in this morning. *Kazan's* killer was Alexander Coleman, now commanding USS *Bluefish*."

"Fascinating." Katerina tapped her fingers against the arm of the chair before she could stop herself. "Excuse me."

Mikhailov waved a hand. "No matter. I am more interested in your skills than your manners. The commanders of the first two *Pictors* have friends in high political places. I could not prevent their appointments, but I do not expect much success from them. From you, however, I expect differently."

"And that is?" she asked, her back straightening.

"I expect you to be the face of our new submarine tradition. Like Russia, you will rise from ignominy to become something better. We have retaken our place in the world, and you will lead our submariners to do the same. Are you willing?"

Katerina met his eyes. "Yes, sir. I am."

Perth, Australia

Ursula found the lack of reaction disappointing. It was petty, but stealing *Alex Coleman's* stores warmed her heart. She had needed the food onload, so what Ursula didn't feel was guilty. *Bluefish* wouldn't do much with them. That boat was the dregs of the American barrel, always avoiding combat. The previous CO—whatever his name was—had been a bloody coward. Ursula doubted Coleman would be much better. He wasn't a weakling, but the man had a habit of blundering right into situations where he didn't belong.

Except for Convoy 57. That had been a nice piece of work. She could admit that, at least to herself. But the bastard had *still* ruined her best shot at getting Rochambeau. If Coleman wasn't so terminally idiotic, she would've sunk the French swine months earlier! And now *Gallant* wouldn't be getting underway at four in the morning.

Never you mind that getting underway before dawn was Ursula's preference. She liked to keep the enemy jumping. Only an idiot thought French, Russian, or Indian satellites didn't have eyes on Perth twenty-four hours a day. Cloud cover plus darkness disguised *Gallant's* departure nicely.

"Where to, Captain?" James Harrison asked as they cleared the channel outbound from Perth.

Her orders provided Ursula with a great deal of latitude. In fact, they were simple: *Find and destroy FNS* Barracuda. The question was where Jules had bloody gone. No word about *Barracuda* had surfaced in the last week except that stupid tweet that Jules sent in his normal immature and bombastic way. Still, Ursula was starting to get a very bad feeling. With an effort, she stopped gritting her teeth.

"Head northeast. *Barracuda* likes to prey on carrier battle groups or on the edge of the Australian patrol sectors. Since the Americans trashed their own carriers in the First Battle of the BIOT and we don't have anything big enough underway, that leaves lurking around our patrol sectors."

"Assuming Captain Rochambeau is conforming to his normal pattern," James finished for her.

"Assuming." Ursula managed not to snarl out loud. "Sooner or later, the bugger has to head *somewhere* to resupply and rearm. If we can't catch him out here, we'll lurk near Mumbai or Réunion." She bared her teeth. "At least we know he's not going to the Seychelles."

James grinned. "Yes, ma'am. We made sure of that."

"Indeed we did. Even if we've only taken the Freedom Union's favorite vacation spot out of the game, I say it's a job well done."

Now if only she could get on with her *actual* job. It was a pity that intelligence had lost Rochambeau. Killing him would be much easier if someone would just find the bastard.

Chapter 12

Solving Problems

19 January 2040, Perth, Australia

Banks didn't have the decency to respond to Alex's email himself.

> *The commodore is of the opinion that one Russian submarine laying mines does not indicate a shift in tactics,* Commander Reyes, Banks' chief of staff, had written. *There is no evidence that this tactic has been used in the past. Since it is likely that the only submarine commander demonstrating this initiative is now dead, there is no need to pass your report onto higher authorities.*

Gritting his teeth, Alex pulled his hands away before he could give into the mounting urge to smash his keyboard into the metal desk. First, Banks ignored his patrol report—which had detailed the two times *Kazan's* commander attempted to lure *Bluefish* into a minefield. Then Banks passed Alex's more pointed email onto his chief of staff because he couldn't be bothered to reply to one of his own captains. Things like this chapped his ass more than his sturdy metal chair with its worn down seat that stuck to his coveralls.

Alex was used to being ignored. He'd even developed a bit of a taste for it on *Jimmy Carter*, but this was just plain stupid. And even the COS was more interested in *Bluefish's* supply shortage than Russian tactics! Sometimes, he wondered if people who stayed on shore even remembered there was a war on.

Was that a fair thought? Alex didn't much care. Consumed by administrative details, Banks had his staff chasing paper trails and rumors to discover which supply weenie sent *Bluefish's* supplies to *Gallant* instead of getting Alex a new onload. Three days had passed. While there remained enough food on board to last a month, that wasn't a margin that left Alex comfortable. Particularly not after what had happened *after* Convoy 57, when his sub needed weeks to limp home from an "unimportant" and "safe" convoy escort.

"This guy understands war about as well as a donkey understands fine art," Alex grumbled to himself. "Probably less. At least a jackass can *eat* a painting."

He turned back to the email, scrolling down. *The commodore is, however, concerned that your supply officer might have inadvertently allowed—*

His phone rang, and Alex grabbed for it, glad for the distraction. "Captain."

"Sir, it's the officer of the deck," Rene said. Rene Shorn was one of Alex's most experienced division officers, and he'd been cool under fire—but now he sounded rattled.

"Everything okay, Rene?"

"Um, no? Or yes." Rene sounded like he wasn't sure what the answer was. "Admiral Rodriquez is here, Captain."

"What?" Alex was out of his seat before he realized he'd moved.

"Yes, sir." He could almost hear Rene cringing. "He's here on the quarterdeck."

"I'm on my way."

So much for being ignored. Heart pounding, Alex grabbed his ballcap and bolted out of his stateroom, scurrying up the ladder leading topside. One quick look took in the situation. Rene stood ramrod straight, nervous as an electrified cat, while Vice Admiral Rodriquez grinned like a loon. The admiral had an aide with him, and there was a pickup truck full of boxes on the pier.

"Captain Coleman!" Much to Alex's chagrin, Rodriquez saluted him first. "Glad to see you're not out of uniform this time."

Alex blanched, remembering to return the salute. "Respectfully, sir, I didn't think I was last time, either."

The man the sub force nicknamed Uncle Marco boomed out a laugh. "I'm glad to see you have a spine when you're not so beat to shit. How's the new boat?"

Son of a misbegotten bitch, was the admiral just there to talk to Alex? Alex wished he could tell his heart to stop the samba, but he didn't *like* attention. And Uncle Marco wasn't known for showing up on submarines just for fun. No, Uncle Marco was known for being a hard ass, for chewing up inept sub COs and spitting them out again. No way in hell he was just there to make nice.

"Well, she's in better shape than the last one," his mouth replied without input from his brain.

Shit, he shouldn't have said that, and Rodriquez's suddenly wide eyes didn't help. Now probably wasn't the time to remind the admiral of the mess Alex made of the last sub the navy gave him, was it? He needed to stop acting like a jackass.

"So far," Alex added quickly.

"She'd damned well better be, Captain," Rodriquez growled. "These babies don't come cheap. Pretty sure they teach you that in the Prospective Commanding Officers' course."

Alex's eyes narrowed. "Sir, I remember you saying something about how the survivors' benefits wouldn't be so good if you were paying us to come back from war."

In for a penny, in for a pound. Alex might not have liked attention, but he wasn't about to get walked all over, either. Even by an admiral. *Especially* this one.

"So I did!" Rodriquez laughed again. "You've got balls. Good. And you haven't fallen to pieces, either. Damn good patrol, by the way, son. The Indians are smarting from the loss of those new *Scorpenes*, and the French are pissed because they weren't fully paid for and now the Indians supposedly don't want to fork over the balance. Nice spot on the *Yasen*, too."

Rodriquez held out a hand, and Alex could have been knocked over by a feather. Rodriquez *wasn't* known for congratulations and handshakes—at least not unless you'd done *really* well. Last time Alex faced him after a convoy escort, he'd promoted Alex on the spot and berated Commodore Banks. Alex had been too exhausted at the time to remember much else, but speaking of his boss...

"Thank you, sir." Alex swallowed. "I, uh, hate to ask, but does Commodore Banks know you're here?"

"Banks can suck it," Rodriquez replied, and Alex didn't want to know who from the quarterdeck watch squeaked in surprise. "Last I checked, he still worked for me."

"I'm not getting in the middle of this one." Alex swallowed. No love lost there, huh? Was that why Banks disliked him? Uncle Marco had given Alex his friend's job.

Great.

Rodriquez's grin returned. "Smart and ballsy. Watch out or you'll end up as an admiral. Assuming you acquire the sufficient ability to kiss ass."

"No, thank you." The very idea of someone wanting to put stars on him made Alex laugh out loud. He'd always been ornery and unconventional; war or no, the navy wasn't looking for admirals like him.

"Don't say that too loudly. With a Medal of Honor, they might do it to you, anyway."

"Admiral, I, uh..."

Rodriquez waved a hand. "Oh, shut your face. I'm not here to make you go all stutter-y."

"Then what *are* you here for?" Alex asked a little plaintively.

"Assemble your crew on the mess decks for awards and pizza, Captain." Rodriquez's grin turned wicked. "I'd have brought ice cream, too, but the base seems to be out of the shit, so you'll have to settle for Pizza Hut."

Bobby walked onto *Bluefish's* mess decks and froze.

That was Uncle Marco standing next to the captain and behind two tables stacked with pizza boxes. The smell was nice, almost nice enough to distract Bobby from the sight of the commander of all pacific fleet submarines standing on *his* boat with *his* captain. But then his mind came back around to the fact that Admiral Rodriquez was on *Bluefish*, and Bobby swallowed.

"Try not to stop in front of me, will you?" Rose shoved him from behind. "Get your ass in gear, Bobby."

"Sorry." Damn it, why couldn't he just be a department head? As acting XO, he'd have to go over and be sociable with the navy's most dangerous animal. No, admiral. Was there a difference? Bobby had never been in a position to meet Uncle Marco before, and he hadn't wanted to change that.

But it wasn't like he had a choice. As the lucky department head who'd won the seniority lottery, he was stuck as the boat's number-two guy. Until they got a real XO, he was just going to have to fake it until he made it. So Bobby squared his shoulders and weaved through the crowd of confused sailors. At least Rose and Lou followed him, joining the knot of junior officers who tried a little too obviously to keep their distance from the admiral. Brigette looked particularly terrified; she probably thought this was about the supply mess a few days earlier.

Admirals didn't solve problems with pizza, though.

"You guys got everybody?" Bobby asked Rose and Lou after doing a quick headcount for the navigation department.

"Everyone who's not on watch," Lou answered for both, and Bobby nodded.

"Crew's assembled, sir," he said to Captain Coleman.

"This the kid you were telling me about?" Rodriquez interrupted before Coleman could answer.

"Yes, sir. Technically, he's my navigator, but Lieutenant O'Kane has been acting XO—for how long, now, Bobby?"

"About four months." Bobby tried not to grimace. It felt *so* much longer, particularly with Peterson.

"Hm." Rodriquez didn't seem pleased. Bobby fought back the urge to babble. "I'll look into that."

The captain started to open his mouth, but Rodriquez waved for silence, turning to the crew.

"All right, you chuckleheads. You're probably all wondering why you're stuck in here listening to an old fart talk instead of getting the hell out of here on liberty, so I'll get this the fuck over with," the admiral said. "This is a little tradition of mine, one I only do for boats that have come back from an outstanding patrol. You've done that."

Rodriquez's grin was infectious. Bobby had to give him that. He could see smiles peeking out on many faces as people realized they weren't in trouble. Even Bobby felt the chill between his shoulders turn to tentative excitement. Could this be...good?

"Pizza isn't the best thank-you an admiral can come up with, but the base is out of ice cream," Rodriquez continued. "And while I'm not sure what kind of fucking douche canoe lets three navies run out of ice cream during wartime, I can't fix that today. I can, however, come bearing gifts. First off, the CNO has authorized the award of the Meritorious Unit Commendation for USS *Bluefish*. I'd read you the citation, but my chief of staff hasn't finished writing it yet."

A surprised laugh burst out of Bobby, which would have mortified him if everyone else hadn't had the same reaction. *Bluefish with a MUC?* The world might end tomorrow. Was Bobby in some alternate universe? He liked it and wanted to stay, thank you very much. The rest of the crew clearly felt the same way; Rose beamed, and Lou grinned hugely. Even Master Chief Baker looked pleased, and she had one of the best poker faces in the world. Bobby'd learned that when he lost three hundred bucks to her in a poker tourney that Peterson shut down just when everyone started having fun.

The captain seemed a little stunned, too. Did he not know this was coming? Bobby cocked his head. Wild.

"Pipe down. I'm not fucking finished." Rodriquez's laugh took the bite out of the words. "Now, onto individual awards—and these citations aren't finished yet, either, but I've got the high points.

"MM1 Tracy Mullins, for timely use of a PECU and destroying the captain's stateroom as little as possible, is awarded the Navy/Marine Corps Commendation Medal, with Combat 'C' device."

A tall, red-haired woman stepped forward, trying to look serious while her shipmates snickered. By now, everyone knew captain's safe. MM1 Mullins had wrecked the safe, but the captain didn't mind. Just thinking about that made Bobby shiver; he'd never been so certain he was going to die before they could shoot back—or so positive that the captain was going to ream them *all* a new one.

Huh. Maybe they *were* dead and this was all a crazy-dead-person fever dream. Stuff like this sure never happened on *Bluefish.*

Admiral Rodriquez continued: "Also receiving the Navy/Marine Corps Commendation Medal with Combat 'C': FT2 Bryan Kay, STC Zenaida Andreas, FTC Min Rhee, MMCS Nori Zhang, and Lieutenant (Junior Grade) Harriet Ainsworth."

Each sailor stepped forward to receive their medals, beaming. *Bluefish* had always had a good crew; they just never got to use their skills the way Bobby knew they could. Seeing them finally recognized made Bobby feel ten feet tall; his chest swelled with pride and keeping a professional mien when a smile wanted to split his face in half was impossible. Thank goodness no one else was standing at proper attention; they were too busy whooping and congratulating their shipmates as the admiral and captain pinned medals on.

Next, Admiral Rodriquez handed out seventeen Navy Achievement Medals, all with the coveted Combat C. Bobby grinned his way through it all. He wasn't the only one unafraid to show his joy, either. Sailors slapped each other on the back, which only made Uncle Marco smirk.

"Next up, the worst of the sinners, or the department heads you all love to hate: Lieutenant Rose Lange and Louis Cooper, you are both awarded the Bronze Star with 'V' device for valor while under fire by the enemy. So is the poor fool who has to wrangle all your asses every day, your unfortunate chief of the boat. Master Chief Ginger Baker, get your ass up here with these lieutenants. I was going to say that I hope to fuck the crew knows how lucky they are to have you, but judging from their smiles, I think they got the memo."

Wide-eyed, Rose, Lou, and Master Chief Baker stepped forward. A weird mixture of confusion and excitement washed over Bobby. If he hadn't been included with the department heads, did that mean…?

"Lieutenant Robert O'Kane, your acting XO—who you probably all doubly hate for that, as any XO deserves—is awarded the Silver Star."

The *what*? Bobby blinked, staring at Admiral Rodriquez like he had a grown a leg out of his face. Surely, he meant someone else. Right?

A hand smacked him between the shoulders, shoving Bobby forward. He didn't have to look to know it was Rose, and he stumbled toward Rodriquez, trying not to trip over his own two feet. This was unreal. So was the way the crew cheered for him and Master Chief Baker, who turned a beaming smile on Bobby he was certain he didn't deserve.

"Cat got your tongue, Lieutenant?" Rodriquez asked.

"More like a whole clowder."

"I'm not even going to ask what that fancy-ass word means." Rodriquez shook his head and pinned the medal on Bobby's coveralls, where it hung looking out of place and suspiciously silver.

Bobby stepped back to where Rose and Lou stood in a daze, but he wasn't so out of it that he missed Rose snickering. Lou just grinned. Bobby felt like he needed to get his head checked. Yeah. This was definitely a fever dream. But it couldn't be his fever dream, because Bobby lost his optimism over a year ago. He'd never dream of successes and medals. He'd only wanted off the miserable hunk of metal *Bluefish* had become under Commander Peterson. Maybe he'd rediscovered hope when they got sunk by that *Akula*. Dying would fix his sense of humor, right?

"And finally, for his many misdeeds—chief amongst them an uncanny ability to find the enemy and shoot the sunzabitches—Captain Alex Coleman is awarded the Navy Cross. Not that it looks all that important compared to his *other* medal, but we won't talk about that one right now," the admiral finished.

The crew snickered, but Bobby spotted a lot of grins. Captain Coleman, on the other hand, went a little green, and he *looked* like he wanted to object. Even lieutenants knew that only idiots argued with Uncle Marco, however, so he let the admiral pin the medal on. Though Coleman's mutinous glare only made Uncle Marco's smirk grow.

"Congratulations to all of you on a job well fucking done," Uncle Marco said as Captain Coleman stepped back. "Now eat your pizza, load up, and go out and do it again."

"Attention on deck!" Master Chief Baker ordered as Admiral Rodriquez walked out, a still-ashen Captain Coleman and his aide on his heels.

That left Bobby in charge, and all he could do was shrug, trying to ignore the weird little Silver Star hanging on his uniform. "Guess that means we can eat, guys," he said with a smile. "Dig in before it gets any colder."

No one had to be told twice—Pizza Hut beat navy food any day, particularly *free* Pizza Hut.

Exiting the Red Sea and Entering the Gulf of Aden, transiting toward the Indian Ocean

USS *Perch* (SSN 868) was so new she still smelled like welded metal, fresh paint, and navy shipyards.

The sleek black attack submarine had commissioned seven months earlier, and she was already in the war. A brand-new Improved *Cero*-class submarine, she was a lean, mean, fighting machine with a great crew and a legacy to build. They'd worked together to get the boat commissioned and out in almost record time, and now *Perch* was ready to get in the fight. Everyone estimated they'd see combat within a few days, even though their current mission was just to transit to Perth. The trip from Norfolk, Virginia, where they'd finished fitting out, was a long one—across the Atlantic, through the Mediterranean Sea, then a tense transit through the Suez Canal, made worse by the fact that no one knew for certain whose side Egypt was on today.

Lieutenant Commander Steven Harper had sort of hoped Egypt would start shooting, if only to break up the monotony of the long transit. He'd been chained to a desk when the war started, then left shore duty to go to the prospective executive officer's course, then to *Perch* to get her ready for sea. Now the boat was finally ready, and he knew the crew was itching for a *real* fight as badly as he was.

Alas, Egypt behaved nicely, and *Perch* was on her way after a long wait for a southbound convoy. Now she was through the Red Sea and ready to find someone, *anyone*, allied with the Freedom Union. Steve couldn't wait to tell those bastards what the real meaning of "FU" was in English.

The very thought made him smile. Steve Harper was the first XO of a great boat, and though he knew the war would probably make his XO tour shorter than normal, he was determined to make his mark.

A slender man, with dark skin, darker hair, and hazel eyes, Steve knew he was photogenic, capable, and ready to be one of the shining stars the navy needed. They had far too few people to look up to, and Steve was ready to assume that mantle. Or he had been, until he got the dreaded "we need to talk" from his captain.

At least Commander Singleton had the decency to have the discussion in private. He sighed, waving Steve into a chair.

"I can't believe I'm having this conversation with you, Steve." Jason Singleton slumped heavily in his desk chair.

The shorter man had been the CO for as long as Steve had been on board, and he wasn't the worst captain to have. He was smart enough to stay out of his hot-running XO's way, and that made them an efficient team. They'd bagged a *Scorpene* and a *Husky* coming down through the Red Sea, which put *Perch* on the Alliance scorecard.

Steve shrugged; he had an idea where this was going. "So don't have it."

"I thought I told you to knock it off." Singleton glared.

"I did."

"No, you went from sleeping with the navigator to sleeping with the engineer. That's not knocking if off!" His CO leaned forward in his chair, his eyes blazing as hot as his red hair. "And now Ensign Contreras said you felt her up in the passageway last night. She said she couldn't get away from you."

"C'mon, Captain, I'd never do something like that." Steve managed to look offended. "I've never had a hard time getting a woman to like me. I'm not going to go after one who *doesn't* want me."

"That's not much of a defense against fraternization," Singleton snarled. "And it's even less of one against sexual assault."

"What can I say? I know I'm guilty of frat, but there's a war on. I've never been with anyone who said no. You know me better than that."

"I'm not sure I do." Singleton's face closed off. "I'm going to have to write this up, Steve. The navy can ignore frat, at least with a war on. But sexual assault is another matter entirely."

"Really?" Steve couldn't believe his ears. "After everything I've done for—"

"Captain to the Conn!" The 1MC crackled, and the officer of the deck's voice filled the captain's stateroom: *"Captain to the Conn!"*

Argument forgotten, Steve and his captain sprinted to control, only to find *Perch* in Rochambeau's crosshairs.

Alex waited until they were topside to speak. He might have kept his mouth shut if not for the shit-eating grin on Uncle Marco's face. Or there was the fact that Rodriquez had just compared him to *Mush Morton*, no matter how obliquely. Mush Morton was one of the most legendary submariners in the world. If a Navy Cross wasn't enough to leave Alex sick to his stomach, that comparison was. He was no Mush Morton. Mush Morton had been brash, photogenic, and an academy graduate. Alex was the first person in his family's history to graduate college and hated public speaking. Never mind how he'd gone to Admiral's Mast a few years earlier!

"Thank you for what you did for my crew, sir," Alex said. "They needed it." He could tell Rodriquez what a piece of trash Peterson had been, but what was the point? Peterson wasn't coming back.

"But?" Rodriquez turned a glare on him. "You not happy with the Navy Cross? Think it should be something better?"

Alex felt the color drain out of his face. "No! Do I look crazy?"

"Son, if someone gave me the fucking Navy Cross, I'd spit torpedoes out of my ass out of sheer ever-loving joy."

"You and I are very different people, Admiral." Jesus, was the man insane? Alex had only met Uncle Marco twice before today, and the president's presence the second time must have muted him.

"No fucking shit," Rodriquez said. "So what are you complaining about?"

"I'm not sure that this patrol was worthy of a Navy Cross." Alex wasn't going to lie to the man; he was an introvert, not a timid coward hiding in the corner. And they'd already slapped *one* medal on him that they wouldn't take back. He knew he'd earned that one, but everything felt so *easy* this time.

"Why the hell not? You sank two frigates, two SSNs, and six SSPs—"

"The *Scorpenes* might as well have been Hondas." Alex rolled his eyes. "They couldn't exactly fight back."

Uncle Marco barked out a laugh. "They still count. And your trick of letting the civilian crews get off the heavy lift ships meant that their owners aren't even that pissed off at us. It was well done, so quit your bitching."

Alex bit his lip. "Sir, Navy Crosses aren't supposed to be this...easy."

"Easy?" That earned him a strange look. "Your patrol report made it sound a bit hairy, particularly given where the firing key started."

Alex shrugged uncomfortably. Shoving his hands in his pockets in front of an admiral was a bad idea, but the stupid things went there anyway, so he might as well own it. "It was a bit exciting, but anyone with half a brain could've outrun those torpedoes."

"A lot of your comrades seem to lack that half a brain, Captain," Rodriquez said, studying him. Surprisingly, his voice softened: "And your first real experience with combat might have been a bit misleading. Not everything is as batshit terrifying as Convoy 57."

That made Alex blink. "I hadn't thought of that."

"Yeah, you just keep doing what you're doing. Like it or not, the navy needs captains like you—and if my little Mush Morton comparison made you want to throw up, that's too damned bad. You're the one doing the work. I'm just talking about it."

"That doesn't make it much better, sir." Alex's stomach heaved, as if it wanted to prove the admiral right.

Marco snorted. "Well, you'd better figure out how to wipe that sick look off your face when people compliment you, Captain."

Alex swallowed. "That sounds ominous."

"To you, probably." A grin. "You're scheduled to do an interview with *60 Minutes* in three days."

"I am *what*?"

"I trust that's a 'what' of objection, not a need to repeat myself?" the admiral asked as Alex tried to swallow the sudden flock of butterflies in his throat.

"Admiral, I'm—I'm not really good with things like that. That's not— Fuck, I don't know what it's not, but you really don't want me talking about *current* sub operations, do you? That's all still classified."

"Of course it is," Marco replied. "This is about Convoy 57. *60 Minutes* and HBO are getting together to do a full-scale documentary on the thing, and you're their star interviewee. Make sure to wear your dress uniform."

Alex wanted to vomit.

"Oh, and update your ribbons to include that new medal, will you?"

What the hell was Uncle Marco doing on *Bluefish*?

Bud did a double take, but COMSUBPAC was still standing on the deck of his old submarine. Maybe Commander Peterson had finally done something nasty or cowardly enough to get himself fired, although Bud had always expected that Commodore Banks would cover for his best buddy if that happened. He'd probably been the only person in the world who was freaking delighted to move from a practically-brand-new *Cero* to the oldest submarine in the navy, but transferring to *Jimmy Carter* had saved more than his career. It had saved his sanity.

And somehow or another, it had turned him into a bona fide sonar technician, too. He'd done well on *Kansas'* underway, even if the XO really didn't like the fact that he could identify enemy ships and subs faster than the computer could. He wasn't sure what had crawled up Lieutenant Commander Song's fourth point of contact, but she really had a hard-on for following the book. Which was weird, considering—

"Hey, STS1!"

Turning, Bud faced Master Chief Casey, *Kansas'* chief of the boat. Casey had been a sonar tech—Bud supposed that technically, he still was—and hadn't exactly been subtle about keeping an eye on Bud. Not that he was surprised, what was with how his reputation circled the fleet and all. With his luck, Casey had talked to Master Chief Baker and knew *all* of the stupid shit Bud had gotten up to.

"What's up, COB?" Bud contemplated stuffing his hands in his pockets to look extra casual, but he was trying to be good on *Kansas*, so he didn't. It wasn't against the rules, but some COBs still hated it.

"Got a moment?" Chindu Casey was a big man, tall and broad enough to make Bud look small. He'd have made a hell of a linebacker. Bud had always preferred hockey.

"For you, Master Chief, any time." He grinned cheekily; being on the straight and narrow didn't mean he had to lose all of his attitude, did it?

"You know, that mouth of yours is going to get you in trouble if you run it around the old man," Casey said, gesturing so that

Bud headed aft with him, away from prying ears. "He's not so big on the attitude."

Bud scowled. "Yeah, and the XO's even more of the straight-n-narrow type. I got the memo."

"Not good enough, if what Miss Hewitt tells me is true."

"Man, are there no secrets on this boat?" Bud sighed. "I only asked a few questions that anyone with gray matter between their ears would ask." On the bright side, he guessed that his division officer was smart. She knew when to go to the COB for help, which was better than most junior officers.

"She was worried that you'd run your mouth and get yourself in trouble. She's a good kid," Casey replied. "I told her you should be bright enough to keep your trap shut, which had better be true."

"Master Chief, I'm just a lowly first class and all, but shouldn't somebody say *something* about the boat wandering out of our assigned sectors?" Bud wished he could make himself shut up, because he knew that it wasn't his business. But it kept eating at him, and Casey had brought it up.

"The captain's patrol report says we left our boxes chasing a contact. That's acceptable enough."

Bud rolled his eyes. "Yeah, except for the fact that I'm not sure we ever even dipped a freaking toe in those boxes."

"And in your word against the captain's, who do you think some flag officer is going to believe?" The master chief stopped, looking Bud dead in the eye. "You might have the Silver Star, but there ain't a sailor in Perth who hasn't heard about the stunts you've pulled."

"Yeah, my credibility is shit. I gotcha." Bud shook his head. "I ain't gonna say nothing, Master Chief. I'm not stupid, 'least not when I'm sober."

"You'd better stay sober, too." A glare. "You're a damned fine sonar tech, Wilson. You've got a better ear than I ever did, and I used to be pretty good at that shit. Don't ruin it."

"By getting drunk or picking fights I can't win?" Bud couldn't resist asking.

"Take your hands out of your fucking pockets," was all Casey said before walking away.

Sighing, Bud followed him. He had work to do before he could go on liberty. And he wasn't going to drink, either, no matter what the assholes thought.

Staying dry was pretty miserable when all his friends liked guzzling beer, though. Maybe he'd try an Alcoholics Anonymous meeting. Better than watching other sailors drink.

In hindsight, *Perch* hadn't stood a chance. Their young OOD—by chance, the newly qualified Ensign Contreras who Steve was accused of feeling up—stumbled right into FNS *Barracuda's* sights, and the fight was short. What saved them in the end was the emergency blow the COB ordered, which rocketed the damaged submarine to the surface, bleeding air and water.

Crash! Lights flickered and sparks flew; Steve clung to the navigation table for balance as Commander Singleton tripped and fell. There wasn't time to see what had happened to his CO, though; he was too busy dodging a battle lantern as it tore itself out of the overhead and sailed toward his head. The lantern bounced off Steve's shoulder; he yelped, and then it hit someone else with a nasty *squishing* sound Steve tried to ignore.

"We're taking on water fast!" the COB shouted. "The bow is staying up, but I can't keep her level. She's not gonna stay on the surface long!"

The lights flickered one more time and then died with a final *whuummm* that didn't sound good. A few more battle lanterns blinked on, filling control with eerie yellow light. Then the navigation table and the helm console went dark.

That was bad.

Steve leaned into the squawk box. "Maneuvering, Conn, do we have power?"

If they had any sort of propulsion, they could get the hell away from the French submarine. Rochambeau was still out there, and he'd only put one torpedo into them. Steve knew that *Requin*-class submarines like *Barracuda* had six tubes, and Rochambeau was not known for rationing his torpedoes.

No one in the maneuvering room answered. The deck was starting to slope under his feet, pitching *Perch's* nose up and stern down. Steve hit the button a little harder than necessary, snapping:

"Maneuvering, Conn! Is anyone there?"

Silence.

"XO, we've got to start getting people off," the COB interjected. "I think we've got major flooding back aft, and—"

Crash!

Part of the left-side weapons console twisted away from its sisters, pivoting in its brackets as *Perch* started rolling right. Binders rained down from overhead shelves, and then two pipes burst together, spraying water and firefighting foam.

"*Shit!* Pass the word to abandon ship, COB!" Steve matched actions to words as the COB grabbed the 1MC. He wasn't sure where the officer of the deck was, and he didn't want to trust an ensign with this, anyway. He hit the switch on the squawk box. "All stations, Conn, abandon ship! I say again, abandon ship!"

Creak...

Perch rolled back to port, settling further down by the stern. Steve leaned forward to remain upright. He could feel the boat slipping backward like an escalator gone wrong. Whatever had happened, the torpedo hit them back aft. He felt a moment's regret for Lieutenant Parker, the engineer. Annie had been a nice girl, and he'd enjoyed their time together. She was probably dead now.

"Leave that!" he barked at a sailor trying to secure the water spraying all over the radar console. "Get out of here!"

Boom!

The deck bucked under Steve's feet, almost throwing him to the deck.

"What the hell was that?" someone asked. He couldn't tell who in the dark; everyone looked the same in the sickly yellow battle lantern light.

"Back aft. Sounded like a crankcase explosion," another voice answered.

"Let's go!" the COB shouted, shooing sailors out.

Someone scrambled up the ladder toward the sail, wrenching hatches open as they went. At least the sail was still out of the water, even with *Perch* rolling to starboard. Two petty officers ran aft out of control, probably aiming for the hatch that led to the top deck. It was a shorter climb than going out the sail, but Steve refused to chance it. That hatch might be underwater, and then escaping would be twice as hard. Sure, they'd trained for it, but one person getting out at a time would be—

"Sir, what about the captain?" the COB asked he shoved sailors up the ladder to the sail. Steve waited his turn. He'd forgotten all about Commander Singleton.

Steve's feet took him back to the captain before conscious thought intervened, and he knelt next to Singleton. Singleton bled from the head, definitely unconscious. Was he breathing? It was so hard to tell in the dark. Slowly, Steve reached out a hand to feel Singleton's neck for a pulse.

"XO?"

Thump thump. Thump—thump. The beat was slow and weak, but there. He was still alive, but for how long? Steve stared at Singleton's unconscious face for a long moment. They couldn't get him up the ladder in time. Strapping Singleton to a stretcher would need precious minutes they didn't have. How many lives was Steve willing to risk saving one?

He'd tell me to go. Was that true or was it just wishful thinking?

"XO!" the COB shouted.

Steve rose, heading for the ladder. The COB was the only one left. "He's dead! Let's get out of here!"

Steve and the COB barely made it out before *Perch* went under, taking Jason Singleton and his reports straight to the bottom. Steve and the master chief swam to a life raft together, then set to work organizing what remained of *Perch*'s crew.

The tweet hit before *Perch's* crew was picked up.

Captain Jules Rochambeau
@JulesRochambeau
@USNavy, your newer Ceros are as easy to sink as the old ones. What is so improved about them? That makes 3 I have sunk.
#Barracuda #UUSPerch #thatmakesfourthis-month

Chapter 13

Man of the Hour

22 January 2040, Perth, Australia, Submarine Squadron 29 Headquarters

Lieutenant Commander Maggie Bennett had learned the hard way not to make snap judgments about people while on *Jimmy Carter*, but adhering to that mantra was a challenge. More so today than usual.

She'd been on the ground in Perth for about sixteen hours, long enough to check in at the bachelor officers' quarters, get a room, take a nap, and stuff food in her face. Then a friendly call from the chief of staff told Maggie both her check-in time and that the commodore insisted on people reporting in their dress uniform, something even that COMSUBPAC didn't care about during a stinking war. So Maggie frantically ironed what she could of her service dress whites, arrived at the appointed time, and then was made to wait almost an hour.

She loved bosses like this. They were always great about letting you know your place.

"Frankly, I don't know why anyone would send an inexperienced intelligence officer to the front." Commodore Banks pinched his nose and stared at an expensive painting of a sailboat on his office wall. "Particularly when you've so recently transferred to the community. You said this was your *first* tour as a staff intelligence officer?"

Maggie bit her tongue. "Yes, sir. But it isn't my first time working in the submarine community."

"Obviously. I see you're wearing dolphins." Banks gestured at the submarine warfare pin on her dress whites. "What is your background, again?"

She didn't miss the way he eyed the dark curls trying to escape her tidy bun, either. Banks one of those obsessive neatniks in love with uniform standards, and while Maggie knew she cut a nice image with her uniform since she did gymnastics for fun, at least when her wrist wasn't in pieces, the jerks always zeroed in on her hair. She squared her shoulders and folded her hands, giving off her best professional image. Maggie was used to being near the top; she had no problem presenting herself well.

"My division officer tour was on *Parche*, where I served as collateral duty assistant intel officer," Maggie replied. "Then I was navigator on *Jimmy Carter*. After she was decommissioned, I applied for a lat transfer, and here I am."

Now wasn't the time to mention that she'd been assigned to Admiral Rodriquez's staff before he'd decided she'd be more useful out here. He hadn't made serving Banks sound like a picnic, so Maggie *thought* she knew what she was getting into. Still, she hadn't expected the sudden sneer on Banks' face, or the way his way his words dripped with derision.

"You served under Captain Coleman."

Maggie bit the inside of her cheek. "I did."

"Tell me about him."

Maggie hesitated. Any idiot could tell her new boss didn't like the old one, which meant she should proceed carefully. Yet the idea of lying just to gain Banks' favor stuck in her craw like ten-day-old fish. She met the commodore's eyes. "He was the best captain I've ever had, sir. We wouldn't have made it through Convoy 57 without him."

"I see." Banks' lips curled. "One might argue that a single attack sub had no business attempting to stay in that fight. Particularly not alone."

"Respectfully, sir, our duty was to protect the convoy." Maggie folded her hands.

"Not to the point of insanity. Engaging at those odds was reckless, Commander, and I do *not* like reckless captains." Banks leaned back in his large leather chair. "And I don't like intelligence failures, either. I won't have them, not in my squadron."

"I'm not especially fond of them, either, sir. I lost good friends in that battle," she replied, Marty Sterling's face flashing before her eyes. But Maggie pushed the thought aside. Marty had made a choice to go to war, just like she had. Just like they all did.

She could best honor him by continuing the fight and keeping others from being left on the short end of the stick.

"I said that I won't tolerate intelligence failures when you're working for me, Miss Bennett. Is that clear?"

Being called "Miss Bennett" like she was some Southern Belle made her want to slap him. "Sir, all I can promise is to do my best. As you've pointed out, I'm a relatively junior intelligence officer, and I won't be performing every analysis we need. However, I will do my damnedest to get you the information you need before you need it."

Banks' eyes narrowed. "Convoy 57 was an absolute intelligence failure. No one notified the navy that the Fogborne Research Team would be among the evacuees *or* that the Indians would target them."

"No, sir, they didn't." Maggie hated admitting that. It was a damned stupid reason for Marty and the others—including nearly everyone on *Ticonderoga*, *Bull Run*, *Jason Dunham*, and *Billings*—to have died. Worse yet, she should've guessed the Fogborne Team was with the refugees, because *Jimmy Carter* had been the submarine that rescued that same team from the South China Sea and *brought* them out to Diego Garcia.

But she'd been a navigator and not an intelligence officer, so Maggie had been focused on her job, not someone else's. And no one ever imagined that India would send a goddamned armada after the Fogborne Team, anyway.

"Well, then. I suppose you'll prove your usefulness. Or not." Another sneer; Maggie stepped on her temper.

"I'm glad to be aboard, sir," she said with the best smile she could muster.

Banks glared. "Dismissed."

Maggie rose and let herself out of the commodore's office. Only once she exited into the rest of the staff's office area—which was less plush than Banks' art-lined office with its big oak desk and comfortable leather chair—did she look down at her hands. They weren't shaking. Six months ago, maybe less, they would've been.

Sighing, Maggie squared her shoulders. Meeting her newest boss could've gone better, but she wasn't here to make Banks happy, was she? With a war on, priorities changed. She needed to get the right intelligence to the right places, and sometimes that might mean torquing her touchy boss off. That might be easy, given how determined to hate her Banks appeared. Maggie could live with that. The nice thing about the war was that he'd have to try hard to kill her career. If Maggie did her job well, she'd probably be safe.

She hoped.

22 January 2040

The television producers put him in goddamned *makeup.* The layers caked on his face felt like a crackling sort of armor, but it provided no comfort. The lights were bright and the chair looked fancier than it felt, leaving Alex feeling like a statue who'd been ordered there in his best dress uniform.

Listening to the interviewer summarize a battle that she'd never understand made it hard not to cringe. He tried to tune it out; Alex had enough nightmares about protecting Convoy 57, and he didn't need to give them more fuel. At least the fucking thing wasn't live, even if it was scheduled to broadcast in two days. They'd probably cut out any extraneous grimaces, wouldn't they?

And at least Jenny Carson, the stunningly beautiful reporter-turned-narrator for this documentary, spent her time beaming at the camera instead of him.

"...By now, the world knows the story of Convoy 57," Carson said. "Five surface ships and one submarine were tasked with defending thirty-two ships of evacuees from Samar Station. After the Indians attacked without warning, four of the five surface warships were sunk, one civilian ship was destroyed, and HMAS *Paramatta*, the last warship, was severely damaged. Only USS *Jimmy Carter* remained to take the fight to the enemy, one submarine against nine enemy surface ships and six submarines."

Alex felt a camera focus in on him and tried to look calm. That's what the public expected of navy captains, right? God help him, he'd never expected his face to be on *anything* for the navy. Who in their right mind wanted *Alex Coleman* as their poster child?

Even worse, he had an appointment with navy photographers after this for some sort of "glamor shots" that he was pretty sure would be turned into actual goddamned posters. Fuck his life.

Carson continued, oblivious to Alex's internal conflict:

"No one expected *Jimmy Carter* to survive. With those odds, who could? And for three weeks after the battle, as reports of heroism and sacrifice rolled in, we all thought the submarine and her crew were consigned to the bottom of the Indian Ocean, never to rise again. Yet here we sit today with Captain Alex Coleman, the former commanding officer of USS *Jimmy Carter*. He received the Medal of Honor for his actions that day and now commands a new submarine, USS *Bluefish*."

Alex struggled not to cringe as she turned to him. He hated public speaking, and the only good thing he could say about this interview was that it wasn't in front of a crowd. Still, the bright lights from the cameras made him queasy, and butterflies danced a jig in his stomach. Combat was easier than this. But he couldn't shoot a reporter to make her go away.

Unfortunately.

"Captain, let's go back to the beginning of the battle. The navy generously provided us with the video logs from *Jimmy Carter*, so tell me what you were thinking at this point."

She gestured toward a screen. Alex followed her gaze, surprised the navy had declassified the attack center video logs from *Jimmy Carter*—but then again, why wouldn't they? There weren't any *Seawolf*-class submarines left with secrets to protect.

The video flickered on, and there was *Jimmy Carter*. The scene was from her attack center, which looked impossibly cramped on screen. Alex—notably lacking the reading glasses he needed these days—stood center stage, holding a radio handset.

"All ships in Convoy 57, this is Killer Rabbit Actual," his younger self said. "Am coming around to intercept the Indians. Recommend new convoy course one-three-five at max speed available. Out."

"Battle Stations set, Captain," Maggie reported. She'd had the deck that day, and damn had he needed her.

"Very well. Make your depth four hundred feet, smartly. Keep the wire up and increase speed to flank once our scope is under."

Maggie nodded. "Make my depth four hundred feet smartly, aye—"

"Captain, I have ignition sounds—!" STS1 Wilson's voice came out of sonar as a shout.

"Ignition—?" George Kirkland echoed the words uselessly, but Alex spun to the periscope again, yanking the radio mike up.

"Vampire, vampire, vampire! *All ships stand by for missile barrage!"*

The screen shifted to the periscope video from *Jimmy Carter*, and Alex looked away. He didn't need to watch. He remembered watching the Indian's surface-to-surface missiles crash down. *Jason Dunham, Ticonderoga, Bull Run,* and

Billings were destroyed in less than a minute, and the personnel carrier, SS *Morning Star*, followed when the Indians got her by mistake. *Paramatta* suffered damage, too, too much to continue the fight, so Alex had taken his submarine in alone against overwhelming odds.

Jenny cleared her throat, clearly waiting. What had she asked? Oh, right. She wanted to know what he'd been thinking. Alex almost laughed aloud. Yeah, he'd have to watch himself. HBO didn't mind profanity, but the navy wouldn't like it if he said what *actually* had been on his mind. Alex let out a slow breath, considering his words.

"My priority was to protect the convoy. To do that, I had to get in torpedo range of the enemy." Alex shrugged. "I'm afraid I wasn't thinking anything inspirational or particularly clever, just that I had a job to do."

"Much has been said about your decision to leave the Australian frigate, *Paramatta*, behind. Can you explain why you did that?" Jenny asked.

At least this was familiar territory; Alex nodded. "*Paramatta* had eaten a few missiles, but she remained capable of air defense for the convoy. Submarines can't shoot down incoming missiles. We're not defensive weapons; what we do is go out and kill the enemy. *Paramatta* could defend the convoy, and at the end of the day, that was still the most important part of our job."

"So you chose to engage the enemy alone, even though you were vastly outnumbered."

"It was either that or run away, and running wouldn't have saved anyone." *Especially us*, he didn't add. Alex was glad they were going to edit this thing. At least then if he said something stupid, some producer would cut it.

The interview went on for several more hours, covering Convoy 57 in nauseating detail. Jenny was better informed than Alex expected; he'd never really talked to a reporter at length, and most of the ones who'd tried to interview him before were woefully uneducated in submarine warfare. But Jenny was smart and sharp as hell. Several of her questions left him distinctly uncomfortable, but at least she didn't delve into the mess that had happened with his XO. She made a big deal out of how he'd smashed his submarine into the ocean floor twice, picking her up again to keep in the fight. Alex had tried not to fidget at that. It had seemed necessary at the time, but listening to someone else talk about it made the idea sound ludicrous.

Finally, she asked him how he felt about winning the Medal of Honor.

"I'd give it back if I could." His big mouth struck again. At least he managed not to tell her that you didn't *win* a prize for surviving the most terrifying day of your life.

"Really? Why?"

Alex took another deep breath. "I did my job. I got lucky, more than once, but a lot of people still died that day. Some of *my* sailors died in that battle, following my orders. You don't look back on a fight like that and think about 'winning' anything."

Jenny stared. "Surely you're not saying that you don't deserve that? Both the U.S. and Australian navies are calling you the most talented submarine commander of this century."

"I'm not sure I'd go that far." Alex chuckled uneasily. "Ursula North and Jules Rochambeau both have better overall records than I do. I...I wouldn't say that I didn't earn the, um, thing, but it wasn't just me. A submarine's crew fights as a team. One person can make a difference, but it's not a one-man show."

"Well, we'll certainly have to keep an eye on you and your team on *Bluefish*." Jenny beamed. "I'm certain this isn't the last we'll hear about you, Captain."

She ended the interview there, and Alex escaped as quickly as he could.

Naval Base Pearl Harbor, Hawaii

The late afternoon storm raging outside did nothing to dull his mood; Marco Rodriquez liked being as sharp as lightning and twice as fast. Lightning zig-zagging across the black sky did ruin the breathtaking view of the waterfront from his corner office, but perks of his rank mattered little with a war on. Despite what the sub force called him, he wasn't "Uncle" Charlie Lockwood, the legendary holder of his office from the Second World War. Uncle Charlie had much more freedom than Marco; today, technology made it easier for his boss to crawl in his pants and play him like a puppet.

Thank Christ that Freddie Hamilton really wasn't interested in what was inside Marco's pants. Never had been, which was probably why they had been best friends for so long, even back in the day when stuck-up twats tried to drive Freddie right out of submarines. She was one of that first generation of homegrown submarine officers who happened to have their plumbing on the inside instead of the outside, and while Marco didn't give two shits about that, a lot of his fellow officers had, back in the day.

It was nice knowing that those numb nuts were pretty much all washed up on the beach. They'd mocked her for her sex and Marco for his heavy Hispanic accent, but now those assholes worked for skeevy recruiting firms or did battle in corporate America while he and Freddie ran the war effort.

"You see the preliminary footage?" Marco asked, carving designs into his desk calendar with a pushpin and ignoring Freddie's face on the video call.

"It looked acceptable." How little Freddie wanted to admit that came through loud and clear with her scowl. "At least he didn't swear as much as you do."

Marco snorted. "Kid did pretty good for someone who claims he doesn't like that shit."

"Stop preening, will you?" she snapped. "We have bigger concerns."

"Like what?" Why did those words generate a sinking feeling in his stomach? Marco had been in this business for too long.

"Senator Angler wants to go for a ride."

"*What?*" Marco dropped his pushpin. "You've got to be fucking shitting me."

"Do I sound like I'm shitting you, Marco? This is the crap I deal with every day." Freddie groaned. "He wants to go out on a war patrol."

"Fuck no. We're not a taxi service, and it's definitely not time for show-and-tell."

"He's the head of—"

"I don't care if he's God, Freddie. He'd be a distraction." Marco glared at his stapler, imaging Senator Benjamin Winthrop Angler III. He been in the service at one point—either army or marines—and claimed to be the navy's friend. Marco didn't like him.

"God doesn't control the purse strings. Angler can get us funding. Aircraft carriers are sexy *and* expensive, Marco. We need the money to go into the *Cero*-follow on class you're so keen on, instead of building another damned flattop."

"It's a *submarine* war." How the fuck could Congress be stupid enough to forget who did the lions' share of bleeding and dying?

"He's a politician. Your point?" Freddie asked.

Marco scowled. "So send him on one of your boats."

"He wants to go where the action is."

"Tell him the Russians are getting frisky up by Alaska. That's not even a lie." Marco bit back a groan. He knew where this was going, knew he was going to get shafted with this political hand grenade.

"So says the admiral who bleats about how he's at the pointy end of the spear? Give me a— Shit, I've got to go. Meeting with the CNO just moved up." Freddie rolled her eyes, not speaking ill of their aviator-flavored boss who *always* told the secretary of the navy that they needed another damned aircraft carrier. "Think on it, okay?"

"No." Admirals did not pout.

Freddie Hamilton hung up, leaving him thinking about which boat he'd saddle with this monument to assclownery.

The Gulf of Aden, near the Horn of Africa

They were in the water for three days before anyone found them. Luckily for *Perch's* crew, the sub tender who finally responded to their short-ranged radio calls was American, and within an hour of establishing communications, Lieutenant Commander Steve Harper stood on the deck of USS *Nereus*. Much to his surprise, the tender's captain met him as he climbed over the rail.

"Thanks for picking us up, sir." Steve tried not to yawn; they'd drifted for three days, and two of *Perch's* life rafts had been leaky. Keeping everyone dry was impossible, but at least he'd been able to keep sixty-seven survivors alive. Almost no one got out of engineering, which meant Annie Parker was constantly on his mind. He kept seeing her face, her cute freckles and her red hair, every time he tried to sleep. Still, Steve told himself that she'd taken her chances, made her choices. He supposed he couldn't begrudge her that.

Besides, there were always other fish in the sea, even if he currently felt waterlogged. He'd never thought about the downside of going back to naming submarines after fish. It was a nice old tradition but felt a bit too on-point at the moment.

"Of course." *Nereus'* captain offered him a hand, which Steve took. A second look at the guy made Steve do a double-take; this was John *Dalton*, the guy who'd won the Navy Cross at the Third Battle of the SOM. He was one of the best in the business. "Your people tell me you got off *Perch*?"

"Yeah." Steve swallowed hard. He'd also spent the last three days thinking about that battle and about his choice to leave Commander Singleton behind. Steve wasn't sure they would have been able to get Singleton up the ladder in time, anyway, not with him unconscious and the boat going down. At least this way no one else had to feel guilty.

"Your buoy didn't go off, did it?" Dalton asked. "I didn't see a SUBMISS/SUBSUNK message for *Perch.*"

Steve blinked. "You didn't?"

"Yeah." Dalton's grimace was sympathetic. "You the senior survivor?"

"XO." Steve let out a breath. "The captain—Commander Singleton—didn't make it. He hit his head when the torpedo hit us."

"Shit. I'm sorry to hear that." Dalton looked over the crowd of *Perch* sailors as the *Nereus'* crew herded them below for dry clothes and warm food. "Looks like about half of you got off. Not bad for a torpedo hit."

"Not bad for fucking Rochambeau, you mean," Steve snarled. "We got a good read on *Barracuda* before she killed us."

"No kidding? People don't usually get off when he slams a torp or two into you." Dalton gestured him forward. "Come on. Let's get you in something dry, and then we'll call it in."

Steve nodded numbly. He didn't look forward to telling his superiors about *Perch's* loss, but so long as he kept to the same story, he'd be fine. The SUBMISS/SUBSUNK buoy not deploying was a surprise, but not an unpleasant one. Still, even if someone did recover *Perch's* video/voice data recorder, no one would be able to tell that Singleton hadn't been dead when Steve checked his pulse. He'd left his CO behind...but he'd done the right thing. He was certain of it.

Bobby was reviewing charts in the wardroom when the captain returned. A flicker of relief ran through him when he heard the words, *"Bluefish, arriving,"* over the 1MC, accompanied by the correct number of bells. He'd already incorrectly bonged Captain Coleman on board once, and Bobby felt like he'd never live that down. Max even mentioned he'd heard the captain telling his wife that story, which made Bobby feel about a thousand times worse.

But why was the captain in dress uniform again? Bobby'd caught a glimpse of him through the open wardroom door, and it made him do a double-take. Maybe he'd been wrong?

Nope. Captain Coleman stuck his head in the door, his jacket already unbuttoned and his cover tucked under his arm. "Anything come up while I was gone?"

"Uh, no, sir. Rose has been running torpedo-loading drills all morning. Other than that, I finally got ahold of a Lieutenant Commander Kirkland over on the supply side, and he's promised us our stores onload tomorrow."

"Lieutenant Commander Kirkland?" The captain stopped cold. "As in, *George* Kirkland?"

"I think so?" Bobby hadn't made a note of the man's first name when he'd talked to him on the phone. "Why?"

"If it's the same guy, he was my XO on *Jimmy Carter*."

"Really? How'd he end up moving over to the supply community?" Bobby asked. He couldn't imagine any situation where the XO from Convoy 57 couldn't write their own ticket to success. Had Kirkland *wanted* to be a suppo? Unlikely.

"Let's just say that he fell apart when it counted. Freaked out, tried to surface the boat in the middle of the battle." Alex grimaced. "I ended up sending him to his stateroom to wait it out."

Bobby's jaw dropped open. "No shit?"

"No shit." Alex shook his head. "It was a bad day all around. Still, he was an administrative monster, so if he says we're getting an onload tomorrow, we'll be getting it."

"That's good to know." Bobby hesitated and then gestured at his captain's dress uniform. "Was there, uh, some ceremony I didn't know about?"

Alex snorted. "No, I got to go be a TV star."

"What?"

"An interview for some documentary about Convoy 57." Alex rolled his eyes. "Uncle Marco made me go."

"Oh. Um, I guess that sucked?" Bobby's first instinct was to laugh, but he suspected that wouldn't be welcome.

"In a word, yes." A sigh. "Is there anything I need to care about before I get out of this monkey suit?"

This time Bobby couldn't stop his grin. "I've always thought of it more as a milkman's suit, but unless you want to go pose for pictures or something, I think we've got it handled, sir."

"Spare me. Please." Alex disappeared down the passageway, leaving Bobby alone.

A moment later, the doubts hit. Who the hell was he to start joking around with the captain like that? Yeah, Captain Coleman hadn't minded, or at least hadn't seemed to, but Bobby knew how quickly things could change. Peterson seemed normal sometimes—okay, no, he hadn't. Not unless pedantic and nitpicky was normal. Bobby's CO on his first sub hadn't been, but Bobby hadn't dared joke like this around her.

There was a war on, and he liked his CO. The world was upside down.

24 January 2040, French Submarine Base, Île Amsterdam

Like it or not, the world's oceans were sailed in English, which meant Jules Rochambeau spoke the language well. Better than many native speakers, in fact; he took pride in that, as he did in most things he did well. It was a useful skill, particularly when listening in on communications that other nations did not want Frenchmen to understand.

Today, *Barracuda* was snuggled up next to a brand-new pier in Île Amsterdam, one of the French Southern and Antarctic Lands in the southern Indian Ocean. Until the war started, Île Amsterdam had sported one tiny settlement of about thirty researchers; now the island was home to France's newest and most secret submarine base. The climate was miserable—the island *was* in the Antarctic—but the base was far closer to Australia than any other option. Jules was a child of warm Mediterranean beaches and mild summers, and he hated the cold. But if it gave him the opportunity to kill his country's enemies, he would endure whatever hardship he had to, bundling up in three layers and not bothering to hide his misery.

Luckily, the island was outfitted with the latest in communications technology, so his submarine could tie in without anyone suspecting her presence. He hadn't planned to pull into port, but a shipment of F27 "Rafale" torpedoes were enticement enough. The Rafales were derivatives of the Russian Shkval, a high-speed, super-cavitating torpedo. The French version was longer ranged and had a better seeker than the barely-aimable underwater missile the Russians loved, although they sacrificed speed to gain accuracy. Rumors said that the Shkval could top three hundred knots. Rochambeau had only seen it manage around two hundred, but that was still faster than his new Rafales. But he would not be disappointed. Each of the twenty Rafales loading onto his submarine could reach 139 knots, making them the second-fastest torpedo in the water.

They were beautiful, too. Each Rafale was six meters of polished black metal, sleek and deadly. The Rafales *did* have a slight downgrade from the old F21 torpedo, however; the new motor and fuel required more space, so the warhead had to shrink to fit the torpedo in the same tubes. That meant a medium-weight PBX B2211A polymer-bonded explosive warhead instead of the old heavyweight, but Jules didn't mind. Submarines still didn't stand a chance against that explosive punch. An aircraft carrier might require two or three torpedoes, but they'd still do the job, and get there so much faster. Perhaps an old battleship might have survived, Jules mused, but not a modern warship.

Voices from his computer made him turn his head. The American documentary *Convoy 57: Against All Odds* was streaming, and now Alex Coleman was on his screen. It was nice to put a living and breathing face to the name, particularly one who looked so uncomfortable on camera. Jules enjoyed the so-called expert breakdown of the battle provided by some historian or another, even if he'd seen a few holes in their analysis that made him curious.

But he was much more intrigued by this American captain who'd been no one and nothing prior to that battle.

"What made you go to periscope depth in the middle of the enemy formation?" the interviewer asked. Normally, Jules would pause to admire to her looks—which were certainly worth the attention—but he was too interested in his enemy.

Coleman smiled wryly. "I was out of torpedoes and needed a quick way to get the Indians' attention. I could have gone active, but it's a lot harder to disappear when you do that. A periscope is just a visual observation, and the mark one, mod zero eyeball is prone to error."

The interviewer cocked her head. "Wasn't that a significant risk?"

"Yeah." Coleman chuckled. "But I had to do something to make them concentrate on me instead of the convoy, so I didn't have a lot of choices. Besides, the best way to put the fear of God into a surface officer is to have a submarine appear in the middle of his or her formation and then disappear again."

"Oh, I shall have to remember that one," Jules whispered to himself, grinning. He could imagine how much that would terrify some poor destroyer driver—or better yet, the captain of an aircraft carrier.

He'd always enjoyed playing with his prey. Jules watched the rest of the interview, taking a few notes. How could anyone not enjoy being the man of the hour? He relished every bit of attention the media gave him, because Jules knew their regard was fleeting. To keep it, he had to remain on top of the game.

Speaking of which, it was time to redirect that spotlight, so he pulled up Twitter on his computer.

Captain Jules Rochambeau
@JulesRochambeau

@USNavy Tell your Captain Coleman that I will sink him when I am done with Lady North. He should get his affairs in order.

#Barracuda #HMSGallant #USSBluefish #BattleoftheCentury

Of course, there was another interview. Alex couldn't be lucky enough to get away with just *one*; he'd been stupid to think that he could. Intellectually, he knew *why* Uncle Marco kept signing him up for the damned things. The navy needed all the good press it could get, particularly after news of *Perch's* fate broke via Rochambeau's tweet. Alex could only imagine how the families felt. No official notification, no navy chaplain, no kind friend with the news: just a tweet by a jerk Frenchman who wanted notoriety. It made his blood boil, made him wish he'd taken a snapshot all those months ago when *Jimmy Carter* stumbled right between Ursula North and Jules Rochambeau. Could he have ended this then? He hadn't known what enemy he faced that day, but the missed opportunity ate at him.

Alex hadn't missed the tweet directed his way, either. He didn't have a Twitter account, but both of his daughters *did*, and talking Bobbie out of trolling the French captain was almost impossible. Bobbie—Roberta, for her grandmother—Coleman was his older daughter, and she was just as much of a hothead as her father, which meant her first instinct was to shoot and ask questions later. Alex was a bit more tempered by experience. Bobbie was still full of fire.

Fortunately, the fact that the Naval Academy would *not* approve of Bobbie making a fool of herself on Twitter brought his little girl around better than Alex ever could.

"I'm not sure how long she'll hold her tongue—or keyboard, I guess—if he keeps up with this crap, though," Alex admitted to his wife.

"Probably about five minutes." Nancy sighed, reaching out to brush invisible lint off Alex's shoulder boards. He was in dress whites again, getting ready for the second interview—and even worse, this one was live.

Alex wanted to hide under the nearest rock. Or, better yet, get his submarine underway until this media fascination died down.

"She's your daughter, too. You've always been the go-getter," he whined.

"And look at you, Mister Big Bad Medal of Honor winner," she retorted. "You even managed to polish your shoes this time."

Alex rolled his eyes, trying not to glance down at the pale blue ribbon on the upper right of his ribbon rack. Just *looking* at it made him feel strange, like he was some sort of phony. "I did last time, too, you know. But the camera isn't interested in my shoes."

"No, it's probably going to be fascinated by this." Nancy tapped the ribbon.

"Gee, Nance, I needed that reminder. Thanks."

"I can always go back to my Q room if you want." Her smile said that she wouldn't, however, and Alex was grateful for that. Hell, he was damned glad she'd come with him. Or maybe he wasn't. With Nancy here, he couldn't run away.

He shook his head, trying not to straighten parts of his uniform that didn't need straightening. "No, that's okay."

"I'm sure it is." She grinned. "You know, I ran into your Commander Peterson at the Q again yesterday. His wife seemed nice, though he wanted to be buddy-buddy with me."

Alex glared. "He's not 'mine.'"

"He's a submariner, dear. That makes him yours, even if your crew is terrified of him."

Alex stuck out his tongue; Nancy laughed.

"Two minutes!" A crew member stuck her head into the dressing room to make the announcement, and Alex grimaced.

"You sure you have to go back to the boat tonight?" Nancy asked. "It's already past eight..."

"Yeah, I'm sure." Alex sighed. "I can't expect my crew to sleep on the boat if I flout that."

"I know. I just miss having you around."

"Me, too, babe."

Juggling their marriage and war was hard enough. They'd both decided to stay on active duty, and neither regretted it, but being stationed in the same port and unable to spend the night together still burned. Particularly since Nancy was days away from assuming her *next* job and heading out to the cruiser, which meant they'd end up juggling underway schedules once more. Normally, Alex and his crew would have been given a week or two off after a successful war patrol, but Commodore Banks was stingy with relief crews. *Bluefish* was still on hot standby, and that meant the crew needed to sleep on board. Including the captain.

Nancy squeezed his hand, and then it was time to jump into another interview and pretend that he didn't want to run away instead of looking into a camera. Who the hell had decided it was a good idea to put him on *Good Morning America*? Alex still wanted to vomit.

Why the hell were they trying to turn him into some sort of national hero?

In total tonnage sunk, USS *Razorback still* led the American pack. Of all Alliance subs, only HMS *Gallant* could top their number or tonnage of ships sunk, and *Razorback's* crew was justifiably proud of that. Master Chief Machinist's Mate Bryan Morton—COB to the crew—had been on board for two months now, and he was quite pleased to see the crew living up to that reputation. Commander Patricia Abercrombie had been the boat's XO under Captain John Dalton, and so far, she was following right in his footsteps.

Which was why he found this conversation so unsettling.

"What do you think we can do to up our readiness, Master Chief?" Abercrombie asked the question evenly enough, but it wasn't the words that worried Bryan. It was the way she kept wiping her hands on the legs of her coveralls, and the slightly wide green eyes. Abercrombie had proven herself in combat time and again. Why was she worried?

"Not much left to do, ma'am. We've drilled and drilled, and the boys n' girls have done a bang-up job every time we've asked them to." Bryan shrugged. "Not sure what else you're looking for."

Abercrombie chuckled uneasily. "I'm not, either, I guess." She swallowed noisily. "The stakes just keep getting higher, and Commodore McNally called last night."

"That why you're so nervous?" he asked.

"Yeah." She let out a breath. "The commodore said that we're the best bet for equaling Ursula North...and that if she can't get Rochambeau, we're going to get sent after him."

"Shit."

Bryan took a deep breath; that was getting into some deep fucking waters. Rochambeau had become a legend in the submarine community. Even Ursula North didn't quite reach his level, though from what Bryan had seen, she was annoyed by that herself. Rochambeau topped the charts by a *wide* margin, and everyone knew it because he tweeted about every damned kill. There had been speculation that he was taking credit for other Freedom Union subs' kills, but Bryan doubted that. There were some people that were just that good.

He'd worked for one of them, and Commander Abercrombie had the potential to be another. Assuming she didn't let her nerves get the better of her.

Shit, if he was in the command seat and got told he was going after that French fucker, he'd be nervous, too. Particularly since the French *Requin* class of submarines were quieter and better armed than even the Improved *Ceros* like *Razorback.* The *Requins* had more tubes, carried more torpedoes, and could dive deeper. *Razorback* was faster by about ten knots, but that only mattered if you were sprinting.

"See why I'm a bit nervous?" Abercrombie's laugh sounded more natural this time. "The commodore said that we'll go after him next patrol if North doesn't get him first."

Bryan made himself smile. If the chief of the boat couldn't calm the captain down, who could? His job was to pretend everything was all right, though looking into Abercrombie's worried blue eyes made that hard. "Well, then everything's normal for this one, right, ma'am?"

"As normal as war gets, anyway." Abercrombie shrugged and then rose. "All right, enough fretting from me. Let's get back to work and go find that Indian battle group that intelligence says should be lurking around Mauritius."

"Right behind you, Captain."

Bryan was glad that Abercrombie hadn't lost her nerve—or her ambition. A good sub CO had to be at least one part crazy, otherwise they'd never take the risks necessary to succeed in wartime. Being conservative and careful worked in peacetime, but a wartime captain had to know when to do something unexpected. Abercrombie was pretty damned good at it, and they'd bagged a pair of *Akulas* on their last patrol. And, well, if she needed shoring up every now and then, that's what master chiefs were for.

But going after Rochambeau?

Damn.

Chapter 14

Unexpected Allies

30 January 2040, Naval Base Pearl Harbor, Hawaii

Every now and then, Marco actually had to talk to his squadron commanders. He was enough of a jerk to admit he enjoyed end-running around them, but professionalism demanded he try to keep that to a minimum. Which was why he sat behind his desk, disassembling a wind-up elephant that Freddie gave him for his last birthday, waiting while his aide talked to Commodore Banks' aide. Why the rigmarole? He was too damned important to call his subordinates and his subordinate was too damned important to answer his own phone. Traditions multiplied during peacetime like a rabbit on crack, and almost two years into a mother-loving navy war, they still couldn't shake them.

Fed up, Marco growled: "Oh, just give me the damned phone."

Lieutenant Katie Greco blanched but handed the phone over without an argument. She was his third aide so far—Marco went through them like socks—but by far the sturdiest. She didn't even flinch when he yelled at people. Marco liked her.

"Her name is Lieutenant Barrera," Katie said, and Marco nodded thanks.

The girl had nerve and brains both. Maybe he wouldn't break this one. He turned his attention to the phone. "Lieutenant Barrera, this is Admiral Rodriquez. Do me a fucking favor and walk in on whatever circle-jerk your boss is involved in and tell him that I want to talk to him *now*."

"Sir, he's in a briefing with the squadron—"

"I don't care if he's making out with the goddamned tooth fairy. Just get him." Marco rolled his eyes. Barrera was loyal but dumb; he wouldn't poach *her* any time soon.

Katie shot him a Mom Glare. Did that work on her kid? Marco thought she had one. But he'd been bulletproof for a long time, even if his ninety-seven-year-old mother didn't think so. He ignored her as Barrera gulped loudly from the other end.

"Yes, sir."

"Thank you. I'll hold." Marco rolled his eyes at Katie. "Stop giving me that look. I'm not an unruly child."

"Of course you aren't, sir."

"Hmpfh." Marco sat back in his chair and waited for Banks. Fortunately, it didn't take long.

"Good afternoon, Admiral," Banks said, sounding like his always perfectly composed self. It was one of the things that Marco hated most about him. Banks was *too* perfect, too much a product of a predictable, peacetime navy. It was a pity that the dickwad was so competent. Otherwise, Marco would've fired him months ago.

"Took you long enough. What the fuck were you doing? Never mind, don't tell me—I don't want to know," Marco said. "I've got a fun job for a sub in your squadron."

He could hear Banks take a deep breath. "What might that be, sir?"

"Senator Angler wants to do a war patrol ride on an attack boat. I'm sending him to *Bluefish*," Marco replied, reaching for his stapler. He'd reassemble the poor elephant later, but now he needed something else to play with. Removing the stapler's springs was always tricky, but he was in the mood for a disassembly challenge. Some presidential hopeful wanting to make political capital out of his submarines still left him pissy, but if it got the navy funding...

He fucking hated politics. Paying attention to the stapler—who the hell swapped out his silver one for a red one?—meant he ignored the pregnant pause on the other end.

"Wouldn't you prefer another boat, sir?" Banks asked.

"No, but you clearly would." Marco snorted. "Convince me."

"I simply think you've provided enough distractions to Captain Coleman and his crew with these interviews." Banks shuffled papers in the background, grating on Marco's nerves. "You've had him do two interviews so far this week, with another scheduled for next week, and adding to the spotlight can only make things worse."

"What kind of things?"

"Sir, he already came into port with a broomstick—"

"He did?" Marco cut him off with a booming laugh. "Good for him! He must have taken it down by the time I got there." That Mush Morton comparison had been even more on point than he'd thought.

How the hell did someone who wanted to throw up when he got the Navy Cross do shit like this? Alex Coleman was a walking contradiction. Marco wanted to shake the kid and be his sea daddy all at the same time.

Teeth ground together on the other end. "I don't want one of my sub commanders turning into a prima donna, sir."

"A prima donna might be just what we need, Commodore," Marco replied. "Besides, Coleman just about shat himself when I gave him the Navy Cross. He ain't no prima donna."

"I do wish you'd remember to tell me about those little visits of yours."

Oops. He'd forgotten to tell Banks about that one. Marco liked to visit successful subs—so far, *Razorback* was leading the pack in pizza parties—and warning their respective squadron commanders was a pain in the ass. "I'll put my aide on that for the future," he promised. "She's smart. She'll figure it out."

Katie shot him that look again, but he could see her making a note.

"Thank you, sir." Banks wasn't done arguing. "Surely you'd rather put a more experienced commander in the limelight? Captain Coleman hasn't been on board *Bluefish* very long, and you already have him running ragged with those interviews."

"He's also has the fucking Medal of Honor, Commodore. And he's proven that he's not a one-shot wonder, so Senator Angler's going to *Bluefish*. Understood?"

Put like that, Banks couldn't refuse. Fortunately, he didn't even try another bureaucratic ass-grabbing dance, either; he rogered up and got to work. Why the hell didn't he put Coleman on a boat in McNally's squadron? She'd be singing hosannas and conspiring with him already. Unfortunately, *Bluefish* had been the available boat, and Marco wasn't stupid enough to wait. If Commodore Banks didn't like that, well, that was just tough titties. Marco didn't much like the arrangement, either.

"Well, that was an unexpected ending to the brief," Commander Dana Pratt of USS *Sailfish* leaned over to say quietly to Alex.

Alex suppressed a smile. "You can say that again."

The captains of SUBRON 29 had been assembled for a lessons learned session, but so far, it just consisted of Commodore Banks talking. Banks hadn't said much that Alex could one hundred percent disagree with, but damn, the man was conventional. His idea of good tactics remained a stalk from below or above the layer and a quiet kill, which was a grand idea if you could pull it off. These days, opportunities like that were rare. Alex knew more than one sub CO who'd died trying to get that perfect kill.

Now Banks rushed out to take a call from Admiral Rodriquez, and Alex could finally relax. Being the senior CO in the room was weird, particularly since he hadn't had a chance to get to know any of his fellows...except for Chris Kennedy of *Kansas*, who pointedly ignored Alex, which Alex was more relieved by than he cared to admit. Their last encounter hadn't exactly been cheery, had it? He'd called Kennedy a glory-minded fuck and Kennedy called him a coward.

Yeah. No one thought the way their partnership on *Kansas* ended had led to a lasting friendship. Or even respect. Kennedy probably wouldn't piss on him if he was on fire, and Alex wasn't sure if he'd return the favor.

Fortunately, most of the other sub COs in SUBRON 29 seemed welcoming.

"So, speaking of interesting tactics, I saw your writeup on that mine-laying *Yasen*," Dana said.

Alex blinked. "You did?"

"Yeah, the squadron intel officer sent your report out yesterday," Dana replied. "How the hell did you figure out what they were up to?"

"Probably blind luck." Alex felt his face trying to go red and stomped on his old fear of public speaking when every head turned his way. "That TACMEMO about their low-acoustic mines had just come out, and it was on my mind when we found the *Yasen*."

"Pretty ballsy of them to try it mid-chase," Commander Randall Littman of *Halibut* said.

"Or desperate." Alex shrugged. "My best guess was that they had their torpedo tubes full of mines already. Probably was faster to shit them out in our path than try to swap them for torps."

A few people chuckled at that one. Everyone but Kennedy, really. He scowled: "You said in your patrol report that you thought they were trying to disable subs with the mines instead of sink them. What in the world made you think of that?"

"Mostly the fact that the *Yasen* led us straight toward the frigate, which was DIW and waiting for someone," Alex replied, trying to keep his voice level. Everyone in the room knew subs detected surface ships through their screw noise. Sitting dead in the water was the best way to hide from a sub, particularly one focused on a moving enemy. It was an old tactic, straight out of the Second World War, but that didn't make it less effective.

"You mean when you almost sailed right into their trap." Kennedy's thin smile was smug, and Alex wanted to wipe it right off his face.

But he didn't need to, did he? Gone were the days when Kennedy had any influence over his career. Hell, now *he* outranked the man whose XO he'd once been. Kennedy was still in the same boat, while Alex was on his second command. That thought helped Alex give Kennedy his best smile and a casual shrug.

"Which is why I wrote it up so that no one else does the same thing," he said.

Kennedy frowned, but the conversation moved past him as Dana spoke up again:

"The Aussies are missing a *Shortfin. Dumaresq* failed to make port on schedule three days ago, and she was assigned a patrol area not far from where you sank the *Yasen*."

"No buoy?" Alex's heart sank. The Australians used the same SUBMISS/SUBSUNK system as the U.S. Subs had sunk without it deploying, but...

Dana shook her head. "Nothing."

"Damn." Alex swallowed hard. He'd hoped that *Bluefish* was the first one to spring that trap. *Dumaresq* was one of the newest *Shortfins* in the Royal Australian Navy. She had all the bells and whistles of the second flight of that class submarine, and if the enemy had nabbed her...

"If they've got her, they've got a lot of our best technology," Littman echoed Alex's thoughts quietly. "She's got the Mark 84s, and their sonar system is almost identical to what's on the Improved *Ceros.*"

"*If*," Kennedy interjected. "I think it's a lot of worry for no reason. Like it or not, *Dumaresq* is probably on the bottom with an intact buoy. We've all seen it happen before."

No one could argue with that, but Alex still couldn't shake the sinking feeling in the pit of his stomach.

The phone in Bobby and Lou's stateroom rang. Lou, sitting at his desk, picked it up. "Engineer." He listened for a moment. "Wait one." Turning toward Bobby, Lou extended the phone with a lopsided smile. "This one's a job for the acting XO."

"Gee, thanks." Bobby was so ready not to be acting XO; the paperwork never ended, and all the best people wanted to talk to him. He grabbed the phone. "Nav here, what's up?"

"Hey, sir, it's Harri. I'm on watch as OOD, and the XO from *Kansas* is here."

Bobby sat up straight, trying to remember if he knew the XO from *Kansas*. They weren't usually berthed near each other, though, so he drew a blank. "What for?"

"She won't say. Just says she wants to talk to the XO right now." There was a bullish edge to Harri's voice, one that said she was pissed off and trying not to show it.

"I'm on my way." Hanging up the phone, Bobby rose and grabbed his ballcap.

Lou looked up from the logs he was reviewing. "Something wrong?"

"Apparently *Kansas'* XO wants to make friends. Since I'm still Acting Some Things, it's all my show."

"Have fun. Call if it's something engineering, will you?"

"You'll be first in line," Bobby promised. Peterson had a habit of giving spare parts or help to other boats without consulting Lou, who might have needed said parts or people. It drove Lou crazy.

Reaching the quarterdeck didn't take long. Nothing did in a 389-foot-long submarine. When his head popped up above the ladder, however, he spotted Lieutenant Commander Song.

She was shorter than Bobby—which wasn't hard, since he topped six feet—with black hair and dark eyes. None of those traits caught his attention, however. Song stood like she had a titanium rod lashed to her back, and her eyes blazed with the anger that would come along with someone shoving that rod up unmentionable places.

Bobby felt his cheerful smile freeze in place, and he saluted her in hopes that it would soften the storm. "Commander. What can I do for you?"

Song's answering salute was razor sharp. Her eyes narrowed. "I asked to see the XO."

"Yeah, uh, I'm afraid I'm what you get." His left foot started wiggling, but Bobby stopped it with an effort. He would *not* fidget now, even if creepy crawlies were swarming all over his spine. "Lieutenant O'Kane, acting XO."

He tried to gesture her aft, to get her away from the quarterdeck watch, but Song ignored the invitation.

"Where is your *actual* XO?" She spoke slowly, as if trying to make a point to a small child.

"I'm it. Sort of. Which is to say that we don't have one." Bobby swallowed. "Commander Vanderbilt broke his leg a few months back, and we haven't gotten a relief yet."

"I see." Her eyes swept over *Bluefish*, her disapproval plain. "That explains everything."

Bobby bristled. The boat looked good. They'd worked hard to make sure she did. "Is there something I can do for you, ma'am?"

"Pier sweepers. Your people are doing a terrible job of it." Her glare dared him to challenge her, and Bobby fought the urge to swallow again.

"Really?" He'd figured she was here about something important: parts, weapons, sailors, food...the things a sub needed to go to war. Instead, Song was here about trash on the pier.

And there was trash on the pier, too. Seven big blue bags of it, not far from *Bluefish's* brow. Bobby frowned. That hadn't been there an hour ago.

"Yes, really," Song snapped. "You may take no pride in your surroundings, but some of us do. And that"—she gestured at the trash bags he'd just noticed—"is a disgrace."

Bobby blinked. "I don't have any problem cleaning up after ourselves, Commander. I just didn't know that—"

"Clearly you need to do some reading of the SORM to figure out what your responsibilities are," she cut him off. "Then again, with *Bluefish's* reputation, I suppose I shouldn't be surprised."

"I'm not sure what you're insinuating, but—"

"I'm insinuating that your boat is known for skating out of things." Song met his eyes, a small smirk playing over her lips.

Bobby wilted. So much for turning *Bluefish's* reputation around. Every boat on the pier was responsible for sending out pier sweepers. *Bluefish* sent them out an hour ago, right on time! Bobby even walked the pier near the boat afterward. He'd been yelled at for this same stupid thing one too many times by Peterson. He supposed that meant he should be used to it.

"I'll, uh, get it taken care of, ma'am," he said, forcing a smile. It wasn't worth arguing.

"Good."

Spinning on her heel, Song strode down *Bluefish's* brow without a further word. He stood and watched for a long moment, eyeing the offending trash bags, before turning back to face the quarterdeck watch with a sigh.

Bobby didn't speak until he could trust himself to do so levelly. "Get someone down there to take those stupid trash bags to the dumpster, will you, Harri?"

"Not a problem, sir." If that was pity in her eyes, Bobby didn't want to see it.

There were times when he really hated the navy.

Commodore Banks caught Alex on his way out of the SUBRON 29 headquarters. "Hold on a moment, Captain."

Alex stopped. "Sir?"

He didn't have to like Banks to respect him. The man was his boss, and Alex had had enough problems with bosses over the years to know that at least fifty percent of the issue was his own big mouth. Banks, however, was an annoying contradiction. On one hand, he was conservative tactically, prickly, and old-fashioned. On the other, he ran his squadron well: subs got the repairs they needed, personnel replacements happened on time—a rarity in the wartime navy—and concerns were addressed quickly.

"How soon can you get underway?" Banks asked. "*Halibut*'s ballast tank issue leaves a gap in our patrol schedule."

Patrol schedule. That meant something other than a convoy escort, which piqued Alex's interest. Even if it wasn't, his answer had to be the same: "We're loaded out. Theoretically, we're ready now, but I'd like to give the crew at least twelve hours' notice."

More would have been better, but there was a war on. Alex and the rest of *Bluefish's* crew had signed up for this, and they weren't going to shrink away from duty. Besides, they'd been in port for eighteen days. Under the circumstances, that was probably the best they could ask for.

"There's no need to be quite that quick off the mark." Banks' smile was thin. "*Halibut* was scheduled for Wednesday at ten hundred. Can you make that?"

He grimaced. "I'm scheduled to do an interview on *First In* Thursday."

First In was a news program on NBC. Although only in its second season, it had already won one Emmy and was an early favorite for a second. The show had astronomically high ratings, and Alex was terrified of being a guest. Not that he'd admit that out loud. Or that it would have stopped Uncle Marco from scheduling it.

"Operational necessities come first." Banks pursed his lips. "I'll talk to Admiral Rodriquez. Surely even he would rather you out on patrol than on TV."

"I hope to hell he does," Alex breathed and then caught himself. "I would, uh, appreciate that, sir."

For a moment, Alex thought understanding flashed between himself and his squadron commander. Then Banks sneered. "These media distractions are silly, but they *are* your duty, Captain. Surely you understand that."

Alex flinched, until hot rage surged up to replace any lingering embarrassment. "If I didn't understand duty, I would have turned tail and run during Convoy 57."

"I...suppose you would have." Banks seemed like he was going to say more, but he shook himself instead. "Send a report of your readiness to get underway at your earliest convenience."

"Of course, sir."

Alex took that as an invitation to walk away and did without a further word. He was grateful Banks had gotten him out of doing a third damned interview, but he still had no idea why the man hated him so much.

Unfortunately, that wasn't the kind of thing you could ask your boss, even if you were a Medal of Honor winner.

Pearl Harbor

Marco Rodriquez was neck deep in reviewing personnel transfers when his cell rang. He let it go to voicemail. Juggling subs' commanding officers was hard enough without interruptions, and the fact that USS *Arkansas* and USS *Kraken* had gone missing in the last week didn't help matters. *Kraken's* buoy had activated, but something went wrong with the accompanying data upload and they had no idea who or what sunk her. *Arkansas*, on the other hand, had vanished without a trace. The only correlation between them was that both were in northeastern patrol sectors, but in war, that didn't mean much. Even worse, *Kraken* had their prospective commanding officer along, and *Arkansas'* XO was slated for a boat of her own. Now Marco had to find replacements for both of them, not to mention shit out submarines to cover *Kraken* and *Arkansas'* assignments.

His cell rang again, belting out the theme from *The Lion King*. Marco glared before recognizing the number and then grudgingly answered.

"I don't have time for this, Freddie." Marco's head was pounding like some munchkin living behind his left eye had three hammers and knew how to use them. Brenda Lu of *Kraken* was an up-and-coming star. How the *hell* was he going to find someone to replace her?

"Well, I don't have time for your antics, either, but you don't hear me complaining," Admiral Hamilton replied. "You didn't answer your office phone."

"So?" He rubbed his temples.

"Are you sending Senator Angler out to *Bluefish*?"

"Jesus, woman, can you complain about everything? You wanted me to send him to my best. Coleman is my best."

Marco snorted. "Better than anyone you've got rolling around in the Atlantic, that's for sure."

He could *hear* her scowl. "The CNO disapproves, Marco."

"Fuck the CNO. Until he can do my job, he's welcome to walk off a cliff."

"You know I'm not telling him that," Freddie said. "Neither are you."

"He's a fucking aviator. He doesn't know jack about submarines." The chief of naval operations was also a political-minded busybody who wouldn't know combat if it bit him on the ass. No way had he been a good pilot, and Marco knew for a fact that he hadn't seen the inside of a cockpit in at least ten years. "Shit. Banks whined to him, didn't he?"

"You *know* Banks was his aide. They talk all the time. Would it kill you to make nice with one of your own squadron commanders?" Freddie sounded ready to tear her hair out. Or his.

Marco chucked his stapler into the trash can. "He doesn't like Coleman."

"*I* don't like Coleman. The man's not a saint."

He rolled his eyes. "Even you admitted he was right at Armistice Station. *Both times.* Get over it."

"If he does something insane, or disregards orders like he did at Armistice Station, this will be on *your* head, Marco."

"Roger that. Big fucking deal." Coleman seemed like a pretty level-headed kid, and sure, he'd disregarded orders before the war at Armistice Station, but he'd been *right.* Hell, they'd *punished* the guy for preventing the war from starting a year early, and yet here he was. Still rising to the top.

Freddie would handle the CNO. She didn't like the idea, but she didn't believe in micromanaging Marco, either. Now he just had to hope that Alex Coleman didn't prove him wrong.

After leaving the SUBRON 29 headquarters, Alex stopped by the pier to discover a rancorous volleyball game in progress. But a captain's presence always dampened the fun, so he left after waving hello to both sides and was rewarded with smiles. Morale was improving, and that was enough—for now. *Bluefish* was definitely a work in progress.

Instead, he met Nancy at Bathers Beach. Alex wasn't the sun-and-sand type, but Nancy loved it. He usually preferred to be *in* the water rather than next to it, but while Nancy enjoyed swimming, she hated wearing tanks or even a snorkel, and swimming around the surface left Alex bored out of his mind. He was a certified rescue diver with multiple *real* rescues under his belt, mostly thanks to the war, but he couldn't quite wrap his mind around *sunbathing.* But he loved his wife, so sun-and-sand it was.

Today, Nancy was settled under a giant purple umbrella when Alex arrived, wearing a two-piece suit she'd bought months earlier but never had the chance to use. Her grin grew when she caught him muttering about sand between his toes and ill-fitting board shorts.

"Here." Nancy extended a bottle of sunscreen. "Or you'll burn to a crisp."

"Yes, ma'am." Alex shot her a teasing grin and dropped down onto the empty towel to her left. He slathered the sunscreen on obediently and leaned in to kiss her. "How's leave?"

"Boring. I don't even have enough time to go home and see the girls, but there's nothing to do without a ship." She pouted. "And you were underway for my change of command."

"You're a workaholic, Nance."

She shrugged. "You already knew that."

Alex flopped back on the towel and squinted when the sun crept around the umbrella. "And people think I'm crazy."

"That's because of what you did with your last submarine." Nancy laughed but sobered quickly. "The girls want to come out, but the academy won't sign off on leave for Bobbie so close to spring break. And Emily has finals."

Alex burned to see his daughters—two months already felt like a lifetime—but he nodded. "Maybe during summer break."

Not that June in Australia was particularly warm; April was the tail end of summer, and by the time both girls were out of school, the weather would be cooler. But they could live without beach time.

"Yeah." Nancy extended a beer bottle as she sipped her own drink. "I got my official orders today."

"Already?"

She shrugged again. "I report in five days. Time to be an XO again."

Alex put the beer down and stared at the sky. "You sure you want to do this?"

"I can't say I'm looking forward to stepping back and being an XO again. It's going to suck big time after having my own command...but if that's what it takes to punch my ticket, that's what I'll do."

"I wish you wouldn't," he whispered.

"Don't you get worked up about this, Mister I Took Command of a Second Sub Without Telling My Wife," she replied.

His jaw dropped. "I didn't exactly have a lot of time to decide!"

"Neither did I." She glared.

"I thought you said Admiral Rosario gave you an option—"

"You were presumed *dead* for six weeks. Let's not turn this into a competition." Nancy snorted. "You'll lose."

Alex's mouth snapped shut. He wanted to shout at her, wanted to demand Nancy stay out of danger, but he had no right to say that, did he? Sure, he hated it when she was in combat and he wasn't back in the early days of the war, but now they were *both* on the pointy end doing dangerous things. Should one of them stop? Should one be safe?

Logic said one parent should work to survive for their kids, but war screwed everything up. And it wasn't like *Alex* had any particular reason to say *he* should be allowed to take risks that Nancy wasn't. Hell, she'd always been better at her job than him. His recent elevation was...well, maybe not going to his head, but something. Nancy was ready to go to the mat over this, too. Her brown eyes gleamed, her shoulders were squared, and she looked ready to throw her beer in his face.

Fuck it. He was okay with being a hypocrite.

"I just want you to be safe." He sighed. "I love you."

Nancy's smile turned sad. "I wish you wouldn't run headlong into danger, too. I think we deserve each other."

"Probably." Alex sighed. "I hate this."

"Same." She moved to put her head on his shoulder. "I've never felt more alive, but it's terrible. I worry about the girls all the time. About you."

"Yeah."

He *wanted* her to be safe, but Alex would never *ask* Nancy to stay behind, to take orders somewhere shoreside or back home where the missiles and torpedoes didn't reach. And she didn't, either. They just laid on the beach in silence as he wrapped an arm around her.

They both knew their duty.

31 January 2040, Indian Ocean, inbound toward Perth

USS *Nereus* was still underway. Picking up *Perch's* survivors hadn't dented her schedule; she still had a damaged destroyer to repair. She'd left USS *Ernest E. Evans* (DDG-169) limping alone to pick up the *Perch* crew, but John couldn't abandon the destroyer, even if sub tenders weren't designed to help surface ships. He hated tooling around the Indian Ocean at six knots and making himself a target, but that was the maximum speed *Evans* could manage with a locked shaft. *Evans* had taken damage during the Battle of the BIOT, but her crew Band-Aided it up well enough to continue fighting until a skirmish with a pair of Indian destroyers off the Agalega Islands.

Evans managed to make it across half of the Indian Ocean before she'd called for help, and *Nereus* had been the only ship available. John's machinists got the destroyer up to ten knots shortly after he'd picked up *Perch's* crew, but it was still a big ocean to sail that slowly, particularly on the surface.

John missed the freedom of being *under* the waves instead of on top. Sure, this job was career-enhancing—even Uncle Marco had told him it was the ticket he needed to punch before putting on stars and becoming a SUBRON commander. It was even challenging. But it wasn't the same as taking the fight to the enemy in an attack submarine. For a tender captain, exciting moments generally came when you were in the wrong place at the wrong time.

He'd had his one bout of fun with *Nereus*, too. No one in their right mind wanted him to sink another submarine with the fat tub he'd come to love. John wasn't an adrenaline junky, but he missed submarine command more than he'd ever imagined.

Even eating in the wardroom was less personal. *Nereus* had seventy officers, which was half of an attack submarine's entire crew. The wardroom, or officers' mess, was a cavern compared to the tiny one on *Razorback*, and sometimes John felt lost. *Nereus* was almost twice as long as *Razorback* and had a total crew of over six hundred. John thought he managed both well, but there were times that he still felt like a fish out of water. He'd been in command for more than four months, however, and he was good at faking it.

"I just sent a message to your tablet that you might want to see, Captain," his communications officer said as she walked in the wardroom for breakfast.

John felt his eyebrows shoot up. "Then sit and tell us all about it, Commo."

She grinned, plopping into a chair. "*Razorback* bagged a French carrier, along with two destroyers. All three sank before the rest of the escorts chased *Razorback* off."

"I'll be damned." John laughed aloud. "That *is* good news to have over breakfast!"

"*Razorback* was your old boat, wasn't she, sir?" Steve Harper asked from a little further down the table. *Perch's* XO sounded merely curious, but John didn't miss the way his commo's face went a little pink when he spoke.

"Yeah. They gave her to my old XO after my planned relief crapped his pants." John hadn't liked leaving *Razorback* and liked his replacement's failures even less. Fortunately, Commander Santos hadn't passed his check ride on another boat, and Patricia Abercrombie was took the boat straight out of John's hands. "Pat's good. One of the best. I'm not surprised she bagged herself a carrier."

"We definitely need more wins like that one, yeah." Steve's face grew a little dark, but *Perch's* XO brightened after a moment. "I never quite understood why they pulled you out of *Razorback*, sir."

John shrugged. "Ours is not to reason why."

He didn't want to explain it was his own ambition as much as anything else. John knew what he wanted to be, and the end of that career had at *least* as many stars as his mother had earned. She'd outranked his father with three stars to his two. John had grown up as the child of an admiral and a general, and he'd always known he wanted to go straight to the top. He could've stayed on *Razorback* if he tried, probably. Dug his heels in and asked for more time. But who was John to lie to himself? He took *Nereus* because this was the way up. That thought didn't make him miss the old life any less, but John was at peace with his decisions.

Usually.

Now, however, he studied Lieutenant Commander Steve Harper. He was clearly on the fast track. His reputation in the sub community was pretty good, or at least *Perch's* had been, which said a lot about an XO. It was a pity Singleton hadn't made it off, but at least one of them did. The navy lost far too many subs with all hands, robbing the sub community of valuable combat experience. Hopefully, Harper would use his experience to keep another sub from suffering *Perch's* fate—but first, there was something John needed to address.

He caught up with Harper just outside the wardroom after everyone else left. "Have a moment, Steve?"

"Of course, sir."

John gestured for the younger officer to follow him, heading toward his cabin. A few minutes later, the door was shut, and they were in private. John sighed and then decided to be blunt. "Is there something going on between you and my communications officer?"

"I'm not sure what you mean, sir."

"I'm asking if you've formed any sort of relationship. You've been on board for twelve days, and this seems...awfully fast."

Steve had the good grace to turn a little pink. "I know that it's a bit frowned upon, sir, but we're not in the same chain of command, and..." He trailed off.

"I take it that's a yes, then." John sighed. He knew that during a war no one cared if a submarine lieutenant commander got together with a surface lieutenant (junior grade), but it still went against the grain. The old rule of *one up, one down* meant they were a bit too far apart in rank to make him comfortable. The age gap was around ten years, too.

Stop being such a stodgy old grouch, he told himself. Wartime had different rules. Officers who couldn't wrap their minds around that didn't go far.

"It is, sir." Steve met his eyes. At least he had guts.

Well, it wasn't like Lieutenant Highly seemed unhappy. In fact, she was bouncy and better at her job than John had ever known her, so who was he to intervene? Besides, Steve Harper was too good of an officer to trip up with this. John sighed.

"Then I expect you to keep it professional on board my ship. What the two of you do once we're on shore is up to you, but for now, you're both officers. We'll make Perth in about a week. Can you behave yourselves that long?"

"That won't be a problem," Steve said.

"Glad to hear it."

Chapter 15

Quiet Hours

31 January 2040, Perth, Australia

If it was Tuesday, Lieutenant Commander Song was back. This time, the OOD had called Bobby when she was still on her way up the brow—Harri must have told the others about Song's last visit—so Bobby met her on the quarterdeck.

Clearly, that did nothing for her mood.

"*Certain* members of your crew violated quiet hours last night." Song's eyeballs might as well have been lasers.

Bobby flinched. "Quiet hours?" he repeated and then kicked himself. He remembered reading some base policy about observing quiet hours after twenty-three hundred, but no one listened to it. "What were they doing?"

"Playing *volleyball*," Song spat. "The sound carried all the way to *Kansas*."

"So they were...shouting or something?" Bobby asked.

"No." Her glare intensified.

Bobby wanted to ask if she'd stood outside her boat waiting for someone to make noise, but he thought the better of it. Maybe she had super hearing. But if she did, she could probably make a much better living than as a submariner. Maybe Song would make a great sonar tech? Until depth charges started exploding and made her ears bleed.

Ow.

"There is no reason to play sports of any sort on the pier—this is a secure area!" Song continued. "At that time of night, they should be sleeping."

"I'll pass that along." Bobby had so many better things to do than micromanage the crew's sleep schedules, but he wasn't dumb enough to say that to Song. Maybe she liked micromanaging?

She'd probably graduated from the Wade Peterson School of Leadership. With honors.

"You'll do better than that, *Lieutenant*." She glared again. "You'll put a stop to that horseshit immediately. It's unbecoming, and I won't have your crew of hooligans infecting *Kansas* with their asshattery."

"Yeah. Sure. I'll, uh, try to cut down on the midnight volleyball games, ma'am." Part of Bobby felt like crawling into his shell and never coming out; being bullied was no fun, and he hated saying *yes ma'am, no ma'am, six bags full ma'am* to this would-be tyrant from another boat. But the other part of him was kind of proud. *Bluefish's* crew had come a long way if they were playing volleyball on the pier in the dark.

A couple of weeks of R&R—and a captain who didn't bully them—really had done wonders for the crew.

"You do that." Spinning on her heel, Song stalked off *Bluefish*, barely pausing to salute the national ensign on the way.

Sighing, Bobby headed down to the wardroom for breakfast. How was he going to figure out who the volleyball players were without asking everyone?

Île Amsterdam

His orders had changed. Jules Rochambeau knew that happened in war. National pride had been damaged. Thus far,

France had been the only combatant *not* to lose an aircraft carrier during the war...until USS *Razorback* came to call. *Razorback* had dared to sink one of France's four precious carriers, and that could not be forgiven. World War III was the War of the Submarine, but nuclear-powered carriers still carried the most visible flags. *Arromanches* was one of two carriers in this theater of war, and without her presence—which consistently overshadowed the lesser carriers the Indians built with French help—France's prestige in the region decreased.

Jules hoped whatever submarine was attached to *Arromanches'* battle group had been chastised. *Barracuda* was generally assigned to independent operations, but the first tenet of protecting a carrier battle group was to not let anyone get within torpedo range of the carrier! Slamming a hand against a cabinet in his stateroom only stoked his rage. Jules strode out and banged on the door next to his own.

His first officer, Commander Camille Dubois, opened it right away, her beautiful brow creased with concern. "Captain? Is everything all right?"

"No. USS *Razorback* sank *Arromanches*, *Lorraine*, and *Bretagne.*" Jules scowled.

"*Arromanches?*"

"Yes." Taking a deep breath, Jules passed an old-fashioned hardcopy of their orders to her. "Our assignment has changed. We are to hunt and kill *Razorback* before she can return to port."

Camille blinked. "We are a long way from where *Arromanches* was sunk, *mon capitaine*."

"Then we must be fast. Get us underway as soon as possible."

"*Oui*." She nodded and headed toward control.

For the first time, Jules was happy Île Amsterdam provided nothing in the way of entertainment for his crew. They would all be near the boat, meaning he could get underway as soon as the reactor was ready.

He would not tweet about this. Providing Lady North with warning was one thing, merely an extension of the cat-and-mouse game they learned to play while their nations were still friends. But *Razorback* had assaulted French pride, and he would not gloat until he had avenged *Arromanches*, *Lorraine*, and *Bretagne.*

Then he would tell the world.

Alex finished an email to his younger daughter when Bobby knocked on the open door to his stateroom. "What's up?"

"There's, uh, something I should probably tell you about, Captain." Bobby fidgeted. "Do you mind if I close the door?"

"Sure." Alex hadn't seen Bobby so worked up since his early days on *Bluefish*, and it made his heart sink. He'd thought they were getting somewhere. The crew seemed more relaxed, and he'd returned from dinner with Nancy late last night to find an impromptu volleyball game in progress on the pier. "Sit down."

Bobby sat, and his left foot started twitching out a rhythm that Alex couldn't identify. "So, uh, yesterday Lieutenant Commander Song—she's *Kansas'* XO—came by. She didn't like the way we'd done pier sweepers, and there were seven bags of trash on the pier I swear weren't there earlier. I told her I'd get it cleaned up, but she was pissed off, and she said a lot about *Bluefish's* reputation—"

"Hold up a sec," Alex finally managed to cut in. "Why did *Kansas'* XO come over about pier sweepers?"

"I guess she didn't like the way the pier looked?" Bobby shrugged.

Had Kennedy put her up to this? "I don't give a rat's ass what she likes or dislikes on the pier. *Kansas* isn't pier SOPA."

The pier SOPA, or Senior Officer Present Afloat, was the senior captain whose command was tied up at any given pier. In the case of their pier, that was Alex, and therefore *Bluefish*. Not *Kansas*.

Bobby blanched. "She's senior to me..."

"But Commander Kennedy isn't senior to me. A fact that I'm sure he's painfully aware of," Alex replied. "So I don't care if she doesn't like a couple of trash bags hanging out on the pier—you don't think Song put them there, do you?"

"No." Bobby shook his head. "She seemed too angry for that."

"Hm." It wasn't worth wasting time on. "Next time she comes over here to raise a shitstorm, remind her that I'm senior to her CO and she can kindly pay attention to her own boat and responsibilities."

Bobby's grimace made him look even more miserable. "She came back today."

"Oh, *did* she?" Alex sat back in his chair. Was Kennedy behind this bullshit? Was he that petty? Alex hadn't worked for Kennedy for that long, but he knew the answer.

"Yeah." Bobby's shoulders slumped. "Apparently, some of the crew was playing volleyball during quiet hours last night."

"And Lieutenant Commander Song has a problem with that." Alex rolled his eyes.

Bobby must've been too nervous to realize who Alex was annoyed with, because he babbled onward:

"I thought I could ask the COB if she knew who was involved. I mean, I know the usual troublemakers: MM2 Krennick, MM1 Borreson, and HM2 Gary are always there if anything goes wrong. Sometimes, STS2 Walkman, too. The first three used to hang out with Wilson, and I think Wilson wore off on Walkman. There are some others who might have been instigators, but I'm not sure anyone is going to admit it if we yell at them."

"Which we're not going to do," Alex said and then chuckled. "No one takes quiet hours seriously. I passed a cruiser having beer on the pier and a regular old party last night on my way in. That was a lot louder than our volleyball game."

"You—you saw it?"

"Yeah. Engineering beat Navigation four out of five games." Alex grinned.

Bobby rocked back in his own chair, eyes wide. "You...don't have a problem with it?"

"Not in the slightest. I'd rather they mess around here than out in town. At least we know where to find them on the pier."

No major naval bases had been attacked, but it paid to keep your crew close. Alex knew some COs didn't mind if their crew wandered far and wide, but that was the one rule he insisted everyone follow. He didn't care if they got drunk: he just wanted them to sleep on the boat and be back before midnight.

"Oh."

Alex tried not to sigh. "I know she's senior to you, but you're the acting XO. That means—rank or no—you're her equal. Would you go marching onto another boat to try to tell them how to run things?"

"Of course not." Bobby scowled. "That would be...really rude."

"Yeah, that's the nice word for it." Alex quirked a smile. "So if she comes by again, tell her to get lost. Politely, if you can manage that."

"What if I, uh, can't?" Bobby asked.

"Then I'll deal with the fallout. Commander Kennedy already doesn't like me, so it's not like I'll miss out on any Christmas cards."

That finally made Bobby smile. "Oh. I guess not."

"You know they actually send people to school to be XOs, and for someone who missed out on all of that *stimulating* curriculum, I'd say you're doing fine."

"I keep worrying I'm letting the boat down." Bobby's voice was barely above a whisper.

"If anyone let *Bluefish* down, Bobby, it wasn't you."

1 February 2040, Perth, Australia

Bluefish got underway the next morning...or tried to.

"You did warn me, I suppose." The captain sighed. That didn't keep him from glaring down at where *Bluefish* was still snuggled against the pier.

Bobby wanted to sink into the ground. Or, barring that, straight through *Bluefish's* HY-80 steel to the ocean floor. "I'm really sorry, Captain. I thought we had the damned thing fixed this time."

Bluefish's outboard motor—or, in a less casual parlance, her bow thruster—had been on the fritz ever since Bobby reported as Navigator in July of 2038. It was the only piece of equipment Peterson never lied about when he said it needed fixing. In a crazy fit of desperation, they'd even traded STS1 Wilson for parts for the outboard months ago. It hadn't helped.

"All right, call Port Ops and get tugs." Alex didn't sound happy, but maybe Bobby didn't have to brace himself for a chewing out. "I guess it's a good thing we tested the fucker before getting underway."

"Yes, sir." Bobby tried not to gulp. Thankfully, Peterson was a stickler for every checklist ever made, so he'd always insisted they test the outboard when they set the Maneuvering Detail, too. Otherwise, it would have been...bad.

Things could've been worse. He *had* told Captain Coleman that the outboard broke frequently, and while the captain might have been unpredictable in some ways, he seemed happy enough to use a checklist when there was time. So they were still tied to the pier instead of drifting around like idiots.

Fortunately, he'd remembered to ask for a pair of tugs to be on standby in their request to get underway, so Port Ops was happy to help after a short phone call. *Bluefish* got underway a half hour behind schedule, which would have sent Peterson into a frothing fit and set the crew to hiding as well as a hundred-plus sailors could in an attack submarine. Captain Coleman just took the conn and headed into the Cockburn Sound without *quite* breaking the local maritime speed limits.

"Ready to get this show on the road?" Alex asked as they passed Beacon Head light.

"Sure." Bobby was surprised to find his smile wasn't forced. "Sounds like a piece of cake. Find enemy ships and sink them. Nothing to it."

Alex grinned. "Yeah, it's the first time I've gotten orders so vague, too. Makes you feel kind of special."

"If it's all the same to you, sir, that's not the kind of special I was looking for."

"What did you want, an engraved invitation?" Alex asked.

They laughed and then headed below. If things went according to plan, none of them would see daylight again until they were headed back into Cockburn Sound, but that was the life of a submariner.

Picking up speed, *Bluefish* sprinted toward her operating area. They needed the better part of two days to get there, looping north around Australia and through the same waters where they'd found *Kazan* laying mines three weeks earlier. Intelligence reports placed three merchant contacts of interest in that area, and *Bluefish* found the first pair on February 4th. Again, Alex gave the crews a chance to abandon ship before sending them to the bottom and then snapped a few old-school periscope pictures that made the crew grin.

Bobby felt the final bit of tension eking out of the crew as days passed. Everyone found the shift a little surreal, but damn it if things hadn't *changed* on *Bluefish.* They were a real submarine, fighting a real war. The war had always been present, like an albatross riding on their backs, taking friends away and destroying lives, but they'd always been on the outskirts. *Bluefish* never mattered, until now.

The three merchant ships were only the start of the patrol. The next day, *Bluefish* headed further north into the Java Sea. Those congested waters were full of noisy merchants carrying flags of a hundred nations—none belonging to active combatants, which meant *Bluefish* couldn't shoot without actionable intelligence. Then they stumbled into the path of an Indian *Akula III.*

The *Akula* got the drop on them, but luckily, Harri had the watch and Rose's top division officer had nerves of steel. She fired a snapshot at the *Akula* and then ran like hell before ordering the boat to battle stations. Her torpedo didn't hit the *Akula*, but the *Akula's* didn't hit them, either. By then, Bobby had raced into control with Captain Coleman right on his heels.

Somehow, Master Chief Baker beat them both there. Did she ever sleep? "Captain's in the Conn!" she sang out.

"Carry on. Talk to me, Harri," Alex ordered, shoes in hand. Bobby noticed he'd forgotten his reading glasses, but now wasn't the time to mention that.

Not when Bobby had left his left sock and his ballcap behind. At least he had both his shoes, and the general alarm clanging through the hull was only sort of loud enough to wake the dead.

Harri looked both terrified and elated. "Sir, we've got an Indian *Akula* close aboard. I think he was hiding under the layer when we came around to two-eight-five. The sonar conditions are crap, and he must not have been able to hear us until we were within three miles. I got off a snapshot, but all I think it did was interfere with the torp he sent our way. We peeled off to the west while he went the opposite direction."

"Good job." Alex's smile seemed to put Harri at ease. Things were always better when no one got yelled at. And no one was going to. This was the new *Bluefish.* The bad old days were over...right?

The captain turned to the plot as Bobby stepped over to Harri. "Anything else I need to know before I relieve you?"

"That's probably it." She shook her head, her eyes still a little wide. "That dude came out of nowhere, Nav," she whispered.

"We're all still alive, so don't sweat it." Bobby reached out to squeeze her shoulder. "Now let's see if we can shoot this guy for good, yeah?"

"You got it." Harri grinned. "I'll be in Sonar."

"Off you go, kiddo."

By the time Bobby turned back to look at his captain, Alex was rubbing his eyes tiredly. He caught Bobby watching and smiled. "I guess my wife was right about me needing glasses."

"I would've thought the prescription could help you figure that out, Captain," Bobby said.

Then his stomach dropped. What kind of idiot was he? Making fun of the captain during—

Alex laughed. "Yeah, good point. The raging headache I had through half of Convoy 57 was probably a dead giveaway, too." He waved a hand. "But my infirmaries can drive the conversation another time. Let's figure out which way this guy jumped and shoot his ass."

"I like the sound of that, sir." When the hell shooting the enemy had started to feel normal, Bobby didn't know.

Unfortunately, what a potentially quick shootout turned into a twenty-six-hour search through the Java Sea. There were a hundred other ships in the vicinity *Bluefish* had to be careful *not* to shoot, lest they torque off an international incident—or, better yet, add to America's list of enemies. Luckily, the *Akula* seemed to feel the same constraint. Accidents had happened in the war, but so far, combatants in the Third World War had tried very hard to be civilized—if one ignored the messy civil war between China and Taiwan. A few innocent merchants had been sunk, and two hospital ships accidentally targeted, but it seemed like every involved nation wanted to keep things from getting worse than they already were.

Was this the new world? Was it modern war? Was everyone just too terrified of going *too far* and someone going nuclear? Bobby didn't know, but as wars went, it was...civilized.

Twenty-five hours in, Bobby returned to control yawning and feeling drunk. Catching small naps every now and then while he and Rose rotated on and off hadn't done much for his mental state; sleeping was hard when Bobby felt like he should be in control. So he hung out there even when he *should've* been sleeping, only to count the shuteye he'd achieved in minutes instead of hours. The captain rotated crew off every watch station to let people eat, sleep, and take care of necessities—something Peterson *definitely* wouldn't bothered with—but one look at the drawn faces around him told Bobby that they all felt the burn.

"Conn, Sonar, I think I've got something." STS2 Walkman's voice sounded wrung out, even through the squawk box. "It's a bottom bounce contact, a bit further out than our friend is supposed to be, but it's definitely submerged."

"Conn, aye." Alex rubbed his face. He'd drunk more coffee than Bobby, and Bobby was damned sure that the captain hadn't slept a wink. He did have his glasses, now, though they were dangling out of his mouth instead of on his face where they should be. "You sure it isn't another supply hauler?"

"The system is saying it's a *Los Angeles*-class submarine, sir, so I'm not *sure*, but I think it's the *Akula*," Walkman replied.

"Conn, aye." Alex spotted Bobby and waved him over. "Looks like we might be in the homestretch."

"If we're not, will you get some sleep, Captain?" Bobby asked. "Zombie captains are only good on TV."

"Yeah." A grunted laugh. "I tried to earlier, but I drank too much coffee."

"I'm not sure I want to know how much that is."

"I'm sure I don't." Alex's smile was lopsided. "I thought this cat would be easier to find. Shows what overconfidence gets you, I suppose."

"I'm not sure I'd call it overconfidence, Captain," Bobby said. "But this guy *does* seem to have nine lives, so the cat analogy seems solid. It's better than him being the Roadrunner, anyway, because that makes us the Coyote, and you know what happens to the Coyote."

"Yeah, thanks, Bobby. I needed the image of Acme-brand anvils dropping on my head today." But Alex laughed, so Bobby counted it as a victory.

"Even when the Coyote catches Roadrunner, it never goes well," he continued. "I remember that one time—"

"Conn, Sonar, got him! Estimate course one-eight-three, speed six. I think we're in his baffles!" Walkman was so excited that Bobby could hear her through the open door to sonar. "Range approximately seven nautical miles."

"Conn, aye." Alex sounded a lot more awake now, too. "Let's go back to battle stations, Bobby. Silently."

"Aye, sir. Chief of the Watch, pass the word to re-man battle stations, torpedo."

Master Chief Baker grinned and passed the order along. Manning battle stations silently meant no use of the general alarm or general announcing system; they were close enough that the *Akula* might hear that with passive sonar. Given how noisy the Java Sea was, that wasn't likely, but who wanted to take chances?

Bluefish's sailors woke up and raced to their stations as Bobby resumed his watch as Officer of the Deck. Rose shot him a tired grin as she returned to the weapons corner, where Chief Rhee dialed the *Akula* in, muttering obscenities with every key strike.

"All right, Bobby, bring us around to stay behind him," the captain ordered. He was chewing on his glasses again, and Bobby wanted to make a face.

Bobby took a deep breath and then raised his voice: "Left standard rudder, steady course two-two-seven. Ahead standard for twelve knots."

Twelve knots was well below *Bluefish's* silent speed, but with the *Akula* moving slowly, there was no reason to run around like idiots. Maybe that coyote reference wasn't so good after all. Bobby glanced at the captain, but Alex only nodded. Being given a free rein was invigorating—and downright terrifying, too. It was a lot easier to let the captain make the mistakes and just carry out orders, but Alex Coleman wasn't that kind of captain.

5 February 2040, Perth, Australia

The bad news was that Uncle Marco scared the ever-living crap out of Commander Abercrombie. The good news was that he'd scared her with the Navy Cross, a reward for sinking the first French aircraft carrier in the war. Master Chief Bryan Morton was less surprised by the Silver Star he'd received, but mainly because this was his second. The first had come from Convoy 57 and probably left more than a few nightmares in its wake.

He figured this one might be a little friendlier to keep.

"You keep doing shit like this, ma'am, and they'll remember you before they remember Captain Dalton," he told his CO after the admiral left.

She turned red right to the roots of her hair. "Cut that crap out, Master Chief. I'm not the one destined for stars."

"Captain, you bagged a carrier, two destroyers, and those two *Scorpenes* who tried to creep up on Christmas Island in one patrol," he replied, leaning on the bulkhead in her stateroom. "That's right up there with the best."

"Says the guy who came off of *Jimmy Carter* and didn't even bother to take leave," she shot back.

Bryan laughed. "Be fair, ma'am. I took two weeks' leave. Long enough to show my kids I'm alive but still avoid my ex-wife."

"Yeah, if I had an ex, I'd avoid her, too." Abercrombie shook her head. "I'm not saying I'm unhappy with the patrol, Master Chief. Just don't go sticking it in the annals of the all-time greats yet, okay?"

"Sure, Captain. But it's worthy of *Razorback*. And if you play your cards right, you'll get to keep her longer than Captain Dalton did, too." Bryan didn't mention that this meant they'd probably have to go after Rochambeau; there was no reason to rain on his captain's parade. Besides, she was pretty good. He figured they had a better than even chance of downing the French asshole-in-chief.

Abercrombie smiled wryly. "You mean if I don't go to pieces first. You hear about what happened to the CO of *Bumper*?"

"Yeah." That sobered him up quickly. "I'm friends with their COB. Said Commander Dennison folded right in the middle of a shooting match and the XO had to take over. Luckily, the XO shot the destroyer depth charging them and dove deep enough that the helos couldn't find *Bumper*."

"I know Tonya Dennison." Abercrombie studied the blue-and-white speckled deck. "She was in my class at the Submarine Commander's Course. Best of the best."

Bryan grimaced. "You never know what combat's going to do to someone. Or what too much combat will do to someone." He sighed. "Remind me sometime to tell you about my XO on *Jimmy Carter*."

"I've heard stories about that."

"They're all true."

Submarines were called the Silent Service for the reason, but that didn't mean they weren't gossips with *each other*. Bryan knew that better than most; with more than thirty years wearing this uniform and a bunch of them shepherding young kids around the boats, he'd heard more than one whopper of a sea story that absolutely *couldn't* be true...except he knew they all were.

War had changed those stories from sometimes scary and usually *oh shit you did what* to frequently terrifying and full of grief. Bryan Morton had lived through both types, and he was old enough to worry about how many submarine commanders—and executive officers—were still melting down in combat. But he didn't know how to stop it. Maybe no one did. He was just a crusty old master chief petty officer. He could mentor them, console them, and be their sounding boards. He couldn't do their job for them.

Another hour crept by while *Bluefish* snuck up on the *Akula*, slowly but steadily closing the distance. Alex didn't want to risk shooting at long range in these waters; there was too much of a chance their torpedo might tag an innocent. He was pretty sure the navy would forgive him, but he knew he wouldn't forgive himself. *Collateral damage* and *acceptable civilian losses* looked reasonable on a PowerPoint slide, but they weren't things his conscience could accept. In waters like these, he needed to be extra careful with where he put torpedoes—and that meant he had to fight contrary to his instincts and experience.

At least his crew wasn't on pins and needles, waiting for an explosion Alex had no intention of indulging in. Yeah, he was a bit testy; lack of sleep never made Alex charming, and his eyes burned like they were full of sand. Convoy 57 taught Alex that he sucked at sleeping when the pressure was on, though, and he knew how to push through it. So far, he'd managed not to snap at anyone.

"Right standard rudder, steady course one-eight-eight," Bobby ordered from the center of control. Alex left the driving to his acting XO as he watched the plot. And Bobby had done well, closing the distance to the *Akula* to less than two nautical miles without being detected.

The *Akula* still trucked along at six knots, carrying out what looked like a standardized search pattern. *Bluefish* had been doing much the same until she sniffed out her enemy, and that had only been by virtue of luck and better sonar. The Indians had bought the *Akula III* design from the Russians in the early 2020s, but there was a reason why the Russians stopped building them. They were good boats, but they'd been outclassed. It took some careful driving to be silent in an *Akula*, and whoever was in charge over there just wasn't quiet enough. Odds were, the *Akula* had been just as surprised as *Bluefish* when they'd stumbled into one another. Now it was a game of patience.

Fortunately, the *Akula* didn't seem to realize they'd been located first. Bobby conned *Bluefish* closer and closer to her over the last hour, creeping up in the *Akula's* baffles, the blindest spot in any submarine's sonar coverage. The gap could be overcome by putting out a towed sonar array, but doing that in shallow and congested waters was always a risk. Most submariners chose not, particularly since the winch noise could give their presence away. *Bluefish*, on the other hand, had streamed her towed array on a short stay before she'd even entered the Java Sea.

Alex liked having ears, and the array cost a lot less than a new boat. Sure, there was a risk that some merchant might run it over and get the hydrophones caught in their screws, but as long as *Bluefish* stayed deep enough, that worry was small.

Speaking of worries, not being henpecked did wonders for Bobby's confidence. Should Alex just ask the squadron to give him a new navigator instead a new XO? The three emails he'd sent on that topic received a "we're working on it" response from Banks' chief of staff, and Alex was pretty sure that Commander Reyes wasn't slow-rolling him. Not on this.

If the navy's admin-heavy personnel system had been up to managing wartime assignments, *Alex* wouldn't have ended up on *Bluefish* in the first place. Unanticipated losses were tough, even in peacetime. Boats sinking—and people dying—wreaked havoc on planned assignments. It was almost a miracle that the only crewmember he lacked was the XO.

Bobby could do it, Alex decided. He was young—just thirty—but he was sharp. And now that he wasn't so nervous, his competence was creeping out from beneath the surface. It was worth thinking on.

"Range is down to thirty-seven hundred yards, Captain," Bobby said. Somehow, he'd crept up next to Alex, and his proximity made Alex jump. Bobby grinned.

"Scaring the shit out of your captain is generally frowned upon." Alex rolled his eyes. "But if you're hinting that it's time, I think you're right. We're not going to get any closer to this guy without him noticing. As it is, we're practically close enough to read his license plate." Alex glanced to his left. "How's your solution look, Weps?"

"Ready and updated, Captain," Rose replied.

"All right. We'll need to wire guide these two in. If we're not certain of the target, we self-destruct the torps. We're not sinking some neutral merchant today, ladies and gents. That clear?"

"Yes, sir," Rose said for her team, nodding vigorously.

Time to dance. "Open the outer doors for tubes one and two," Alex said. If the *Akula* was going to hear them and increase speed, now would be the time. Unless Alex didn't give him that chance. "Fire."

Rose slapped the buttons. "Tubes one and two away!"

Bluefish shuddered slightly, firing one torpedo from each of her top two tubes. Firing one starboard torpedo and one port torpedo left Alex's options open for a snapshot. Maybe the *Akula* had an unseen friend. The *Ceros* off-bore firing capability was decent, but he still couldn't shoot very far to port from a starboard tube or vice versa. Only having four tubes still made him feel half crippled, but at least there were twenty-two weapons left in his torpedo room. If anyone jumped out at them, *Bluefish* was prepared to deliver a world of hurt.

"Conn, Sonar, two fish running hot, straight, and normal," Chief Andreas reported a moment later.

"Very well." Alex looked back at Rose. "Estimated time to impact, Weps?"

Rose didn't even have to look at the display. "Less than three minutes."

"Conn, Sonar, the *Akula's* kicked it up," Walkman reported. "Twenty knots and increasing fast."

"Conn, aye." Alex remembered to put his glasses back on to watch the plot. The icons representing *Bluefish's* torpedoes sped outward, chasing after the *Akula* as the Indian submarine twisted and turned. He didn't look up before saying: "Match her course and speed, Bobby."

"Aye, sir." Bobby gave the appropriate commands, and *Bluefish* sped up in the *Akula's* wake. That did nothing to help the torpedoes—the Mark 84's top speed was eighty-seven knots no matter what the firing submarine did—but at least it kept the guidance wires from getting too long.

More importantly, if they stayed in the *Akula's* baffles, the Indian sub couldn't shoot back.

"One minute until impact!" Rose no longer sounded ready to bounce away in excitement; she'd gotten past that after their first engagement. Now she was cool and professional. Alex liked her focus; Rose was a laser. All he had to do was point her in the right direction.

She'd go far. Probably further than Bobby, and maybe further than Alex, too. Rose had ambition Alex lacked, and he had a feeling Bobby wasn't the rocket-to-the-top type, either.

"Very well." Now all Alex could do was sit back and wait. At least he didn't have to wait long. The *Akula* spat out noisemakers and dove, but it was too late.

"Both torpedoes in terminal homing," Chief Rhee said.

Alex grimaced. Diving meant that the *Akula* wasn't going to—

"Impact! Good impact on both torps!" Chief Rhee interrupted his thoughts, and sonar chimed in a moment later:

"Conn, Sonar, two explosions bearing zero-six-three! Whoa—*big* implosion, I think we got her, Captain!"

The deck under Alex's feet rumbled as Bobby put *Bluefish* into a hard right turn. No one wanted to drive through an explosion that used to be a submarine, particularly one loud enough to hear from three thousand yards away. *No one's getting off that* Akula. *Not with them a thousand feet down.* An *Akula III* had a crew of seventy-four. That was seventy-four enemy sailors he'd just killed. He didn't quite feel guilty, but a bit of regret bubbled up before he could stop it.

The *Yasen* was easier. At least that boat reached the surface; some people got off. He'd been too busy to think about the other side dying during Convoy 57, and the first *Akula* he'd killed in command of *Bluefish* put up such a fight that all he felt was relief. Now, however, Alex found himself all too easily imagining how it must have felt to be on that other sub in its last few moments. Water rushing in, metal buckling—

"Where to now, Captain?" Bobby asked, and Alex shook himself.

"Secure from battle stations," he replied. "And have Charlie gen up a message to report this sinking." Charlie was *Bluefish's* communications officer, and he knew the drill. Commodore

Banks was a sucker for being kept in the loop. So Alex would provide information overkill if it kept his boss happy. All he wanted was to be left alone enough to do his job.

"Aye, sir." Bobby threw him a concerned look. "Is...everything all right, Captain?"

"Yeah." Alex made himself smile. "Just wool-gathering. I think I need to get some sleep before I turn into a drooling idiot."

"Well, I wasn't going to say it, but..."

Alex laughed. "I get the message. Get the captain out of control so you can all party. I see how it is." He waved off Bobby's attempt at a response. "Don't answer that. You win."

Most of the watchstanders laughed, which made Alex smile as he walked out. His boss could hate him, but his crew didn't. If he had to pick one of the two, he was damned happy with what he had.

Chapter 16

Curiouser and Curiouser

Perth, Australia

Reporting to a ship during peacetime could be a nerve-racking affair, even for senior officers. However, with a successful command tour under her belt, Nancy felt *better* coming to a new ship than she had in the past...which wasn't to say that there wasn't a mess of Alex-like butterflies racing around in her gut.

Nancy considered herself a sturdy and self-sufficient individual. She didn't sweat the small stuff, and even better, she knew she was on the fast track. Now, with two Silver Stars and assorted lower medals on her dress uniform—and an admiral's promise—she was certain to make captain before nearly everyone else in her year group. Her husband, of course, was the distinct exception to that, but Nancy didn't mind. It was nice to see Alex make rank ahead of her for once, even if he was mortified by it.

Still, it was nice to be back in the world of the surface navy, where no one asked if she was related to *that* Coleman. Nancy hated being anyone's appendage. She was a naval officer and a professional warfighter, not a wilting flower. Which wasn't to say that she didn't like flowers just fine, but roses belonged in a vase, not on a warship.

"Ready to go, Commander?" the dark-eyed coxswain asked. His nametag read *Silverio,* and he was a short, barrel-chested man who looked like he ate barbells for fun.

"Let's roll," Nancy replied, settling into the small boat that would take her out to where USS *Cape St. George* swung at anchor. The navy's newest class of cruiser was lean, mean, and bursting with weapons, which made them too big to sit alongside most of Perth's piers. That meant anchoring out in the harbor, where anyone coming or going had to take a boat.

In this case, it meant Nancy had to haul all her stuff out with her, too. It wasn't much fun, but it was the surface warfare officer life.

She let her eyes trace over *Cape's* smooth lines as they approached. The cruiser was a beast, bigger than any surface warship built since the days of the cold war. She boasted of two twin five-inch gun mounts, two hundred vertical launch cells for various missiles, and two CIWS, or Close In Weapons Systems, for point defense. *Cape* was the first in America's newest class of guided missile cruiser, barely a year old. She was tougher and meaner than even Julia Rosario's *Belleau Wood*, and Nancy knew from experience how good the former was in a fight.

Cape was, by all metrics, the best cruiser in the world. Was that despite—or because of—Captain Rowlings? No one knew. Helen Rowlings was competent, even brilliant, but Nancy took one look at her string of fired or otherwise discarded XOs and shuddered.

Not that *she* planned on being added to that list.

The boat slid alongside *Cape* easily as Nancy watched with a critical eye, half listening to waves slap lazily against the cruiser's metal hull. That sound screamed *home* to her, and she smiled. Yeah, she'd miss *Fletcher*, but if this was the way up, Nancy would climb that orange Jacob's ladder hanging down *Cape's* side, endure whatever Captain Rowlings threw at her, and bide her time until she could command this gorgeous machine of war.

Ding ding, ding ding. Bells rang out as she stepped on deck. "Commander, U.S. Navy, arriving."

Nancy managed not to frown. There was no stinger, no final bell, and she was no longer announced as *Fletcher*. No, that was reserved for captains in command, which she was not. It burned a little, disappointment digging around in her gut for purchase, but she pushed the feeling aside as her eyes swept over *Cape's* aft missile deck.

There were grills on the starboard side, with paper plates, buns, and sodas stacked nearby. Two cooks stood behind the grills, preparing fixings and laughing.

Nancy blinked.

"Welcome aboard, XO," a voice said from her right, and she spun to find a short, gray-haired woman smiling at her.

On first glance, Helen Rowlings looked more like someone's kindly grandmother than the hard-assed and brilliant captain her reputation called her. Her smile was infectious and a touch naughty, and her brown eyes gleamed warmly. When Nancy saluted, Rowlings' return salute was just on the right side of casual, the kind of salute Nancy expected from someone who had spent a career at sea instead of one sucking up to some pencil-pusher or another in the Pentagon.

"Thank you, ma'am," she said, accepting the offered hand to shake.

"Steel beach picnic," Rowlings said before Nancy could ask about the activity on the missile deck. "Starts in about an hour. You've got just enough time to get your gear stowed and change into something more comfortable."

Nancy tried not to grimace and look down at her dress whites. She looked good and knew it, but climbing out of the boat and on board hadn't done her any favors. She'd be surprised if her pure white trousers had survived the experience unstained, and she refused to check.

"Do you want to do a check-in interview or anything, Captain?" she asked as sailors lugged her seabag and other assorted gear out of the boat.

Rowlings shrugged. "We can do it over burgers. It's the CMC's birthday today, and I thought that was a good excuse to break out the grills."

Well, that didn't fit what she'd heard about "Hardass Helen," but Nancy could roll with it. "Sounds good to me. Let me just stow my gear, change, and I'll be back out."

Rowlings grinned and shooed her off, leaving Nancy to think that maybe things weren't as bad on *Cape St. George* as the rumor mill suggested. It wouldn't be the first time that fleet scuttlebutt was wrong, after all. If Hardass Helen was just brilliant and badass, well, Nancy was good with that. She had her own reputation on that front, after all.

Or maybe that was the source of her casual greeting? Nancy, unlike Rowlings' past XOs, had come fresh from her own successful command. She had two silver stars on her ribbon rack and plenty of combat experience on *Fletcher.* No one doubted her nerve or her skill. Maybe that was what Rowlings wanted?

It didn't matter, Nancy decided as she grabbed her seabag and followed a young officer to her new stateroom. No matter what, she had a job to do.

Sending a message to announce their success in killing the *Akula* turned out to be a bad idea. Commodore Banks was entirely too much like Peterson. No wonder they'd been friends. New instructions arrived before *Bluefish* could go deep and out of communications range, sending them back toward Australia's coast and away from places Indians subs might be found.

"It's almost like he doesn't want us to kill anything," Rose muttered to Lou when he came forward to control to visit her on watch.

"It's almost like you're paranoid for no good reason," he replied.

Rose glared; *Bluefish's* engineer smiled and poked her in the shoulder. She rolled her eyes. "There's no other reason to send us here. Intelligence says there's nothing but merchants we can't shoot at."

"I'm okay with not shooting civilians unless we have to." Lou shrugged, leaning against the chart table. "Most of them are just trying to go about their business."

"I know." She scowled. "And I don't want to kill innocents, either, but World War II was simpler. Then you just could shoot anyone who was providing 'aid or comfort' to the enemy, and no one cared."

"The world's a different place." Lou gestured at the high-tech consoles surrounding them. "And I don't know about you, but I enjoy the modern technology-driven, *air-conditioned* submarine. You wouldn't catch me dead being Eng on one of those old sweat factories."

"I'd do it." Rose figured she'd get used to the smell of sweaty bodies soon enough, and after that, who cared? The point was to take the fight to the enemy, not personal comfort. Sometimes, she dreamed about being on board *Wahoo* with Mush Morton or *Tang* with Dick O'Kane. Those were the days when submarine warfare was in its infancy, where men like Morton and O'Kane took actions that changed the world. She could only imagine what it must've been like to sail with those legends.

Lou laughed. "I know."

She scowled. "Shut up."

"Conn, Sonar, new contact, track 6027. Sounds like a high-speed ferry," STS2 Walkman announced via the intercom.

"Conn, aye." Rose glanced at the plot but didn't pay it much attention. Walkman knew her shit. If she said it was a ferry, it was a ferry. Passenger ferries were off-limits, anyway, no matter which flag they flew. Sighing, she glanced at Lou. "Pity it's not something more interesting."

"You crazy weapons types can keep your 'interesting,'" he replied. "I'm content when my plant runs well."

"You're also content not to have Peterson breathing down your neck every five seconds," she shot back.

"Hey, I was his favorite department head."

Rose rolled her eyes. "That's like saying you have a favorite plague."

"Good point." Lou chuckled. "Still, I can handle a quiet night. We tagged that *Akula* two days ago. You're just greedy."

"So?"

"So be glad that no one wants to cork off the kind of atrocities that happened during World War II. You really want to be remembered for shooting up civilians?"

"Of course not." Rose scowled and then walked over to take a closer look at the plot. The ferry was heading toward Australia, which wasn't odd, but it wasn't on any of the normal ferry routes. Weird. Rose walked over to the open door to sonar. "You got a better I.D. on that ferry, Walkman?"

The young sonar operator looked over her shoulder. "Not really, ma'am. Sounds like she's waterjet, so probably one of those car-carrying types that the Aussies love to build. You want to go up and take a looksie?"

Rose shrugged. "Why not?"

She headed back into control proper, where Lou let out a long-suffering sigh. "You're going to go to P.D. and take a look, aren't you?"

"No reason not to." Rose tried to sound casual, but ants were crawling up her spine. She wanted to *do* things, not creep around and hope an enemy came her way. War made her feel alive. She had no intention of doing something terrible, but sinking the enemy was her job. She was *good* at her job, thank you, and Rose wanted to go straight to the top.

Though maybe not Medal of Honor straight. Reading the patrol report on Convoy 57 was hairy enough. Rose liked to think that she'd do well in that kind of situation, but not finding out sounded smarter.

"You going to call the captain?"

Rose shook her head. "He's napping. Besides, standing orders say we don't have to." That was a welcome change.

"What, you mean we can fart without permission?" Max Goldberg, Rose's piloting officer on watch, spoke up.

"Hush when your betters are talking." Rose grinned. Life on *Bluefish* had relaxed a *lot* since Peterson left, and Rose reveled in the newfound freedom.

She also wanted to live up to Captain Coleman's trust, which was a new feeling. She hadn't given a rat's ass about what Peterson thought about her, not after he'd micromanaged the life out of everyone. Captain Coleman was different, though. He wasn't a screamer—though Rose suspected he could blister the sound-deadening patches off the hull if he wanted to—and he actually *trusted* people to do their jobs. It was a heady feeling. Even her first CO, on *Redfish*, hadn't been like this. And Commander Goddard was pretty damned good.

"You want me to hush or to take us up to periscope depth, Weps?" Max asked.

"You let your divos get all kinds of uppity, don't you?" she said to Lou, who was Max's boss. Max was *Bluefish's* electrical officer and therefore worked for the engineer. He was a pretty good kid, and decent at his job, particularly for someone who'd been on board less than a year.

"Yep. I tell them to be like you." Lou's smile was lazy.

"Flattery will get you nowhere." Rose turned back to Max. "Of course I want you to take us up to P.D. Don't ask silly questions. But take us up quietly, will you? It wouldn't do to be *another* watch team that almost rammed the enemy by accident."

Max nodded emphatically. They all knew Harri would have a hard time living the "surprise *Akula*" down. "Yes, ma'am."

Bluefish slowly rose toward the surface, pausing periodically to check for contacts. Surfacing—or nearly surfacing, which was what going to periscope depth meant—was one of the most dangerous times for a submarine. Even with modern filters to dampen out the sound of her own screws, a sub was half blind while working her way to the surface. There were plenty of historical examples of submarines surfacing underneath fishing boats, warships, and merchants—usually to the detriment of the other ship. Fishing boats sank, merchants complained about giant holes in the hull, and warships generally survived the experience. Subs usually ended up with a bent periscope—at best—and others ripped their entire sails off.

Rose remembered an incident with USS *Moray* five or six years ago. *Moray* had surfaced right underneath the cruiser *Sacket's Harbor. Sacket's Harbor's* keel hadn't quite been broken, but *Moray* glanced off the hull and tore open several of her own ballast tanks. Only her CO's quick surfacing saved the boat. Then the limping cruiser had to tow *Moray* back into port. Talk about embarrassing.

It took *years* for the sub force to live that incident down. Their surface brethren—whom submariners usually called targets—mocked them for months. Only the war starting had—

"Officer of the Deck, the boat is stable at eight-zero feet." Max's formal report made Rose crawl out of her headspace.

"Very well." She took a breath. "Up scope!"

She was glad that the *Ceros* got rid of the always-up periscopes the *Virginia* class still had. With those scopes, everyone knew you were there the moment you hit periscope depth. There was no way to lurk shallow and listen without your scope breaching the surface, because the idea of driving *so* perfectly that you could keep the scope under the waves was ludicrous. Rose was crazy. Not stupid.

The soft sound of hydraulics greeted her as the number two periscope slid upward. Rose waited until it was fully extended before pressing against the eyepiece. Once upon a time, she thought the attached monitor was just as good, but there was something to be said for doing things the old-fashioned way.

"Range and bearing to ferry?" she asked. Max relayed the question to sonar.

Carefully, Rose walked the periscope in a circle, checking their surroundings. By the time she was done, Max had her answer.

"Zero-zero-six, eleven thousand yards," he said.

"Aye." Rose twisted to the appropriate bearing. Her eyes needed a moment to pick out the ferry. It was almost six miles away, and that was about the maximum you could see out of a periscope. Surface ships had a greater height of eye and could see out to the horizon, but a periscope only stuck a few feet out of the water.

The ferry looked depressingly normal. Blue and red in color, it stuck out against the morning sky like a sore thumb, chugging along. Its wake wasn't very big, either. Rose frowned. Waterjets weren't her thing, but she'd seen the giant rooster tails of water they could kick up.

Rose frowned, stepping away from the periscope to speak into the squawk box. "Sonar, Conn, are you sure this guy is a waterjet ship?"

"That's affirmative, Conn."

"What's his speed?"

"Um...twenty knots?" Walkman sounded thoughtful. "Seems to be slowing."

"Maybe he's got something stuck in one of his jets?" Max asked.

Lou shook his head immediately. "No, those jets can eat aluminum stepladders and keep going. Unless he sucked up a whale, he's fine."

"If he ate a whale, he's going to start calling for help really soon." Rose shook her head. Stranger things had happened, and while a sub wasn't a good search-and-rescue platform—even when there wasn't a war on—they'd do what they could to help if civilians were in danger. Probably. Someone would have to do a risk-reward calculation. There was a war on, after all.

"No radio transmissions, Weps," the communications watch reported two minutes later.

"Probably not a whale, then." Rose looked at the periscope view screen again. The ferry had slowed further, but why? He was still over fifty miles out from Australia. Tooling around like this burned money. Fuel was expensive with the war on, and no company liked waste.

"You think he's up to something?" Lou asked.

"I think he's weird. That's as far as I've gotten." Rose bit her lip. She wanted to know more, wanted to have a complete package to tell the captain...but maybe that was just her desire not to earn a condescending lecture.

Peterson would've complained about the lack of information if she called him. Peterson would've looked down his bumpy nose and implied Rose was an incompetent worrywart. But Peterson was gone. Rose let out a breath.

"Guess it's time to call the boss," she said, earning an approving nod from Lou.

"Guess it's time for me to go back aft and pretend to do my job," he replied, winking. "Call me if you need anything, though preferably not a PECU, okay?"

"If I need a PECU, it'll be to cut through your thick skull," Rose retorted automatically as she picked up the phone.

She couldn't stop from bracing for a bad reception, though. No matter how hard she tried.

The Northern Indian Ocean, HMS **Gallant**

The days felt like they were getting longer on board Britain's most famous submarine.

So far this patrol, *Gallant* had found and sunk a pair of Indian *Akulas*—they had to be running short of those boats, which was unfortunate, because Ursula preferred her enemy with less effective submarines—and a trio of destroyers. It was a good accounting for by any measure, but still not *Barracuda*. Not the boat she *needed* to find, the one her country, and their allies, were desperate to sink.

Even better, now she found herself surfaced to take a phone call from Rear Admiral Collins, the submarine force commander to whom *Gallant* was assigned to. Their conversation was one of the *least* productive chats she'd ever had with a superior officer, and it left Captain Ursula North wanting to punch someone or something.

Unfortunately, she was surrounded by metal and sailors who she liked, which left her with nothing to hit but her own pillow once she reached her cabin. How disappointing.

"All settled, ma'am?" James Harrison, her first officer, asked as she squeezed her way out of the radio room.

Ursula scowled. "The damned Americans want to send one of their own after Rochambeau."

"Whatever for?"

"Apparently, we're not finding him fast enough," she spat. "I'd like to see them bloody well do better."

"Whoever they send is likely to get killed." James's eyes grew dark with worry. "The Americans don't have anyone good enough, do they?"

It wasn't ego that prompted that question; it was experience. No one knew better than Ursula and James how bloody *good* Rochambeau was at this business. They'd drilled against him before the war, and now they were tasked with finding him as he sank Alliance submarine after submarine. Jules Rochambeau had a gift. One that couldn't be quantified or explained because it wasn't just the sum of his training or his experience. Hell, Ursula wasn't always sure *she* was good enough to kill her old ally and acquaintance. She just knew she was better than everyone else, which meant the job fell to her.

"No." Ursula walked over to the navigation table, zooming the chart out so she could look at most of the Indian Ocean. Icons danced across the display, most of them merchants grouped together in convoys for protection or warships protecting said convoys. A plan started to form as she chewed her lower lip. "Perhaps it is time to create bait that my old friend can't refuse."

"What are you thinking?"

"He likes the grand targets. Ones there is 'glory' in killing. Or interviews with the bloody press." She rolled her eyes. Ursula did interviews when her nation told her to, but she'd never found much joy in it. Perhaps she would relish them after sinking *Barracuda.* "So...we give him something he cannot refuse."

It was a dangerous idea, and might end with a lot of dead Alliance sailors, but what other choice did they have?

Naval Base Perth, Australia

Nancy spent the steel beach picnic getting to know *Cape St. George's* crew. At first glance, they seemed professional and cheerful, but she could sense an ugly undercurrent raging. What caused it? No one was going to tell the new XO. Tradition said the XO was the Designated Bad Guy, which meant Nancy was assumed to be the enemy until she proved otherwise.

No, she'd have to earn their trust before anyone told her anything of note. For now, she just introduced herself to as many people as she could, stuffed her memory full of names and faces, and listened.

Eventually, that listening paid off. Just as she piled onions on her burger—a habit Alex *hated* and said made her breath stink to high heaven—she overheard two junior officers talking. One was the fire control officer, if she remembered correctly, and she hadn't met the other one, though he was just an ensign and looked wet behind the ears.

"Watch out or she'll make you walk her dog," FCO said. "She's got this little yappy thing that she's in love with, but it bites everyone else. I've got a mark on my ankle from a month ago that still hasn't faded. Baby Doc said it got infected, but he wouldn't report it because it'd just piss her off."

Nancy cocked her head, stared at the impromptu game of catch happening on the flight deck, and pretended not to listen as Ensign Gallagher replied:

"You're joking, right?"

"Nope." FCO shook her head. "She usually keeps the damn thing on board, but she sent it ashore since we got the reporter."

"I thought Jake was joking about the Rowlings' Ravings Log."

"Ha. No. I wish. She wants to be Lord Fucking Nelson, but the bitch was born in the wrong century."

Nancy blinked. That was ominous. The dog thing more than Nelson; ambition was a fine thing in a naval officer. However, hearing junior officers disparage their captain so openly was...well, even with a war on, *bad*. Still, she had to keep an open mind. FCO seemed levelheaded when Nancy talked to her, but who knew for certain?

So she turned away from that conversation and made her way back over to her new captain. Command was lonely; Nancy knew that from experience. Her job was to be Helen Rowlings' right hand—and sometimes her left—and if that meant keeping her out of trouble, well, Nancy knew how to do that, too. It had been a long time since she'd been an XO, but the rust should fall off easily enough.

"What's this I hear about a reporter, Captain?" she asked.

"Oh, I forgot to tell you." Rowlings beamed like a grandmother who was proud of her family. "Eric Armstrong from ABC Washington is on assignment with us. *Cape* was chosen to be one of the first ships with an embedded reporter so that the public can see the war up close and personal."

"I assume not too personal? We get to clear what he transmits, right?" Nancy's heart hammered for a moment as she thought about all the security concerns involved in keeping a reporter out of sensitive and classified events, not to mention areas on the ship. God, how could they police what the crew *said* to Armstrong?

This was going to be a nightmare.

Rowlings chuckled. "Every second of it. That'll be your fun job, of course. You and CSO."

"I look forward to it." Nancy didn't, of course, but the XO usually got all the odd jobs, and most of the unpleasant ones, too. So the nightmare belonged to her. No big surprise.

"Excuse me, Captain, XO." A watchstander approached, his eyes a little too wide for Nancy's tastes.

"What is it, French?" Rowlings' smile snapped into a scowl.

French swallowed, his Adam's apple bobbing. "We got flash orders. *Lexington* is down an escort, and we're to join her ASAP."

"How soon is ASAP?" Rowlings curled her nose. "And take your hand out of your pockets when you talk to me, you son of a bitch."

Nancy stared, but French just yanked his free hand out of his pocket, wearing a resigned expression. "Chat from the strike group says no later than sunset, ma'am."

"Very well." Rowlings turned to Nancy. "Time for you to earn your keep, XO. Navigation brief in three hours, and underway within two hours after that. Can you manage?"

Three hours to make a nav plan and then two hours to get underway on a ship she didn't know with people she'd barely met? That sounded like the kind of challenge Nancy lived for, so she pushed her worries about Rowlings' short temper aside and grinned. "You bet I can, Captain."

"What do you think, Bobby?"

It took Bobby a moment to realize the captain was speaking to him, that Alex *wanted* to hear his opinion. That was the most unsettling thing about all of this, even more than the lack of yelling. Rubbing his hands together, Bobby snuck one more look at the periscope display. The ferry was still tooling around on the surface, looking normal.

Innocent.

"I think it's odd that he's not calling for help if he's just sitting there at five knots," Bobby said. "I mean, why waste the money? I suppose he could be doing lifeboat drills or something, but I think ferries are supposed to do those pier side, and they wouldn't take this long anyway, right?"

"Merchants aren't exactly my expertise, but I'd guess you're right." Alex started playing with his glasses instead of chewing on them, but Bobby just knew they'd go into his mouth before long.

Maybe he could get the captain's coffee a refill. Maybe that would keep him from chewing on them. More comfortable or not, Bobby *refused* to tell the captain how much that grossed him out.

"It's more likely Rose is right," Bobby pointed out, and Alex inclined his head.

"Point. Good eyes, Weps." He turned to the assembled watch team. "Anybody find a picture of this guy on the internet yet?"

"I got a close match, Captain." It was Chief Andreas. "She looks a lot like *Spirit of Kangaroo Island II*, but this guy's got a lot more antennas."

Bobby shifted to peer over one of Andreas' shoulders while Alex looked over the other. The chief held a tablet showing a good side view of *Spirit of Kangaroo Island II*. The hull shape was right, the paint job was spot on...and there were far too many antennas.

"And radars," Bobby said, counting spherical radar domes. "Way too many of those, too."

"That one looks a lot like Top Plate radar." Rose pointed at a dish on the top of the ferry. Typical that Rose would remember that; she had all kinds of weapons and radar odds and ends stored in her skull. *Top Plate* was the codeword for an older Russian 3D radar, the Fregat MR-710. It was on a lot of their destroyers and, as far as Bobby knew, was never sold for civilian use.

Alex blinked. "It does."

Silence reigned in control for a long moment; everyone waited for the captain to make a decision. And now he was chewing his glasses again.

Bobby sighed. He'd just have to get used to that.

"What do you want to do, sir?" he asked when he couldn't take the quiet any longer.

"Unfortunately, we don't have much of a choice. Let's get in close and watch him." Alex shook his head. "I don't think he'll have organic sonar, but just in case, let's creep in at ten knots."

"You're thinking he's military." Bobby looked back at the ferry on the periscope display. There were cars on deck. Were those part of a disguise?

The captain frowned. "I'm thinking he's something. More is just speculation at this point."

"And if you were going to speculate?" Bobby asked. "Me, I'd guess that he's trying to disguise himself, just like Elmer Fudd used to do so he could hunt Bugs Bunny. But if he's only got a shotgun, that's not going to do him much good."

Crap, he was babbling again. Bobby had hoped that habit vanished with Peterson.

"I'd guess that he's an intel gatherer in disguise. But the real question isn't what he's pretending to be," Alex said. "It's whether or not he's carrying passengers."

Bobby's jaw dropped. "You think the Russians would actually put *civilians* on a ship they're sending to spy on us?"

"I think we're not going to be the first navy to sink a passenger ferry, so yeah. I do." Alex scowled. "Let's get in close."

"You got it, Captain," Rose replied, since she still had the watch. Bobby didn't bother to observe while she coached Max through the drill of bringing *Bluefish* close in on the ferry's heels. He was more interested in the idea of the Russians using their super-secret spy ship as a ferry.

It was dirty, and it endangered civilians...but they weren't *Russian* civilians, were they? Those ferries ran between Australia, Paupa New Guinea, and various Indonesian nations. If the Russians managed to spoof up a fake one or just talk the owners into playing a double game, they wouldn't endanger their own people. Crap, that could change the entire war, couldn't it? Bobby shivered. So far, everyone had been careful not to target civilians. Nations were doubly willing to pay reparations when non-combatants got hurt by accident. What happened if the Russians no longer wanted to play by those rules?

"Captain, we're getting a message from the SUBRON to wrap things up and come on in," the radio watch reported, making everyone turn to look at her.

"What?" Alex asked. "We're not due back for two weeks."

"That's what it says, sir. Change of orders, apparently."

Alex's scowl spoke volumes, and Bobby braced himself for an explosion. They'd only been underway for six days, and the standard patrol was at least twice that.

"You sure about that?" Bobby asked.

The young electronics technician bobbed her head. "I asked for confirmation from the tactical watch, sir. They said come on back."

"All right." Alex let out a breath. "Let's snap a few pictures of this would-be ferry before we head out."

Bobby caught his captain's eye, but Alex only shook his head. Whatever was going on, the captain had no more idea than Bobby did.

Submarine Squadron 29 Headquarters, Perth, Australia

Steve was glad to be on dry land again. Once *Nereus* pulled into Perth that morning, *Perch's* crew scattered to the winds. They'd all received orders before the sub tender made port, which Steve supposed was one of the few good things about being on a surface ship. *They* got regular email. He hated to see the crew fall apart, but that was the name of the game.

He had orders, too. Steve's first reaction was disappointment: he was headed to the no-load submarine of Perth, USS *Bluefish*, the dregs of the fleet. But Captain Dalton dropped a bug in his ear. *Bluefish* had a new CO in Alex Coleman, and that made Steve sit up straight. Going to a boat commanded by the only living submariner Medal of Honor winner would be good for his career. If half the game was getting noticed, this could get him there!

Unfortunately, *Bluefish* was underway, which meant he was off to report to SUBRON 29. That meant going to a brick building instead of a boat, but at least they'd arranged for a room for him at the Combined Bachelors' Quarters, or CBQ. Steve had already filed for his survivors' allowance to replace all the uniforms he'd lost on *Perch*, and being in port gave him the opportunity to go shopping. And take a few days' leave. First, however, he needed to get to know the staff at his new SUBRON, since *Perch* had been assigned to SUBRON 13.

As a bonus, the first woman he ran into was cute, with fuzzy hair and a slender gymnast's build. She was a lieutenant commander, like him. "Looking for someone?" she asked with a smile.

"I'm here to check in for temporary duty." Steve smiled, holding out a hand. "Steve Harper."

"Maggie Bennett. I'm the staff intel officer." She shook his hand. "What boat are you headed to?"

"*Bluefish*. I was *Perch's* XO...before." He repressed the urge to shudder, thinking of the water coming in and the boat going down, thinking of people left behind and—

"Damn. I'm sorry." Maggie grimaced.

"Me, too." For some reason, Commander Singleton's face flashed through his mind. Steve pushed that aside. *Perch's* chapter in his life was over. Now he was headed toward *Bluefish*, and where he'd be the best XO in the fleet. Shaking himself, Steve changed the subject: "How'd the staff intel officer end up with dolphins?"

"I was a submariner before I saw the light." Maggie chuckled. "Now I try to keep you lot out of trouble."

He grinned. "Some of us need more of that than others. Maybe even a bit of a personal touch?"

"If that's a come on, it's a pretty clumsy one." Her eyebrows rose.

"What can I say? I'm a bit out of practice." Though the communications officer on *Nereus* hadn't thought so. Still, she was going to be out of reach soon, and she'd been a bit young for Steve's tastes, anyway.

"I doubt *that*." Maggie rolled her eyes.

"Maybe not." Steve grinned. She seemed amused, if a little sassy. He liked sassy. "But a little modesty never hurts."

"And a little fraternization never helps, either." She crossed her arms. "You might want to find another tree, Steve. But I'll take you to admin to get checked in."

"It's not really frat between two lieutenant commanders," he objected as he followed her. "Besides, I'll be on the boat soon enough, and—"

Maggie stopped, turning to glare at him. "And I'm not the kind of girl who likes being come onto like a freight train, either. Please stop."

"Sure. Sorry." Steve blinked. "Didn't mean to offend."

Maggie flashed him a grin. "If you'd offended me, you'd know. You're just not my type."

"Right." Shrugging, Steve followed her to get his paperwork sorted out. At least he wouldn't be at the squadron very long, and he *did* still have his last girlfriend to fall back on.

Going in early made no sense to Alex, but orders were orders. He wasn't going to shoot the messenger. The SUBRON watch in Perth didn't have answers, so he brought his boat around and headed back home. While she was still shallow, he shot an email off to Commander Reyes, the squadron chief of staff.

> *If getting a new XO for BLF is a problem, I recommend that we spot promote Lieutenant O'Kane and put him in the job. He's the navigator and senior department head, and he's been filling in as acting XO for months. He's doing well and has command potential.*

> *I'd be satisfied with a new navigator to replace him and letting him do the XO's job full time. Let me know if this helps with the SNAFU of the bureau's personnel difficulties, and I'll write up the spot promote letter ASAP.*

There. It was done. Alex supposed that he should've done it sooner. After his last experience with a "real" XO, he should've known that getting someone educated in the schoolhouse to fill the job wouldn't guarantee someone who could actually *do* it. Bobby held himself together well in combat and had good instincts. He had a bit to learn about management, and maybe he freaked out a bit when a neighboring XO came over to bully him, but he was still doing a good job. And Alex didn't have to send him to his room when the shooting started.

George Kirkland would've flipped his lid when the firing key was missing, and everything would've gone downhill from there. Yeah, this was the right call. With his luck, the squadron would give him someone like Lieutenant Commander Song. Better the devil he knew.

Chapter 17

The Short Patrol Season

Alex conned *Bluefish* into port with the help of one tug. He hated needing a tug, but Bobby was right about the damned outboard. Every American attack sub possessed one screw or propeller. In *Bluefish's* case, the screw was a propulsor wrapped in a metal shroud to diffuse the noise of the blades moving through the water. The rudder's placement in front of the screw complicated maneuvering on the surface, where *Ceros* were notorious for driving like drunk hippos. Having only served on *Virginias* and *Jimmy Carter* prior to his new boat, Alex hadn't believed the stories. Now he knew they were true.

Needing the tug to push the bow to the pier made him scowl. Alex imagined *Bluefish* could get off the pier alone if offsetting winds helped them, but onsetting winds would pin her there no matter what he did. Thankfully, that was a problem for another day. His lines were across and *Bluefish* back against the same pier. *Kansas* was noticeably absent.

Not that Alex minded. Every confrontation he didn't have with Chris Kennedy was a victory.

"All right. Once the plant spins down, give the crew as much liberty as we can afford," Alex told Bobby.

Bobby started. "You don't want me to put out in-port worklists, Captain?"

Alex shook his head. "There'll be plenty of time for that if we're in port as long as we were last time. For now, let 'em loose."

"No problem, Captain." Bobby headed back down the ladder from the sail to put down liberty call, but Alex stayed up there for a few minutes.

Coming back into port after sinking only one enemy was strange. Sure, he'd only had six days to do it, and they'd also sank two merchants who supplying India, but it still felt like failure. Logic said otherwise; Alex knew that a lot of subs came back into port without a single kill to their name. Hell, that had been his life on *Jimmy Carter.* But he couldn't quite overcome the feeling in the pit of his stomach.

On the bright side, no one important was waiting on the pier. Alex would take that while he could. Maybe he wouldn't have to do any more interviews, either.

That was an even happier thought.

Kansas headed out as *Bluefish* headed in, this time assigned to an outer patrol sector. Bud hoped that meant they'd actually do the job they were supposed to do, instead of wandering off wherever the captain wanted to go, but his hopes were dashed before they'd been underway for more than a day.

It wasn't his fault that he had good ears. It was practically a job requirement for a sonar operator, and Bud had always been too good at eavesdropping. It was why they'd called him The Menace in high school, but it had gotten him a lot of dates, too. Unfortunately, overhearing this conversation wasn't going to get him the girl. Particularly since the girl in question was Commander Song, and Bud wasn't dumb enough to come on to his XO. Particularly not when he was pretty sure she was part dragon.

"We got lucky that no one pressed the point of us not being in our box when that *Yasen* sucked *Bluefish* out, sir," Song said quietly. The respectful way she spoke identified the other party to the conversation, and Bud's heart sank. If anyone found him listening in on the captain and XO, he was toast.

He'd been trying so damned hard to be the model sailor. He hadn't had a drop to drink during their last in port period, and given his previous drunken habits, that was saying something. Hell, he'd tried out an Alcoholics Anonymous meeting, too, but that really hadn't been for him.

"Then we'll be more careful this time. Luckily, our patrol area is bigger." Kennedy sounded pensive but not worried. "If there's no good pickings where we're assigned—which there probably won't be, since they put us lowly *Virginias* closer in—we'll drift east. Rumor says that the French are building a new sub base out of Île Amsterdam, and I bet we can catch someone coming our way from there."

"Île Amsterdam is a long way from our boxes," Song objected.

"Would you rather sit at home and let hotdogs like *Bluefish* get all the glory?"

"Of course not." He could hear her scowl. "That entire crew is an undisciplined mess. I could train monkeys to behave better than they do."

"It's not a surprise." Kennedy sniffed. "I know Coleman from before the war. That medal he's wearing came from a combination of really good luck and an utter disrespect for anything resembling a tactical norm."

"Not given their 'acting' XO, either. He's a child."

Were they talking about Commander Vanderbilt? Bud remembered *Bluefish's* XO, and he'd been a pretty solid dude. He'd had to be, to stand up to Commander Peterson— Wait a minute. Coleman? Medal? Who they were talking about sank in. Captain Coleman was on *Bluefish*? Bud almost laughed out loud. The irony of that assignment was thicker than *Bluefish's* hull. Why the hell couldn't he go back there? Oh, no, he was stuck on board a boat where the CO felt like following some rules and breaking others.

Had Kennedy ever even heard of irony? The man was the biggest hypocrite Bud had ever met.

"Back to my point," Kennedy said. "We'll drift east. If anyone calls us on it, we'll chalk it up to gyro failure—just stay deep enough that we can't get a GPS fix and that'll work out fine. But I don't think Commodore Banks will object if we bag ourselves a few French ships. He's not happy with *Bluefish* taking all the limelight, either."

Song hesitated. "Maybe we should ask him if we can expand our operational area?"

"No. Half of the assignments come straight from COMSUBPAC, and 'Uncle Marco' loves to play favorites. Until we get lucky, we'll be left out in the cold—so I intend to make our own luck."

"Yes, sir." She sounded doubtful, but she wasn't really arguing, was she?

Bud wanted to growl. Song seemed like a by-the-book sort, so why was she playing long with this idiocy? And more importantly, how long did they have until this idiocy got Kansas—and everyone on board—killed?

7 February 2040

Perhaps she was wrong about needing to bait a trap. *Barracuda* was right here, and Ursula was fairly sure he'd yet to detect *Gallant*.

"You're certain that it's *Barracuda*?" she asked her leading sonar chief, leaning over his shoulder.

His glare was just on the polite side of annoyed. "Look for yourself, Captain. The computer concurs: this is *Requin* 722. That's her, undoubtedly."

"Very well." Ursula straightened, ignoring the twinge in her back. "Range?"

"A touch over eleven nautical miles, ma'am. I have him via bottom bounce."

"And does he have *us* in these conditions?" Ursula was no sonar expert, but she knew enough to understand that sound gradients weren't always where you expected them to be. However, they usually were quite predictable once you found them.

"Perhaps." Her chief chewed his lip. "We will know when we move in closer, I hope."

"Indeed." Nodding her thanks, Ursula headed back into *Gallant's* attack center. "Pass the word to man action stations," she told her senior watchkeeper.

"Yes, ma'am!"

Gallant's crew rushed to their battle stations, an exercise made quick by years of practice. Most of the crew had been together since the war's start in April 2038. Only a few officers got replaced along the way, which was an unavoidable result of the Royal Navy's personnel system. Ursula avoided personnel rotations like the pox; her best were *the* best Britain had to offer. She had no intention of ruining her crew's integrity merely for the sake of career progression. She let some officers go when she was ready to lose them and not a moment before.

Sooner or later, she'd have to let go of her first officer, but today was not that day. James met her in the attack center, wiping sleep out of his eyes and drinking a cup of tea.

"Something unexpected, Captain?"

"Yes. It seems my friend on *Barracuda* decided to make an appearance after all." She snorted. "After all the work you and I put into planning a trap for him, he obliges us early. Bloody typical of him, isn't it?"

"It would appear to be so, ma'am." James' smile was more serious than Ursula's bared-teeth grin, but she could see the excitement in his eyes.

The bastard wasn't getting away this time.

Steel coiled around Ursula's spine. She was done with this chase. It was time to *end* things, once and for all.

Like clockwork, Bobby put in yet another order for outboard parts. Lou's engineers thought the seals were leaking again, so a new set was on the way, along with an expert to install them. Unfortunately, neither the contractor nor the parts would arrive for another week, which seemed fine until *Bluefish* received orders to get underway two whole days after getting back.

"You know what's going on, Captain?" Bobby asked Alex over breakfast the morning after they'd pulled in.

"Not a clue." Alex was on cup of coffee number two. Did he inhale the stuff? But Alex was a lot less grouchy after he had caffeine in his system, so Bobby wasn't complaining. "Commodore's on leave and COS has no idea."

"That's just awesome."

"Tell me about it."

"The outboard's still going to be broke, sir." Bobby surprised himself by not flinching.

"Fucking beautiful." Alex sighed. "Guess you'd better schedule a tug, then."

Bobby nodded. "You got it."

The next two days flew by. *Bluefish* loaded stores—thankfully, they didn't need much food, although Bobby laughed when their long-overdue ice cream finally arrived. Peterson would've been pleased, but at least now the crew would benefit. However, they got no new torpedoes, which would annoy the *current* captain. According to Rose, the weapons depot wouldn't pony up reloads when *Bluefish* still had twenty-two torps, a fact she announced at their weekly department head meeting with the captain. That was the first time any of them ever heard Captain Coleman raise his voice outside combat.

"You've got to be fucking kidding me," he said.

"I wish," Rose scowled. "Apparently, we squeak in just under their rule about minimum percentage of weapons capacity required to get underway."

The captain's eyes narrowed. "And let me guess, they won't give us Harpoons to fill in the empty slots?"

"No, sir." Rose let out a breath. "They say they're backordered. So are the torpedoes, actually. They're putting ADCAPS on some subs because there aren't any ASVs available."

"How the hell can *weapons* be backordered during a war?"

No one wanted to answer that, so the department heads remained uncomfortably quiet while the captain glared at no one in particular. Finally, Bobby decided that he shouldn't let someone else fall on this sword.

"We've still got twenty-two—"

"That'll be fan-fucking-tabulous comfort if we run out of torps in the middle of an engagement," the captain snarled. Then he shook himself. "But short of yelling at the weapons depot, there's not a damned thing I can do, is there?"

They all exchanged glances. Brigette, the junior person in the room, looked ready to sink into the deck. Lou and Rose only looked resigned. Master Chief Baker appeared unworried. Bobby wished he felt that way, too.

"Not really, sir," he said.

"And yelling at you lot won't make things better." Alex sighed. "My apologies. My experiences with running out of torps ranges from bad to absolute shit, but none of you deserve to be targeted for it."

Bobby stared. To his left, Rose, Lou, and Brigette did the same. None of them knew what to make of a captain who didn't berate them for things outside their control.

"Worse things have happened, sir," Bobby finally said for all of them. "I mean, if you targeted us with a nuke, at least it'd be over quick."

Alex barked out a laugh. "Yeah, and I'd be left with the fallout. No thanks."

"I was thinking more of mutually assured destruction, sir."

"Wow, that paints a happy picture." Alex shook his head. "You guys react this happily when Peterson bitched you out?"

"Mostly we just took it." Rose shrugged, looking like she didn't know what to make of this but was determined to be brutally honest. "Wasn't much use in mouthing off to him. He always won."

"That's the perk of being the boss." Alex smiled crookedly. "But being an asshole isn't. Or shouldn't be. So feel free to tell me if I start being one."

Realization hit Bobby like lightning. They were in the Twilight Zone! That explained everything. Somehow, they'd tripped and fallen into the wrong timeline, one where *Bluefish* was normal and successful. Somehow, Bobby stopped himself from saying that aloud. Unfortunately, that gave Rose a moment to grin and say:

"That's Bobby's job, sir."

"He's the high-and-mighty acting XO and all," Lou added.

Brigette just watched with wide eyes. Bobby, however, couldn't let that stand.

"Watch yourself, Rosie. I can make you all kinds of miserable as the acting XO, you know." He grinned, turning to Lou. "And I know where *you* sleep."

Lou shrugged. Rose laughed. "Sure, you can."

"All right, children," Alex interrupted before they could continue bickering. "Behave yourselves. We've got a boat to get underway, lack of torpedoes or not. So let's get to work."

His grin took any sting out of the order, and Bobby realized with a start that he'd been enjoying himself. On *Bluefish*. What had the world come to?

9 February 2040, The Arabian Sea

Tension ratcheted up; *Gallant* crept in. Oblivious, *Barracuda* coasted onward, seemingly unaware of their enemy. But Ursula knew that couldn't be the case. If her navy provided her with the best watch keepers they had, the French had undoubtedly done the same for Rochambeau. Otherwise, any fool could have killed *Barracuda* by now.

Steadying herself with a deep breath, Ursula planted herself in the middle of the attack center instead of prowling like a trapped tiger. Her chest was tight and her spine stiff; she was so ready for this to be over. The closer she got, the more the thought of killing her onetime ally, the man she'd almost called a friend, rankled. She bit the word out: "Range?"

"Down to nine nautical miles, Captain."

"Very good." Ursula resisted the urge to grind her teeth as numbers marched through her mind. *Gallant* carried the same Mark 84 ASV torpedo as her friends in the Alliance. While it was the fastest torpedo invented by Britain or America, its range was somewhat limited. Fortunately, the longer-legged French F21 Artemis torpedo was slower, which evened the playing field nicely.

"Captain, I have multiple surface contacts at long range," Sonar reported. "Likely range thirty-plus nautical miles, along the same bearing as *Barracuda.*"

Ursula nodded, looking at the chart. That was probably a convoy. Under other circumstances, she'd investigate. Ursula preferred not wasting torpedoes on merchants unless they were high-value targets, but some of them could be. And they'd have escorts, which were always worth sinking. But no. Her orders were to sink Rochambeau. The convoy might be friendly, anyway.

Of course, that meant he'd turn toward it if Rochambeau was unaware of *Gallant* closing his position. She knew where this led, so Ursula glanced at James.

"Work up an intercept solution assuming *Barracuda* heads for the convoy," she ordered.

"Aye, ma'am," James replied. "Do you think he's missed us, then?"

"I think discounting any possibility where Captain Rochambeau is concerned is folly." Ursula squared her shoulders. "Stay under fifteen knots if possible."

James nodded. They both knew that *Gallant's* builders claimed she could run silently at up to twenty-four knots...and they both knew that was a lie. *Gallant* was reasonably quiet up to fifteen knots. After that, her reactor coolant pumps ran loud. Loud enough for detection. *Barracuda* probably couldn't hear them at this range, but why find out?

Ursula shivered. Her enemies—and maybe even her friends—might say she had nerves of steel, but the closer she got to killing Jules Rochambeau, the more her stomach churned with a mixture of anxiety and...what? It wasn't fear. Maybe it was regret. Or sorrow for how the world *should* have been.

This war, this world war, ought never have been. Ursula knew that. She'd grown in up a world that thought itself too advanced for a world-spanning navy war, one where powerful nations might fight proxy wars elsewhere but never really went toe-to-toe. Yet the advent of undersea exploitation had changed *everything*, and now here they were. Submarines hunted submarines in the pursuit of one country or another owning more underwater territory.

Was there territory to be gained from her current fight? Of course not. Like every war ever fought, mission creep snuck through the cracks. So here Ursula was, out to sink a man who was supposed to be a friend just a few short years ago, back when British and French submarines squared up for friendly matches in the Channel.

Today would not be friendly.

A tug eased *Bluefish* away from the pier on the morning of 9 February. Alex's crew was in reasonably high spirits; he could see a new spring in most sailors' steps. There was more laughter, and the enlisted crew members no longer jetted out of a space the moment Alex arrived. Earning the officers' trust was tricky, but even that trickled downhill. Particularly after word got around that Alex was only an ogre *before* his second cup of coffee.

He hid a smile behind his coffee mug. Bobby had the conn to take them out of Perth, and Alex wasn't surprised that he was a talented ship handler. He'd make a good XO. Yeah, Bobby would have to grow a little, but war did that to all of them, didn't it? Even thinking back to his *own* career and actions before the war was a little mind-boggling, wasn't it?

Alex stayed on the bridge until *Bluefish* cleared the channel and prepared to submerge. By then, the sun was fully up, and he'd had those two cups of coffee, making him suitable to co-exist with real humans. Early morning underways weren't his forte, and Alex had skipped breakfast to catch as much sleep as possible.

"Feeling more social now, Captain?" Bobby asked after he turned the watch over to Rose, who was the normal morning officer of the deck.

Caught walking to the control coffee pot to refill his mug, Alex grinned. "Noticed that, have you?"

"I'd have to be blind to miss it, sir. I mean, being one of the three blind mice could be cool and all, but that would kind of suck on a submarine. I'd run into everything."

Alex laughed, almost spilling his new coffee. "Making your captain dump coffee on himself is frowned upon, you know."

"If was *trying* to make you spill your coffee, I'd do something really diabolical, like have Rose make a sudden turn—"

"Into a seamount?" Alex cut in, gesturing at the chart. *Bluefish's* current course held her squeaking between two underwater mountains.

Bobby shrugged. "We'd do a *Hunt for Red October* and turn at the last minute. You'd spill your coffee, we'd outfox the torpedo, and we'd be set."

"There's a torpedo in this mess now, is there?" Alex laughed. Now that Bobby wasn't a ball of tension likely to explode at any moment, his logic was always fun.

"I'm sure it's around somewhere, sir. Probably back in the weapons depot, since they wouldn't give us any new ones."

"No shit." Alex shook his head. "All right. We've had enough fun. Let's head out to our patrol area and see what we can find."

"Enough fun?" Bobby grinned. "I thought being in the navy was supposed to be an *adventure*. Or at least that's what they told me at the academy."

"XO, if you haven't figured out that the academy lies to you by now, you're in the wrong business."

The intercom beside Jules Rochambeau's computer crackled softly.

"Captain, *Gallant* is closing for an intercept at fifteen knots."

Jules sat up straight. He'd left the control center to do a little paperwork—a strangely calming activity—but now it was time to rejoin the game. "I will be there momentarily," he told the officer of the watch. "Continue as before."

"*Oui*."

The *Requin*-class design was a good one, and Jules was out of his stateroom and into control within seconds. A quick glance around told him his crew was ready. They'd closed up to battle stations and were poised to sink *Gallant* the moment she came close enough. Technically, the British submarine was in range now, both of their old Artemis torpedoes and the new Rafales, but Jules did not believe in taking chances. The Rafales were fast enough to have difficulty turning. That meant the only certain way to kill *Gallant* was to get in close and take a straight shot. If Lady North couldn't dodge, her boat couldn't survive.

"What is the range to the convoy?" he asked.

"Seventeen miles and closing."

Jules stroked his chin. "Continue to close at fifteen knots." He would not make it too easy for Ursula. He needed her to think he was here for the convoy, not for her.

Jules had chosen his position carefully and scouted the convoy before allowing *Gallant* to close with him. It was an Alliance convoy, and a lightly defended one, at that. With only two frigates and a littoral combat ship to protect twelve merchants, Ursula would feel obligated to take action, particularly after he sunk the frigates.

While she was busy racing to the rescue like a lady knight, Jules would sink *Gallant.* He smiled sadly. Hopefully, Ursula would survive. If not, she would understand. He would in her place, anyway. They were not close, but Jules knew that Ursula understood duty. It was a pity—and a welcome challenge—that fate and France's territorial ambitions placed them on opposite sides of the war.

"Distance to *Gallant*?" he asked after *Barracuda* settled onto the new course.

"Holding at nine miles, Captain."

"Very well." Jules took a deep breath. They would need seven hours to reach the convoy due to their speed and his. Alas, that made for a long wait. Would Ursula get impatient and fire? There was no knowing with her. Still, it paid to be cautious when leading the enemy into a trap. "Increase speed to eighteen knots. That will keep her further back."

His officer of the watch grinned. "It is a pity that the *Gallants* are so loud over fifteen knots, *mon capitain*."

"Indeed. Such a pity." Jules knew Ursula would wish to remain undetected. She'd allow *Barracuda* to increase the range as long as she could keep them on sonar. Of course, he'd need to change course to shoot at the convoy's escorts, at which point she would be able to catch him.

Assuming he did not sink *Gallant* first.

Twelve hours later, *Bluefish* settled into her patrol sector and started looking for targets. With no contacts in the area, Alex ordered *Bluefish* to come up in satellite Link 18 with other Alliance warships, which gave them a long-range view of other ships in the area. Link 18 was the Alliance's newest version of radar, fire control, and sonar sharing software. It allowed ships, aircraft, and subs to exchange tracks and even fire on one another's data. Using Link was significantly less detectable than active sonar, although Alex still preferred to remain passive and allow no emissions to leave his submarine. In a situation like this, with no one nearby, Link was a useful way to find targets.

"OOD, looks like we have a convoy at long range. Picking up Link tracks from *Fitzroy*. Other escorts are *Buckley* and *Oakland*," the fire control tech on watch reported.

"Very well." Harri nodded, looking jittery. She'd been jumped by that *Akula III* on their last patrol, and now her captain breathed down her neck on this watch.

Not that Alex was there to watch her. If Alex lacked confidence in Harri's abilities, he'd just take her off of the watchbill. But the navigation plot and chart display was in control, and he needed to be there to plan *Bluefish's* next move. His patrol sector was a big one, and it was up to Alex to decide where to go. Too bad the area they found that suspicious ferry in was far away. He grimaced. Alex wasn't stupid enough to go prancing into someone else's sector. That was a quick way to accidentally kill a friend.

The three Link tracks popped up on the display, and Alex clicked them for details. *Fitzroy* and *Buckley* were both frigates, whereas *Oakland* was an older littoral combat ship. Seeing that made Alex grimace. The last time he'd worked with a littoral combat ship, he'd watched *Billings* blown into tiny pieces by the missile attack that kicked off Convoy 57. This twelve-ship convoy was a big one, too, and it reminded him uncomfortably of the one he'd protected with *Jimmy Carter*.

"We got a convoy number for these guys?" he asked.

"Today's random number is 487," FT2 Kay replied, grinning. Most of the navy found it silly that convoy numbers weren't assigned chronologically. Someone, somewhere, thought that was a good security precaution.

"Thanks, FT2." Moving over to the classified computer in control, Alex looked up the Convoy 487 formation message. Sure enough, there was a sub assigned to the convoy, too. "Any word from *Pacu*?"

"Nothing yet, sir. They may be running silently."

"Aye." Alex nodded. That was what he would do. Logic said there was nothing to worry about. *Pacu* was another *Cero*, commissioned a year before *Bluefish*. Alex didn't know her CO—*Pacu* was based out of Pearl Harbor—but the boat didn't have a bad reputation.

No reputation usually meant competent but not flashy, Alex reminded himself. There'd been a time when he'd fit into that category, and he was still trying to figure out how the hell he'd left it.

Flashy? He'd never wanted to be flashy. Just good at his job.

"What's our range to them?" he asked.

"A bit over two hundred nautical miles, sir." Harri's answer showed that she was paying attention, and Alex shot her a smile.

"All right. Keep an eye on them and let me know if anything changes," he ordered. "I'm heading down for the night. Don't be afraid to call."

"I won't be, sir," she promised, and Alex believed her.

Maybe he'd finally broken Peterson's invisible grip on the crew.

The convoy changed course, turning their seven-hour chase into fifteen hours. Now it was well into *Gallant's* night, and Ursula secured from action stations to get her crew some rest. Like all Royal Navy submarines, *Gallant* remained on local time to her homeport, regardless of where she was physically located. Ursula was a harsh taskmistress, but she refused take an exhausted crew into battle. Particularly against *Barracuda.*

Unfortunately, she didn't think Rochambeau would be that stupid, either.

Staring at the ceiling did not help her sleep. Jules Rochambeau was clever, which meant he was up to something. Otherwise, why creep up on the convoy so slowly? Was he wary of an unseen submarine escort? *Gallant* had good reads on the three surface escorts, but she hadn't seen any sign of an American attack sub along for the ride. Sometimes the Americans didn't send one, which she thought was the height of arrogance, but—

Knock, knock.

"Enter!" Ursula sat up, twisting to face the door as James walked in, his dark face pinched with concern.

"Captain, I've looked up the convoy formation message for the ships *Barracuda* is tracking. They're supposed to have an American boat along." The worry in James' voice made Ursula cock her head; he was too unflappable to fret over small things. Unlike her.

"And?" Ursula asked.

"They have an escort. *Pacu.* She's a *Cero*-class boat, original build." James frowned. "But there's no sign of her."

Ursula scowled, following his train of thought. "If another bloody American pulls an Alex Coleman and gets in between me and—"

"I worry she's already been sunk," James cut her off. He never did that, and Ursula felt her eyes go wide.

"You think Rochambeau is hoping to trap *us*," she hissed between gritted teeth.

"I cannot discount the possibility, Captain."

"Which would mean he's been leading us toward the convoy the entire time. And that he knows we're here." Ursula wanted to spit fire and was on her feet in an instant.

"He might not." James chewed his lip. "There's no way to know."

"Oh, there's a bloody way," she spat. "Jules Rochambeau does nothing by accident, James. He's the canniest son of a bitch you'll ever encounter, and worse yet, he likes to *play* with his food before he eats it. This is all a game to him."

"*If* the American is sunk," he reminded her. "Do you want to contact the senior frigate to ask?"

Ursula growled under her breath. "No, then he'll know we're here."

She was out of good options, so which bad one to take? The repeater plot in her stateroom told Ursula the convoy's range was down to twelve miles. They—and *Barracu-*

da—were overtaking the convoy from astern. The slow way. Melting glaciers felt faster than this, and worse yet, any shot they took would be a bad one. Yet that worked in her favor, since Rochambeau would have to sprint to close the distance before shooting, but it also meant *her* shot at *him* was also a stern shot. Even worse, *Barracuda's* maximum speed was almost ten knots greater than *Gallant's.* He could outrun her, if he wanted to.

She had to change the odds. "Come."

Without waiting for James to answer, Ursula slipped her feet in her shoes and stalked out to the attack center. A few minutes of playing with courses later, she had her answer.

"Come right to zero-one-six and increase speed to thirty-five knots," she ordered. "Once we're twelve nautical miles away from him, come down to five knots and drop beneath the layer."

That would open the distance between *Gallant* and *Barracuda*, a move she didn't enjoy making, but it would also force Rochambeau to stop following the convoy to keep pace with her. And if she made the move quickly enough, she might make *Barracuda* lose her track when she hid underneath the thermal layer. If she timed it right, *Gallant* could wait for *Barracuda* there, and then it would be over.

After another bloody hour of waiting.

Ursula burned for a drink.

Alex was in the middle of a dream about space shuttles shooting torpedoes when the knock on his door woke him up.

More accurately, a *pounding* on his door woke him up.

"Um...?" One eye blinked open. "Come in!"

A harried looking Master Chief Baker glared at him as she flipped the light on. His COB waited a moment before speaking, but Alex's brain flipped into high drive and started working. A knock in the middle of the night meant something had happened, although he couldn't figure out why no one had used the stupid phone. Wasn't that why it was there?

"You knocked your phone off the hook," Baker said as Alex stared at her dumbly.

"Oh." Sure enough, the offending thing was lying on the floor next to his rack instead of hanging on the wall. "What's up?"

"We just got a SUBMISS/SUBSUNK message in for *Pacu*."

"Shit." Alex rolled out of bed and grabbed for his coveralls. "What time is it?"

"Zero four."

Alex groaned. "I'll be in control in a sec. Start closing the convoy. Sprint and drift like our lives depend on it."

Baker left, leaving Alex to hurriedly dress and follow her. They were still almost two hundred miles away from Convoy 487, which meant a whole lot of nothing was going to happen fast, but he still had to see what he could do.

"Son of a bitch!"

Ursula had guessed wrong. USS *Fitzroy* ate a torpedo five minutes after *Gallant* received news of *Pacu's* sinking, and Ursula slammed her fist against the nearest padded bulkhead. She wasn't angry enough to hit something she could damage, and she'd broken her hand smacking a metal support two years ago. She wasn't dumb enough to do that again, but punching things made her feel better, at least in tiny and insignificant ways.

"Ahead flank," she ordered. "Close the convoy, Commander."

"Aye, aye, Captain." James's face was as white as it ever was, and when their eyes met, she felt the anger radiating from his bones.

She'd arsed this up. Now they were sixteen miles away from the convoy and out on its starboard side. *Barracuda* had followed them for a few miles and then they lost one another in the thermal layer. She assumed that Rochambeau continued searching for *Gallant*, but she'd been wrong. No, the bastard had been *humoring* her. Playing with her.

Again.

This was all a game for him, wasn't it? Lord, she felt stupid for her earlier regret. Now she just wanted to shank his arse and watch that infernal submarine implode. No mourning. No sorrow. Just good, old-fashioned warfare leading to a cold and dark end.

Ursula bared her teeth at the tactical display. She was not finished. Yes, thanks to her mistakes, Rochambeau would hear her coming. Yes, there was nothing she could do about that. But she would still find a way to end him.

Hours ticked by as *Gallant* raced to the convoy's defense, and Ursula's temper just spun higher and higher. Perhaps it was exhaustion. She could tell herself that a thousand times, and it might even be true.

"No track on *Barracuda*, ma'am," the sonar supervisor reported, his voice quiet.

Ursula punched the padded bulkhead again and ignored it when several sailors flinched. "Keep searching," she snapped.

A few minutes later, James approached and spoke quietly. "Sonar has another contact, Captain."

"Oh?" Ursula twisted to face him, resisting the urge to swear. The fact that sonar had told her first officer and *not* reported the contact in the traditional way meant someone didn't want to get yelled at...and that meant it wasn't *Barracuda*. "Tell me it's *Pacu* and the bloody Americans stuffed this up in spades."

"No, ma'am." He swallowed. "It's *Bluefish.*"

"Alex *fucking* Coleman?" The words rolled out of her with the force of an explosion. "Again? Why the *hell* is that bastard *always* around when I lose Rochambeau?"

No one answered.

15 February 2040, the Indian Ocean

Fitzroy sank before *Bluefish* was even in spitting distance, and much to her crew's chagrin, they picked up the escort duty from the late and lamented *Pacu*. Six days later, they made port in Bahrain, spent eighteen hours resupplying, and then headed back south. By then, Bobby could sense everyone's frustration. They hadn't managed to engage the enemy, and there was no time for liberty in Bahrain. When Bobby asked the captain why they'd had such a quick turnaround, he only shrugged and handed over their orders—which contained nothing that couldn't wait a few days.

Bobby tried not to feel hemmed in when *Bluefish* got underway again, and the feeling vanished within a few days like it always did. This time, their first order of business was to check in on the Agalega Farmstead, a series of underwater stations off the coast of the Agalega Islands. They had the misfortune of being part of the Alliance and located in predominately French and French-Alliance waters, but when *Bluefish* arrived, things seemed moderately secure. The farmstead's owners had purchased three German Type 214 submarines to stand guard over their property, so *Bluefish* just checked in on them and continued onward.

Most of the crew hoped that some French submarine might stumble upon them, but unfortunately, they weren't so lucky. The great big goose egg earned during the impromptu convoy escort left no one satisfied, and grumbling started by the time *Bluefish* headed toward Armistice Station. At least action was likely *there.*

"Great big nada, sir," FT2 Kay reported as Bobby paced. Harri slept off a stomach bug while Bobby took her watch. It wasn't like he could to sleep on the approaches to Armistice Station, anyway. He was glad for something to do.

"Really?" Bobby asked. "This has been one of the biggest repeat battlegrounds of the war. There's *nothing* here?"

Armistice Station was the biggest and oldest independent station in the world. A combination fishing, farming, and mining station, Armistice Station was worth *billions.* Between the manganese mining and the oil well, its owners had done very well for themselves before going public in 2035. Both sides wanted to own the station, which tried to remain neutral. The Freedom Union killed that notion when they invaded the station last year, but the Alliance took it back in January with much fanfare.

"Station says all is fine and they're secure, sir." Kay shrugged. "I can ask again if you want."

"No, that's okay." Bobby bounced on his toes. This was stupid. Boring was supposed to be good in wartime, and *Bluefish* was supposed to be used to it. When had he started craving action?

Alex sounded equally annoyed when Bobby called with that report. Still, they'd done their job, so it was on to a trio of Australian stations so close to Australia that no one needed to check on them. Apparently *someone* wanted *Bluefish* to do that, though, so Bobby sent the boat in that direction, skirting between operating areas and hoping no one decided to shoot them thinking they were an enemy.

It was so much fun it hurt.

Chapter 18

Good Subordinates

1 March 2040, the Indian Ocean

Two merchants. That was all *Bluefish* sank before she headed back into Perth and then, much to Alex's surprise, spun around and headed back out again. That pattern held for the rest of February and the beginning of March: six or seven days underway followed by a day or two in port, rinse and repeat. *Bluefish* didn't catch much, aside from a Russian *Husky*-class guided missile submarine they sent to the bottom toward the end of February. Alex found a SSGN's presence heading toward Australia unsettling, and apparently Commodore Banks agreed with him. The next few weeks were spent looking for *Huskies* between in-port periods and coming up dry.

It was like the world's worst job of whack-a-mole. Meanwhile, he fielded frustrated emails from his wife about *her* new boss, who seemed twice as capable but three times as pedantic as his own—assuming that was possible—and irate messages from crew members' families who wanted to know why *Bluefish* was suddenly the busiest boat in the fleet.

Alex knew how to commiserate with Nancy's situation, but how the hell did he explain the feeling of makework to his crew, let alone their friends and families?

"I feel like a California burger joint, Captain," Bobby said as *Bluefish* got underway for the sixth time in seven weeks.

"What?" Alex blinked.

"In-N-Out. You've never heard of them?"

"No. Should I have?"

Bobby shrugged. "The name's pretty self-explanatory. The burgers are good, but the menu's limited." He hesitated, glancing around, and Alex followed his gaze. They were alone on the bridge except for the lookouts, which seemed to reassure him. "The crew's pretty tired, Captain."

"I know." Alex sighed. *Bluefish* had spent a grand total of twelve days in port out of the last forty-nine. One long underway would be no problem, but constantly going in and out of port was another matter. Turning the boat around to get underway less than eighteen hours after making port meant loading stores instead of sleeping, and everyone was exhausted. "Hopefully this is the last one."

"Do you know something I don't know, sir?" Bobby sounded hopeful.

"No." Alex shook his head. "But the pace is fucking untenable and doesn't give us long enough to settle in and find the enemy, so it's hurting our efficiency. Sooner or later, someone's going to figure that out."

"I sure hope so." Bobby slumped against the side of the sail.

"Me, too," Alex said quietly.

The day they returned from that underway—after sinking a single *Scorpene* and chasing numerous sonar ghosts reported by surface ships—Alex's schedule finally synced up with his wife's.

"Sorry for not figuring out somewhere fancier," he said as he and Nancy squeezed into an empty table at the Perth Officers'

Club. "The way things are going, I never know when a call will come in."

Nancy cocked an eyebrow, looking him over. "You look exhausted."

"Yeah." Alex shrugged. "It's been a long six weeks."

"Everyone on our crew look this bad, or you just running yourself ragged like an idiot?"

"I hope the crew's doing better than I am," Alex replied. Not having an XO was getting old. Bobby did his best, but he was still the navigator. That left Alex liaising with the SUBRON over things his XO usually handled. Between that and *Bluefish's* insane patrol schedule, Alex was beat.

"You want to get a hotel room tonight?" Nancy asked. "We're in port for a week."

Alex sighed. "I wish. But we're still on a twelve-hour alert."

Technically, he could sleep away from the boat. Hell, Alex allowed his sailors to when they weren't on duty. A twelve-hour alert meant *Bluefish* was expected to keep her reactor hot and be underway within twelve hours, *any* twelve hours, which meant half the crew needed to stay on board. Still, he could get back to the boat from any hotel in Perth in under an hour, but the idea of sleeping elsewhere left Alex uncomfortable. No matter how much he missed his wife.

"We aren't, but we might as well be." Nancy shook her head. "First underway *should* have been quiet—*Lexington* needed someone to ride shotgun, and we got the call. But that morphed into chasing down and boarding three merchants. Our boarding teams were busy, let me tell you."

There was something in her face, something in the way her eyes narrowed, that told Alex there was more to the story. He cocked his head, curiosity chasing away his fatigue. "Bad kind of busy?"

"We've only got two qualified teams. The one we left on the third ship as a prize crew was..." Nancy grimaced. "They're good kids, but I wouldn't have left them alone over there."

"Wait, Rowlings actually put *prize crews* on merchant ships? Like, to steal them? What is this, the age of sail?"

"Felt like. But the reporter we've got on board loved it. Did an entire video blog about how *Cape* is 'creatively sourcing the war effort.' It'll release next week."

"Jesus."

"Tell me about it." Nancy scraped her hands over her face. "It's not illegal. It's not immoral. It's just...not done? I don't know what to make of her, Alex."

He might've snickered if Nancy didn't seem so lost. "I thought she was the demon who chased XOs away. Kind of like people say I did to George."

George Kirkland had been *Alex's* first—and thus far only, unless one counted Bobby—XO. He'd come apart under fire, and Alex had more or less kicked him out of control so he could get on with the fight, but Rowlings' reputation said she chewed up XOs and spat them out again.

"I'm starting to wonder if some of my predecessors weren't George-esque," Nancy replied. "But I know Cat Markham. She's not incompetent, and she's not a coward. So it makes no sense."

"You're getting along with Rowlings okay?"

"Most of the time. Just getting to know her, and yeah, she's a hardass who doesn't like the word 'no,' but she sure knows how to get the job done." Nancy shrugged. "I've worked for worse. She's not Admiral McNally, shooting the wrong guy and then cocking it all up when shit hits the fan, that's for sure."

"It'd be hard to match that standard, babe."

Nancy chuckled.

"Hey, wait, did you say *reporter*?" Alex's mind finally reeled in one of Nancy's other comments, and his jaw dropped. "Why do you have a reporter on board?"

"You haven't heard of the new initiative? They're calling it 'View from the Front,' and *Cape's* one of the pilot ships. We've got a guy from ABC on board. He'd been pretty decent so far."

Alex snorted. "Wow, what a ringing endorsement."

"Says the man who looks ready to fall asleep at this table." Nancy grinned. "My captain might be aggressive, but we're doing better than you on work-life balance, I think."

"It's the job. Ours is not to reason why."

"Your sense of duty will be the death of you," she said.

Alex snorted. "Commodore Banks' inability to plan ahead will get me first."

Except he knew that wasn't true. No other boat assigned to SUBRON 29 had these problems. Just his. Was he that good at making friends?

"You going do something about that?" Nancy crossed her arms.

"He's my boss, Nance."

"That doesn't give him license to be stupid." She glared. "Someone needs to speak up. Exhausted people make mistakes."

Alex squirmed. Banks already hated him for not being Peterson. "Even if I said something..."

"You're not just a sub CO now, Alex." Nancy's eyes narrowed. "No one can ignore that medal, even you."

"I know." He slumped. "Waiting for sanity to break out hasn't gotten me very far."

"How someone as argumentative as you can hate confrontation, I don't know." She smiled, reaching across the table and squeezing his hand. "I suppose I'll keep you, anyway."

"If I buy you a drink, will that sweeten the deal?" Alex grinned. Damn, he wanted to drink himself into oblivion, but that was a terrible idea as a sitting CO.

"One's my limit. My captain may be logical than your boss, but I'm not sure I'd want to head back to the ship tipsy, if you know what I mean."

"Yeah, I hear you." Rising, Alex headed to the bar. The O Club was crowded with naval officers who wanted to drink without leaving the base. Unlike the U.S., the Australians kept their Officers' Clubs open, and Perth's had doubled in size since the start of the war. Alex spotted a trio of *Bluefish* division officers over in one corner, laughing and joking with their counterparts from another boat. They looked tired, but more at ease than they had since his arrival, and—

Another shoulder jarred his. "Excuse me," Alex said automatically.

"You really are good at bumbling into places you aren't wanted, Commander Coleman," an accented and biting voice said.

"What?" Dumbfounded, Alex turned to face Captain Ursula North. They were both in civilian clothes, but any submariner would recognize her, with how the Brits plastered her face on every other recruiting poster. Still, he was surprised she'd recognized him. They'd only met once.

A sudden thought hit: had her boat commandeering *Bluefish's* supply onload *not* been an accident?

She rolled her eyes. "You're bloody blind, too, aren't you?"

"Not last I checked." Alex gritted his teeth. "And it's Captain Coleman now, by the way." He didn't like throwing his rank around, but the way North looked at him like he was dirt on her shoe rankled.

"Oh, congratulations. Did they promote you for ruining someone else's shot like you ruined mine?"

"Not exactly." He'd been promoted after Convoy 57, but Alex still remembered the day *Jimmy Carter* had encountered *Gallant.* He met her angry glare. "I see they didn't promote *you* for standing by while Rochambeau sunk another Alliance submarine."

North loomed close, her face suddenly inches from his. "I was doing my job!"

"So was I." Alex refused to flinch.

"Terribly, as it turns out." She snorted, leaning back against the bar again. "Stay out of my way, Coleman. Including at sea."

"Oh, gladly. I wouldn't want to stumble in the Sea Witch's path." Spinning on his heel, Alex headed back to Nancy. He didn't need a drink badly enough to deal with Britain's darling.

Even if the way Ursula North gnashed her teeth and swore at his backside made him want to get flaming drunk.

Fortunately, he didn't give into that urge, because Bobby O'Kane stuck his head in Alex's stateroom ten minutes after

Alex's alarm went off the next morning. He hadn't gotten out of bed yet; lying there, staring at the overhead and missing his wife, had seemed like a superior option until the knock on the door startled him.

Bobby, fortunately, had grown enough that he didn't even wait for an invitation to open it. "We're a ping pong ball again, Captain."

Alex sighed and sat up. "What time?"

"Underway sked for noon. I've already initiated a crew recall," his acting XO said.

"That's flexing a twelve-hour alert pretty hard." Alex frowned. "When did we get the call?"

"Twenty minutes ago." Bobby scowled. "No tugs provided, either. Some nincompoop thinks the outboard's going to work."

Alex chuckled. Three months on *Bluefish* put him in the never-trust-the-bow-thruster club. Maybe Bobby was right, and it was possessed. Most *Ceros* had a reliable thruster. *Bluefish* didn't. "Someone going to dance in the moonlight and sacrifice to the outboard gods?"

"It's a little early for moonlight, Captain, but I'll get Weps to dance." Bobby grinned.

"Weps? I'll believe that when I see it."

Bobby snickered. "Okay, maybe Master Chief Baker?"

"Oh, get out!" Laughing, Alex shooed Bobby back through the door. "Let me know if someone can't be contacted."

"Aye, sir." Still grinning, Bobby headed out, leaving Alex alone with his thoughts.

Damn, Bobby had come a long way. The nervous stutter was gone, replaced by an irreverent sense of humor Alex treasured. He hoped the squadron got back to him soon. Alex didn't need an XO; he had one. But it would be nice if they'd fork over a new navigator.

Speaking of the SUBRON, he had a call to make. Luckily, Banks was a morning person, and Alex reached him before eight.

"What can I do for you, Captain? Is there some reason you can't get underway?" As always, Banks sounded like there was something stuck under his nose.

"No, sir, we're on track."

"Good." Banks paused. "I realize you were on alert twelve and we only gave you five hours of warning. I appreciate the flexibility."

Alex grimaced. Hating Banks was harder when he acted reasonably. "Sir, about that... These short patrols are exhausting my crew. We're good to go today, but *Bluefish* is going to need some downtime soon."

"I see." The sound of Banks pursing his lips was audible.

"We need a few weeks to do major maintenance. I've had to defer—"

"I hear you, Captain," Banks cut him off. "Frankly, I'm surprised that crew of yours hasn't fallen apart already. From what I understand, they're not particularly reliable."

"*What?* No, they're a good group." Alex bit off the urge to blame Peterson for the mess he'd inherited. He knew Peterson and Banks were friends, so it didn't take much imagination to know how well that would go over. "But tired people make mistakes, and we've been underway twenty-three out of the last thirty-two days."

"I'll see what I can do," Banks said as if he wasn't the one who approved schedules for his squadron's boats.

Good subordinates didn't point shit like that out. Alex swallowed. "Thank you, sir."

8 March 2040, the Indian Ocean approaches to Australia

Bud Wilson didn't like chiefs, but he sure as shit wished he had one right now. Under normal circumstances, he could ask

Master Chief Casey for advice, but they were at battle stations and the COB was busy. Besides, him wandering off station to go talk to the COB would be noticed by both the captain and the XO, and that wasn't the kind of attention Bud wanted. Not on this boat, and not with those two being as shady as a pair of palm trees.

Sure, he could suck up like the rest of the hopeless idiots on *Kansas*, but Bud had always been contrary. Did he blame the others for playing the game and pretending they didn't know what tricks Commander Kennedy pulled to get more kills? Nah. But the idea of twisting himself into a knot to playing along left him cranky. Problem was Kennedy's habit of wandering had already netted them two *Huskies* and an *Akula*, which meant everyone on board felt pretty good. Bud didn't mind killing the enemy, and he'd been the one to detect the *Huskies*, but doing it this way still felt wrong. Probably because being *there* meant not being where they were *supposed* to be, and that meant someone else could be sneaking in the back door to rob the Alliance blind.

Damn strategic thinking. Being a half-drunk drone was so much simpler.

Worse, he knew how lucky they'd gotten lucky with that second *Husky*. It had been creeping up on the *Saratoga* battle group when Kennedy had felt the need to return to the edges of his own sector, and they'd managed to sink it before the *Husky* could launch more than two of its forty 3M22 Zircon hypersonic cruise missiles. *Saratoga's* escorts shot the incoming missiles down, but it had been a near thing. Commander Kennedy was praised by the battle group commander for his quick actions, but Bud knew the truth. If *Kansas* had been in her own stupid boxes, she'd have detected the *Husky* sooner, and the Russian might not have launched *any* missiles.

Bud sighed. That had been a week ago, and they were finally scheduled to head into port. Maybe now that Commander Kennedy had made a name for himself, he'd be more open to doing what he was supposed to do.

Yeah. Bud shook his head. Fat fucking chance of that, wasn't there? Kennedy was chasing glory, and he was going to get everyone on the boat killed if he wasn't careful. Bud didn't have to be a navigation tech to know that they'd left their own sectors yet again. Was this the fourth time, or the sixth? He'd lost count and didn't dare taken notes. Still, the internal nav system fed right into his integrated sonar plot, and Bud could read a chart. They were in sectors belonging to USS *Lionfish*, tooling around the northeastern edge where Indians were more likely to encroach.

Not swearing out loud was hard. He had a job to do no matter how he felt about his captain, so he turned in his seat, missing *Jimmy Carter's* separate sonar space. Whatever kind of idiot decided to put the sonar consoles smack in control where the command team could watch sonar techs drooling needed to be shot.

Bud scowled at his waterfall screen. "Captain, Sonar recommends decreasing speed due to poor sonar conditions."

"How poor?" Kennedy asked, walking in Bud's direction right away. He was a loomer, and Bud hated that about him.

"Piss poor," Bud said before he could stop himself. He could feel Song's eyes burning into the back of his neck but continued: "Detection range on the passive arrays is down to six thousand yards, sir, and decreasing."

"Why?" Song demanded, still glaring. "And keep it professional, STS1."

"Aye, ma'am." Bud managed not to scowl at her. "A sh—*significant amount* of background noise is impacting detection ranges. Bunch of biologics to starboard, and that underwater volcano bubbling at two-one-one isn't helping, either. The filters can't do jack about it."

Kennedy and Song exchanged a look Bud couldn't read, so he turned back to his console again. Even a sonar operator knew that jetting around at twenty-two knots when you couldn't hear a stereo at six thousand yards was just stupid.

"Maintain course and speed," Kennedy ordered a moment later. "Keep your ears open, though, STS1."

"Sonar, aye." There wasn't much else Bud could say. A first class petty officer couldn't tell his captain that he thought he was stupid, particularly not *this* captain. And definitely not with Song waiting to pounce.

Except Song kept throwing concerned glances Kennedy's way, as if she wasn't quite sure of his tactics. Maybe that meant she thought this was a bad idea, too. Not that she'd say it. Lieutenant Commander Song wasn't the type to contradict her commanding officer. Oh, no. That might look less than perfectly military and disciplined. Bud stuck his tongue out at his screen. At least it wouldn't complain when he described things accurately.

An hour ticked by, an hour of mind-numbing boredom complete with a sonar system that couldn't filter crap out from the squawking whales and bubbling volcano. Bud slipped one headphone off so that the noise level didn't give him a pounding headache, chewed two Motrin, and then noticed that the operator to his right, STS3 Maddie Cruz, had her volume cranked all the way down.

"Turn your volume up, kid," he said in an undertone.

"I can't hear jack over the background noise, STS1," she replied. "Why bother?"

"Cause sometimes the system is dumb and the human ear is better." Reaching over, Bud twisted the knob back up. "Take one ear off if it starts to bother you."

She rolled her eyes. "It's freaking pointless."

Bud snorted. "Welcome to the navy."

Cruz giggled and opened her mouth to respond, only to be cut off.

"Is there a problem over there, STS1?" Song demanded, striding over to the sonar corner.

Bud stepped on the urge to be an ass. "No, ma'am. Just doing a little training."

Even she couldn't argue with that, could she?

"Keep it professional," Song said for the four thousandth time.

Bud rolled his eyes at his console. At least she could only see the back of his head. Cruz coughed out what sounded suspiciously like another laugh, but something *thrum-thrum-thrummed* in Bud's left ear, and he stopped caring.

Slapping his right headphone back into place, Bud quickly turned up the volume on both headphones, working his filters to try to exclude more of the volcano noise. It only worked so well; the constant rumble just wouldn't go away, and the sizzle of lava meeting seawater came on too many frequencies for him to block them all. The constant explosions were headache inducing despite the pills, too. Some of them sounded like gunshots, others like an incoming train.

Squeezing his eyes shut, Bud concentrated on the *thrumming* noise. It was too rhythmic to be nature. Whatever it was, this sound was manmade, and it was growing louder and—

Silence.

"I asked if you *understood*, STS1." Song was standing right over him when Bud opened his eyes, glaring. Had she turned his volume off?

Bud gritted his teeth. "Yeah, sure, ma'am. Can I get back to listening now?"

"'Yeah, sure' is not a proper form of military address. If you think that Silver Star is going to carry you through insubordination here—"

"XO, I'm not trying to be insubordinate, but I *am* trying to listen to something, okay? There's something manmade out there, and I'm trying to isolate it," Bud cut her off.

That finally seemed to take her aback. "Let me know when you have something," Song ordered as if she hadn't just been an ass.

"Yes, ma'am." If this was what he got for *trying* to be a well-behaved, conventional sailor, he wasn't sure he wanted to bother. There it was. *Thrum-thrum-thrum-thrum...*

"You got this, Cruz?" he asked.

A moment passed. "Something out to starboard?"

"Yeah. I think it's fading back aft, moving right to left behind us." Bud took a breath. "OOD, can we put the tail out? I can't isolate this without—"

"In combat conditions with a potential enemy nearby to hear? I think not." Song cut in before the officer of the deck could answer. When Bud twisted to look over his shoulder, the lieutenant on watch as officer of the deck just shrugged helplessly.

"Can we come right some, then? I need to get the starboard lateral array a better chance at detecting this."

The two officers conferred, leaving Bud to go back to his console. The signal was stronger, but it kept blinking out on him. Whatever it was, the contact was moving, too, and was now in their baffles. Then an explosion from the volcano filled his ears, completely blanking out the contact. *Fuck these sonar conditions.* Bud sighed.

"Sonar recommends new course two-eight-five to unmask the starboard array," he said after a few moments of tense silence.

"Conn, aye." The officer of the deck started to order the course change, but Song shook her head.

"Come around to a reciprocal course," she said, shooting Bud a triumphant smirk that said she knew better than him. "That will unmask the starboard array in our turn and then give the bow dome the best shot at detection."

Stupid officers always thought they knew best. Yeah, the XO was right. Technically. But flipping around on an unidentified contact was dangerous, too.

Still, Bud supposed it was their risk to take. Officers drove. He just listened.

"Sonar designates new contact as track number 6874," he announced, struggling to find it again. "Tentative classification as submerged." Bud grimaced; no way was she gong to listen to his next recommendation: "Sonar recommends decreasing speed to eight knots for better detection."

"Negative. Maintain speed." Kennedy's voice made Bud's head jerk up. The captain had left control earlier, but now he was back, and the Shady Sisters (shady duo just didn't sound good enough for the captain and XO) were side by side.

"OOD, aye." Poor Lieutenant Hanson sounded like he thought they weren't being smart, and Bud would be dipped in shit if he was wrong.

"System evaluation?" Kennedy demanded.

"Nothing yet, sir," Cruz answered as Bud listened.

If he could extrapolate the missing sounds, assuming the *thrumming* came in a pattern led him to blade count—

"What do you mean, nothing yet?" Kennedy asked. "Is the sonar computer down?"

"No, sir," Cruz replied. "There's just a lot of background noise. It can't hold the track."

Kansas swept into the turn, which was tighter and faster than it probably should have been since the OOD used too much rudder. Bud just turned his attention back to sonar, decreasing his filter power as *Kansas'* starboard side lateral array gained the contact. It was still *thrumming* away, no longer fading in and out, just being overpowered by the rumbling volcano.

Bud tweaked another few settings with his left hand, scribbling notes on the monitor in grease pencil with his right.

There. That should be enough for the system to chew on. It would need a few minutes, but Bud didn't. The sound was still getting louder, though, not drawing off to starboard like he'd expected. *Thrum-thrum-thrum...* Was that a tick on the sixty-six hertz line? Bud squeezed his eyes shut again. Nothing in the Indian inventory sounded like that, and the Russians didn't—

"Shit!" His eyes flew open. "Captain, I think we've got a *Cero* close aboard. Range hard to guess, something less than four thousand—"

"What? Are you sure?" Kennedy rushed over, but Bud didn't look up.

Where the fuck was the guy? Bud watched the sonar trace jumping on his screen as the system tried to hold the track. Another gunshot sound pierced his left ear like a hot poker. *Shit, shit, shit, shit.* "I can't hold this guy with the background noise. Sonar recommends coming left to course zero-zero-zero."

Zero-zero-zero was a safety course. Any American submarine would see a quick turn to the triple goose eggs and do the same, and two subs on the same course *couldn't* hit each other.

"What?" Kennedy sounded more incredulous than worried. Bud wanted to shake him, but his hands were too busy.

Thrum-thrum-thrum-thrum-thrum. "Captain, I've got no bearing drift. Sound incoming but not moving laterally—"

"Set battle stations!" Kennedy barked.

Bud ignored the wailing of the general alarm. "Sir, we've got to—"

Screech!

Metal kissed metal, ending in a snap. A strange tinkling sound, almost like breaking glass, filled Bud's ears, growing louder and louder. *Kansas* rocked left as Bud tore his headphones off, sure they were going to collide with *something.* Cruz yelped, and Kennedy staggered. Song managed to keep her balance, but her voice shook as she demanded:

"What happened? What was that?"

Hell if Bud knew.

He just knew it was bad.

Chapter 19

Ping Pong

Kansas rolled back on an even keel as Bud clung to his console for balance. Then a vicious thought hit him, and Bud hit the sonar feed onto the speakers. A scraping sound overrode the constant background rumble, high-pitched and awful. He flinched away from the speaker, cringing and really glad that he was sitting at the console instead of struggling to remain upright as the boat did her best impression of a bucking bronco.

"What the fuck did we hit, man?" Cruz demanded.

Bud just shook his head. "Nothing good. But if it was another boat or a torp, we'd be dead by now."

"Maybe a depth charge?"

"No way." Memory made Bud shudder. "Those are a lot louder and don't sound like metal hitting metal. We'd also be deader than dead if one bounced off the hull."

"What the hell did you let happen, STS1?" Song stalked over, her glare up to a couple thousand megawatts and growing. "What hit us?"

Bud shot a glare over his shoulder. "Fuck if I know, ma'am. Probably the *Cero* I told you about a few moments ago."

"Don't you—"

"I'm not interested in assigning blame, XO." Much to Bud's surprise, Kennedy stepped up in his defense. "Let's assess the damage and get back to our sectors."

Oh, great. *Finally* the captain decided to do the right thing. Bud managed not to say that aloud, instead pulling his headset back on and turning back to his console. He could do nothing to help with this copper-plated clusterfuck. He was just a freaking sonar tech, and his job was to give recommendations, not make decisions. He'd never wanted to be anything else, not before now. Now, however, for the first time in his career, Bud started to wonder if maybe he wanted to be a decision-maker.

Could he do worse than these glory-hunting chucklefucks? God, it would be hard.

Reports flowed in; despite the rocking and rolling she'd done, *Kansas* seemed to be in okay shape. There was a strange thumping sound out to starboard that kept blanking out parts of their lateral sonar array, but that was the worst of the damage. A few people were hurt, but nothing serious, which left Bud both relieved and a little bit bummed. If someone had a real injury, like something serious, Kennedy might've learned his lesson. That was a horrible thought, but Bud was pretty sure he'd take that one for the team if it made *Kansas*' command team pull their respective heads out of their asses.

A concussion would be all right. He'd gotten a few playing hockey, and it wouldn't be the end of the world, but it would get him the hell off this crazy boat. Even a broken leg. He'd heard that worked for Commander Vanderbilt, formerly of *Bluefish.*

Finally, *Kansas* crept a dozen miles away from the sight of the collision and surfaced. Bud wasn't qualified as a lookout on this boat—he was senior enough that no one cared to make him requalify—so he didn't expect to get a look at what had happened. At least not until Song came back down into control, storm clouds dancing across her eyebrows.

"STS1, join us on the bridge." Her imperious gesture belonged on some old world queen, not a naval officer, but who was he to argue?

"Yes, ma'am." There was no point in further antagonizing her. Bud scrambled up the ladder and squeezed into the small bridge area up in the sail.

At least the weather was nice. The last time Bud had been topside on a submarine underway, he'd been swept half overboard and almost drowned. *Kansas* was a lot less fun than *Jimmy Carter*, but there was that.

There was also something caught on *Kansas'* barely visible starboard bow plane, scraping against the hull where it stuck out of the water. "Ah, shit."

"You have a concise way with words, STS1." Kennedy looked unhappy with Bud's language, but at least he didn't chastise him.

Not like a lecture or two was going to fix him, no matter how much they complained.

"I do what I can, sir." Bud grinned briefly before cold sobriety hit him. "But yeah, that's a hydrophone array, or most of one. Looks like a TB-34."

A TB-34 meant a *Virginia* or one of the earlier *Ceros*, like one of Bud's previous boats. But it wasn't their array—Bud was pretty sure you *could* twist around stupidly enough to get your array wrapped around your own bow plane, but only if you really fucking tried. But *Kansas'* array hadn't been out because Song hadn't wanted to deploy it.

"Looks like we got an extra tail," he quipped before he could stop himself. Kennedy glared.

"That's inappropriate, STS1."

"Sorry, sir." Bud was even a little sorry, but only because some poor bastard out there had just gotten his towed array ripped off by *Kansas*. Right after he'd told his CO and XO that there was another American submarine out there. "We have any idea whose it was?"

"No." Kennedy's expression grew stormy. "We'll send out divers and get rid of the thing. You don't think it still works, do you?"

"No, sir." Bud could see innards of the acoustic module and the nose cone was cracked, too. "Cheaper to buy a new one."

"Very well." Kennedy swung to face Bud, looking him right in the eye. "This doesn't leave the boat. Understood?"

Bud tensed. "Captain?"

"The last thing the navy needs right now is reports of our subs making physical contact with one another." The captain crossed his arms, his voice suspiciously calm. A distant part of Bud noted that Kennedy had avoided saying they'd *collided,* even though they had. "This did *not* happen."

"Someone's gonna be missing that array, sir." Bud had to try common sense. Even if it wasn't his best color.

"You leave that to me."

Bud hesitated. He could buck these orders and raise a stink...but to who? Who would believe a sonar tech on his last fucking chance—or a couple of chances past that, if Bud was going to be honest—with a reputation for drunken antics? Sure, he had the Silver Star, but most folks thought that just meant he'd been lucky once.

"You're up for chief this year, aren't you, STS1?" Kennedy asked when Bud didn't answer.

Fuck. A year ago, Bud would have told Kennedy that he didn't care about making chief. But now he did. Now he wanted to make a difference, and this asshole was going to hold his fucking career hostage over *Kennedy's* own stupidity.

"Yes, sir," Bud said.

To give Kennedy credit, he didn't try outright bribery or threats. He just waited. Bud sighed.

"Ain't no one going to believe me, anyway, sir. You write it up however the fuck you want." *And you don't screw me when it comes to writing my evaluation, either, thanks,* he didn't add.

Kennedy nodded, and Bud headed back into the skin of the submarine as quickly as he could get away with it.

"There she is again, Captain."

Chance put *Bluefish* was back in the vicinity of the strange ferry. Most ferries stuck to the same route, and *Spirit of Kangaroo Island II* remained in the same general area as before, miles away from any of the normal ferry routes. Yet Alex's instincts told him there was something off about this cat. She still sported too many antennas.

"What do you think, Bobby?" Alex asked.

"Now that our ESM antenna is up and listening?" Bobby grinned. "I mean, it's theoretically possible that she's a yacht for some super-rich dude who bought a bunch of Russian radars when their navy discovered capitalism, but she's a really ugly yacht, and no one's got that many cars. Particularly cheap Fords."

Alex suppressed a smile. "So a spy ship."

"Sure looks like, Captain." Bobby shrugged. "No car carrier wants that many radars. They take up too much space you could put cars in. You want to sink her?"

"I'd love to, but those are definitely passengers." Alex gestured at the periscope viewscreen.

Bobby blinked. "They could just be military dressed up in civies."

"There are different cars on board this time." Alex held up a tablet showing the periscope pictures they'd taken a month ago. "That leads me to civilians."

"Damn." At least Bobby caught on quickly. "You think they're *also* transporting passengers."

"It's smart, if diabolical." Alex sighed. "We'll track and report. Maybe someone from intel can figure out what she's doing and trace her history."

"You always pick the *boring* option, Captain." Bobby's grin undermined his sarcasm so well that Alex laughed. "If only we could do something *exciting* sometime. Then everyone would be happy."

"Tell you what, Bobby," Alex retorted. "Next time someone needs to use a PECU, I'll let you volunteer."

"Oh, no, sir. I couldn't do that. I might break a nail."

Alex threw his head back and laughed.

Watching the spy ship turned out to have interesting unintended consequences. Alex was ninety percent done writing his patrol report—easy enough, since they were scheduled to head back toward Perth the next day—when his phone rang.

"Captain."

"Good evening, sir, it's the officer of the deck," Rene said. "Sonar's got a whiff of something they think you might want to take a look at."

"I'm on my way." Alex clicked *save* and then headed out of his stateroom. Odds were his report would go straight into Banks' trash bin, anyway. The one about the Russians trying to capture submarines with submarine-laid minefields had been similarly dismissed. Why should this one be different?

Alex would write it anyway.

"What's up, Rene?" he asked, walking into control. The space hummed with energy, and Rene was near to sonar doorway.

Rene's face lit up. "I think we might have a *Requin*, Captain."

"Really?" No American boat had sunk a *Requin* yet. The Brits nailed a few—although not the one that really mattered—and a lucky Japanese CO killed three before she died. The *Requins had* turned out to be a better submarine than anyone ever imagined, deadlier even than the Russian *Yasens.* Maybe they were the best attack subs in the world, though no American wanted to admit that.

Rene pulled the curtain leading to sonar aside for him. "Yeah. Chief Andreas is on it."

"All right, then. Stay on your toes." Alex ducked through the curtain, waiting quietly for Chief Andreas to ease one ear of her headset off.

"I think we've got one, sir. *Requin* 657 or 674, system can't decide which."

Alex nodded. "So one of the earlier flight."

"Yes, sir."

Pity. The late-flight *Requins* were the real prize, but the older ones were still less than ten years old and desirable targets. Alex wasn't too proud to want to join the club of COs who'd killed a *Requin*. God knew enough *Requins* had killed his friends, even if this one wasn't the worst offender of the bunch. He'd have to be crazy to want to go after Rochambeau, anyway. His one brush with him was enough.

"Range?"

Chief Andreas' eyes slid up to meet his. "Looks like around ten thousand yards. He's headed inbound toward the ferry."

"Really?" Now that was interesting.

"CPA is zero. Looks like an intercept to me."

"I'll be damned." Alex let out a breath. "All right. I'll be in control. Call me if anything changes."

"Aye, sir."

Alex headed back into control, his mind whirling. He couldn't sink the ferry, even if he had ironclad evidence it was collaborating with a French attack sub. There were civilians on board. And if he demanded they abandoned ship before sinking them, Alex risked the ferry calling in friends. He was all right with taking small chances to save civilians, but risking his boat was another matter.

Hello, rock. The hard place is right over there.

"I hear we got something fun, Captain." Bobby's voice made him jump; Alex hadn't even realized his acting XO was in the space.

"Fun like a land mine, yeah. One we already stepped on."

Bobby grinned. "Sounds great. Can I step on it, too?"

"Jesus, Bobby." Alex shook his head, trying to stifle a laugh. "You're a strange cat sometimes."

"Honestly, sir, I generally prefer dogs. They're more loyal and less likely to take a crap on the furniture."

"You know that's what litter boxes are for, right?" Rene asked from over by the helm.

"Please don't tell me you're a cat person, Rene." Bobby flailed like he was dying as Alex watched in ill-concealed amusement. "I might need a new assistant navigator. What's Harri doing these days? I know *she* likes dogs."

Rene laughed. "Weps won't let you have her. It's a losing battle."

"I'd look great falling on my sword, though. Assuming I had a sword." Bobby shrugged. "Which I don't. Oops."

"You can borrow mine," Alex said. His was somewhere back in Groton. Keeping it on the boat was stupid, but a sword was one of those things you were supposed to have after you made a certain rank. He also owned an old cavalry saber from his alma matter, but no way would he hand a Norwich University sword to some academy grad. Even if he liked him.

"Gee, thanks, Captain. I didn't know you were so nice."

Alex gave up on trying not to laugh. "Me, neither," he said and then sobered. "But nice or not, I have a decision to make. Shoot this guy now, or wait to see what he does after he meets with the spy ferry?"

"Safer probably just to do it now." Bobby made a face. It wasn't his old uncertainty; instead, Bobby was looking at the tactical picture and *thinking*. The last month of short patrols might have worn Alex's crew down, but they were a team now.

"But no one signed us up for safer," Alex agreed. "All right. Let's go to battle stations and watch this cat for as long as we dare."

Perth, Australia

"Underway. Shift Colors."

Nancy didn't look up from her chair on the port side *Cape St. George's* bridge; she already knew that any bridge team trained by Helen Rowlings was going to be on the ball at all times. They were too on-edge not to be.

She hadn't *really* told Alex about how uneasy she was in her current role; one look at her husband's dragged-down and exhausted expression meant she kept her bitching to a minimum. If there was anything eighteen years in the navy had taught her, it was that there'd always be another chance to complain.

Speaking of complaining, it was the *lack* of complaining that struck her on *Cape*. If a bitching sailor was a happy sailor, her current crew was at rock bottom. Oh, she heard some whispers, all right. Things that left her stomach clenching, like that "Rowlings Ravings Log" Nancy overheard mention of on her first day on board. No one talked about it in *her* hearing—the XO was assumed to be the captain's stooge—but she knew it existed.

Even worse, Nancy had witnessed just enough...odd things to guess that there was a great deal of truth in that log. Like the fact that there was no coffee available on the mess decks during this underway. A shortage in Perth meant that *Cape* got less than half her usual loadout, which resulted in only the officers and the chiefs' mess being "allowed" to brew coffee. Lucky enlisted sailors who stood watch on the bridge might snag a cup, but the others either had to bring a personal stash on board, which was hard with their limited living space, or go without.

Nancy didn't love navy coffee—and wasn't the addict Alex was—so she'd always brought her own. She was old enough now to ignore being ribbed for liking frou-frou flavored coffee and senior enough to afford the good stuff. But watching sailors scramble before their underway left her feeling odd.

It wasn't right. Was it entirely wrong? Probably not. Not enough against regulations that anyone would care during wartime, anyway. Nancy knew that, too. She'd commanded a destroyer for the first year of the war and knew how little oversight successful captains received. Like it or not, Rowlings was successful.

Even if she did throw coffee mugs at people when she was angry.

Before long, *Cape* was outbound from Australia, hunting high-value merchants.

"How's it hanging, XO?"

Nancy looked up to find Eric Armstrong, the ABC reporter, standing next to her chair. Pasting on a smile was annoyingly easy; the short man was personable, and everyone on board liked him. Of course, that was his job, wasn't it?

"Same stuff, new day," she replied, glad he wasn't recording but still not willing to swear. Armstrong was a vlogger, or a video blogger, so almost all his reporting was done via "in the moment" videos, but the guy was smart and wrote good opinion pieces, too. She couldn't count how many times she'd told officers and sailors to watch what they said around him or told him he couldn't transmit this or that information.

"I hear we're hunting merchants again," he said.

Nancy narrowed her eyes. "Who told you that?"

"The captain." He shrugged. "But a little bird at the strike group told me that *someone* up high liked how we took prize vessels last time around, and now it's official tasking." Armstrong wore a hell of an innocent smile. She had to give him that.

If she felt truthful, Nancy didn't see the real downside to stealing ships serving the ULP's war effort as long as they put experienced enough people on the ships they "borrowed." That was just smart. As for the rest... Well, it was her turn to shrug.

"I'm sure some lawyers somewhere are getting warmed up to argue about it," she replied. "But that's above my paygrade. If the navy wants us out there snapping up resources so the ULP can't use them, I'm not going to complain when their beans and bullets become ours."

Armstrong laughed. "Sounds practical."

"I'm a practical woman."

"So what happens, do we just grab a bunch of merchants and lead them into port like lost ducklings?"

"Maybe. Depends on how cooperative they are." Nancy didn't relish the idea of sinking merchants, but putting a few five-inch rounds into one or two misbehaving ones wasn't going to make her lose sleep, either. "A cruiser's pretty scary, you know."

"Probably scarier than submarine because you can see us coming, yeah?" he asked.

"Don't tell my husband that." She grinned.

Armstrong laughed. "I've been meaning to ask if you're willing to do a piece on that. You're no longer the only couple in command, but you're still one of the most highly-placed marriages in the navy. People find that relatable."

Our daughters don't, Nancy didn't say, thinking back on her last email from Bobbie. Bobbie wasn't struggling at the academy these days—rather the opposite—but she got angry at the world every time one of her parents stepped into what she perceived as extra danger. As for Emily... Well, at least she was on track to go to Norwich, where Nancy could be certain people would look out for her.

"Sure," she said, because it was her job. Nancy didn't hate the spotlight like Alex did, but she really hoped Armstrong's questions focused on *her* career. She wasn't here to play second fiddle to anyone, including her maddening, wonderful, and Medal of Honor–winning husband.

"How about this evening? It'll fill the gap before we find some action."

"Let me clear it with the captain first." Nancy wondered if Rowlings would be bothered by the spotlight moving off her. Usually, Armstrong's little cameo pieces focused on Rowlings or people she chose. Would she dislike her XO suddenly filling the limelight?

No time like the present to find out.

The French sub surfaced and remained next to the ferry for an hour, unaware *Bluefish* was tracking them. Alex knew that meant he'd gotten lucky; the *Requin's* sonar suite might be better than *Bluefish's*, but they hadn't heard his boat. *Bluefish* hovered near the ferry while the *Requin* approached, with her reactor cooling pumps off line, making like a hole in the water.

Bluefish was shallow, too, sneaking her ESM mast up and catching every signal she could. Everything passed between the *Requin* and the ferry was encrypted, but Alex figured the intel bubbas would have a field day with it.

The trick, however, turned out to be getting behind the *Requin* and tracking her once she submerged again. Alex still didn't know if the spy ferry had sonar, but the last thing he wanted was for the ferry to realize that an American boat was onto her games. That would mean he'd have to sink her—and the civilians on board—or let her go, all without knowing what the ferry was up to. Talk about a lose-lose situation.

Alex didn't like this mystery. It ate at him like bad pizza, churning around in his gut. He couldn't think of anything specific a spy ship would do all the way out here, but surely the Russians—or maybe the French?—had a purpose. His enemy wasn't stupid. If they were, the war would be a lot less close.

So he waited until the *Requin* was six nautical miles away from the ferry before turning to Rose. "Make tubes one and two ready in all respects, including opening the outer doors."

"Make tubes one and two ready in all respects, including opening the outer doors, aye," Rose echoed immediately. "Outer doors open, tubes one and two ready to shoot!"

"Fire."

Bluefish was less than a mile away from the *Requin*, and the French sub only had seconds to react once two torpedoes rocketed out of *Bluefish's* tubes at eighty-seven knots. Those seconds were not enough; within two minutes, the deck rocked under Alex's feet.

"Primary and secondary explosions, Captain," sonar reported. "Breakup noises. She's not surfacing."

"Very well." Part of Alex felt a little guilty, but not enough of him. It was war. Fair was making the other guy die first. "Good job, folks. Now let's tie things up and go home."

The smiles were no longer hesitant as Alex headed back to his stateroom. He had a patrol report to finish. Maybe now he had enough evidence to make Commodore Banks pay attention. *Someone* had to figure out what this spy ship was up to, and that was intelligence's job. Alex didn't have enough information, and shoot first and ask questions later was such a bad idea here.

Unfortunately, the answers he hoped for were not in his inbox. Instead, he had an email from Uncle Marco waiting for him, one whose subject line made Alex go white in the face:

BLF selected for War Patrol Ride with Senator.

Chapter 20

Truth or Dare

15 March 2040, Perth, Australia

"You got yourself in one fucking pickle this time, didn't you, STS1?"

Bud wiggled out from under a console to look at *Kansas'* chief of the boat. Master Chief Casey had cornered Bud in the sonar room after they'd made port, doing equipment checks while his sailors went on liberty. Bud still wasn't sure if the starboard side lateral array was damaged, and he wanted to be sure before he had to use the thing during another one of their captain's harebrained schemes.

Yeah. Like staying underway for another seven days after the collision they "didn't have." So smart.

"Not sure what you're talking about, COB." Bud shoved himself back under the console to hide his face. He wasn't sure he couldn't say something about how fucking stupid the captain and XO had been between them, and there was no reason to be an idiot about this. Not now.

"Bullshit you don't. I was in control, kid, and I heard you singing out. Wasn't your fault the XO ignored you."

"Don't matter now." Bud stuck a flashlight in his mouth, hoping it would make the master chief go away.

"No? You're not going to complain to someone?"

Bud huffed, sliding back out from under the console to glare at Casey. But he didn't get up off the deck; the feel of metal under his back was grounding, somehow. "Who the hell's going to listen to me, Master Chief? I'm just a disposable sonar tech with a reputation for being drunk, stupid, and destructive. I've racked up more bar bills and damage than most people have teeth. Besides, *you're* the one who told me to keep my fucking mouth shut last time. I'm just taking your advice."

He could afford to mouth off, right? What the hell was the COB going to do to him that Commander Kennedy couldn't?

"Good." Casey snorted. "The captain's got friends enough to screw you over if you run your mouth."

"Great. Not like he needs lots in the way of friends to screw over a first class." Maybe it would take more to torpedo a master chief's career, but Bud knew no one would really notice if he stayed a first class petty officer forever. Or got demoted to second class. Again.

"Probably not, no. But you've got a gift, Wilson, so don't fuck it up. Even if you have to endure this asshattery."

Bud grimaced. "Seems like a piss-poor way to fight a war."

"It is." At least Casey didn't try to sugarcoat things. "But your day will come, so long as you don't fuck it up by fighting battles you can't win."

"I'm no Don Quixote." Bud laughed. "Ain't no windmills in my future, Master Chief."

"Smart of you. Patrol report says that we had a near-miss with a torpedo, by the way. Just in case anyone ever asks you." Casey gave him a hard look, one that made Bud want to snap back at him, but even he could tell that the master chief was trying to protect him.

"That'll explain the bow plane damage, at least." Bud rolled his eyes.

Casey shook his head. "If you're ever going to make chief, you're going to have to learn to polish a turd better than that."

"Whatever happened to just doing my job and finding the enemy first?"

"Even in war, it's not that simple," Casey said before turning and walking out of the sonar room, leaving Bud to stew.

Sometimes, he wondered if he wanted to stick around in a navy that played these stupid games, but it was the only life he knew.

What the hell else was he going to do with himself and his stupid "gift?"

Alex's unenthused response to Uncle Marco's email earned him a phone call from COMSUBPAC right after *Bluefish* made port. Once radio notified him of the call, Alex scrambled down from the bridge and headed for the privacy of his own stateroom, acid rolling through his stomach. Who the hell wanted an audience for this?

"Don't even start complaining," Admiral Rodriquez said by way of greeting. "You're one of the best we've got, even with this jerkoff of a patrol schedule Banks has had you on. And you'd have to be fucking crazy to think that I'd put a senator on another boat when I've already given yours to a goddamned Medal of Honor winner."

Alex felt the color drain out of his face. "Admiral—"

"No one expects you to be out for long. That would be utter fucking stupidity. Just take him out for a week and then come back. Try not to offend him, either. The man might be our next president."

His heart hammered into his throat so hard that Alex wanted to vomit. How the hell did he tell Rodriquez how nervous this made him? "Sir, I'm not exactly, uh, good with, uh, anything like this."

"Yeah, I watched your fucking interviews. Not that they were *complete* shitshows," Rodriquez said. "So you're not the most photogenic asshole to ever grace a television with your presence. You're better in person. And I'll send someone along to ride herd on him and hold your hand."

"Why not *Razorback*?" Alex asked. Guilt welled up immediately; who was he to wish a senator on Pat Abercrombie? She wouldn't like this much more than he did, if at all. But

Razorback still led the American pack, even though *Bluefish* was catching up. Which was a strange thought.

He really wished John was still in command of the other boat. John Dalton would have *loved* this assignment. Alex was terrified.

"Can't use her. I'm sending them after Rochambeau. Ursula North screwed the goddamned pooch again, and it's time we got some of our own back."

"Oh." Alex swallowed. So far, Ursula North had been the only one to go after Rochambeau and survive. Sending a senator on a one-way trip was probably frowned upon. "This doesn't mean we're going to be relegated to convoy escorts and—"

"Fuck no. If Senator Angler wants to go for a ride, he can take risks like the rest of us," Rodriquez replied. "Now, do you have any other objections, Captain?"

"None you'd listen to, sir," he said before he could stop himself.

Rodriquez laughed before hanging up.

Slumping in his chair, Alex stared at the phone for a long time before scraping his hands over his face. Was there a bright side of this? He couldn't think of one. Getting *more* attention would just be another way for the world to remind him of the fact that he was no longer allowed to slip into the shadows. Alex Coleman wasn't anonymous anymore, and what was he supposed to do with that?

A *senator*? Alex still wanted to vomit. Or maybe scream. How the hell had a guy with a crooked sense of humor from a little military college in Vermont squeak his way to the top?

The Indian Ocean

Nancy's relationship with her captain *had* cooled slightly after Armstrong's spotlight piece on her. Of course, Rowlings didn't *say* anything; she was proper and encouraging and everything a captain should be. But Nancy sensed a little frost entering their conversations after the interview, even though Rowlings approved it for transmit and eventual publication. Stepping on her desire to talk the problem out with her CO was hard, and Nancy reminded herself three times a day, every day, that she wasn't *Cape's* captain.

Not yet, anyway. She just had to do her job and bide her time without going insane. It helped when they had a mission to do.

"This one should be an easy one," Rowlings said as they sat down for an afternoon chat in the captain's cabin. "If intelligence is right, this Indian convoy consists of nine heavy load ships, but only one frigate defending them. Easy peasy."

Nancy pursed her lips. "Assuming the intel is correct."

"I'd think even the satellite gurus know how to count ships by now." Rowlings shrugged. "And if they're wrong and it's more of a challenge, I have every confidence that we're up to it." She bared her teeth. "If there's *one* thing you can count on this crew to do, it's fight well."

"Given what we're up against, that's what matters." Nancy had other feelings—*lots* of other feelings—but she couldn't deny the truth. Her navy was at war, and the odds weren't getting better. Being good in a fight trumped everything else; otherwise, Rowlings would've been kicked to the curb the moment she snuck a dog on board.

Nancy still hadn't met the dog in question. Apparently, Rowlings left the yapper at a friend's house while they embarked a reporter, lest the colorful parts of her personality be *too* obvious.

"Someone should tell our wardroom that." Rowlings' expression darkened. "You've seen it, haven't you?"

"Captain?" Nancy asked carefully.

"I'm sure they've talk to you. They talk to *everyone*, including that fucking reporter," Rowlings snarled. "The log. You've heard of it."

"I didn't give it much thought." Nancy knew this was the time to be cautious; though she'd been told about the Rowlings' Ravings Log, she hadn't seen it and didn't want to. Her job as XO was to support the captain, take care of the crew, and make sure the ship was in fighting shape one hundred percent of the time. She couldn't afford to get sucked into silly high school drama games.

Even if she was pretty sure the officers' objections were based very firmly in reality. Nancy could only base her actions off what *she* saw, and so far, Rowlings had been careful not to go ballistic where Nancy could see her.

"There's a small group of disgruntled officers in our wardroom. They're spreading rumors throughout the crew and convincing others that the command climate *and* my demeanor are far worse than they actually are." Rowlings scowled. "Sooner or later, Armstrong's going to eat that up for dinner."

"He seems pretty logical to me," Nancy replied. "For a reporter, I mean."

"Yes, but reporters love drama. That's why I hate having him here—he encourages the bad apples."

Nancy cocked her head. "I thought you'd requested an embarked reporter?"

"I did. It gets us extra funding and puts *Cape* on the tip of the spear. I'd be a fool not to." Rowlings sipped her coffee. "But Eric Armstrong is a smug, opinionated, and anti-war son of a bitch. If I could get away with throwing him overboard, I would."

"I haven't found him to be particularly anti-war." Nancy felt like she was walking through a field of buried landmines, none of which were flagged and all of which were ready to explode.

"That's because you haven't had to lug him around for months." Rowlings scoffed. "You'll see. He's a prick of the highest order, and I'm *certain* he's working on a major hit piece about me. Those ungrateful shits in the wardroom are probably making up tales left and right."

Oh, that was a stack to unpack, wasn't it? Nancy sat back, wishing for coffee of her own, but Rowlings hadn't offered her any. It just another power play in a long line of petty actions, like the way Rowlings had kept Nancy's *Cape St. George* ball-cap in her cabin until her third day on board, or how she *still* insisted on reviewing messages that should be approved by the XO. Six weeks after reporting on board, Nancy was fully up to speed, but Rowlings continued micromanaging...even though she knew Nancy just came from a successful command of her own.

"I'll keep an eye out for anything funky, ma'am," Nancy said. Threading this crazy needle was going to be fun, wasn't it?

Her first instinct was to go talk to a few of the officers after escaping Rowlings' cabin, but Nancy had a feeling that the captain would notice. Did Rowlings have a few loyalist spies? She wouldn't put it past her.

Nancy shivered. She hated thinking like this, hated bracing herself for insanity every time the captain opened her mouth. Rowlings was an excellent strategist and a top-notch tactician, but her paranoia was only growing. Shaking away from it was hard, so Nancy headed up to the bridge, nodded a greeting to the officer of the deck, and then stepped out into the quiet of the port bridge wing.

"You look like you've got the weight of the world on your shoulders," Eric Armstrong said.

Nancy jumped. She hadn't seen him wedged between the Nulka and a spotlight a little aft of her, probably because her mind was still doing laps around her captain's crazy.

"Sorry, didn't mean to startle you." Armstrong grinned. "Long day?"

"Long war, more like." Griping about the war was always safe; there was no way she'd tell Armstrong about the captain saying he wanted to assassinate her in the press.

"It feels like a stalemate." He pulled up a map on his tablet, gesturing at land won and lost. "The Freedom Union—forgive me, ULP—has taken all the islands and stations near India. We've got everything near Indonesia and the Strait of Malacca. The coast of Africa is split, and for some reason the ULP is moving south toward Antarctica. But right now, we seem to be hunting enemy ships more than territory."

Nancy sighed. "You're not wrong. But cruisers don't take territory. Strike groups and marine expeditionary forces do that. Our job is to destroy the enemy's ability to fight."

"That didn't work out well at Diego Garcia. I hear they stormed the place and took it. Not to mention the outright destruction of Samar Station."

"Nor the ongoing battle for Nepal." Nancy shook her head. World War III had not really been a land war so far; however, India kept nipping out and snatching territory. Rumors of brutal battles were rife, but the same common theme emerged on the land side of the war, too: no one wanted to expand the war into the civilian population if they could avoid it. Fighting for Nepal was harsh, but both sides steered civilians clear of the front lines whenever possible. Even Russia, up north, did the same as they spread into previously Japanese-owned waters with terrifying purpose. It was hard to keep track of the battles taking place in other theaters; sometimes, Nancy envied her past counterparts in World War II. At least then the news cycle had been slower and less overwhelming.

"I can't help but wonder what the hell we're doing out here," Armstrong said quietly. "Sure, hunting convoys makes sense, but..."

"Denying the enemy resources is one of the quickest ways to end them," Nancy replied.

"Yes, but if they take territory faster than we can sink their ships—or sink just as many of *ours* as we do theirs—does it even matter?"

"I wish I knew."

"They're starting to call this the War of the Submarine, you know." Armstrong pulled an article up on his tablet to show her. "Because submarines are the last true stealth weapon. People also say they're making a difference, but..."

"Submarines don't hold territory, either."

"No, but they seem able to take underwater stations, if Armistice Station is any indicator."

She smiled despite herself. "I know who was responsible for that one. Colonel Swanson is...creative, to say the least. I'm not sure I'd count that as *normal* until it's done again."

It had been too long since Nancy talked to Paul. Maybe she should drop him a line, see how life was treating him in the marines. She'd been so focused on her job, her daughters, and Alex's revolving door of successes and media attention that Nancy almost forgot she had friends all over the military. Maybe talking to them would make the war make sense.

"All the information in the world at my fingertips, and I still feel like I'm in the dark," Armstrong said. "There's just so much going on, man."

"I hear you." Nancy was usually too busy to catch up on the news; she'd had more free time as *Fletcher's* captain than she did now. Nowadays, she spent her time trying to predict what odd thing Rowlings would want next. Maybe she should spend more time paying attention to the war as a whole. After all, she wanted to move up in the navy someday. That meant thinking big picture. She needed to get her head in the game.

Or maybe she just reported to a captain who was determined to make everything about her, and Nancy just would have to gut it out until *Cape* became hers.

Bobby hadn't expected a visitor, but when the quarterdeck called to let him know that the squadron intelligence officer was there, he hurried up to meet her. *Bluefish* was on rocky ground with SUBRON 29, though Bobby wasn't sure why. He thought that the commodore should be happy with their successes, but that was way above Bobby's paygrade. Maybe Banks just missed Peterson. Regardless, antagonizing one of Banks' staffers was suicidal, so he scooted up to the quarterdeck with more enthusiasm than usual. He arrived within two minutes, whistling cheerfully—and then stopped cold.

Lieutenant Commander Bennett was a slender woman with frizzy black hair, olive skin, and dark eyes, but she was familiar. She was cute, too, for someone who dug dimples, which Bobby did. And she wore dolphins, which was weird for an intelligence puke. Had she been a submariner? Bobby shook himself.

"Welcome aboard. I'm Bobby O'Kane, Nav and acting XO." He held out a hand, which she shook firmly. "What can I do for you?"

"Maggie Bennett. I came to ask about that passenger ferry you guys found."

Bobby's eyebrows shot up like twin rockets. "That was fast."

"Fast?" She frowned. "You found it several patrols ago."

"Yeah...we found it again this patrol. Not sure if the captain's sent that one in or not yet." Bobby had endorsed Alex's patrol report, which was one of the more fascinating parts of his job as acting XO, but it was probably smarter to assume the squadron hadn't gotten it. Accusing them of not reading captains' patrol reports wasn't nice.

"I'm sure he did." Maggie's face twitched. "I'll have to check that out when I get back."

"I can show you our logs, if you want." Bobby shrugged. Why couldn't he remember her?

She smiled. "That'd be great."

"C'mon." Bobby led Maggie below, heading toward control, which was quiet when they were in port. But he paused at the bottom of the ladder. "Look, Commander, I don't mean to be rude, but have we met before?"

"Depends on how long you've been on *Bluefish*."

"Since July 2038."

She snorted out a laugh. "Shit, you were the navigator when I came over here to yell at you about Wilson."

"Huh?" Then the memory hit Bobby like a ton of bricks. "You were *Jimmy Carter's* navigator!"

"Right in one." Maggie's grin was infectious. "I lat transferred to intel after Convoy 57, but I still remember your refusal to call the brig to get Wilson out."

"In my defense, that was *so* not my call to make. And it's not like that guy isn't a liberty incident waiting to happen. He *was* in the brig," Bobby pointed out. "*Again.*"

Maggie waved him off. "He's not my problem now. He's on *Kansas.*"

She'd been pretty when she yelled at him. Bobby remembered that. Still, war wasn't a good place for romance—he'd learned that lesson the hard way one embezzling girlfriend back.

"Right. Let me show you our logs about *Spirit of Kangaroo Island II*," Bobby said, walking over to the nearest computer station. "We got some great periscope shots last time when she met up with a *Requin*—"

"A *what*?"

"Yeah, it was kind of the jackpot. Problem is that it looks like they've got genuine passengers on board, too, and who wants to shoot up Mom, Uncle Suzie, and Aunt Nattie's Ford Explorer?"

Maggie giggled. "That's...an interesting description. Okay. Show me these pictures and walk me through what happened. If these guys are using a false flag operation to gather intelligence, I need to get this written up in a hurry."

Pulling up the photos, Bobby obliged.

"You've got to be bloody kidding," Ursula growled. She wanted to hit something, but with only her own officers present, that was a terrible idea. Not to mention piss-poor leadership.

Ursula North was a practical woman. She knew her birth shielded her from a host of hazing, stupidity, and other bullying over the years. People she worked for didn't want to antagonize an earl's daughter, particularly when she was destined to someday inherit said title as a countess. But she'd watched bad or abusive leadership in action enough times to swear to herself that she'd never be the type. Sure, she growled and barked and swore, but she never crossed the line.

"No, ma'am. My, uh, friend in Commodore McNally's squadron confirmed it an hour ago." James spread his hands. "*Razorback* has orders to locate and destroy *Barracuda*."

Ursula ignored the reference to James' so-called friend. She didn't care who her officers screwed, provided it wasn't anyone on her crew. Lord knew the boy was pretty enough to pick up whomever he wanted. He could have a girlfriend or boyfriend of every nationality if he wanted to. She was more concerned with the fact that an *American* had been sent after her prey.

"And our own admiralty can't pull its head out long enough to work things out with the Americans." Her lips twisted into a sneer. "Cunts."

James grimaced. "Captain, the Americans are our allies..."

"Never you mind." Ursula waved a hand. "I'm sure their lordships' displeasure won't rub off on you if it ever comes to visit me. Now, what *is* our next assignment, since the Admiralty's great and mighty wisdom has decided to send an American to death?"

"No word yet, ma'am. Just rumors about a mission to take back the Indian Ocean Territory."

"Oh?" Ursula felt her eyebrows rise.

That was interesting. Diego Garcia, home to the British Indian Ocean Territory, was one of the few pieces of colonial real estate Britain never gave up. Granted, they'd leased it to the Americans—for a nice profit over the decades—but the Americans were almost family, despite Ursula's complaining. They'd shared the BIOT amicably for almost seventy-five years...until five months ago. Then the Indians bombed the naval station to oblivion and turned the island into a parking lot.

Even worse, the first attempt to take it back gutted an American battle group, sinking one carrier and nearly destroying another. But if the rumors were right... Ursula grinned.

"Perhaps being pulled off of Rochambeau will be worthwhile," she said, sitting back in her chair. "Talk about a target-rich environment."

"Assuming they defend it," James said.

"After the media mess they've received for attacking Convoy 57 *right there*?" Ursula scoffed. "And defeating the Americans once? The Indians *must* defend Diego Garcia, or the Indians will have a devil of a time explaining the blood and treasure they expended to acquire the dull set of rocks."

Dull set of rocks was something of a misnomer. The sixty islands of Chagos Archipelago weren't all useful, but several of them were big enough to support human habitation. Diego Garcia, of course, was the largest, supporting both a military base and an airfield. Both were critical to the war effort. Ursula knew her superiors didn't care about much else, so why should she? Well, there were also abundant resources on the ocean floor scattered across the Great Chagos Bank, which meant underwater stations and exploitation...

Yes, the Indians would defend Diego Garcia. Ursula's mind whirled. Subs were usually sent in ahead of the battle group, and if *Gallant* had a free rein to wreak havoc, she could make a difference. That was all Ursula wanted in the end. Yes, being the Alliance's premier submariner stroked her ego. Yes, she reveled in being compared to past greats of the Royal Navy. Being on the same bloody page in a history book as Nelson? She burned for that. However, in the end, she was in uniform to serve and protect her nation.

"Let's start planning," she said, and they got to work.

16 March 2040, Submarine Squadron Twenty-Nine Headquarters, Perth, Australia

The SUBRON 29 building was still a dump. Yeah, there was a war on, but Alex knew for a fact that there were *always* spare sailors around. Couldn't the commodore—or his staff officers, really; Alex knew how this game worked—find the time to slap a coat of paint on the place? He was usually the last person to nitpick stupid cosmetic details, but Banks was the kind of leader who scowled when subordinates didn't iron their khakis properly.

Was there just no paint available? Maybe the supply system just couldn't keep up with the war. What a surprise that would be.

"I don't like this in the slightest." Banks glared at Alex while they waited in the foyer, which looked a little better than the outside but still needed paint. And mopping.

"You and me both, sir." Alex hoped his casual shrug hid the butterflies doing laps around his colon. "But Admiral Rodriquez didn't make it sound very optional."

Banks glowered. "As I am aware. But don't pretend you won't enjoy another opportunity to showboat."

"Commodore, I'm not—"

"Don't think I've forgotten about that broomstick episode, either, *Captain.*" Banks poked a pointed finger into his chest.

Alex sighed. "No, sir, I imagine you haven't." Not saying more took all the self-control he had, but what was the point? If Banks was determined to hate him, so be it. At least that hadn't hurt his career. Yet.

Alex was still getting used to being a bit bulletproof. A bit? Maybe entirely. Grimacing, he resisted the urge to look down at the left side of his chest at a certain ribbon. He wished he hadn't put khakis on for this, but they were hosting a senator, and Banks was a stickler. Alex was lucky not to be in his goddamned dress uniform.

Why the hell couldn't they do the dog-and-pony show on the boat?

"I have an XO for you, by the way," Banks said suddenly.

"Beg pardon?"

"*Perch* was sunk. The XO survived. He's yours."

Alex's jaw dropped, working soundlessly. Then he shook himself. "I shot an email off to the chief of staff over a month ago about Lieutenant O'Kane staying in the—"

"Yes, I am aware." Banks cut him off again, his eyes glittering with malice. "Lieutenant O'Kane is far too inexperienced to become your XO, *particularly* since you're hosting Senator Angler."

"He's damned good at the job, sir," Alex objected. "And having a VIP along is hardly the time for change, I'd think."

Banks glared. "O'Kane is too junior. I'm not prepared to discuss this further, Captain."

"Yes, sir."

Alex bit his tongue. God, he wanted to be anywhere but here. He thought about telling Banks how he knew Benjamin Winthrop Angler the *Fourth* but discarded the notion. It wouldn't help. Sure, Benji Angler had been Alex's weapons officer back on *Jimmy Carter*, but Senator Angler hadn't wanted his son to stay in the navy when the war started. Would that ire rub off on *Bluefish*?

Alex had the best fucking luck.

The door opened, and Admiral Rodriquez led a group in. "You lot look like you're at someone's funeral. Try to fucking smile, will you?"

Banks' audible gulp made Alex suppress a snicker. The sight of Senator Angler close on Uncle Marco's heels, however, sobered him right up. Damn, he looked like an older version of Benji. How the hell had Alex been roped into this?

"Senator, allow me to introduce you to America's leading submariner: Captain Alex Coleman," Rodriquez said, and Alex's stomach dropped.

Good God, did he *have* to say that? Yeah, he was ahead of Patricia Abercrombie in enemies sunk, but without Convoy 57, they'd be neck and neck. Alex swallowed, forcing his shoulders back and pretending he didn't notice Angler's eyes tracking immediately to *that* ribbon.

Everyone's did.

"It's a pleasure to meet you, sir," Alex said, proud of how level his voice remained.

Angler shook his hand with a politician's charm. "Likewise, Captain. My son speaks highly of you as a leader and a warfighter. I look forward to getting underway with you next week."

"Thank you, sir," Alex replied, ignoring the poisonous look Banks shot him. "I hope Benji's doing well."

"He is, and we're very proud of him," Angler said. There was no hint of the man whom Benji complained wanted him to leave the navy, but Alex hadn't expected that. Angler *was* a politician, and rumor said he wanted to run for president in 2044.

Yeah. Having a politician on board was *exactly* what Alex needed. Joy.

"Well, there's no missing that message is there, Captain?" Master Chief Bryan Morton looked up from the orders Commander Abercrombie handed over and shrugged.

Razorback's captain let out a breath. "I'd say it's pretty explicit."

She looked nervous, but not like she was going to go to pieces. *Thank fucking God.* Morton had served under ten different COs at sea in his thirty-two-year naval career, and he'd been lucky enough never to find a coward. Patricia Abercrombie was only his second wartime CO, however, and he hadn't been certain that this wouldn't set her off the edge. There was enough pressure on sub captains to make anyone crack. Between the responsibility for 130 lives, tactical decisions, and the safety of the boat, a lot of captains went to pieces. No one really knew why, just that it happened.

Rumors on the waterfront spiked every time another captain went off the deep end. Some took their crew and boats to the bottom with them. Others just did things like drunkenly smash cars into the main base gate or have "accidents" while gliding and never come home. There was also the guy who went diving and ran out of air; rumor said that one was due to a mental meltdown rather than suicide, but all Morton knew was that the pressure kept mounting and some people couldn't keep up.

Lord only knew if *he* would've been able to stand up to it as a captain. There was a reason he was happy to be chief of the boat. Plenty of responsibility, but never the end of the line.

He re-read their orders. Now *Razorback* was up for the hard job: sinking Rochambeau. Replacing Ursula North was a hell of a compliment, but it gave Morton the jitters. He was just better at hiding them.

"When do we leave?" he asked.

"Tomorrow, before dawn." She squared her shoulders. "I'll take every advantage we can get. We know he's been operating down south, so we'll work our way down there and see if anything crops up that looks like a good target."

"You're going to use Alliance ships as bait to pull him out?"

Abercrombie grimaced. "I don't like it, but unless you have a better idea...?"

"No, ma'am. Just thinking."

"We won't let him get close enough to sink anyone. We just need a way to bring him to us. The Brits spent over a year trying to chase him down, and that hasn't worked. I want to try something new."

"You want me to go grab the XO so we can start planning?" Morton asked, gesturing toward the closed door of her stateroom.

"No time like the present." Her smile seemed forced, but Morton tried to ignore that and headed out.

Orders were orders, after all, and there was a certain kind of backhanded compliment in being handed a mission that had killed everyone else.

Lieutenant Commander Steven Harper looked like a go-getter. He shook Alex's hand firmly and didn't seem to have a nervous twitch. He even met Alex's gaze levelly. Maybe having a real XO—not a panicky pencil pusher like George Kirkland—would be a good thing. Part of Alex was still sorry that Bobby hadn't gotten the job, but the navy wasn't the kind of profession where you could pick your team.

"Welcome aboard," Alex said, waving the newcomer into a seat in his stateroom. "Do you go by Steven or by Steve?"

"Steve is fine, sir." Harper sat like a flagpole was attached to his spine, but that was probably nerves. How had Alex become someone who could make people nervous?

"Steve it is. I assume the squadron brought you up to speed on our current ops sked?"

"Yes, sir. I'm ready to roll—doing nothing on *Nereus* for the better part of a month was torture."

Alex chuckled. "I have a hard time believing Captain Dalton didn't put you to work."

"It's not the same. And survivor's leave was almost worse. I was bored out of my mind."

"I hear you there." Alex felt the same restlessness when he'd been on leave after *Jimmy Carter*, but he hadn't expected to scratch the itch with another boat. "Don't worry. I'll keep you busy."

"I look forward to it," Steve said.

The eagerness in his eyes was almost off-putting, as was the way he leaned forward in his chair. But that was a stupid thought, wasn't it? Alex just wasn't used to having a real XO.

"Nav—Lieutenant O'Kane—has filled in as acting XO since October, so he'll provide the minute details. My expectations are simple: do your job, be honest with me, and don't sweat the small stuff. We're at war, and our job is to kill the enemy. If it doesn't help us get that done—or get in the way—I don't much care about the details."

Steve finally smiled. "I can live by that, sir."

"Then we'll get along just fine." Alex hesitated. "Is there anything I need to know about you?"

"Not much that matters. I'm not a fu-fu academy grad. I'm just here to do my job and do it well."

Alex laughed. "Well, I'm not from Canoe U, either, so no worries on that front."

"Do you think there's any chance we'll get a shot at Rochambeau, sir? He killed *Perch*. I lost a lot of good people that day."

"And you want to sink him in return."

Alex studied his new XO. There was no denying the fire in Steve's eyes. Nearly every Alliance submariner shared it;

Rochambeau had killed a *lot* of Americans. Everyone had lost friends to the French hotshot. But for Steve, it was personal, wasn't it? *Perch* had lost more than a third of her crew to *Barracuda.*

"Yes, Captain, I do."

"I can't make any promises, but if we get a shot, we'll damned well take it." Not a shot like last time, either, when Alex didn't know what he was bumbling into. That incident still burned.

Steve nodded. "That's good enough for me."

Dangerous times called for dangerous measures, Chris Kennedy decided, putting the finishing touches on his patrol report. There was no knowing for certain which sub's towed array *Kansas* had ripped off, although he suspected *Lionfish*. He'd been on the edges of *Lionfish's* sectors when the near-collision took place, not that he'd admit to that. Logs and inertial navigation records were only pulled when boats sank or after major battles. No one would be interested enough in *Kansas'* last patrol to pull them, and his XO would endorse his report faithfully. There was nothing to worry about.

Except for STS1 Wilson. Damn it if the young sonar operator hadn't been right, and Chris had to admit that he'd been too reckless. Song hadn't helped with that, a fact he'd made blisteringly clear to her—in private, of course—but the bulk of the blame rested with him. And now he had a too-sharp first class petty officer who knew far too much about what had happened. He thought Wilson would behave himself, but what if he was wrong? Chris knew what boat Wilson had come from, and the sonar tech had apparently done well during Convoy 57. Having no love for Alex Coleman didn't blind Chris to Wilson's skills. He was pretty sure that Wilson had gotten the hint, but playing it safe was smarter.

The temptation to hammer the kid was hard to resist. Wilson's disciplinary record meant no one would look twice if

Chris dropped the book on him...yet instinct told him that Wilson wouldn't go quietly. No, he'd use that Silver Star of his to raise a stink, and *then* people might start asking questions.

Bribery was better.

Not old-fashioned bribery. That was against regulations in ways Chris found repulsive. No, he'd just have to shepherd Wilson's career along, make sure he was always one of the top sailors on board, that he knew he was a valued member of the crew. Wilson had the talent to be the number one first class petty officer on *Kansas*, and if he kept his mouth shut, Chris Kennedy would make that happen.

Hell, he'd make sure the kid made chief petty officer if it kept him out of his business. Then they could *all* win. Chris could take the risks necessary to enhance his career and reputation, and Wilson would get the promotion every enlisted sailor dreamed of.

That would do it, he decided. Perhaps a quiet word with Master Chief Casey was in order. He already seemed interested in mentoring Wilson, so it was time to make it official. He'd have the COB take the reckless-but-brilliant sonar tech under his wing. Then Wilson would be too busy—and have too much of a personal stake in *Kansas's* success—to create trouble for one Christopher A. Kennedy.

He sat back in his chair with a smirk. This was how the game was played.

Chapter 21

Early Warning

17 March 2040, Perth, Australia

"Anything else?" *Bluefish's* new XO asked.

Bobby shook his head, and the other department heads followed suit, glancing at each other before coming up empty. It was their first *real* executive officer's call since Commander Vanderbilt broke his leg, and everything felt...funky. It wasn't the meeting itself. Lieutenant Commander Harper knew what he was doing, and nothing dragged on. He also liked holding department head meetings in the wardroom, which meant they could sit in comfort instead of cramming into the XO's stateroom like Vanderbilt used to make them do. So it was even comfortable.

Yet it felt weird to be *normal* again after so long. Good weird? Bobby wasn't sure. Either way, Harper ended the meeting quickly and the department heads filed out in silence.

Once in the passageway, Bobby turned to Rose.

"It's a beautiful day, isn't it, Rosie?"

"It's storming like a bitch."

"Yeah, but I'm back to being just the navigator. We could be stuck in a sharknado for all I care." The weight on his shoulders felt a thousand pounds lighter.

Rose rolled her eyes. "Only you."

"Yep." He grinned.

"Don't get your panties in a happy twist yet. This one might fall down a ladder, too."

"You know what the actual likelihood of that is?" Bobby rolled his eyes, passing by a pair of engineers hurrying toward Lou's departmental quarters, or morning meeting. "I mean, I know we have a crap track record between the old XO breaking his leg and Commander Peterson's appendix, but we really aren't cursed. Or are we?"

"You're a flaming turd sometimes, you know that?"

"Hey, I'm not the one with the flexible interests here."

Rose scoffed. "Speaking of which, your girlfriend called me."

"She is *not* my girlfriend." Bobby stopped cold. "I changed my number for a reason. Why haven't you blocked her yet?"

"Okay, your *stalker* called me." Rose's smile was diamond-sharp. "She wants you to testify on her behalf."

Bobby shook his head hard enough to make himself dizzy. "Oh, hell no. No way. Not happening in a million years."

"Hey, it's only embezzlement. I thought you liked her."

"I thought you said I had horrible taste," he said.

Rose leaned lazily against the bulkhead. "You do."

"Well, I've learned my lesson. Crazy embezzling stalkers need not apply to be Bobby O'Kane's girlfriend. Will it make you feel better if I ask your approval for future girlfriends?"

"Maybe." Rose snickered. "Though I might be tempted to steal them."

"Geez. No one's safe with you."

They laughed together.

USS **Cape St. George** *(CG 108), the Indian Ocean (approximately 300 nautical miles from Perth, Australia)*

"Birds away, track seven-seven-oh-niner!" Nancy heard the voice ring out over *Cape's* internal net from her chair on the bridge, and her eyes instinctively snapped to look at the cruiser's forward vertical launch system.

Two SM-6 missiles erupted from *Cape's* missile cells, roaring into the sky to meet the enemy. The rocket motors burned bright against the early morning sky, illuminating the bridge and making Nancy squint. The sixth iteration of America's reliable standard missile travelled at around Mach 3.5, carried a one-hundred-and-forty-pound fragmenting warhead, and had a range of up to two hundred nautical miles against air targets. Its range for surface targets, like ships, was much shorter, but that didn't really matter once your opponent ran out of missiles.

"Good hits!" their air warfare coordinator reported a few moments later. "Drone footage shows the frigate listing to starboard."

"Captain, aye." Rowlings' voice sounded dead calm and professional, just like it should.

In fact, everything about this small battle had gone just right. *Cape* tracked down the Indian convoy in under a day, and for once, intelligence was correct. The eight merchant ships had just one escort, the *Talwar*-class frigate *Pathan*. *Pathan* was a new ship, almost as new as *Cape*, but she just didn't have the throw weight to stand up to a cruiser in a fight. *Cape* had over a hundred more missile cells than Pathan, and while the cruiser didn't have a full complement of missiles—Nancy didn't know of any surface ship that did—she had more than enough to doom *Pathan*.

"It was nice of the Indians to send her out without any Brahmos missiles," Nancy murmured to *Cape's* operations officer,

Lieutenant Commander Austen Sullivan. Austen had the deck at general quarters, or battle stations, and he seemed a solid sort. If jumpy.

Now Sullivan grinned. "It does even the odds."

"Better than even." Nancy sat back in her chair, watching the drone footage on the monitor near her left foot. *Pathan's* list grew worse with every passing minute, and the drone was close enough to pick up sailors jumping overboard. "It's nice to have the range on the enemy for once."

"Yes, ma'am, it is." Sullivan grimaced. "We've been on the receiving end of enemy long-range missiles enough times already. Nice to see that *they're* finally having supply problems, too."

"From your lips to God's ears." Nancy glanced at the monitor again. *Pathan* was done for, which meant it was about to be her turn. She grabbed the phone attached to the internal net. "Captain, XO, visual looks like enemy frigate is sinking. Request permission to transmit on bridge-to-bridge to the convoy."

"XO, Captain, go ahead."

"XO, aye."

Nancy put the phone down and shot Sullivan a look. "Time to be on your toes, Ops. If any of these guys try to run away, we'll be chasing them down."

"Helo is on Alert Five. Give me the word and we'll go to green deck and launch, ma'am." Sullivan knew his stuff, and Nancy was grateful for it. Crew members on a cruiser tended to be more senior and more experienced, which made day-to-day operations a lot easier. Even when they were out of the ordinary.

Nancy didn't need to glance right to see that Armstrong was on the bridge, recording everything he could get away with. No one was ready to let him be in CIC—there was too much classified information down there!—but the public loved video clips from a warship's bridge in battle.

Not that there had been much of a battle. Once Captain Rowlings guessed that *Pathan* lacked the longer-range Brahmos NG missiles that so often gave the U.S. Navy headaches,

Cape just pickled off standard missiles until enough of them hit the frigate. Now their enemy was sinking...right next to an eight-ship convoy that was ripe for the stealing.

Lifting the bridge-to-bridge radio handset, Nancy checked to make sure it was on channel sixteen before speaking. "Attention all ships in Indian convoy. I say again, attention all ships in Indian convoy, this is U.S. Navy Warship One-Zero-Eight. Your escort is sinking. You will form up on my unit for immediate transit to Perth, Australia. Any refusal to do so will be met immediately with deadly force, over."

How did Nancy feel about stealing merchant ships? Pretty good. Rowlings' reputation said she often came up with crazy ideas like this, but Nancy thought this one was stellar. Hopefully, those ships would be full of raw materials or even foodstuffs, things the Grand Alliance could use. It would be less helpful if the loaded containerships were full of Indian weapons, which weren't compatible with Alliance technology. Still, that would deprive the enemy of weapons, which would be a hell of a lot better than letting India have them.

The long pause felt heavy on the airwaves. Finally, one ship's master replied in accented but good English:

"Warship One-Zero-Eight, this is Motor Vessel *Willow's Song.* We understand and will reply, out."

Acknowledgments crept in from the other seven ships, and Nancy sat back in her chair as Sullivan changed *Cape's* course to close with the convoy and the sinking frigate.

"Not a bad day's work," she said, smiling.

"Now we just have to get them home, ma'am." Sullivan glanced at the radar, where the eight civilian ships clumped together like it might protect them from the big, bad cruiser. "Shouldn't be that hard, since they're cooperating."

Merchant ships didn't like tangling with warships, a fact that was doubly true during war. Nancy didn't doubt this bunch would behave, but *defending* their impromptu convoy from an enemy might be another matter entirely. She grabbed the internal net handset again.

"Captain, XO, all merchant ships acknowledge change in ownership."

"Captain, aye. Close with the convoy."

"Already in progress, ma'am."

"Aye."

Nancy cocked her head and looked at the radar screen. Maybe they could steal one of *Lexington's* escorts to help herd their new charges once the carrier got underway. That would make the transit back to Perth a lot safer for everyone—particularly if they could steal a good anti-submarine warfare destroyer. *Cape's* one real weakness was in sub hunting. She sub hunted about as well as Nancy's last ship, which wasn't saying much. *Fletcher* hadn't been designed to take the war to ultra-quiet submarines, and while Nancy might've hoped the navy learned their lesson when designing their newest cruiser class... Well, she was glad she hadn't put money on that hope.

She'd talk to Rowlings about borrowing a destroyer before reaching out to the *Lexington* Strike Group. Rowlings was smart and reasonable about combat; Nancy doubted she'd disagree. And their course to Perth would take them right past the boxes where *Lexington* was scheduled for her brief post-repair sea trials after her last battle, which made the rendezvous easy.

They had time. The convoy was still seventy nautical miles away, which meant *Cape* needed two hours to reach them, even at her best speed. Fortunately, it never occurred to the merchant ships to try to run away.

Nancy didn't have to ask to know that Rowlings would sink them in an instant.

Finding a target sweet enough to lure Rochambeau in was the easy part. Like all good COBs, Bryan Morton was plugged into the waterfront chiefs' mess, the navy's most powerful grapevine, and there were no secrets between chief petty officers.

"You're sure she's getting underway today?" Commander Abercrombie asked while *Razorback* lurked right outside the exit lanes leading out of Perth, trolling along at five knots.

"Master Chief Jenkins is their command master chief, ma'am. He'd know." Morton knew that his captain wasn't really that worried, just fretting. The idea of using a multi-billion-dollar aircraft carrier as bait would make any commander rethink their sanity.

But Petey Jenkins had been Morton's neighbor way back when they were idiot third class petty officers, and they shared a few drunken escapades, one memorable date with Morton's now ex-wife, and they and several friends split an annual casino vacation every year. Or at least they had, before the war ruined things.

"Right." Abercrombie's smile grew strained. "I'm sure we'll see her soon."

"She's due to get underway right at dawn." Morton checked the notes he'd scribbled on his tablet. "Time-distance says we should see her within the next hour."

Abercrombie rubbed her eyes. "Then it's a long stalk and probably a longer hunt. We best make sure people are rested."

You should rest, too, Morton didn't say. Not in control when surrounded by their crew. He'd nab the captain later, talk to her in private about the fact that she didn't have to look over their shoulders for every moment of their hunt for Rochambeau. Abercrombie wasn't usually a micromanager, and he knew this was just the stress eating at her, but saving the captain from herself was the COB's job.

Maybe it was time for Abercrombie to take a page out of John Dalton's book. No one on this boat would blink if they found her passed out and drooling on the wardroom table.

"You want to come up in Link with her when we find her, ma'am?" their weapons officer asked.

"No." Abercrombie shook her head after a slight hesitation. "Going receive-only won't help much, and there's always a chance of detection if we broadcast."

Morton nodded. The chance of detection for a slender comms wire communicating to satellite Link 18 was low—the techs said about one in twenty—but they were going against the best. No need to gift Rochambeau the upper hand.

It was easier to pretend his heart wasn't pounding when the captain made good decisions, too.

"Conn, Sonar, broadband contact on the tail! Long range, four screws, moving fast—sounds like *Lexington*, ma'am."

"Conn, aye." Abercrombie met Morton's eyes. "Looks like your network was right, Master Chief."

"It always is, ma'am." His grin was cockier than he felt, but appearing confident was half of a COB's job. The good ones could lie like Satan, and Morton would look good in horns.

"Here we go, then."

Razorback swept into a lazy turn, her towed sonar array trailing behind. She'd shadow *Lexington* while the carrier headed out for sea trials, testing repaired equipment. Rumor said *Lexington* would spearhead the next big offensive, wherever that was ended up, and everyone on *Razorback* knew they couldn't afford to lose the carrier. Carriers weren't *quite* the queens of the ocean these days, not with several sunk during the war, but they were hellaciously expensive and packed a hell of a punch.

Carriers were still capital ships. Politicians loved them, and they flew admirals' flags. They were symbols in a way submarines were not. Priceless symbols.

None of that would stop *Razorback* from using *Lexington* to draw Rochambeau in.

SUBRON 29 Headquarters, Perth, Australia

The best thing about their short patrol season was how *Bluefish* managed to miss most of the weekly squadron briefings. Unfortunately, Alex couldn't skip this one; *Bluefish* was in port, and he had a new XO to bring along. On the bright side, Steve seemed more interested in Banks' long-winded briefings than Alex. He even took notes, the picture of an industrious XO.

By an hour in, most of the COs were fidgeting, and Kennedy was back to glaring at Alex. Banks posting squadron rankings didn't help, because *Bluefish* was on top. All but two of *Bluefish's* twenty kills were with Alex in command, a fact that left him feeling funny. He hadn't done the math, maybe on purpose, and was surprised to see that number so high. He still felt guilty adding the six *Scorpenes* to his total, but the other hand, the four SSNs, one SSGN, five surface combatants, and four merchants were worth being proud of. *Kansas* and *Halibut* were tied for second with ten kills each, but the idea of his boat having double their kills made Alex's innards dance. It was almost as bad as knowing that a senator would join them on their next underway.

Things didn't get better when Banks turned the briefing over to his chief of staff, Commander Reyes.

"We have a few major taskers coming down the line," she said. "*Bluefish* has been selected to provide a wartime ride-on for Senator Benjamin Angler. *Sailfish* is scheduled to join the *Saratoga* Battle Group next week. *Halibut* has already CHOPed to the *Lexington* Battle Group to support an upcoming offensive. *Sole* completed a major overhaul and will commence sea trials next week. Finally, *Iowa* made it onto the combatant scorecard with two frigates killed last patrol."

The assembled captains and XOs applauded, although Kennedy shot Alex another poisonous scowl. Alex just slumped in his seat and wished for a less important assignment. He'd rather a boring convoy escort over hosting a politician busy chasing glory. Steve seemed happy, though.

Reyes continued: "Also, we'd like to recognize *Bluefish* for preservation of civilian life under extenuating circumstances. Two months ago, *Bluefish* was ordered to sink two heavy lift ships—each carrying three *Scorpenes* bound for India—and their escorts. Captain Coleman gave the civilian crews time to abandon ship, and today, we were notified that Dockwise Shipping, the owner of the heavy lift ships, will no longer provide services for the Union for the Freedom and Prosperity of the Indian Ocean."

Alex sat up straight. He'd spared the civilians because he hated killing innocents in the name of "collateral damage;" he hadn't expected results. But talk about results! Dockwise Shipping owned ninety percent of the heavy lift ships in the world. How would France ship new submarines to India without them? Could Russia find another carrier? Damn.

Alex suppressed a smile as Reyes handed out the less-glamorous assignments. Kennedy's glower deepened when *Kansas* got handed a pair of convoy escorts; he exchanged rolled-eyes glance with his XO, whose laser-sharp gaze said she wanted to kill someone. Alex ignored both as best he could, until the meeting ended, and Kennedy approached. His smile would've looked at home on an alligator.

"I didn't take you for someone who kissed ass so well, Alex," Kennedy said. "I guess times have changed."

A few years ago, an asinine comment coming from his old CO would've made Alex freeze. But Kennedy wasn't senior to him now. He was just a whiny child. Alex shrugged. "I'm here to do a job. The rest is just details."

"Sure you are." Kennedy snorted and then turned to Steve. "Be careful of this one. His last XO's career didn't survive him."

Steve blinked. Alex's chest felt tight. Did Steve know the story? Kennedy had heard too much; his smile widened.

"Saint Alexander has a nice ring to it, but it doesn't really fit, does it?"

Alex's jaw dropped. "I—"

"Captain Coleman, a minute?" Banks' nasally voice carried past several cubicles from his office doorway. He stood there glaring at Alex like he was at fault for global hunger, climate change, and the war itself, but at least a conversation with him beat talking to Kennedy.

"Of course, sir." Taking a deep breath, Alex followed Banks into his office, enjoying Kennedy's sudden scowl. Hopefully Steve could hold his own against Alex's old captain.

The door clicked shut, and Banks' frown deepened. "I would like to hear your rationale for providing those heavy lift ships time to abandon."

Alex blinked. "Your chief of staff just—"

"Yes, it turned out well. But what were you *thinking*?"

"That I don't like killing civilians unless I have no choice."

Banks pursed his lips. "You risked your boat."

"Not really." Alex shrugged, glancing around the well-appointed office. Banks had the standard I-love-me wall covered in mementos from the boats he'd been on, but the furniture was downright luxurious. And almost new. There was even a crystal decanter and glasses set over by the window. Did Banks drink on duty? Damn, that might make him more human and Alex might almost like him.

He returned his attention to his boss. "We sank both escorts. Neither got a helo off. We were out of range for Indian air cover, and I gave the crews a very short window to abandon ship."

"I see." Banks' lips formed a thin, white line.

"Is there a problem, sir?"

"I don't like your methods, *Captain*. You're unpredictable and prone to reinterpreting instructions to suit your fancy."

Alex wasn't sure what to say. "I'm just trying to do my job—"

"I'm well aware of that," Banks snapped. "And you're Admiral Rodriquez's fair-haired boy, so you'll get away with it. For now."

Alex swallowed. He knew Banks disliked his methods, but did Banks *want* him to fail? How had he earned such vitriol from his boss? First Kennedy, now him. Alex was just great at making friends today.

Almost three hours later, *Cape* slowed to five knots in the vicinity of *Pathan's* grave. The oil slick on the water was visible in the pre-noon light, and life rafts dotted the waves. Most of the sailors seemed to have found a spot in one of the bright orange rafts; Nancy couldn't see anyone treading water, though there were some bodies bobbing in the waves here and there.

She swallowed. Looking at their handiwork was never fun or pretty, but war was war, and they had a job to do.

"You want to pick them up, Captain? I imagine some of them could have some useful intelligence," Nancy said, looking over at Rowlings.

They stood side-by-side on *Cape's* starboard bridge wing as the cruiser approached the convoy and the site where *Pathan* sank. Rowlings' eyes remained on the survivors in the water, studying the debris around them while she frowned. A long moment passed in silence before Rowlings said:

"I don't trust it."

"Trust what?" Nancy arched an eyebrow.

"Any of them. Bringing them on board would be trouble." Rowlings's scowl deepened. "I'm not interested in prisoners."

"International law says we have to pick them up if able." Nancy licked her lips, trying to put thoughts of her *last* at-sea rescue out of her mind.

That had been the day *Enterprise* sank, along with two of her escorts, killing hundreds and kicking off the war that became World War III. Nancy hadn't asked for a front seat to the pain and chaos, but she'd been there from moment one. *Fletcher* had been right in the thick of things, and Nancy launched missile after missile to defend the carrier until her ship had nothing left. It hadn't been enough.

Rowlings sneered. "International law has no understanding of tactical realities."

Nancy felt her jaw working as she tried to come up with a coherent argument against that. It wasn't *un*true, and yet... Fortunately, Rowlings shook her head.

"Make it happen, XO."

"Aye, ma'am." Nancy turned to shout through the open door to the bridge proper. "Ops! Find yourself a relief and start coordinating recovery efforts."

"Ops, aye." Sullivan bobbed his head. "Nav is ready to relieve me, if the captain agrees?"

Asking the captain permission to be relieved as officer of the deck was naval tradition, but Rowlings turned to glare at where the operations officer and navigator stood side by side. "You should have known this was necessary and already turned over, Ops. What use is a second tour department head if you can't anticipate *legally* required operations?"

Sullivan blanched. "Captain, I—"

"Shut it. This is why I hate you," Rowlings snapped as Nancy stared. "Turn your watch over and get the hell below."

"Aye, Captain." Sullivan's voice went quiet, and he disappeared after the navigator took the watch.

For her part, Nancy stood rooted to her spot at Captain Rowlings' side, flabbergasted at her superior's sudden heel turn. She'd heard officers muttering about how nothing mattered more in a given day than the captain's mood—not the tactical situation, not what ships were near them, and not even if battle beckoned—but this was something else.

The XO was more than the captain's tactical deputy. She was her sounding board and, if need be, her conscience. Talking the captain off a ledge was part of the XO's job, but how the hell was she supposed to tell her CO that bullying people only made the ship miserable and less effective? Rowlings would just tell her that *Cape* was the best cruiser in the navy and had never participated in a losing battle.

Worry churned in Nancy's gut. Rowlings didn't want the Indian survivors on board. How awful would she make their stay? Heading straight to Perth meant a transit of less than a day, but bringing on dozens of survivors would overcrowd the ship. Cruisers weren't designed to carry passengers, which meant they'd have to either keep the prisoners on deck or stuff them on the mess decks. If they did the latter, where would the crew eat? A thousand questions crowded through Nancy's mind, each begging for attention and solutions, but her eyes kept flicking to Captain Rowlings.

"Do you want me to handle recovery operations so you can report this in?" Nancy asked. Maybe getting Rowlings away from the situation was a coward's answer, but it might also be better for the crew.

Not to mention safer for their incoming prisoners.

"I appreciate that." Rowlings cracked a smile. "I'll call the boss and get clearance to return to Perth early."

Neither mentioned that their operations officer could do that, assuming Rowlings didn't want to talk to Admiral Franklin directly. Knowing her, she probably did.

"Captain, permission to place the RHIB at the rail?" The navigator stuck his head out the door. Billy Connors was a short but lanky kid who looked about twelve, but he knew his job well. So far as Nancy could tell, Nav was the one officer Rowlings *didn't* hate.

Rumor said he hated her extra for that.

"Granted." Rowlings sniffed the air like a dog hunting. "The XO has point for all boat ops today. I'm going below."

"Officer of the Deck, aye," Nav replied as Rowlings marched past him into the bridge.

Nancy leaned over the bridgewing rail, watching the RHIB, or rigid hull inflatable boat, swing out to the rail of the ship as the davit pivoted. Sullivan was on deck already, rigging ladders up forward for the survivors to climb, but they needed to put the boat in the water to tow life rafts close to the ship. The boat could also rescue any swimmers, though Nancy didn't see any and doubted anyone would survive the two-plus hours it took *Cape* to reach the frigate's grave.

Unfortunately, putting her attention on the boat meant Nancy was looking aft when a *crack* split the air. It came from somewhere to her left, somewhere forward of amidships, and she spun to look just as Rowlings surged back onto the bridgewing.

"What was that?" Rowlings demanded. "Are they firing?"

"What?" Nancy scanned the water for any sign of resistance, but she didn't find any before Rowlings shouted down to the boat deck:

"Ops, get that boat back in the cradle! We've taken fire!"

Another *crack* split the air, and bright light caught Nancy's eye as something pinkish red erupted into the sky.

"Was that a flare?" she asked, but Rowlings ignored her, grabbing the phone for the internal net and saying:

"All stations, Captain, we have taken fire. Batteries release, all starboard side crew served weapons. I say again, batteries release for all starboard side crew served weapons."

Nancy's jaw dropped "Captain—"

"Not now!"

Her eyes traced the sky desperately as *Cape* twisted into a turn, water boiling at her stern as her screws churned. Why would they shoot a flare? Why would anyone be so stupid?

Finally, Nancy spotted the tiny outline of a helicopter on the horizon. Was it Indian? There was no way to know at this range, but if the Indians in the water were signaling...

The firing of machine guns shattered the stillness as the forward fifty-caliber mounts obeyed Rowlings' command.

Chapter 22

No Quarter

Two mounts opened fire as Nancy gaped; she only needed seconds to react, but by then, both fifty-caliber mounts had overlapping fields of fire on the nearest rafts and had fired several short bursts. Heart hammering in her chest, Nancy grabbed Rowlings' shoulder, shouting to be heard over the din.

"Captain, stop! That was a flare!"

"Fuck that! Even shooting a flare at us is hostile intent," Rowlings snarled, jerking away.

Screams and shouting carried across the water; survivors jumped out of the first shredded life raft, diving underwater to try to escape the hail of bullets. Panicked voices screeched pleas, insults, and objections in both Hindi and English, and finally someone raised a pistol and started shooting back.

"This is against the law!" Nancy grabbed the handset out of Rowlings' hand. "Order them to cease fire or I will."

"Get the fuck out of the way so I can kill the enemy." Rowlings' eyes blazed as she leaned right into Nancy's face.

"Surrendering prisoners are not the enemy," Nancy spat. This had gone on too long. People were dying and because of *what*? Rowlings' hair trigger? This was wrong in more ways than Nancy could count.

"Step aside." Rowlings' voice was a growl, but Nancy met her fury head-on, looking the older officer in the eye as she lifted the handset.

"All stations, XO, cease fire. I say again, *cease fire*!" she barked. "All mounts, cease fire!"

The third repetition did the trick; the rhythmic *burr* of machine gun fire died. Only then did Nancy realize how silent *Cape's* bridge was; she could hear Indians protesting from the water and splashing. But she had to deal with Rowlings first; her captain's glare was a fierce and bloody thing, and Rowlings looked ready to rip Nancy's throat out.

Nancy refused to back down. "We cannot shoot survivors in the water. All rules of war prohibit it. We are supposed to be *better than this*."

"Returning fire is our duty." Rowlings gestured menacingly at the sailors in the water.

"Not when a survivor shoots off a *flare*!" Nancy couldn't believe her ears. "Captain—"

"Give me the handset. We're not done here," Rowlings cut her off. "The enemy can still fight."

"The *what*?" Nancy's jaw dropped.

"Give me the handset, XO, and I *might* forget your insubordinate behavior."

"I cannot and will not do that, Captain. Neither of us has the authority to break the law. Naval regulations are clear on this."

Rowlings' face went bright red. "Give me a fucking break! Our job is to kill the enemy before they can kill us! Now give me the goddamned handset or I will have you relieved!"

She grabbed for the handset, but Nancy took a step back. A feeling of cold washed over her, like she'd been dumped in snow in the middle of a Vermont winter. She couldn't believe this was happening, couldn't wrap her mind around the reality of a *modern* cruiser captain shooting at defenseless survivors in the water. The world was *better* than that now. Butchering civilians was never acceptable! Rowlings' actions were unthinkable. Indefensible.

But she knew what she had to do.

Taking a deep breath, Nancy squared her shoulders and pitched her voice so that every staring crew member could hear. "Captain Rowlings, by the authority granted to me by

U.S. Navy Regulations, I relieve you of command for violation of both our rules of engagement and the laws of war."

"You *what*?"

Nancy ignored her fire-breathing captain and turned to the navigator, who stood gaping a dozen feet away. "Lieutenant Connors, please log the date and time and that I have relieved Captain Rowlings of command."

Connors' eyes flicked back and forth between them once, twice, and then a third time before he nodded sharply. "Log it, aye, ma'am. Commander Coleman has assumed command."

"Captain Rowlings, if you would be so kind as to retire to your chair here on the bridge, I will inform the strike group after we have recovered *Pathan's* survivors."

Nancy just squared her shoulders as Rowlings hissed curses under her breath; she watched her (former?) captain look around the bridge for support, only to be met with stony faces. Thank *God.* Nancy wasn't enjoying this moment, not at all, and terror still coiled around the back of her mind as she reflected upon the fact that she, the newcomer, had just stirred up one almighty hornet's nest.

But no one else on the bridge seemed to have an appetite for killing sailors clinging to life rafts for survival, either.

Rowlings stalked to her chair as Nancy leaned over the railing. "Ops! Get that boat back at the rail and get ready to launch!"

Lieutenant Commander Sullivan stared up at her with wide and confused eyes before shouting: "Put the boat at the rail, aye!"

Nancy grabbed the handset again. "All gun mounts, XO. Hold fire. Do not fire unless fired upon or upon *my* order. Captain Rowlings has been relieved of command."

A long moment of silence passed before acknowledgments rolled in; Nancy's heartrate slowed to something approaching normal. She turned back to the navigator.

"Nav, please pass the word. I don't want any confusion over the chain of command," she said and then turned back to look at the Indian sailors bobbing in the waves.

Getting them on board was going to be a mess, wasn't it? Lord only knew how hostile they'd be after being shot at—Nancy knew what a foul mood that put *her* in—and yet it was her duty to rescue them. Then she'd have to call her captain's superiors and let them know what she'd done.

"XO?" a quiet voice came from her right and made her turn to face Eric Armstrong.

"Yeah." Nancy tried a smile on for size, but it itched like an ill-fitting Halloween mask.

"I got a video of everything. Been here the whole time." The reporter gestured at his camera and grimaced. Then he glanced at the people in the water who clung to rafts, some bleeding. "Glad you stopped her."

"Me, too." Nancy didn't want to guess how many of those floating bodies were dead or dying. They'd have to find out once they got the survivors on board, but... She shuddered.

"I'll help however I can. No one deserves to get away with murder." Armstrong swallowed. "There's got to be a difference between war and butchery."

"There should be," Nancy whispered, sneaking a glance back at Captain Rowlings.

Rowlings was silent now, staring out the bridge window with a thunderous expression. Nancy half expected her to try to take command back, or to yell at the bridge watch team, but so far, that hadn't happened. Was Rowlings in shock? God knew Nancy was. She had never imagined being in a situation like this. Never in her career had she so much as had a nightmare of a captain trying to shoot survivors in the water.

Taking a deep breath, Nancy shook the thoughts away and went to work.

Hours ticked by as *Razorback* crept along on the edges of the *Lexington* Battle Group's formation, undetected even by the other American ships. Since they weren't up in Link and trading contact information, neither *Lexington* nor her escorts knew *Razorback* was there. That was a risky choice but probably the best one. There was no way of knowing whether Rear Admiral Zurcher would try to assume operational command of the attack sub and make them part of the carrier's defensive screen. Technically, Zurcher *could* do that, since *Razorback* was being rude enough to sneak into his operational area, but it would hurt their chances of finding Rochambeau.

Unfortunately, there was a price to that tactic. Yes, staying out of Link reduced their chances of detection, but *Razorback* was also limited to her own organic sonar range. Theoretically, receiving sonar operation from *Lexington's* escorts would extend that range by dozens if not hundreds of miles, but Master Chief Bryan Morton still felt Abercrombie made the right choice in sailing solo.

Still, it meant their hunt had been a mind-numbing six hours of nothing so far. The sub had tracked *Lexington* out of Perth and into her operational box, where *Lexington* was scheduled to test everything repaired since the last battle. From what Morton had heard, that included one engine, several catapults, two radars, and a dozen other critical systems that couldn't be tested alongside the pier. But it really just looked like *Lexington* was sailing the same straight line over and over again from a submarine's perspective. Now the carrier was down to five knots, doing lord knew what.

Aviators and surface pukes were weird. The former were worse than the latter, if that was possible, and Morton never quite understood what the heck they got up to on a carrier all day when they weren't launching planes. Which *Lexington* definitely wasn't doing at five knots.

Morton was wasting time in Sonar when the end of that sixth hour passed. Everything was quiet, maybe too quiet, until the sonar supervisor—who was the third best sonar operator he'd ever met—sat up straight in his chair.

"What the...?"

"What's wrong?" A sinking feeling settled in Bryan's gut and wouldn't go away.

"I've got an explosion at long range, bearing one-niner-niner." Chief Ferguson's frown wrinkled his bald head. "Makes no sense all the way the hell out there, though."

"A destroyer eat a torp?" Morton frowned.

They knew there was an enemy out here, but it wasn't Rochambeau, which meant it was *Lexington's* problem. *Boone*, one of the new *Constellation*-class frigates, had got herself shot an hour earlier when *Razorback* was on the wrong side of the battle group formation, but three destroyers were out on that bearing searching for the submarine who did the deed. *Razorback* had detected faint tonals of an *Akula*-class submarine and stayed away; Rochambeau wouldn't partner with an Indian submarine, which meant their prey would be elsewhere.

Now, however, *Lexington's* maneuvering brought her—and the *Akula* who killed *Boone*—miles closer to *Razorback*.

"No way. Wrong bearing for the *Akula*, Master Chief," STS3 Sue Boxer—the *second* best sonar operator Bryan knew—interjected. "He's diddling around at zero-four-two, way too far away to do shit."

"You're saying we've got two bad guys out there."

"Bingo." Boxer stuck a Twizzler in her mouth.

"Shit." Shaking his head, Bryan headed back to control. Chief Ferguson already had passed the word up, but the heavy feeling in his gut wouldn't go away.

The captain caught his eye as soon as he'd closed the sonar curtain behind him. She still hadn't figured out how to nap, and Abercrombie beckoned him over. "You think the second one is Rochambeau?"

"Might be." Bryan didn't like playing chicken like this; that distant explosion might have been *Halibut*, the *Cero*-class boat assigned to guard *Lexington*. He hoped not. He had friends over there.

Using *Lexington* as bait seemed like a great idea until that fucking *Akula* showed up, too.

"Our mission is unchanged." Abercrombie shook her head. "*Lexington* has escorts to protect her."

"Two less, now." Morton scowled.

She looked away, sighing. "I know. But if we can get this asshole, there'll be a lot *less* American ships and subs on the bottom."

"You're right about that one, ma'am." He took a deep breath. "You want to start working around to the north?"

"A little. Let's put ourselves out on *Lexington's* starboard quarter and see what happens."

Watchstanders carried out Commander Abercrombie's orders, but Morton didn't miss the way the XO's eyes narrowed. Lieutenant Commander Debbie Keys had only been on board three weeks—her predecessor left early for a command of his own—and she wasn't what Bryan considered a tactical genius. Keys was no coward, but a dunce cap would've fit her perfectly.

Watching her frown worried him.

SUBRON 29 Headquarters, Perth, Australia

Alex spotted a familiar face when he stepped out of Banks' office following that impromptu and unpleasant lecture. He stopped cold. "Maggie? What are you doing here?"

"Hey, Captain." His former navigator turned with a grin, and they shook hands. Maggie looked the same as always, with wavy black hair in a tight bun. Now she wore the uniform of a lieutenant commander, and she looked a lot happier than she did leaving *Jimmy Carter*. "I'm the squadron's intel officer. I came by your boat a bit ago to say hi, but you weren't around."

Alex's jaw dropped. "You're the reason that report on the minelaying got out."

"Guilty as charged." Maggie laughed. "Though I won't brag too loudly about that here."

Both glanced at Banks' closed door. Alex shrugged. "I'm already in the doghouse for being unconventional."

"Say it ain't so." Maggie's eyes danced. "Still, I hear you're doing well with *Bluefish.*"

"She's not *Jimmy Carter*, but I've got a damned good crew," Alex said. Together, they walked out of the office area and into the foyer. "They were pretty messed up, but I'm getting there."

He was damned proud of them, too, but this wasn't the place to badmouth his predecessor.

Maggie nodded. "I met your new XO the other day. Someone more different than George Kirkland would be hard to imagine."

"That's not hard."

"I mean *different*, Captain." Maggie hesitated. "He came onto me like a freight train."

Alex missed a step. "Come again?"

"Like, I don't mind being flirted with, but I got the impression that he already had a bed picked out and sheets cleaned, if you know what I mean."

"Huh." Alex chewed his lower lip. Steve hadn't struck him as anything worse than ambitious. "Did he take no for an answer?"

"Yeah. Barely."

"This is...just what I need with a senator coming on my next under way." Alex let out a breath. One more thing to keep an eye on. Joy. "Thanks for telling me, Maggie."

Her smile was lopsided. "Sorry to complicate things."

"You're just calling it like it is." Alex couldn't blame her. So he shrugged and changed the subject to how Maggie liked life as an intelligence officer. Maggie was one of the finest officers he'd ever had the privilege to serve with; she'd been a rock during Convoy 57, his sounding board when George fell apart. It was a damned shame she'd left the submarine community. He would have taken *her* as his XO in a heartbeat. Maybe shorter. Maggie was one of the best.

Still, she was happy, and he supposed the intel community needed people like her, even if it was a loss for submariners.

The *Cero*-class submarine never saw him coming. *Barracuda's* computers thought it was *Halibut*, but Jules was content to wait until the United States Navy helpfully announced its identity. He could tweet about it later. He had more interesting targets to track right now.

No one seemed to notice *Halibut's* death. The Indian *Akula* he'd followed in helpfully sank an American frigate, and now the entire battle group was racing about as if they were having a fit. Ships danced left and right while the carrier's torpedo evasion maneuvers sent her north—and right into Jules Rochambeau's waiting arms.

He bared his teeth. This kill would make him the only submarine on both sides to sink more than one carrier. It would be yet another accolade in a long list, but Jules Rochambeau was the best in the business, and he wanted to set every record. There weren't many left; he had to keep inventing them. But that was the peril of being on top, was it not?

Jules smiled to himself. There would be more interviews after this one, for certain. And maybe then dear old Ursula would finally find him and they could put their rivalry to rest.

He half hoped he didn't have to kill her. *Living* with defeat would infuriate Ursula, wouldn't it? And while Britain might give her another submarine if he sank *Gallant*, the stink of having lost would never fade. Ursula wouldn't forget, and neither would Jules. Nor would the world.

"We are down to four torpedoes, Captain," Camille Dubois muttered in his ear, disrupting his daydreams.

"*Oui*." Jules nodded. He always kept count of torpedoes. One did not become the best attack submarine captain in the world by being careless. "That leaves three for the carrier and one for the way home."

She cocked her head. "Only one?"

"Supercarriers are hard to sink. Better we use too many torpedoes than not enough." He turned his attention to the plot. *Lexington* continued closing *Barracuda*, blissfully unaware of the French attack submarine in her path. The *Akula* was stalking her, too, but the fool had fired too soon. The Americans would find him, and for what? A frigate was nothing next to a carrier.

"Helicopters launched from multiple platforms," his sonar lead reported.

Jules gestured absent acknowledgment. They'd search for the *Akula*, not him. All he had to do was do his best impression of a hole in the water, staying silent and ready. All he had to do was wait. "Range?"

"Fourteen miles. Best course for interception is two-seven-three."

"Make it so." Jules tapped his fingers against the plot. "Keep your speed below ten knots. I do not want to be detected."

"*Oui, mon capitaine*."

Soon.

"Bearing and range to the *Akula*?" Abercrombie asked.

"One-zero-six, range nineteen thousand yards," Boxer answered over the speaker.

Hearing her voice made Master Chief Bryan Morton smile again. That girl was a double handful of trouble on liberty—she had a habit of bringing marijuana-laced brownies back to the boat, too—but damn her ears were good. At least she hadn't stolen an airplane recently, he thought. The incident at the fire station was nothing compared to that.

"The helo at zero-eight-one is starting to get returns off us, Captain," Boxer continued. "He don't got us cold yet but will soon."

Commander Abercrombie scowled, but when she glanced at Lieutenant Commander Keys for ideas, the XO only shrugged. Morton tried not to groan. New or not, now wasn't the time for Keys to sit back and watch!

"You want to come up in Link 18 now, ma'am?" Morton asked. They'd decided not to join the satellite data-sharing network earlier, but feeding the ASW helos their position would keep *Razorback* from being shot by accident.

"I'd love to, but I still don't think we can risk detection going against Rochambeau." Abercrombie sighed. "Let's duck below the layer and see if we can lose the helo instead."

"COB, aye." Morton didn't agree with the decision, but it wasn't his to make, so he sent the boat down another three hundred feet.

Razorback snaked under *Lexington's* formation as the destroyers formed up protectively on the carrier with the helos delousing water forward, port, and starboard of *Lexington's* course. Fortunately, the helo that been close to detection a few minutes earlier didn't follow them. Instead, it wandered over to where a destroyer was busy fishing *Boone's* survivors out of the water. That was close to the estimated position *Razorback* held on the *Akula*, but hopefully not close enough that the destroyer would die during their rescue efforts.

So far, there was no sign the *Akula* had heard the American submarine. It was busy trying to creep up on the carrier from the south but had to swing wide to avoid sonobuoys dropped by the helos.

"I think we have to kill this guy." Abercrombie crossed her arms and chewed her lower lip.

"What about using the carrier as bait?" Morton asked. "*Halibut* didn't sink herself. Someone else is out there, and it might be Rochambeau."

Abercrombie scowled. "It probably is."

Neither needed reminding what their mission was.

Keys finally spoke up. "We can't let the *Akula* sink another American ship."

Morton rolled his eyes. "Better to let Rochambeau sink another, instead?"

"We don't *know* Rochambeau is here." The XO glared. "We have a track on the *Akula*. We can kill it."

"Conn, Sonar, high-speed screws bearing one-one-five! Torpedo in the water, not in bound own ship!"

"Shit!" Abercrombie spun around. "Right full rudder, steady course one-two-zero. Ahead full for thirty-two knots!"

"Right full rudder, steady course one-two-zero. Ahead full for thirty-two knots, aye." Morton watched the helmsmen carry out the orders as he spoke. "My rudder is right thirty degrees, coming to course one-two-zero. Ahead full for thirty-two knots."

"Very well." Abercrombie sounded nervous, which made Morton swallow.

This was a shit situation for sure. Now that the threat was plain, *Razorback* had little choice but to race for the *Akula*, closing the range a hair faster than her own best silent speed of thirty knots. Was that wise? Being a tactician wasn't Morton's job, but he figured if you were going to be noisy, you should just go for broke. The boat could do better than twice that. Why try for *sort of* quiet? This speed only gave *Razorback* ten knots of overtake. A glance at the plot indicated that they'd be in ideal range of the *Akula* in eight minutes.

Eight minutes could be forever. Particularly when a torpedo hit another destroyer.

Chapter 23

Retribution

USS **Lexington** *(CVN 84) Battle Group, mid-Indian Ocean*

Four hours after relieving her captain, Nancy found herself on a Knighthawk helicopter speeding toward USS *Lexington.* Rowling sat to her right, a scowl etched into her face but otherwise silent. She had barely spoken a word to Nancy since Nancy stopped her from shooting on *Pathan's* survivors, but Nancy could see the fury boiling beneath the surface.

Was Rowlings just waiting for her chance to talk in front of Admiral Zurcher? Probably. But any argument of innocence on her part would be countered by the man strapped to the seat on Nancy's left.

She met Eric Armstrong's eyes briefly. The reporter, or "vlogger," as he preferred to be called, had a video of the entire disaster. Nancy had watched parts of it before getting in the helicopter, and she was still surprised by how calm and collected she seemed in the video. But questions plagued her. Had she waited too long? Would more Indians be alive if Nancy had stopped Rowlings right away? Could she have seen it coming?

The silence in the helicopter—enforced by the loud *thrumming* of the rotors, which kept anyone from talking—did her racing mind no favors. Nancy preferred action to second-guessing herself. She was good with making decisions, not so much with pulling them apart afterward and figuring out what went wrong or what went right. But here she was trapped with her thoughts, trapped with the knowledge that *Cape* and her stolen convoy were closing *Lexington's* position to join the battle group. But the admiral had explanations out of Nancy sooner, which meant a helicopter ride.

She'd barely had time to finish recovering the survivors and call Alex before the helicopter arrived. Fortunately, the conversation with her husband had been encouraging...at least after Alex got over his shock. Nancy couldn't blame him; the idea of an XO *actually* relieving their captain while the latter was in the process of committing a war crime was absurd.

"Landing in two mikes," the pilot said over the intercom.

Nancy glanced out the window as *Lexington* grew in size, her heart pounding like drums in her ears. Was she confident? Could she explain her actions? Absolutely. Truth was on her side, and she had proof.

Then why did she feel so nauseous?

Less than ten minutes later, Nancy, Armstrong, and Rowlings followed a junior lieutenant away from the helicopter and its still-spinning rotors. Unsurprisingly, the trio was led immediately to Admiral Zurcher's cabin, where both the admiral and his chief of staff waited for them.

For her. Rowlings and Armstrong were asked to remain outside, while Nancy was led right in by the admiral's aide.

The admiral's cabin was more austere than she expected, with just the standard navy decorations: an ugly painting on one white-painted bulkhead, monitors showing the tactical and navigational plots, and an old-fashioned clock that looked like a compass. It had one small porthole that showed blue sea and sky, but few personal knickknacks. Admiral Zurcher didn't even have the standard *I love me* wall where most senior officers displayed their awards, deployment souvenirs, and farewell gifts from past ships. This was a room meant to be worked in, one much like Nancy's own stateroom back on *Cape*.

Admiral Zurcher was a tall and slender man with dark skin, intense eyes, and short-cropped hair. Nancy only knew him by reputation—he was an aviator, not a surface warfare officer—but he'd been more successful than most so far in the war. And he hadn't gone to pieces like the *last* carrier admiral she encountered, so that had to count for something.

Granted, now that former admiral was a senator, so Nancy wasn't sure what to feel on that front.

"Admiral." As casual as the navy was, now was a time to pop to attention, so Nancy did.

"Commander Coleman." Zurcher nodded stiffly. "As much as I'd like to welcome you aboard, it seems now is not the time for pleasantries."

She swallowed. "No, sir, I don't believe it is."

"Then take a seat and tell me what happened." His dark eyes bored into her own. "Your reputation precedes you, as does Captain Rowlings', so tell me the truth."

Steeling herself, Nancy began to speak.

Barracuda continued humming along her course, her crew working quietly and professionally. Jules's ambitions might've brought them here, but for his top-notch crew, this was just another mission. One more chance to strike at the enemy; one more chance to put France on top.

France had withered for too long, and every French sailor felt the tug of national pride driving them on, just as much as Jules Rochambeau did. They knew that territory in the Indian Ocean, and the riches therein, could change France's future forever. Sooner or later, their enemy would give way and make peace. France would not get to keep all of her gains, but enough underwater territory would remain theirs to upend the old balance.

Jules Rochambeau savored being one of the people responsible for that change.

"Captain, there's another *Cero* out there," Sonar reported.

Jules looked up. "Oh?"

"Sounds like an Improved *Cero*. Moving at thirty-two knots, range thirteen-point-five nautical miles."

Ah. Jules sat back in his seat. An Improved *Cero* was quite the prize. Not quite as good as a carrier, but...he would not mind getting both. Perhaps it was time to reevaluate his torpedo priorities.

"Preliminary identification is USS *Razorback*," sonar continued.

His head snapped around. "*Razorback*?"

"*Oui, mon capitaine*."

Grinning, Jules turned to his first officer. "Fate is a tempting mistress, Camille," he said. "Now I must choose."

"I would normally say the carrier, but it is *Razorback*," Camille agreed. "She is being very kind to stumble into our sights like this."

"*Oui*. And I have no intention of allowing some fumbling Indian *Akula* to accomplish *our* mission and gain the glory of killing *Razorback*." Jules frowned. He was the best in the world, but *Razorback* killed a French carrier on her last patrol. National pride was at stake. Besides, *Razorback* was America's most successful submarine. Between Dalton and Abercrombie, she'd sunk thirty-one warships. If anyone else from the Freedom Union killed her, their reputation would grow.

No. Jules would not allow that.

"Well, that was something." Eric Armstrong looked as pale and drawn as Nancy felt; his normally chipper face was creased with worry, making him look ten years older than his thirty-three years as he leaned against a railing on the carrier's O-4 level.

Nancy's smile was crooked, though she had to wait for an F-35 to finish taking off before she replied: "Never been on the receiving end of an admiral's ire before?"

"I'm still glad I just took an indirect blast. Maybe shrapnel?" He shook his head, looking as dizzy as if someone had punched him.

She chuckled. "It was just a glancing blow. Captain Rowlings took the worst of it, thanks to your video."

"It's what I do."

Nancy couldn't lie; going before Admiral Zurcher to explain herself left her so nervous she could barely breathe. Relieving Captain Rowlings wasn't something she'd done on a whim, and she knew it was the right thing to do, but that didn't mean this wasn't a monumental event. Relieving the most successful cruiser captain in the navy for cause *in the middle of a war*? It was unthinkable. Rowlings' combat record was more impressive than Nancy's, and while she was known for being a hard ass who chewed up her XOs and spit them out again, no one had ever even hinted that she might do something against the laws of war.

But shooting an enemy who could no longer fight back, at enemy survivors in the water, was a war crime. There was no debate.

Thank goodness Admiral Zurcher agreed.

"Now what?" Armstrong asked. He'd been present to provide his video, but Zurcher asked the reporter to leave for the bulk of Nancy's testimony.

Nancy took a deep breath. "Now we return to *Cape*...and Captain Rowlings stays here on the carrier, pending disciplinary action."

"Please tell me she'll go to courts martial."

"It would be hard not to. There are fourteen dead Indians." Nancy grimaced. "I should have stopped her sooner."

"You needed about three seconds to react. I'd say that's pretty human," he replied. "You were faster than the rest of us, that's for sure."

"People still died that shouldn't have." She watched sailors running back and forth on the flight deck as they prepared to launch a wave of F-35 fighters. Nancy didn't envy a carrier's crew; everything on this floating city revolved around the air wing. She preferred ships with a mission to shoot and fight.

Two helicopters lifted off as she watched; rumor said an Indian sub was harassing *Lexington*. Nancy made a face. Sub hunting was the name of the game these days, but that didn't mean she enjoyed it. Though she'd enjoy it a lot more from on board *Cape*. Warfare sucked as a spectator.

"And Captain Rowlings will pay for that," Armstrong replied.

"True." She sighed. "I'll have to testify when it goes to trial, I'm sure."

"I'll make myself available if the navy needs me, too."

Nancy snickered. "And cover the trial in your vlogs while you're at it?"

"Hey, I'm not one to pass up an opportunity. Once the admiral okays this for release, this one's so hot it'll spontaneously combust."

"I'm not sure I should get behind that."

Armstrong shrugged. "The navy asked for embedded reporters. I'm just reporting what I see, and what I *saw* was you not letting Rowlings commit war crimes. That's not a black eye. That's good."

Her smile felt forced. "If you say so."

"Trust me. This is what I know."

Before Nancy could reply, a young-looking ensign approached. "Commander Coleman? I'm here to escort you to your helo."

"Thank you." Nancy's knees felt weak with relief. She hadn't liked leaving *Cape* at such a critical juncture; the cruiser had sixty-eight Indian POWs on board and was now without a captain or an XO. Thankfully, Nancy had been confirmed in *acting* command, which would at least take care of things for now.

Would she assume permanent command after this? Nancy wasn't sure. She was still a commander, and a cruiser was a captain's billet. The idea of stepping over the corpse of Rowlings' career to get a promotion made acid do laps in her stomach, but Nancy knew she was already slated to be *Cape's* next commanding officer. Was it too soon? Admiral Zurcher hadn't said one way or another, and she didn't know the man well enough to make a bet.

"Ready to get back?" Armstrong asked.

"You know it," she replied. "If my hair isn't gray by then, I'll consider myself lucky."

Razorback shuddered.

"Tubes two and four fired electrically," Weps reported.

"Two fish running hot, straight, and normal," Sonar added.

Abercrombie nodded. "Very well."

Master Chief Morton's earlier worries appeared unfounded. The *Akula* hadn't detected them; hell, it didn't even start maneuvering until twenty seconds after *Razorback's* torpedo launch. Then it put on speed and ran like hell, but simple math said that wasn't going to help.

He grinned. *Bye, Charlie.*

That *Akula* was doomed. Commander Abercrombie had closed to twelve thousand yards before firing, and a Mark 84 ASV covered that distance in eleven minutes and change. By the time the *Akula* turned and started running, the proverbial snowball would've had a better chance in hell than the Indian sub would've had to outrun that torpedo.

"Ten minutes to impact," Weps announced.

"Very well. COB, come right to one-four-five," Abercrombie ordered.

"Aye, ma'am." Morton nodded and relayed those orders to his team. One-four-five brought them back toward *Lexington*, who'd turned south to open the range with the *Akula*. It also kept *Razorback* between the enemy and the carrier, which was always a good idea.

Maybe he'd worried over nothing. Yeah, someone else was out there, but if that someone wasn't quick to act, *Razorback* would rule the seas. Morton liked the sound of that.

The minutes flew by.

"Two good hits!" Weps pumped her fist, grinning.

"Conn, Sonar, implosion and breakup noises from the *Akula*," Chief Ferguson said.

That made even Keys happy, though Morton didn't miss the *I-told-you-so* look the XO shot him. He shrugged. The nice thing about being a master chief was not needing to worry about petty—

Boxer's voice thundered out of the speaker: "Conn, Sonar, torpedo in the—*shit*, two torpedoes in the water bearing zero-two-five and zero-two-three! Range nine thousand yards!"

"All ahead flank!" Abercrombie snapped, and the helmsman slammed the throttles forward before Morton could respond. "Full rise on the planes!"

"Full rise, aye," Morton echoed. There wasn't time to wonder how the enemy had gotten so close. "Planes at max, passing nine hundred feet."

"Very well." Abercrombie jerked her head at Keys. "Stand by countermeasures."

"Standing by!" For once, the XO was on the ball, her hand poised over the button.

"Snapshot tube one, bearing zero-two-three!"

The weapons team raced to comply, shooting a torpedo down the approximate bearing of their attacker. *Razorback* didn't know who'd shot at them, but a snapshot could disrupt the enemy's firing solution—or just kill them outright.

"Weapon away!"

"Range seven thousand yards!" Boxer shouted.

"What?" Morton felt his eyes go wide, even as Abercrombie demanded:

"Say again, Sonar!"

"Seventy-five hundred yards!"

Chief Ferguson chimed in: "Torpedo speed one hundred thirty–plus knots!"

"Holy shit." The whisper escaped before Morton could stop himself. The Mark 84 was the best torpedo in the Alliance arsenal, and it topped out at a sprightly eighty-seven knots. There was a mythical, almost legendary, Russian three hundred–knot torpedo, but he'd never seen one. Most everyone he knew had only talked to someone who knew someone who'd seen it. This sucker, however, was real as death.

Crap, that was a bad analogy.

"Left full rudder!" Abercrombie ordered. "Drop first countermeasure!"

Razorback rolled into her turn, up to fifty knots and heeling hard. Her deck sloped upward at the same time as the submarine shuddered and shook, leaving the crew climbing a mountain sideways.

"Passing five hundred feet!" Morton grabbed a pipe in the overhead for balance.

"Level off at two hundred." Abercrombie's eyes were locked on the plot. "Range?"

"Conn, Sonar, five thousand yards." A few tense seconds passed; Morton leveled the boat out at the ordered depth and held his breath. The speed indicator ticked its way to sixty-three knots, and then slowly to 63.4.

That was the best *Razorback* had, but the torpedo was still seventy knots faster.

Boxer continued: "First torp is at the countermeasure... Yes, it's foxed it! First torp is circling."

Someone cheered. Abercrombie looked grim. "Very well. What about the second one?"

"Thirty-five hundred yards out and still on our tail!"

Morton swallowed. He'd been outright terrified more than once on *Jimmy Carter*, but even when they'd bounced off the bottom, he'd never thought they were done. Now, there was a cold shiver stealing down his spine that wouldn't go away. There was too much goddamned overtake. The three-minute rule said that torpedo would gain seven thousand yards every three minutes, and *Razorback* was only nine thousand yards away to begin with.

"Hard right rudder! Drop two countermeasures!"

"My rudder is right thirty-five degrees, no new course given," Morton repeated automatically.

Twenty-three hundred yards a minute. Shit. Morton couldn't stop thinking about his kids. Damn, he didn't need this distraction, but how was his ex-wife going to explain this to them?

"Countermeasures away!" the XO said.

"*Sonova*—Captain, the torp ran right through!" Boxer shouted. "Range two thousand yards!"

Less than a minute. He'd been trained for this; Morton didn't wait for an order. They had one chance, and just one. "Hit the roof!" he barked at the planesman, a petrified petty officer second class. "Planes to the max!"

Morton blew every ballast tank, initiating an emergency blow. They were at two hundred feet. Was there time? Their only chance of surviving a torp strike was to be near the surface and hope some watertight bulkheads held through the blast. Even then, *Razorback* might go turtle, and even their escape airlock might be breached—

"Launch countermeasures!" Abercrombie ordered again.

Keys hit the button hard enough to break the plastic. "Third set away!"

"Brace for impact!" Morton lunged for the collision alarm. It was the only way to warn the entire crew, and he'd waited too long.

Boom.

He yanked the alarm handle down just as a wall slammed into his back and everything went dark.

Jules disliked missing, even when the odds said about forty percent of the newest French torpedo, the sleek and fast F27 Rafale, would miss. So far, *he* had a hit rate of almost sixty percent, ignoring the fact that this last miss would decrease that. Fortunately, his second torpedo had done the job. He smiled.

"Well done, people," he said to his crew. "Now, let us kill another aircraft carrier."

"With only two torpedoes?" Camille arched an eyebrow.

Jules shrugged. "Better to merely damage it than leave it alone. Close the range, *s'il vous plaît*."

It went without saying that a fortuitous shot would take even a super carrier down. Two torpedoes were less than doctrine required, but Jules was paid to make decisions. *Barracuda* quivered and sped up, racing after *Lexington* and her escorts. The helicopters were headed in the wrong direction, probably still looking for the *Akula*. Had they heard *Razorback* explode? He did not know.

They would find out there was additional trouble in the water soon enough.

Jules sat down in his tiny fold-down chair in the attack center and folded his hands. He had time to relax. No one had detected him, not even *Razorback*, and they were supposed to be America's best. Winning was almost boring, or would have been, if not for all the allocates and internet fun. Oh, he was going to enjoy tweeting this evening. The Americans would be bitterly offended by the time he was finished today.

"Captain, it sounds like *Razorback* is close enough to the surface to abandon," Sonar reported.

"Oh?" Jules cocked his head. The American battle group was miles away. Had they even noticed? Perhaps the helicopters would find *Razorback's* survivors. "Record the position in case our American friends forget to pick them up."

Jules saw no reason to butcher survivors, or even to abandon them. His countrymen and their Alliance would love to question the crew of an Improved *Cero*, wouldn't they? Perhaps someday he could thank the commander of *Razorback* for the abbreviated chase in person. Wouldn't that be entertaining?

There had been very few prisoner exchanges so far during the war. No one wanted to return highly trained military personnel, not in a war where *people* were one of the limiting factors. Who would have thought it was easier to build a technologically complicated nuclear attack submarine than it was to find qualified sailors to man her? France faced problem after problem keeping her ships and submarines manned. The latter were particularly difficult, as more submarine sailors went down with the ship than their surface counterparts.

Jules could not imagine a situation in which the Americans, even with their vast population, did not have the same problem. They were so bitterly against conscription, with war protestors—oh, how he loved to watch them on television—saying that even the *suggestion* of a draft impinged upon their freedoms. Their infantile posturing made Jules laugh. How could so powerful a nation live with people like that within her ranks? They were just another example of how America's time was done.

He returned his attention to the plot as *Lexington* increased speed. Pity for her that she was running in the wrong direction, assuming she wanted to live. *Barracuda* was almost parallel to her course and closing fast.

Perfect.

USS Lexington *(CVN 84) Battle Group, mid-Indian Ocean*

After what felt like hours of waiting, a Knighthawk helicopter lifted off with Nancy and Eric Armstrong on board a few minutes before sunset. The aircraft banked right, and she could see *Edward Byers*—named after a Medal of Honor winner from her own alma mater—listing to port and limping along far back in *Lexington's* wake. Flames licked at the front of the destroyer's superstructure as ant-like sailors fought the fire, racing back and forth. Their figures grew larger as the helicopter swept down *Byers'* starboard side. From Nancy's perspective, her bow looked crooked, almost like she had a broken nose.

Torpedoes were supposed to snap ships' spines. Had this one missed and ended up with her nose?

The helicopter circled, waiting for clearance to depart *Lexington's* vicinity. It was no formality; the carrier's airspace was busy with fixed-wing fighters and anti-submarine warfare helicopters. The former were on guard against any enemy attack from the air, while the latter were hunting for the submarine everyone knew was out there. Trying not to tap her foot impatiently, Nancy watched the battle group with curious eyes. This wasn't her normal vantage point, and the ships seemed so tiny from here, even *Lexington.* The cruisers and destroyers surrounding her looked even smaller.

Despite her chosen career path, Nancy liked flying. Seeing the power of a carrier battle group from above was enough to give her chills. By dawn, *Cape* would join up with *Lexington,* turn her prisoners over, and then—

"What the—" the pilot's voice buzzed in her ear, breaking into Nancy's thoughts.

Suddenly, the helicopter banked hard right, throwing Nancy against Armstrong, who squeaked. Below them, *Lexington* turned hard, water boiling at her stern—

Two explosions, one right after the other, geysered out of the water on *Lexington's* port side. The carrier rocked forward—no, the bow and stern both dipped as her midsection reared up—as Nancy watched in horror. Then the ship settled back toward the waves again, seeming to move in slow motion, water churning as *Lexington's* deck trembled. Two helicopters spinning on deck lifted frantically, and one F-35 fighter rolled right off the starboard side.

Ant-sized figures raced across the flight deck, some jumping into the water and others heading into the superstructure. Empty minutes passed in silence; hundreds more people appeared on deck, releasing life rafts and racing for other helicopters. Pilots jumped out of their fighters, and the carrier developed a dangerous port list, making people and aircraft slide in that direction. Suddenly, *Lexington's* middle dropped, and kept dropping, right until the flight deck dipped into the ocean, disintegrating while her screws spun uselessly in the air.

"Oh my God," Nancy whispered.

Armstrong grabbed her arm with a shaking hand. The reporter's eyes were wide, lost. But Nancy knew her own expression matched his. There were four thousand people on the carrier. Four *thousand* people. Nancy's stomach lurched.

"We have to go back for survivors!" The pilot's voice sounded like a gasp over the intercom.

Nancy shook her head. "Put us down on *Byers* first."

"But—"

"You'll have more room. Do it."

"Yes, ma'am." The poor kid looked like he wanted someone to tell him what to do, and Nancy outranked a junior lieutenant by a mile.

Within five minutes, Nancy and Armstrong stood on board *Byers's* flight deck, there greeted by the destroyer's operations officer. By then, *Lexington* had slipped beneath the waves, leaving hundreds of survivors bobbing amid jet fuel and debris.

Nancy just squared her shoulders and headed toward *Byers's* bridge. She had a cruiser to contact and would help however she could.

Chapter 24

Into the Valley

Jules wished he had time for some old-fashioned periscope photos. The sight of an American supercarrier sinking must have been a thing of beauty—but he could not afford to tarry. It was such a pity; he would have loved to see *Lexington* slipping beneath the waves. Listening to the litany of explosions and implosions over sonar was not the same.

"They are buzzing like angry hornets up there," he said to Camille with a grin.

Her smile was smug. "Our helicopters would be much the same."

"*Oui*." Still, one had to only be able to do simple math to know that the three American carriers lost so far in the war equaled the total number of carriers France had in service. Two more were under construction, but the Americans still had ten others. Still, they had to cover three oceans, where the Jules's nation was concerned with far less.

"Will you tweet about this, Captain?" Her eyes gleamed.

"*Bien sûr.*" Of course. "But after we are free of the hounds." Jules gestured overhead, where American anti-submarine aircraft circled, hunting. He felt confident that he could elude them, but encountering another Alliance submarine now could be just as deadly. *Barracuda* was out of torpedoes. Care was in order.

Per usual, Camille read his mind. "Admiral Sauvageau will be annoyed that we did not find Captain North."

Jules shrugged. "An aircraft carrier and *Razorback* should mollify him."

He was not truly worried about what his superior thought. The Americans had sent their best to defend *Lexington.* Patricia Abercrombie had been out racking up kills whilst Captain Coleman did television specials. But she, too, fell to *Barracuda*. Ursula North was the only competition left. Jules would make a point of finding her before long. Sooner or later, Lady North would end up in his sights. Jules could wait.

Perhaps in the meantime, he'd antagonize an additional American or two. That would be fun.

Perth, Australia

The ringing of eight bells echoed across the water. *"Commander, Submarine Forces, Pacific, arriving!"*

Eight more bells.

"Senator from the State of Maryland, arriving!"

Alex fidgeted. Of course, Commodore Banks had decided at the last minute to shift *Bluefish's* underway time to before dawn tomorrow. That meant embarking Senator Angler tonight, along with an aide who would displace Rose's roommate for the duration of the patrol. Leaving his supply officer behind wasn't ideal, but Steve was able to jump through seventeen administrative hoops and send her to some useful schools in the meantime.

At least he hadn't had to host a senator for dinner.

And his new XO was earning his keep.

Maybe if he kept thinking about the silver linings, he wouldn't go to pieces with nerves. That was a good strategy, right? Alex wanted to ask who'd signed him up for this dog-and-pony show, but he knew exactly who was at fault and why. It all started with Convoy 57, and there were days he really just wished he'd left *Jimmy Carter* sitting on the bottom. It would've been a hell of a lot more peaceful.

But he'd had the audacity to live, so there was no getting away from the ceremony. Stepping forward, Alex dredged up his best smile and held his hand out.

"Welcome aboard, Senator," Alex said to Senator Angler, hiding the butterflies racing around his midsection.

Angler was a tall man, with an eagle-beaked nose and graying hair. He looked like his son, assuming Benji Angler ever wanted to wear such a high-and-mighty expression. Oh, Alex doubted Angler *wanted* to look snotty, but he definitely held himself like he was someone important.

"Thank you, Captain." Angler smiled and made way for Rodriquez.

"Captain, I hope you don't mind if I ride along, too." Marco Rodriquez's grin sucked the air right out of Alex's lungs. "No need to put me anywhere fancy. Stick me in the J.O. Jungle or enlisted berthing."

Alex gulped. "I'll...see what I can do, sir."

Sweet Jesus, why me? The thought of staying on the bottom during Convoy 57 was looking better and better. Alex wanted to sink into the deck and disappear. Steve's eager smile to his left didn't help, either. Alex didn't mind his XO's ambition, but man, he missed having Bobby as his right hand. Bobby would feel his pain and babble his way through it.

Come to think of it, maybe there were benefits to not having Bobby's babbling ass out here.

"Good man." Rodriquez slapped him on the shoulder hard enough to hurt, but Alex's mind wouldn't stop whirling.

Should he oust Steve out of the XO's stateroom and put the admiral in with the senator? That would make sense. But Bobby approached before Alex could open his mouth.

"Captain, you got a sec?"

"Sure, Bobby," Alex said, watching with half an eye as Steve offered to escort Angler to his stateroom. Meanwhile, Rodriquez struck up a conversation with the officer of the deck under Rose's watchful gaze. Thankfully, Rene could usually be counted not to stick his foot in his mouth. At least when he was sober, which the young lieutenant (junior grade) had been ever since that debacle at the Mediterranean.

"Didn't you tell me that your wife was over on *Lexington*?" Bobby asked.

"Yeah?" Alex turned to face him, remembering how he'd mentioned Nancy's crazy circumstances to Bobby. His wife had called him after the debacle on *Cape St. George* and told him she was bringing her war crime–committing captain over to the carrier to face the admiral. The situation left Alex's mind whirling; for all the problems he'd had with his old XO, at least George Kirkland had never tried to shoot survivors.

"Then you're going to want to read this." Bobby's knuckles were white as he handed over the message tablet. Something in his expression made Alex's heart start pounding.

Alex pulled up the top message, scanning past the header information and to the subject. He froze.

> USS LEXINGTON TORPEDOED AND SUNK IVO 30°39'02.4"S 94°02'56.1"E. RESCUE IN PROGRESS.

Alex's stomach heaved, and the tablet tumbled to the deck, falling out of his nerveless fingers. It hit sound absorbent tiles and the screen shattered, despite the "tough" case, but Alex didn't notice. He didn't even remember dropping it. He didn't remember speaking, or Bobby guiding him down to his stateroom while fending off Admiral Rodriquez's curiosity. It was a carrier, Alex told himself again and again. Lots of people got off carriers when they sank.

But Nancy was on that goddamned carrier, there because her supposedly hotshot captain felt the need to *shoot at survivors in the water* and no one else had the guts to stop her. She'd called him hours ago, nervous—Nancy, nervous!—about reporting to the battle group admiral, worried that Rowlings' get-the-job-done reputation would overshadow this obvious war crime.

Now *Lexington* was on the bottom or headed to it. Talk about an event that would overshadow everything. Alex felt sick.

Somehow, he wound up sitting numbly at his desk, scrolling through message traffic and hoping for a list of survivors.

Steve dropped the senator off in his stateroom and turned his mind to the problem of Admiral Rodriquez. No way was he sticking COMBSUBPAC in enlisted berthing. That left the Junior Officers' "Jungle," one of the six-person staterooms the ensigns and junior lieutenants slept in. That was a terrible idea, too, but judging from Admiral Rodriquez's reputation, he'd probably enjoy it.

It'd do those kids good, too. The environment on *Bluefish* was too casual—a fact proven by the way Lieutenant (j.g.) Hill answered the phone in the forward junior officers' six man. "DCA, what's up?"

Steve scowled. "DCA, it's the XO. I need you to clear a rack in your stateroom for Admiral Rodriquez. He's getting underway with us."

"You want him in the J.O. Jungle?" Wally repeated.

"Did I stutter?" Steve wanted to strangle the kid. Where did he get off talking to a senior officer like that?

"Sorry, sir. Sure. I guess I can do that."

"You 'guess' you can?" Steve snapped. "Lieutenant, I expect better than that out of one of the so-called 'top' division officers on board."

"I'll get it done, sir." Wally sounded stung, as well he should.

"You do that." Steve hung up, growling under his breath. These kids took everything for granted and flitted their way through every task like it was a game.

He needed to find a way to enhance discipline to this boat. That was his *job* as XO. Steve was still stoked to be here—being the second-in-command to Alex Coleman would make his career, particularly with *Bluefish's* record—but Coleman was surprisingly casual. His attitude wore off on the rest of the crew, and Steve blamed Bobby O'Kane for that. He'd let the crew go, let them do whatever they wanted as long as they got the job done.

Not that Bobby knew any better. He was only the navigator. Steve supposed he shouldn't blame him; he was young and needed mentoring, too. At least Bobby seemed competent, as did everyone on board. He could work with that, though Steve had a feeling he'd really need to shake things up first. Some sailors—some crews—needed to learn a leader was *serious* before they buckled down and remembered they were in the military.

Steve had a few ideas in mind to put fear and discipline back into *Bluefish's* crew, but they'd have to wait. No way was he making waves with a senator and Admiral Rodriquez on board. He'd just have to hope no one did anything super casual or embarrassing in the meantime, because there was no way this side of hell that Steve would allow anyone on this boat to get in the way of his career rocketing right to the top.

He'd always known he just needed a break. Now he'd gotten one: he was at Alex Coleman's right hand, sitting beside the submarine service's *only* living Medal of Honor winner. No one was going to get in his way.

USS Lexington *(CVN 84) Battle Group, mid-Indian Ocean*

Edward Byers wasn't just swamped by *Lexington's* survivors; the destroyer was in the middle of repairing her own battle damage. A quick trip to the bridge and a conversation with her captain—who Nancy was inconveniently senior to—led to Nancy volunteering to help fight the damage and find *Byers's* own wounded while the destroyer's captain coordinated with other ships performing search-and-rescue for the sunken carrier.

As senior officer present, Nancy might've stood on ceremony and insisted on doing the "sexy" job; however, she didn't know the captains in the *Lexington* battle group and there wasn't time for her to butt in and figure things out.

Nancy was a practical woman, and her nation was at war. Her job was to help as best she could, and until *Cape* arrived at midnight, Nancy would do her best. No way would a helicopter be available before then, either. Not with four thousand people to pull out of the water and find homes for on the other ships.

Nancy glanced at *Byers's* damage control plates and grimaced. She'd taken station on the mess decks, coordinating repairs in conjunction with the destroyer's damage control assistant. The ship's chief engineer was dead, along with a third of the engineering department, which left a young lieutenant scrambling to put the lamed engineering plant back together while the rest of the team fought both fires and flooding.

After two hours, Nancy was fairly sure they had the fires out and most of the water out of the people space, but after two reflashes, she wasn't going to bet her life on it. *Edward Byers* hadn't taken a direct hit from the torpedo, but it exploded close enough to wrench her bow around and tear watchstanders apart in three separate spaces. The resulting fire engulfed her forward engine room, leaving her with only one working propeller and at least twenty-five dead sailors...plus thirty still unaccounted for.

A phone talker grabbed the DCA's arm, and she watched Lieutenant (junior grade) Costello go pale.

"What is it?" she asked

Costello gulped. "There's people trapped up forward in sonar and anchor windless."

"Go on." Nancy gestured for him to continue when he stuttered to a halt.

"They're hurt. They can't get out."

Nancy looked around and took a deep breath. "You got a team to send?"

"Not really." Costello grimaced. "Two stretchers. Brody and Reyes are qualified stretcher bearers, but no one else in here is."

"Then I'll take them and two non-quals." She glanced around, catching sight of the white-faced and frozen corpsman sitting in the corner. "I'll also take HM1 Lopez. You've got things here."

Costello blinked. "Ma'am, don't you want to send someone, um..."

"Younger?" Nancy's grin dared him to say something else.

"More junior?" Costello shrugged.

Nancy shrugged. "I'm what we've got." She turned to the four sailors with the last two stretchers. "Let's go."

A lifetime passed before Alex started thinking. Then he read the message again. *Lexington* was sunk. Rescue efforts were underway; that meant the carrier hadn't just exploded into smithereens. Should he call the girls? What about Nancy's mother? Bobbie was at the academy, but Emily hadn't graduated high school yet. Quick math told him both should be heading to class soon, if not already there. He took a shuddering breath. *Nancy might be fine.* Was this worth ruining their day? The navy would sit on the news as long as they could.

Unless some asshole tweeted about it.

That thought made Alex's chest seize up; *Lexington* had been torpedoed. The Freedom Union had a hundred-plus submarines in the war, but odds were fair he knew which one was responsible. Suddenly, Alex understood why Steve hated Rochambeau so much. And he'd been within *spitting* distance of the bastard with *Jimmy Carter.* If his failure then... Alex couldn't finish the thought.

He wanted to throw up. Nancy couldn't be dead. A 110,000-ton warship didn't sink in seconds. There would be time to get people off. Carriers weren't submarines. They were *on* the water, not in it. Alex knew the statistics: roughly half of any warship's crew escaped a sinking. Sometimes more. He cheerfully bet his own life on worse odds than that every time he got underway, but it was different for someone he loved.

Alex gave up on message traffic and dropped his head into his hands. He'd been a clueless and shy freshman when he and Nancy met at Norwich University, skinny and looking like he'd been assembled out of spare parts. She'd been athletic and gorgeous, even then, with a mile-long line of recruits who wanted to invite her to the Navy-Marine Corps Ball. Somehow, however, Nancy picked him. And somehow, he'd made it through the humiliating experience of "serenading" her in the mess hall, had weathered the not-so-good-natured ribbing from her training cadre and the marathon run they'd made him do.

Decades later, Alex still marveled at the fact that she chose him. Alex wasn't handsome or athletic; he'd been all knees and elbows and David to his roommate's Goliath. Those nicknames stuck for four years, through two breakups with Nancy and a senior-year pregnancy that scared both out of their wits and made Nancy's parents refuse to talk to her for three months. Her father never had come around, but her mother had, courtesy of a quick wedding in White Chapel and a howling baby girl they named after Roberta Petretti.

Their early years in the navy were a mess of learning to be parents and officers at the same time. They weathered separations while Alex went to numerous schools for nuclear reactors, invested in base daycare when Nancy was underway as a junior surface warfare officer, and finally gave in and asked Roberta to move in when USS *Virginia* spent three weeks out of every four underway during Alex's first year on board. His mother-in-law forgave him for the ill timing of Bobbie's conception after Emily was born, and somewhere along the way, Roberta filled some of the void left by his own parents' deaths while Alex was in college. Their family grew more solid over the years, strong enough to withstand a war that pulled both Alex and Nancy halfway around the world from home.

Could it withstand this?

A knock came on his door, followed by Bobby O'Kane's voice: "You okay, Captain?"

Shit. He was supposed to get underway tomorrow morning. *Bluefish* had a senator and a three-star admiral on board, and Alex was the fucking captain. He just wanted to be there for his daughters when—*if!*—they heard the news. Alex scraped his hands over his face before he could make himself speak.

"Yeah." He swallowed. "Come in."

Bobby crept in with the enthusiasm of a chicken on its way to slaughter, then closed the door. "Can I, um, do anything, sir?"

Great. He was back to *um* and *uh*-ing. That said a lot about how Alex looked. He shook his head. "Not unless you've got a magic wand and can make news get here faster."

"Sorry, they were fresh out of magic wands at the uniform store," Bobby replied. "I could get you a pink tutu, though."

"A *what*?" Alex surprised himself by laughing. "Christ, Bobby."

"Sorry, Captain. I didn't—"

Alex waved a hand. "Don't apologize. Not you." He ran his hands over his face again. "Not right now."

"Sure."

Silence reigned for a few moments; Alex still felt empty, if perhaps a little more human. He still didn't know how to cope, had no idea how to face this, but at least he had a friend to talk to.

A friend. When had Bobby O'Kane become a friend?

"Not to be the bad news bear, but there was a SUBSUNK on *Razorback*, too," Bobby said. "Wasn't your old master chief there?"

"Shit." Alex felt like a mule had kicked him in the stomach. *"Yes."*

"They were near *Lexington*," Bobby added, and they dropped into silence again.

Nancy's odds were better than Bryan Morton's, math that made Alex feel guilty. Would crying make him feel better? Probably not. Numbness inched down his spine. Maybe he'd burn for revenge later. At some point, he'd start feeling again, right?

Another knock came before Alex could pull himself together. Bobby gestured at the door.

"Do you want me to...?"

"No." *You wanted another command, asshole. Act like it.* Alex took a deep breath. "Come in!"

Steve stuck his head in, pausing when he spotted Bobby. "Sir, I've got the senator settled in the spare rack in my stateroom, and Admiral Rodriquez in the forward J.O. Jungle. I've set up a tour for Senator Angler in fifteen minutes. Do you want to come along?"

A proper captain would. Alex *should*. "I think you'll be all right, XO," he said. "Try not to let the admiral scare anyone."

"He already wandered off, sir." Steve looked befuddled. "Said something to DCA about sneaking up on another boat."

Well, that was one thing out of his hair. Alex nodded listlessly.

"Better them than us, right?" Bobby asked.

Steve shot him a strange look. "I'd prefer a warning in their shoes, Nav."

"Duh, but beggars can't be choosers." Bobby shrugged.

"Anything else you want me to deal with tonight, Captain?" Steve asked, making Alex aware of his conspicuous silence.

"No, nothing right now." Alex knew he sounded duller than an unsharpened pencil, but his mind was anywhere but there. Shit. If he couldn't get out of this fog, he wasn't fit for command. That thought should have scared him, but right now, nothing did.

"I'll help with the tour, XO," Bobby said, jumping to his feet. "Never hurts to have someone else wrangle a politician, right?"

"Wrangle?"

"Sorry, I'm from Texas." Bobby grinned and ushered Steve out of the room.

Alex just stared at the wall.

Picking their way through wrecked passageways took longer than Nancy expected. She prided herself on her fitness, and she still liked to run—unlike her husband, who rolled his eyes at running shoes and went for a swim—but climbing over downed equipment proved challenging. They needed twenty minutes to travel less than one hundred and fifty feet, finally reaching *Byers's* anchor windless. The space was as far forward as you could get on the destroyer's main deck, and Nancy was pretty sure you didn't usually hang a right to get inside.

But the watertight door leading into anchor windless was warped and wrenched that way, so she stepped through, walking right into a wave of warm air, blood, and burned metal.

There were five sailors, two women and three men. All looked shell-shocked and one was unconscious, with her leg bent at a horrible angle and bones sticking out. The others were bruised and bleeding; they looked like the explosion had merrily used them as ping pong balls.

One of the stretcher bearers retched, adding to the already poignant smell.

"The windlass got unseated when the torpedo exploded," one of the men said. He was a third class petty officer, probably an engineer. He only used one arm to gesture at the windlass as the other held a wound on his abdomen closed. He'd stuffed rags in the wound—Nancy hoped they were clean, unlike half the oil-soaked rags hanging around in *Cape's* anchor windlass—and seemed the most coherent of the group. "It bounced around like a fucking Frisbee."

Nancy didn't know exactly how heavy the windlass was, but she imagined a wrecking ball trapped in a tornado. The purpose of the anchor windlass was to raise and lower the anchor without letting the chain get tangled up...and it wasn't supposed to bounce.

Speaking of chain, there was a lot of it on the deck, some on top of one of the other petty officers. He looked alive but uncomfortable, and while a destroyer's anchor chain was nowhere near as heavy as a carrier's, Nancy bet on a handful of broken ribs. She took a deep breath, twisting to look at HM1 Lopez, the corpsman standing a few feet behind her. He hadn't said a word.

"All right," Nancy said, gesturing at the stretcher bearers. "You two start getting that chain off him. HM1"—she shot a glare at Lopez when he stood frozen—"check out your unconscious shipmate. Get a splint above and below that compound fracture and keep it clean."

"Yes, ma'am." Lopez sounded shocked but followed instructions; that was all she could ask for. Nancy knew enough about injuries to know what she didn't know, but what she couldn't do was treat broken bones or determine if someone needed surgery. HM1 Lopez would have to do that, but the poor kid was shell-shocked to his core and didn't seem able to think without direction.

She took a deep breath. Nancy might not be able to *heal* people, but she could help them. She walked over to the sailor with rags sticking out of his wound. "So you going to tell me how you cut your belly open, or are you going to make me guess?" she asked.

His nametag read Deveaux, and his face was pale, his breathing rapid, and he looked like he'd vomited on himself already. At least that hadn't gotten in the wound.

"I...I'm not sure I remember, ma'am," Deveaux whispered.

"That's all right," Nancy said. "You're going into shock, so I'm going to start by lying you down and elevating your feet a bit. Then HM1 will look at your wound." She matched actions to words, trying to be gentle. He still hissed in pain.

"So did you use clean bandages for this, or are we going to be scrubbing oil out of the wound?" Nancy asked, mostly to keep Deveaux talking.

"Clean." He coughed. "Not stupid. Ma'am."

She made herself smile. "Well, that's one-up on most of the engineers I know."

"You know a lot of engineers?"

"I'm the XO on a cruiser." Maybe the captain; Nancy wasn't sure and if Admiral Zurcher was dead, who was left to make that call? Anxiety churned around the base of her spine. Had Zurcher forwarded his decision upward? Was Rowlings alive? What impact would *Lexington's* sinking have on *Cape St. George's* future?

Shaking her head, Nancy pushed those thoughts aside and focused on the sailor in front of her. She didn't think she should remove the rags; pressure on the wound was good. Deveaux wasn't bleeding much, which had to be something.

His smile was brave. "Guess no one's perfect."

She laughed. "I guess not. I think you'll be okay, though." Nancy squeezed Deveaux's hand, gestured the stretcher bearers over, and helped ease him onto the stokes board. Then she moved onto helping free the next sailor, pushing away thoughts of her ship and crew.

She couldn't help *Cape* right now, but there was a mess on *Byers*, and Nancy would do what she could. Then she'd help recover as many of *Lexington's* survivors as possible, and *then* and only then would she be able to head back to *Cape.* Sometime after that, probably days if not weeks, she'd find out her fate.

No, that wasn't nerve-wracking. Not at all.

Naval Station Perth, Australia

Someone else did most of the talking when the XO gave a tour. Luckily for him, Bobby volunteered to tag along after Steve had already wrangled a few division officers into doing the job. It was a good learning experience for the kids, so Bobby didn't object. It also gave him a chance to keep an eye on things from the back.

Keep an eye on things? When had he started thinking like a senior officer? It was like having cooties, and Bobby didn't like it.

Much to his surprise, Senator Angler seemed like a decent sort, at least for a politician. He appeared more interested in asking sailors questions than learning how the boat operated, however. Politicians were always more interested in people than machines, a feeling Bobby understood. He'd completed nuclear power school and qualified in as an engineer back aft, but he preferred leadership over equipment management. Judging from Angler's webpage, he didn't have much of a technical background. So at least he wasn't faking it.

"This is the weapons room," Harri Ainsworth said from the front of the group. "*Bluefish*, like all *Ceroes*, can carry up to twenty-eight torpedoes or Harpoon anti-ship missiles in here. Land-attack missiles, like the Tomahawks, are stored in the vertical launch tubes and fired from there. We don't have any missiles right now, but we're loaded out with twenty torpedoes."

"Impressive." Angler looked around. "Do you fire torpedoes often?"

"We do now that Captain Coleman's here." Harri beamed. "It's not like it was—"

"I think what Lieutenant Ainsworth is trying to say is that we've been pretty busy lately," Bobby interrupted. He couldn't let her trash talk Peterson, even if he deserved it. Steve looked confused, but Bobby ignored him.

Harri, fortunately, showed that she got the hint with a rapid nod and a set of too-wide eyes. "Yes, sir. We've been lucky enough to make a difference the last few months."

"And how do you like being on board, Lieutenant?" Angler asked. At least he didn't stumble over ranks. Hadn't Bobby heard something about his son being in the navy?

"It's hard work, but it's worth it," Harri replied, but when she stuffed her hands in her pockets, Bobby wanted to bash his head into the wall. Of all the captain's habits for her to pick up...

"Don't you miss your family?"

"I do, but I didn't join the navy just for when it's easy." Harri smiled. Then she said something else, but Bobby was distracted by a hand on his arm.

"What was that about?" Steve hissed.

Bobby grimaced and led their new XO several feet away from the senator. "Our last CO wasn't really...good at taking chances."

Or leading. Bobby shouldn't say that.

"I see." Steve frowned. "Speaking of the captain, what's up with him? He seemed really detached."

Crap. What was Bobby supposed to do? Did he respect the captain's privacy, or did the XO need to know? Instinct told him to keep his mouth shut. Alex had enough to deal with already, but—

"Detached?" A new voice interjected as Harri led the group out of the torpedo room. "What the fuck is wrong with Captain Coleman?"

Admiral Rodriquez stomped over to join them, and Bobby wanted to sink into the deck. He gulped. "Wrong, sir?"

"You tell me, XO." Rodriquez turned his glare on Steve, who shrugged.

"Nothing I'm privy to, sir. That's why I was asking the navigator."

"It's kind of...uh, complicated, sir." Bobby bit his lip.

"Well, then simplify the fuck out of it."

Bobby squirmed. Would a sudden enemy airstrike be too much to ask for?

"Now would be a great time to pop your head out of your ass and answer my goddamned question, Lieutenant." Rodriquez crossed his arms.

Bobby couldn't escape. He felt horrible for blabbing when the captain wasn't here. He took a deep breath. "You know the captain's wife is in the navy, sir?"

"Yeah, I flew my flag from her destroyer for months. She's a fucking rockstar. What of it?" Rodriquez asked.

"She, uh, flew over to *Lexington* earlier today. Something about an issue on her cruiser. But then *Lexington...*" Bobby bit his lip. Steve looked confused, but Admiral Rodriquez got the message.

"Shit."

Steve frowned. "People get off carriers. It's overreacting to—"

"He hasn't heard from her." Bobby boiled at the insensitivity. "We got the message hours ago."

"Don't be an ass." Rodriquez glared death at Steve. Then he looked back to Bobby. "Let me see what I can find out."

"Sir?"

"Sometimes, it's good to be an admiral. And Nancy Coleman's my friend, too." Rodriquez grinned. "You're the navigator. Get your radio pukes to put me up in chat and I'll handle the rest."

"You got it, Admiral." Bobby *had* thought about trying to see if anyone was in chat, but he figured what was left of *Lexington's* battle group was busy. No way would they answer a lieutenant's questions, but an admiral was something else.

So he led Rodriquez to a classified computer and prayed the news wasn't bad.

He should stop being a coward and call home.

Alex sighed, scraping his hands over his face. It was almost nine a.m. back home, and he was out of excuses. He'd waited almost two hours for news to come in, betting *Lexington's* killer would be too busy dodging angry escorts to tweet about the sinking. But he knew Bobbie kept up with the news; hell, she followed Rochambeau on Twitter! Emily probably did, too, although she was less vocal about it. And no father in their right mind wanted either of his daughters to learn of their mother's death via tweet. Alex couldn't avoid this.

Was this how Nancy felt when *Jimmy Carter* went missing for six weeks? He'd brushed off her concerns in the immediate aftermath, too exhausted and relieved to comprehend how hard it had been for his family. Alex had never experienced this mind-numbing emptiness, the feeling that a piece of your soul was missing and never coming back.

Taking a deep breath, Alex lifted the phone, only to drop it as the door to his stateroom slammed open without even the courtesy of a knock.

"Time to drop the misery ball, Captain, and get the fuck back to work," Admiral Rodriquez said.

Alex blinked in confusion. "What?"

"I just got out of chat with *Edward Byers*. She's a destroyer, in case you're not keeping score." Rodriquez smirked. "Your wife's on board. Apparently, she was in the air before *Lexington* got her ass shot off and landed on the tin can."

The whirlwind of emotion almost knocked Alex flat. His mouth flopped open, jaw numb, wordless.

"You hear me, son? Nancy's fine." Uncle Marco tapped his foot. "I told that destroyer driver to set her up with an email so you can talk to her yourself. Half their comms are out, and they're still picking up survivors, but they've still got satellite internet."

"But why was she on a destroyer?" Alex asked, his mind whirling. Nancy was *alive*! Forming coherent thoughts beyond that was hard.

Rodriquez snorted. "Fuck if I know. I'm not a goddamned surface warfare officer. I just pretended to be one for about six months."

Alex grimaced. "Sorry. I just..."

"No need to apologize. Back when I still gave a damn about my ex, I'd have been pretty fucked up about this kind of thing, too." Rodriquez leaned back against the bulkhead. "You should've said something earlier. We take care of our best."

Alex stammered wordlessly, his face heating. "I'm not—"

"The fuck you're not. Don't be stupider than God made you." Rodriquez shifted uneasily. "Particularly now that *Razorback's* sunk."

That made his stomach twist into a new knot. "Any news on survivors?" Thinking about Master Chief Morton tempered Alex's relief. He knew the statistics. More than half the subs sank so far in the war had gone down with all hands.

"None yet. A helo sent over by the battle group saw some life rafts, though, so we're investigating."

"I suppose that's the best we can hope for," Alex whispered.

Shit. How had this happened? How had he gone from *Admiral's Mast* as an XO to the most successful living submariner in America? A few months earlier, Alex would have shied away from the thought, but not now. Now, even if you took away the Medal of Honor, he'd done well.

What the fuck was he supposed to do about that?

"You gonna sit here and mope, or you going to get off your ass and remember that you've got the man who might be our next president on board?" Rodriquez asked.

Alex shuddered and then stood. "I'd rather avoid the politics, to be honest."

"No doing that at your level, Captain. That little blue ribbon of yours says you'll wear stars someday, like it or not." A barked laugh. "Just don't let them pin them on you too soon."

"Shit, sir, I never expected to be a *captain*. I can live without being an admiral."

"If you live, son, you're not going to get a choice. Now come on. We've got a politician's ass to kiss."

Alex groaned and followed him. Nancy was *alive.* If playing kiss ass with a senator was the price to pay for that, he'd do it gladly.

Chapter 25

Good Order and Discipline

18 March 2040, USS Lexington (CVN 84) Battle Group, mid-Indian Ocean

Stopping got her.

Fourteen grueling hours of saving lives and repairing damage kept Nancy from thinking about *Lexington*. Who had died? It was too soon for a roster of survivors to be compiled. Dawn was an hour or two away, and *Byers's* port list was still heavier than anyone wanted, but they'd recovered every *Lexington* survivor the battle group could find. That left even the lamed destroyer overloaded, but *Cape* would be with them in an hour or so, which meant they could transfer some survivors around and then head toward Perth at the formation's best speed.

Nancy felt like she was floating, despite being anchored firmly to the seat on *Byers's* mess decks that she sat in. Too much stress and not enough sleep left her euphoric and testy, and while she knew she'd come down from the artificial high soon, for now, she clung to it. Otherwise, she'd think about everyone who'd been on board *Lexy* when those two torpedoes hit.

It was far too soon for a list of survivors. They had a count, however, which told Nancy that a quarter of *Lexington's* crew was dead. Another four or five hundred were injured or waterlogged. None of that counted the dead or wounded on *Byers*, and there were rumors of a sunken submarine—

"Commander Coleman."

She jumped, twisting to look at Commander Simjian, *Byers'* CO. "Captain?"

"You just saved too much of my crew for formality. Call me Adam." Simjian slumped against a nearby bulkhead decorated by pictures of places *Byers* visited before the war.

"Nancy." She nodded, noticing that someone had patched up Adam Simjian while Nancy was busy with others. His arm was in a sling and gauze was taped to his forehead.

"Can I ask you for a favor?" Adam asked.

Nancy smiled wryly. "Sure. I might not be much good at the moment, but I'll try."

"I just need you to get an irate admiral off my back. COMSUBPAC wants you to email your husband ASAP." Adam shrugged. "I expect I'm missing something here. He was pushy as all hell."

"Oh, shit." Nancy wanted to smack herself. "My husband's in command of a submarine, and I told him I was going to the carrier. He probably saw the message about *Lexington* sinking and is freaking out."

"Come on, then. You can borrow my computer."

That was how Nancy found herself sitting at the desk in the captain's stateroom of a destroyer, struggling to find words to tell Alex she was okay. Was she? Physically, sure.

> *Hey babe,* she started the email. *Sorry for not emailing sooner. Things are chaotic here. In case you couldn't figure it out from the header, I'm on board* Edward Byers. *I was on a helo to head back to the ship when LEX went down, and I had them*

land on the destroyer so they could get rid of us and help recover survivors.

I don't know what happened with anyone on the carrier. I did talk to the admiral before leaving, and he confirmed his intention to level charges against Captain Rowlings. He confirmed me in temporary command of Cape *for now, too, though I don't know how long that will be for. And now I don't know if Admiral Zurcher is alive or dead, so your guess is as good as mine.*

Have you talked to Mom and the girls yet? I know the girls both have news alerts on navy sinkings, so they probably saw the news the moment the navy released it. Mom's less technology happy, thank God, or she'd worry all the time. I didn't tell anyone other than you that I was headed here, so I hope they're not twisted up over this. If so, please let them know I love them and I'm fine. I'm tired and loopy and I've been up more hours than I can count, but I'm okay. I didn't let the water in the people space, either, so you can tell Bobbie to quit asking.

I love you, and I'll try to write something more coherent when I'm more awake.

Morning underways always left Alex in a bad mood, particularly when he had to get up at the ass crack of dawn. Playing host to a talkative senator only made things worse; Alex tried foisting Senator Angler off on Marco Rodriquez, only to find that *both* of them wanted to squeeze into *Bluefish's* tiny sail for the surface transit out of Perth. For Angler, it was a salutary experience; he'd never been underway on a submarine and was fascinated by everything. Rodriquez, on the other hand, just closed his eyes and inhaled the salt spray, clearly missing his days at sea.

Still, their presence left Alex and Bobby squeezing in between the lookouts. No one was comfortable with six people crammed into space meant for four, but Alex judged it a bad moment to complain.

Thankfully, Bobby, back to being the officer of the deck for the maneuvering watch now that he wasn't acting XO, needed about as much micromanaging as a fish in the ocean. So Alex could pay attention to the politician and the admiral who'd come along to make things "easier."

"I owe your crew another awards ceremony, Captain," Rodriquez said after *Bluefish* passed Beacon Head light. Alex jumped.

"Come again?"

"Your sins have caught up with you again. I don't have pizza this time, but I did bring a politician." Rodriquez jerked a thumb in Angler's direction.

Much to Alex's surprise, Angler grinned. "Might not be a fair trade. From what my son tells me, junk food is treasured on a submarine."

"Benji's not wrong." Alex chuckled. "We used to say he ran the wardroom black market on junk food. No one knew where he fit it all, and Marty"—Alex gulped and then continued quickly to cover the sudden surge of grief for *Jimmy Carter's* late engineering officer—"used to say that their stateroom held more candy than uniforms."

"Much to his mother's despair," Angler said.

"Who's got the junk black market cornered here, Captain?" Rodriquez asked, his eyes sparkling.

Alex hesitated. "I'm not sure we've gotten one yet."

"What? Every sub has a wardroom black marketeer." Rodriquez snorted. "What, you crack down on it like some goddamned nun?"

"Not me," Alex said before he could stop himself.

Rodriquez's bushy eyebrows shot up. "Do tell."

There his big mouth went again. Shit. "Anything I've got is just speculation..."

"Which means it was your predecessor." Rodriquez rolled his eyes. "Stupid fucking waste of time, particularly at war."

Alex shrugged, his eyes on Angler. The senator watched their conversation with gleaming eyes, saying little. Was that his way, or would this come back and bite Alex in the ass?

The idea of a politician hurting his career was still a little out to lunch. Alex pushed it out of his mind. Instead, he gestured for Angler and Rodriquez to head down the ladder.

"Officer of the Deck, submerge the ship," Alex ordered after reaching control, tuning out Bobby's repeat back. That left him free to turn to Angler, who was trying too obviously not to fidget. Alex suppressed a smile, asking: "Never submerged before?"

"Is it that obvious?"

"Everyone's nervous the first time." Even Alex had been—he'd been ridiculously excited, too, since he'd spent a lifetime dreaming of being a submariner before finally getting underway on a midshipmen cruise. "We've got a saying: as long as your surfacings match your sinkings, you're doing okay."

"Benji said something like that." Angler chuckled. "I'm stupid to be nervous, right?"

"*Bluefish* is a fairly new boat, and she's in good shape," Alex said. Not like the mess he'd left *Jimmy Carter* in, that's for sure. "So you don't need to worry about sudden leaks taking us to the bottom. And she's not a World War II diesel, either—we're not going to hit pipes with mallets until they start spraying water."

"I always thought that was just for effect in the movies."

Alex grinned. "It is. We aim to keep the water out of the people space."

"That's good to know!" Angler still looked nervous, but before Alex could say anything else, Rodriquez cut in.

"You're almost the poster boy for that one, Captain." Rodriquez waggled his eyebrows. "Given how you bounced *Jimmy Carter* off the bottom like a fucking jack in the box. Twice."

Alex cringed. Just when he started feeling comfortable, Rodriquez brought that up. Even worse, Senator Angler's son had been Alex's weapons officer on board *Jimmy Carter*, which meant that Benjamin the Fifth had also been presumed dead for three weeks. Did Angler blame Alex? God, this patrol was going to be miserable.

"I didn't exactly do it on purpose, Admiral." Alex swallowed hard. "Except the second time. Sort of."

"Damn straight you didn't. Bet you're still telling stories about that one."

Alex snorted. "Only when I'm drunk."

"That kind of thing isn't...normal, is it?" Angler asked Rodriquez.

"No, it isn't," the admiral replied. "Convoy 57 was a unique situation. We try not to let our boats get outnumbered like that, or..."

Alex tuned out the rest of Rodriquez's response. At least he had the grace not to mention that most subs wouldn't survive it. Alex couldn't forget how much more fragile *Bluefish* was than the decades-older *Jimmy Carter*; she couldn't dive as deep and wouldn't take half as much punishment. Not that he intended to ever do anything that crazy again. He was perfectly content shooting the enemy without getting the shit kicked out of his boat in return.

Movement caught his attention, and Alex turned his head to watch his XO talking to his weapons officer. Rose looked unhappy; her eyes were narrow and her posture tense. Steve, however, wore a smile big enough for Alex to see from across control. What was going on there?

It wasn't his problem. Alex finally had a competent XO. He didn't need to micromanage the man. Steve would let him know if it was something the captain needed to care about.

"You okay, Rose?" Bobby caught his fellow department head on the arm after *Bluefish* secured the maneuvering watch, pulling her into his stateroom.

Rose slammed the door shut. "That fucking pervert propositioned me!"

"What? Who?" Bobby's heart hammered in his chest. "You don't mean Senator Angler? Or *Admiral Rodriquez*?"

Bobby's eyes went wide with the last question. If the senior submariner on this end of the world—

"No! Of course not." Rose scowled. "Angler's old enough to be my father, and I'm not sure Uncle Marco knows women exist. I'm not even sure he's noticed his aide is a chick or that she's hot."

"Then who?"

She punched a standup locker. "The goddamned XO."

"No way." Bobby couldn't believe it. Steve Harper seemed like a decent guy. And why would any XO with half a brain proposition a department head? Sure, Steve was only a lieutenant commander, which was just one rank above Rose, but *one up, one down* didn't count when they were in the same chain of command. "That's fraternization."

"No shit." She rolled her eyes. "I said as much."

"And?"

"And he said it's wartime, so no one gives a damn." Rose slumped against Bobby's rack. "I could practically see him drooling."

Bobby blinked. Sure, Rose was good-looking; hell, she was gorgeous. He'd even kissed her once, at the academy's annual

Navy Ball. And Steve Harper wasn't half bad looking himself, not that Bobby was looking. "That's...problematic."

"He's not my type. Not by a fucking mile. Even if he wasn't the XO." Rose glared.

"Hey, I'm not the enemy here." Bobby held up his hands in surrender. "I gave up on you years ago. It was like kissing my sister."

That finally made her chuckle, shaking her head. "And neither of us is into incest, yeah. Your brother's cute, though."

"Don't you start. He's married."

Rose's grin was wicked. "I didn't say which one."

"You're a horrible person, you know that?" Bobby laughed, though. It was good to see Rose fuming less and smiling again.

"Not as horrible as the XO." Rose's frown returned. "This can't be the first time he's tried this. He was too confident. Hell, he did it in the middle of fucking control, like he thought I should be honored by his proposition."

"You know, the logistics of it mystify me." Bobby chewed his lip. "You're rooming with Admiral Rodriquez's aide, and he's got the senator in with him. Where'd he think the two of you were going to get it on, the wardroom table?"

"Ew, Bobby, I didn't need that thought. We *eat* there." She made a face. "And I didn't ask. I just politely told him I wasn't interested and tried to move on."

"I can't see you being terribly polite about that, Rosie." He didn't want to think about how that would sour her working relationship with the XO. Steve could make Rose's life miserable in a thousand ways.

"I *tried*. I'm not used to having a senior officer insist that I'd have a great time in his bed. I did manage not to tell him that I wasn't interested because he didn't have boobs," she said.

Bobby grimaced. "Did that help?"

"I also told him I wasn't interested in committing frat and I liked my career intact." Rose crossed her arms, hugging herself. "I didn't know what to say, all right?"

"Even if you pissed him off, it's not your fault." Bobby wished he believed Steve's displeasure wouldn't make this even worse. "Talk about a no-win situation."

"Yeah. I can sleep with him and risk my career—and he isn't my type, even if I am bi—or say no and risk him ranking me as the worst department head on board." Rose sighed. "No matter which way this goes, I come out of it looking like shit."

"The captain's not going to believe it if the XO says you're suddenly turned into a bad department head," Bobby said, hoping he was right. Alex was fair and knew Rose better than he knew Steve. Surely that had to count for something?

"I hope not," she whispered.

Bobby ached to hug Rose, but she'd never been the hugging sort. Trying now would probably just get him hit and upset her more. So he put on his best smile. "You know I've got your back. Lou does, too."

"Yeah." Rose swallowed. "Thanks."

"You...want to tell the captain about this?" Bobby asked after a moment's hesitation.

"And have the XO say I came onto him? No thanks." She growled a curse under her breath. "In any 'he said, she said' situation, the higher rank always wins. Do I look like an idiot?"

"I'm not sure the captain would believe him over you."

"Yeah, I'm not taking that chance. My career can survive a bad FITREP better than it can someone thinking I'm making false allegations. No one would ever trust me again."

Bobby opened his mouth to argue, but Rose cut him off with a raised hand.

"The sub community's a *lot* better to women than it was, but that doesn't mean people won't believe him over me," she said. "They'll assume I led him on, or I was flirting, or whatever. I'm not dealing with that."

"Okay. Your call."

Bobby almost volunteered to bring it up to the captain for Rose, but he wasn't the acting XO any longer. He'd been so glad to be rid of that job, but now he almost wished he had it back. Still, he could keep an eye on things. Maybe having a witness would help encourage Rose to speak up if it happened again.

HMS Gallant, *Naval Station Perth, Australia*

The attack submarine's wardroom was quiet; Captain Ursula North sat in the corner, sipping tea and reading message traffic. Across from her sat her first officer, Lieutenant Commander James Harrison, doing the same.

They'd started the tradition of sitting down for tea every day shortly after James was promoted from principal warfare officer. Often, they said nothing, simply sitting in companionable silence. Rarely, they discussed tactics or strategy or home and families. They kept to the same schedule, even in port, for the most part, and Ursula found the routine comforting. Not that she'd ever admit it.

Today—not unusually—Ursula wanted to break something.

"He's bloody done it again." If Ursula glared at the message tablet long enough, would it spontaneously combust? She hoped so.

"Ma'am?" James cocked his head, his dark features a touch apprehensive.

"Jules flaming Rochambeau." She bit off every word, trying not to swear. Why? She wasn't sure. "The cunt. He sunk an American aircraft carrier, along with the Americans sent to sink *him*."

The tweet was as bold as brass; she only wondered why he'd waited a day. Was Jules worried about the Americans finding him? If only they could be so lucky. With *Razorback* gone, none of those fumbling fools stood a chance. Fuming, she tilted the screen so James could see:

Captain Jules Rochambeau
@JulesRochambeau

@USNavy Did you think @USSRazorback would do the job? I also hear you are missing an aircraft carrier. Perhaps you should look on the bottom of the Indian Ocean.
#Barracuda #USSRazorback #USSLexington

The second tweet sent her blood boiling to a fever pitch:

Captain Jules Rochambeau
@JulesRochambeau
@RoyalNavy, did you lose Lady North? I thought she was coming for me.
#Barracuda #HMSGallant #CatchMeIfYouCan

James sighed. "That man is a menace."

"You have no idea." Ursula's lips curled into a sneer. "I am *done* with this. Make preparations to get underway."

"Captain?" James looked confused, as well he should. "Aren't we assigned to the BIOT task force?"

"The Yanks no longer have a carrier to form the center of that task force." She stabbed a finger at the second tweet. "No one's going to take back the *British* Indian Ocean Territory without one. And I refuse to let that wanker keep on like this."

"We can't get underway without—"

Ursula wheeled to glare at him. "And who will stop us? Make the preparations, Commander."

"Aye, aye, Captain." James' shoulders slumped, but he obeyed.

Ursula, meanwhile, headed for her cabin, fury gnawing at her bones. She felt no grief for *Razorback*, save for the fact that the Americans were brother and sister submariners who deserved better than going to the bottom. Nor did she rage over *Lexington*. It was the waste that ate at her. *She'd* been sent after Rochambeau and failed, and now others paid the price. It would not happen again. She'd launch land attack missiles at *Barracuda* pier side if she had to.

That was a thought; heart racing, Ursula wrenched open her cabin door and shouted:

"James!"

"Ma'am?" He appeared almost like magic.

Ursula bared her teeth. "Find me charts for the French Southern Antarctic Islands and everything else down there."

James blinked. "You think that's where he's hiding?"

"I think we've looked everywhere else, and no one will give a good goddamn if we throw some missiles that way. They're practically uninhabited." Ursula could feel her blood singing. She knew she was right. No one had looked at the half-dozen islands off the northern coast of Antarctica because no one in their right mind would build a submarine base in an arctic environment. Not in peacetime, anyway.

But the French had taken the Heard and McDonald Islands off Australia months ago. Why do that if they didn't want to protect their flank? France already owned four island groups in the area, and if *she'd* wanted to hide somewhere that gave her excellent access to the Indian Ocean's sea lanes, Ursula couldn't think of a better place. Perhaps the rumors of a base *being* built out at Île Amsterdam were out of date. What if the base was already there?

"I'm on it." James looked more cheerful, and Ursula stalked back toward the attack center to study their electronic charts of the area.

Roughly two thousand miles of ocean stretched between Perth and Île Amsterdam. Judging from the position where *Lexington* was sunk, Rochambeau had roughly the same distance to cover with a day's head start. He wouldn't dare sprint the entire way, but he had to be heading home. Jules would've sunk more of that American battle group if he'd had sufficient torpedoes. She knew him, knew that. No, any situation where he chose to slink off like a coward—waiting a day before tweeting!—meant he thought hiding was safest.

Indeed. Ursula nodded to herself. Running with an empty weapons room meant Jules would run quiet.

If the stars aligned, she might beat him there. Worst case, she could arrive before he got underway again.

Ursula licked her lips and started plotting a course. She'd call her superiors later.

Two days into the patrol, Alex wanted to shut himself in his rack and never come out again. Some of his crew seemed to enjoy the novelty; Senator Angler was genuinely interested in their profession, and Admiral Rodriquez crawled all over the boat like an excited, profanity-laden puppy. But the attention made Alex's skin crawl. He cringed every time Rodriquez referred to his Medal of Honor. Sly references to Convoy 57 re-awakened nightmares he thought banished. Worse yet, Rodriquez's aide was pretty good with a camera, and she snapped "candid" shots every two minutes.

Closing his eyes, Alex tipped his chair back so he could lean against the wall. He needed to get his head in the game. The dog-and-pony show was just a distraction; *Bluefish* was on war patrol. Technically, he should be in control. They'd come shallow to check the mail, and doing so was always a dangerous gamble. Steve could supervise that, but Alex was the captain and really should be there. He just didn't have the energy.

A knock on his open door made him jump. "Asleep on the job, Captain?"

"No, sir," Alex said, bringing his chair back down onto an even keel as Rodriquez walked in. "Just thinking."

"Well, it's time for you to use that sneaky brain of yours, because I've got a new job for you."

"That sounds ominous." Alex took a breath; Rodriquez didn't intimidate him quite as much as in the beginning, but he still didn't like having an admiral on board, let alone in his stateroom. Alex was in command, but having his boss's boss along for the ride was weird.

"Should be right up your alley." Rodriquez grinned. "Ursula fucking North cottoned onto a good theory: Rochambeau might be working out of Île Amsterdam. She's headed that way, but I want you to block him before he can return to port."

Alex did some quick math. "That'll take a hell of a sprint."

"No compunctions about trying to sink everyone's worst enemy?" Rodriquez cocked an eyebrow.

"Plenty." Alex tried to bite back a nervous laugh without much success. "But that doesn't really matter, does it?"

"You've got a fucking strange sense of courage, Coleman," Rodriquez replied. "You make absofuckinglutely no sense to me at all."

This time, Alex grinned. "The feeling's mutual, Admiral."

"You're still not getting out of that next awards ceremony, you know. I've noticed how it keeps falling off your schedule."

"We've been busy."

"Bullshit."

Alex hadn't noticed the delay. He didn't relish the idea of another personal award, but his crew deserved recognition. "I'll talk to my XO."

"Damn straight you will."

Alex's phone rang before he could answer, and he grabbed it. "Captain."

"Sir, it's Radio. You've got an outside line call. It's one of your daughters."

"Standby." Alex lowered the phone and looked back toward Rodriquez, his heart clenched with worry. "You mind if I take this, sir? My daughters still aren't taking their mom being out of touch well. Usually I'm the hard one to get ahold of."

Rodriquez flashed him a grin. "Consider me gone."

Before Alex could blink, the admiral vanished, closing the door with a *click*. Meanwhile, Alex took a deep breath and steeled himself. He loved his girls, but this call could get ugly. He brought the phone up again. "Put her through, Radio."

"Radio, aye."

Two beeps and a bit of static later, Alex's phone completed its dance with the satellite. "Daddy?" Emily's voice asked.

"Hey, sweetie." Alex couldn't help smiling; his younger daughter, a senior in high school, wasn't quite the stubborn spitfire the elder had become. Emily was smart and strong, but a little more sensitive than her sister.

"I see how it is. Emmie gets the hello while I just sit here," another voice said.

Alex sat up straight. "Bobbie? What are you doing home?" His elder daughter was a sophomore at the Naval Academy, and she should—

"It's called spring break, Dad. Jeez," Bobbie replied; Emily snickered.

"Well, I apologize for not keeping up with your academic calendar." Alex rolled his eyes. "So, since I've got both of you, what's up?"

"We were wondering if you'd heard from Mom," Emily said. "Is she okay? I saw the news release on *Edward Byers*, and one of Bobbie's old upperclassmen is on board. She says it's bad."

"Yeah, Ensign Goodman was my company commander last year," Bobbie added. "She's their auxiliaries officer, and *she's* had time to email me, unlike Mom."

Damn, he could see where this was going. Alex took a deep breath. "Girls, you know we're at war. Communicating isn't always easy."

"That doesn't mean we have to like it," Bobbie snapped.

"Dude, you're the one who tells me to 'suck it up and drive on,'" Emily said before Alex could answer. "Quit your bitching."

"Language!" Alex finally got in.

Emily laughed. "You say worse, Daddy."

"And you're supposed to be better than me," Alex said, trying not to sigh. Commanding a submarine was far easier than parenting teenagers. Thank God he had his mother-in-law back in Groton to keep an eye on his two hellions.

Both girls giggled. "How are things on *Bluefish*?" Bobbie asked. "You get any more awesome kills? I've been following Rochambeau's twitter feed, and now that *Razorback* is gone, they're going to send you after him, right?"

"I hope not," Emily said.

Alex barely heard her. He hadn't thought much about *Razorback* since learning she'd sank; *Lexington's* fate had been far more distracting. He'd heard nothing about survivors from *Razorback.* He hadn't known Patricia Abercrombie well, but Bryan Morton had been his left hand on *Jimmy Carter*—

"Dad? Did we lose you?" Bobbie's voice broke through his grief.

"Yeah. I'm here." He shook himself. "Sorry, command can be distracting."

"That sounds like an excuse," Emily said.

Alex swallowed. "You guys remember me mentioning my COB on *Jimmy Carter*?" Affirmative answers came. "He went to *Razorback.*"

"Oh, shit. Ouch," Bobbie, the future submariner, said.

"Yeah." Alex didn't have the energy to reprimand her.

"I'm sorry, Daddy," Emily said into the silence. "You okay?"

Better than Razorback's *crew,* he didn't say. A father didn't say that to his daughters, no matter how old they were. "Yeah." Alex forced his grief aside. "So tell me what you've both been up to and how much trouble you aren't getting in."

Over the next ten minutes, his daughters regaled him with stories of parties—*without* drinking, they claimed, though Alex wasn't an idiot—Emily's graduation preparations, and stories of touring the dozen colleges Emily had been accepted to. Bobbie told stories about her friends at the academy, particularly Mike, who was absolutely *not* her boyfriend, no matter what Emily said. Listening to them helped Alex remember what he was fighting for, admirals and ambition be damned.

Chapter 26

The Race

21 March 2040, Naval Base Perth

"Do you think he'll beat us there, ma'am?" James asked from her right.

Both officers stood on *Gallant's* forward deck, watching as a crane lowered the last Tomahawk Land Attack Missile into the submarine's weapons hatch. Unlike some American classes, British attack sub didn't possess vertical launch tubes; they fired missiles from torpedo tubes. British designers felt VLS was unnecessary in a submarine designed to kill other submarines, and at the time, Ursula North hadn't disagreed. Better to leave land attacks to the Americans with their TLAM obsession.

Now, she grimaced. This was taking too damned long. "He might. He won't hurry, but he's got a big head start. We're going to have to run like our britches are on fire to catch him."

"So you want the TLAMs."

"I always knew you were a bright boy." Ursula bared her teeth, making James chuckle. She continued: "Even Jules' magic can't load a torpedo room faster. *Barracuda* has room for thirty-six weapons. He won't leave again until it's full."

Gallant needed half a day to load six Tomahawks. Jules would require longer, even if he just loaded torpedoes.

"I hope you're right, Captain." James grimaced. "If he catches us roaring in—"

"We'll be dead meat." Ursula shrugged. "You have to throw the dice to win. Playing cautious gained us nothing save dead Alliance sailors."

She didn't want to count how many Alliance sailors were on the bottom, British or otherwise. The war had become a bloody stalemate, even if no one wanted to admit it. The admiralty talked about *the path to victory* like a miracle was right around the corner, but Ursula just saw empty berths were submarines commanded by colleagues would not return to.

"Aye. It has."

The crane's wires released, leaving the missile in the loading cradle. Her weapons people would need an hour or so to get the last Tomahawk properly stowed, but Ursula believed in multi-tasking. She strode to the edge of *Gallant's* sloped deck, yelling at the crane operator:

"Take the brow before you go! I want that contraption off my deck within twenty minutes!"

"Yes, ma'am!" the operator responded, but she'd already turned away.

"Get the engineer dancing, James. I want to get underway as soon as the brow is clear." She'd kept the reactor hot just for this reason. She glanced at the submarine moored aft of her command. "Call *Kansas* and tell them to send line handlers over yesterday."

"Aye, aye, captain." James vanished down the hatch, leaving Ursula to stew on deck alone.

Now was not the time to think about the three-hour delay before the pier was cleared for a weapons onload. Nor was it time to think about the prick in command of the boat across the pier and how he'd drag his heels in sending her line handlers, hoping someone else would do it first. Ursula wanted to be underway two days ago, and she had an enemy to find. She didn't care who she pissed off in the meantime.

Senators didn't hand out medals every day, and Admiral Rodriquez had done the last round. This time, there was no pizza to make the party even better, but the novelty of having a politician pin their medals on and announce the awards seemed enough to win Alex's crew over.

Everyone not on watch had assembled in the crew's mess for the impromptu ceremony. Alex heard sailors teasing each other and a few card games broke out once the ceremony was finished; he stayed to watch for a few minutes to get the pulse of the crew and wasn't disappointed. Rodriquez's aide took a thousand pictures, of course, but Alex managed to avoid being caught in most. At least Lieutenant Greco was a submariner and knew not to take pictures of classified stuff.

"Come down in the world, Captain?" Bobby asked, grinning as he approached.

Alex blinked. "With what?"

"Well, this time you only got a Silver Star. That's not nearly as nifty as the Navy Cross the admiral pinned on you last time."

"It's a bizzaro world if you're using the words 'only' and 'Silver Star' in the same sentence," Alex replied. He still wasn't sure what to make of being the guy who won awards instead of the guy stuck holding the short end of the stick.

"Hey, you're the one with the big damned medal, sir."

"Don't remind me." Looking down, Alex pulled the Silver Star off where it was pinned to the front of his coveralls and stuffed it in his pocket. Bobby still sported the Bronze Star he and the other department heads were awarded for their last few patrols, and he gestured at it with a wicked grin.

"Get one of these and you can have the whole collection," Bobby said.

"Jesus, Bobby." Alex laughed, shaking his head. "Really?"

Bobby shrugged. "It's not my fault you lack a sufficient sense of humor, sir."

"Sense of the ridiculous, you mean."

"Same difference."

Damn, Alex wished he had this easy rapport with Steve. They still tiptoed around each other; sometimes, Steve seemed more worried about impressing Alex than doing his job. But Steve's reaction wasn't like Bobby's early nerves. Bobby had been intimidated by Alex's damned Medal of Honor and still suffering from Peterson's so-called leadership. Steve didn't have any hang-ups about the medal, and *Perch* had a good reputation, so why was he determined to impress?

Steve reported on board six days ago, he reminded himself. Steve was a good officer, and they had time to gel. Alex should be patient.

Bobby grimaced. "So, uh, speaking of humor—or I guess lack thereof—can I talk to you about something?"

"Of course you can." Alex turned to face his navigator. If Bobby's was uh-ing again, something was wrong.

"Rose came to talk to me a couple of days ago, and she kind of doesn't want me to say anything, but I can't really not." Bobby groaned. "I'm babbling, aren't I, Captain?"

"A little," Alex said. Now he was worried. "But it's okay."

"It's about—" Suddenly, Bobby cut off, his eyes going wide. Alex twisted to follow his gaze, only to find Steve approaching.

"Congratulations, Captain." Steve held out a hand, smiling.

Alex shook the offered hand, holding back a frown. "Thanks."

He glanced after Bobby, but the navigator retreated without a word. Steve scowled. "I know you said he was hot shit as the acting XO, sir, but he's been off the last few days."

"Has he?" Alex hadn't noticed, but he'd been occupied by an admiral and a senator, plus Lieutenant Greco's five thousand candid pictures.

"Yes, sir. He's been strangely quiet at department head meetings," Steve replied.

"Odd." Alex chewed his lower lip. Did this have to do with whatever Rose told Bobby? Or that something he didn't want the XO to know?

Steve looked around, his eyes narrowed. "You can tell Suppo isn't underway with us. The menus posted are still yesterday's."

Alex shrugged. "If that's the worst you can find, XO, I'm a happy captain."

"It's my job—"

"Relax, Steve," Alex said. "You're doing fine. I wasn't being sarcastic, and I'll trust you to deal with this small oversight while our friendly neighborhood supply officer is at school."

"I will, Captain." Steve looked determined, not cowed, which meant he hadn't been beaten down or intimidated by his CO on *Perch*.

"How's your first underway with us so far?" Alex asked.

"Good, sir. I think I'm getting the hang of things here." Steve's smile was engaging, but Alex sensed reservations behind it.

"Yeah?"

"It's a bit different than *Perch*." Steve shrugged. "We were a bit more...spit and polished."

"You missed our worst days," Alex replied quietly. "When I got here, things were rocky."

Steve nodded. "Lieutenant Ainsworth told me a bit about that."

"She did?"

"I ran into her at the O Club our last night in port." Steve didn't say more, but Alex could guess Harri had been drinking.

Harri was a damned good officer, a good leader, and had potential to be an excellent tactician. But when she drank, she *talked*. Lord only knew what she'd said.

"I'd rather a hard-drinking and hard-fighting crew than one that doesn't do either," he said.

"That's a change from the old navy way." Steve's eyes followed Harri and Rose as they spoke off to one side.

"Peace gives you time to worry about the stupid shit." Alex shrugged. "God knows we fucked up enough in the early days because we couldn't let go of the old mentality."

Steve laughed. "Yeah, I don't miss the endless admin and inspection cycles, either."

"On that we can agree." Alex glanced at the clock. "You'd best get some shut eye if you're going to be awake come midwatch."

"I'm headed that way, sir."

"Good." Nodding a farewell to his XO, Alex headed for his stateroom. If Rodriquez was determined to send them after Rochambeau, he had homework to do.

Perth, Australia

Cape St. George returned to port with what was left of the *Lexington* Battle Group. *Byers's* damage kept the formation's speed down to about twelve knots, which meant the transit took almost three times as long as it should have, during which time Nancy's stressed crew had to guard almost a hundred Indian prisoners of war in addition to keeping the cruiser ready to fight all comers. That included the frantic hunt for the submarine that sank *Lexington, Boone,* and—they later learned—*Razorback.*

Despite activation of *Razorback's* buoy, which Nancy knew would tell the tale of her sinking, there had been no survivors at the designated location when USS *Andrews*, a destroyer, sprinted over to try to save anyone they could after recovering the last of the *Lexington* survivors. Alex would take that hard, Nancy knew; the thought left a knot in *her* stomach, even though she'd never met anyone on board the submarine. Yet at first, they thought the price might *almost* be worth it.

For a few blissful hours, the battle watch on *Michael Monsoor* thought that *Razorback* achieved a double kill with the submarine that sank *Lexington*, but a second look at the sonar records showed that there had been *another* enemy submarine in the area. Then the inevitable tweets from Rochambeau rolled through the next day, solving that mystery for good.

Cape and her fellows pulled into port the day after that on March 19th. Now, two days later, Nancy had finally offloaded her prisoners and given them to the appropriate authorities—thankfully, several of the Alliance's fast-growing POW camps were located in Australia—and turned their stolen convoy over to local authorities to offload the goods and decide what to do with the civilian ships. They'd probably be returned to their owners, who, war or no, were likely to sue to get them back if the Alliance tried to keep them. But that wasn't Nancy's problem. As far as she was concerned, life was back to normal.

Or at least as normal as it could be on a ship whose captain had been relieved for committing war crimes.

"I can't believe she got off easy by *dying*," Bobbie Coleman said from thousands of miles away in North Stonington, Connecticut.

For once, her daughters were together, sharing a tablet screen so they could video call with Nancy across the world. Bobbie was home from the academy on spring break, which miraculously lined up with Emily's high school. They looked like they were getting along, too, which was a minor miracle. Nancy was used to breaking up petty squabbles between her strong-willed daughters, who loved each other but didn't always *like* each other.

"Dying isn't exactly easy," Nancy replied with a sigh.

Bobbie sneered. "Yeah, but it means she'll be a historical footnote."

"And it means that the navy can't show they mean business by prosecuting Captain Rowlings for trying to kill unarmed survivors," Emily added.

Nancy cracked a smile. "You really are thinking about being a lawyer, aren't you?"

"Not everyone wants to play copy-cat." Emily grinned.

"Hey!" Bobbie stuck out her tongue at her sister. "I resemble that remark."

"I'm hurt that neither of you want to be surface warfare officers," Nancy said before they could start sniping.

"Mom, no offense, but this war is rapidly becoming a *not*-ship war," Bobbie replied. "It's really obvious from the sidelines. More surface ships are getting sunk than doing the sinking, and missile shortages are all over the news. Pretty soon, it's going to be World War II all over again—you'll have nothing but guns, but you don't *have* big guns, do you?"

Nancy grimaced. "Not if you mean battleship-grade sixteen inchers, no."

She couldn't argue with her navy-mad elder daughter, much though she wanted to. Even a cruiser like *Cape* received fewer and fewer missions that didn't revolve around chasing convoys—which, fortunately, *did* have to move on the surface, because every country knew that building cargo submarines was dumb, expensive, and wasteful. The early days of the war had been full of ship-on-ship action, with missile battles and air defense dominating the narrative. Now? Now *Cape* was lucky to have duked it out with one Indian frigate.

"See? Told you so," Bobbie said.

"Don't be rude." Emily scowled, brushing blond hair out of her face to glare at her sister.

Bobbie just rolled her eyes. "The truth isn't rude. All the seniors here who chose surface are regretting it. They want to swap to subs or, even worse, aviation. Though on one's really keen on *that* with a second carrier sunk, unless they want to be rotor heads."

"It's not that bad out here," Nancy said, but the objection felt hollow.

Was her profession a dying breed? Or were they just overcome by missile shortages and a war that dominated a medium surface ships had a hard time projecting power into? Sure, even Nancy's cruiser carried over the side torpedoes, but tracking modern submarines with a surface ship was at least twice as hard as it was for another submarine to do the job. Maybe four or five times as hard.

She smothered a sigh and returned her attention to her daughters. Whatever came, Nancy would do her duty. But for now, she had two beautiful girls and limited time to talk to them, so she would take advantage of every moment.

"Are we losing the war, Mom?" Emily whispered.

"I don't know." Nancy swallowed. "But I'm not sure anyone's winning."

The two sides traded blow after blow. Ships and submarines sank; nations built new ones. Territories were taken and retaken. The only solace after two years of war was that no one had gone nuclear, despite the claims of prewar experts.

Nancy remembered how everyone used to talk. The old assumption was that any world war would end in an *early* nuclear explosion or two, leading straight to the end of the world. Nancy didn't have words to describe how glad she was that they were wrong. All the major players had nuclear weapons, but everyone knew the first nation to use one wouldn't be the last nation standing.

Still, no one trusted another country not to pull that trigger. American *Colombia*-class ballistic missile submarines were underway constantly. So were their British counterparts. Nancy had heard the French did the same, although the Indians seemed more conservative with their patrols. No one wanted to know which side of China's three-cornered civil war controlled their launch codes, but so far, no one had launched from there, either.

But Nancy knew that nukes couldn't win the war. Not when the territory in dispute was underwater, a place few nuclear weapons could reach. They just had to slug this out until one side or the other sued for peace.

How long would that take? There was no way to know.

Bluefish's mess decks were still noisy, with two groups of sailors playing cards, one playing cribbage, and others competing in a video game tournament on the biggest screen TV. All the conversations gave Rose Lange and Harriet Ainsworth the ability to get lost the crowd, an opportunity for which Harri was grateful.

"Just watch out for yourself, okay, Harri?" Rose said, sounding more worried than Harri had ever seen her.

It wasn't like Lieutenant Lange to fret; Harri's boss had a spine of steel and everyone knew it. Rose just wasn't the fussing sort.

"Roger that, Weps." She nodded. Harri wasn't dumb enough to ignore the warning, even if she was pretty sure the XO had zero interest in her. *Rose* was gorgeous, particularly if you went for blondes. Harri, with her dark skin and eyes, didn't stand out like Rose did.

Rose glared; Harri shrugged.

"I'm pretty sure the XO thinks I'm still in high school, ma'am," she said. Not that Lieutenant Commander Harper was hard on the eyes. Harri and her fellows rated him number three on their boat hotlist, right behind Chief Payne and Lieutenant O'Kane.

"Let's hope it stays that way," Rose said before walking out of the crew's mess.

Harri watched her go, an uneasy feeling stirring in her stomach. Yeah, the XO coming onto anyone on the boat—Rose hadn't said who—was skeevy. But Harri was sure it wouldn't be her. She'd never been considered beautiful, and she spent a lot more time reading books than she did looking in the mirror. Rose was just paranoid.

Shaking her head, Harri headed out of the crew's mess and toward the forward ladder. A hand touched her arm before she could mount the first step.

"You okay?" Rene asked.

"Yeah." Harri shook herself, pushing doubts aside. "Peachy keen. What's up?"

"Wallie and I were going to play cards in the wardroom. Want to join?" he asked.

"Nah." Harri shook her head. "I think I'm going to study up a bit on *Requins*."

Rene snorted. "You passed your qualifications board. You can quit that now."

"I just want to be ready." Harri figured they'd be sent after Rochambeau. Aside from Ursula North, who else did the Alliance have? *Bluefish* was the obvious answer.

"Right." Rene drew the word out by adding several syllables in the middle that didn't belong. "Have fun with the boring, then. Let us know if you'd rather the simulating mental challenge of poker."

Harri rolled her eyes. "Although it'd be better than watching you and Max try to play cribbage, I'll pass."

"Have it your way." Rene walked past the ladder and into the wardroom while Harri went up a deck, heading for her own stateroom. One of her roommates was on watch and the other was probably sleeping, which meant Harri could use the computer to study without disturbing anyone.

Harri wasn't going to be caught by surprise again. At least the other junior officers had stopped teasing her about the "surprise" *Akula* that snuck up on her months earlier. She didn't like being the butt of jokes, and—

"Everything okay, Harri?"

Harri jumped. Somehow, she'd missed the XO standing near her stateroom. "Yes, sir."

"You look like something's bothering you," he said.

"No." Harri frowned. "I was just going to get some studying in..."

Steve laughed. "You know what they say about all work and all play."

"That it makes a good submariner?" Harri tried to inch around him, but he shifted casually to block her. Passageways on a submarine were narrow; to pass, people had to turn ninety degrees and accept that they'd brush one another, anyway. Standing straight meant he could stop her without even trying.

"People burn themselves out that way," Steve said. Why was he looking at her so strangely?

Belatedly, Harri realized that this was the first time he'd ever used her first name instead of her rank. She swallowed. "I think I'm okay, thanks."

"You could be better than okay, you know." Steve leaned forward. "Particularly if you're looking for...company."

"Company?" Harri felt her eyebrows shoot up to meet her hairline. "I just told the guys I didn't want to play cards."

"I'm not talking about playing cards." Steve smiled. "You're a beautiful woman, Harri."

"...*What?*" she asked. She couldn't have heard that right. But Steve stepped forward again, his face angling toward hers. Harri stumbled back a step. "Sir, I don't think this is a good idea."

"It's always lonely—"

A new voice interrupted from behind Harri. "Damn, XO, I didn't think you bounced back from rejection so quickly."

"Weps." Steve's eyes narrowed, and Harri twisted to look at Rose, tension pouring out of her like a waterfall.

Rose had warned her, not *five minutes ago*, and she hadn't listened. Gulping, Harri took a shaky step toward Rose, whose eyes blazed as she glared at Steve, arms crossed.

Silence reigned. Harri fidgeted; had she led the XO on? Had she made him think she might *want* him like this?

"What do you want, Miss Lange?" Steve finally asked.

"Lieutenant Ainsworth owes me a spot check in Sonar." Rose glanced at Harri. "Coming?"

"Uh, yes, ma'am?" Harri licked her lips.

Rose led her back down the ladder without glancing at Steve. Harri did look back, even though she knew she shouldn't, catching a glimpse of Steve's pursed lips. His eyes lingered on her. Harri's skin tingled like there were ants biting every inch of her. Her stomach heaved, and her mouth watered; she wanted to throw up.

Did she owe Rose a spot check? If so, Harri was going to get her head ripped off. Maintenance spot checks were part of navy life, even during wartime. But Harri hadn't told any of her sailors to be ready for one, which meant this was going to be a disaster. *Better her yelling at me than him trying to kiss me.* The XO *had* tried to kiss her, right? Harri didn't think she'd been imagining that.

Neither said anything until they were safely in the weapons room, deep down in the bow of the submarine. Harri didn't own this space. Maybe that meant she hadn't forgotten a spot check.

"You okay?" Rose asked.

Harri nodded, trying not to let her relief show. "Yeah." She winced. "I mean, yes, ma'am."

Rose waved a hand. "Fuck that shit. It's not the time to stand on ceremony," she said. "You sure you're all right?"

"I think so." Harri didn't know what to make of any of this and stared at her feet. "I mean, I'm supposed to be flattered, right?"

"Flattered that the XO just did his best impression of a dog in heat? I don't think so." Rose rolled her eyes. "Once was stupid; twice is too much. I'm telling the captain."

Harri's head snapped up. "Please don't mention me," she whispered.

"Why not?"

"I...I don't want him to think less of me." Harri hugged herself, feeling tiny. She hadn't cared what Commander Peterson thought of her, but Captain Coleman was different.

Rose sighed. "All right. I won't mention your name."

"Thanks, Weps." Harri squared her shoulders with an effort. She was a naval officer, not a scared teenager—she was twenty-four! She'd be fine.

"Any time." Rose's smile was fierce. "You know I've got your back."

Harri nodded, steeled herself, and headed up to study. Thankfully, the XO was nowhere in sight, and she made it into her stateroom without incident.

22 March 2040, Île Amsterdam, French Southern and Antarctic Lands

Île Amsterdam was the northernmost volcanic island within the Antarctic Plate, located approximately 1,700 nautical miles from both Australia's Cocos (Keeling) Islands and the British Indian Ocean Territory. Discovered in the 1500s by the Spanish and originally named *Deseperanza*, or "Despair," due to the lack of safe landings and natural resources, the island remained largely untouched for centuries. A small island with an area of only about twenty-one square miles, the two stratovolcanoes of Mont de la Dives and Le Mount du Fernand dominate the island, which led few to travel there, even in the busy days of exploration.

Eventually, seal hunters began using the island as a base, and the British even investigated using it as a penal colony in the late 1700s, though they would eventually settle on Australia, instead. By the early 1900s, the island became part of the French colony of Madagascar; then, the French Southern and Antarctic Lands were formed in August of 1955. Around that same time, the first French base was established, then called Camp Heurtin. Pre-war, it had been seasonally populated by a research staff of around thirty who studied geomagnetic, meteorology, and biology.

In the late 2030s, however, France realized that additional submarine bases would be needed in its quest to dominate the resources of the Indian Ocean, and Île Amsterdam was ideally located. So the research base—renamed Base Martin-de-Viviès—was expanded, floating piers were built, and resources were shipped in.

By 2040, Île Amsterdam was the first secret French submarine base in the Indian Ocean. It would not be the last.

Barracuda moored at Île Amsterdam's pier one shortly after four in the morning of March 22nd. Contrary to accepted wisdom, Jules had raced his submarine to the secret base, barely pausing to search the surrounding seas. He was willing to risk being heard so long as he avoided a shooting confrontation; with nothing to shoot *with*, his best option was running. And fast. While French intelligence indicated that the Alliance suspected the base's existence, Jules knew anyone hunting him would expect him to proceed with caution.

Fools. Caution was not in Jules' nature. Killing the enemy was.

He caught up with the base commander as soon as the brow connected with *Barracuda's* deck. "I need a full load of Rafales. *Immédiatement*."

"My instructions are to ration the new torpedoes. Production has slowed, and there are two other submarines here that—"

"*Non*. You may do so to everyone but me," Jules cut him off. "Call Admiral Sauvageau if you do not believe me."

"It is midnight in Marseilles!"

Jules shrugged. "I will call if you insist. Ursula North is on my tail, and I am certain you do not wish to be the man who denied me *that* kill."

That earned him a glare. "Fine. I will provide the onload. Be it on your head if the admiral objects."

"I will take that risk." Jules knew Admiral Sauvageau would not object. And Ursula *was* coming. He'd designed his last tweet to enrage her, and the Alliance had no one else to send.

"Be it on your head," the commander repeated, but Jules walked away. He had more important people to concern himself with.

Chapter 27

Blue-on-Blue

Bluefish was halfway to Île Amsterdam and Alex was thinking tactics, shifting through the known capabilities and limitations of a *Requin*-class submarine on his computer. He'd scheduled a skull session with his senior officers for that afternoon, but he knew the important decisions would be his. Would Rodriquez stay the hell out of the way? The admiral was *everywhere*, talking to sailors and entertaining Senator Angler. By now, the fact that they'd be sent after Rochambeau was the worst-kept secret on board, and you could taste the tension. The only bright side was that Angler didn't appreciate the danger they were—

"Can I talk to you, sir?" Rose stood in the open doorway to Alex's stateroom, paler than he'd ever seen her.

"Sure, Weps. Come on in." Alex gestured her into a chair, but Rose closed the door before she sat down. Her movements were jerky, *angry*, and her blazing glare could've melted the iceberg that sank *Titanic*.

A lump rose in his throat. Was this related to whatever Bobby had tried to tell him yesterday? Alex pushed his chair away from his computer to face Rose. She sat without moving a muscle, perched on the edge of the chair like she was sitting at attention with a frown making her features tight.

"I didn't want to talk to you about this." Rose grimaced. "I thought I had it handled."

"That sounds ominous."

"It's the XO, sir." Rose took a deep breath. "He...propositioned me."

Alex's heart stopped. "He *what*?"

"Not just me. One of the divos, too." Rose grimaced. "We both said no, even though he's persistent as a sex-starved emperor penguin."

Alex swallowed. "I needed that mental image," he said and then shook himself. "Is there...anything else I need to know?"

"The, uh, division officer he went after is pretty shaken. Even if she won't admit it." Rose scowled.

"The division officer you don't want to name?" Alex asked. *Bluefish* only had nine division officers, ten junior officers if he counted the supply officer, who wasn't on board. That knocked her out. A third of the divos were women. Which one had Steve been stupid enough to proposition?

"She asked me not to, sir," Rose replied.

Alex bit back a groan. Rose hadn't wanted to come forward, either. Did they think he'd step on them? That he'd take Steve's side? "Thank you for telling me. I'll deal with the XO."

"Yes, sir." Rose still looked uncomfortable.

"Is there something else you're worried about, Rose?" Alex hesitated. "Has this happened before on *Bluefish*?"

"No." Rose snorted and then rolled her eyes. "Things weren't that interesting here before, sir. It's just that...the XO said there was a war on, so no one would care."

"War on or not, that shit doesn't belong on my boat," he replied. Alex wanted to strangle Steve. He didn't want to wrap his mind around how his XO could have so little self-control, but Maggie had warned him, though, hadn't she? And he hadn't done a damned thing. Shit, he owned this. "It'll stop. I promise."

"Thanks, Captain."

Rose smiled wanly before walking out. Seeing his fiercest department head so drained left Alex sick. How had he not seen this? Why had Rose felt she couldn't come to him? Asking that question rarely resulted in an honest answer.

Pinching the bridge of his nose, Alex stepped on the urge to hunt Steve down and yell at him. That would make *him* feel better, but this wasn't about him. This wasn't what his boat needed right now! He groaned. This could divide his crew on the verge of going against the deadliest submariner in the world. How the hell was he supposed to trust a tactical deputy who couldn't keep his pants zipped?

God, what if Steve had tried propositioning *enlisted* sailors? That was even worse for discipline.

Taking a deep breath, Alex picked up his phone and called Steve's stateroom. The phone rang and rang, but there was no answer. Alex scowled, imagining what Steve was up to. An hour ago, he'd have guessed Steve was mentoring someone, giving Angler a tour, or checking on the watch in control. Now, he was afraid to find out.

He hung up and dialed control.

"Control, Officer of the Deck," Harri's voice answered.

"Harri, it's the captain. Is the XO up there?" Alex asked, hoping Steve hadn't found trouble.

A moment passed in ominous silence. "No, sir."

Shit, had Harri heard? Did everyone know but him? Alex pushed those worries aside. "Please pass the word for the XO to come to my stateroom."

"Aye, sir," Harri replied.

"Thank you." Alex hung up, sitting back in his chair. A moment later, he heard the word passed over the 1MC:

"Executive Officer, your presence is requested in the captain's stateroom."

Minutes passed; Alex stewed. He wasn't the type of CO who liked barking out orders or passing the word for people, particularly his second-in-command, but there was nothing pleasing about this situation. A submarine was a family: a dysfunctional, rough-edged, and crazy family. Their success depended upon trust and training. Fraternization ruined that.

Finally, Steve knocked on the door, and Alex bade him enter.

"You passed the word for me, Captain?" Steve cocked his head.

Could Rose have been wrong? No. Alex knew her better than that. "Take a seat, XO," he said.

Steve's eyebrows went up, but he sat. "Everything all right, sir?"

"No." Alex waited a moment to judge Steve's reaction, but Steve appeared relaxed; either he didn't feel guilty, or he had no idea what was going on. "I've been told that you've propositioned two officers. Is this true?"

"Well, not at the same time." Steve's smile was lopsided, like an invitation to share some joke.

"You're not even denying it." Alex stared.

"I wouldn't want to call anyone in the wardroom a liar." Steve shrugged. "And I'll never deny being a ladies' man."

"That's...what you have to say for yourself?" Alex wished he sounded more intimidating, but he was too stunned. Steve had been in the navy for almost fifteen years. How the hell had he missed the memo that fraternization was bad?

"I'm not going to lie, sir."

"That's the *only* point in your favor," Alex growled. "Let me put this simply: you will stop. Immediately."

"It's wartime." Steve didn't quite roll his eyes. "No one cares."

"*I* care, XO, and that should be more than enough for you," Alex said, leaning forward and spearing Steve with a glare. "This is my boat, and if you think you can fuck with my officers, you need to reevaluate your priorities in life."

Steve finally flinched. "Meaning?"

"Meaning that if you want a future on this boat—or in the navy—you'll recalibrate yourself and cut this shit out. Understood?"

"Yes, sir."

"Any questions?" Alex asked, biting off each word.

Steve shook his head.

"Good." It was nice to see Steve could get the hint when it was spelled out to him in small words. "Now—" The phone ringing cut him off, and Alex bit back the urge to swear. "Captain."

"Sir, it's the officer of the deck," Harri said. "Sorry to interrupt, but we've detected a Russian intelligence trawler at about ten thousand yards."

Alex blinked. An intelligence trawler wasn't Rochambeau, but it was still a juicy target. Spy ships always were. "Close to intercept and I'll be right there."

"Aye, sir!" Harri hung up, and Alex twisted to face Steve again.

"If we have to discuss this again, XO, it'll go badly," he said. "You're a good XO, and you've got good tactical instincts. But if you don't learn self-control, you've got no business commanding a submarine."

"That's hardly fair—"

"Neither is the fact that you're using your rank to try to get women in bed with you!" Alex stepped on his temper with an effort. "So figure out which is more important to you: your ambition or your inability to keep your dick in your pants. Got it?"

Steve frowned. "Yes, sir."

"Now let's go do our goddamned job." Rising, Alex headed out of the stateroom, expecting Steve to follow him.

Île Amsterdam, French Southern and Antarctic Lands

The base commander was still a trifle annoyed. *Barracuda* had loaded thirty-four torpedoes—two less than her full capacity, but all the Base Martin-de-Viviès possessed—in record time. If they had disregarded safety regulations to do so, well, that was not Jules' concern. No one had been hurt, unless he counted the base commander's pride. Or perhaps the ire of his fellow submarine commanders who could acquire no more torpedoes. Jules did not care.

The torpedoes were all F27 Rafales, exactly as he had asked. *Barracuda* was ready to fight again, and Jules would not wait. His crew could rest once they were underway.

Ten hours after her arrival, *Barracuda* eased away from the pier, heading out to sea. Once she submerged, Jules gestured for his second-in-command to join him at the chart table.

"You are certain she will chase us, *mon capitaine*?" Commander Camille Dubois asked.

"*Oui*." Jules felt a smile tug at his lips, thinking back on the way he had baited his old friend. "She will not be able to sit still."

"Surely she knows this is a trap."

Jules chuckled. "*Bien sûr*. But she will think she is good enough to avoid it."

"Is she?" Camille looked him in the eye.

"Perhaps." He shrugged. "We shall find out, shall we not? Either way, it will be a battle for the ages, and surprise is on our side."

"Unless she does not know about Île Amsterdam," she said, looking down at the chart. "I think you assume too much."

"Says the woman who accepted the *Neyk* mission all those years ago," Jules retorted, grinning.

Camille shook her head. "That was lower risk. This is counting upon the enemy to do as we wish."

"And *that* was counting on an American submarine commander to be deceived into believing an innocent submarine was carrying terrorists." He waggled his eyebrows. "I remember only a *partial* success on that front, do I not? I seem to have maneuvered into position to shoot torpedoes and fool the world into thinking it was the Americans."

She glared. "As was the plan."

"Sneaking up under the belly of USS *Kansas* was not without risk, my friend." He gestured at the chart, where *Barracuda* sped away from Île Amsterdam at her best silent speed. "We lose nothing if she does take the bait. If dear Lady North does not arrive within a few days, we will move elsewhere to hunt. Perhaps the approaches to Perth will be more to your liking, no?"

"Only if you mean *inside* their outer patrol areas." Finally, Camille grinned back, and Jules bowed his head in respect for her point.

Yes, Ursula could waste her fury on other targets. Or she might not find them at all. Attempting to manipulate an enemy was always risky, but Jules felt it was worth the effort. Shooting up a convoy to suck Ursula in would not work twice. He had to try something new.

It was a shame Captain Coleman was so good at his job.

Steve *never* let someone talk to him like that, not since his academy days. He'd always been one of the best. Even Commander Singleton, back on *Perch*, hadn't been this rude. Or so damned blind! There was a war on; who cared what happened between consenting adults? It wasn't like Steve would ever play favorites because he slept with a woman. He was too professional. Captain Coleman, however, couldn't seem to understand that. Hell, he was pissed because Rose had said *no*! Steve rolled his eyes. If either woman said yes, neither would've run to the captain. Not that Harri had actually come out and said no. Things would have been different if Rose hadn't shown up.

"Firing point procedures, tubes one and two, track 7898." Hearing the captain's order jerked Steve back to reality, and he headed over to the weapons corner to do his job.

Let Coleman complain about him now, Steve thought. He'd show him who was the best.

"XO." Rose's voice was downright frosty.

"Weps." Steve smiled. He knew she'd ratted him out. Maybe rumors were right, and she was a lesbian. If so, she should have said so right off the bat. He would've left her alone.

She didn't reply, instead concentrating on calculating a firing solution for the Russian intelligence trawler. Sonar reported the ship was a *Yantar*, one of Russian's older and more reliable classes of spy ships. Technically a research vessel, the *Yantars* could carry mini subs, splice underwater cables, lay mines, and find sunken submarines. No one in the Alliance knew much about them aside from what could be found online, because no one had captured one to look inside it. The one thing they *did* know was that *Yantars* were armed. *Yantar* herself had sunk a pair of subs with depth charges earlier in the war.

Bluefish set battle stations while Steve and the captain made their way to control, their first time since Admiral Rodriquez and Senator Angler came on board. Both were in control, too, along with the gorgeous aide who was Rodriquez's shadow. Should Steve appeal to one of them? Rodriquez was the king rule breaker, consistently avoiding regulations he didn't like. On the other hand, Angler was a politician who wouldn't have the traditional navy hang up over fraternization. Steve was willing to bet that Angler had boinked an intern or two over the years. *Even better, he's my roommate.* Steve would have time to talk to Angler in private, and—

"Solution set," Rose announced.

"Solution checked," Steve echoed as quickly as he could. He needed to look impressive. Trying to use a politician's influence to counter his captain would be tricky. Coleman was a Medal of Honor winner, and Steve couldn't forget how much weight that carried.

How the hell could someone so unconventional give a damn about this?

"Very well." Coleman was as cool as a cucumber; Steve wished he didn't respect the man. Maybe he could convince him that Rose had overreacted.

Steve headed over to stand next to the captain. Angler and Rodriquez were both watching; Angler was mildly curious, but Rodriquez's eyes sparkled like firecrackers. Of course, the old man had never been in sub combat; he'd already been an admiral when the war started. He looked ready to jump out of his skin with excitement.

"Sonar, Conn, what's the range?" Coleman asked over the squawk box.

"Nine thousand yards," Chief Andreas answered from sonar.

"Conn, aye." Coleman studied the plot as *Bluefish* crept in closer, moving at a silent ten knots. The *Yantar* was on a nearly perpendicular course, approaching from starboard.

Maintaining a slow speed let the *Yantar* cross her own "T." It was the perfect shot, and they were already in range.

"Make tubes one through four ready in all respects, including opening the outer doors," Coleman said. "Standby for snapshot tube three or four."

The weapons team raced to comply, but Steve frowned. "You think someone else is out here, Captain?"

"I think the odds of a Russian spy ship running around alone are low. Particularly this far south," Coleman replied. Then he shoved his hands in his pockets like he had no idea an admiral was watching.

Steve chewed on the idea for a moment. "Between this guy and the intel gatherer disguised as a passenger ferry, I think we're looking at a shift in tactics."

"Good point. The ferry was visited by *Requin*, too, which indicates cooperation between Russian intelligence and the French sub force." Coleman started chewing on his glasses and then turned to Admiral Rodriquez. "You hear anything about stuff like this, sir?"

Rodriquez scowled. "Nothing more than what you've just said. I assume your squadron commander *accidentally* neglected to fucking tell me the details."

"Ah." Coleman was the only one in the room who didn't flinch at the admiral's caustic tone; even Angler looked concerned. The captain leaned over to speak in the squawk box: "Sonar, Conn, any other customers around?"

"Conn, Sonar, negative. Unless you count the fish. There's a pod of whales out to port at about four miles."

"Aye." Coleman straightened; Steve tried not to scowl. He should have been ahead of the captain and asked that question. He'd always been ahead of Commander Singleton.

Being outthought annoyed him.

"Going to shoot without playing 'Saint Alexander,' Captain?" Steve asked.

"*What*?" Coleman's head snapped around, and Steve fought back a smile. Did the captain think he hadn't noticed the nickname Commander Kennedy pinned on him?

Served him right. Steve shrugged. "I just thought you might want to offer them the chance to abandon."

Rodriquez's bark of laughter forestalled any answer the captain might have managed. "Saint fucking Alexander. I love it," he said. "That what people are calling you after letting those heavy lift ships abandon?"

"I hope to hell they're not." Coleman was a bit red; Steve wanted to laugh, too. Even if he hadn't meant it as a compliment.

"Beats being 'Uncle' Marco." Rodriquez's grin made Steve wonder if the admiral had somehow missed the reference to Admiral Charles—"Uncle Charlie"—Lockwood, World War II's legendary COMSUBPAC. Was he that dense? Steve didn't think so. "Not bad at all."

"If it's all the same to you, sir, I think I'll get back to work," Coleman said, clearly trying not to fidget.

"I'm not going to stop you from shooting the sons of bitches, Captain."

No, Rodriquez clearly understood the World War II reference, given that he'd just thrown out one of his own. Did Coleman know he'd just been compared to Mush Morton? Steve would have given his left leg to hear an admiral say that about him, but his CO just turned back to Rose and her team.

"Tubes one and two, fire!"

Yantars weren't built to hold prisoners, but Master Chief Bryan Morton supposed he shouldn't be picky. They were alive, and although the Russians left them topside, they'd provided cold weather gear. That mystified *Razorback's* survivors, who'd been picked up in the middle of the Indian Ocean, until the spy ship headed *south*.

"Where the hell do you think we're going?" Commander Abercrombie asked. She and Master Chief Bryan Morton stood a bit away from the rest of the crew, including the injured-and-surly XO, Lieutenant Commander Keys. Somehow, two-thirds of *Razorback's* complement made it off the boat when she went down. Most of them were huddled together as far from the tip of the bow as they could get, lacking shelter or warmth.

"Fuck if I know, ma'am." Morton took a deep breath. "About the only thing down there are the French Southern and Antarctic Islands. That, and the Australian islands they took off them at the beginning—"

The world went wild. A giant hand smashed up from underneath the *Yantar's* hull, throwing Morton off his feet and into Abercrombie. She yelped, and both crashed into the deck together as a pair of geysers erupted out of the water on the ship's port side.

The deck sloped immediately, spilling American sailors and their Russian guards toward the middle of the ship. People howled and metal screamed, cracking and bending. Water roared, rearing up to lap at the *Yantar's* top decks within seconds. Meanwhile, the air filled with an ominous *glugging* sound that Morton knew all too well. He'd heard it five days ago as water filled *Razorback*, drowning every sailor unable to escape in time.

Morton's helpless roll continued until he crashed into a capstan. Pain raced through his shoulder and back—he was far too old for this bullshit—but he lurched to his feet, anyway. He'd lost Abercrombie in the chaos, but most of the crew was still within the barriers the Russians set up, clinging to the flared sides of the bow for balance. Somehow, the explosion had thrown Morton clear of those barriers, but he sprinted for them now.

It was like running uphill; the deck's slope was over twenty degrees and deepening quickly.

"Get over the side!" he shouted, waving frantically. "Get over and swim as hard as you can!"

"Are you crazy?" Keys was the closest, her eyes wide and terrified. Where the fuck was the captain?

Morton wished there was time to look for Commander Abercrombie.

"That was two torpedoes, ma'am, and ain't no way this tub's going to survive that!" Morton pushed the XO toward the side, noticing that their Russian guards were already running for the lifeboats. Idiots. No davit would launch a boat at this angle. Swimming was their best bet, along with hoping that the Russians did decent maintenance on their life rafts. If none of the rafts auto-ejected, they were in deep shit.

"Let's fucking go!" Petty Officer Boxer shoved two young officers to the rail before jumping over herself. That seemed to give the pair courage, and they followed suit.

"The water's nearly freezing here, Master Chief!" Keys objected.

"No shit." Morton was done with the XO's fretting; he grabbed the woman by her coveralls and heaved her bodily over the side.

Keys screamed.

Something exploded; Morton detected the faint whiff of diesel fuel before the deck jerked out from under his feet. Catching himself on the temporary barrier, he watched several *Razorback* sailors tumble down toward the ship's rapidly disintegrating midsection. There wasn't even time to swear.

Another explosion ripped through the *Yantar*, throwing the bow back down on a somewhat even keel.

"Go, go, go!" Morton shouted, hauling himself to his feet and sprinting for the rail. Sailors scattered like the wind, lunging for the side.

He threw himself over just as a third explosion rolled the *Yantar* onto her starboard side.

Morton missed hitting the keel by inches. Then the water rose to meet him, and for a moment, everything went black. Then he sputtered his way to the surface, coughing up seawater. The water felt like a thousand icy needles stabbing into his skin, but Morton forced himself to swim away from the sinking *Yantar*. He didn't want to look back; he just needed to get far enough that the suction didn't get him.

A long two minutes of swimming relieved him of the need to think. Once he stopped to tread water, the enormity of the situation hit Morton. He'd survived two sinkings in five days.

Was that a record? He hoped not. Either way, he'd just been sunk by friends, and didn't that suck?

Voices drifted his way, carried by a cold wind. Twisting in the water, Bryan spotted four inflatable life rafts peppering the area around where the *Yantar* had been. Little of the ship was left save some debris and an oil slick; Morton tried to avoid that as he took a deep breath and swam toward the life rafts. Worst case, the Russians shot him. That beat drowning.

When Morton reached the raft, his limbs were growing sluggish. But the first face he spotted was the angry Russian in charge of guarding them. Vova? Bryan thought that was his name.

Morton grabbed for the side of the raft, only to have his hands slapped away.

"You wait," Vova said, sneering.

"Sure." Morton managed not to swear. But it was the damned Russians' life raft.

What a pity they didn't leave the *Razorback* crew floating around for the Alliance to rescue. By now, they'd have been warm *and* safe, instead of caught in the middle of this shit-show. Christ on a cracker, Morton was getting colder by the moment.

More *Razorback* sailors arrived as Morton treaded water, looking ragged and half frozen. A dozen Russian sailors clambered right into the life raft, but they made the Americans wait for several agonizing minutes. Finally, Vova looked at another man—the one who introduced himself to the prisoners as Colonel Nikolin, Bryan thought—and got a nod in return.

"Up," Vova said.

Bryan didn't need to be told twice. Climbing into the raft with limbs that didn't want to work was hard; he had to try twice before his feet would kick hard enough to propel him out of the water. He really was too old for this—why oh *why* had he volunteered for *another* tour again? The Russians offered no help, so Morton turned to haul Boxer into the raft behind him. Next up was Lieutenant Commander Keys, who sat there with chattering teeth but didn't mention the way Morton had thrown her overboard.

"I count thirty-nine of us, now, Master Chief," Boxer said quietly.

Morton cringed. "Same."

"What?" Keys finally found his voice. "Seventy of us got off *Razorback*."

"Yeah." Morton didn't need to say more. A Russian—not Vova, but one of the sailors off the *Yantar*—offered him a blanket. Stripping off his wet coveralls, Bryan wrapped himself in the blanket, noticing how others did the same without regards to modesty.

Hell, it wasn't like anyone was looking. They were all too cold and wet, Russians included. Except Vova. He was leering at everyone.

Morton wanted to smack the Russian but knew better. At least the fucker was an equal opportunity asshole. He drooled over everyone, including his Russian comrades. None of them had the guts to call him on it, either.

"Maybe this time we'll get picked up by the Alliance," Boxer muttered, glancing at Vova. "Would serve the assholes right."

"From your lips to God's ears," Morton replied.

Maybe this time they'd be lucky.

Chapter 28

The Hunt

24 March 2040, USS *Bluefish*

What Uncle Marco wanted, Uncle Marco got. Even if it delayed *Bluefish's* date with Rochambeau.

Still, Alex hadn't expected Admiral Rodriquez to show up in his stateroom, tablet in hand and closing the door firmly behind himself. "I got the download of *Razorback's* logs," the admiral said. "Thought you might want to see them before I throw you off the fucking deep end."

"That...might be useful." Alex swallowed, his mouth suddenly dry.

"Yeah. It's like goddamned grave robbery, I know." Rodriquez dropped into the chair across from Alex, putting the tablet on the table. "But if I'm going to send you after that asshat, I owe you every tool I've got."

"I appreciate that, sir." Alex tried not to think about how *Razorback* carried Master Chief Morton to the grave, or how Patricia Abercrombie had been his best friend's old XO. John had to be taking this hard, and Alex hadn't even called him. What kind of terrible friend was he?

"All right, quit your fucking wool gathering and let's get to work." Rodriquez hit the play button.

Watching the video log from *Razorback's* attack center was like peeling back the curtain to the afterlife and spying on someone's biggest regrets.

Video Data Recorders—not-so-affectionately called "Vaders" by the sub and surface fleet—were a relatively new addition to submarines. Surface ships started the trend with *voice* data recorders in the early 2000s, but submariners resisted them for decades, convinced that the old paper deck log was enough. Coupled with electronic charts that recorded a submarine's position to the second, the U.S. Navy of the early twenty-first century felt like they were on the cutting edge. Other nations started using VDRs on their submarines in the early 2020s, but the U.S. resisted.

Until the Neptune Memorial Station disaster.

In April 2032, USS *South Carolina*, a *Virginia*-class submarine, ran headlong into an underwater station off the coast of Florida. Her deck log was incomplete, and crew members contradicted one another, claiming mechanical issues, navigation problems, and drunk officers. The submarine survived the collision; the station did not. Two hundred people drowned without adequate explanation from the U.S. Navy. From that day forward, American ships and submariners sailed with continuously-recording VDRs even their COs could not disable.

Those logs automatically uploaded to the nearest satellite when a SUBMIS/SUBSUNK buoy activated. Alex had received emails from dead friends triggered by the buoy, but he'd never watched a dead submarine's logs. It made his stomach heave.

But on the video, *Razorback's* crew crackled with energy. Pat Abercrombie was the center of the maelstrom, caught between the proverbial rock and Rochambeau. She chose to go after the *Akula* after it sank a frigate and targeted a destroyer, all because they weren't certain Rochambeau was caught in their trap. Was that trap so good it lured two enemies in, or was Rochambeau so canny he followed the Indian *Akula* in to use it as cover? The French bastard was cold enough to let *Razorback* sink his ally.

Then Rochambeau fired a pair of impossibly fast torpedoes. *Razorback* ran for her life, dodging and dancing and launching countermeasures. Master Chief Morton sent her to the roof, and Alex watched his old COB turn to do something else—

The image danced wildly, sparks and people flying. Screams filled the background, coupled with the screech of breaking HY-80 steel. Something exploded, and water rushed toward the camera before everything went black.

Alex wanted to throw up. "Fuck," he whispered.

"Took the words right out of my mouth." Rodriquez's eyes were wet, too.

"She should have left the *Akula* alone," Alex said softly. "She threw away her shot at Rochambeau to kill it."

"Takes a piss-ton of cold blood to watch your own allies get sunk," Rodriquez replied. "Could you do that?"

Alex swallowed. "I don't know."

But I think I'm going to find out. He'd railed at Ursula North for letting *Illinois* sink while she laid in wait for Rochambeau. Patricia Abercrombie had made the opposite choice and died. Was there a middle ground? Could there be?

French Southern and Antarctic Waters

Gallant settled into a patrol just off the entrance to Île Amsterdam's harbor. Creeping along at four knots with her coolant pumps offline made *Gallant* as quiet as any other Alliance submarine, but her crew remained uneasy. *Gallant* hadn't detected any traffic in the area; this seemed like a sleepy island without a care in the world.

Ursula was damned sure that was a lie.

"Nothing yet?" she demanded, walking into control three hours after their arrival. James had convinced her to take a nap, but now she was on her feet and burning to shoot someone.

"No, ma'am." James took a deep breath. "It's possible he beat us here, Captain."

"Then we'll catch him on the way out." Ursula gritted her teeth. Math was on Jules' side, much though she hated to admit that. In his shoes, Ursula would've proceeded with caution. Sailing with no torpedoes was worse than being naked in public. But Jules might not care. He'd always been reckless.

"Yes, ma'am."

Ursula stopped pacing to look at him. "You have doubts."

"Not doubts." James shook his head. "Just...concerns. We've very alone out here, Captain. What if the French base is better defended than intelligence believes?"

"Then that's why we have torpedoes and missiles, Commander." She flashed him a grin.

"Captain, we have a patrol boat incoming at zero-four-four," Sonar interrupted. "Looks like they're heading for the channel."

"Mark their course," Ursula ordered. "The more we learn about the base, the better."

She tuned out the reply, moving over to the plot. Was Jules already here, or was the patrol boat out there to clear a path for him? The French were protective over their submarines, doubly so out here. Putting a submarine base on a barely-defended island was an excellent idea while that base was a secret, but once the enemy knew about it, your options became limited. Should she proceed to periscope depth and look around? She'd need to put eyes on the base in order to lob Tomahawks at it.

It would wait, Ursula told herself. Her desire to turn a French submarine base into flaming wreckage must take backseat to her duty. Jules Rochambeau was her target, not the base. No matter how her blood boiled.

Common sense won; Ursula waited until after dark to sneak *Gallant* in as close as she could. Using the low light setting on her periscope allowed Ursula to see almost as well as in daylight, and spotting a camouflaged periscope in the dark was almost impossible. Two French security boats patrolled the approach to the small harbor, but neither noticed the periscope.

Probably because no one else was crazy enough to remain submerged with only four meters beneath the keel. Ursula bared her teeth. She didn't dare creep in any closer, but careful maneuvering kept her from bottoming her boat.

Not that it made her watchkeepers any less nervous.

"I see two *Requins* pier side," James reported. Her best watch officer was on the periscope while Ursula watched the feed on the monitor. Sticking her eye to the damned thing always gave her a headache, and one of the privileges of commanding His Majesty's warships was delegating tasks you hated. "One on the east pier, the other two piers down."

There were four piers total, with an empty one on the west end and patrol boats between the two submarines. Ursula had six Tomahawks—all she could get on short notice—which meant two per sub and two extra for the base. Not that she really needed to double up with GPS-guided missiles, but Ursula did not believe in taking chances.

"Both subs look like they're on shore power," James added.

"Good eyes, James." Ursula smiled. Shore power meant the base provided power for the subs' electrical load instead of their own reactors. *That* meant they'd have to start their reactors before getting underway, something any nuclear submariner knew was not a quick or easy proposition.

"Do you want to begin firing procedures, Captain?" he asked.

Ursula sighed. "Not yet." She hated hesitating, but... "We need confirmation either of these *Requins* is *Barracuda.* If we destroy the base prior to his arrival, Rochambeau will run. We must wait."

"How long, ma'am?"

"A day or two. But further out." Ursula was not an idiot; staying this close might get her boat run over by a patrol boat with nowhere to dive. The patrol boat wouldn't survive the experience, but the element of surprise would be ruined, and then where would she be?

"Yes, ma'am." James sounded relieved. Truth be told, Ursula was, too. She just couldn't say it.

Gallant lowered her periscope and crept away from the harbor, settling back into her patrol pattern.

Thanks to Steve, that "Saint Alexander" nickname got whispered all over the fucking boat. Hiding in his stateroom didn't shield him from the unholy glee his crew displayed. In some strange way, the low-key mockery almost felt good. He knew they'd hated Peterson, but the crew was *proud* of Alex's stupid new nickname. Proud of him. That left him giddy and wanting to vomit; the attention was horrible, but knowing his crew trusted him was priceless.

Unfortunately, Uncle Marco was never going let Alex live it down. Was that a bit of petty revenge on Steve's part? For some guy labeled a hot runner, Steve's actions sure fell short of his reputation.

That was a problem for another day. Today, Alex needed to figure out how to catch the war's most successful submariner—and he needed to decide if he could trust his XO. *You're either going to give him a second chance or you're not. And if you aren't, you need to talk to the admiral about firing him.* Of course, that entailed going right over his boss' head, something guaranteed to enrage Commodore Banks. But could he torpedo someone's career? Particularly when Steve *hadn't* committed fraternization?

For some COs, trying to sleep with someone on their crew would be enough. Alex, however, had once been the victim of a torpedoed career, and he couldn't bring himself to do the same thing to Steve. They were at war. If Steve could do his job, Alex would let him.

Sighing, he rose from his desk and headed toward control. He was too keyed up to sleep, even though it was past taps on *Bluefish's* internal clock. The sub's passageways were quiet; anyone awake was on watch or on the mess decks, probably watching the football game the radio watch downloaded at periscope depth. This was one of Alex's favorite times to wander the boat. Back in his own XO days, it was when he'd discovered *Kansas'* aches and pains. A well-maintained submarine emitted a certain set of healthy noises; when you knew a boat well enough, you could hear problems. You could also feel a crew's tension when everyone was too tired to hide their worries. Night watches aired their grievances when they thought senior officers weren't around to hear.

The soft murmur of voices greeted him when he reached the open hatch to control. Rene had the watch, and Alex spotted him before the officer of the deck noticed the captain walking in. Rene's posture was alert but relaxed as he chatted with the diving officer of the watch. The helmsmen and planesmen were both standing since autopilot was engaged. The curtain to sonar was open, too, a dead giveaway that no one in there was asleep. Nodding, Alex slipped his hands in his pockets and stepped into the space.

Steve stood by the navigation plot, his eyes riveted on its display. Alex headed over there, waving for Rene to be quiet when he opened his mouth to announce Alex's presence. He'd never been big on standing on ceremony, and everyone with eyes knew the captain had wandered in.

"Evening, XO," he said. "You're up late."

Steve's smile was strained. "Thinking about Île Amsterdam."

"You and me both." Alex sighed. "Unfortunately, none of our charts are good."

Alex spent hours poring over charts for the island and its surrounding waters, but he found nothing helpful. Île Amsterdam had been claimed by France in 1843 and had been home only to a lonely research station before the war. No one cared much about the place—Antarctic islands with active volcanos were low on the tourism index—so information was scarce.

"Do you want to get in close, sir?" Steve asked.

"I don't think we need to. Either Rochambeau's beat us here—which I'd bet on—or he hasn't. Either way, lying in wait is our best bet," Alex said, chewing his lower lip. "The problem is that's been tried against Rochambeau before."

"Is that what *Razorback* did?" Steve grimaced. "We never saw him coming on *Pacu*."

"*Razorback* tried hiding around a target they knew he couldn't refuse."

Steve snorted. "That worked out great for them."

"They were on the money until they went after an *Akula*." Alex pulled his glasses off; maybe then he could stop staring at the plot. Besides, he needed something better to chew on. "The *Akula* sank a frigate and went after another ship; *Razorback* sank the *Akula*."

"And then Rochambeau sank *Razorback*," Steve finished for him, groaning. "I've seen this episode before."

"Yeah." Alex sighed. "Now we have to rewrite—"

Ping!

"Conn, Sonar, active sonar, close aboard!" a voice shouted through the squawk box. "Approximate bearing three-one-five true!"

"Right full rudder, all ahead flank!" Alex snapped, stepping away from the chart. Three-one-five was almost the reciprocal of *Bluefish's* current course, which meant their enemy was right off their bow. "Snapshot tube one, bearing three-one-five!"

"You want to head toward the island?" Steve asked as *Bluefish* rolled into a sharp turn, the deck vibrating slightly as the submarine picked up speed.

Rene hit the general alarm before Alex could respond, passing the word for the crew to go to battle stations.

"If this is Rochambeau, he's got a new torpedo that's ungodly fast," Alex replied. "We're not going to outrun it, so going closer to the island gives us a chance to lose it in the bottom topography and—"

"Conn, Sonar, we've got a call on the Gertrude claiming to be HMS *Gallant*," Sonar reported.

Alex spun to the squawk box. "Sonar, Captain, say again!"

"Captain, the active pulse matches signature to the Thales 2076 sonar suite installed on *Gallant*."

"Fuck! Weapons, you still have that torpedo on a wire?" Alex demanded.

"Yes, sir," Rose replied. How had she reached control so fast? It didn't matter; she was hard at work. "Range approximately fifteen thousand yards, closing at eighty-seven knots. Time to impact five minutes."

"Self-destruct the torpedo." Alex hated giving that order—it was a waste of a weapon that cost several hundred thousand dollars. But he wasn't about to shoot an ally, either.

"Captain, are you sure you want to—" Steve started.

Alex held up a hand to forestall him. "Kill the torp, Weps."

"Weps, aye." Rose grimaced and hit the button. Moments later, the explosion's shockwave rocked *Bluefish*.

"Conn, Sonar, *Gallant* Actual wants to talk to the captain." Now it was Chief Andreas' voice, rough and tight.

Great, Admiral Rodriquez just walked through the hatch. Jesus, could Alex have fucked this up worse?

"Rene, slow to five knots and come back to base course." Alex scraped a hand over his face. He felt like such a fool—but what the hell kind of idiot said hello with active sonar when they had multiple *voice* communications circuits to use? Alex turned to Steve. "I'll be in sonar."

"Aye. I'll hold down the fort." Was Steve pleased? Alex wasn't sure, but the glint in his XO's eyes left him uncomfortable.

Stalking into the small sonar room, Alex grabbed the handset for the Gertrude, or underwater telephone. Every submarine in the world had one. Technological advances amplified voice quality over underwater telephone, but communications were still in plain voice and unencrypted. It was like talking on an open radio circuit; anyone who had the right frequency could listen in.

Theoretically, Alliance Gertrude frequencies were classified. But *Gallant* could have called *Bluefish* on a secure comms circuit, too; Alex didn't believe in continuously transmitting his submarine's position, but his boat always monitored Alliance Subsurface Secure.

It just had to be *Gallant*, didn't it?

Not growling obscenities at the British submarine took a herculean effort. "*Gallant*, this is *Bluefish* Actual, over."

"*Bluefish*, this is *Gallant* Actual." Ursula North's familiar buzz saw of an accent came through loud and clear. "What the bloody hell do you think you were doing? You fired at me!"

"Perhaps then you should think before lashing someone with active sonar, over." Alex bit his tongue to avoid saying more.

He wanted to scream that North was a flaming moron. They were *at war*. Active sonar painted a target. Any submariner with half a brain would fire at someone who pinged them!

"*You're* the one who bitched about my using another Alliance submarine as bait, Captain," Ursula retorted. "Perhaps next time I will not try to save you."

Alex snorted. "I wasn't aware that I required *saving*."

"Get out of my way, Coleman," she said, and he could almost hear Ursula rolling her eyes. "I have work to do."

"And you think I don't?" His stupid big mouth struck again; the question was out before Alex could stop it.

"Yes, you're doing an excellent job of being in my way. *Again.*"

"Look, clearly we have conflicting orders," Alex replied as calmly as he could. One of them had to be the adult here, and it wasn't going to be her. "So why don't we work together and—"

"When pigs fucking fly. Over."

Are you fucking kidding me? Alex couldn't say that with every eye in sonar riveted on him. While he hesitated, Ursula continued:

"I wouldn't trust you not to fuck a porcupine. Stay clear of my boat. You bloody well know why I'm here, so get the hell out of my way and let me get on with it!"

Alex closed his eyes, resisting the urge to bash his head into the nearest bulkhead. Here they were, two of the Alliance's top submarine captains—with *Razorback* and Patricia Abercrombie gone, Alex found himself in the top American spot, a scary thought he didn't need right now—fighting like children. Hell, he'd grounded his daughters for less! He sucked in a deep breath.

"I think we need to kick this upstairs, *Gallant*," Alex said. "It's a damned shame you can't pull your head out long enough to cooperate with an *ally*, but that's your call."

"I am *not* letting you ruin my shot," she replied. "Talk to whoever you want to. I already have my orders."

Alex rolled his eyes. She wanted him to continue sniping at her, didn't she? Fuck that. "This is *Bluefish*, roger, out."

He hung up the handset, careful not to slam it down like a petulant child. Chief Andreas looked like she expected him to explode. Alex just shrugged.

"I suck at making friends sometimes, but I didn't mean to piss in Captain North's Wheaties."

Andreas snorted out a laugh. "She sounds pretty rip shit, sir. Maybe she doesn't like Wheaties. Do they have those in England?"

"Hell if I know, Chief." Alex smiled. "Well, it's time to make people better paid than I work out this thorny mess, so if you'll excuse me."

"Good luck, Captain."

"Thanks, I think."

"This is the grandest entertainment I've had in years," Jules said to his XO, chuckling.

French intelligence had identified the Alliance's preferred Gertrude frequencies years ago; listening in was easy. Once *Barracuda* detected the single active sonar pulse from *Gallant*—which he was already tracking—they found *Bluefish*. *Barracuda* now had both in her sights, yet Jules preferred to be closer before he shot. Technically, the F27 Rafale's maximum effective range was twenty-seven nautical miles, but practice proved it was best fired up close. Those torpedoes did not turn fast, and with a large island as a backdrop...well, it would not do to drop a torpedo warhead on a French base.

Particularly not a base situated on an island over an underwater magma chamber. Jules studied geology as a hobby when he was young, and that sounded like a *terrible* idea to him.

Jules had not survived so long by picking fights he could not win, either. Shooting at both *Gallant* and *Bluefish* guaranteed both would shoot back. Dodging torpedoes from two angles might end *Barracuda*, not to mention Captain Jules Rochambeau. Perhaps he might try if *Bluefish* hadn't opened the distance between herself and *Gallant* so expeditiously. That American clearly had no desire to cozy up to his British counterpart.

Camille smiled thinly. "I believe I recognize one of those voices. From my time on *Kansas*."

"Oh?"

"*Oui.* Commander Coleman was the executive officer during the...incident at Armistice Station." She scowled. "In fact, he was the one who ruined everything."

"Was he?" Jules perked up. "I did not know that."

"He was a nuisance then as well." She rolled her eyes. "Such a pity. It nearly succeeded."

"I admit I do not know much about your end of that mission." Jules shrugged. "And it is a minor matter now."

Jules had enemies to sink, not schemes to rehash. Which to target? *Gallant* and *Bluefish* were too far apart to sink together, yet close enough to offer mutual support. Would they? Both captains seemed...irate.

It was nice to know the Alliance had warts, too. Jules heartily despised most of his Indian counterparts, who thought themselves so sophisticated using gifted French and Russian designs. Half of his Russian comrades were barbarians; the other half were too enthusiastic or too timid. Only Katerina Revnik stood out from the rest, and she'd been buried somewhere unknown for months.

"Now we concentrate on the present," he continued. "And we wait to see what our old friends will choose to do."

Camille nodded, her lips pressed tightly together and posture stiff. She disliked Americans more than Jules did. He wanted to *best* them; Camille wanted to destroy them. He enjoyed her fire, but sometimes it needed reining in.

Pity that Ursula and Coleman didn't resume their discussion via Gertrude. Jules suppressed a smirk. *Lady North does speak so...well.* Jules sat back and waited. He had time, and his preferred target was within his sights. *Bluefish* didn't matter, not yet. *Gallant* and Ursula North did.

An hour ticked by; *Bluefish* drifted further from both *Gallant* and *Barracuda*, reorienting to face northeast and slowing to a crawl. *Bluefish* clearly wanted in on the hunt, but could the so-called Alliance cooperate? Jules hoped not. Camille despised the all-too-clever Alexander Coleman. Jules had studied him, however. He admired Coleman's actions in defense of Convoy 57; tenacity and guts went a long way in their business. Jules could not afford to ignore him.

Particularly since *Bluefish* was hard to track. The *Ceros* were almost as quiet as Jules' own *Requin* class. *Gallant* was noisier, even though Ursula parked her boat under a thermocline to disguise her emissions.

"Dial *Bluefish's* signature in," he ordered his sonar watch. "I want to know her if we see them again."

"Yes, sir."

Jules smiled. He would complete the *Razorback-Gallant-Bluefish* trifecta before 2040 ended. Then who would the Alliance send after him? They were running short on heroes.

Bluefish started moving, slowly at first and then building speed up to twenty knots. But she didn't turn, instead heading away from Île Amsterdam. Jules' jaw dropped.

"He is *leaving*?" Camille gaped.

"So it would seem." He shrugged. *"Après la pluie, le beau temps."* Every cloud had a silver lining. Taking them out separately was easier, anyway. "Perhaps she offended him."

Camille laughed. "If only we are so lucky. Shall we engage *Gallant* now?"

"No. Lady North does not know we are here, so let us make her wait. She won't leave while she thinks we are pier side." Jules grinned again; he had figured out Ursula's game. "We will follow *Bluefish* to make sure this is not a ruse; Captain Coleman is a clever rat, and I refuse to be sandwiched."

Camille nodded, and Jules gave the orders for his submarine to fall in behind *Bluefish*, tracking her silently. Fortunately, the American remained below *Barracuda's* own silent speed. A silent and still submarine always had the advantage, but *Barracuda* was one of the quietest submarines in the world.

Perhaps the Russians' new *Pictors* might someday equal her, but until then, Jules Rochambeau commanded the queen of the seas.

Chapter 29

The Better Part of Valor

Alex wanted to break things. Smashing valuables into tiny pieces would mollify his temper. Being dismissed like an errant child *burned.*

Orders were orders. *Bluefish* lacked Tomahawk cruise missiles. Ursula North's plan to blow Île Amsterdam into oblivion was solid, particularly if Rochambeau was already pier side. No matter how much Alex liked the idea of emulating *Wahoo* and Mush Morton, driving his submarine into Île Amsterdam's harbor was lunacy. Even if he did, the Mark 84 ASV had trouble targeting subs tied up at the pier. And then he'd have a bitch of a time getting out again.

Groaning, Alex headed into the wardroom to get coffee. He was too angry to sleep. It was almost one a.m.; *Bluefish* had secured from battle stations and headed away from *Gallant* after an hour of dickering with the higher-ups. Admiral Rodriquez had taken care of that, leaving Alex feeling like a fifth wheel unable to make decisions on his own submarine. Why the hell had he ever agreed to bring an admiral and a senator—

"Did that coffee pot fucking wrong you in another life, son, or are you just going to glare it into submission?" Admiral Rodriquez asked.

Fuck. Alex hadn't noticed him sitting off to the side, mug in hand.

"Neither. I think." Alex filled his trusty Darth Vader mug, trying to school his features into neutrality. A navy-issued coffee maker would have been a stupid thing to throw, anyway. The damned thing was made of steel and designed to survive a nuclear apocalypse.

Rodriquez snorted. "I can tell."

"If you'll excuse me, sir." Alex managed a polite nod and turned to leave.

"I know you're pissed off, Captain. But you might as well take it out on me instead of your crew," the admiral said, stopping Alex in his tracks.

"I'm not Wade Peterson," he snapped before he could stop himself, twisting back to glare at Rodriquez.

"Oh, so he was the unabashed fucking train wreck I suspected? That's good to know."

Throwing his mug at COMSUBPAC was a terrible idea. It might crack Darth Vader's face.

Rodriquez rose, his expression grave. "I'm sorry to deny you a shot at Rochambeau. He's the holy fucking grail, and you deserved it. But the Brits were right about Tomahawks being the game changer here."

Alex blinked. "I don't give a damn about having a shot at him, sir."

"No? And here I thought you wanted to be the best. Fight the good fight and fly a damned broomstick for clean sweep."

"I don't care about *glory*, Admiral." Alex fidgeted, Commodore Banks' voice echoing in his mind. *Glory hound.* "I just want to make a difference."

Rodriquez snorted. "You've done that. Or did you forget that medal the president pinned on you?"

"The war's still on." Alex did want to forget about that medal, thank you very much. "And someone has to *keep* doing it, right?"

"I suppose so." Rodriquez looked him up and down. "Please tell me you have *some* ambitions, son."

"Hell, sir, I never thought I'd be a captain. After what happened at Armistice Station the first time around, I never thought I'd get command. Everything else feels like gravy. Or a fucking nightmare."

"You're probably the only submariner on the planet who'd call that medal a nightmare. It's unnatural." Rodriquez shook his head.

"With respect, the only people who *wouldn't* haven't been there. They don't give you the fucking thing for the best day in your life," Alex replied. "I still have nightmares from Convoy 57."

Rodriquez stared at Alex in silence. The scrutiny was unnerving; Alex knew he was almost the polar opposite of the brash and outspoken admiral—at least until someone torqued him up. Alex didn't *like* attention; Marco Rodriquez reveled in it. The only thing they had in common was their inability to shut their damned mouths.

"I imagine I would, too, if I'd been there," Rodriquez finally said. "It looked hairy as fucking hell from your logs."

Of course he'd watched them. By now, half of the sub community had. It still left Alex feeling small and vulnerable. "Some of it." He shrugged. "The rest was...terrifyingly exhilarating."

He waited for Uncle Marco tell him he was insane. But the admiral only grinned.

"I told you there was a bit of Mush Morton in you."

Alex rolled his eyes. "I'd rather be like Dick O'Kane, thanks."

At least Mush Morton's XO—a legend in his own right and commander of *Tang* during World War II—hadn't been a brash, oversized wrestler. Alex studied both their tactics, even in a pre-war navy that despised the idea of a submarine CO running straight into an enemy formation and firing everything he had. Both were brilliant, and they'd made an unbeatable team on board *Wahoo* before O'Kane left for his own command. But Alex preferred to emulate the quieter O'Kane rather than someone so loud he'd been nicknamed "Mushmouth."

"Too bad for you that you're the one blazing trails." Rodriquez laughed. "Stay alive and we'll talk about who you want to emulate when it comes to your next command."

"My *what*?"

Rodriquez just grinned and sauntered out of the wardroom, leaving a confused Alex in his wake.

"Missiles ready," James announced.

Ursula smashed a fist into her open palm. "Fire."

Gallant shuddered; seconds ticked by. Finally, the weapons tech reported: "Tubes one through six fired. TLAMs broaching the surface."

Turning to her periscope monitor, Ursula watched six jets of flame shoot out of the otherwise calm and cold waters off Île Amsterdam. The missiles burned into the sky, breaking through the water at a ninety-degree angle before arcing toward the island. Tomahawks were the old reliable of the cruise missile world. First deployed in 1983 and improved incrementally ever since, its conventional warhead was 1,000 pounds of high-explosive material. The latest version of the TLAM ranged up to nine hundred nautical miles. With a speed of about five hundred knots, Ursula's missiles would reach Île Amsterdam in less than a minute.

Firing from so close to the island also meant Ursula could watch.

"Target package engaged," the weapons tech said. "Impact in thirty seconds."

"Very good." Ursula squared her shoulders, her eyes never leaving the screen. *Gallant's* periscope pointed at Île Amsterdam's harbor, where two *Requins* slumbered. Local time was almost four in the morning; only the night watches would be awake.

It was a pity Jules would never know who killed him, but Ursula had not been trained to play fair.

"Fifteen seconds."

A shiver ran down Ursula's spine. When the Admiralty sent her after Rochambeau, she hadn't thought the task would be easy. Jules Rochambeau was too talented and *Barracuda* too technologically advanced. But she had never imagined it would take a year. Nor had she expected it to become an obsession.

Ursula knew she was not the kindest woman in the world. Her profession did not require kindness. Command of a wartime submarine was not for the gentle. Yes, she was short-tempered, but she was about to become the woman who sank *Barracuda* and ended the march of submariners who died at Jules Rochambeau's hands.

Light flared on the monitor, and Île Amsterdam's night ended.

"Impact!"

Ursula could not track the explosions as six Tomahawks hit simultaneously. One hit each of the moored *Requins*—James convinced her that two per submarine would be overkill—one took out the patrol boat pier between the attack submarines, and the other three hit the base. Tomahawks were precision-guided warheads, which meant they struck *exactly* what they'd been told, provided that target's position remained unchanged. GPS was a beautiful thing, no matter how many times opposing navies had worked to deny each other access to its dedicated satellites. They could, and did, always launch more.

Fire ripped across the screen, secondary explosions rocking the landscape. Pieces of submarines sailed into the air. Ursula tried to watch both *Requins* but couldn't track which pieces belonged to which. One bow went up as a boat sank by the stern. The other rolled sideways and turned turtle, a gaping hole open amidships. That one took part of the pier with it, burning furiously until waves extinguished the flames. Tiny figures emerged from the first *Requin*, scrambling away.

Perhaps Jules was among them. Perhaps he was not. That was not Ursula's problem, not unless they gave him another bloody submarine.

"You did it, Captain." James' grin was bright in the dim lights of control.

"We did, Commander." Ursula looked at her crew, nodding. "Well done to every one of you."

She pretended not to notice as crew members exchanged high fives. *Gallant* had just made history. They could afford to celebrate.

Turning back to the periscope monitor, Ursula smiled as Île Amsterdam burned. She would look for other targets later.

"Is it just me, or did the XO seem pissy?" Bobby asked Lou as they headed back into their stateroom after the morning meeting. Each had their own departmental officers' meetings to head to, but Bobby had left his tablet on his rack, and Lou wanted his sweater.

Lou shrugged. "After our middle of the night adventure, I'd be pissy, too."

"I dunno. He was glaring at Rose more than ever." Bobby scowled.

"Better than drooling."

"Yeah." Bobby picked up his tablet and tried to turn the screen on, only to find that it was dead. But the power cord was in.

Not that the cord was connected to the wall. Instead, Lou's personal laptop occupied that outlet.

"Dude, did you unplug my tablet?" Bobby asked.

"It's bad for it to be plugged in all the time." Lou's voice was muffled by his sweater.

"It's bad for it to have *no* charge, too." Bobby rolled his eyes. "You didn't even check the charge. I disown you as a roommate."

Lou laughed. "Fine, I'll invite Rene in here. You can go to the J.O. Jungle."

"I'm senior to you!"

"Oops. I called it first." Lou grinned. "You could always go room with the XO. You were almost-XO forever, and he wouldn't hit on you. Probably."

"Eww. Yuck." Bobby shuddered dramatically. "Even if I liked guys, he's not my type."

"No, your type is the new squadron intel officer. I saw the emails you're exchanging with her."

"You've *never* heard of privacy, have you? Not ever?"

Lou rolled his eyes, grabbing his old-fashioned notebook off the desk. "The stateroom is five feet wide, Bobby. When you sit at the computer, you're practically in my lap."

"Fair enough." Bobby sighed. "But I still think the XO was acting weird. He was as angry as a Hulk who missed breakfast."

"I think it's just Steve Harper being Steve Harper." Lou opened the door, effectively ending the conversation. "Not everyone's as bright and sunny as you. You keep complaining and I'll start wondering if you miss the job!"

"Do I look crazy?" Bobby demanded as Lou walked away. His roommate didn't answer, instead heading aft toward engineering.

Sighing, Bobby headed out of their stateroom. He supposed he could remember his to-do list, and if he couldn't, Steve would surely remind him. As pointedly as possible.

Bobby hadn't ever thought he'd *miss* being XO. However, between Steve trying to crawl in bed with female officers and his nitpicking Bobby's every move, the freedom of only answering to the captain sounded sweeter and sweeter.

"Are you satisfied, Captain?" Camille asked. "Can we shoot him now?"

Jules sighed. "One of these days, you're going to tell me the story of Armistice Station and why you remain so angry."

"I am not angry." Her beautiful face closed off. "I just don't like leaving loose ends."

"Of course." Camille was the best second-in-command he'd ever had. Besides, she had an excellent point. He needed to get on with completing his trifecta.

Barracuda had followed *Bluefish* for five hours. Had he surfaced, the sun would now be in the sky. Jules' crew was well-rested, and everyone had finished breakfast. This was his favorite time to engage. His enemy was probably bogged down by administrative minutiae—the bane of any navy—and not ready to fight. Giving them another hour would decrease their reaction time, and Jules did not want that.

"You are correct," he said, rising from his seat at the wardroom table. "First the American, and then my old friend Lady North."

"Excellent." She beamed. "Today we will make history."

"Oui." Jules liked that idea. He'd intended to sink *Gallant* first, but *Bluefish* was right there.

If he could sink the best of the Alliance's remaining submariners, his country might finally break the gridlock of this war.

Jules took a moment to refine their firing solution. The American submarine was six miles ahead of *Barracuda*. Her speed of twenty knots meant she travelled approximately a third of a mile every minute. The F27 Rafale could cross two miles every minute, but a *Cero's* top speed was close to sixty knots. The 139-knot Rafale couldn't catch up if *Bluefish* sped up the moment Jules fired.

But every minute *Bluefish* took to increase speed was a minute the Rafale travelled 2.3 nautical miles. Would that be enough? Theoretically, *Bluefish* could run the Rafale out of gas. Fast though it was, France's best engineers had not been able to squeeze more than twenty-seven nautical miles' range out of torpedo's engine.

"Come up to thirty knots," Jules ordered. That was *Barracuda*'s top silent speed, and it would let his submarine gain ground. He would wait until they were two miles closer. The *Requins* were the quietest submarines in the world, and *Bluefish* shouldn't hear him.

Then it wouldn't matter how quickly *Bluefish* accelerated.

Jules hated waiting. Even composing tweets in his mind did not make the time pass faster. *Barracuda* needed six long minutes to gain two miles on *Bluefish*. It felt like an hour.

Worse, now he was over a hundred miles from Île Amsterdam. "Lord only knows what she's doing," he grumbled.

"Pardon?" Camille turned.

"Our lovely Lady North." Jules scowled. "*La dame est trouble.*"

"We'll be with her soon enough." Camille grinned. "The range is down to four-point-three nautical miles."

"*Oui.*" Jules sighed, leaning against the chart table. He was not enough of a fool to shoot out of impatience, but did it have to take so long?

"Captain, *Bluefish* has increased speed to forty knots," the sonar watch reported.

In just another minute—

"What?" Jules jerked upright.

"The American is up to forty-three knots and climbing." The young woman at sonar twisted to face him, shrugging.

"Did they *hear* us?" Camille demanded.

"No indication, ma'am," Sonar replied.

The hard hand of fate gripped Jules' innards. He shook his head. "That one will shoot first and ask questions later." He threw Camille a dark look. "Armistice Station probably taught him that."

She scowled. "Do we chase?"

"No. The *Ceros* are five knots faster than we are, and he will hear us," Jules replied. "We cannot gain enough ground to justify wasting the torpedoes."

"We still might catch him." Camille's frown etched lines into her face.

"I said no." Jules gritted his teeth. "Bring us around to a course for Île Amsterdam. *Immédiatement.*"

Jules did not wait to see if Camille carried out his orders prior to leaving control.

He wanted to slap himself. Only once safe in his stateroom could Jules admit that he should have acted sooner, should have shot the moment *Bluefish* was out of *Gallant's* sonar range. Or even once they were both out of range of *Gallant's* torpedoes. Instead, he tried for secrecy. *Fool.*

Now he would have to find *Bluefish* and her clever American commander another day. Jules lived for a good challenge, but this was annoying.

This paperwork wasn't going to chop itself, but Steve couldn't concentrate.

Being told they weren't *good enough* to go after Rochambeau burned. Admiral Rodriquez had kicked it upstairs to the theater commander when *Gallant* tried to poach their kill, and somehow or another, the Brits won. The Royal Navy couldn't hold a candle to the United States Navy, and Rochambeau killed *far* more Americans than Brits. Ursula North had her chance—it was their turn!

Unfortunately, someone wearing more stars than Admiral Rodriquez disagreed, which meant *Bluefish* got told to hurry back to port and drop off Senator Angler. Their patrol had netted only one kill, the spy ship sunk three days ago. Not exactly a patrol that got an XO his own boat. Steve scowled. He'd been certain serving under Alex Coleman would make his career. Now he had to deal with the fact that the submarine community's only *living* Medal of Honor winner was a prude who didn't have the balls to insist they stick around and kill Rochambeau.

A knock sounded against the metal of his open stateroom door. Fortunately, Angler was off on a tour of enlisted berthing—Rose was giving it, and Steve wouldn't touch that with a ten-foot pole—so he was alone.

"Yes?" Steve looked up from the safety instruction he was reviewing.

"Sir, we just finished sorting through the morning message download," ET2 Kowalski said. Her usually pretty smile was strained as she held out *Bluefish's* urgent message tablet. "I thought you might want to see this one."

"Just give me the highlights." Steve hated the way the radio watch assumed he wanted to read through a hundred headers to get at the body of a message.

"*Gallant* reports six missile strikes on Île Amsterdam. Two *Requins*, one presumably *Barracuda*, have been sunk," Kowalski replied.

Cold washed over Steve. Was that it? *Pacu's* killer got an inglorious end and Steve played no part?

"Sir?" Kowalski asked.

Steve shook himself. "Thank you. That's all."

Kowalski disappeared, leaving Steve to stew. *Barracuda* was gone, all because Ursula North made a better argument to her admiralty than Steve's own captain. Did Coleman even care? Oh, he said he did, but Steve had his measure now. Despite his reputation, Coleman was smarter than he was brave. He didn't pick fights he couldn't win. Of course he hadn't wanted to go after Rochambeau. He might've lost.

Steve wished his punching bag hadn't gone down with *Pacu*. He'd planned to buy a new one after this patrol, but the damned patrol was on track to be the *shortest* patrol in the war. *Bluefish* got underway from Perth on 18 March. At their current speed, they'd be back in ten days with nothing to show for it.

Snarling out a swear, Steve rose from his desk, slamming the draft safety instruction down. It could wait. He needed to work some excess energy off, and he knew how. Fuck Alex Coleman's prudishness. He knew Harri wanted him. She'd been full of blushes and flattered by the attention. If Rose hadn't interrupted, this patrol would be *much* better.

Exiting his stateroom, Steve hung a right and went three doors down to the female junior officers' stateroom. It was a small stateroom shared by the three female division officers, shoehorned between larger staterooms as a compromise in the navy's first attack submarine designed from the keel out to accommodate women. He knocked.

Ensign Tanya Chin opened the door. "Sir?"

"I need a word with Lieutenant Ainsworth," he said. He could see Harri at the computer over Chin's shoulder. Her head shot up, wide-eyed.

"What can I do for you, sir?" Harri asked, rising slowly.

"Finish up with what you're working on and come by my stateroom." Steve favored her with a smile.

"Yes, sir." She sounded remarkably composed.

Nodding to Chin, Steve headed back to his own stateroom. Angler would be busy for the next hour. A shiver ran down Steve's spine. That gave Steve and Harri plenty of time. Besides, the thrill of danger always added spice to any relationship.

A few minutes passed before Harri showed up. He closed the door behind her.

Harri gulped. "You wanted a word, sir?"

"I wanted to pick up where we left off the other day." Steve smiled. "Before we were so rudely interrupted."

"I, um, don't think that would be a good idea." Harri glanced at the door, as if worried someone would come in.

"No one has to know. It'll be our secret."

Steve hadn't expected her to be so shy. Harri was a smart and outgoing girl. She'd noticed his interest. They'd spent hours talking at the O Club one night, and he'd made his intentions plain not long ago. What was her game?

Chapter 30

Trust

Harri didn't know what to do. It was supposed to be *over*. Rose said the captain promised to talk to the XO, and who in their right mind ignored Captain Coleman? She gulped again.

"*I* would know." Crap, how did she tell him that he was ten years older than her, and she wasn't interested? Harri backed up a step. "And I...I really need to get back to work. I've got watch in an hour."

Her right heel hit the standup locker by the door. Harri wanted to shrink into herself. Could she flee? The door was right there. Steve was close enough to block her if he wanted. He wasn't that kind of guy, right?

"I've seen you watching me." Steve's smile sent a chill down her spine. "There's no one here to interrupt. You don't have to pretend you're not interested."

Harri wished someone would knock. Or the senator would come in. Anything! "Sir, you're the XO..."

"Not right now. Forget all that. Ranks don't matter in romance, right?"

"But I'm not—I mean, I don't—" Harri cut off. Steve was the *XO*. He'd remember if she pissed him off. He could make her life miserable.

Steve leaned in, and there was nowhere to go. Panicking, she shoved him back, but he had six inches on her and suddenly his arm blocked her from twisting away. His face was only inches from hers, coming closer and closer. Steve was still smiling, but Harri didn't know what to do. Then he wrapped his other arm around her and squeezed her ass.

Harri jumped. "I'd like to leave now, sir." Her voice squeaked, and she felt like a little girl.

His lips touched hers, and Harri tried to jerk back. But he was too close, and she couldn't get away. So she slammed her left knee into his crotch. Hard.

Squeaking, Steve stumbled back and doubled over. He tried to say something, only to lose it in a wheezing cough. He still had one hand on her, but Harri brought her knee up again. It hit his jaw with a *crack*, and he toppled backward, unbalanced. She didn't watch him hit the deck, bolting for the door and wrenching it open.

Only to run headlong into Bobby O'Kane, whose hand was raised to knock.

"Harri?" He skipped back a step. "Everything okay?"

"Yes—no—I..." Harri glanced over her shoulder, to where Steve struggled to pick himself up off the floor.

Steve staggered to his feet. "She hit me!"

"She what?" Bobby gaped.

"No!" Harri gasped. This situation was spiraling out of control quickly. "I didn't—I mean—it wasn't like that!"

"The fuck it wasn't!" Steve snarled, blood dripping down his chin. "I was trying to counsel her, and she hit me for no reason!"

Harri backed up another step, eyes wide and darting back and forth between Steve and Bobby. Her heart pounded in her ears, and she knew she should have said something, *anything*, except now Steve had gotten in first and everyone would believe him. Even Bobby, who was the nicest of all the department heads, would think Steve was telling the truth. Bobby twisted to face her, his brows crinkled in confusion.

"Harri?" Bobby asked again.

She had to get her shit together. Swallowing, Harri tried to square her shoulders, but it was hard when you were a lieutenant (junior grade) and the freaking executive officer said you'd hit him. Worse, she *had*.

"I did hit him," Harri whispered, watching Bobby's eyes go wide. "After I kneed him."

"See?" Steve sneered. "I want the captain to know—"

"*After* he tried to kiss me," Harri cut in. She was too angry to shout; every word felt like razor-sharp ice. "After I said no."

"You can't prove that," Steve said.

"What?" Bobby gaped. "*That's* what you have to say?"

"That's not how you address a senior officer, Lieutenant O'Kane," Steve retorted, and Harri's stomach dropped.

"Yeah, there's a lot of wrong going on here." Bobby's hand landed on Harri's shoulder, and he steered her away, toward the stateroom he shared with the engineer. "C'mon, kid."

Oddly, Steve didn't say a word.

Harri made herself stop glaring. She wanted to rip his face off, to cry, to shake and hide and tell the world what a piece of shit he was. But she didn't. Did Bobby believe her? What if he didn't?

Finally, they reached Bobby's stateroom. He shut the door, and Harri flinched.

"You want me to get Rose?" Bobby asked.

"Isn't Weps on watch?" Her whisper felt tiny again.

"I'll go relieve her if you'd rather talk to her," he said.

"No, it's okay." Harri had known Bobby for a year and a half. He was goofy, smart, and everyone's unruly older brother. She could trust him. Couldn't she?

"You want to sit down and tell me what happened?" Bobby sat down on the bottom rack while Harri sat at the computer. That felt safer, somehow.

Safer. She was the one who'd just kneed a senior officer in the gonads. Harri swallowed a giggle that would make her sound insane.

"It's...pretty much what I said," she managed after a moment. "He said he wanted to talk to me...but he didn't want to talk." Harri swallowed. "I didn't want to, but he tried to kiss me, anyway. So I kneed him."

Bobby grimaced. "Did anything else happen?"

"He grabbed my ass?" Harri frowned. "I, um, kneed him in the face, too. After the crotch."

When had her hands started shaking? Harri stared at them, not wanting to look at Bobby. He'd believe she kneed the shit out of the XO—there'd be bruises to prove that—but would he buy her story? The navy always believed the senior person.

"Good for you," Bobby said, making Harri's head snap up.

"Huh?"

"Good for you. If you're up to it, I want you to type up a statement right now, saying what happened. Then we're going to take you down to see Doc and make sure you're okay."

"He didn't hurt me." Harri grimaced. "He didn't get the chance."

"Damn straight." Bobby's grin was lopsided as he gestured at the computer. "You okay with making that statement?"

"Do you think it will help?"

Bobby nodded. "I think it'll sink his horny ass."

Hope flared; Harri nodded slowly. "Okay. I'll do it."

Île Amsterdam, French Southern and Antarctic Lands

Ursula felt empty. Eighteen months she spent chasing Jules Rochambeau, almost the entire war. She'd shot and missed, watched him kill friends and allies. But today, she'd damned well done it.

Now she could relax while Île Amsterdam burned. *Gallant* snapped three dozen pictures and a video, but watching a tiny naval base wreathed in flames grew old. After three hours, Ursula directed her submarine to head for deeper waters, loping away from the island at a leisurely twenty knots. Mission done, Ursula could choose her own hunting grounds. For a moment, she contemplated dogging *Bluefish* and annoying her least favorite American. No. Destroying *Barracuda* was better revenge, even if tweaking Coleman's tail would be fun.

The destruction of Île Amsterdam would take the French out of the submarine game in the Indian Ocean, at least in the short term. Perhaps she should turn her attention to the Indian bases up north? Ursula smiled thinly. That was a topic to discuss during her next strategy session. For now, she would put her feet up, relax, and enjoy a good—

Gallant's general alarm blared. Ursula launched out of her chair like a rocket, racing for the attack center as her submarine trembled. By the time she got there, *Gallant* was up to thirty-four knots and leaning into a sharp starboard turn.

"What the hell happened?" she barked.

"Torpedoes in the water, bearing zero-two-two!" sonar replied.

Ursula's eyes zoomed in on the navigation plot. The angry red icon of an enemy torpedo was only three miles away, racing toward *Gallant.*

"Who fired?"

"*Requin*-class submarine off the port bow! Computer ID is...*Requin* 722?"

Ursula's blood went cold. "*Barracuda?*"

"Yes, ma'am." James stood over the watchkeeper's shoulder, checking the information himself.

That's impossible. Ursula wanted to scream. She couldn't believe this. Couldn't—

No. She would not lose her mind. She had a battle to fight. "Increase your rudder hard left! Prepare decoys." Ursula twisted to look at James. "Torpedo speed."

"One hundred and thirty-nine knots." His dark face was pale.

"Shit," Ursula whispered.

Every cell in her body was tense. Ursula had never faced such a fast torpedo. Compared to many of her counterparts, she'd been shot at relatively few times. She was famous for not giving an enemy the chance.

So much for that.

"Shift your rudder!" she ordered. The torpedo was in a tail chase, less than two minutes away. "Drop decoys *now*!"

Gallant swung into port turn, snaking back toward her original course. Her top speed was forty-two knots, but the digital display read *43.7.* Either there were favorable currents or Ursula's engineers knew how much danger they faced. But an extra knot couldn't help against a torpedo almost one *hundred* knots faster. But a torpedo that fast had to go through petrol like a drunk sailor did whisky. It couldn't turn fast. Could it?

"Decoys away!" James reported.

"Minute thirty to impact!" sonar announced.

Everyone was pale. Ursula's stomach was a gordian knot of nausea and fury, sprinkled with shame. Turn now or later? Turn *again* or maintain her course? The angry red icons were far outside her wake. Given their overtake speed, they could afford to blow the turn. Instinct told Ursula that she couldn't turn enough times to run them out of gas.

No, she would have to dodge.

"One torpedo chasing the decoy, Captain!" her sonar chief reported. "One still on us!"

"Very good." *The second one is going to be harder to outfox.* Rubbing her hands together, Ursula tried to pretend she wasn't sweating. She twisted to look at James. "Do you have a firing solution?"

"Yes, ma'am!"

Where was *Barracuda*? The firing bearing put her off *Gallant's* starboard bow, soon to be port as they continued their turn. "Match bearings and shoot, tubes two and four!"

"Weapons away!"

Ursula swallowed. "Very good. Rudder amidships." Now she had to wait.

"One minute to impact." Her sonar operators sounded nervous; Ursula couldn't blame them.

She met James' eyes, silently beckoning him over. He was at her side within seconds.

"The question is when we turn," she muttered. "We'll have one chance to skip aside, and if we turn fast enough..."

James frowned. "If we don't, the torpedo will strike us broadside."

"Point." Ursula grimaced. "Make your depth eighty feet. Smartly."

James gave the orders; Ursula watched the plot. Her hands shook. *Gallant's* speed ticked up another knot as the engineers disabled safety mechanisms, but it could never be enough. *Gallant* settled out at eighty feet as Ursula's butterflies grew worse.

"Thirty seconds!"

She dared wait no longer. "Hard left rudder!" Ursula ordered. "Emergency blow!"

Gallant rocketed upward as her diving officer blew water out of every ballast tank. High-pressure air screeched in to replace it, and the submarine bucked under Ursula's feet as she clawed her way into a turn mid-blow. It was horrible shiphandling under any circumstances, and put an ungodly amount of strain on her beloved submarine, but Ursula needed to get out of the torpedo's path. *W*ar had taught submariners to drive for the surface if their decoys didn't work. It was the only way to survive.

Unless you wanted to be like HMS *Ambush* and sit on the cold ocean floor for days, waiting for rescuers who arrived too late. Ursula shivered, clinging to the navigation table for balance.

Gallant's bow broke the surface, still rushing forward at forty-four knots. A giant wave heralded her arrival, made even larger when the hand of gravity slammed the submarine down. Ursula's midsection crashed into table, and she bit out a swear, coughing for air.

"Captain, do we slow down?" James asked, picking himself off the deck. Ursula's stomach burned.

"No! Burn up the goddamned shaft for all I care!" Ursula straightened with an effort. She didn't care that modern attack submarines weren't made for high-speed surface ops. The Admiralty would forgive her if she managed not to sink her bloody submarine. "Give me time to impact!"

"I don't know! The sonar picture is—"

Boom!

The floor jerked out from underneath Ursula's feet, pitching upward and sending her flying. She crashed into the ballast control panel, clipping something metal on her way past. Crying out—and vaguely aware of her crew's screams and sparks filling the air—Ursula tried to get up, but something heavy landed on her legs. She managed to kick her right leg free and shove the weight aside.

That was a body. God. The face was half burned; she couldn't tell who. Bile rose in her throat.

Another explosion rocked *Gallant* as Ursula struggled to her feet. Her right ankle didn't want to support her, but she had to get *moving—*

"Abandon ship!" There was smoke in the air; Ursula coughed the words. "Everyone go!"

Someone wrenched the lower hatch open. Ursula leaned against the periscope housing, grabbing people and shoving them toward the ladder. There was no water in the attack center yet, but she could feel *Gallant's* nose pitching up at a dangerous angle. Had the torpedo broken *Gallant's* back? The attack center was too far forward to tell.

The outer hatch was open. James grabbed her arm. "Let's go!"

"You first!" Ursula shoved him forward.

"Captain—!"

The third explosion threw Ursula off her feet again. Something *cracked* and someone screamed—was that her? Landing hard on her back, Ursula had just enough time to realize that the periscope housing had broken before it crushed her and everything went black.

Still no news on who will command Cape, *though I suppose that's not a surprise,* Nancy wrote in an email dated the day before. *Admiral Zurcher is dead, but apparently he did get off an email about Captain Rowlings' actions before* Lexington *sank, which means Seventh Fleet knows what happened. That's something. Eric Armstrong—our embedded reporter—still has a copy of the video, too, so it's not like we don't have proof of what she did. Sitting in limbo like this just sucks.*

Speaking ill of the dead feels wrong, but Rowlings really was a stand-up tyrant. Did you know she had junior officers walking her dog? I'll send you a copy of the log they kept now that they trust me enough to let me see it, and holy shit is that some reading. Armstrong keeps asking them to let him see it, but everyone knows that'll mean a blog about it, and for now, the navy wants him to sit on the news.

I did tell the girls about it, and Emily gave me a lecture on war crimes and the law of armed conflict. I think she's serious about this JAG business. Is it bad that I'm relieved? With Bobbie ready to jump headfirst into the first submarine that will take her, I'd love one of them to be out of the line of fire.

Alex scraped a hand over his face. Damn, one of their daughters choosing a non-combatant role would be nice. He'd never say it to the girls—and he was proud of their accomplishments, no matter what career path they picked—but with no end in sight for the war, he worried for them all the time. Bobbie concerned him most, since she was two years older than her sister and that much closer to becoming a naval officer. Even worse, she wanted to follow in his footsteps as a submariner, and Alex knew firsthand how many submariners didn't come home.

A knock on the door saved him from spiraling further. "Come in!"

Steve walked in, slamming the door and sporting a growing bruise on his chin. "Sir, I need to talk to you."

"Take a seat." Alex found Steve's formal tone worrisome. "What happened to your face?"

"That's the problem, sir." Steve took a deep breath. "I listened to what you said, and I haven't made romantic advances toward anyone. But Lieutenant Ainsworth came to my stateroom earlier, and she propositioned me."

Alex narrowed his eyes. "She what?"

"I thought she was interested in me, and maybe I was wrong to act on that before, but, well, you can see what happened when I told her we couldn't be together." Steve smiled and gestured at his chin.

"What exactly is it that I'm supposed to be *seeing*?" Alex felt cold. There was something off in Steve's casual smile, and his attempt at sincerity set Alex's teeth on edge.

"I said no, and she hit me." Steve's eyes were wide, but the feigned innocence smelled like dogshit. "I admit I didn't expect it, and I shouldn't have been in private with her, but..."

"Is that so."

"I know it's hard to believe, but—"

"Yeah. It is," Alex cut him off. "I've known Harri Ainsworth for a while now, and—"

Now the phone ringing cut *him* off. Alex wanted to throw the stupid thing across the room. Bad enough that his XO was lying to him. Worse, he couldn't figure out *why*. And now something else needed his attention. He grabbed the phone. "Captain."

"Sir, it's the navigator," Bobby said. "Is the XO in there with you?"

Bobby's uneasy tone made Alex sit up. "Yeah. Why?"

"Harri's here with me," Bobby replied. "I don't know what the XO said, but I bet his story is as crooked as a fishhook."

"Tell me what you know." Alex glanced at Steve. His XO looked mildly curious but not concerned. Hopefully, he thought this was something tactical.

"Harri's written up a statement. She says the XO tried to kiss her and didn't quit when she said no. So she kneed him in the crotch and then the face," Bobby replied. "He looked like trash trending toward shit."

"That's accurate." Alex eyed Steve's growing bruise.

"What do you want me to do, sir?" Bobby asked. Alex heard him swallow.

Breaking the phone would be a bad idea. This wasn't what he'd signed up for. He didn't mind a leadership challenge, but how the hell had the "hotshot" XO turned out to be a scumbag? Was he? Bobby could be lying. But Bobby was the same officer who'd stuttered nervously, whose confidence had been so hard to win.

He took a deep breath. "Stand by. I'll get back to you."

"Yes, sir." Bobby hung up, leaving Alex to face Steve.

"I want to press assault charges," Steve said.

Holy fuck, the man had gall. "You what?"

"I'm guessing that was the navigator on the phone," Steve continued. "You don't want to listen to him, Captain. I'm pretty sure he put her up to it—probably with Weps' help. Or it might have been Rose's idea in the first place."

Alex scoffed. "You're casting that net pretty wide, aren't you?"

"Sir, I can only—"

"You're going to want to think *very* carefully about the words coming out of your mouth, Commander." Alex said. "You've now maligned *three* officers on this boat, all of whom have proven themselves time and again in combat. Furthermore, your recent history tells me there probably isn't some giant conspiracy against you."

"I resent that! My reputation is stellar. I've been on the fast track for years." Steve glared.

"Anyone with a pulse has been on the fast track since the navy started building up in the late 2020s." Alex rolled his eyes. "Try not to think you're too special."

Steve jumped to his feet. "You have no right to disparage me!"

"Sit down, Commander." Alex didn't bother rising; he just waited.

"I will not—"

"Sit. Down."

Steve sat, his face red and eyes narrowed with fury. Alex remained silent for several seconds, counting to ten to rein in his temper. His heart thundered in his ears, and his chest was tight. This douche canoe tried seducing *two* officers junior to him, then in case that wasn't enough, he sexually assaulted a division officer. Alex would believe Harri over Steve any day. She was the smartest and most contentious of the division officers, even if half the junior sailors on board had crushes on her.

"You may consider yourself confined to quarters until I've investigated this," Alex said. What he couldn't ask was what kind of fucking idiot tried to sexually assault someone with an admiral *and* a senator on board. "You will have no contact with Lieutenant Ainsworth. Is that clear?"

"Yes, sir." Steve's glare hadn't abated. "Allow me to say that I find your lack of trust in me insulting, both personally and professionally."

Alex smiled thinly. "Let's not talk about professionalism right now. It's not a conversation you'd enjoy." He nodded toward the door. "Feel free to see yourself out."

Steve rose and stalked out; a moment later, the door to the next stateroom slammed shut. Only then did Alex head out, hanging a right and heading aft. He knocked on the door to the forward J.O. Jungle, hoping one of the officer of the deck–qualified division officers would be in there.

Luck was with him; Rene opened the door. He jumped. "Captain?"

"You in the middle of anything?" Alex asked.

"Nothing that can't wait."

"Good. Head up to control, relieve Weps as OOD, and tell her to come talk to me."

"Yes, sir!" Rene hurried off without asking more questions. Unfortunately, the stateroom's *other* occupant wasn't so kind.

"Something the matter, Captain?" Admiral Rodriquez asked from where he sprawled in one of the top racks.

Shit. Uncle Marco was the last person he wanted to talk to right now. He hadn't even thought about how to tell his boss about this. Now his boss' *boss* was here. This was seventeen shades of fantastic.

Then again, the senator would be worse.

He had to do something about that, too, didn't he? The last thing he needed was Steve whining to a politician and getting Angler on his side. Alex took a deep breath.

"We may have a...problem, sir," he said. "An internal one. Is there any way you can keep Senator Angler occupied until I've investigated it?"

Was he asking too much? Rodriquez arched an eyebrow.

"That sounds pretty fucking ominous," the admiral replied.

"It is." Alex saw no reason to lie. "But I'm not positive what direction. Not yet." He had to give Steve the benefit of the doubt, even if he wanted to stuff him down a toilet and pump waste overboard.

"All right." Rodriquez twisted out of the rack, landing on his feet. "You've earned some trust. Don't abuse it. How long do you need me to keep our friendly neighborhood senator entertained?"

"An hour or two should do."

Rodriquez barked in laughter. "I'll teach him to play cribbage. That's a fine submarine tradition, and it'll take at least that long."

"Thank you, Admiral." Alex swallowed, watching Rodriquez go down the aft ladder. Who was he to use an admiral as a distraction? Admirals were halfway to god-dom.

Gods of the Greek variety, anyway. Did that make Uncle Marco the Zeus of the sub force? At least he didn't try to sleep with everyone in sight.

Apparently, that was Steve's job.

"You wanted to see me, Captain?" Rose's voice made him jump.

"Yeah. Come with me." Grimacing, Alex led her toward Bobby's stateroom. He could feel Rose's worried gaze on his back. She probably didn't know what had happened, but she could tell something was wrong.

Her angry hiss when Harri opened Bobby's door gave that away.

"Let's have this conversation where the XO isn't right next door." Alex gestured Rose into the room. Harri stared at him with eyes as wide as hubcaps, and Bobby swallowed.

Arguing with Ursula North was peachy compared to this.

"You okay, Harri?" Alex asked after the door clicked shut. He leaned against the wall instead of sitting down, gesturing Rose into the other chair. Bobby perched on the bottom rack, and Harri lowered herself back into the desk chair.

"Yes, sir." She glanced at the floor instead of meeting his eyes. "I'm sorry I kneed the XO. I didn't— I just didn't know what else to do."

Alex couldn't tell her Steve deserved that. Damn it, Harri reminded him too much of his daughters right now, but his job was not to be a protective parent. "Tell me what happened."

Harri did, from Steve showing up at her door to his attempt to kiss her. She looked to Bobby for reassurance a few times, but Alex wasn't worried about Bobby O'Kane being some Machiavellian puppet master. Not with the sick look on Bobby's face or the muttered curses coming from Rose's direction.

Harri's story hung together better than Steve's did, particularly when coupled with how Steve tried to proposition Harri a few days earlier. Not reacting to the story was hard; Alex's job required impartiality, but he was furious. He was the idiot who thought Steve would take no for an answer. If he hadn't—

Screw that. Counting might-have-beens was as effective as shooting spitballs at enemy submarines.

"You have that statement you wrote up?" he asked.

She nodded. "Yes, sir. Am—am I in trouble?"

"No. Not you." Alex bit off each word. "The XO wants to press assault charges, but I will sink his ass before I let that happen."

"He *what*?" Rose hissed. There was murder in her eyes. Bobby looked devastated, and Harri terrified, but Rose came out of her chair, fists clenched and face flushed.

"I'll handle it, Weps." Alex turned his glare on her. "If you act, you'll taint the case against him, so you'll sit on your fucking hands. Understood?"

Rose blinked. "Understood. Sir."

"Good." Alex looked back at Harri, forcing his tone to gentle. "I need a signed copy of that statement. The XO's confined to his quarters, so you won't have to see him. If you want off the watchbill for a bit, talk to Bobby—he'll be acting XO again until I say differently."

"I'm okay." Harri's nod was spastic.

Meanwhile, Bobby's mouth dropped open. "Me? Again?" He groaned theatrically. "Great. All the fun."

"Quit your bitching." Rose rolled her eyes. "Better you than a drooling dickwad."

"I can drool, but it wouldn't be over anyone in this room." Bobby grinned. "Sorry, ladies. And you, Captain. You're not my type."

Coughing out a laugh, Alex shook his head. "You're a lunatic, Bobby."

"Sir, you're still not my type, so you should stop complimenting me like that."

Even Harri giggled that time.

Chapter 31

Consequences

"We should have picked up the survivors," Camille said as *Barracuda* glided up to periscope depth outside Île Amsterdam's harbor.

Jules rolled his eyes. "And put them where?"

She sniffed. "I'd still prefer confirmation Captain North is dead."

"If she is not, she's still lost the game." Jules shrugged as the officer of the watch reported that the submarine was stable at periscope depth. "And I have won."

"*Oui*." His second-in-command didn't roll her eyes, but Jules could hear the exasperation in her tone.

"*Gallant* broke up quickly." He pulled up the periscope's camera view. The *Requins'* periscopes were of the always-up variety, which meant there was no physical eyepiece to use in the attack center. A few French attack submarines had damaged their non-retractable periscopes operating close to the surface, but Jules was not foolish. Overall, he approved of the design. "There were few survivors, and even if so— *Mon Dieu!*"

Gulping for air, Jules stared at the fiery conflagration of Île Amsterdam. Three of the four piers had vanished, leaving only shards visible above the waves. One *Requin's* bow stuck out of the water at a sixty-degree angle, burned red where her paint and sound-absorbent tiles had been scorched off. Her sonar dome was barely visible, and only the starboard side of her sail remained above water. Jules thought he saw the top of the other sub's rudder peeking out next to a broken-but-somehow-floating bollard—and then realized that the bollard was perched on top of the sunken submarine.

The patrol craft were in shambles. One was mostly afloat but burned to the waterline; the other's stern was shoved up on top of the quay wall with no evidence of where the bow had gone. Several shoreside buildings were in flames. Another two were craters. People peppered the landscape, trudging back and forth, fighting fires and pulling others out of the rubble.

"*That's* what she was doing," Camille snarled. "That bitch!"

"She always did have a hot temper." Jules sighed. So much for their secret submarine base. He'd told Admiral Sauvageau that someone would find them eventually. "Did she think she'd killed us?"

"Probably." Camille bared her teeth. "I hope so."

"Hm." Jules watched the picture, but his mind raced elsewhere. His hurried torpedo onload hadn't allowed much time to onload food. *Barracuda* carried perhaps two weeks of food for her crew before they were limited to expired Indian crackers.

"Shall we go ensure there are no survivors from *Gallant*, Captain?" Camille asked.

Jules rolled his eyes. "No. Of course not." He smiled thinly. "Snap some periscope photographs of the destruction. I have a better idea."

"Better?"

"*Oui*. More humiliating for our foes, and less disregard of the Geneva Conventions." Jules believed that the ends justified the means, but he had no desire to break the international laws governing warfare and the treatment of survivors or prisoners. Yes, he enjoyed mocking them. Yes, he disrespected the dead. But there were lines he would not cross.

Only a fool deprived himself of protections he might someday need.

She scowled. "As you wish." Camille took the required stills.

Meanwhile, Jules directed his watch officer to dive and turn the submarine northwest. His choice was between

French-owned islands near Madagascar or an Indian port further north. Given the choice, he would always aim for French territory. The faces were friendlier, and the food was better.

Helping the beleaguered people on Île Amsterdam never crossed his mind. Even had there been a pier to tie his submarine up at, Jules' duty lay elsewhere. The base could fend for itself.

He sent his next tweet when *Barracuda* returned to periscope depth six hours later. It featured two pictures side-by-side: Île Amsterdam burning and *Gallant's* few survivors bobbing in life rafts. It was a pity he didn't have a picture of the torpedo breaking *Gallant's* back, but underwater drones were expensive.

Captain Jules Rochambeau
@JulesRochambeau
@RoyalNavy There are consequences for every action. You may have destroyed our base, but Gallant proved très spineless.
#Barracuda #HMSGallant

Rose was too angry to trust with a sensitive task, so Alex grabbed Bobby and left Rose with Harri. Harri seemed disappointed to see Bobby go, which left Alex queasy. Was there a relationship there? Or was he jumping at shadows? No. Alex refused to look for enemies among his crew.

Luckily, Bobby was a talker and not at all intimidated by Senator Angler. They met Rodriquez and the senator in control, where the admiral was explaining how to drive a submarine. Bobby did one better and plopped the politician in the driver's seat, much to the helmsmen's glee. Alex met Rodriquez's eyes and gestured him out of the space.

"You going to enlighten me about whatever clusterfuck you've uncovered?" Rodriquez asked once they were in the passageway.

Alex glanced around; it was dinnertime, so the passageways were empty. He sighed. "My XO just sexually assaulted one of my divos."

"He fucking *what*?"

"He propositioned her—for the second time—and she said no. When he tried to kiss her anyway, she kneed him in the junk. And then in the face for good measure." Blunt was the best route; he hoped Rodriquez felt as strongly about this as he did.

Heaven help them all if Rodriquez wanted to turn a blind eye.

"That kid's supposed to be a goddamned superstar." Rodriquez's eyes narrowed. "You sure about this?"

"Yeah." Alex forced himself to stop gritting his teeth when his jaw started hurting. "I want him off my boat."

Rodriquez crossed his arms. "Back the fuck up, Captain, and tell me the story."

"He propositioned Weps and the same divo before. Weps told me about it, and I gave him a chance to pull his head out of his ass and not commit frat," Alex snarled. "Today, he shut the same divo in his stateroom and didn't want to take no for an answer."

"And she popped him in the nuts and the jaw?" Rodriquez' grin was bloodthirsty. "Good for her."

"Yeah." Alex's blood boiled too hot for him to think about the next words before they came out: "I want him gone, Admiral. Any son of a bitch who thinks he can abuse his rank like that needs to take a long walk off a short pier."

"You got a statement from the girl?"

"She's already signed one. Weps'll write one up, too." Not glaring at the navy's second-ranking submariner was hard enough that Alex didn't try.

Rodriquez snorted. "That weps of yours looks ready to eat nails on a good day. I'm surprised she didn't rip him to shreds."

"Keep him on board and she just might," Alex said. And he'd hold her goddamned coat.

"All right, he's gone." Rodriquez shrugged. "Hell, you deliver and you don't ask for much. This is easy."

This didn't taste like victory. Should it? "The asshat wants to press assault charges."

"Of course he fucking does. It's the only thing he can do." Rodriquez looked thoughtful.

Alex's jaw dropped so hard he thought it might fall clean off his face. "Only thing he *can* do? Are you serious?"

"Good. You've got bite to you after all. I was starting to wonder."

"Sir, if this is some fucked-up sort of test—"

Rodriquez held up a hand. "It isn't. Sorry; I'm a jackass. I'll step on the pervert, don't you worry. And I'll slap Banks if he gets any bright ideas about listening to him."

"All right." Alex sucked in a few deep breaths. "Thanks."

"Like I said. Easy."

"So it's just like driving a car?" Senator Angler asked.

Bobby let Master Chief Baker answer. "As far as turning the wheel goes, yes, sir." *Bluefish's* COB wore a strained smile. "Aside from that, it's pretty different."

"There aren't a lot of lines on our road, either." Bobby gestured at the digital navigation display over the helmsman's console. "Some people like to try to draw pictures with the track history."

Baker chuckled. "Some of those pictures are less than politically correct."

A hand landed on Bobby's elbow, making him turn before he could hear Angler's laughing reply. It was ET2 Aspen. "Sir, radio just picked this up."

Bobby took the extended tablet, scanning the message header. "*Shit!*"

"Everything okay, Nav?" Baker asked, and great, everyone was staring at him.

"You want me to take it to the XO, sir?" Aspen said before Bobby could answer.

"No." Bobby shook his head and then kept shaking it before he realized he looked like a fool. "I've got it."

Now wasn't the time to explain that the XO had been sent to his room like an errant sex offender. Bobby still wasn't sure what the outcome of that disaster would be. But he knew the captain needed to hear about this. Yesterday.

"Thanks, Aspen," he said and then glanced at Baker. "I'll be back in a few, Master Chief."

"I'll hold down the fort, sir."

Bobby hurried out of control, heading down the ladder toward Officers' Country. He passed a few sailors along the way, squeezing past a pair busy tagging out a panel for maintenance. How would they react to the shitstorm Steve's actions could ignite? Bobby didn't give a damn about Steve, but Rose and Harri didn't deserve to be caught in the crossfire.

He found Alex and Admiral Rodriquez outside Alex's stateroom. "Sir, you're going to want to see this," Bobby said.

"More good news?" Rolling his eyes, Alex took the tablet.

"*Gallant* went down." Bobby let out a shaky breath.

"What, she have a reactor accident to top off this fine navy day?" Rodriquez asked.

Bobby shook his head.

"Worse," Alex said, looking up from the message. "Rochambeau got her."

"*What?*" Rodriquez's eyes went wide. "I thought she put that fucker out of our misery!"

"We're not that lucky." Bobby swallowed. "He tweeted about it."

"False flag?" Rodriquez demanded.

"Probably not," Alex picked up where Bobby left off. "*Gallant's* buoy deployed not far from where we saw her last."

"Shit." The admiral groaned.

So much for that missile attack on Île Amsterdam. A small base destroyed weighed nothing against the loss of Ursula North.

"Reverse course and head back for Île Amsterdam," Alex ordered.

Bobby blinked. "Say again?"

"If there are survivors, we need to pick them up before the French can," Alex said, handing the tablet back. "Ursula North is one person we can't afford to have sit the rest of the war out as a POW."

"Yes, sir." Bobby nodded, unsurprised. Bad blood or not, the captain would always—

"I guess you're earning your nickname today, Captain." Rodriquez grinned.

Alex colored. "Please don't start."

Rodriquez laughed. Bobby hurried off before Uncle Marco could come up with a nickname for him, too.

News of *Gallant's* sinking hit the boat like lightning. Every conversation Marco overheard centered on the fact that Rochambeau sank Ursula-fucking-North, and God help anyone else who tried to get in his way. Sure, Marco had met the woman a few times, and he'd found her brilliant if temperamental. He'd been impressed by her tactical savvy and her grit, but she wasn't a giant. Just a legend.

Legends were in short supply this war, but Marco found one of his own. He hadn't expected that after meeting Alex Coleman—the man was shier than a spooked elephant—but spending the last week on *Bluefish* told him otherwise. Coleman wasn't a conventionally charismatic leader, but this crew would follow him anywhere. Everyone but that fucktard Banks made his XO. Marco scowled. It was probably time to pay more attention to Commodore Banks. He'd let *Bluefish* out of Convoy 57 in its pre–Alex Coleman days and now sent a predator out as XO. No way was this Steve Harper's first offense. *Banks* had called him a superstar.

Banks also called Coleman a prima donna, something Marco hadn't understood until he saw the man's teeth. Maybe he'd finally get to see Coleman in combat. He had guts; it took that to turn around and rescue the person who'd told you to fuck off when you offered help.

Bluefish burned holes in the water for five hours to reach *Gallant's* survivors, then slowed to a crawl. Marco was in control when they arrived. Angler was asleep, but not before Marco had a word with him about Steve. The last thing they needed was the navy's not-so-favorite politician taking up Steve's case. Fortunately, Angler was smart. He wouldn't let something toxic splash on him.

"Captain, we're at *Gallant's* last known position," Bobby said. The kid was doing a pretty good job being both navigator and XO.

"Very well." Coleman was all business, lifting the 1MC microphone to speak to his crew. "*Bluefish*, it's the captain. Everyone knows by now that *Gallant* sank. We're here to find our British friends before the enemy can, but there's no knowing who else we'll find. Stay on your toes."

Marco nodded to himself. Coleman had set battle stations thirty minutes earlier, but no one complained about how that arsed up their sleep schedule. *Bluefish's* clocks read almost midnight, but every sailor was primed and ready. He bet Steve Harper was wide awake, too, kicking himself for missing a shot at Rochambeau.

Marco hoped the fucker was here. *Someone* had to take his ass out, and Marco wanted to be around to see it.

A voice crackled over the squawk box. "Conn, Sonar, still no contacts."

"Conn, aye." Coleman's expression didn't change, but he chewed on his glasses, hands buried deep in his pockets.

Patience was the name of the game. Marco's own days as a sub CO were like that; the objective was always to creep somewhere you weren't supposed to go. He'd snuck *Washington* into some hairy situations, delivered SEALs twice into places he still couldn't talk about, but Marco never fired a torpedo outside of practice. This wasn't the game he knew.

"Make tubes one and two ready in all respects, including opening the outer doors," Coleman ordered.

Rose's head snapped up. "Someone might hear the doors, Captain."

"I'm counting on that, Weps." Coleman's grin was fiercer than Marco expected.

"Yes, sir." Rose grinned right back. She was one worth watching—but so was Bobby O'Kane, who Marco found surprisingly competent. "Tubes ready, doors open."

"Very well." Coleman waited.

Marco reminded himself to keep breathing. If Rochambeau was out there, he had ice water in his damned veins—and he *had* to shoot now. Only an idiot would let his enemy prepare to shoot without getting in first, and Rochambeau was anything but that.

Five minutes. Ten. Still nothing. Finally, Coleman broke the silence:

"OOD, come to periscope depth. If no one's going to shoot at us, it's time to find our friends."

Bobby gave the orders before turning to say quietly: "Finding them in the dark is going to be a bitch and a half, sir."

"I know." Coleman put his glasses on. "But at least no aircraft will spot us on the surface."

"You can say that again." O'Kane looked down at his tablet. "There's only twenty percent illumination."

Coleman shrugged. "That's what NVGs are for."

"You—you want to surface. Of course you do. I'll have someone break them out." Bobby didn't even try to hide his wide eyes, but at least he hadn't called Coleman crazy.

Marco wanted to. Surfacing in a war zone *was* a bit off the reservation...but it was also the only way to pick up survivors. He caught Coleman's eye.

"Damned if you do, damned if you don't."

"I think *Gallant's* the damned one here, sir," Coleman replied without blinking. *Bluefish* slid up to periscope depth, and he turned to the scope without another word. "Scope's up."

Stepping forward, Marco watched the periscope display screen. The camera on the scope was in low-light mode, but that didn't mean it did a great job. Coleman walked the scope around carefully as *Bluefish* glided along at five knots. Picking anything out against the dark horizon was hard—

"Got something." Coleman froze the scope, pulling away from it to look at the screen. "Zoom in on that," he told the fire control tech.

"Zoom, aye. Bearing three-four-niner."

Slowly, the picture swam into focus. Barely visible against the dark horizon, two life rafts bobbed in the waves. Make that one and a half. Were there people in the water?

"I'll be damned," Marco whispered. He'd agreed to head back, but he hadn't thought they'd find anyone. "Poor bastards."

"Surface the ship," Coleman ordered. "Stand by rescue and assistance detail."

Bobby cleared his throat. "Captain, usually the XO..."

"I'll go topside. You stay down here and shoot anything that moves. Ask questions later."

"Aye, sir," Bobby replied. Marco expected the young man to flinch; he hadn't.

"I'll tag along if you don't mind, Captain," Marco said. Part of him wanted to stay and watch Bobby, but nah. The kid was sharp. They made a good team. *I've got my Mush Morton... Why not add a literal O'Kane to the mix?* Not snickering was hard.

"Not at all," Coleman replied.

Liar. But why call him on it? Marco followed Coleman up the ladder, watching him carefully conn the submarine up to the survivors. Marco's eyes needed a few minutes to adjust to the darkness; no one offered him night-vision goggles, and he didn't ask.

Squinting, Marco finally spotted the life rafts a hundred yards off *Bluefish's* starboard bow. His initial impression was right; one of the life rafts failed to inflate and was three-quarters sunk. Part of it remained above water, lashed to the fully inflated life raft, with survivors clinging to each. The Brits used enclosed life rafts, but the roof of the good one was punctured on one side, lying against the bottom of the raft like a demented slip-n-slide. How many people did each British life raft hold? Marco couldn't remember. U.S. submarines carried six thirty-man life rafts, but the U.K. might use a different model. That didn't look like thirty people, and they didn't all fit in the raft, either.

Coleman lifted the sound-powered phone. "Conn, Bridge, what's the water temp?"

"Sixty-two degrees," Bobby's voice answered.

"Bridge, aye. Come right to three-five-two."

Marco ignored the repeat back, thinking back to the days when he'd given a damn about hypothermia tables. Sixty to seventy degrees Fahrenheit was the big box, wasn't it? *Gallant* sank eight hours ago. Hypothermia would set in by now, but probably wouldn't kill anyone.

Hopefully.

Bluefish crept forward, a black shadow silently gliding toward the survivors. There was a slight vibration under Marco's feet, but the submarine was largely silent on the surface. Several long minutes passed before the survivors spotted them. The sound of splashing and frantic whispers carried back to the submarine.

"Fuck me sideways," Marco whispered. "From their angle, we might as well be Rochambeau."

One nuclear submarine looked much like another on the surface, particularly in the dark. No nation painted hull numbers on their sails during wartime, and while *Bluefish* sported the distinctive flared sail edge of all modern American submarines, that was hard to see head-on.

Coleman glanced over his shoulder. "Unless you speak French, I think we're okay."

Marco snickered. "Bi-lingual is enough for me. I take it you weren't some liberal arts weenie?"

"Civil engineering. I wanted a PhD in naval architecture, but the navy had other ideas."

"Damn straight. You'd be wasted as a desk jockey." Marco filed that away. His top captain was full of surprises, and there was a project underway needing a shooter's perspective.

Coleman shook his head wryly, picking up the sound-powered microphone again. "All stop."

The speaker crackled. "All stop, aye. Engines all stop."

"Very well," Coleman replied. "Station the recovery detail."

Looking aft, Marco watched *Bluefish* sailors emerge from the hatches. Each wore a lifejacket and tied themselves off to the deck of the submarine; even in wartime, no sailor walked around topside on a surfaced submarine unless they had to. Submarines didn't have life rails, and their sound-absorbent tiles were notoriously slippery. Ten years ago, Marco would've been dumb enough to volunteer. Today, he stayed on the bridge and listened as calm seas lapped against the metal hull.

"That was quick. You drill that?" he asked. Most sub COs didn't.

Coleman shrugged. "Never hurts. Besides, it beats another pier security drill, and I used to do a lot of this on *Jimmy Carter*."

Bluefish glided to a halt a few feet from the British sailors. "Nice driving."

Was Coleman a little red? Marco didn't get a chance to ask before Master Chief Baker called from *Bluefish's* deck:

"Ahoy, *Gallant*!"

"Who asks?" a distinctly British accent demanded. A *man's* voice. Not Ursula North. Worry gnawed at Marco's gut. The Alliance needed that pain-in-the-ass woman.

"*Bluefish!*" Baker replied. "Stand by to receive lines!"

"Aye!" There was a pause. "We're going to need stretchers for the wounded!"

Baker twisted to look up at the sail; Marco saw Coleman nod. He picked up his sound-powered handset again as Baker's team threw lines across to the waterlogged life rafts, hauling the Brits toward the submarine's hull.

"Conn, Bridge, have stretcher bearers lay to the forward hatch and pass their stretchers up."

"Conn, aye," Bobby replied. "Still no sonar contacts, Captain. A few distant aircraft on radar, but nothing nearby."

"Very well."

"Stretcher bearers are on their way!" Coleman shouted. He was surprisingly loud for a skinny guy.

"Many thanks!" the same Brit yelled back.

The rescue took almost an hour. *Gallant's* able-bodied sailors jumped from the rafts to *Bluefish's* deck, but six wounded were transferred by stretcher. Getting them across the gap was a challenge, but maneuvering a stretcher down the vertical ladder leading into the submarine was the real copperplated bitch. Finally, the last stretcher went down, a dark-skinned Brit bringing up the rear. Master Chief Baker flashed a thumbs-up.

"Clear the deck!" Coleman ordered. *Bluefish's* sailors scurried to comply, sealing the deck hatches behind them. Coleman turned to the lookouts. "You guys, too. It's time to leave this party."

"Yes, sir." The senior lookout grinned, and both headed down the ladder.

"Ahead one third," Coleman said into the sound-powered phone and then looked at Marco. "After you, Admiral."

"Don't have to tell me twice." Marco took one last look at the sky. They were damned lucky not to be spotted; it was time to get back to the haven of deep water.

Marco scurried down the ladder, followed by Coleman, who secured the hatch.

"Green board!" Bobby said.

Coleman nodded. "Submerge the ship. Resume your nav plan for Perth."

"It's already loaded. You want to kick it up and get there faster?" Bobby asked.

"Yeah. Good call." Coleman glanced around control. "Call if you need me. I'm going down to see the survivors."

He glanced at Marco, who grabbed accepted the silent invitation and followed. He'd counted thirty-four survivors, barely a third of *Gallant's* ninety-one sailor crew. At least ten of them were walking wounded, and six stretcher-bound.

A sick feeling welled up in Marco's stomach and wouldn't let go.

Chapter 32

Ice Water

Alex heard shouting before he even reached the wardroom. Most of *Gallant's* survivors were on the mess decks with warm drinks and wrapped in blankets, but the injured went to the wardroom, which doubled as overflow for the boat's small medical area. Much to his surprise, the door was open—and blocked by a tall, dark-skinned British man wearing the two and a half stripes of a lieutenant commander. His uniform was still wet, but he seemed oblivious to his own shivering.

"Captain, you need to listen to their corpsman," the Brit said.

Alex's heart skipped a beat. He hadn't seen her among the survivors, but—

"I am not letting some fucking American amputate my bloody leg!"

Yeah, that was Ursula North. Shit.

"Pardon me." The British commander swung to glare at him before spotting the captain's insignia on Alex's coveralls.

"Thank you for picking us up, Captain," Lieutenant Commander Harrison said.

The naked gratitude on the other man's face made Alex swallow. "Please don't thank me for doing the right thing."

Harrison nodded. "All the same..." He grimaced. "Captain North isn't at her best."

"I wouldn't be, either." Alex worried for his corpsman. Chief Bethany Waskow was a tough cookie, but Alex had been on the receiving end of Ursula North's wrath and wouldn't wish it on anyone.

He slipped past Harrison and into the wardroom. Most of the wounded were seated in chairs, but two were flat on the table. One of those was Captain North.

"Captain, the only reason you feel like you're this side of dead is because your crew pumped you full of painkillers," Chief Waskow snapped. "If your corpsman was alive, she'd tell you the same thing I am, and—"

"He." Ursula glared. "Chief Tennant was a *he*."

Shit, she looked awful. Alex barely recognized Ursula through the bruises covering her sheet-white face. Her lower left leg was caked in blood and bent sideways below the knee, mangled beneath a tourniquet made from someone's belt. A makeshift sling held her left arm tight to her chest, and her right ankle wasn't supposed to turn that way, either.

"Then *he'd* tell you the same thing I am. If I don't amputate that leg soon, you're going to lose a lot more than below the knee," Waskow retorted.

"Piss off." Ursula slurred the words, but her head still snapped around when Alex arrived. "And double piss off to you, Coleman. Your twat of a corpsman here isn't chopping my fucking leg off."

Waskow twisted to look at Alex. "Captain, she might bleed out if I don't."

Ursula snorted out a laugh, spraying blood all over Waskow's coveralls. "Isn't that what tourniquets are for?"

"A tourniquet *slows* blood loss, particularly when it's as sloppy as this one," Waskow snapped. "If I remove it, you *will* bleed out. If I don't, it'll just be slower. *Ma'am.*"

"Captain, you need to listen," Harrison pleaded from behind Alex.

"I'll wait for a proper British doctor." Ursula tried to cross her arms, only to hiss in pain when she moved the left one. "Fuck."

"How long to Perth?" Harrison asked Alex.

"Two days," Alex replied. "Maybe a bit less." That depended on how many risks he wanted to take—and if they found no more enemies.

"She can't wait that long," Harrison whispered.

"The fuck I can't." Ursula started slurring again. "I can..."

"Ma'am, I don't even know how you're conscious with the amount of morphine your crew shot you up with," Waskow cut in.

Ursula glared; Chief Waskow glared right back. Alex felt like a bystander who didn't belong, but goddamn it, he was the captain. And by virtue of his training as a search-and-rescue diver, he knew more about emergency medicine than the average layman. Not nearly as much as a corpsman, of course, but enough to understand how dire this situation was.

"Knock her out and do it," Alex said before anyone else could speak.

"What?" Ursula snarled.

"Aye, sir." Waskow didn't hesitate before stabbing Ursula with a needle, and seconds later, the British captain passed out.

"Thank you, Captain," Harrison said. "I know there's bad blood between the two of you, so...thank you."

"I don't have to like her to want to save her, Commander." Exhaustion penned Alex in; he just wanted to sleep, wanted to be alone. There were a thousand things he needed to do, but for once, Alex gave in to the desire to retreat. "Excuse me."

Harrison nodded; Waskow went to work on Ursula's leg. Admiral Rodriquez shot Alex a strange look when he slipped out of the wardroom but said nothing. Alex didn't wait for him to change his mind, heading toward his own stateroom and ten minutes of peace.

26 March 2040

Eating breakfast on the mess decks was an adventure Marco hadn't experienced since his division officer days, way back in the prehistoric past. Fortunately, the crew was comfortable with him and didn't run away screaming when an admiral happened to sit down at a table next door. Everyone knew the wardroom was full of British survivors; the rest were sleeping in the torpedo room and on the mess decks. Attack submarines didn't have extra berthing; squeezing in thirty-four Brits strained *Bluefish* to the gills.

They weren't so accustomed to the senator, however, which meant the neighboring tables evacuated when Angler showed up. Except for the Brits. They didn't give a good goddamn about some American politician, and Marco loved them for it.

"You slept through all the fun last night," Marco said around a mouth full of pancakes. God, he'd missed sub food.

"I thought I'd be in the way and could get the Cliff's Notes version from you this morning." Angler didn't grimace at Marco's lack of table manners, but it was a close thing.

"Rescue was boring. Lady North cursing out *Bluefish's* doc and Captain Coleman was much more fun," Marco replied. He'd been impressed with Coleman again. Too bad he hadn't seen the man in actual combat.

Angler's eyebrows mated with his hairline. "That sounds...interesting."

"You got that fucking right." Swearing at senators was so much fun. They never knew what to do with him. Marco was at his terminal rank, anyway. No one in their right mind would give him a fourth star. Freddie Hamilton was the highflyer from the sub community, not him.

"So...speaking of Captain Coleman, I have to wonder how long you're going to keep him here," Angler said after a moment of silence.

Marco frowned. "Here? You know that we're running like a scared skunk for Perth, right?"

"I mean on *Bluefish*."

"Oh. Long enough to kill Rochambeau. Probably longer." Marco shrugged. "He's got a touch for this business. We need someone like him."

"We need admirals like him, too," Angler replied.

Marco chewed some more pancake before replying. Angler wasn't wrong, but he wasn't right, either. Alex Coleman had put on captain five months ago. Yeah, he was a Medal of Honor winner—still the only living one the sub community had—and he was sharp. Marco shook his head. "We need him in the seat more."

"The seat?"

"In command." Marco sighed. "We don't have a lot of COs like him. Ask your son if you don't know what I mean. Coleman ain't afraid to shoot but damn well knows when not to. It's a hard balance. He's also got balls of fucking titanium."

Further profanity made Angler wince. "Staying out here might kill him, too."

Marco snorted. "You think he doesn't know that?"

"I imagine he does." Angler grimaced. "Benji admires him, you know."

"Your son's a damned good officer." Marco didn't like saying that; it felt like ass licking. But it was true. Benjamin Angler IV was a hot shot, two months into his XO tour and everything Steve Harper *should* have been. Along with not trying to boink the help. Pity he hadn't sent the younger Angler to *Bluefish*, but that would've looked like favoritism. "He's got a bright future."

"I almost wish he didn't." Angler scratched his chin. "But he's made his choices, and I have to be proud of him."

Marco didn't ask if he *had* to because Benji was his son or because it was political suicide not to approve of the navy in wartime. Marco didn't want to know. And Freddie said he didn't know when to keep his trap shut.

"I've learned a lot," Angler said after a moment. "I want you to know that I'm grateful for the opportunity to see what life on a sub is like."

"Thank Admiral Hamilton. She's the one who set this up."

"I will. But I want you both to know that if you need a friend in Washington, you have one." Angler smiled.

"Sir, if you think that's why I'm doing this, you're dead wrong." Marco leaned forward. "I didn't come along to kiss your ass. I came along because a, I wanted a wartime ride myself, and b, I wanted to make sure you didn't get in the way. You've been a shit-ton more reasonable than any of us expected—which we're grateful for—but no admiral with a lick of sense would send you out alone."

To Angler's credit, he didn't bristle at the implication that he needed a babysitter. "My point still stands, Admiral. For whatever it's worth."

"Shit, at least I don't have to wonder where your kid got his balls from." Marco sighed. "I'm no politician, and won't ever be, but hell, I'll take the friend if it gets us the funding we need."

Angler's eyes narrowed. "Funding?"

"Project 971 is the sub we need to fight this war. CNO is sitting on the money to fast-track the construction." *Sorry, Freddie.* Freddie thought she could talk the chief of naval operations around, but he wasn't going to wait for the golden goose to take a shit in his lap.

"A new sub class?" Angler wasn't stupid, thank goodness.

"Yeah. The design started years ago, got overtaken by bean counters, and we built the *Ceros* instead." Hamstringing the navy's future in the name of saving a few billion dollars was such a great idea.

"Has the keel been laid?"

"Not yet. Final design is awaiting funding."

Angler frowned. "You think you can get a whole new class of sub out before this war is over?"

"Shit, sir, if we can't, we're fucked." A list of names rolled through Marco's mind. He'd memorized the name of every CO of every boat lost, and that list kept fucking growing. "The

French *Requins* are quieter than our boats, and their new torps are faster than ours. The Russian *Yasens* are the best fucking subs in the world—we're lucky they quit building them because they're so damned expensive. But rumor says they're going back to that quality with their next class, and the *Huskies* are about as good as our *Ceros*, anyway. We're supposed to be the best in the world. But we're fucking not."

"Is it that bad?"

"Worse."

Wide-eyed, Angler nodded.

Staring at the horizon rarely accomplished anything, but Captain John Dalton enjoyed it. Seeing the sky was the perk of having moved to a submarine tender. He relished those few moments on the surface when commanding *Razorback*; commanding *Nereus* (AS 43) meant he could see the sea and sky every day. Unfortunately, his view of the horizon was marred by the knowledge of two subs hunting his ship from beneath the surface.

"The only question is why they haven't shot us yet." John crossed his arms.

"They probably don't know we're on to them," his new XO, Commander Sheldon Fisher, pointed out. "We wouldn't be if we didn't have the tail out."

John scowled. Sheldon was a surface warfare officer. He was an engineer, too, which explained how he'd ended up as the second-in-command of a submarine tender. John, however, was a submariner, only on this surface ship because it was the quickest route to admirals' stars. He'd commanded two attack submarines, done well in the war, and had a Navy Cross. None of that mattered when there were two Russian submarines dogging his sub tender.

"Which means they're waiting for our next customer." He wanted to swear. "We're the bait."

"I think so, sir." Sheldon scowled. "We've got some depth charges..."

John shook his head. No way would these subs let him sink them like he'd sunk an *Akula* on his first underway with *Nereus.* He knew he wouldn't get that lucky twice. "They're not close enough, and you know it. The moment they hear splashes, they'll retreat, and we'll lose them in the clutter."

Man, he missed the days of being able to dive deep and listen where it was quiet. The surface duct was too noisy for good detection ranges, even with the navy's newest Tactical Towed Sonar Array. Why had John come here, again?

His ambition. Right.

"What do you want to do, Captain?" Sheldon asked.

"I want to change the rules." John looked out the bridge window, staring out at the horizon. "If we're going to be bait, let's be bait for someone friendly."

Sheldon started. "You think you can find a friendly submarine to come take them out?"

"Someone's bound to check in if we come up in PACIOSUB Battle Chat."

"We could just call for help on the surface combat circuit," Sheldon said.

John scoffed. "And have some idiot cruiser roll in here to save the day? They'd get shot, too." One look at his XO's face told him that he'd offended Sheldon's surface pride, so John softened his tone. "Those *Yasens* are quiet, XO. It's a miracle we're tracking them at all. If they know we've asked for help, the one lurking shallow and listening to our radio chatter will go deep. And then we'll never find them again."

"Point." Sheldon frowned. "So if we can't shoot them and we shouldn't radio for help, what do you want to do, Captain?"

"Hold down the fort. I'll be back," John told Sheldon, heading to his at sea cabin just aft of the bridge. Unlike attack submarines, the CO's cabin on *Nereus* was downright palatial. A bed that didn't fold down and the ability to use his rack and his table at the same time remained novel.

John logged into the Pacific-Indian Ocean Submarine Battle Chat, scanning usernames of underway submarines. Most subs didn't stay in chat unless they were attached to a battle-group, but John only needed one. He scratched his chin and started to type.

All de NER. Anyone underway in the south IO?

An ominous minute passed.

NER de RHI. What's your w/c/s?

My posit 30°03'18"S 92°01'49"E, course 090 speed 15. Have two Yasens tracking me. Looking for an ambush partner.

John's heart pounded. Could this work? Getting someone to shoot the subs tracking his tender beat getting sunk. He preferred a *Cero*, but a late-model *Virginia* like *Rhode Island* could do the job just as well.

At best speed I need nineteen hours to reach you. Can you lead the Yasens west and meet me?

Nineteen hours. Shit. Speeding up to flank would alert the Russians; if John turned toward *Rhode Island*, he could only cut that by a few hours. Would the Russians wait that long? In their shoes, he wouldn't.

Standby.

John scratched his chin, hoping for someone else. But several more minutes passed without another sub speaking up. John sighed. Time for his next plan.

One of the good things about commanding a submarine tender was that sub COs liked to email him. John had no idea which boats were underway—keeping that kind of database on an under-defended tender was an invitation for the enemy—but he could shoot out a group email. Subs that didn't come up in chat would still check email. Getting a response would take longer, though. Was the nineteen hours *Rhode Island* needed to reach him the best John could expect?

Sheldon's depth charge idea looked better and better.

Ding. Someone new entered the chat; John checked without much hope it would be a nearby sub.

NER de BLF Radio. We are about two hours from your posit. Standby while I ask the captain, k.

John whooped. Not only had he gotten a *Cero*, but the one his best friend commanded. Alex would say yes. Now John just had to sit on his own nerves long enough to find out. Thankfully, the response came quickly.

NER de BLF Actual. Your captain around?

NER Actual here. You want to kill 2 Yasens for me?

I thought I might kill them because they're the enemy, but if you want a personal gift, sure.

Grinning, John started hatching a plan.

The acting XO's job was never done. Bobby would've complained about that last month, but the position felt like it weighed less today. It was hard to believe Steve Harper had been *Bluefish's* XO for a grand total of nine days. That had to be some sort of record.

At least Steve had the sense to stay in his stateroom since he'd been relieved. From what Bobby heard, Steve wasn't happy, but the captain coldly cut his yelling off with the news that Admiral Rodriquez already approved Steve's detachment for cause. A DFC was a career ender, even with a war on, and Bobby would've felt sorry for the guy if he hadn't been such a sleezeball.

Bobby found Harri in the sonar spaces with three of her sailors and an electrician. She came out to join him in the passageway once she spotted him.

"How's the forward array looking?" Bobby asked. Rose had mentioned a problem with it during their morning meeting, and Bobby figured he should be the adult and check it out.

"Looks like it was just a busted fuse." Harri shrugged. "Should be good in a few."

"That's good news, because we're going to need it in about two hours." As Navigator, Bobby owned the radio room and knew about *Nereus'* call for help.

She cocked her head. "Rumor says a tender acquired a couple of leeches."

"Rumor's right," Bobby said. Rumors traveled faster than the speed of sound on a submarine. If only they could power sonar with them.

"We going to help?" Harri asked. "Even with *Gallant's* survivors on board?"

"Can't see why the captain wouldn't." Bobby knew Alex by now, and he wasn't the sort to leave an American ship in trouble.

Harri didn't seem surprised, either. "I heard the Sea Witch's leg got cut off. Is that true, too, sir?"

"Since when did you become the Rumor Queen?" Bobby scowled.

Harri shrugged. "It's a good distraction."

"C'mon." Bobby led her into a quiet corner, wedging between a load center and the outer bulkhead. "You okay?"

"Good as I can be." Harri studied her green-and-gray sneakers. "I'm glad I don't have to see him. Is he really getting fired?"

"I had admin finish the detachment paperwork this morning," Bobby replied. "He's gone."

"Good." Harri's sigh was almost a shudder, and Bobby wished he could be a real big brother and give her a hug. But he couldn't, not as acting XO. She looked up, her glare suddenly fierce. "I hope those bruises last."

Bobby tried not to laugh. Really, he did. "They're still there last I checked." When Bobby brought Steve the paperwork, his face remained purple.

"Good," she repeated, as if daring him to disagree.

"Speaking of our illustrious former XO, the captain wanted me to ask you if you want to press charges." Bobby swallowed. *He* knew that Steve was pissed enough to retaliate with assault charges, but did Harri?

Harri scowled. "I just want this to go away so I can go back to doing my job. I'm not some weepy little girl."

"No one things you are." Bobby chuckled. "The only one weeping is Steve."

"Not hard enough." She sighed, against the wall. "What would happen if I did press charges? I'd have to leave the boat, wouldn't I?"

"Probably. You'd stay on shore for the courts martial, at least."

"Can't someone just take him to Mast? I don't care if he gets kicked out of the navy. I just want to keep him from doing it to anyone else." Harri's glare was back.

"Admiral Rodriquez is willing to take him to Admiral's Mast. Couple that with a DFC and his career is done."

"That's good enough for me."

A voice over the 1MC cut him off. *"Man Battle Stations Torpedo. Man Battle Stations Torpedo."*

"Time to get back to our glorious day job, kiddo." Bobby grinned.

"Can you quit calling me that? It makes me feel like I'm your kid sister or something." But Harri still smiled.

"You're about my sister's age, so nope," he replied. "Not gonna happen."

She laughed before shooting up the nearest ladder. "You're the worst, Nav."

"And don't you forget it!"

"Commence hover," Alex ordered.

"Commence hover, aye," Master Chief Baker replied.

"Make tubes one through four ready in all respects, including opening the outer doors," he said next. Rose responded immediately; within seconds, *Bluefish* was ready to fire. Unfortunately, the enemy was still far out of range.

Bluefish's two-hour sprint put them fifteen miles ahead of *Nereus* along the sub tender's track. Given *Nereus'* current speed, the tender wouldn't reach them for another hour, but this was the best plan Alex and John had.

"Feeling timid today, Captain?" a voice asked from behind him.

Turning, Alex managed not to grimace. God, why did he *still* have to have an admiral on board? "No, sir," he replied. "Just trying not to get *Nereus* sunk."

"Well, I appreciate that, since I own the fucking tender." Rodriquez grinned. "And here I was thinking I wouldn't get to see you in combat."

"The *Yantar* wasn't enough?"

"Boring." Rodriquez smirked. "I've come to expect more from you."

"Pardon me while I go blush," Alex replied. Or vomit in a bucket. Here his big mouth went, running away with him again. Damn it.

"You're still a strange fucking cat." Thankfully, Rodriquez laughed. "But don't let me stop you from executing the battle plan you didn't clear with me."

"You're the one who said you're just along for the ride, sir." Rolling his eyes was a mistake, but, well, *oops.*

"And I'm an old fart while this is a young man's game. Carry on," Rodriquez said. "I'll be as quiet as a mouse."

Alex laughed. "If that was going to happen, your nickname would be 'Uncle Mouse.'"

"My name's not Mickey, so don't you give people fucking ideas, son."

Was this conversation for real? Alex couldn't believe he'd gotten away with snapping at an admiral. *Jesus, I must be bulletproof.* Worse yet, it was intoxicating. Most captains ran and hid when Marco Rodriquez glared. Alex talked shit back at him. The world was upside down.

"Conn, Sonar, we have a bottom-bounce contact on the first *Yasen* that matches the Link track from *Nereus*," Chief

Andreas reported via the net. "No track on the second one. She might be obscured by *Nereus'* screw noise."

"Conn, aye. What's the range?" Alex asked.

"Thirty-four thousand yards, closing us at fifteen knots."

"Conn, aye." Alex leaned away from the squawk box and met Bobby's eyes.

Bobby grinned and slid his gaze toward Rodriquez. His question was obvious: did Alex need him to distract the admiral? Alex shook his head. Pity they couldn't take silent bets on how long Rodriquez could keep his mouth shut.

Damn, having Bobby back in the job was nice. Steve was competent, but he'd barely waited a week before trying to sleep with Alex's officers. That was one career Alex wouldn't regret sinking.

"Out of the mildest of fucking curiosity, what *is* your plan?" Rodriquez asked.

Thirty seconds. Not bad. Alex turned back to face his boss' boss.

"We'll sit pretty until *Nereus* runs over us and the *Yasens* don't have a chance to shoot her. Until then, we're receive-only in Link so *Nereus* can feed us track data," he replied. Receiving *Nereus'* tracks on the enemy subs would let *Bluefish* know if the Russians changed course before she could detect them. That was doubly important since they still didn't have a track on one *Yasen* using *Bluefish's* own sensors.

"You're going to shoot when you're between them." Rodriquez crossed his arms. "Dalton signed off on this even though he'll have no clue where you are?"

"He did, sir." Alex hadn't needed to talk John into it, either. John knew how important it was for a submarine to remain undetected.

Rodriquez's eyes narrowed. "You're one of those captains who think any transmission is a bad transmission."

"We know the Russians have better toys than we do. I'm not taking chances." Alex made no apologies.

"Son, I'm not here to second-guess you. You're the one with the habit of kicking the shit out of the enemy. I'm just along to learn what I can," Rodriquez replied.

"That's...good to know, sir."

Who the hell was he to explain current tactics to the navy's second most senior submariner? Unfortunately, Alex spent the next forty minutes doing just that. They gained track on the second *Yasen* eighteen minutes after the first, which confirmed both Russian submarines followed *Nereus* at a range of about ten thousand yards.

Alex didn't like the idea of firing from that far away, however. If these Russians had the Shkval torpedo—or even the slower but still ridiculously fast French torpedo—they could kill *Nereus* before Alex's torpedoes could kill them. He needed to be in close.

Besides, if they had the hundred-plus-knot French torpedo or the *three* hundred–knot one Russian supposedly had, being in close would be *Bluefish's* only hope. Torpedoes needed time to fire, and if the Russians didn't pull the trigger fast enough...

"*Nereus* is at closest point of approach," Bobby announced.

"Very well." Alex took a deep breath. "How're your solutions looking, Weps?"

Rose grinned. "Dialed all the way in, Captain."

"Very well." Alex leaned over to speak into the squawk box. "Sonar, Conn, range to the *Yasens*?"

"Ten thousand yards for track 7819. Eleven thousand for track 7820."

"Conn, aye." Alex took a deep breath. Ten thousand yards meant five nautical miles. He was well within the Russians' weapons' effective range.

"How long do you want to wait, Captain?" Bobby asked.

"Five thousand yards."

Someone coughed to cover their surprise. Alex didn't need to glance at Rodriquez to know Uncle Marco thought he was crazy. The confident atmosphere in control grew tense; he could feel his crew's collective blood pressure rising. Even Master Chief Baker looked over her shoulder, questions all over her face.

"You sure you don't want to ask them out first, Captain?" Bobby's giggle was a tad high-pitched. "That's intimate."

Alex chuckled. "We'll consider a full spread of torpedoes our invitation." He glanced at Rose, who was the only one not disconcerted by his decision to wait so long. "Your reload crews are going to have to be on point, Weps."

"They will be, sir," she promised.

"Good." Alex grinned, feeling his confidence infect his crew. They were a good bunch, and he'd earned their trust. Now he just had to not lose it by screwing up.

If he kept thinking those happy thoughts, he'd lose his nerve. Crossing his arms, Alex returned to studying the plot. *Nereus* was past *Bluefish* and opening; the range to the leading *Yasen* decreased to nine thousand yards as he watched.

Ten minutes until the second *Yasen* was at his preferred range. Would anyone freak out if he mentioned that he was going to let the first one get to four thousand yards? Alex decided not to mention that.

Minutes ticked by; Alex let his battle plan roll through his mind another time. Shit, he was a bit of an idiot. No one had called him on it, either. Lacking speed through the water put *Bluefish* at a serious disadvantage if she had to run from enemy torpedoes. Time to fix that.

"Ahead two-thirds," he ordered. Ten knots wasn't much but was better than starting from a standstill. Of course, that increased the closure between *Bluefish* and the *Yasens* to twenty-five knots, cutting the intercept time by four minutes.

"Conn, Sonar, the leading *Yasen* is at five thousand yards."

"Very well," Alex replied.

Every eye was on him. No one spoke.

Except Admiral Rodriquez. "Damn, son. You've got fucking ice water in your veins," he whispered.

"Nothing ventured, nothing gained." Alex surprised himself with a smile.

Rodriquez muttered something under his breath; Alex didn't catch anything that didn't sound vile.

There.

"Firing point procedures, tube one and three, track 7819; tube two and four, track 7820," Alex ordered.

Rose waited less than a second. "Solutions set!"

"Solutions checked," Bobby added.

"Fire." Alex hadn't raised his voice, but he heard Admiral Rodriquez jump.

"Tubes one through four fired electrically," Rose reported.

A few seconds passed before Sonar said: "Conn, Sonar, four fish running hot, straight, and normal."

"Very well." Alex leaned away from the squawk box and squared his shoulders. "Cut the wires, close the outer doors, and reload all tubes." Turn right or left? The *Yasen* to starboard was closer. Either way, a turn would present his broadside to one enemy. Crossing his own "T" seemed like a shitty way to die. Up or down? "Twenty degree up bubble, make your depth one hundred feet. All ahead flank."

Too many people forgot submarine warfare worked in three dimensions. Alex's torpedoes could fend for themselves. Now it was time to complicate the Russians' firing solutions.

"Conn, Sonar, both contacts are maneuvering! Torpedo in the water, single torpedo, bearing three-four-one!"

"Hard right rudder," Alex ordered. The further *Yasen* got a shot off. Time to dodge.

"My rudder is hard right, no new course given!" Master Chief Baker said. "Steady at one hundred feet, all engines are ahead flank for fifty-nine knots."

"Very well." Alex took a deep breath, checking the range to *Nereus* on the plot. *Six thousand yards. Sorry, John.* "Continue right, steady course one-seven-zero."

"Continue right, steady course one-seven-zero, aye," Baker replied. "My rudder is hard right, coming to course one-seven-zero."

"Conn, Sonar, one explosion on the bearing for track 7820! Torpedoes one and three still in acquisition!" Chief Andreas' voice boomed out of the speaker. "Enemy torpedo bears three-four-zero, range four thousand yards!"

Thank god he'd turned. "Torpedo speed?"

"Sixty-five knots!"

"Very well." The relief was crushing. The chance either *Yasen* had the Shkval torpedoes was always about fifty-fifty, and while Alex *thought* he could dodge one of those under these specific circumstances, he wasn't positive. But a sixty-five knot torpedo meant it was one of the old Futlyars. Maybe the Russians still had trouble with the targeting package on the Shkvals, or they still had to run down their inventory of the old torpedoes.

Either way, Alex knew he'd gotten lucky.

"Conn, Sonar, impact! Multiple explosions for track 7819!"

"Conn, aye." Alex grinned. "Good job folks. Now let's dodge this torp so we can go home."

His crew's reactions were a world apart from the first time *Bluefish* killed an enemy; no one high-fived, no one cheered. They were seasoned professionals now. Their satisfaction was a fierce but quiet thing.

Bluefish reached *Nereus'* wake.

"Bobby, start corkscrewing your way across *Nereus'* course. Don't get closer than one thousand yards from the tender, but let's see if we can use her wake to confuse the torpedo."

"You got it, sir," Bobby replied.

Fortunately, John knew his stuff. *Nereus* sped up when she heard the torpedoes launched, up to twenty-five knots and straining at the seams. Heaven help him if Alex ever took command of something so slow. He'd go insane.

"You better be good fucking friends with Dalton to pull this shit," Rodriquez said. Alex had almost forgotten he was there.

He grinned. "He owes me one for introducing him to his wife."

Rodriquez shook his head.

Driving back and forth along *Nereus'* wake did the trick. Like most modern torpedoes, the Russian Futlyar was wake-homing. With its mother submarine unable to guide it, the torpedo couldn't choose between the two wakes and eventually circled hopelessly until running out of gas. By then, *Bluefish* and *Nereus* were over two miles away.

Chapter 33

A Bad Penny

The Indian Ocean

Three hours after sending two *Yasens* to the bottom, *Bluefish* surfaced five hundred yards off *Nereus'* port side. Squinting in the light of the blazing blue sky and bright sun, Alex conned the submarine up to nest against the tender. Under normal circumstances, he hated the idea of leaving his submarine tied up and vulnerable, but he had passengers to offload.

If only he could ditch the admiral and the senator. Unfortunately, they'd be miles more vulnerable on a surface ship.

"Thank you for taking good care of our people, Captain," Commander Harrison said as they stood on deck together. Most of the *Gallant* survivors were able to climb the long ladder up to *Nereus'* deck on their own. For the others, the tender rigged a pulley to hoist the stretcher-bound patients on board.

Including Ursula North, still sedated post-amputation.

"I'm just glad to get your injured people to a real doctor," Alex replied as the last stretcher disappeared onto *Nereus'* deck.

Harrison chuckled. "And to ditch the most troublesome of us?"

"I think it's safe to say that we'll never be friends." Alex smiled wryly.

"Aye, Captain North may be a master at holding grudges, but the rest of us won't forget," Harrison said.

Alex held out a hand. "Good luck to you, Commander."

"Thank you, sir." Harrison saluted and headed up the ladder. Alex watched him go before turning to Bobby.

"Try not to let Uncle Marco do something crazy while I jump over to *Nereus* for a sec, okay?"

Bobby cocked his head. "Unless you're Superman, I don't think you're jumping that tall tender in a single bound."

"Jesus, Bobby." Alex almost choked on his own laughter. "It's a figure of speech."

"Of course it is, sir." Bobby grinned.

Rolling his eyes, Alex grabbed the bottom rung of the ladder and looked up. *Nereus* towered over *Bluefish*. The submarine's deck only cleared the wave tops by a handful of feet, but *Nereus'* was over twenty-five feet above the waterline. It made for a long climb.

Four bells sounded as his right foot found the first rung. "*Bluefish*, departing!"

Ding! The stinger followed, because Alex was in command of *Bluefish* and that was navy tradition when he departed his own submarine.

A sailor helped him over *Nereus'* railing a moment later as two bells rang over the tender's 1MC. "*Bluefish*, arriving!"

John waited for him on deck. "You've got a lot of nerve, you know," he said, saluting.

"I hate it when you do that." Alex returned the salute with a grimace.

"What, follow navy regulations and salute a Medal of Honor winner?" John grinned.

"Yeah, that." Alex sighed. John made captain about the same time Alex put on *commander* and was several years senior to him. But John was right about regulations. Six months after getting the damned medal, he still wasn't used to all the honors attached to it.

"You know, you could have mentioned that you were going to use me as bait for that torpedo," John said.

Alex shrugged. "I didn't exactly plan on it."

"You never do, do you?" John shook his head, slapping Alex on the shoulder. "For a guy who was such an obsessive pre-planner as a junior officer, you really do fly by the seat of your pants in combat."

"As if you didn't." Alex didn't mention that he always had a plan and at least two backup plans. He *did* usually end up going with plan D.

"Guilty as charged." John gestured toward the tender's superstructure. "So, do you want a tour, or are you planning on running away now that you've dumped the Brits on me?"

"Running away. I need to get Senator Angler back to Perth ASAP."

John shuddered. "Better you than me. How's Nancy? I heard what happened on *Cape*."

"She's okay. Still not sure if she's inheriting *Cape* now or later, or if the shit's all going to fall on her." Alex swallowed. "How're you after *Razorback*?"

"Okay." John looked away. "Pat was a good friend. I'm going to miss...all of them."

"Yeah." Alex didn't need to mention Master Chief Morton; John knew.

They stood in silence together, staring out at the setting sun. The list of friends they lost only grew longer as the war continued. Who was winning? No one knew. The Southern Theater, as the conflict in the Indian Ocean was recently named, remained a giant game of tug-of-war. Aside from the islands invaded early on by the Freedom Union, underwater stations were taken and retaken, bouncing back and forth between the two sides like ping pong balls. The Union's most recent victory at Diego Garcia made momentum seem to be in their corner, but the massive territorial gains of World War I and II were a thing of the past.

Two years in, World War III was an uncoordinated mess. Was this what modern war between significant powers looked like when no one wanted to go nuclear?

Alex hoped they didn't find out the alternative.

"So I hear you're ditching your XO on me, too," John said a little too lightly.

Alex scowled. "Yeah, he turned out to be a dickweed who can't keep it in his pants."

John frowned. "He was chummy with my communications officer when he was here, but I didn't think he was that bad."

"I should have taken the hint when he propositioned my weps." Alex still hated himself for that. "Instead, I was the idiot who let him grope one of my junior officers."

"Quit blaming yourself." John glared. "You can't fix stupid."

"I can at least kick it off my boat." Alex sighed.

"You keep this up, you're going to get a reputation for being murderous on XOs." John chuckled. "First George, now Steve."

Alex snorted. "Assuming they send me someone who can keep his dick in his pants and doesn't shit himself when combat starts, I think I'll be fine."

John laughed.

28 March 2040, Naval Base Perth, Australia

Bobby wasn't sure how Uncle Marco acquired a caretaker crew for *Bluefish* on such short notice, but he wasn't going to argue. *Bluefish* made port in Perth at nine a.m.; by noon, the caretaker crew arrived and liberty call went down. He found Rose and Lou drinking coffee in the wardroom after most of the crew departed.

"Come on, boys and girls, it's time to get a celebratory drink," he said.

Rose rolled her eyes. "Your use of the plural is disjointed."

"By which she means grammatically incorrect," Lou added.

Bobby scoffed. "You party-poopers plan on staying on board to bitch about my grammar instead of taking advantage of the Q rooms the *navy* has paid for and the barbeque already set up?"

"Do we look stupid?" Lou chuckled. "We're just taking a moment of quiet reflection."

"Translation: we're wondering how the hell *Bluefish* went from being the dregs of the navy to super successful in less than four months," Rose said.

"Well, if you want to sit with coffee and contemplate, far be it for me to stop you. But I'm heading over for steaks and beer."

"Are you cooking?" Rose asked.

"Sure, if no one's beat me to it."

"Then we're coming." She looked at Lou. "He's crazy, but he's a damned good cook. I learned that back at the academy."

"They let you cook at the academy?" Lou asked.

"Let...?" Bobby snickered. "Not exactly. It's a long story. C'mon."

The department heads headed off the boat and piled into one of the duty vans reserved for *Bluefish's* use. Uncle Marco had blocked off an entire section of the Combined Bachelors' Quarters for *Bluefish's* crew, including a barbeque pit, volleyball court, and access to the pool. *Bluefish* had never been so lucky, and every sailor on board was rushing to be the first one there. Before Captain Coleman, no one considered *Bluefish* worthy. Lately, they'd been too busy.

Five minutes later, they reached the CBQ. Bobby, Rose, and Lou picked up their room keys—each got a room, much to their surprise—and headed out into recreation area. Most of *Bluefish's* crew was already there, along with a smattering of local girlfriends, boyfriends, and everything in between. Two dozen sailors were in the pool, while others played volleyball and various other sports. A few engineers tossed a football back and forth, making Bobby yearn for his old college sport. But he'd promised to cook, so he headed over to the deck where two grills were set up.

Master Chief Baker already had both going, but she handed over her spatula with a smile. "Have fun, Nav." She grinned. "I'm going to play volleyball."

"Skater." Bobby laughed as she retreated, turning to his fellow department heads. "You guys going to cook with me?"

"Not a chance," Rose replied. "I'm playing soccer." She gestured to the group next to the volleyball net. "Enjoy."

"I'm going to work on my suntan," Lou deadpanned, hopping up on a picnic table, resting his feet on the seat.

Laughter shook Bobby hard enough that he almost flipped a burger into the atmosphere. "Yeah. *That's* what you need."

Lou snickered. "Anything that's not radiation from my reactor is an improvement."

"And we've got two weeks off." Bobby nudged the chicken with the tongs; it needed longer.

"Amen to that."

Bobby grinned again, until something caught his eye. Across the recreation area walked a familiar figure in khakis. Bobby would know that straight-backed, pigeon-toed walk anywhere, even if it hadn't been accompanied by the world's grouchiest glare. Directed at *Bluefish's* sailors, of course. Did he recognize them?

"Don't look now, but our personal demon is glowering," he said.

Lou twisted to look just as Harri's squealing laugher split the air, followed by a large splash.

"Gotcha!' Rene shouted, dancing by the pool's edge while Harri swam to the surface, sputtering. "I'm going to— *Umph!*"

He flew into the water, too, almost hitting Harri, as Max cackled. Then Max jumped into the water to join his fellow division officers. All three were oblivious to the fact that their old captain found their antics Not Amusing.

Commander Wade Peterson stood with his arms crossed, radiating Senior Officer Displeasure. The fact that no one paid him any mind only furthered his fury. Peterson crossed his arms, scrunching his nose up as *Bluefish's* sailors partied. Someone turned the stereo up, playing the week's top hundred country songs, and Peterson scowled.

Lou grimaced. "He's like a bad penny."

"The kind that gives you bad luck for seven years, you mean." Bobby scowled.

"He's not a broken mirror."

"Are you kidding? He looks like someone broke a mirror over his head under a ladder while a black cat scratched him." Bobby rolled his eyes. "Watch him come over here and say something."

"Nah, he's walking away." Lou shrugged. "He's a dick, but he's not our problem."

"Yeah." Bobby pushed aside the year-plus worth of anxiety-ridden Peterson experience. "Gimme another beer, will you?"

Lou handed over another cold one, and Bobby went back to grilling.

Alex wished he could partake in barbeque and fun with his crew, but he had bigger problems. Like his boss.

"Admiral Rodriquez seems satisfied with his underway." Banks sniffed, his expression still pinched and unhappy. "As did Senator Angler."

"I'm glad to hear it, sir." Alex was also glad that Uncle Marco hadn't bitched about Alex mouthing off to him, but if Banks didn't know, Alex wasn't going to share.

"Hm. I see he's already provided a caretaker crew and two weeks' liberty."

A response didn't seem required; Alex kept his mouth shut.

"I had planned to assign you a convoy escort next week, but I suppose I can send *Kansas*," Banks finally said.

He'd probably tell *Kansas* why, which would make Chris Kennedy like Alex just that much more. Great.

"My crew is grateful for the down time," Alex replied as diplomatically as he could.

"Of course." Banks folded his hands. "And *I* am grateful you didn't see the need to showboat and fly a broomstick again."

Alex shrugged. "We didn't get everything we went after."

"Yes, I know you're going to be assigned to go after Rochambeau next." Banks scowled. "Don't let it go to your head. Ursula

North's the only one who survived *that* so far, and your patrol report says where that got her."

"I have no intention of letting it 'go to my head,' sir," Alex said. *Deep breath. Don't be an ass.* He wasn't Ursula North's biggest fan, but Banks was a pencil-pushing micromanager who'd never seen the inside of a submarine on war patrol. "However, I do need an XO."

"Yes." The scowl grew deeper. "I've endorsed your detachment for cause for Lieutenant Commander Harper. Had I known he would act in such a despicable manner, I never would have approved his assignment."

Hot damn, did he and Banks *agree* on something?

"Thank you, sir." Alex took a deep breath. "Since I assume we're getting underway after our R&R is over, may I suggest promoting Lieutenant O'Kane into the job? He did very well as acting XO, and finding another navigator should be easier than an XO."

Banks remained silent for far too long. "The idea may have merit," he said, scratching his chin. "The Bureau *did* inform me that the wait time for an XO would be months. But he's awfully junior." Banks' eyes narrowed. "Are you sure you want him?"

"What I want is continuity." Alex didn't want to sing Bobby's praises too loud; Banks was still Peterson's friend, and Peterson still hated Bobby.

If he had to kiss some ass to get the XO he wanted, Alex could brown nose with the best of them.

"I'll investigate it," Banks said.

"Thank you, sir," Alex said and actually meant it.

4 April 2040, Saint Dennis (French Territory)

Saint Dennis was a nice little island, but one tropical island might as well have been another. After partaking in enough sea, sun, and excellent views, one grew bored with them. That didn't stop Jules Rochambeau from spending a day or two at the beach, but he was no longer excited by it. Still, Saint Dennis was warmer than Île Amsterdam, and it had a small television studio.

Alas, the anchor was a portly, middle-aged man.

"Captain Rochambeau, now that you've sank HMS *Gallant*, where will you go?" he asked.

Jules smiled. "That depends upon the needs of the nation, *bien sûr*. I am merely a servant of France."

He could afford to be modest now that he was the undisputed king of the seas. He'd killed the best Britain and America had to offer, held records of every sort. No one could touch him.

"Perhaps an admiral's stars are in your future?" the anchor asked.

"Perhaps." Jules sighed. "I would prefer to remain with *Barracuda* for now, but I will go where my nation calls."

He didn't mind the idea of being an admiral, but junior admirals rarely had the kind of authority he enjoyed on *Barracuda*. He would have respect, but he would have to mark time until he gained the rank to make a difference. Jules misliked being a nobody.

"Rumor says you'll take part in a new offensive designed to turn the tide of the war." The anchor's eyes begged for Jules to give him a hint. "Can you comment on that?"

"Of course not." Jules chuckled. "It would be irresponsible."

He did not mention that *Barracuda's* food onload would be complete in six hours. Nor did Jules say he planned on getting underway four days from now—just enough time to let his crew have some fun. Jules might've been done with the beaches, himself, but Saint Dennis *did* have a thriving population of gorgeous women. He checked his watch. Assuming this interview got out on time, he had a date.

"What can you tell us, Captain?"

"Only that you have not heard the last of me yet." Jules smiled, thinking of the blonde in his hotel room.

The interview continued with a few bland questions and an overview of the war Jules found blindingly boring. The more interesting news came when he walked out of the news building to find his second-in-command waiting for him.

"She's not dead," Camille said, her face pinched with fury.

"What? Who?" It would be such a pity if something had happened to Eloise—

"*Ursula North.*" Camille shoved a message tablet into his hands. "She's *alive.*"

"Ah." Jules' heart hammered against his ribcage. Was he happy or sad? He had not relished the idea of killing his former ally, but he had enjoyed beating her. Ursula would feel the sharp edge of humiliation now, both from the sinking and the pictures he'd taken.

"Is that all you have to say?" Camille snapped.

Jules read the message instead of replying. It contained the official U.K. press release concerning *Gallant's* sinking, but the most startling reveal was near the bottom. "*Mon Dieu.* She's lost a leg."

"She has?" Camille perked up. "*Bien.* That will keep her out of a submarine."

"*Oui.*" Jules blinked, staring up at the sun. A strange numbness stole over him. How was he supposed to feel? What was he supposed to do? Thank God the interviewer had not known to ask about this.

"Your afternoon plans?" Camille asked as if nothing monumental had happened.

Jules shook himself. "Private, I'm afraid." He smiled, pushing aside the thought of how it would feel to lose a leg and never command a submarine again. He could not imagine a worse fate. "And you?"

"Much the same." Her grin was sly. Jules knew Camille's tastes were as vociferous as his own, but they'd never slept together. Perhaps someday, when she was not under his command.

Perhaps he should call Admiral Sauvageau. He did not want to lose her, but Camille would go far in her own command. If Jules was to be an admiral someday, it was time to start building support with his fellow officers.

Ten days into their fourteen-day leave, Alex stayed in his room at the Q while Nancy headed back to *Cape* with orders to prepare for an underway. She still didn't know if she'd be in command when the cruiser left port, but that wasn't Alex's problem. His crew needed time off, and Alex had, too, but now it was time to get back to the boat and go to work.

He started with the survivors' reports and VDR data from every sub Rochambeau sank. He'd gotten as far as *Los Angeles* before he had to stop, emotion welling up when he thought of Teresa O'Canas. A few minutes later, knuckles rapped against the door. Blinking, Alex rose and padded over to open it.

Bobby O'Kane stood in the doorway, looking awkward in a pair of board shorts and a worn *Lion King* T-shirt. "Wow," Bobby said. "You look weird in civilian clothes."

Alex chuckled, looking down at his sweat pants and old Norwich University shirt. "You should talk."

"That was kind of silly, wasn't it?" Bobby grinned. "I thought I should drop by and see how things were going, since we all kind of ran off the boat without looking back."

"Come on in." Stepping aside, Alex gestured Bobby into the room. "We needed to talk, anyway."

"That sounds ominous."

"Probably." Alex laughed and shut the door. "I was watching Rochambeau's greatest hits."

"Ouch." Bobby grimaced. "Need some company?"

"Wouldn't be the worst idea." Alex took a deep breath. "Bobby...I intended to talk to you about this after we got back on board, but..."

"Now we're getting to double ominous, Captain."

"You've got no idea," Alex replied. "How do you feel being the actual XO?"

Bobby's eyes went wide. "Like I'm too young, too junior, and the navy'll never go for it?"

"Funny you say that, because I got approval yesterday."

"What?" Bobby's jaw dropped. "You're kidding, right?"

"Take a seat and think about it." Alex flopped into a chair at the little round table; after a moment, Bobby lowered himself into the other. "It'll mean an immediate promotion to lieutenant commander, which should be at least six months early for you."

"More like a year."

Alex leaned forward, his elbows braced on the table. "You did a damned good job when we didn't have an XO, and the way you handled the mess with Steve was spot on. More importantly, you've got the trust of the crew—and after what just happened, they need that."

"You mean after Commander Harper." Bobby grimaced.

"Yeah." Alex wouldn't forgive himself for not noticing sooner, but *Bobby* had. And he needed an XO he could trust.

"I'm not sure I'm XO material, sir. I mean, did you see my fitness reports from Commander Peterson? He thought I was incompetent, and—"

"Screw that. I've seen you in action. I *asked* for you," Alex said. "You can say no if you want, and I won't think less of you, but don't think someone's trying to dump you on me, okay?"

Alex wasn't sure how to go about this if Bobby *did* say no; the navy didn't really work like that. He was also the idiot who'd put his own reputation on the line before asking Bobby what he thought. Had that been a mistake? Maybe calling Uncle Marco to underline the request he'd made to Banks had been too much.

"Captain, I knew you were crazy, but this kind of takes the cake." Bobby laughed, fidgeting.

Damn. Alex thought he'd broken that habit out of him.

He shrugged. "Sometimes crazy does the job."

"You really want me?" Bobby asked, and Alex nodded. "Okay, then. I guess."

"You guess?" Alex arched an eyebrow.

"If I say no, do I get out of going after Rochambeau?"

"No, but I have to send the new navigator to another boat." Alex had noticed the orders in message traffic that morning, but he was probably the only one on the boat reading messages. Everyone else wanted to have fun.

Bobby gaped. "What, I don't also have to be the navigator?"

"Nope."

"You should have said that in the first place." Bobby grinned. "Sign me up."

Alex laughed.

Chapter 34

Stolen Moments

Jaylen Banks considered himself a reasonable man; however, this situation was anything *but* reasonable.

"You told my chief of staff it was urgent," Vice Admiral Hamilton said, settling herself down in front of the camera on the other end of the line.

"Yes, ma'am." Banks chose a video conference with COMSUBFOR to show his sincerity; in his experience, people had a harder time saying no to someone when looking them in the eye.

Freddie Hamilton was a tall woman whose brown hair had yet to go gray. Today she wore glasses. Opinion in the sub fleet was split over whether she needed them. Most people thought she wore them to make herself look older, but some said she was blind as a bat. Having served under her when Hamilton commanded *Kentucky*, Banks still didn't know.

"Well?" Freddie crossed her arms. "Get to the point, Jay."

Banks took a deep breath. "You know I hate to go around the chain of command, ma'am, but..."

Freddie sighed. "What'd Marco do this time?"

"He's gone over my head to approve a new XO for *Bluefish*," Banks replied. "He ordered me to accept Captain Coleman's request that Lieutenant O'Kane be promoted and given the job."

"Is O'Kane up to it?"

"There are some...questions concerning his performance. His previous CO didn't think highly of him." Banks folded his hands.

"This being Wade Peterson?" she asked.

"Yes, ma'am." Banks resisted a smile. Unlike him, Wade never served under Hamilton, but he *had* been the chief of naval operations' aide. Friends in high places helped.

Freddie's eyes narrowed. "I know you and Wade are close, but his lack of success on *Bluefish* doesn't put him in the brightest light."

"Alex Coleman is a prima donna." Not sneering was hard. "He's a show boater who takes advantage of being in the right place at the right time and is going to ride that Medal of Honor until the day his reckless tactics get him sunk."

"He gets results."

"That's what Admiral Rodriquez said, ma'am, but I have to consider the welfare of all the crews in my squadron. O'Kane is immature, inexperienced, and—"

"*And* I'm not Coleman's biggest fan, either, but I'm not going to interfere in Admiral Rodriquez's bailiwick just because you don't like O'Kane. Or Coleman." Her brown eyes were ice cold. "Frankly, I'm surprised you've jumped the chain of command like this."

"I wouldn't unless I felt it important, ma'am." Banks took a deep breath. He *knew* O'Kane was a terrible choice—but maybe that was what *Bluefish* needed.

Banks trusted Wade Peterson. They'd served together twice, and he asked for Peterson's boat in his squadron after war broke out. No, Peterson's record wasn't the best, but his crew was a bunch of immature hooligans. Their conduct under Coleman only proved that.

Perhaps he needed to let them fail. Then Peterson would be exonerated, and he could remind Freddie that he'd been right all along.

"But I understand why you don't wish to overrule Admiral Rodriquez," he continued before she could answer. "I simply wanted to voice my objections."

"Consider them noted," Freddie replied and then changed the topic to ask about his wife and family.

The rest of the conversation was pleasant. Banks didn't bring up *Bluefish* again, didn't mention that he'd found a medically-cleared Wade Peterson a place on his staff. Eventually, he'd get Peterson another submarine. COs frequently departed without warning in wartime. There'd be another opportunity. He'd make sure of it.

Rain seemed appropriate for Alex's mood. Six days from getting underway—and one away from his crew reporting back on board—Alex still wasn't sure how he was to succeed against *Barracuda* where everyone else failed. And died. He shouldn't forget that awesome bit.

Except for one.

Nancy met him in the doorway of the base hospital. "I thought you two hated each other."

Alex shrugged. "It's more like a cordial loathing."

"*Cordial* doesn't describe her almost punching you at the O Club." Nancy rolled her eyes. "But far be it from me to stop you when you've got your mind made up. Just so long as we're still on for lunch afterward. You clear it with her doctors?"

"Yeah. It'd be stupid to have come all this way and be told no."

"Sometimes the stupid finds you." She smirked. "I remember that time our senior year, with the coffee creamer fire balls back on Goodyear Beach—"

Alex chuckled. "You don't need to remind me!"

Together, they walked down several long hallways, all decorated with soothing art in pastel colors. The smell, however, made Alex shiver. It was too clean, too *crisp*. Hospitals gave him the creeps. Submarines, even modern ones, acquired a personality over time; no scrubber could fully remove the scent of food, people, lube oil, and hydraulic oil mixed with the occasional spritz of diesel fuel and pizza. Something so sanitized felt suspicious.

Finally, they reached a door to a private room. "I'll wait here," Nancy said. "No use riling her up extra."

"Nice to be the one on the chopping block." Taking a deep breath, Alex knocked. A moment later, a familiar British accent answered:

"Enter!"

She couldn't put it down, could she? Shooting Nancy one last smile, Alex walked in to face Ursula North.

Ursula looked better than she had on *Bluefish*, though that wasn't saying much. She still seemed tiny lying against the white sheets of the hospital bed, like lying quietly somehow reduced her. Color had returned to her features, however, and her left arm was in a cast instead of a sling. The deep purple bruises had faded to a sickly green, and her eyes burned with intensity that made Alex shiver. Her left leg was still gone; Alex had ordered Chief Waskow to amputate it over Ursula's objections.

"You going to fucking *stare* at me, Captain, or are we going to talk about Rochambeau?" Ursula growled.

Alex blinked. "I...understand you were expecting me."

"No shit." She struggled to sit up and hissed in pain. "Believe you me, you don't want to talk about the *other* subject on my mind."

"Probably not, no." Alex shoved his hands in his pockets, glad Nancy wasn't there to scold him. Ursula scowled.

"God, you *are* my polar opposite, aren't you? How the fuck did a dodgy git like you end up as our best hope?"

Alex wasn't going to ask what a "dodgy git" was. He shrugged, trying not to dwell on the surge of terror her words induced. "Guess I was in the right place at the right time."

She rolled her eyes. "Well, you're sure talented at making *my* life miserable. May you wear off on him."

"I was hoping for a bit more advice than that," Alex replied.

"Advice? A sub CO who wants to swallow his pride and ask for help?" Ursula's bark of laughter turned into a cough. "I'll be damned."

Alex bristled. "I don't give a fuck about pride. I want to bring my crew home alive."

"Yes." Suddenly, she sobered, looking away. "I imagine you do."

"I—" Shit, he'd gone and been an ass, hadn't he? Alex gulped. "Sorry."

"Don't. If I'd been a hair less overconfident, I might've done the same." Ursula's eyes focused on some horizon Alex couldn't see. "The arrogant shit is *sneaky*, and every time you think you've got him, he slips away." She gestured with her good arm. "Sit down."

"I remember what you did with *Illinois*," Alex said. He needed a deep breath to keep his voice level. "You laid in wait and let Rochambeau sink her. Did you not have a shot yet, or were you waiting for a better one?"

"I had a shit shot, and with him, you only get one," she replied. "It would have been better had you and that whale of yours not stumbled in." Ursula's glare held little heat; were her meds that good? "You were setting up on both of us, weren't you? Ballsy little nobody, ready to take on the two best in the world."

Alex flushed. "I didn't know who either of you were. If I had, I'd have pissed myself."

"Bullshit. I saw the logs from Convoy 57."

Wasn't that fucking embarrassing? Nah, it had probably been a hate-watch.

"You won't get a second shot against him," Ursula repeated. "He's an expert at making you think he's somewhere he's not and then killing you while you're looking the wrong way."

"That's why you tried to make him come to you."

"Aye. 'Till I was a fucking pillock and let him sucker me into thinking he was at that fucking base. Bastard got underway before I arrived." Pale faced, she leaned back against the pillows, focusing on the ceiling for several seconds before continuing. "If you chase him, you die. That's what your Abercrombie never understood. Or the others."

"Pat Abercrombie came out of hiding to kill an *Akula*, yeah." Alex grimaced. "She knew she was wrong but must've felt she had to."

"Watched her logs, did you?"

"Yeah."

The silence that followed was surprisingly companionable. They'd never *like* each other—Alex wasn't sure he could stick around much longer before someone lost their temper—but understanding flitted between them.

"You've got to be a cold-blooded bastard to do it," she said, turning to look Alex in the eye. "I know I am. Are you?"

"I think I have to be," he whispered.

Alex didn't like the idea. He'd joined the navy to serve his country and to *protect* people, not to stand by and watch them die. But Rochambeau had sunk seven Alliance submarines, three frigates, and one carrier in just the first four months of this year. Hell, he'd sank two subs and three frigates in *April*, and the month wasn't over yet. That put the Frenchman at almost sixty warships sunk since the war started. Thousands of sailors who lost their lives because of him.

"Now you're getting it." Her smile held no humor. "You know what you have to do."

"Yeah."

Alex didn't thank her. This wasn't the kind of thing you thanked someone for. Instead, he wished her a speedy recovery and left, wanting to dive into Nancy's arms. Would his wife understand? She'd seen combat and watched friends die, but the idea of potentially sacrificing others was anathema to her, too.

They went to lunch together, and he steered the subject away from Rochambeau and the war. He didn't like thinking he might die, but if he was going to, Alex wasn't going to spend his last days talking about his killer.

By some miracle, the caretaker crew didn't make a mess of their beautiful submarine. Not that Bobby wasn't sure they'd find something, probably hidden under a toilet in the forward head or something. Or stuck to an angle iron in an out-of-the-way place. The nasty surprises were never where someone would look for them, and they hadn't had much time to look, anyway. The crew had only been back on board since zero-seven hundred that morning.

Rose's bony elbow dug into his side. "Quit fidgeting."

"I *can't*. What if this is all some sort of bad dream? What if we wake up and Peterson is back, or some giant shark has—"

"You're giving me a migraine, Bobby," Lou cut in from his other side. *Bluefish's* engineer grinned. "Or should I call you 'sir'? You're about to be the real XO."

"That's going to be so weird." Bobby shook his head. He still felt numb. Was it all some cosmic joke? Captain Coleman wasn't mean enough to do something like that.

Yet here they were, standing on the mess decks waiting for *his* promotion to lieutenant commander. Becoming XO without finishing his department head tour and without attending the senior officers' course at the sub school was unheard of. The world had gone mad.

"You think it's going to be weird? I'm the one getting a new roommate," Lou replied.

Rose snickered. "Make sure you change the mattress before moving into your new stateroom, *XO.*"

"Oh. Ew. Gross." Bobby gagged, earning himself a few strange looks from the assembled crew.

"You know, I hear disinfectant isn't—" Rose started, only to be cut off by Master Chief Baker.

"Attention on deck!"

Bobby popped to attention as Alex walked in, waving a hand. "At ease, folks." Then Alex's eyes found Bobby. "Except you, XO. Get your ass up here."

Several people snickered. Bobby knew rumors floated around the boat about his pending elevation, but he hadn't told anyone other than Rose and Lou. Peeking a look at the rest of the crew revealed smiles—were they *happy* he was becoming the XO? Must've just been relief for the devil they already knew.

Bobby stepped forward, trying and failing not to smile. He felt like a giant goof, minus big floppy ears and a tail.

"All right," Alex said. Was it Bobby's imagination, or was the captain fidgeting, too? What did he have to be nervous about? "As I'm sure you've all noticed, Lieutenant Commander Harper is no longer with us. And since it's a bit too late to add a new member to the band, today Lieutenant O'Kane becomes Lieutenant Commander O'Kane, our new XO."

Someone started the applause; Bobby thought maybe Lou. He still felt like he was in the Twilight Zone. When would the other shoe drop? *Bluefish* wasn't a place where good changes happened.

Except Alex unpinned the silver lieutenant bars from Bobby's collar. Holy cow, those were a lieutenant commander's gold oak leaves. Bobby always thought that the navy had its precious metals backward, since gold ranks fell under the silver ones (a full commander got silver oak leaves). But here he was, moving up the ladder. Peterson would've had a fit.

"You can sign the paperwork later." Alex grinned.

"Thanks, Captain." Bobby couldn't verbalize everything he wanted to thank Alex for—thank you for not being an asshole, thank you for trusting him, thank you for not running *Bluefish* into the ground—but he thought Alex understood.

Alex patted his shoulder. "You've earned it."

His face heated. "I—well, I guess?" Bobby said. "Can I ask you a favor?"

"Sure."

"Never use that band joke again. It wasn't as good as you think it was."

Alex laughed—and so did the everyone else, because dang it, Bobby said that louder than he'd meant to.

"I'll keep that in mind." Alex turned to the rest of the crew, and Bobby faced them, too. "Since we're short a navigator, young Mister Shorn will be the acting Nav until the new guy reports next week. No more dual hats for the XO."

"But what if I like wearing two hats?" Bobby asked before common sense could rear its fair head.

Alex eyed him archly. "I can always change my mind. Unless you mean actual hats."

Bobby grinned. "I'm partial to Mickey Mouse ears."

The crew laughed again until Alex waved for silence. "So this was the good news. The *other* news is that we're being sent after Rochambeau."

The compartment fell silent. A shiver ripped down Bobby's spine. But he shouldn't be surprised, not after being sent to Île Amsterdam. Particularly since Ursula North hadn't managed to do the job.

Six months ago, *Bluefish* had dodged Convoy 57 and they all felt secretly glad despite the shame. Peterson probably would've gotten them sunk in the first five minutes of that battle. Now, they were the go-to sub sent to kill the best submariner in the world.

Had the temperature on the mess decks dropped, or was that just him?

Alex skipped lunch and headed over to the SUBRON 29 headquarters near pier seven. The weather was nice, so he walked. Was he feeling sentimental? He'd lost two good friends to Rochambeau and a dozen acquaintances. Wouldn't a rational person want revenge? No, a rational person should be terrified.

He wasn't. Focused, yes. Resigned, a little. But not completely terrified. Perhaps he'd feel fear in the moment. Convoy 57 had been full of sheer terror, and his first action on *Bluefish* had been almost as bad when he'd discovered he couldn't even shoot back. Somehow, however, his talk with Ursula

North helped. Rochambeau was good. Probably better than Alex. But he wasn't unbeatable.

You just couldn't afford to play by his rules.

Entering the squadron headquarters aroused the same odd mixture of feelings in him that it always did. The building looked like a World War II relic assembled of spare parts on the outside, and the staff cubicles were vintage, 1990s crap that no self-respecting office would use, but the closer one got to Banks's palatial offices, the nicer the furnishings got. Wood floors, nice carpets, new paintings on the walls...Banks went for the whole nine yards when decorating areas *he* looked at. The quarterdeck was shined up and inspection ready, too.

Not that Alex expected a pedant like Banks to accept any less from his team. Fortunately, the petty officer on watch knew him, so the young lady just snapped to attention, let Alex sign in, and waved him through. From there, finding his destination was easy.

Uncle Marco had claimed a corner belonging to some member of Banks' staff. The desk looked like it had seen better days, but it had stickers from Australian craft breweries decorating the upper drawers, so at least it had a little character beyond peeling paint and a mismatched color scheme.

Rodriquez was due to depart for Pearl Harbor in the morning, so Alex had one chance to pin him down. Technically, he should talk to his boss. But Banks would hem and haw, and Alex needed a decision. So he wandered up to that stolen cubicle.

"You have a minute, Admiral?"

"You get bolder by the fucking day, don't you?" Rodriquez looked up and grinned. "Pull up a shitty chair."

Alex grabbed one that was puke green with a torn seat. But it had four legs—two of the others didn't.

"Spit it out, son. I've got a telcon in twenty minutes with Freddie Hamilton, and she's a copper-plated bitch when I'm late," Rodriquez said. "For some reason, she's got you in a category with the likes of Scott Waddle and fucking hates you."

Alex blanched. "I've never surfaced a boat under a fishing vessel, thanks."

"You know that. I know that. Freddie's a mite unreasonable about you." Rodriquez snorted. "Give her time. For now, just tell me what you need."

"I need bait," Alex replied. "Something high value enough that Rochambeau can't resist it. I want to force him to come to me."

"You want to play Abercrombie's game?"

"Yeah, but I'm going to see it through." Alex met the admiral's eyes. "Pat was right, and so was Ursula North. You can't chase Rochambeau. He'll kill you every time."

Rodriquez's eyes narrowed. "You've got to have ice water in your veins to pull that off, Captain."

"I don't think I have a choice." Alex shrugged, surprised by his own calm. "His sonar suite is better than ours, and his boat is quieter."

"So you want to dangle another carrier in front of the bastard? NAVAIR will *kill* me if I suggest it, and he's a four star."

"Not a carrier, sir. Rochambeau's already sank two of those. He'll only go for something novel."

Rodriquez sat back and crossed his arms. "You seem to have crept inside his fucking head, so what do you have in mind?"

"It depends on what you'll let me risk. The bigger, the better." Alex might as well go for broke. He was no Ursula North; he wouldn't get a second chance at Rochambeau. He took a deep breath. "Whatever happened to that long overdue shipment of torpedoes?"

"You are sky-fucking-high if you think I'll agree to that."

Bingo. "I take it the shipment's on the way?"

"Fuck your smartness. Yes." Rodriquez shook his head. "You're not even dumb enough to promise to save it, are you?"

"I don't make promises I can't keep, Admiral."

"Shit, son, you pull this off and you'll be the first captain who gets to call me by my first name."

That sent a weird thrill through Alex. He didn't want to die, and he *did* want to be the best, but holy shit, why him? How the fuck had he risen to the top so fast?

"Is that a yes?" he asked.

Rodriquez heaved a sigh. “You go shadow the damned weapons carrier. I’ll see what I can’t do about leaking its position.”

A bull kicked him in the stomach; Alex thought he wheezed aloud.

“You didn’t think I’d agree, did you?” Rodriquez laughed.

“I had my doubts.” Alex swallowed. “I’ll try not to let him sink the thing, sir.”

“You’d better. If not, I’m taking the torpedoes out of your pay.”

How had Bobby amassed so much *stuff*? Submarine staterooms were small. Yet he had twenty-seven pair of socks, nineteen undershirts, eight pairs of board shorts—two of which he hadn’t seen in at least a year—four hardback self-help books, and three bags full of other stuff. And his uniforms. He shouldn’t forget those.

He hadn’t brought friends to *Bluefish*—they wouldn’t have fit in the tiny drawers of a department head’s stateroom. They couldn’t even hide under a desk, since both “desks” in his and Lou’s room were just little shelves that folded down enough for a laptop. The racks weren’t big enough for two, either, despite the shenanigans some junior sailors tried. But Bobby had found one of his best friends on board in Lou and been reunited with Rose. Their presence made even Peterson mostly bearable. How would things change now that he was the XO?

“Earth to Bobby.” Rose poked him with *Building your Brain Trust* by Emilia Desai.

“Huh?” Bobby looked up from the single green sock he held. Why did he have a green sock? He couldn’t wear them in uniform and wouldn’t wear them with real clothes. He gestured with the sock. “Lou, is this yours?”

Lou’s nose wrinkled. “I am truly worried about the state of our relationship if you can see me in green socks.”

"Great. Now we have the Mystery of the Green Sock. I wonder—"

"Quit writing new *Cecilia Serra* books and help me fold this monstrosity you call a comforter," Rose cut in.

"Your character flaw of not liking the Cowboys does not make my comforter a monstrosity." Bobby snorted. "But I'll help because I'm a gentleman."

Rose laughed. "You'll help because it's your fucking comforter." She moaned, flopping against the locker. "I still don't know how you convinced the captain to pick a clown as our new XO. We're all going to die."

"I didn't ask him. I swear." It was still a mystery to Bobby. Bobby could do the job, sure, but there had to be some real XO who wanted to come to *Bluefish*! They weren't even the dregs of the navy these days.

"Sure you didn't." She shoved the comforter in his face, and they spent several minutes folding it.

"Hey, where'd you get these old ranks?" Lou asked, gesturing at the golden oak leaves on Bobby's collar.

"Old?"

"Yeah, they're not new. They're worn on the edges." Lou frowned. "Someone give them to you?"

Bobby blinked, turning the question over in his mind. He hadn't asked where the ranks the captain pinned on him came from; the boat always bought new one for people when they got promoted. "I guess?"

"Are you blushing because someone pinched your ass, or did the captain give you his old ranks?" Rose asked.

"I...think he did." Bobby's face was on fire.

Rose cracked something about him looking like a blowfish, but Bobby felt...odd. Honored, but odd. The captain gave *him*—Peterson's favorite punching bag!—his old ranks. Maybe he was doing okay. Okay? Better than okay. He'd made lieutenant commander a year early. Even in wartime, that was quick. None of his classmates had put that rank on yet. Their first shot was the selection board three months away. Wow.

So much for being less than halfway competent.

"We're *not* getting drunk tonight," Harri told Rene and Wally while they waited for some last-minute supplies to be loaded on the submarine. All three were in civilian clothes and ready to go. Their other usual liberty buddies, Max and Andrea, were on duty, so that left the three of them to go out for one last drink. "We're not going to that shitty restaurant, either."

"C'mon, it's tradition." Rene grinned. "We had a great patrol after that."

"*And* we had to fork out thousands to the Mediterranean," Wally said. "I'm with Harri."

"I don't know why you two aren't good with owing a few thousand bucks if it means we survived Rochambeau." Rene spread his arms. "Clearly, we're meant to take one for the team."

"God, could you be any more pathetic?" Harri rolled eyes. "Two to one: no drunken sailors tonight. I'd rather not be hungover for whatever comes."

"C'mon, we're not going to run into Rochambeau when we get underway tomorrow," Rene said.

"Probably not," Harri conceded. "But I think I've had enough hangovers for a while."

Her last hard drinking had been in the O Club with the old XO. Nothing happened, but had that made him think she was interested? Harri scowled. Screw Steve Harper.

Rene sighed. "So says the wardroom drinking champ. You're disappointing, Harri."

"Learn to live with it." She smiled sweetly.

"I'm wounded! Wally, back me up here. Harri needs to keep her crown, only so we can be—"

"Hey, Harri, you got a minute?" a new voice interjected.

Harri turned to face Bobby— Crap, no, he was the XO now. For real. Bobby had always been the most approachable department head, with Lou buried in engineering and Rose someone easy to emulate but difficult to relax with.

He'd earned everyone's trust, which was why Harri found him when everything went to pot.

"Yes, sir?" she said, heading over to join him on the other side of the quarterdeck.

"You guys heading out?" he asked.

"Yeah, but you don't have to worry about us being drunk and stupid this time. I promise." Harri knew her smile was sheepish, but they *had* made quite a mess of the Mediterranean that time.

Bobby smiled crookedly. "Actually, I just wanted to see how you're doing."

Harri swallowed. Would this ever go away? "I'm okay, sir."

"You sure?"

"Yeah." Harri took a deep breath; she didn't like thinking about what happened. She *hadn't* been assaulted. *Harri* left Steve bruised, not the other way around. "Really, I'm fine. My mom's a psychologist, anyway, so she wouldn't let me be stupid."

"I'll take your word for it." Bobby fidgeted. "I don't want to push, just wanted to make sure you're okay."

"Thanks, Nav—XO. Sorry." Harri laughed. "That's going to take some getting used to."

"Yeah, for me, too." He grinned. "Head out and have some fun. Just please don't make me have to write a report on you guys, okay?"

"No promises, sir." She grinned back and headed off, grabbing Rene and Wally on the way. Just because they weren't planning on being stupid didn't mean she shouldn't make Bobby fret. He was the XO now, and worrying was his job.

Sunrise crept later in Australia's April, which meant *Bluefish* was scheduled to get underway in the dark. Nancy got up before four to be there, glad that no one on *Cape* questioned why she needed a boat to shore before dawn. She hated that Alex wouldn't sleep off the boat the morning before an underway, but she understood...and she still wanted to say goodbye.

They didn't kiss. First, they were both in uniform, and second, a trivial display of affection seemed unworthy of the moment. They just stood side by side, their shoulders brushing against one another. "Everything on track?" Nancy asked.

"Yeah." Alex's voice sounded heavy. Was he tired, or as terrified as she was? "Line handlers should be here in twenty minutes."

Nancy swallowed. "Great."

"You sound like you're excited for your own funeral," Alex replied.

"Can you blame me?" Not snapping was hard. Nancy rubbed her hand over her face. "I'm proud of you, Alex, and I *won't* be the hypocrite who tells you not to go. But still wish they'd picked someone else."

"They did." His quiet tone reminded her of how many friends they'd both lost, particularly to Rochambeau.

She remained silent for a long moment. "You think you can get him?"

"I've got a good crew and a good plan."

Fingers touched hers; Nancy didn't look down, just squeezed his hand in her own. "I hope that'll be enough," she whispered.

"If it isn't—" Alex's voice caught.

"I know," she said.

They'd said goodbye before, and Nancy would send him a dozen emails until she knew what happened one way or another. Yet this was different. Nancy didn't want it to be, but it was.

"Is there a problem, Captain?" a nasal voice asked from behind them.

Nancy turned to see a tall commodore walking toward them. He towered over her, and she was two inches taller than Alex, who looked up at Banks with ill-concealed impatience.

"No, sir," he replied, returning the salute Banks seemed annoyed to give. "Just taking a few moments before we get underway."

"I see." Banks pursed his lips. "I came by to make sure you don't plan on any...stunts after this."

"Stunts?" Alex sounded innocent.

Banks glared. "No *broomsticks* this time, Captain."

Nancy resisted the urge to laugh. She knew enough about submarine history and traditions to know that a broomstick stood for a clean sweep. She also knew that her attention-fearing husband wouldn't ever tie one to his boat's periscope unless they'd done something extraordinary—or he thought his crew needed it.

"Admiral Rodriquez may enjoy that kind of hotdogging, but *I* do not," Banks continued. "Is that clear?"

"You can be assured I understand your feelings on the matter, sir," Alex replied. Nancy managed not to giggle at the careful answer.

"Hm." Banks frowned. "Good luck."

"Thank you." Alex's eyebrows shot up when Banks offered him a hand to shake but took it. "I hope we'll see you soon, Commodore."

"I'm sure you will." Banks sounded resigned.

The commodore glared at *Bluefish* for another few minutes before stalking back down the pier toward a waiting car.

"He's a friendly sort, isn't he?" Nancy asked. "Nice of him to introduce himself."

Alex chuckled. "I've come to the conclusion that he likes things 'just so' and can't handle it when they aren't."

"Can't handle you, you mean." Nancy shook her head fondly. "You're too unorthodox for him."

Alex grinned. "Didn't I just say that?"

Eventually, Nancy found herself standing on the pier as a tug eased *Bluefish* out to sea. By the time she left, Alex was reduced to a dark silhouette against *Bluefish's* darker outline. She thought about going to a church to pray, but Nancy hadn't done that since college. Perhaps she'd call their old college chaplain instead. He wasn't Catholic, but he'd been there for Nancy when she'd been pregnant, unmarried, and terrified of her parents' reaction.

She hadn't expected to feel like that again. Not as an adult with a successful naval career, good marriage, and a life that made her happy. Even watching *Lexington* sink hadn't filled her with such helplessness.

Nancy shivered and walked away.

Chapter 35

Wait for It

25 April 2040, USS **Bluefish,** *the Southern Indian Ocean*

"Motor Vessel *Titan Uranus*." Bobby only managed to keep a straight face by pressing his lips together as tightly as he could, but he could feel his chest vibrating with the effort. "Seriously."

"Someone at Titan Limited has a sense of humor." Alex's eyes danced. "Three times, apparently."

"There's been *other* ships with that name?" Harri smothered a giggle further down the wardroom table. "You've got to be kidding. Is English their first language?"

"Probably not." Alex shrugged, but his seriousness didn't keep everyone else from snickering.

Bluefish's officers gathered in the wardroom two days after they got underway. By then, *Bluefish* was over two thousand miles from Perth and churning toward a rendezvous point in the central Indian Ocean. Everyone knew they'd been sent after Rochambeau, but what they were going to do beyond flail in the dark was up to the captain. At least Alex wasn't Peterson. Peterson hoarded secrets like ice cream.

Every officer not on watch was there. Lou had even crawled out of his black hole in engineering to take the watch in control so everyone who would be in a tactical position against Rochambeau could come. Lou, of course, had laughed and pointed out that they were in real trouble if the engineer needed to be tactically engaged. Rose would brief him later, anyway.

"Joking aside," Alex continued, "MV *Titan Uranus*"—Bobby snickered—"carries over two thousand Mark 84 ASV torpedoes, inbound to Perth. The plan is for some intel bubba or another to leak that information to the French. Our hope is that Rochambeau goes after the ship with the truly unfortunate name."

"You think he will, Captain?" Bobby asked. It was time to put his XO pants back on. "It seems like we're betting on him and not someone else."

Alex shrugged. "That's a risk we have to take. My read on Rochambeau's character is that he wants to strike the big, flashy blows. That means he'll want to do it himself."

"Assuming he's in position." Rose chewed her lip. "Do we know where he went after Île Amsterdam was destroyed?"

"No clue." Rene was *Bluefish's* collateral duty intelligence officer, and he shrugged. "The French have little torpedo depots squirreled away on every island they own in the Indian Ocean, and there are a lot of little islands."

"Half of which they've stolen." Rose scowled. "And that doesn't even count the underwater stations."

"Trying to dock a submarine with an underwater station is like a cat trying to mate with an elephant in the dark." Alex shook his head. "Loading torpedoes that way would be worse."

"Ew. Great mental image, Captain." Bobby made a face. "I need some brain bleach."

Everyone chuckled. Bobby enjoyed playing class clown, but that wasn't why he wanted to insert levity into the conversation. The atmosphere on *Bluefish* had been tense since they got underway. Everyone knew they'd been sent out to do something dozens of boats failed to do...and they might be next.

"Ask Suppo for some when she gets off watch," Alex replied, grinning. Brigette Sonnen was with Lou in control.

Bobby mimed taking a note on his tablet. "I'll do that, sir."

"*Anyway*," Alex said without any actual rancor, "let's assume Rochambeau finds *Titan Uranus*. As far as the ship's master knows, their cargo is a secret. We're not going to change that."

"We're not warning them?" Harri asked.

"No. We don't want them to do anything that might give our presence away," Alex replied. "Any deviation in their normal steaming procedures—or whatever passes for normal during war for a merchie—might be noticed. We're going to lurk nearby and wait."

"Just wait?" Rose almost looked offended. "Nothing else?"

"Not another thing. No matter what we hear or see." Alex's eyes swept around the table, all mirth gone. Bobby had seen this side of his captain before, but only in combat. Mouths clicked shut. Alex continued: "We can't out-quiet Rochambeau. We can't hunt him. He will hear us—and sink us—if we do. We have to outsmart him."

"You want to make him come to us," Bobby said.

"Yeah. *Titan Uranus* is the bait. We wait, and when he comes to sink her, we sink him."

"What if he shoots a torpedo at the merchant before we have a solution on him?" Bobby was afraid he knew the answer, but he needed to hear it out loud.

Particularly since his captain was the same man who refused to needlessly kill *enemy* merchant sailors. *Titan Uranus* was flagged out of Panama, a neutral country.

"We let him shoot." Alex stayed silent for a long moment, and Bobby felt those words sink in. "Make no mistake, ladies and gentlemen. Saving *Titan Uranus* is a bonus. Sinking Rochambeau is the mission."

Bobby swallowed and then said what everyone else was thinking: "We're going to be in a world of hurt if all those torpedoes go to the bottom, Captain."

"I know." Alex sighed. "But it's going to hurt more if Rochambeau can keep sinking our subs. Frequently with full torpedo rooms."

No one could argue that. Bobby'd lost friends to Rochambeau, too. He wasn't Steve, who had a hard on for killing the Frenchman, but he'd attended too many memorials. Someone had to take *Barracuda* out, and *Bluefish* was up to bat.

All the same, maybe Bobby should send his brother a farewell email to forward to their parents in case they didn't come back. Derek had a secret clearance and could be trusted to keep his mouth shut, and Bobby didn't want Mom and Dad always wondering. His family had enough rotten traditions already.

Rose stopped right before walking into the torpedo room. Eavesdropping was rude, but it was a good way to catch gossip since sailors didn't like lordly lieutenants knowing what they talked about in private. Usually, Rose was more than happy to let them keep secrets, particularly concerning who slept with who. She didn't *want* to know that shit, but now there was a different buzz around the boat.

"You know he sank *California*, too," Petty Officer Luke Gemba told Petty Officer Flora Walkman. Walkman was a sonar tech and Gemba a machinist's mate (torpedoes). But Rose hadn't expected the pair to hang out. Walkman was as high speed as Gemba was trouble. Oh, Gemba wasn't in Wilson's league, but he was still Rose's favorite problem child.

"No one's proved that," Walkman replied, scoffing.

"Yeah, but no one can prove why she went down, either. She just *disappeared*," Gemba said. "You can't tell me that wasn't Rochambeau."

"You can't tell me it was, either." Walkman sounded like she'd rolled her eyes.

"*North Dakota, Illinois, Albacore, Pacu, Moray, Skate, Razorback, Flasher, Sea Tiger,* and *Perch* can. Did I miss any?"

Walkman sighed. "Probably a dozen Brits. I think he sank more Aussies, too. And was there a Canadian? Plus *Razorback.*"

"It's almost impossible to remember," Gemba growled. "The guy sank an entire convoy single-handedly. What choice do we have?"

"There's no use bitching unless you're going to shoot yourself out a torpedo tube and swim home," Walkman shot back.

"Hey, I'm just being a realist here, Flora." Was the troublemaker's voice shaking? Rose couldn't be sure if he was scared or being a jerk. Maybe both.

"At least we don't have Needledickerson on board," Walkman replied. "He would've been too busy crying about ice cream or paint on someone's coveralls to kill Rochambeau."

Needledickerson? Rose almost laughed. That had to be Peterson. She'd remember that one. But she also needed to step in before her people started disparaging a senior officer. Despise Peterson though she did, this kind of shit was bad for discipline.

So was Gemba's attitude. Rose squared her shoulders and ducked through the hatch into the torpedo room.

"It would also be good for you two slackers to remember that Captain Coleman sank an entire Indian task group by himself," she said. Rose threw a pointed look at both sailors, who were leaning against one of the torpedo racks instead of cleaning it. "I think that if anyone's going to take out Rochambeau, it'll be him."

She was impressed by the captain's plan. Horrified, too. It took some serious balls to put the long-awaited shipment of torpedoes in the line of fire. How *had* the captain talked Commodore Banks around?

"Weps!" Walkman had the grace to look embarrassed. Gemba straightened slowly.

"Glad you recognized me." Rose crossed her arms. "You two hiding in here to escape work or because you want to bone each other?"

"No!" At least they both looked horrified. Even Gemba was red. "We're just here to talk. Nothin' else."

"Right. I'll believe that when I see it." Rose gestured at the hatch. "Do I have to yell at you, or you two going to get back to work?"

Both vanished like magic, leaving Rose alone in her torpedo room. *Bluefish* had twenty-one torps, not a full load, but hopefully enough to do the job. *Barracuda's* torpedoes were faster—ungodly fast, if reports were right—but the Mark 84 ASVs were pretty good.

Thank God she'd talked the weapons depot out of loading ADCAPS. The Mark 48 ADCAP went out of service in 2008, but the weapons shortage was getting bad. Torpedoes had expiration dates; no way was Rose loading ADCAPS. Supposedly, they'd been retrofitted and would explode on time, but Rose wasn't buying. Even the Mark 48 CBASS was better, and *those* torps were old news! She'd read more than one report of "refurbished" Mark 48s cooking off inside a torpedo tube. Rumor even said a hot run sunk *California*, not Rochambeau. Not that anyone could prove it.

Rose ran a hand over the nearest torpedo, studying its sleek green metal. Only warshots were green. Yellow dummy torpedoes were everywhere before the war, but not now. Sometimes, Rose couldn't remember being in a peacetime navy. Thinking of that made her feel stupid; she'd been in the navy for nine years, and the war started just two years ago. Yet somehow that seemed a different lifetime.

"Don't you fucking fail," she told the closest torpedo and then headed out. She needed to put a bug in Harri's ear in case Walkman was screwing Gemba. No one wanted their top sailor in bed with a dunce.

26 April 2040, Saint Dennis

Saint Dennis had a nice casino, and Jules always enjoyed poker. So far, he was two thousand Euros up, enough that the casino's security looked a little askance when he entered the building. Not that he stopped. His sixth hand put him another five hundred Euros above his original budget, and the seventh looked even sweeter, with two aces and a king dealt to him right way. Unfortunately, his phone rang to recall him to *Barracuda* before he could start bidding. Sighing, he collected his wins and departed. It was probably for the best. *Barracuda* would get underway at midnight, and he had work to do.

Much to his surprise, Commander Camille Dubois waited for him on the quarterdeck. Camille had left detached from *Barracuda* three days earlier, sent to temporary duty while Admiral Sauvageau found a submarine for her to command. Rumor said she'd receive a brand-new *Requin*, one of the last built before France's next class of attack submarines came on line. A variant of the *Requins* would be built for India, but France was ready to transition to a newer, quieter, and faster submarine.

Jules did not want to leave *Barracuda*, but he had seen the design. The idea was tempting.

Not nearly as much as Camille's proposal that he hunt this American torpedo carrier, however. As a rule, Jules did not trust the intelligence community, yet the idea was still tempting. Camille was a good example of how they always thought themselves clever. His previous second-in-command was a smart woman, but her tendency to over-complicate things grated on his nerves.

"It is good information, Jules." Camille looked him in the eye with boldness she would not have displayed while under his command.

"*Oui*, like the information that sent the Indians after the Fogsborne team on Convoy 57." Jules scowled. "*Tres bien*."

"That intelligence was correct. It is not our fault that the Indians ran into an unstoppable force."

"Our?" Jules said. "My dear, you are wasted in intelligence."

Camille laughed. "I must do something while I wait for a submarine."

"Must it annoy me so much?" Jules chuckled. He did not regret orchestrating Camille's sudden departure from *Barracuda.* It was high time she got her own command. He would miss her, but she was his third executive officer. The other two already moved onto successful command, and he intended for her to be no different.

"But of course, *Capitain*." Her smile was razor-sharp. "The information is good. If you wish to cripple our enemies, you know how."

"The loss of two thousand torpedoes would not *cripple* them, Camille. Not with the American industrial complex behind the Alliance." Jules sighed, shaking his head. "I have told Admiral Sauvageau that we must take the war to them instead of merely defending our new territories, but she is hesitant."

"No one wishes to strike the first blow on the mainland of a former ally," she replied. "Not when Britain is so close to France and so ready to strike back."

"Nothing ventured, nothing gained." He shrugged. "This is not our department."

Alas. The Freedom Union was winning the war by any objective measure: more enemy ships sunk, more territory—mainly underwater stations, but also strategic islands such as Sri Lanka and the Maldives—taken, and more allies made. Yet there remained a stalemate of sorts. The Alliance could not take back that which the Union had taken, but nor could the Union drive them out of the Indian Ocean.

Things were worse in the north, where the Royal Navy doggedly took the fight to the Russians in their own backyard, preventing the bulk of the Russian Navy from joining the southern fight. No one wanted to resort to World War II's fire bombings or massive amphibious assaults; the world would not stand for such atrocities. Nor would the world accept the use of nuclear weapons. So how to break the paradigm?

Perhaps removing American torpedoes from the equation *would* be a good start.

"Will you do it?" Camille asked.

"*Bien sûr.*" Jules's smiled lazily. He had a reputation to live up to. "I cannot allow someone else to steal such glory, can I?"

Camille chuckled. "This is more like the Jules Rochambeau I know."

"But first I will taunt someone else into trying to kill me." He was already composing tweets in his mind. "I must finish my trifecta."

"I am sorry I will not be there for that." Camille sighed. "Are you certain that Solenne is ready?"

"*Oui*. You know she is." Jules waved a hand. Solenne Chappelle spent a year on board *Barracuda* already as Jules' operations officer. She was competent, smart, and ready to be Jules' next protégé.

"*Bonne chance*, then," Camille said, offering him a hand to shake.

Jules shook it, returned her salute, and watched his former second-in-command leave *Barracuda* forever. He turned to Solenne, who approached silently.

"Prepare for our underway," he ordered. "We have Americans to hunt."

Solenne smiled.

Jules had a tweet to write. Not about the weapons carrier—what was it called? *Titan Uranus*. Jules would not give the Americans opportunity to protect such a prize. He was a gambler, not a fool. But he would tweak Alexander Coleman's nose a little. That would be fun.

"Shit," Alex whispered. "Confirm that."

"Emissions match *Burrfish* across the board, Captain," STS2 Walkman reported from sonar. "Range twenty-eight hundred yards. She's trailing *Titan Uranus* at about a mile."

"Conn, aye." Alex released the talk switch and slumped against the plot table. Another submarine *Titan Uranus*' vicinity was the last thing he needed. Risking the weapons carrier was one thing. Another American sub could shoot back.

"Isn't *Burrfish* homeported in Groton?" Bobby asked from his left.

"Is she?" Alex cocked his head. He hadn't been stationed in Groton since *Kansas*, a lifetime ago.

"Yep." Harri looked up from the tablet she'd searched. "Just finished workups in January, no word on her deployment. Probably so new she squeaks."

Alex chuckled. *Burrfish* was a *Cero-I*, the generation after *Bluefish*. The newer boats were quieter, faster, and had a slightly smaller crew. Incremental improvements supposedly made a much better submarine, but he'd never set foot in one. And *Burrfish* wasn't supposed to be here.

"You think he's just hanging around hoping someone will try to shoot *Titan Uranus*?" Bobby asked.

"Probably. SUBFOR might've sent her down as an escort without telling anyone." Alex chewed his glasses. "Would've been nice to know that."

"No kidding." Bobby glanced around control. *Bluefish* hadn't set battle stations. So far, they'd simply waited along *Titan Uranus'* projected track until the giant merchant ship arrived, unexpected escort in tow. "What do you want to do, sir?"

Alex sighed. "Let's stick to the plan. *Titan Uranus* is still miles out, so we'll go shallow to check the mail. Maybe Uncle Marco's sent something useful."

"That'd be great." Bobby combed a hand through his hair. "Trying to coordinate with a crew we've never met is going to be like trying to get Batman and the Hulk to work together."

"Whatever that meant, I agree it won't be fun." Alex rarely tried to keep up with Bobby's pop culture references. "Officer of the Deck, proceed to station and then to periscope depth."

"OOD aye," Harri replied. Alex didn't watch her work. Harri didn't need supervision.

He didn't like *Burrfish's* presence, but what did it change? Only Alex's comfort level. He was prepared to sacrifice *Titan Uranus* if need be. Could Alex do the same for another American sub? They'd signed on to fight the same war he had, didn't they? Risks were part of the game.

He hated Ursula North for letting *Illinois* die.

Fuck.

Maybe *Burrfish* would go away. Coincidences happened, even in war.

A few minutes' unpleasant rumination later, *Bluefish* reached periscope depth. The miracles of modern technology meant they only needed to stream a slender communications wire to download gigs and gigs of emails and message traffic instead of sticking the entire scope up, which decreased detectability by a landslide. The entire process took about ten minutes, after which Harri dove the submarine back to six hundred feet.

"Sonar, Conn, depth on *Burrfish*?" Alex leaned into the squawk box to ask.

Walkman didn't hesitate: "Right on one thousand feet, sir. There's a sonic layer at nine hundred."

"Very well." Alex chewed his lip because his glasses were on his face; he expected the message tablet as soon as radio finished sorting traffic. "He's playing it safe."

Bobby handed him the tablet. "Just got this from radio. And we wouldn't have heard him if we hadn't been sitting so quiet, either."

"Nope." Alex really liked it when Bobby used his brain, a much commoner occurrence with Steve gone. "He's being smart. Here's hoping it doesn't get him killed."

"You think he's heard us?"

"If I was *Burrfish*, and I'd heard another American boat, I'd phone a friend," Alex replied.

"Not that we're going to," Bobby said.

"Not that we're going to. Let's take position under *Titan Uranus* as planned. Make your depth four hundred feet," Alex said, flipping through messages. "Nothing useful, here—except an email from Uncle Marco. Maybe he's got something to say about *Burrfish*."

Alex didn't think Rodriquez would send someone else to watch *Titan Uranus*, but he could've been overruled. Freddie Hamilton was no cowboy, and she wasn't Alex's biggest fan, either. Neither of his encounters with her had been pleasant.

Come to think of it, while she might have enjoyed *giving* him a tongue-lashing, Alex hadn't enjoyed receiving it.

He skimmed the email. The information had been leaked, but Rodriquez couldn't promise it would get to Rochambeau. Nothing new, there. No mention of an extra escort. No change in plans.

"Huh."

"Captain?" Bobby turned to look at him.

"Looks like someone has the same idea we do. Take a look at this," he said, extending the tablet. Rodriquez included a screenshot of a tweet in his email:

Captain Jules Rochambeau
@JulesRochambeau
@USNavy You should tell Captain Coleman to get his affairs in order. I have a trifecta to complete.
#Razorback #Gallant #Bluefish #onemoreleft #Barracuda

"Wow, he's subtle." Bobby glanced up as if to gauge Alex's reaction. "A trifecta? Really?"

"Crass, too." Alex shrugged. "Certainly banishes any lingering regret I'll have for sinking him."

A few people snickered, and Alex was glad. He'd said that for the crew's benefit; Alex would never be the bombastic sort—or at least he hoped he wouldn't.

"So, still the same game?" Bobby asked.

Alex nodded. "No use changing it. We'll just have to hope *Burrfish* stays out of the way."

He didn't say that *Burrfish* might be good bait, too. Alex didn't want to think it. But he thought Bobby heard, given the sober expression his XO wore.

Alex watched quietly as *Bluefish* settled into position right underneath *Titan Uranus*, drafting into the container ship's noisy shadow. Detecting them with passive sonar would be difficult, and what sane attack sub CO nestled so close to a clumsy container ship?

COMSUBPAC Headquarters, Pearl Harbor, Hawaii

Marco Rodriquez got the news of *Burrfish's* assignment an hour late. His frustration led to three disassembled pens, a broken stapler, and a keyboard with seven keys missing. After he rushed off another email, of course, but Marco knew that would do little good.

"What was her estimated rendezvous time again, Katie?" he asked his indefatigable aide.

"Two hours ago, sir," she replied. Again.

"Damn it." Marco slumped in his chair. He didn't even have the energy to swear creatively. It was eight p.m. in Hawaii, which made it one o'clock in the morning on the East Coast. Did he care? Snarling, Marco pulled out his cell and dialed Freddie Hamilton's personal number. At least he'd do her the courtesy of letting her know who was calling when she saw his name on the display.

It took forever and a day before COMSUBFOR picked up. Did she even have voicemail configured? Marco wanted to throw things.

"This had better be good," Freddie said in greeting.

"You sent another boat along with *Titan Uranus*," Marco snapped.

He could picture her shoving sleep aside. "What?" A moment of silence passed. "Why do you care? Did *Burrfish* get sunk?"

"Not yet." Marco growled under his breath. "You missed my fucking memo about using *Titan Uranus* to bait Rochambeau in, didn't you?"

Now was probably not the time to mention to her that he'd hidden said information in a long status update Freddie didn't have time to read. Marco didn't want her stopping him or changing the weapons carrier's course. Freddie meant well, and she was pretty fucking bright, but she was also as straight and conventional as a steel rod.

"You fucking what?" Now Freddie was awake and mad enough to swear. Glorious.

"*You're* the one who told me to kill the French fuckwad at any cost."

"Not that one!"

"Too late. My little hunter is already out there and out of communications. Can you raise *Burrfish* and tell them to stay the hell out of his way?" Marco asked.

Freddie sighed. "Tell me you didn't send Coleman."

"Okay. I won't tell you." He also wouldn't lie to her.

"God*damn* you, Marco." Movement; Freddie got out of bed. "What do you want me to pass to *Burrfish*, or do you just want her to CHOP to you so you can call the shots?"

CHOPing was a Change of OPerational command, or a fancy way of saying a submarine answered to a new boss. The navy had an acronym for everything. "Yeah, give her to me," Marco said. "I'm still in the office, so I can send orders out in a hurry. Who's got command?"

"Commander Shizue Kanda. She's smart."

Typical Freddie, keeping all that in her head. Not that Marco didn't know the names of the COs of submarines assigned to the Pacific side of the world. He grimaced before asking:

"She the type to stay in comms, or does she dive and go silent?" He knew which he'd be if he'd been a wartime captain, but a lot of COs found comfort in the ability to talk to someone. The submarines he'd grown up in had even less connectivity than his most paranoid COs wanted. This was a new world.

"She should pop up every so often," Freddie replied.

"Here's hoping it's often enough." Marco hung up. He drafted a quick email to *Burrfish's* captain, relaying orders to clear the area and then contact COMSUBPAC directly. He wanted that sub out of the line of fire. A quick look at the sub school's notes on Commander Kanda said that she was *Burrfish's* first captain, commanding the submarine through builders' trials and commissioning. She probably knew her boat and crew well, but *Burrfish* had commissioned just two months earlier.

Green as fucking grass.

The last thing Marco wanted to do was lose another brand-new sub to Rochambeau. The assclown would just love that.

Unfortunately, *Burrfish* didn't answer his email that night. Nor the next day.

28 April 2040

Two boring days later, *Bluefish* remained in *Titan Uranus'* shadow, tooling along at a lazy eighteen knots. Keeping the sub positioned there was a challenging at first, but after the first few watches, everyone got the hang of it. They were still over a thousand nautical miles—three-plus days—from Perth, and the crew's initial nerves gave way to frustration.

Burrfish continued to track *Titan Uranus* like a particularly clumsy shark, remaining below the layer and scissoring back and forth along *Titan Uranus'* wake. A less-cautious CO would put themselves out on the flank from which they expected danger, and a ballsy one would be in front of the container ship. Unfortunately, Alex's counterpart on *Burrfish* seemed conservative. Alex could tell Shizue Kanda was new at this game. *She's good enough to get an Improved Cero, which should say something.*

Alex sure hoped it did.

The idea of raising *Burrfish* on the underwater telephone was tempting. But Alex had blown his chance to do that already. Rochambeau hadn't been around when *Bluefish* arrived, but Alex hadn't known that. Now he couldn't risk the Frenchman listening in. Alex knew *Barracuda* was quieter than his own boat, which was why he stayed hidden. Transmissions of any kind would give the game away.

"You think he's going to take the bait, Captain?" Harri asked over dinner that night. "His tweet didn't say anything about torpedo shipments."

Alex put down his fork. "There's no knowing." He chuckled. "But if I knew he wanted to come after us so badly, I would've just asked him to meet us somewhere."

Uneasy laughter filled the wardroom. Bobby filled the silence. "Probably would've been easier to take an ad out on Twitter, sir. He seems obsessed with it."

"Yeah, he's got that in common with my oldest daughter." Alex grinned. "That's an idea for next time."

"Could be fun to watch you get in a tweet war with him, Captain." Harri's eyes gleamed.

"Don't get cocky, young lady." Alex softened the words with a smile. "I might know *how* to tweet, but you won't catch me dead doing that kind of shit."

"I doubt anyone would mind," she replied. "Uncle Marco seemed pretty cool."

Alex and Bobby exchanged a glance. Alex shook his head. "You won't say that when you're more senior."

"What, you mean she'll get a stick up her butt?" Rene snickered.

"It's called *responsibility*, Rene," Bobby drawled. "It's not much fun, kind of like growing up, but you get used to it."

"Bah. I plan on staying cool."

"Good luck with that." Alex grinned. He remembered being that young and optimistic. He'd clung to that until—

The phone to his right rang, and Alex grabbed it. "Captain."

"Sir, it's the officer of the deck," Rose said. "Chief Andreas is in sonar and says she's got something wonky out to port."

"Something wonky?" A chill raced down Alex's spine.

"Yes, sir. She's not sure she wants to put a name on it."

"Man battle stations silently. I'll be right there."

His officers were up and moving before Alex even hung up the phone, dinner of pizza and wings forgotten. They even left their fake beer—nonalcoholic, because the navy trusted them with weapons but not adult beverages. It would end up on the walls if someone didn't clean up before *Bluefish* started maneuvering, but fake wood paneling meant easy cleanup.

Alex left the wardroom on Bobby's heels, pausing in the doorway to let a pair of sailors rush pass. The general alarm hadn't sounded, but sailors passed the word from space to space, rousing their fellows from their racks and interrupting meals or training. Silence was life in a chase like this...assuming the contact was Rochambeau. With Alex's recent luck, it might just be a whale. But he had to treat every possible contact like the enemy, because Rochambeau didn't give second chances.

Hanging a left, Alex scurried up two ladders to control, pausing in the doorway. Tension tingled in the air; sailors bent over their consoles, eyes intent and expressions blank. Bobby took the watch while Rose headed to the weapons corner. That was the one concession Alex made to not having a true navigator. Rene could do the day job well enough, but there wasn't time to train him to be officer of the deck in combat. So Bobby got to put his two hats back on for battle stations.

Alex's chest was tight. Was this it? God, he was so not ready. Had Ursula felt so out of her depth? She certainly never seemed like it. He'd just have to fake it until he made it.

Alex ducked through the hatch, closing it behind him. At least the metal of the handle was reassuringly cool and normal. He turned to face his team.

"What do we have, Bobby?"

"Chief Andreas calls it 'twitchy,' sir, but it's definitely a contact," Bobby replied. "No luck holding it yet."

So much for looking at the plot. He leaned into the squawk box instead. "Sonar, Conn, report bearing and range to contact."

"Conn, Sonar, somewhere between two-six-five and two-nine-zero, almost directly astern of us. I *think* it's moving from left to right." Chief Andreas' voice was low and frustrated. "Range is about twenty thousand yards. Maybe more."

"Conn, aye." Alex took a deep breath. "Let me know if anything changes."

Could he say something less useful? Alex hadn't been so nervous in combat since Convoy 57.

"You think it's him, sir?" Bobby asked.

"Either that or whales farting."

Alex shrugged, and they settled in to wait. Sooner or later, something had to give.

Chapter 36

Tenacity

Minutes turned into hours, dinnertime to midnight, and finally into breakfast. Still the unknown contact remained distant and unidentified. *Burrfish* puttered along aft of *Bluefish* and *Titan Uranus*, far closer to the mystery submarine and seemingly unaware. Aboard *Bluefish*, despite Chief Andreas' best efforts, the contact kept slipping out of their grasp.

Staying at battle stations this long was suicidal, so Alex stood the crew down by cutting manning at each station in half, allowing people to get food and sleep. He and Bobby took turns in control, keeping *Bluefish* hidden under the container ship. Everyone was tense. Was it Rochambeau? They all knew he liked to toy with his prey. Combined with how quiet a *Requin*-class boat was, logic said this had to be him. But how to get him to come out of hiding without getting shot at?

Submarine-on-submarine engagements were usually decided by whoever got the first shot off. But they had to see the enemy to shoot him, and so far, Rochambeau was doing a damned good impression of a hole in the water.

"Hope you like eggs and toast, Captain," Bobby said from behind him, making Alex jump.

"Jesus, Bobby." Heart pounding, Alex turned to face his XO. He caught a nap from midnight until about four, sending Bobby to catch four hours after that. Now Bobby was back, extending a breakfast plate. Alex smiled. "Thanks."

His stomach growled; Alex hadn't realized he was hungry until he smelled the eggs. Eating while balancing the plate in one hand wasn't the most graceful thing he'd ever done, but Alex didn't care. His crew wasn't going to think less of him.

"Still boring and more boring?" Bobby asked.

"To the nth degree." Alex chewed and swallowed. "We can't detect him without getting closer, and if we get closer, he'll hear us. Catch 22."

"Awesome. That's what I wanted to do with my day." Bobby heaved a sigh and leaned against the nav table.

"Me, too." It beat being sunk, but Alex preferred shooting to waiting. Not that he planned on twitching. He'd make Rochambeau come to him.

"*Burrfish* is still oblivious, too," Bobby whispered. "You think they have any idea?"

Alex shook his head. "If they did, they'd have tried shooting." He'd thought about it a hundred times during the too-quiet night. "Even the greenest CO would've shot by now."

Finishing the eggs, Alex stuffed the toast in his mouth and then walked over to shove the plate in an angle iron near the coffee pot. Master Chief Morton would've yelled at him for that. Grief made his throat tight; Bryan Morton was another victim of Rochambeau's who needed avenging. Master Chief Baker might yet give him a disapproving look, but she'd gone to off sleep and wasn't back yet.

Alex refilled his coffee and returned to Bobby's side. "Nothing we can do to change the game. We've got to out-wait him."

"I'm not really good at patience, in case you haven't learned that about me."

"Yeah, I hate it, too."

Another three hours flowed by like molasses. Alex contemplated pacing, but that wouldn't help and would make his crew nervous. Bobby cracked jokes, pop culture references falling left and right, but Alex tuned him out when he started in on the similarities to some hunt in the latest *Star Wars* movie. He studied the plot, watched the icon representing *Barracuda* flicker in and out. What was the bastard waiting for?

He had to change the game. But how?

Alex started another cup of coffee and studied the plot. Moving out of *Titan Uranus'* shadow was out of the question. He'd lose the only thing keeping him quieter than his enemy. He supposed he *could* slow to a crawl and hope Rochambeau would overtake them, but if that didn't work, he'd have no momentum to dodge French torpedoes. Turning would put him broadside to Rochambeau. Right now, the contact seemed to be aft and a bit to port. The geometry sucked. If Rochambeau stayed on this course, Alex would have to turn before shooting.

Damn it.

"Conn, Sonar, *Burrfish* is maneuvering," Chief Andreas reported.

Alex straightened out of his slump and keyed the intercom. "What's she doing?"

"Coming up in speed and heading to starboard, I think." Andreas paused. "Hard to tell with her in our baffles, sir. Even with the tail out. *Titan Uranus* makes a lot of noise."

It didn't help that *Bluefish* wasn't quite matching *Titan Uranus'* course; Alex had ordered her into a corkscrew pattern hours earlier. Constant course changes kept anyone from getting a firm solution on *Bluefish*, but it didn't help them detect Rochambeau, either.

"Conn, aye." Alex took a deep breath, butterflies dancing in his stomach. *Please open the range,* he thought as loudly as he could. *Get the hell away from here.*

Would Rochambeau shoot? Knowing he could do nothing to help *Burrfish* made Alex feel sick. If Rochambeau opened his torpedo tube doors, *Bluefish* might hear. They'd definitely detect a torpedo launch. That would give Alex the drop on Rochambeau, but would *Burrfish* die?

"Reman battle stations," Alex ordered, twisting to look at Rose. "Standby for a snapshot from tube two, Weps."

"This is a really bad angle to shoot from, sir," she replied.

"I know. I'll try to turn to give you a better shot." Theoretically, the Mark 84 possessed an off-bore firing capability. *Bluefish's* towed sonar array trailed behind her, giving her the ability to see the normally blind zone astern, but Alex still had to turn to get anything other than a crap firing solution.

Rose and her team went to work as Bobby materialized at Alex's side. "Something happening, sir?"

"Might be. *Burrfish* is maneuvering." Alex chewed his glasses, watching the plot. Chief Andreas was right; *Burrfish* had turned to starboard and the range was opening. "I think she's going home."

Bobby frowned. "Groton is northwest of here. She's heading south."

"Home as in not here." Alex waved off Bobby's objection. Now the question was if Rochambeau would let an enemy sub—

"Conn, Sonar, sounds like *Burrfish* is going shallow. I've got hull-popping noises."

"Damn." Alex wanted to punch something. He knew what that meant. "Checking the mail is only going to make her a better target."

Bobby grimaced. "That means she's got no idea Wile E Coyote is out there, too."

"Yeah."

Being the best in the world at this game did not mean Jules did not find it irritating.

"Any change?" he asked sonar, not bothering to rise from his chair. The sonar station was mere feet away.

"No, sir." There was a pause. "The contact near the container ship continues to fade in and out. We cannot hold it."

Jules blew out a sigh. "*Merci*."

Commander Solenne Chappelle arched an eyebrow. "Will we wait, *Capitaine*?"

"*Oui*." Jules scowled. "We wait."

"*Capitaine*, the first American is moving toward the surface," Sonar reported.

"Oh?" Jules perked up, heading over to look at the navigation display. *Barracuda* was unable to positively identify the sonar contact they *did* hold, but it was clearly an Improved *Cero*. The fact that its particular sound signature was not in *Barracuda's* library meant the enemy submarine was new.

"*Oui*. Depth now five hundred feet and increasing. Her speed remains eighteen knots."

Of course it did. All three submarines—*Barracuda*, the Improved *Cero*, and the mystery contact—were at eighteen knots because that was the merchant ship's speed. *Titan Uranus* continued in a straight line, blissfully unaware of death stalking her. But now one of the enemy submarines was going shallow. Was that to communicate with the merchant?

If so, they weren't talking with their hidden counterpart. Detecting that would have been easy, particularly this close. Jules frowned. Did they know he was here? Probably not. The *Cero-I* would not go shallow in that case.

"Do you wish to shoot her now, *Capitaine*?" Solenne asked.

"No." Now he grimaced. "Shooting gives our position away. Without a good firing solution on the *other* submarine, that would be suicide."

"Sonar is not positive that is not an echo of the merchant."

"Would you stake your life on that?" Jules asked. "I will not. A clever American would hide under the merchant."

"If we shoot fast enough—"

"No. One of them will make a mistake if we wait." Jules smiled thinly. "Keep a solid solution on the shallow submarine. Increase speed by two knots and close to six nautical miles." Perhaps that would get a better track on the mystery submarine. If not, it would still help his firing solutions. The Rafale torpedoes were fast, but their legs were short. They also turned like drunk donkeys, which meant a smart enemy could dodge and run them out of gas.

Not that his enemy knew that. Jules needed to be in a range where his first shots killed the Americans so they never found out.

Solenne nodded and headed to the weapons table. Jules folded his hands, leaned back in his seat, and forced himself to appear calm. "Wait and hope" was a good French maxim, and he had made it his own. Overconfidence and overenthusiasm would not force him into making mistakes.

Americans were impatient. One of them would make the first mistake.

Burrfish remained shallow for too long. Alex knew how quickly a submarine could upload and download messages, and *Burrfish* should have submerged fifteen minutes ago.

He wanted to shake his younger counterpart. *Younger.* Alex almost laughed out loud. She was probably his age. At thirty-eight, Alex was young for an honest-to-goodness captain, even in wartime. Peacetime said that attack sub COs were commanders, O-5 in military parlance. Alex was an O-6, commanding his second submarine because wartime made different rules. And he felt ancient.

Pinching the bridge of his nose did not banish the rising headache. *Dive,* he thought toward *Burrfish. Dive and hide, damn it.* How long would Rochambeau wait? Alex couldn't risk being the next Patricia Abercrombie. He had to make Rochambeau shoot first, but must *Burrfish* make themselves such a pretty target?

"They're taking forever," Bobby whispered.

Alex glanced at his XO, a lump forming in his throat. "They're going to get themselves killed."

"We can't do anything without dying with them, can we?" Bobby asked.

"No." Alex shook his head. "The only thing keeping those idiots alive right now has got to be Rochambeau knowing we're here."

"He what?" Bobby's eyes went wide.

"Otherwise, he would've already shot them." Alex felt cold and sick, tense and exhausted. His neck kept cramping, too. "But he knows that if he takes the first shot, we'll know where he is."

"So he waits."

"Yep." Alex groaned and checked his watch. "Eighteen hours and counting."

This debacle started at dinner the night before. Now it was almost lunchtime. Alex scraped his hands over his face. How long would they wait?

As long as he had to.

"You want to catch a nap, sir?" Bobby asked. "You've been up since four."

"Not while *Burrfish* is doing their best impression of a bulls-eye. Maybe after."

"You say so, sir." Bobby eyed him. "And maybe it's just me, but we all think better when we're not exhausted."

"Point taken." Alex chuckled. "You've really come a long way, you know that? Four months ago, you'd never have tried bossing me around."

"Oh, this isn't bossing. You'll know if I get to bossing you around, Captain." Bobby grinned. "This is just gentle nudgery."

"Nudgery? Is that a word?"

Bobby shrugged. "It is now."

Alex shook his head. But his amusement faded when he looked back at the plot. *Burrfish* remained at periscope depth. They'd been there for almost an hour. In a *warzone*. "For fuck's sake, someone send them a tactics manual or something while they're up there."

"We could try from down here, but..." Bobby trailed off.

"But that would require painting a target on ourselves. I'd rather not. Besides, it's hard as hell to get red paint off the sound-absorbing tiles."

"You know that from experience, sir? I thought you were better at blasting paint *off* than putting it on," Bobby said.

"Fuck you, too, XO." Alex grinned. "You're not supposed to make your CO look like an idiot."

"They must teach that at the Prospective Executive Officers course, Captain, which as you know—since you set me up for this shiny job—I skipped."

Alex snorted. "Hm."

Bobby laughed.

An hour later, Alex relented and went to the wardroom for lunch. He was halfway through pretending to like a chicken salad sandwich when *Burrfish* finally dove back down to eight hundred feet. She ended up eight thousand yards off *Bluefish's* starboard quarter, paralleling *Titan Uranus*. Her position completed a lopsided triangle, with *Bluefish* to the right, *Burrfish* at the bottom, and *Barracuda* further back to the left. Somewhere.

He was too keyed up to sleep, but Alex forced himself to lie down for a few hours, turning the intercom in his stateroom up to the max. His crew needed to think he was calm and confident, not a bundle of nerves trying to shake itself apart.

Logic said impatience would kill him. Besides, what could he do? He could pickle off a torpedo or two in *Barracuda's* general direction, but *Burrfish's* position made that dicey. Rochambeau was smart enough to sprint behind *Burrfish* to complicate Alex's firing solutions. Worst-case scenario, his torpedoes hit another American submarine and committed the first friendly fire incident of the war. No fucking way was he doing that.

Staring at the ceiling didn't help. Could he outwait Rochambeau? *Should* he? There had to be another option.

Alex was still mulling that question when he fell into a fitful sleep.

Standing in the middle of *Burrfish's* control center, Commander Shizue Kanda frowned. New submarines were prone to problems—everyone knew that—but *Burrfish's* communications glitches were dangerous.

"Anything?" she asked her radio watch.

"No, ma'am." The petty officer manning the radio console shook her head. "I'm pretty sure our packet uploaded, but nothing came down. We can't receive anything from the satellite."

"Thank you." Not swearing was hard. Shize glanced at her XO, Lieutenant Commander Vick Monfils. "We'll try again in a few hours."

"I'll get Chief Candless up and see if he can fix it," Vick replied, heading toward a phone. Vick was short, freckled, and blond, the stereotypical midwestern American. Shizue, on the other hand, had the hair and eyes of her Japanese ancestors coupled with her mother's height.

Shizue nodded. Chief Candless, their best electronics technician, was probably sleeping. This was worth waking him up for, however. Being unable to receive new orders left Shizue uncomfortable, even if escorting *Titan Uranus* was boring. She'd hoped for a little action deep in the Indian Ocean, but apparently intelligence kept a lid on *Titan Uranus'* cargo. *If anyone knew what she was carrying, the French and Indians would be all over us.*

Pacing across control, Shizue stopped by sonar. The curtain was open, and STS1 Penny Blackman's expression was perplexed as she tapped the gain controls.

"Something wrong, STS1?" Shizue asked.

"I think we've got a glitch in the sonar system, too, Captain," Blackman replied. "*Titan Uranus'* signature keeps echoing on me."

"Weird." This was just what Shizue needed. Sonar ghosts and *three* broken radio systems. Although the latter was probably a computer problem. That was the only explanation for their complete inability to download message traffic and emails.

"It's almost like there's two ships there, ma'am." Blackman scowled. "Do they have prairie or masker?"

"No, only warships have those." Shizue shook her head. Prairie and masker were systems designed to obscure the sound a surface ship made by using bubbles in the water, but civilian ships weren't designed that way.

"Right." Blackman tapped her console with a grease pencil, making Shizue cringe. Blackman was an old school sonar operator; she'd been in the service for almost twenty years and was Shizue's age. More importantly, Blackman had grown up in the old 688 class, with CRTs you could write on. Modern monitors didn't like that, but Shizue didn't want to interrupt when Blackman was in the zone.

Instead, she tried not to tap her foot.

"There might be someone else there, ma'am," Blackman finally said.

"What? That's impossible." Shizue stopped herself from swearing. Again. "We've been within eight nautical miles of *Titan Uranus* for days. And now we're only four miles away."

Blackman shrugged. "I just call what I see, Captain. There's something funky going on here. Another sub hiding under her is the best explanation I've got."

"Keep listening and tell me what you find." Shizue returned to stare at the plot. The Improved *Ceros* had even better sonar and targeting integration than the original subs. If a second sub showed up, they would've seen her. Wouldn't they?

Unless there was a glitch in sonar, too. Damn this new submarine. *Burrfish* was her baby, but Shizue knew how much the yard left unfixed after builders' trials. There was too much of a rush to go to war. All the primary systems passed testing, but now there were gremlins everywhere.

Still, the idea of a second submarine sneaking right past them was ludicrous.

Alex's alarm buzzed at 1600. Blinking blearily, he forced himself to sit up and turn the stupid thing off. A few moments passed before he remembered why he'd gone to sleep on top of his rack with his shoes on, but then reality crashed back in.

Butterflies came with it.

Dropping his head into his hands, Alex took a minute to contemplate the enormity of the decision he made before drifting off. Was it crazy? Sure.

But he wasn't Ursula North. He *could* sit there and watch Rochambeau shoot at Americans, but why do that if he could change the rules? If he was smart—and a little lucky—they could finish this before dinner. He just had to be crazy enough.

Standing, Alex grabbed his glasses, heading to control without looking in the mirror. He exchanged greetings with a few sailors along the way, but *Bluefish's* passageways were largely empty. They'd been at modified battle stations for twenty-three hours. Anyone not on station was eating or sleeping. *We can't do this for much longer.*

How the hell had he ended up with this job again?

The hatch to control was open, and Alex looked his crew over before stepping through. Bobby's jokes had some laughing, although Master Chief Baker—who looked freshly showered—was deep in conversation with Chief Andreas near sonar. Tension still bubbled under the surface, but no one looked ready to fall apart.

That would have to be good enough.

Alex cleared his throat. "XO, pass the word to reman battle stations."

"Reman battle stations, aye." Bobby passed the word to all other controlling stations via the squawk box.

Fifteen minutes later, *Bluefish* was ready for combat. Alex tried to pretend his heart wasn't pounding in his chest as he studied the plot. The three submarines' positions remained unchanged. *Burrfish* continued obliviously, and *Barracuda* was back there somewhere, fading in and out of contact. Sighing, Alex walked forward to duck in the sonar room.

"Anything I can do to make finding *Barracuda* easier?" he asked.

Chief Andreas shook her head. "The tail's out and I've fiddled with every setting we have. Those *Requins* are quiet, sir. We're trying, but she's too far away."

"What's your best guess on range?"

"Something between ten and fifteen thousand yards." Chief Andreas shook her head. "Sorry I don't have better, Captain."

"No need to apologize. Thanks." Nodding, Alex walked out of sonar, making sure the curtain closed behind him.

Too far away was still too close for comfort. Rochambeau probably had those ridiculously fast torpedoes, which meant Alex had to get the first shot off. And it had to be a *good* shot.

"Is it just me, Captain, or do you have something on your mind?" Bobby asked when Alex reached his side at the center of control.

"Yeah." Why hesitate? "We've got to break this logjam. Otherwise, we'll keep sitting here, wearing everyone down, for another day or two."

Bobby frowned. "I thought you wanted Rochambeau to make the first move?"

"I did. But now I'm thinking that's not such a good idea." Alex stared at the plot, judging angles. "If you chase him, you die."

"Huh?"

"That's what Ursula North told me," Alex said. "We can't let him take the initiative. Hiding until he does something isn't going to work and might get *Burrfish* killed. So we change the rules."

Bobby looked thoughtful. "To what?"

"Join us, Weps." Alex gestured to Rose, and she bounced over, her eyes bright and fascinated. He knew everyone in the compartment was listening. Might as well get Rose's input. "We go active and shoot as soon as we have a bearing. Snapshot with a torp from tube two, followed up two more the moment we have a firing solution. We keep the fourth in reserve and reload as fast as we can."

"You want to cut the wires on the pair instead of guiding them in?" Rose asked.

"Yeah. We're going to maneuver too much to keep them on the wire." Alex had no illusions. Rochambeau would shoot back. However, French accuracy would suffer from maneuvering, too. And torpedoes sometimes committed fratricide. If Rochambeau fired down a reciprocal bearing from Alex's first shot, the two torps might decide to kill one another.

"You're *really* going to go *Hunt for Red October* on this guy and go active?" Bobby's eyes were comically wide.

Alex smiled crookedly. "You got a better idea?"

"Well, no." Bobby grinned. "But if you say 'one ping only,' I might need a video."

"Not happening, thanks." Alex shoved his hands in his pockets, his mind tripping through possible outcomes. He looked at Rose again. "We'll come left before we shoot, the snapshot, then shift our rudder and come around to the right before firing the pair."

"You want to turn back toward our original course?" Bobby scratched his chin. "Why?"

"Because those fast torpedoes the French have can't turn on a dime. Not if they're based off the Russian model we know about," Alex said, praying physics would be his friend. "So when he shoots at where he thinks we'll be, we'll be going the opposite direction."

Rose frowned. "That'll delay our second and third shot."

"I know." Alex let out a breath. "Once we've got two tubes reloaded, we'll shoot again. And we'll keep at it until we sink him or run out of torpedoes."

Or he sinks us, no one said. Rose nodded.

Bobby asked: "What about *Burrfish?*"

"I want you to warn her off the moment we shoot. Get her on the Subsurface Secure and tell her to stay clear."

Bobby made a face. "You think she will?"

"I'm senior to Commander Kanda, so she'd better." Alex hated throwing his rank around, but *Burrfish* could bumble into this worse than he'd bumbled into the engagement between *Gallant* and *Barracuda.* Alex needed the other American sub out of the way.

He'd never expected to feel like Ursula North.

"I can do that, Captain," Bobby replied and then glanced at Rose. "Any other thoughts?"

"No." Rose's eyes narrowed. "Shoot and keep shooting. Pretty simple when you're Weps."

They had twenty-one torps. Alex imagined they wouldn't get the chance to shoot them all before something gave. Part of him wanted to stop everything, to wait awhile, just so he could send another email to Nancy and the girls, but the emails he'd sent ten hours ago would have to be enough.

"Let's get to work," he said. Alex reached for the 1MC microphone, the old terror creeping up his spine. He shoved it aside. "*Bluefish*, this is the captain. We're about to start this dance. I have every confidence in you. Hold tight, do your best, and I'll see you on the other side."

It wasn't terribly inspirational, but it was all Alex had. He put the microphone down and took a deep breath. "This is the captain. I have the conn."

"The captain has the conn," Master Chief Baker acknowledged.

Game time.

"Ready on your end, Weps?" Alex asked.

"Yes, sir! Outer doors are open. Tube two standing by." Rose's finger hovered over the firing button. All they needed was a firm bearing.

"Left full rudder," Alex ordered. Better to start the turn first; Rochambeau wouldn't detect that. Odds were he hadn't heard their outer doors opening with *Bluefish's* stern pointed at him, either.

"Left full rudder, aye," Baker replied. "My rudder is left full, no new course given."

"Very well." Alex's eyes flicked upward. *Bluefish's* original course was one-zero-zero. He needed to come left at least thirty degrees for a good shot. Forty would be better.

"Passing course zero-nine-zero," Baker said.

"Very well." The words were automatic. At eighteen knots, *Bluefish* turned about half a degree per second. A forty-degree turn needed a minute twenty. Could they remain undetected that long?

"Passing zero-eight-zero."

More math. The time required for an active pulse to go out and return was negligible. How long would they need to shoot? More importantly, how long would Rochambeau need to react?

"Passing zero-seven-zero."

Alex continued to stare at the digital course indicator.

068.

066.

064.

Alex leaned into the squawk box. "Sonar, Conn, go active to port." He glanced at Bobby, mouth open, but Bobby already had the red phone for Subsurface Secure in hand.

"Duelist, this is Silent Night," Bobby said, using both boat's callsigns. "Come right and clear the area immediately. I say again, come right and clear the area immediately, over."

"Conn, Sonar, contact bears two-six-five, range twelve thousand yards!"

"Snapshot tube two, bearing zero-six-five!" Alex ordered.

Rose's hand slammed down on the button. "Tube two fired electrically!"

"Sonar, Conn, secure active sonar," Alex said into the squawk box and then turned back to the COB. "Hard right rudder, ahead flank!"

He ignored both repeatbacks, but his head snapped around as STS2 Walkman reported: "Conn, Sonar, designate contact track 7099. Speed twenty knots and increasing, course one-one-zero!"

"*Barracuda* is turning—shit, torpedo in the water bearing two-six-seven!" Chief Andreas broke in.

"Weps, firing point procedures tubes one and three, track 7099," Alex snapped.

"Solution set!" Rose said.

"Solution checked!" When did Bobby reach the weapons corner? Either *Burrfish* wasn't arguing or Bobby decided to ignore them.

Alex glanced at the plot, his heart racing. *Barracuda* was astern of *Bluefish* again, but his sub's rate of turn increased as her speed did. A hard rudder was thirty-five degrees, and the helmsman had thrown the rudder over until it slammed into the hard stops. *Bluefish* leaned starboard now, rolling into her turn at about two degrees per second. She'd already passed her original course and continued right.

That turn unmasked her starboard torpedo tubes. "Match bearings and fire!"

"Tubes one and three fired electrically!"

"Conn, Sonar, three fish running hot, straight, and normal!" Andreas reported. "Enemy torpedo speed one-thirty—I say again, one-thirty-plus—knots!"

Someone swore.

"Relax, folks, we knew this was coming." Alex's heartbeat slowed as his submarine sped up. Her propulsor digging into the water, *Bluefish* was up to forty knots despite the turn.

"Passing course one-seven-zero!" Baker said.

"Very well. Steady course two-zero-zero." That would do for now. Alex wanted to come further right, but he needed to ditch that torpedo first.

"Wires cut, outer doors closed. Reloading all tubes," Rose said before he could ask.

"Conn, Sonar, *Barracuda* speed fifty-two knots, course two-four-five," Walkman's voice said.

"Conn, aye." Alex waited a heartbeat. "XO, stand by countermeasures."

"Standing by," Bobby replied.

"Drop a pair as we turn." Alex's eyes focused on the plot. *Barracuda* was running from his three torpedoes at fifty-two knots. The Mark 84 ASV's top speed was eighty-seven knots with a range of twenty-one nautical miles. Practically applied, that meant the torpedo could run full out for almost fourteen-and-a-half minutes.

Barracuda was slower. Despite her torpedoes' greater speeds, the submarine couldn't match *Bluefish's* sprinting ability. Alex's torpedoes could catch her, even with a six-nautical-mile head start. Barely. Assuming Rochambeau didn't dodge them, or his countermeasures didn't work.

But Alex couldn't do a damned thing about that until his tubes were reloaded, so he concentrated on the torpedoes trying to kill him. Intelligence said that French Rafale torpedoes had a range of about twenty-seven nautical miles. Coupled with their speed, that meant they'd run for almost twelve minutes. But Rochambeau only shot one torpedo. Had Alex surprised him? Alex chewed his lower lip, staring at the plot. The French torpedo was aimed for where *Bluefish* was before her right turn. Now, it circled, hunting. Time to give it something to chase.

Control was eerily quiet.

"Right full rudder, steady course two-four-five," Alex said. That put them right on Rochambeau's tail, with *Bluefish* up to fifty-seven knots. They wouldn't catch *Barracuda*, but who wanted to?

"Countermeasures away!" Bobby said as the COB brought the submarine to the new course.

"Very well." Another deep breath; Alex turned to Rose. "Ready, Weps?"

She held up a hand, listening on the headset connecting the weapons corner to the torpedo room. Alex waited, stepping on his impatience. Firing sooner would be better than later, but—

"Tube two reloaded!" Rose said. "Solutions set and checked!"

Alex barely gave her a chance to finish: "Tubes two and four, *fire*!"

"Weapons away!"

"Expedite reloading tubes one and three, Weps," Alex ordered. "I want to box him in. If he turns right, our old torpedoes will close him. I want to nail the bastard when he comes left."

"You got it, sir." She grinned. "Thirty seconds."

"I think his torpedo's going for the countermeasure, Captain," Bobby said. He moved back to the plot, and soon enough, Sonar echoed:

"Conn, Sonar, enemy torpedo has turned away—I think it's circling the countermeasure."

"Very well." Alex forced down the lump in his throat, watching *Barracuda* tear holes in the water. "He's not done yet. He'll shoot at least one more time."

"You think he's waiting for us to get closer so we can't dodge?" Bobby went pale.

"I would." Alex turned to Baker. "Ahead flank for fifty-two knots."

"Ahead flank for fifty-two knots, aye."

"Ooh, that's nasty." Bobby flashed him a grin. "Matching his speed means he has to slow down if he wants to sucker us in."

Alex tried not to smirk. "Sonar, Conn, report range."

"Steady at ten thousand yards, sir," Chief Andreas said.

"Conn, aye." Alex leaned away from the box. "Shit, that's still close if he shoots. But we'll know if he starts to turn."

Bobby frowned at the plot. "He's got to soon, right?"

"Unless he knows something we don't."

Chapter 37

The Hard Stops

"Who the hell is 'Silent Night?'" Shizue demanded.

Vick bent over the list of call signs, flipping through tablet pages. Several agonizing seconds passed while the other American sub—the one that had somehow snuck *under* the merchant while they weren't looking—maneuvered and pinged away. "*Bluefish*."

"*Bluefish*." Shizue made her mouth snap shut. "As in Alex Coleman."

Commissioning a new submarine was akin to being buried under a rock, but even Shizue had heard of Alex Coleman. *Everyone* had. She'd even studied his tactics.

"Yes, ma'am." Vick's frown mirrored her own. The unspoken question hung in the air: *Now what?*

"Crap." Shizue didn't like swearing, but she almost did. Alex Coleman outranked her by a mile.

"Conn, Sonar, new contact signature matches *Requin* 722," Blackman reported.

Vick jumped. "What?"

Shizue felt cold. She had that hull number memorized. Everyone did. "*Barracuda*," she whispered.

Shizue met her XO's eyes. Everyone knew that Rochambeau had sank Ursula North last month. He'd sunk *so* many submarines, all without a flicker of regret. Shizue had even watched several interviews with the cocky Frenchman; he knew he was the best in the world.

Now they had a ringside seat for America's best trying to kill him. And *Bluefish* had warned them off.

"How can we help, Captain?" Vick asked.

"By getting out of the way." Shizue's chest felt heavy. "Captain Coleman outranks me by a lightyear. It's a legal order. Come right and open the distance."

Vick stepped close to ask in an undertone: "Are you sure?"

"Unfortunately." She sighed. "But stay on the edge of our range envelope. I want to be able to take a shot if we need to."

Or if Rochambeau sinks Bluefish, *too,* she didn't say.

Nodding jerkily, Vick relayed the order.

Shizue stared at the plot.

"It is *Bluefish*," Solenne confirmed.

"That is no surprise." Jules sought to appear unaffected, but it was difficult. He'd never let an enemy outfox him like this, and the experience was not one he enjoyed. Coleman had waited so long that Jules assumed he would get to shoot someone before everything came to a head. Jules forced a smile. "I suppose he read my tweet."

Solenne chuckled, but there was little humor in her eyes. "Your orders?"

Jules frowned. He had to turn to shoot. In *Barracuda's* maneuvers to escape the first three American torpedoes, he'd turned to a course that allowed *Bluefish* to tuck in behind him. Such an amateur mistake. He was not accustomed to being shot at.

Now he had three torpedoes closing from his starboard quarter and two from behind. Meanwhile, his own torpedo continued to circle the American countermeasure—at high speed, to be sure, but useless speed. The only way to shoot again was to turn, but the moment he did that, any captain with half a brain would fire a broadside straight into *Barracuda.* Alas, Coleman had proven himself intelligent.

"*Capitaine*?" Solenne said.

Jules blinked. He had to turn. But when? A cold feeling filled his chest. Even his hands felt numb.

"*Capitaine.*"

"*Oui.*" Jules shook himself. "We must turn before he can reload. *Ceros* only have four torpedo tubes, and he has shot five torpedoes already. He can only reload so fast."

Was he speaking for his own benefit?

"Just say the word, *mon capitaine.*" Solenne swallowed.

Blinking again, Jules focused on the navigation plot. "Range to *Bluefish*?"

"Five nautical miles, *mon capitaine*," Sonar replied. "He has reduced speed to match ours."

Jules hissed. Of course, the American sub was faster. Yet his torpedoes were almost twice the speed of the Americans'. A Rafale would close the distance in...two minutes. American torpedoes would need three-and-a-half minutes.

One weakness of the *Requin* class was their lack of an off-bore firing capability. The later submarines in the class remedied that problem, but *Barracuda* still could not shoot at targets abaft of her beam. Jules would have to turn his submarine at least ninety degrees before he could fire.

That required seventy seconds with all the rudder he dared use at this speed. *Barracuda* was built for silence, not high-speed maneuvering. Using too much rudder at high speeds could cause a loss of depth control. The last thing he wanted was to slam his submarine into the ocean floor.

He could not afford to wait longer.

"Left standard rudder. Standby port tubes," Jules ordered.

Barracuda began to turn.

"Sonar, Conn, she's turning!" Chief Andreas shouted so loudly that Alex didn't need the intercom to hear her.

"Tubes one and three, *fire*!" Alex snapped.

"Weapons away!" Rose said.

"Two fish running hot, straight, and normal," Walkman said.

"Conn, aye." Alex took a deep breath. *Wait*, he told himself. How long did a *Requin* need to unmask her torpedo tubes? If she had the same turning capability as a *Cero*, she'd need forty-five seconds or so.

"Do you want to maneuver, Captain?" Bobby asked quietly.

Alex shook his head. "Not yet."

His eyes fastened on the clock to the right and above the helm. They'd fired twenty seconds earlier. If Alex maneuvered too soon, game over. *Barracuda's* torpedoes could slam right into *Bluefish's* underside.

This was going to be close. Alex turned to Master Chief Baker. "Standby to hit the roof, COB," he said. "When I give the word, take us to sixty feet."

"COB, aye."

Sixty feet was the minimum depth *Bluefish* could manage without broaching the surface. The slight tremor of the deck under Alex's feet reminded him that his sub remained near her own top speed. Driving toward the surface could get messy if Baker missed the ordered depth, but *Barracuda* was too close to sidestep.

"XO, launch a pair of countermeasures once the nose comes up."

"Standing by." Bobby bounced up and down on his toes; Alex glanced that way and wished he hadn't. There were plenty of white knuckles and pale faces in the room. Everyone not focused on a task was watching him. Forty seconds.

Forty-five.

"Impact in three minutes!" Rose said.

When the hell was Rochambeau going to fire? Alex tried not to swallow. A torpedo that ran at 139 knots would need two minutes to close the ten thousand yards between the two submarines. Move too early and the torpedo could follow them. Head for the surface too late...

Fifty seconds.

Bobby glanced his way, concern coloring his features, but said nothing. Thank goodness. If Bobby started questioning him, Alex might crack. He trusted Bobby's judgment like he'd learned not to trust his previous executive officers'.

"Tubes two and four reloaded, solution set!" Rose whipped around to face him, her expression triumphant.

Was there time? Just. "Fire!"

"Weapons away! Wires cut, doors closed."

"Conn, Sonar, torpedoes in the water, three torpedoes dead on the bow! Estimated speed one-thirty plus!" Chief Andreas reported.

The cards were on the table. At her current speed, *Bluefish* needed less than five seconds to get to the new depth. His crew was going to hate him, but Alex had to wait. He glanced at the clock, judging seconds.

"Torpedo range eight thousand yards!"

"We've got to wait until we're too close for the torpedo to maneuver, folks," Alex said, daring to look around control.

Faces went whiter, but he got a few jerky nods.

Alex forced himself to breathe. One minute ticked by; *Barracuda* maneuvered wildly, launching countermeasures as she turned back to the right, aiming for her original course. But her jog left let Alex's first three torpedoes gain on her. Now the French sub had seven torpedoes closing in on her from three directions, and *Barracuda* wasn't fast enough to run any of them out of gas.

Cold relief washed over Alex. Whatever happened, he'd nailed Rochambeau. Now he just had to live through it.

"Conn, Sonar, torpedo range two thousand yards!" Chief Andreas' voice was high and terrified.

"Full rise on the planes! Make your depth sixty feet," Alex ordered. Immediately, the deck sloped upward, and he grabbed for the nav table for balance. "Ahead flank!"

Bobby yanked the lever to launch their noisemakers. "Countermeasures away!"

Bluefish raced toward the surface, leveling out almost as soon as she'd started her climb. The movement was jerky; the sub came back on an even keel with enough force to throw

Bobby forward. Better braced, Alex caught himself and looked at the depth gauge: sixty feet.

His heart almost stopped in relief.

"Good job, COB. Right on the money." He leaned toward the squawk box. "Sonar, talk to me about the torpedoes!"

"Blew right past us, sir. Our torpedoes are homing." Chief Andreas paused. "Can't tell which, but at least three of them are."

Three out of seven made for astronomically bad odds. Alex would take it.

"Holy shit, did we just dodge those torps?" Rose said to no one in particular.

Bobby giggled. "Hold onto your hat, Rosie, because I think we did."

Alex couldn't afford to embrace the euphoria. Not yet. His mind raced through possibilities—maybe they were about to sink Rochambeau. Still, surviving would be nice. Time to act.

Bluefish rumbled up to fifty-eight knots. Not enough if the torpedoes were still coming. Alex keyed the squawk box. "Maneuvering, Captain, if you've got some extra juice, now's the time."

"Standby," Lou replied.

Slowly, the digital speed indicator crept up to fifty-nine knots. And then sixty. Lou didn't bother to say anything, but the indicator stopped at 60.9. Not bad! Giddiness started to creep in; Alex shoved it down.

"Final homing on torpedoes three, four, five, and seven!" Rose said.

Alex's eyes snapped to the plot. *Barracuda* continued writhing, dancing left and right, dropping countermeasures with every turn. Three of the American torpedoes circled noisemakers at uselessly long distance from *Barracuda*, but four of them—no, three, one lost lock—kept on her. All were within three thousand yards. That gave them...thirty-five knots of closure. Rochambeau had less than three minutes to dodge.

On that note, it was time to further confuse any French torpedoes that might forget the noisemakers and go after *Blue-*

fish. "Right standard rudder, steady course zero-four-five," Alex ordered.

Right was away from *Barracuda.* As much as Alex wanted to watch the show, no way was he letting one of his own torpedoes target his boat. Changing course meant that the French torpedoes would have a harder time finding *Bluefish*, and Alex wanted to live.

"How's the reloading going, Weps?" he asked next.

Rose flushed. "We'll get on that, Captain."

"Thank you." Alex let himself smile. "Overconfidence will get us killed. Let's be ready if he dodges those torps."

"You got it, sir." Rose grabbed her headset, but Alex didn't listen to her tell the torpedo room to reload all tubes. He trusted her.

"You think he can dodge them, Captain?" Bobby asked quietly from his side.

Alex shrugged. "I think he's the best in the world for a reason."

"Not if you nail him today, he's not." Bobby grinned.

Alex blinked, his mouth flopping open. He'd been so focused on getting the job done that he hadn't thought—

"Conn, Sonar, *Barracuda* is going for the roof!" Chief Andreas reported. "Two torpedoes in final acquisition!"

"He's good." The words came out before Alex knew he was speaking.

Bobby started. "What?"

"He outfoxed another torp." Alex's eyes remained on the plot; now there were only two torpedoes on Rochambeau's tail.

"Too late to matter," Bobby replied.

"Point." Alex gripped the chart table, glancing at the tracks of the torpedoes following them. Those Rafales only had four minutes of gas left. Alex did the math again. "We're in the clear. Those torps can't catch us unless they learn to teleport."

Bobby stared at him for a long moment before bursting into laughter.

"Surface, surface *immédiatement*!" Jules snapped. The order was too late, but he had to see this through to the end. He looked at his crew, looked at the pale faces staring back at him with a mixture of shock and resignation. "I am sorry."

"It is not over yet." Solenne looked on the verge of tears.

Jules just shook his head. It was not supposed to end this way. So glittering of a career should not end in such disgrace. How had he fallen from the very pinnacle of his profession?

Ursula will laugh at me, was his last thought before *Barracuda* breached the surface. Seconds later, two torpedoes exploded beneath her.

Jules would not remember escaping his sinking submarine. Later, the escape came to him in bits and pieces, memories of water rushing in, pipes breaking, and people screaming. The helm console vanished in a brilliant rain of sparks while his crew raced for the escape chamber. Jules could not remember if someone dragged him through or if he used the conning tower hatch. He *thought* the explosions displaced the hatch enough to force it open, and a few survivors later told stories of escaping that way.

It was all a blur.

Minutes—it felt like hours—later, he found himself in the water, clinging desperately to a lonely life raft. Only one of *Barracuda's* seven life rafts deployed. Had explosions savaged the other ones? He would never know. Jules was a strong swimmer, however, and made it to the raft. Many of his crew did not.

When he finally managed to count survivors, there were fifteen. Fifteen out of a crew of fifty-eight.

Jules crawled into the raft and then helped a cook do the same.

There they sat, waterlogged and shocked, watching the sky turn colors overhead. He'd forgotten sunset was approaching; being underwater was always timeless, controlled only by *Barracuda's* internal clocks.

Those clocks would reach the bottom of the Indian Ocean soon, along with his navy's pride and joy. Perhaps he should not have swum to the life raft. This would go over terribly at home. But no. Jules preferred to live. He would fight again. He would *remember*.

Closing his eyes, Jules willed the shame aside.

Alliance Subsurface Secure was a short-ranged communications circuit, not prone to the difficulties *Burrfish* had connecting with satellites. Still, Commander Shizue Kanda didn't expect *Bluefish* to call them back into the area after *Barracuda* sank. She'd been prepared to be chastised for her refusal to leave the area.

Who wanted to turn their backs on history? She and her crew watched, fascinated, as a legend fell. *Burrfish* had a hard time holding the distant contacts on sonar—for some reason, their fellow American sub was not up in Link—but they saw enough to know when *Barracuda* sank. The explosion was probably heard for miles, anyway.

She still couldn't believe it.

"*Burrfish*, this is *Bluefish* Actual," Alex Coleman said. "Are you able to surface, over?"

Shizue grabbed the phone out of Vick's hand. "*Bluefish* Actual this is *Burrfish* Actual. Affirmative, over."

"It appears *Barracuda's* survivors made it to the surface," Coleman replied. "We would appreciate some assistance in picking them up."

"Picking them *up*?" Vick hissed.

Shizue's own eyes were wide. Was he crazy? "Say again, over."

"I say again, I would appreciate assistance with *Barracuda's* survivors." Even through the distortion, she heard the edge in

Coleman's voice. "I don't know how many of them there are, and I don't want to put them all in one boat, over."

A superior officer *appreciating assistance* might as well be an order, so Shizue pushed back her horror. "We'll need twenty minutes to reach your position, over."

"This is *Bluefish*, roger, out."

She hoped most submarine commanders out here weren't so terse. Shizue swallowed and turned to Vick. "Proceed to *Barracuda's* last known position at forty knots." She squared her shoulders. "Keep a good track on *Bluefish* while we do and stay well clear."

"Yes, ma'am." Vick's expression told the story of his unhappiness, but he didn't argue. That wasn't the *Burrfish* way.

Picking up the survivors—even with an unwilling *Burrfish* along—was simpler than Alex expected. Finding that *Burrfish* hung around to watch the engagement wasn't much of a surprise, either; Alex probably would've twisted those orders into a pretzel in Shizue Kanda's shoes, too.

There were only fifteen survivors. *Fifteen.* He probably could bring them all on *Bluefish*, but Alex sent seven to *Burrfish*, anyway. Attack submarines didn't have brigs. The smart thing would be to let the survivors float around on the Indian Ocean until someone friendly picked them up, but why start being conventional now?

Alex used a satellite phone to call COMSUBPAC while Bobby pulled the French sailors on board. Surprisingly, Harri spoke French, which popped her up on deck to act as interpreter.

The phone rang for too long while Alex watched waterlogged French sailors accepting American help to scramble on board. Most didn't complain when they were searched, although one exchanged some not-so-kind sounding words with Harri.

"SUBPAC, Lieutenant Greco speaking," a woman's voice finally said.

"Lieutenant, this is *Bluefish* Actual, calling for the admiral," Alex replied.

"Standby, sir."

Alex barely had time to draw breath before Marco Rodriquez was on the line. "Coleman! Why the fuck are you calling me? What went wrong?"

"Good evening to you, too, sir." Alex couldn't resist needling Uncle Marco. He'd just sunk Jules fucking Rochambeau. He deserved to have a bit of fun.

"Son, if you keep taunting me, I'm going to make sure you get shit jobs for the rest of this war."

"I can always throw Rochambeau back if you want me to, Admiral," Alex said. "Though that's probably a violation of the Geneva Conventions."

"*What?*"

"*Barracuda* went down about an hour ago." He grinned. "We're picking up the survivors, now. I shanghai'd *Burrfish* into taking half of them."

Shocking Uncle Marco into silence had to be a reward in itself; a long moment passed before the stunned voice on the other end said: "You fucking did it. You sank the bastard."

"We did, sir. *Titan Uranus* is still afloat, too." Alex didn't mention that he'd need to sprint like hell to catch up with the merchant. Letting those torpedoes go to the bottom now would be such a waste.

"Fuck me."

Alex laughed. "No thanks."

"And you *got* the arrogant shit?" Marco seemed to finally realize what Alex had said. "You're picking up French survivors *including* Rochambeau?"

"Yes, sir. There are only fifteen of them, but I've got him on deck now. Luckily, one of my officers speaks French." Bobby seemed to be trying some Spanish on their French guests—not successfully, judging from Harri's amused expression.

"Damn—damn good job, Captain," Marco said. "Bring him back so we can show him American hospitality for the rest of the war, will you? That sure beats the idea of him in a shiny new submarine."

"Yeah, it definitely does."

Harri herded the survivors below, with Bobby on their heels. Rochambeau and his people would spend the next two days on *Bluefish's* mess decks, whether they liked it or not. That was hardly the most comfortable place in the world, but it would do. It was inconvenient, but guarding them was worth it to get Rochambeau out of the war.

Alex hung up, then stood in silence and stared at the setting sun. He'd lost enough friends to Rochambeau. No more.

Now he could head back to Perth. Guarding *Titan Uranus* with *Burrfish's* help would be easy. Within three days, they'd be back. Nancy would be underway, but maybe he'd take some leave when she got back. Hell, maybe they could even head home for a few weeks, reconnect with the girls over summer vacation and pretend they were normal people. The war wasn't over—not even close—but this was the first far-reaching victory the American sub force had scored in a long time.

They'd probably make him do more interviews, but for once, Alex didn't care.

...continue reading Alex's story in *The Stars Shall Burn*, available for preorder now!

Thank you so much for reading! As an indie author, I treasure each and every one of my readers, including you! If you haven't already signed up for my newsletter to get a free short story in the *War of the Submarine* universe, head over to www.rgrobertswriter.com or click right here. If you don't like getting emails (even if they only show up 1-2 times a month), that's okay! You can follow me on Facebook, where I post frequent updates and sometimes sneak peeks. I hope to see you there!

Fun Facts from the Writing of Fortune Favors the Bold

Or, things you might not have known while reading

#1: This was the second book I wrote for the series.

If you are a member of my newsletter or follow me on Facebook, you probably already know this story, so skip on down to #2. If not, strap on in.

I started writing *War of the Submarine* (then under the series title of *Manifest Destiny*) way back when I was at the Naval War College, around 2011. What I *thought* was the first book, then titled *Little Blue Ribbon*, later became Book #4, *I Will Try.* Still with me?

Later, I realized that IWT wasn't a good beginning for the series, and I wrote *Cardinal Virtues* (the one had two working titles, first *The Dictates of Conscience*, and then later *An Unjust Peace*).It became Book #1. Then I wrote *Before the Storm* to be Book #0, the prequel novella. At that point, I turned my attention back to the original book one/now book "two," and realized that it didn't really bridge well from CV.

So, I sat down, reorganized that beast, and wrote the shit out of it. By the time I was done, it was about 300,000 words (*way* too long!), and I realized it was two books. I spilt it in half, wrote an ending and a beginning, and next you know, you have *The War No One Wanted* and *Fire When Ready.* Bam, now we're finally up to *I Will Try*, which had been sitting around for over ten years at that point, waiting for me to get to the poor bastard.

But the story had changed a lot by then. Nancy Coleman was a navy nurse in my original drafts, but by the time I wrote CV, she changed to a surface warfare officer. So, I scrapped her original plots and rewrote them. I also had to update some things, because along the way, I advanced the story nine years in time (it originally took place in the early-2030s) to align with current/future events. I also busted out some mid-story pieces, including *Pedal to the Medal* (originally part of *The War No One Wanted,* but it didn't fit so out it came) and *Clean Sweep* (originally titled *Reef Points*).

Then I finally, *finally* got to *Fortune Favors the Bold.* This baby survived without a title change but there was a lot of nurse Nancy that needed to go—some of which I'm sad to not save, because it was one of my favorite parts—and some other stuff that needed fixing to align with the rest of the story as it developed. What resulted was the longest book in the series, but I think it's a lot of fun...and my story is now finally on track.

Now I can finally continue in order! *The Stars Shall Burn* is up next, and I am very excited to dive into this world without having to untangle my very own Gordian Knot.

#2: Submarine History has inspired more than one event/character in this book.

If you're not up to speed on World War II submariners, I highly recommend jumping into that rabbit hole as soon as you can. I've namedropped both Mush Morton and Dick O'Kane in this book, and it wasn't by accident; they're two of the most legendary submariners of all time. Both served in World War II—together, as it so happens—and redefined submarine warfare almost singlehandedly. Mush Morton was the second, and last, commander of USS *Wahoo*, and Dick O'Kane was his XO and later the CO of USS *Tang*. Morton was loud, brash, and nicknamed "Mushmouth" by his peers, whereas O'Kane was more studious and quiet. Both were superb tacticians and extraordinary leaders.

Will I continue to make historical references throughout this series? You bet. If you're looking for some light reading on either of them—or on other submarine heroes of World War II—I recommend any of the following books: *Undersea Warrior*, by Don Keith; *Wahoo: The Patrols of America's Most Famous World War II Submarine*, by Richard O'Kane; *Wake of the Wahoo*, by Forest J. Sterling; *Clear the Bridge: The Patrols of the USS Tang*, by Richard O'Kane; or *The Bravest Man: Richard O'Kane and the Amazing Submarine Adventures of the USS Tang*, by William Tuohy.

I'm not making money off those recommendations, but I've read all of those books and found them both good resources and good reads.

Other good books on WWII submarines include *Thunder Below*(Eugene B. Fluckey), *Final Patrol* (Don Keith) and *Silent Warriors* (Gene Masters). There are hundreds more, but these are a few of my favorites.

And if I have to recommend just one non-submarine WWII book, it will always be *Last Stand of the Tin Can Sailors* (James D. Hornfischer), which definitely helped inspire the events of *I Will Try*, at least a little.

#3: Odd References? Probably.

There are a few references that might run by you if you blink too fast. Chapters 4 and 6 have references to *The Caine Mutiny*, which was pretty much what life felt like on my third ship. (Much of the crap that goes down on *Bluefish* is based on my experiences there, though thankfully *some* of it gets exaggerated...though not too much).

PFM is mentioned in Chapter 5. This isn't just a navy-ism; it's also an engineer-ism. It stands for "Pure Fucking Magic."

The Arnheiter Affair is also mentioned in Chapter 6. This book is a true story and an absolutely wild ride. It should be required reading for all Surface Warfare Officers, particularly for someone heading to a command where the captain is...we ll, like Captain Rowlings. Suffice it to say that USSTHIRDSHIP was quite like this for me, and it took me years to recover from how it made me feel as a leader and a naval officer. There are a lot of reasons I'm glad I left the service, and that ship is about 90% of them.

Captain Rowlings is also heavily based off of a certain female navy captain who made the news while I was still in the service. She was the first woman to command a cruiser, but oh boy did she screw it up. Turned out to be a terrible tactician, a worse leader, totally toxic, and absolutely abusive to her crew. Including walking her dog. Fun times. I knew a few people who served under her, and they were never the same.

The smell of navy shipyards is also mentioned in chapter 12.If you've been in the service, you 100% know what I mean. Some of my readers will vividly remember contractors taking leaks in corners because the heads don't work when your tanks are being worked on (and thus no flushing water and the heads are locked). If you've never received that particular gift when the ship was turned back over from the yards, you got a unicorn.

Commander Scott Waddle is referenced in Chapter 34. He was in command of USS *Greenville*, a fast attack sub that surfaced underneath a Japanese fishing boat in 2001. Nine died. It was a bad day for the navy, made worse by *Greenville* not following procedures.

Motor Vessel *Titan Uranus* (chapter 35) was real. I had the pleasure of seeing her myself on my first deployment, though she was renamed around 2006 to *Titan Taurus* after the owners figured out what the name sounded like when said out loud. Trust me, there was *so much* giggling on the bridge of the good ship USS *Cape St. George* when we came across her.

And yes, good catch, *Cape* herself is a reference to my first ship, CG 71, who we used to call "Battlecruiser 71." A great ship with a great crew. I was honored to serve on her.

#4: Other Fun Stuff

1. Yes, I've calculated hypothermia tables every time I put survivors in the water.
2. Steve Harper? Yeah, that jerk's based off someone I knew in real life. Fortunately, that guy (who was also an O-4; I served with him as an ensign/O-1) also got his comeuppance.

3. There wasn't room for it in the book, but Rochambeau totally remembers meeting Alex on Armistice Station. Sooner or later, they'll chat about that. They'll never hate each other the way Ursula and Rochambeau do, but they certainly won't be friends. Or even friendly enemies.

#5: Hints for Upcoming Books (don't read this if you haven't finished this book!)

1. Alex should never try to predict the future. He makes at least one solid prediction in this book that is absolutely, horribly, wrong.
2. This book contains a fun part of Alex Coleman's character development: the beginning of him saying things to senior officers that he *really shouldn't*. Keep your boots on: this is only the beginning!
3. Ursula North was originally slated to die, but somehow or another, I couldn't bring myself to kill the Sea Witch. So, she got a reprieve. That turned into giving *Rochambeau* a reprieve as well, since their stories are pretty well tied together. Of course, they'll both be on the beach for a bit: Ursula needs a new leg and Rochambeau is a POW. But I still have plans for our favorite cranky Brit and everyone's least favorite fighting Frenchman.
4. In my original notes, Marco Rodriquez was also slated to die. Originally, he was going to commit suicide. Later, he was due for a heart attack. But the colorful bastard's grown on me far too much, and he'll probably get a reprieve. Particularly now that I've put this in print!

5. In Chapter 36, Alex worries about committing the first friendly-fire incident of the war. He doesn't. But well, someday, someone...stay tuned!

About R.G. Roberts

R.G. Roberts is a veteran of the U.S. Navy, currently living in Connecticut and working as a Manufacturing Manager for a major medical device manufacturer. While an officer in the Navy, R.G. Roberts served on three ships, taught at the Surface Warfare Officer's School, and graduated from the U.S. Naval War College with a masters degree in Strategic Studies & National Security, with a concentration in leadership.

She is a multi-genre author, and has published in military thrillers, science fiction, epic fantasy, and alternate history. She rode horses until she joined the Navy (ships aren't very compatible with high-strung jumpers) and fenced (with swords!) in college. Add in the military experience and history degree, and you get A+ anatomy for a fantasy author. However, since she also enjoyed her time in the Navy and loves history, you'll find her in those genres as well.

You can find R.G. Roberts' website at www.rgrobertswriter.com or find all her links at linktr.ee/rgroberts. From there, you can join her newsletter! Joining the newsletter will get you a free novella or short story, set in either the War of the Submarine or Age of the Legacy universes (or both, if you like both genres). Newsletters are a twice-a-month affair, so there won't be a ton of spam in your inbox, but you'll be the first to hear about sales, get sneak peeks of new writing, and get to read free short stories from time to time, too!

R.G. Roberts is also one of the authors trying the new-fangled site known as "Ream." It's like Pateron, but made for authors and readers – and especially for superfans! There you will have access to exclusive first looks at all of her works, including early access to chapters of novels, short stories, and more! You can find her Ream at www.reamstories.com/rgrobertswriter.

Also By the Author

War of the Submarine

Before the Storm

Cardinal Virtues

The War No One Wanted

Fire When Ready

Clean Sweep

I Will Try

Fortune Favors the Bold

The Stars Shall Burn

War of the Submarine Shorts

Never Take a Recon Marine to a Casino Robbery (subscriber exclusive)

Pedal to the Medal

Age the Legacy

Shade
Shadow (Coming Soon!)

Night Rider
Before the Dawn (Coming Soon!)

Legacy Shorts

Prelude to Conquest (subscriber exclusive)
The First Ride (Exclusive on Ream!)
City of Light (Exclusive on Ream!)

Alternate History

Against the Wind

Caesar's Command

Other Works

Agent of Change (Portal Sci-Fi with an Alternate History Twist)

Fido (Cozy Fantasy Serial, high on humor)
Once Upon a Dragon (Exclusive on Ream!)

Printed in Great Britain
by Amazon

51217478R00364